I'm
我識出版社
17buy.com.tw

I'm

我識出版社
17buy.com.tw

一網打盡
英文單字
15,000

Vocabularies

Point ❶
字彙量夠用一輩子

全書涵括 15,000 個英語字彙，臨時需要的單字，隨手一翻，絕對能馬上找到你要的那一個字彙。

15,000 個單字完全適用於：
全民英檢初、中、中高、高級及國中會考、大學指考學測、統測、新多益、雅思、托福、博思、公職國考等英檢考試。

Point ❷ 實用例句超越英語會話書

單字書除了記憶字彙以外，更發揮其會話書的功能。書中單字搭配生活常用的英語例句，讓學習者透過單字熟習例句、理解例句進而加深對字彙的印象，兩者相輔相成，學習效果倍增。

 fable ~ future

★一網打盡 884 個英文單字 │ 一網打盡 179 句英語會話句　　　◎ MP3 06-01

fable [`febl] 名 寓言，傳說
▶ Most kids are familiar with the fable of the tortoise and the hare.
大部分的孩子都很熟悉龜兔賽跑的寓言故事。

相關衍生字彙

▶ Most kids are familiar with the fable of the tortoise and the hare.
大部分的孩子都很熟悉龜兔賽跑的寓言故事。

fabric [`fæbrɪk] 名 織品，布料
▶ The skirt is made of cotton fabrics.
這件裙子是棉布做的。
相關衍生字彙 fabric conditioner 片 織物柔軟劑、fabric sample 片 布料樣本、fabric softener 片 衣物柔軟精、textile [`tɛkstaɪl] 名 紡織品 形 紡織的

fabricate [`fæbrɪ͵ket] 動 組裝，製造，杜撰　　片 to fabricate an excuse 編造藉口
相關衍生字彙 fabrication [͵fæbrɪ`keʃən] 名 製造，構造物、fabricative [`fæbrə͵ketɪv] 形 造造的、fabricator [`fæbrɪ͵ketɚ] 名 製作者，裝配工、construct [kən`strʌkt] 動 建造，創立（學說等）、assemble [ə`sɛmbl] 動 集合，配裝

Point ④ 一網打盡英文的「聽、說、讀、寫」

免費附贈英語單字完整收錄 MP3。特別邀請專業外籍教師錄製全書主要英語單字，書本不用帶著走也能聆聽正統發音的英語單字。無時無刻、隨時隨地都能隨心所欲的預習及複習。

★本書附贈CD片內容音檔為MP3格式★

---

barley [`barlɪ] 名 大麥
▶ The beer was made from barley. 這啤酒是大麥釀成的。

barometer [bə`rɑmətɚ] 名 氣壓計
▶ A barometer is used to measure air pressure. 氣壓計是用來量大氣的壓力。

◎ MP3 **02-03**

barrel [`bærəl] 名 木桶　　片 a beer barrel 啤酒桶　　◎ MP3 **02-03**

barren [`bærən] 形 荒蕪的，不孕的
▶ After the war, the land became barren. 戰爭過後，這片土地就變荒蕪了。

barricade [`bærə͵ked] 名 路障
▶ There was a fire, so the firefighters put barricades to block off the road.
有火災發生，所以消防人員放置路障封鎖此路。

barrier [`bærɪr] 名 障礙
▶ It takes time to overcome the language barrier.
克服語言障礙是很費時的。
相關衍生字彙 obstruction [əb`strʌkʃən] 名 阻礙、obstacle [`ɑbstək!] 名 障礙（物）、
hindrance [`hɪndrəns] 名 妨礙

barter [`bɑrtɚ] 動 以～作為交換
▶ In the past, the villagers bartered rice for their necessities.
以前，這裡的村民用米去換日常用品。
動詞三態變化 barter - bartered - bartered

base [bes] 動 以～為基礎　　片 be based on 根據～
動詞三態變化 base - based - based

baseball [`bes͵bɔl] 名 棒球
▶ After school, kids like to play baseball.
放學後，孩子們喜歡打棒球。
相關衍生字彙 basketball [`bæskɪt͵bɔl] 名 籃球、soccer [`sɑkɚ] 名 足球、
badminton [`bædmɪntən] 名 羽毛球、tennis [`tɛnɪs] 名 網球、golf [gɑlf]
名 高爾夫球

相關衍生字彙 basketball [`bæskɪt͵bɔl] 名 籃球、soccer [`sɑkɚ] 名 足球、
badminton [`bædmɪntən] 名 羽毛球、tennis [`tɛnɪs] 名 網球、golf [gɑlf]
名 高爾夫球

Point ③ 紮實內容更勝英語辭典

字彙不僅搭配相關實用英語例句外，更結合常見片語、同義字、反義字和相關補充字彙，學習者能舉一反三。豐富且細緻的學習元素，引領學習者探索更多語言字彙的謎漾世界。

學習一種外國語言，總是起頭難。而單字量是幫助你能一躍而上的基石。如果能具備基本的單字來處理基本的生活所需，或學術學習所需，假以時日再透過自己的生活經驗及領域，逐日加深加廣，自然成就出精練的英語能力。

過往，我的學生及自己的小孩在學習英語起步時，會跟我抱怨坊間很多單字書，在他們英語程度未臻成熟時，背一個單字時，還得費力去讀它冗長的例句，而例句裡又不乏有他們不認識的單字，還有尚未學習過的句型，常常讓他們舉步維艱，最後就放棄那本單字書，甚至放棄學習。所以，這次有機會幫各位編寫《一網打盡英文單字 15,000》一書，編者謹記學生們跟自己孩子的建議，以下為此書的特色：

▶ **單字皆彙整於各類英文測驗及考試**

▶ **以生活化的情境來造句**

▶ **單字、例句及所補充的片語均附上中文解釋**

▶ **同反義字及諺語相關小補充**

綜合以上特色，不僅讓讀者容易自學，更能讓學習的焦點回到單字本身。另外，英文單字常常一字多詞性，又多義。編者累積 20 多年教書及旅遊經驗，就個人的生活經驗中常聽常用的英語單字，幫讀者去蕪存菁。除了例句跟片語以外，有些單字碰巧有常用的諺語，編者也幫各位附上耳熟能響的諺語，讀者

若能背上幾句，運用在寫作上也更顯腹中有書氣自華。相關單字的統整與補充，希望提供給讀者更多的學習觸角。

　　本書附上有聲光碟，出版社用心良苦，希望讀者在學習語言時，一定要能正確發音。尤其英文單字是拼音系統，要會唸才會拼正確，並且讓你在與老外交談時有自信的表達。所以，編者建議各位讀者一定要善用有聲工具，反覆聽，跟著複誦，相信可有效協助有心學習者快速累積單字量，並正確地說出英語與人有效溝通。

　　學無止盡，學海無涯，期盼《一網打盡英文單字 15,000》能幫助讀者打開浩瀚的英文世界。

Victoria Lin 2015.06

一網打盡

字母 A

aback ~ awkward

詞性說明

名 名詞　　　副 副詞　　　介 介系詞

動 動詞　　　形 形容詞　　連 連接詞

代 代名詞　　助 助動詞

內文圖示說明

片 片語　　　反 反義字　　同 同義字

一網打盡「英語小知識」｜月份

| January | February | March | April |
| 一月 | 二月 | 三月 | 四月 |

| May | June | July | August |
| 五月 | 六月 | 七月 | 八月 |

| September | October | November | December |
| 九月 | 十月 | 十一月 | 十二月 |

abate ~ awkward

★一網打盡 1721 個英文單字 ｜ 一網打盡 279 句英語會話句

aback [əˋbæk] 副 向後　　片 be taken aback 震驚

abandon [əˋbændən] 動 拋棄，放棄
▶ To support his family, he had no choice but to abandon his dream.
為了養家，他不得不放棄他的夢想。
〔相關衍生字彙〕 abandoned [əˋbændənd] 形 被拋棄的、abandonment [əˋbændənmənt] 名 放棄，放任、forsake [fɚˋsek] 動 拋棄，革除、relinquish [rɪˋlɪŋkwɪʃ] 動 放棄，讓與、evacuate [ɪˋvækjuˏet] 動 撤空，使疏散
〔動詞三態變化〕 abandon - abandoned - abandoned

abase [əˋbes] 動 使謙卑　　片 to abase oneself 自貶身分
〔相關衍生字彙〕 humble [ˋhʌmbl] 形 謙遜的，簡陋的、modest [ˋmɑdɪst] 形 謙虛的、proud [praʊd] 形 驕傲的、arrogant [ˋærəgənt] 形 自大的
〔動詞三態變化〕 abase - abased - abased

abash [əˋbæʃ] 動 使羞愧
〔動詞三態變化〕 abash - abashed - abashed

abate [əˋbet] 動 減少，降低
▶ He was so angry. It seemed nothing could abate his rage.
他是如此生氣，似乎什麼都無法平息他的憤怒。
〔動詞三態變化〕 abate - abated - abated

abbreviate [əˋbrivɪˏet] 動 縮寫
▶ We abbreviate New York to N.Y.
我們會把紐約縮寫為 N.Y.。
〔相關衍生字彙〕 abbreviation [əˏbrivɪˋeʃən] 名 縮寫字，縮寫式、abbreviator [əˋbrivɪˏetɚ] 名 使用縮寫者，縮寫的東西
〔動詞三態變化〕 abbreviate - abbreviated - abbreviated

abdomen [ˋæbdəmən] 名 腹部
▶ She felt a great deal of pain in her abdomen.
她覺得腹部非常疼痛。
〔相關衍生字彙〕 stomach [ˋstʌmək] 名 胃、belly [ˋbɛlɪ] 名 肚子、intestine [ɪnˋtɛstɪn] 名 腸子、anus [ˋenəs] 名 肛門、kidney [ˋkɪdnɪ] 名 腎臟、appendix [əˋpɛndɪks] 名 盲腸

abduct [æbˋdʌkt] 動 誘拐，劫持
〔相關衍生字彙〕 abduction [æbˋdʌkʃən] 名 誘拐，綁架、abductor [æbˋdʌktɚ] 名 誘拐者，綁架者、highjack [ˋhaɪˏdʒæk] 動 搶奪（運輸中的貨物），劫持、kidnap [ˋkɪdnæp] 動 誘拐（小孩等），綁架
〔動詞三態變化〕 abduct - abducted - abducted

abashed [ə`bæʃt] 形 難為情的　　⊜ embarrassed [ɪm`bærəst] 形 尷尬的，不好意思的

---

abbey [`æbɪ] 名 修道院
▶ Jay Chou held his wedding ceremony at Selby Abbey in Britain.
　周杰倫在英國賽爾比教堂舉辦他的婚禮。

---

aberration [ˌæbə`reʃən] 名 過失，偏離軌道
▶ We were all shocked by the aberration in the excellent student.
　我們都對這位優秀學生的脫序行為感到震驚。
相關衍生字彙 aberrant [æ`bɛrənt] 形 偏離正道的，異常的、abnormality [ˌæbnɔr`mælətɪ] 名 反常，異常

---

abhor [əb`hɔr] 動 嫌惡，討厭
▶ All people are born equal. I abhor racial discrimination.
　人人生而平等。我厭惡種族歧視。
相關衍生字彙 like [laɪk] 動 喜歡、dislike [dɪs`laɪk] 動 不喜歡、hate [het] 動 討厭、
　　enjoy [ɪn`dʒɔɪ] 動 喜愛、be sick of 片 厭惡、be fond of 片 喜愛、
　　abhorrence [əb`hɔrəns] 名 厭惡，最討厭的東西、abhorrent [əb`hɔrənt]
　　形 令人憎惡的，背離的
動詞三態變化 abhor - abhorred - abhorred

---

ability [ə`bɪlətɪ] 名 能力
▶ A good secretary should have the ability to organize things well.
　一位好秘書要有統整事情的能力。
相關衍生字彙 able [`eb!] 形 能，可，會，有能力的、capable [`kepəb!] 形 能幹的，有才華的、
　　proficient [prə`fɪʃənt] 名 專家 形 精通的、competence [`kɑmpətəns]
　　名 能力，勝任

---

abide [ə`baɪd] 動 忍耐，容忍　　片 abide by 遵守
▶ I can't abide his rudeness.
　我不能忍受他的粗魯。
動詞三態變化 abide - abided - abided

---

ablaze [ə`blez] 形 閃閃發光的，閃爍的
▶ In fall, the woods are ablaze with colors.
　秋天時，樹林閃爍著各種色彩。
相關衍生字彙 shine [ʃaɪn] 動 閃耀、glitter [`glɪtɚ] 動 閃閃發光、twinkle [`twɪŋk!] 動 閃耀、
　　light [laɪt] 名 亮光、twilight [`twaɪˌlaɪt] 名 微光

---

abnormal [æb`nɔrm!] 形 不正常的，反常的　　反 normal [`nɔrm!] 形 正常的
相關衍生字彙 abnormality [ˌæbnɔr`mælətɪ] 名 異常，畸形、abnormally [æb`nɔrməlɪ]
　　副 反常地，不規則地、irregular [ɪ`rɛgjəlɚ] 形 無規律的，不合法的、
　　eccentric [ɪk`sɛntrɪk] 形（人、行為等）古怪的，反常的

---

aboard [ə`bord] 副 上車，上船，登機
▶ Welcome aboard! 歡迎搭乘（車、船、飛機皆可）！

abominable [əˋbɑmənəb!] 形 惡劣的
▶ Most of the victims are living in abominable conditions.
多數的災民正活在惡劣的條件下。

相關衍生字彙 bad [bæd] 形 糟的、unpleasant [ʌnˋplɛznt] 形 使人不悅的、terrible [ˋtɛrəb!]
形 糟糕的、comfortable [ˋkʌmfɚtəb!] 形 舒服的、enjoyable [ɪnˋdʒɔɪəb!]
形 令人愉快的、pleasant [ˋplɛzənt] 形 令人愉悅的

aborigine [ˏæbəˋrɪdʒəni] 名 原住民
▶ Maoris are the aborigines of New Zealand.
毛利人是紐西蘭的原住民。

相關衍生字彙 aboriginal [ˏæbəˋrɪdʒən!] 名 土著居民 形 原始的，土著的

abortion [əˋbɔrʃən] 名 墮胎
▶ Abortion is illegal in many countries.
墮胎在很多國家是違法的。

相關衍生字彙 abort [əˋbɔrt] 動 流產，（計劃等）失敗、miscarry [mɪsˋkærɪ]
動 流產，（人、事等）失敗、abortional [əˋbɔrʃən!] 形 失敗的，夭折的

abolish [əˋbɑlɪʃ] 動 廢除
MP3 01-02
▶ Slavery was finally abolished in America in 1863.
美國奴隸制度終於在一八六三年廢除。

相關衍生字彙 delete [dɪˋlit] 動 刪除、cancel [ˋkæns!] 動 取消、eliminate [ɪˋlɪməˏnet]
動 消除、remove [rɪˋmuv] 動 除去、destroy [dɪˋstrɔɪ] 動 毀壞、
demolish [dɪˋmɑlɪʃ] 動 撤銷

動詞三態變化 abolish - abolished - abolished

abound [əˋbaund] 動 富足，充足   片 abound in / with 富含～
相關衍生字彙 abundance [əˋbʌndəns] 名 豐富，充足、abundant [əˋbʌndənt]
形 大量的，富裕的、overflow [ˏovɚˋflo] 動 泛濫，充滿、flourish [ˋflɝɪʃ]
動（植物等）茂盛，（事業等）興旺

動詞三態變化 abound - abounded - abounded

abridge [əˋbrɪdʒ] 動 刪減
▶ The classic novel has been abridged for kids'.
這本經典小說已被刪減成兒童版本。

動詞三態變化 abridge - abridged - abridged

abroad [əˋbrɔd] 副 在國外
▶ Studying abroad is a dream for many young students.
對很多年輕學子而言出國留學是一個夢想。

abrupt [əˋbrʌpt] 形 突然的
▶ In order not to run into the cat, the bus came to an abrupt stop.
為了不撞上貓咪，公車緊急停下。

abruptly [ə`brʌptlɪ] 副 突然地，險峻地，魯莽地、abruption [ə`brʌpʃən] 名 分裂、abruptness [ə`brʌptnɪs] 名 突然，意外，陡峭

---

absent [`æbsn̩t] 形 缺席的

▶ Albert got a terrible cold. He has been absent from work for days.
亞伯特重感冒，已經好幾天沒上班了。

---

absence [`æbsn̩s] 名 缺席　　片 absence of mind 神不守舍

相關衍生字彙 present [`prɛzn̩t] 形 出席的、presence [`prɛzn̩s] 名 出席、absentee [͵æbsn̩`ti]
名 缺席者、absent-minded [`æbsn̩t`maɪndɪd] 形 心不在焉的、
absent without leave 片 曠課，曠職、leave without pay 片 留職停薪，無薪假

---

absolute [`æbsə͵lut] 形 絕對的

▶ There is no absolute standard about beauty.
美沒有絕對的標準。

相關衍生字彙 absolutely [`æbsə͵lutlɪ] 副 絕對地，完全地、absoluteness [`æbsə͵lutnɪs]
名 絕對性、thorough 形 徹底的，完善的

---

absolve [əb`sɑlv] 動 赦免，釋放

▶ The judge absolved the suspect from the crime.
法官赦免這嫌犯的罪刑。

相關衍生字彙 pardon [`pɑrdn̩] 動 原諒、excuse [ɪk`skjuz] 動 原諒、forgive [fɚ`gɪv]
動 原諒、blame [blem] 動 責備、accuse [ə`kjuz] 動 指控、charge [tʃɑrdʒ]
動 指控

動詞三態變化 absolve - absolved - absolved

---

absorb [əb`sɔrb] 動 吸收

▶ It's hard to absorb so much information on the Internet.
網路上資訊這麼多很難吸收。

相關衍生字彙 absorbing [əb`sɔrbɪŋ] 形 引人入勝的、absorbent [əb`sɔrbənt]
形 能吸收（水、光等）、absorbency [əb`sɔrbənsɪ] 名 吸收性，吸收能力、
absorbed [əb`sɔrbd] 形 專心一意的

動詞三態變化 absorb - absorbed - absorbed

---

absorption [əb`sɔrpʃən] 名 吸收

▶ Sunshine can help the absorption of vitamin D. 陽光有助維他命 D 的吸收。

---

abstain [əb`sten] 動 戒除

▶ The patient was advised to abstain from alcohol and smoking.
這病人被建議戒除酒和菸。

動詞三態變化 abstain - abstained - abstained

abstract [`æbstrækt] 形 抽象的
▶ Picasso is famous for his abstract paintings.
畢卡索以他抽象的畫作聞名。
相關衍生字彙 concrete [`kɑnkrit] 形 具體的、solid [`sɑlɪd] 形 固體的、fluid [`fluɪd] 名 流質、liquid [`lɪkwɪd] 名 液體

---

absurd [əb`sɝd] 形 荒謬的，不合理的
▶ The legend was so absurd that few people believe in it.
這傳說如此荒謬以至於鮮少人相信。

---

abundance [ə`bʌndəns] 名 大量，豐富　　片 an abundance of 大量的

---

abundant [ə`bʌndənt] 形 充足的，豐沛的
▶ The national park is abundant in wild animals.
這國家公園有非常多的野生動物。
相關衍生字彙 poor [pur] 形 貧乏的、rich [rɪtʃ] 形 富有的、wealthy [`wɛlθɪ] 形 富有的、affluent [`æfluənt] 形 富裕的、insufficient [ˌɪnsə`fɪʃənt] 形 不足的、sufficient [sə`fɪʃənt] 形 充足的

---

abuse [ə`bjus] 名 虐待，濫用　　片 drug abuse 藥物濫用 / child abuse 虐待兒童

---

academic [ˌækə`dɛmɪk] 形 學術的　　片 academic freedom 學術自由

---

academy [ə`kædəmɪ] 名 學院，研究院
▶ The Academy Awards is an annual ceremony honoring achievements in the film industry.
奧斯卡金像獎是一年一度的典禮，用來獎勵電影工業的成就。

---

accelerate [æk`sɛləˌret] 動 加速
▶ To catch up with the ferry, we had no choice but to accelerate our car.
為了趕上渡輪，我們只好加速行駛。
相關衍生字彙 speedy [spidɪ] 形 快速的、rapid [`ræpɪd] 形 快的、hasten [`hesn̩] 動 催促、hurry [`hɝɪ] 動 趕緊、quicken [`kwɪkən] 動 加快、speed up 片 加速
動詞三態變化 accelerate - accelerated - accelerated

---

accent [`æksɛnt] 名 口音　　　　　　　　　　　　　　　　○ MP3 **01-03**
▶ Judging by his accent, he is no local. 從他的口音判斷，他絕不是當地人。

---

accept [ək`sɛpt] 動 接受
▶ I feel so bad. Please accept my apology.
我感到很抱歉，請接受我的道歉。
相關衍生字彙 acceptance [ək`sɛptəns] 名 接受，贊同，承認、accepted [ək`sɛptɪd] 形 公認的
動詞三態變化 accept - accepted - accepted

acceptable [ək'sɛptəbl] 形 可接受的
▶ The dancer's performance was not very outstanding, just acceptable.
這舞者的表現沒有非常傑出，只是可接受而已。

access ['æksɛs] 名 接近，通道
▶ The only access to the village on the small island is by boat.
唯一能通往小島上小村落的管道是搭小船。

accessible [æk'sɛsəbl] 形 易得到的，易接近的
▶ Dangerous stuff should not be kept where it is accessible to little kids.
危險的東西不應放在小孩子容易拿到的地方。

accessory [æk'sɛsərɪ] 名 配件，飾品
▶ My sunglasses are my fashion accessory.
我的太陽眼鏡是我的時尚飾品。

相關衍生字彙 necklace ['nɛklɪs] 名 項鍊、bracelet ['breslɪt] 名 手鐲、scarf [skɑrf] 名 圍巾、earrings ['ɪr.rɪŋ] 名 耳環、ring [rɪŋ] 名 戒指、necktie ['nɛk.taɪ] 名 領帶

accident ['æksədənt] 名 意外事件　　片 by accident 意外地

accidental [.æksə'dɛntl] 形 意外的　　　片 accidental death 意外死亡
相關衍生字彙 accidentally [.æksə'dɛntlɪ] 副 偶然地，意外地、accident-prone ['æksədənt.pron] 形 特別容易出事故的、unintentional 形 非故意的，偶然的、unintended [.ʌnɪn'tɛndɪd] 形 非計畫中的，非故意的、unpremeditated [.ʌnprɪ'mɛdə.tetɪd] 形 偶然的，無預謀的

acclaim [ə'klem] 動 為〜歡呼，喝采，讚美
▶ The scientific community acclaimed Marie Curie's achievement.
科學界為居禮夫人的成就喝采。

動詞三態變化 acclaim - acclaimed - acclaimed

accommodate [ə'kɑmə.det] 動 容納，供宿
▶ The new dormitory can accommodate more than five hundred students.
這棟新宿舍可容納超過五百位學生。

動詞三態變化 accommodate - accommodated - accommodated

accommodation [ə.kɑmə'deʃən] 名 住處，膳宿
▶ You had better call the hotel for accommodations in advance.
你最好事先打電話跟飯店確認住宿。

相關衍生字彙 apartment [ə'pɑrtmənt] 名 公寓、dormitory ['dɔrmə.torɪ] 名 宿舍、building ['bɪldɪŋ] 名 建築物、house [haus] 名 房子

accompany [ə'kʌmpənɪ] 動 陪伴，伴隨
▶ Sadness is often accompanied by depression.
悲傷常常伴隨著沮喪。

動詞三態變化 accompany - accompanied - accompanied

accomplish [əˋkɑmplɪʃ] 動 完成，實現，達到
▶ The teacher asked her students to accomplish the task in two hours.
老師要求她的學生在兩小時之內完成任務。
動詞三態變化 accomplish - accomplished - accomplished

accomplishment [əˋkɑmplɪʃmənt] 名 成就
▶ The invention of vaccine is quite an accomplishment.
疫苗的發明是個了不起的成就。
相關衍生字彙 achievement [əˋtʃivmənt] 名 成就、success [səkˋsɛs] 名 成功、attainment [əˋtenmənt] 名 成就、contribution [͵kɑntrəˋbjuʃən] 名 貢獻、feat [fit] 名 豐功偉業

accord [əˋkɔrd] 動 符合，一致
▶ Parents' opinions do not always accord with their children's.
父母的意見並不總是跟孩子一致。
動詞三態變化 accord - accorded - accorded

accordance [əˋkɔrdəns] 名 一致性　　片 in accordance with 與～一致

according [əˋkɔrdɪŋ] 形 相符的　　片 according to 根據～

accordingly [əˋkɔrdɪŋlɪ] 副 因此
▶ Mark didn't feel good yesterday. Accordingly, he canceled all the meetings.
馬克昨天身體不適，因此取消所有會議。
相關衍生字彙 thus [ðʌs] 副 因此、therefore [ˋðɛr͵for] 副 因此、consequently [ˋkɑnsə͵kwɛntlɪ] 副 因此、hence [hɛns] 副 因此

account [əˋkaunt] 名 帳戶　　片 to open an account 開戶

accountant [əˋkauntənt] 名 會計人員
▶ The accountant helps our company keep and check financial accounts.
這位會計師幫我們公司記帳並核對財務。

accredit [əˋkrɛdɪt] 動 歸功於，授權　　　　　MP3 01-04
▶ The new university has been accredited by the Ministry of Education in Taiwan.
這間新大學已獲台灣教育部的認可。
相關衍生字彙 authorize [ˋɔθə͵raɪz] 動 授權、assign [əˋsaɪn] 動 指派、authorization [͵ɔθərəˋzeʃən] 名 授權，批准、credit [ˋkrɛdɪt] 名 信用，功勞
動詞三態變化 accredit - accredited - accredited

accumulate [əˋkjumjə͵let] 動 累積
▶ With the help of computers, it's easier to accumulate a huge mass of data.
有電腦的幫助，累積大量數據變得容易多了。

相關衍生字彙 accumulator [əˋkjumjuˏletɚ] 名 積累者，聚財者、
accumulation [əkjumjəˋleʃən] 名 積聚，堆積

動詞三態變化 accumulate - accumulated - accumulated

accuracy [ˋækjərəsɪ] 名 精準度
▶ The public questioned the accuracy of the news. 大眾質疑這則新聞的精確度。

accurate [ˋækjərɪt] 形 準確的，精準的
▶ The witness gave the police an accurate description.
這位目擊者給警方精準的描述。

相關衍生字彙 perfect [ˋpɝfɪkt] 形 完美的、correct [kəˋrɛkt] 形 正確的、incorrect [ˏɪnkəˋrɛkt]
形 不正確的、wrong [rɔŋ] 形 錯誤的、false [fɔls] 形 錯的、mistake [mɪˋstek]
名 錯誤

accuse [əˋkjuz] 動 指控   片 to accuse somebody of 控訴某人犯了～
相關衍生字彙 accuser [əˋkjuzɚ] 名 原告，控告者、accusingly [əˋkjuzɪŋlɪ]
副 責難地，指責地、accusation [ˏækjəˋzeʃən] 名 指控，控告、
accusatory [əˋkjuzəˏtorɪ] 形 非難的，指控的、accused [əˋkjuzd] 名 被告
形 被控告的

動詞三態變化 accuse - accused - accused

accustom [əˋkʌstəm] 動 使習慣於～   片 accustom oneself to 使自己習慣於～

accustomed [əˋkʌstəmd] 形 熟悉的，習慣的
片 get / become accustomed to 漸漸習慣於～
同 get used to 逐漸習慣於

ace [es] 名 (骰子的) 么點   片 an ace in the hole 最後的王牌

ache [ek] 名 疼痛
▶ As we get older, we may have all kinds of aches and pains.
隨著我們年紀的增長，有可能會有很多痠痛。

achieve [əˋtʃiv] 動 完成，達到
▶ To achieve her objectives, Anita practices day and night.
為了達到她的目標，安妮塔日以繼夜地練習。

achievement [əˋtʃivmənt] 名 成就   片 sense of achievement 成就感
相關衍生字彙 complete [kəmˋplit] 動 完成、terminate [ˋtɝməˏnet] 動 終結、finish [ˋfɪnɪʃ]
動 完成、conclude [kənˋklud] 動 下結論

acid [ˋæsɪd] 形 酸的   同 sour [ˋsaur] 形 酸的
相關衍生字彙 acidity [əˋsɪdətɪ] 名 酸味，酸性、acidulate [əˋsɪdʒəˏlet] 動 使酸化，使尖刻、
acidulous [əˋsɪdʒələs] 形 微酸的，尖刻的

acknowledge [əkˋnɑlɪdʒ] 動 公認，承認
▶ Mandela was acknowledged as a hero in South Africa.
在南非，曼德拉被公認為英雄。
相關衍生字彙 acknowledgement [əkˋnɑlɪdʒmənt] 名 承認，致謝、
acknowledged [əkˋnɑlɪdʒd] 形 公認的
動詞三態變化 acknowledge - acknowledged - acknowledged

acne [ˋæknɪ] 名 粉刺，面皰
▶ Many teenagers are annoyed by acne on the face.
很多年輕人為臉上的青春痘感到困擾。

acquaint [əˋkwent] 動 使認識　　片 be acquainted with 認識～
動詞三態變化 acquaint - acquainted - acquainted

acquaintance [əˋkwentəns] 名 熟識的人
▶ The professor has many acquaintances in the academic circle.
這位教授在學術圈有很多熟識的人。

acquire [əˋkwaɪr] 動 獲得
▶ I acquire a large number of vocabularies by reading novels.
藉由讀小説，我獲得龐大的單字量。
相關衍生字彙 gain [gen] 動 獲得、obtain [əbˋten] 動 獲得、miss [mɪs] 動 失去、
inquire [ɪnˋkwaɪr] 動 詢問、enquire [ɪnˋkwaɪr] 動 查詢
動詞三態變化 acquire - acquired - acquired

acquisition [ˌækwəˋzɪʃən] 名 獲得
▶ A good student should devote his time to the acquisition of knowledge.
好學生應該投入時間於知識的獲得。

across [əˋkrɔs] 介 跨過
▶ Don't run across the street. It's too dangerous.
千萬不要用跑的穿越街道，太危險了。
相關衍生字彙 cross [krɔs] 動 越過、through [θru] 介 穿越、below [bəˋlo] 介 在～下方、
above [əˋbʌv] 介 在～上方

act [ækt] 動 扮演，行動　　片 to act as 擔任～
動詞三態變化 act - acted - acted

action [ˋækʃən] 名 行動　　片 to take action 採取行動　　◎ MP3 01-05

activate [ˋæktəˌvet] 動 使活絡
▶ The teacher tries various ways to activate her students to learn.
這位老師嘗試各種方式激勵她的學生去學習。
動詞三態變化 activate - activated - activated

active [`æktɪv] 形 活潑的
▶ My grandma is ninety years old, but she is still active.
　我奶奶已經九十歲，但她仍舊很活躍。
相關衍生字彙 energetic [ˌɛnɚ`dʒɛtɪk] 形 精力旺盛的、vigorous [`vɪgərəs] 形 體力充沛的、
　　　dynamic [daɪ`næmɪk] 形 生氣勃勃的、inactive [ɪn`æktɪv] 形 不活動的、
　　　lifeless [`laɪflɪs] 形 死氣沉沉的

activity [æk`tɪvətɪ] 名 活動，活動力　　片 parent-child activity 親子活動
相關衍生字彙 activist [`æktəvɪst] 名 行動主義者、actor [`æktɚ] 名 男演員，行動者、
　　　actress [`æktrɪs] 名 女演員

actual [`æktʃʊəl] 形 實際的
▶ The actual cost of the product is not high. 這產品的實際成本不高。

actually [`æktʃʊəlɪ] 副 事實上　　同 in fact / in reality 事實上

acupuncture [`ækjuˌpʌŋktʃɚ] 名 針灸
▶ Acupuncture, one special skill of Chinese medicine, is often used to stop pain.
　針灸是中醫的一種特殊療法，常用於止痛。

acute [ə`kjut] 形 尖銳的，急性的　　片 acute triangle 銳角三角形

adapt [ə`dæpt] 動 改寫，使適應　　片 adapt oneself to 適應～
▶ The author is adapting his novel for a drama.
　作家正在為一部戲劇改寫他的小說。
相關衍生字彙 adept [ə`dɛpt] 形 擅長的、adopt [ə`dɑpt] 動 採納，收養、adjust [ə`dʒʌst] 動 調整以適應～
動詞三態變化 adapt - adapted - adapted

add [æd] 動 增加　　片 to add up to 加起來總共～
動詞三態變化 add - added - added

addict [ə`dɪkt] 動 使醉心，使沉迷　　片 be addicted to 沉迷於～
動詞三態變化 addict - addicted - addicted

addictive [ə`dɪktɪv] 形 成癮的，沉迷的
▶ More and more youth are addictive to smartphones.
　愈來愈多年輕人使用智慧手機而成癮。

addition [ə`dɪʃən] 名 額外，附加　　片 in addition 此外 / in addition to 除～之外

additional [ə`dɪʃənl̩] 形 額外的
▶ If your luggage is overweight, you have to pay an additional charge.
　如果你的行李超重，你得付額外的費用。
相關衍生字彙 additionally [ə`dɪʃən̩lɪ] 副 此外、besides [bɪ`saɪdz] 副 此外、
　　　moreover [mor`ovɚ] 副 再者、furthermore [`fɝðɚˌmor] 副 再者

address [əˋdrɛs] 名 住址
▶ Please remember to write down your home address on the envelope.
請記得在信封上寫下你的住址。

adequate [ˋædəkwɪt] 形 足夠的
▶ Without adequate proof, you can't charge the kid with cheating on the exam.
沒有足夠的證據，你不可以指控這孩子考試作弊。

adhere [ədˋhɪr] 動 堅持，黏附
▶ Facing difficulties, Mark still adheres to his dream.
雖然面對困難，馬克仍堅持他的夢想。

相關衍生字彙 insist [ɪnˋsɪst] 動 堅持、emphasize [ˋɛmfə.saɪz] 動 強調、stubborn [ˋstʌbən] 形 固執的、determined [dɪˋtɜmɪnd] 形 堅決的、decision [dɪˋsɪʒən] 名 決心、impatient [ɪmˋpeʃənt] 形 沒有耐心的

動詞三態變化 adhere - adhered - adhered

adjacent [əˋdʒesənt] 形 鄰接的
▶ There are three department stores on the two adjacent roads.
在這兩條鄰接的路上共有三間百貨公司。

adjourn [əˋdʒɜn] 動 休會，延期
▶ I suggest that we adjourn the meeting and gather more data for discussion.
我建議暫停會議再收集更多資料來討論。

動詞三態變化 adjourn - adjourned - adjourned

adjust [əˋdʒʌst] 動 調整，適應
▶ After migrating to America, I have to adjust myself to the English environment.
在移民到美國之後，我得調整自己適應英語環境。

相關衍生字彙 regulate [ˋrɛgjə.let] 動 調整、revise [rɪˋvaɪz] 動 校訂、change [tʃendʒ] 動 改變、improve [ɪmˋpruv] 動 改善、alter [ˋɔltə] 動 改變、modify [ˋmɑdə.faɪ] 動 更改

動詞三態變化 adjust - adjusted - adjusted

adjustment [əˋdʒʌstmənt] 名 調整
🅟 to make an adjustment 做調整

administer [ədˋmɪnəstə] 動 經營，管理
▶ To administer the company, the CEO works day and night.
為經營公司，這位執行長日夜操勞。

動詞三態變化 administer - administered - administered

administration [əd.mɪnəˋstreʃən] 名 經營管理
🅟 business administration 企業管理

相關衍生字彙 administrative [ədˋmɪnə.stretɪv] 形 管理的，行政的、administrator [ədˋmɪnə.stretə] 名 管理人，行政官員

admirable [ˋædmərəb]] 形 值得讚美的
▶ The soldiers' loyalties are admirable. 這些士兵的忠心是值得讚美的。

admiration [ˌædməˋreʃən] 名 讚美
▶ The king felt great admiration for his general's courage.
國王十分讚美將軍的勇氣。

admire [ədˋmaɪr] 動 讚美　　片 to admire greatly 大大地讚美
相關衍生字彙 compliment [ˋkɑmpləmənt] 名 恭維，讚美、praise [prez] 名 讚美、flatter [ˋflætɚ] 動 巴結奉承、self-admiration [ˌsɛlfædməˋreʃən] 名 自負
動詞三態變化 admire - admired - admired

admission [ədˋmɪʃən] 名 入學許可，入場許可
▶ Victoria applied for admission to three top universities.
維多利亞向三所名校申請入學許可。

admit [ədˋmɪt] 動 承認
▶ Mark and Alice admitted cheerfully that they were married.
馬克和艾莉絲高興地承認他們已經結婚了。
動詞三態變化 admit - admitted - admitted

admonish [ədˋmɑnɪʃ] 動 告誡
▶ Those who like to bully others should be admonished.
那些喜歡霸凌他人的人應該被告誡。
動詞三態變化 admonish - admonished - admonished

adolescence [ˌædḷˋɛsns̩] 名 青春期　　同 teenage [ˋtinˌedʒ] 名 青少年

adopt [əˋdɑpt] 動 採納，收養
▶ After discussion, the boss finally decided to adopt the employees' suggestion.
經過討論，老闆終於決定採納員工的建議。
相關衍生字彙 accept [əkˋsɛpt] 動 接受、use [juz] 動 使用、adept [əˋdɛpt] 形 熟練的、adapt [əˋdæpt] 動 使適應
動詞三態變化 adopt - adopted - adopted

adore [əˋdor] 動 崇拜
▶ The public adore the president for his leadership.
老百姓崇拜這位總統的領導能力。
相關衍生字彙 adorable [əˋdorəb]] 形 值得崇拜的、adoration [ˌædəˋreʃən] 名 崇拜，敬愛、adoring [əˋdorɪŋ] 形 崇拜的，愛慕的
動詞三態變化 adore - adored - adored

adult [əˋdʌlt] 名 成人　　反 juvenile [ˋdʒuvənḷ] 名 青少年

adulterated [ə`dʌltəˌretɪd] 形 摻雜的
▶ The consumers complained the wine seemed to be adulterated with water.
消費者抱怨這酒似乎摻了水。

adulthood [ə`dʌlthʊd] 名 成年期　　片 to reach adulthood 達到成年期
相關衍生字彙 kid [kɪd] 名 小孩、boy [bɔɪ] 名 男孩、girl [gɝl] 名 女孩、youth [juθ] 名 青年、
under age 片 未成年、elder [`ɛldɚ] 名 長者

advance [əd`væns] 副 前進，進展　　片 in advance 事先地

advanced [əd`vænst] 形 先進的
▶ Germany is advanced in industrial development. 德國在工業發展方面很先進。

advantage [əd`væntɪdʒ] 名 好處，長處　　片 to take advantage of 利用～

advantageous [ˌædvən`tedʒəs] 形 有利的，有助益的
▶ The policy is highly advantageous to the poorer families.
這項政策對較為貧窮的家庭極為有益。
相關衍生字彙 disadvantage [ˌdɪsəd`væntɪdʒ] 名 缺點，害處、drawback [`drɔˌbæk] 名 缺點、
handicap [`hændɪˌkæp] 名 障礙、benefit [`bɛnəfɪt] 名 利益、profit [`prɑfɪt]
名 利潤

adventure [əd`vɛntʃɚ] 名 冒險
▶ Bill plans to set out on an adventure during the summer vacation.
比爾打算暑假出發去冒險。
相關衍生字彙 adventurer [əd`vɛntʃərɚ] 名 冒險者、adventurous [əd`vɛntʃərəs]
形 大膽的，愛冒險的

advertise [`ædvɚˌtaɪz] 動 登廣告　　　　　　　　　　　　　　🔘 MP3 01-07
▶ To promote their new products, the company advertised extensively in
newspapers.
為了促銷新產品，公司在報紙上大規模打廣告。
動詞三態變化 advertise- advertised - advertised

advertisement [ˌædvɚ`taɪzmənt] 名 廣告
片 a classified advertisement 分類廣告

advice [əd`vaɪs] 名 忠告，意見　　片 to take advice 接受忠告
相關衍生字彙 opinion [ə`pɪnjən] 名 意見、view [vju] 名 觀點、sight [saɪt] 名 視力，看法、
vision [`vɪʒən] 名 願景、perception [pɚ`sɛpʃən] 名 看法、
suggestion [sə`dʒɛstʃən] 名 建議、advise [əd`vaɪz] 動 勸告，忠告、
advisor [əd`vaɪzɚ] 名 顧問

advocate [`ædvəkɪt] 名 倡導者
▶ She has been a famous advocate for female rights.
她一直是女權的倡導者。

aerobic [eə`robɪk] 形 有氧運動的　　片 aerobic exercise 有氧運動

aeronautics [ˌɛrə`nɔtɪks] 名 航空學
▶ John has been interested in aircraft, so he decides to major in aeronautics.
約翰一直對飛行器感興趣，所以他決定主修航空學。
相關衍生字彙 aeronautic [ˌɛrə`nɔtɪk] 形 航空學的、aeroplane [`ɛrəˌplen] 名 飛機

aesthetic [ɛs`θɛtɪk] 名 美學 形 美學的
▶ From an aesthetic point of view, the building is a work of art.
以美學的角度來看，這棟建築物是個藝術品。
相關衍生字彙 philosophy [fə`lɑsəfɪ] 名 哲學、anthropology [ˌænθrə`pɑlədʒɪ] 名 人類學、archeology [ˌɑrkɪ`ɑlədʒɪ] 名 考古學、literature [`lɪtərətʃə] 名 文學、geology [dʒɪ`ɑlədʒɪ] 名 地質學、biology [baɪ`ɑlədʒɪ] 名 生物學

affable [`æfəbl] 形 親切友善的　　同 friendly [`frɛndlɪ] 形 友善的

affair [ə`fɛr] 名 事件，事務，風流韻事　　片 state of affairs 局勢

affect [ə`fɛkt] 動 影響
▶ Education can affect a child deeply.
教育會深深影響一個孩子。
動詞三態變化 affect - affected - affected

affection [ə`fɛkʃən] 名 影響，愛慕，感情
▶ Men often show their affection for girls by sending them flowers.
男生常常藉由送花給女生來表達愛意。

affectionate [ə`fɛkʃənɪt] 形 深情的，溫柔多情的
片 an affectionate kiss 深情一吻
相關衍生字彙 love [lʌv] 名 愛情、emotion [ɪ`moʃən] 名 感情、passion [`pæʃən] 名 熱情、enthusiasm [ɪn`θjuzɪˌæzəm] 名 熱忱、eagerness [`igənɪs] 名 熱切，渴望、friendship [`frɛndʃɪp] 名 友誼

affiliate [ə`fɪlɪˌet] 動 聯合，合作，加入
片 to become affiliated with 成為（會員），加入～
動詞三態變化 affiliate - affiliated - affiliated

affirm [ə`fɝm] 動 確認，斷言
▶ The lady was affirmed as the candidate for the next president.
這位女士被證實將為下任總統之候選人。
相關衍生字彙 affirmation [ˌæfə`meʃən] 名 斷言，證實、affirmative [ə`fɝmətɪv] 形 肯定的
動詞三態變化 affirm - affirmed - affirmed

afflict [əˋflɪkt] 動 使折磨，使痛苦
▶ Thousands of people in West Africa were afflicted with Ebola.
西非數以千計的人民受伊波拉病毒之苦。
動詞三態變化 afflict - afflicted - afflicted

affluent [ˋæfluənt] 形 富裕的
▶ The country is affluent in minerals. 這個國家有豐富的礦產。

afford [əˋford] 動 負擔得起，供得起
▶ On his salary, he can't afford a new house.
以他的薪水，他不可能買得起新房子。
相關衍生字彙 affordable [əˋfordəbḷ] 形 負擔的起的、offer [ˋɔfɚ] 動 供應、provide [prəˋvaɪd] 動 提供、supply [səˋplaɪ] 動 供應
動詞三態變化 afford - afforded - afforded

affray [əˋfre] 名（在公共場所）打群架，鬧事   片 to cause an affray 引發口角

affront [əˋfrʌnt] 動 冒犯
▶ I felt affronted by his dirty words.
他的髒話讓我覺得被冒犯。
動詞三態變化 affront - affronted - affronted

afraid [əˋfred] 形 害怕的   片 be afraid of 害怕～
相關衍生字彙 fear [fɪr] 動 害怕、scared [skɛrd] 形 害怕的、frightened [ˋfraɪtṇd] 形 受到驚嚇的、unafraid [ˌʌnəˋfred] 形 無畏的

afterwards [ˋæftɚwɚdz] 副 之後   ◎ MP3 01-08
▶ They got engaged, and got married 3 weeks afterwards.
他們先訂婚，然後三週後就結婚了。

agency [ˋedʒənsɪ] 名 代理機構
片 an advertisement / travel / employment agency 廣告商、旅行社、職業介紹所

agenda [əˋdʒɛndə] 名 議程，流程
片 to draw up a meeting agenda 擬定會議流程

agent [ˋedʒənt] 名 代理人   片 an estate agent 房地產經紀人

aggregate [ˋægrɪˌget] 動 聚集，總計達～
▶ The audience of the concert aggregated more than ten thousand people.
這場音樂會的聽眾總計達上萬人。
動詞三態變化 aggregate - aggregated - aggregated

aggressive [əˋgrɛsɪv] 形 侵犯的，企圖心強的，有進取心的
▶ Boys tend to be more aggressive than girls.
男孩比起女孩較具攻擊性。

相關衍生字彙 offensive [ə`fɛnsɪv] 形 冒犯的、aggressively [ə`grɛsɪvlɪ] 副 企圖心強地、aggressiveness [ə`grɛsɪvnɪs] 名 侵犯、ambitious [æm`bɪʃəs] 形 有企圖心的

aggrieved [ə`grivd] 形 委屈的，不滿的
▶ The customer complained with an aggrieved tone of voice.
這位客人以委屈的口吻抱怨著。

agitate [`ædʒə͵tet] 動 煽動
▶ All of the workers in the factory were agitating strongly for reform.
這工廠的工人激烈鼓吹改革。
動詞三態變化 agitate - agitated - agitated

agony [`ægənɪ] 名 痛苦　　片 in great agony 非常痛苦地

agree [ə`gri] 動 同意　　片 to agree completely 完全同意
相關衍生字彙 disagree [͵dɪsə`gri] 動 不同意、comply [kəm`plaɪ] 動 順從、refuse [rɪ`fjuz] 動 拒絕、reject [rɪ`dʒɛkt] 動 拒絕、consent [kən`sɛnt] 動 同意
動詞三態變化 agreed - agreed - agreed

agreeable [ə`griəbl̩] 形 令人愉悅的
▶ Roses give off an agreeable odor. 玫瑰釋放令人愉悅的氣味。

agreement [ə`grimənt] 名 協定，契約　　片 to reach an agreement 達成協議

agricultural [͵ægrɪ`kʌltʃərəl] 形 農業的　　片 agricultural products 農產品

agriculture [`ægrɪ͵kʌltʃɚ] 名 農業
▶ Agriculture plays an important part in the economy of Taiwan.
農業在台灣經濟方面扮演重要角色。

ahead [ə`hɛd] 副 事先，預先　　同 in advance 提前

aid [ed] 名 幫助　　片 first aid 急救

aim [em] 名 目標 動 瞄準
▶ To realize her aim, Anita devoted all her time to music.
為實現她的目標，安妮塔投入所有的時間在音樂領域。
相關衍生字彙 goal [gol] 名 目標、destination [͵dɛstə`neʃən] 名 目的地、finish [`fɪnɪʃ] 名 終點、aimless [`emlɪs] 形 無目的的、purpose [`pɝpəs] 名 目的，意圖、intention [ɪn`tɛnʃən] 名 意向，目的
動詞三態變化 aim - aimed - aimed

air-conditioner 片 空調設備
片 to turn on / off an air-conditioner 打開／關掉空調（冷氣）

aircraft [`ɛr͵kræft] 名 航空器，飛機　　片 military / enemy aircraft 軍機／敵機

airline [ˋɛrͺlaɪn] 名 航線
片 a domestic / an international airline 國內航線／國際航線
相關衍生字彙 airplane [ˋɛrͺplen] 名 飛機、airport [ˋɛrͺport] 名 機場、airmail [ˋɛrͺmel] 名 航空郵件、flight attendant 片 空服員、airway [ˋɛrͺwe] 名 航線

---

airtight [ˋɛrͺtaɪt] 形 密閉的　　　　　　○ MP3 01-09
▶ An airtight container can keep food fresh. 這密封的容器可保食物新鮮。

---

aisle [aɪl] 名 通道　　片 an aisle seat（飛機上的）靠走道位置

---

alarm [əˋlɑrm] 名 警報器，鬧鐘
▶ To go to work on time, I set my alarm to go off at six in the morning.
為了能準時上班，我把鬧鐘設定在早上六點。

---

album [ˋælbəm] 名 唱片專輯，相簿，黏貼簿　　片 a stamp album 集郵簿

---

alcohol [ˋælkəͺhɔl] 名 酒精
▶ The beer contains only 2% alcohol. 這啤酒只含百分之二的酒精成分。

---

alert [əˋlɝt] 形 警覺的，機敏的
▶ Parents should keep alert to their children's words and behavior.
父母應該對子女的言行保持警覺性。
相關衍生字彙 watchful [ˋwɑtʃfəl] 形 警惕的、nimble [ˋnɪmbḷ] 形 敏捷的、dormant [ˋdɔrmənt] 形 靜止的，休眠的

---

algebra [ˋældʒəbrə] 名 代數
▶ David is good at mathematics, especially algebra.
大衛的數學很厲害，尤其是代數。

---

alien [ˋeliən] 形 陌生的，外國的 名 僑民，外星人
▶ When I studied abroad for the first time, it was all alien to me.
當我第一次出國念書時，一切對我都是陌生的。

---

alienate [ˋeljənͺet] 動 使疏遠
▶ Generation gap alienates teenagers from their parents.
代溝使青少年與他們的父母產生了疏離感。
動詞三態變化 alienate - alienated - alienated

---

alight [əˋlaɪt] 動（從飛機、馬背、車～等）下來
▶ After the bus stopped at the last stop, all the passengers alighted.
公車停在終點站後，所有的乘客都下車。
動詞三態變化 alight - alighted - alighted

---

allege [əˋlɛdʒ] 動 宣稱，據說
▶ A newspaper article alleged that the police had caught the murderer.
報紙宣稱警方已經逮捕殺人犯了。

相關衍生字彙 allegation [͵ælə`geʃən] 名 主張，斷言、allegedly [ə`lɛdʒɪdlɪ] 副 據宣稱，劇傳說

動詞三態變化 allege - alleged - alleged

allegiance [ə`lidʒəns] 名 忠誠　　片 to swear allegiance to 宣誓效忠於～

allergic [ə`lɝdʒɪk] 形 過敏的

▶ She is allergic to seafood. 她對海鮮過敏。

allergy [`ælɚdʒɪ] 名 過敏　　片 to have an allergy to 對～過敏

alleviate [ə`livɪ͵et] 動 減緩

▶ He took painkillers to alleviate his headache.
他服用止痛劑減緩他的頭痛。

相關衍生字彙 abate [ə`bet] 動 減輕、reduce [rɪ`djus] 動 減少、lessen [`lɛsn̩] 動 減少、decrease [dɪ`kris] 動 減少、relieve [rɪ`liv] 動 緩和

動詞三態變化 alleviate - alleviated - alleviated

alley [`ælɪ] 名 巷子，（保齡球）球道　　片 a blind alley 死胡同

alliance [ə`laɪəns] 名 聯盟　　片 a military alliance 軍事同盟

allocate [`ælə͵ket] 動 配置，分配

▶ The charity allocated food and clothes to the needy and the homeless.
這慈善機構將食物與衣物分配給窮困和無家可歸的人。

動詞三態變化 allocate - allocated - allocated

allot [ə`lɑt] 動 分配，撥給

▶ Every students was allotted ten minutes to make an English speech.
每個學生被分配十分鐘做英語演講。

動詞三態變化 allot - allotted - allotted

allow [ə`lau] 動 允許

▶ Smoking is not allowed on campus.
校園是禁菸的。

相關衍生字彙 disallow [͵dɪsə`lau] 動 不許，駁回、permit [pɚ`mɪt] 動 允許、forbid [fɚ`bɪd] 動 禁止，阻止、prohibit [prə`hɪbɪt] 動（以法令、規定等）禁止

動詞三態變化 allow - allowed - allowed

allowance [ə`lauəns] 名 津貼，零用錢　　◎MP3 01-10

片 an education / housing allowance 教育／房屋津貼

allude [ə`lud] 動 暗指，間接指出

▶ The novel alluded to the author's childhood.
這部小說間接描述出作者的童年。

動詞三態變化 allude - alluded - alluded

allure [əˋlur] 名 魅力 動 引誘
▶ He enjoyed sailing. He said he couldn't resist the allure of the sea.
　他很喜歡航行，他説他無法抗拒大海的誘惑。
相關衍生字彙 allurement [əˋlurmənt] 名 誘惑，吸引、alluring [əˋlurɪŋ] 形 誘人的，迷人的
動詞三態變化 allure - allured - allured

allusion [əˋluʒən] 名 影射，提及　　片 to make an allusion to 提及～

ally [əˋlaɪ] 動 使聯盟 名 同盟
▶ North Korea allied itself with Mainland China. They are political ally.
　北韓與中國結盟。他們是政治同盟。
動詞三態變化 ally - allied - allied

almighty [ɔlˋmaɪtɪ] 形 全能的　　片 the Lord Almighty 上帝

aloof [əˋluf] 形 冷漠的，遠離的　　片 to keep aloof from 遠離～
相關衍生字彙 aloft [əˋlɔft] 副 在上面，在空中、alone [əˋlon] 形 只有，獨自的 副 單獨地、
　　　　　　along [əˋlɔŋ] 介 沿著，順著

aloud [əˋlaud] 副 大聲地
▶ The teacher read the story to the kids vividly and aloud.
　老師生動又大聲地朗讀故事給孩子們聽。

alphabet [ˋælfəˌbɛt] 名 字母系統
▶ The English alphabet has 26 letters.
　英文字母一共有二十六個。
相關衍生字彙 letter [ˋlɛtɚ] 名 字母，信件、phonetics [foˋnɛtɪks] 名 語音學、stress [strɛs]
　　　　　　名 重音、syllable [ˋsɪləb]] 名 音節、vowel [ˋvauəl] 名 母音、
　　　　　　consonant [ˋkɑnsənənt] 名 子音

alter [ˋɔltɚ] 動 改變　　同 change [tʃendʒ] 動 改變
相關衍生字彙 altar [ˋɔltɚ] 名（教堂內的）聖壇，祭壇、alteration [ˌɔltəˋreʃən] 名 改變，修改
動詞三態變化 alter - altered - altered

alternate [ˋɔltɚˌnet] 動 交替，輪流
▶ According to the weather forecast, sunny weather will alternate with rain next week.
　根據氣象報告，下周會晴雨交替。
相關衍生字彙 alternately [ˋɔltɚnɪtlɪ] 副 交替地，輪流地、switch [swɪtʃ]
　　　　　　動 使轉換，改變，轉移、interchange [ˌɪntɚˋtʃendʒ] 動 交換，輪流進行
動詞三態變化 alternate - alternated - alternated

alternative [ɔlˋtɝnətɪv] 名 選擇，二擇一選項
片 to have no alternative but to V 除～別無選擇

相關衍生字彙 choice [tʃɔɪs] 名 選擇、option [`ɑpʃən] 名 選擇、elective [ɪ`lɛktɪv] 形 選舉的，選修的、either [`iðɚ] 形 代（兩者之中）任一個

although [ɔl`ðo] 連 雖然，儘管　　同 despite the fact that + 子句 儘管

altitude [`æltəˌtjud] 名 高度，海拔
▶ The captain broadcast that we were flying at an altitude of 12,000 meters.
機長廣播我們正在海拔一萬兩千公尺高。

altogether [ˌɔltə`gɛðɚ] 副 完全，總之
▶ It's all right making friends with him, but marrying him will be a different matter altogether.
跟他做朋友可以，可是嫁給他是另外一件完全不同的事。

altruistic [ˌæltru`ɪstɪk] 形 利他的
▶ The rich man is so altruistic that he often donates money to charities.
這位富翁是如此無私，他常常捐錢給慈善機構。

always [`ɔlwez] 副 總是　　片 not always 並不總是
相關衍生字彙 usually [`juʒʊəlɪ] 副 經常、often [`ɔfən] 副 常常、seldom [`sɛldəm] 副 很少、sometimes [`sʌmˌtaɪmz] 副 有時候、never [`nɛvɚ] 副 從不

amass [ə`mæs] 動 累積
▶ J.K. Rowling has amassed a huge fortune by writing her novels.
J. K. 羅琳藉著寫小說而累積大量財富。
動詞三態變化 amass - amassed - amassed

amateur [`æmətˌʃur] 形 業餘的 名 業餘愛好者
片 an amateur photographer 業餘攝影師

amaze [ə`mez] 動 使驚訝　　片 be amazed at 對～感到驚訝
動詞三態變化 amaze - amazed - amazed

amazement [ə`mezmənt] 名 驚訝
MP3 01-11
片 to one's amazement 令某人驚訝的是
相關衍生字彙 amazing [ə`mezɪŋ] 形 驚人的、surprising [sɚ`praɪzɪŋ] 形 出人意外的、astonishing [ə`stɑnɪʃɪŋ] 形 令人吃驚的、astounding [ə`staundɪŋ] 形 令人震驚的

ambassador [æm`bæsədɚ] 名 大使
▶ The beautiful girl was elected as Goodwill Ambassador.
這位美麗的女孩被選為親善大使。

ambiance [`æmbɪəns] 名 氛圍，格調
▶ The ambiance of the city is relaxing and romantic.
這座城市的氛圍是輕鬆浪漫的。

ambiguous [æm`bɪgjʊəs] 形 含糊的，模稜兩可的
▶ Regarding the affair, the politician has been giving ambiguous answers.
有關這件緋聞，這名政客的回答一直很含糊。

ambition [æm`bɪʃən] 名 抱負，野心
▶ To become wealthy is his main ambition in life. 追求財富是他人生的主要抱負。

ambitious [æm`bɪʃəs] 形 野心勃勃的，有抱負的
同 aggressive [ə`grɛsɪv] 形 侵略的，好鬥的

ambivalent [æm`bɪvələnt] 形 矛盾的
▶ I felt ambivalent about quitting the job. 對辭掉工作，我有矛盾的心情。

ambulance [`æmbjələns] 名 救護車
▶ By the time an ambulance arrived, the old man was dead.
在救護車到來之前，這老人就去世了。
相關衍生字彙 first aid 片 急救、gauze [gɔz] 名 紗布、bandage [`bændɪdʒ] 名 繃帶

amenable [ə`minəbl] 形 願意的，服從的，肯順從的
片 be amenable to 願意順從～

amend [ə`mɛnd] 動 修訂（法律文件）　　片 to amend the constitution 修改憲法
動詞三態變化 amend - amended - amended

amendment [ə`mɛndmənt] 名 修改
▶ The author insisted that his novel didn't need any amendation.
這名作者堅持認為他的小說不需要做任何的修改。

amenity [ə`minətɪ] 名（舒適的）設施
▶ The hotel provides the amenities for guests. 這飯店提供很多設施給客人。

amiable [`emɪəbl] 形 和藹可親的　　同 friendly [`frɛndlɪ] 形 友好的，親切的

amid [ə`mɪd] 介 在～之中
▶ The small bookstore stands amid many skyscrapers.
這間小書店矗立在高樓大廈之中。
相關衍生字彙 among [ə`mʌŋ] 介 在～之中、across [ə`krɔs] 介 跨過、outside [`aʊt`saɪd] 介 在～之外、inside [`ɪn`saɪd] 介 在～之內、beside [bɪ`saɪd] 介 在～旁邊

amnesty [`æmˌnɛstɪ] 名 特赦　　片 to declare a general amnesty 宣布特赦

amount [ə`maʊnt] 名 數量　　片 to figure out the amount 算出總數

ample [`æmpl] 形 大量的
▶ Join our club. Then you can have ample opportunity to communicate with our professor.
加入我們的社團，你就有充分的機會與我們教授討教。

amuse [ə`mjuz] 動 取悅，娛樂
▶ Apparently, the fairy tale amuses kids a lot.
很顯然地，這童話故事讓孩子們很開心。
相關衍生字彙 amusement [ə`mjuzmənt] 名 娛樂、amusing [ə`mjuzɪŋ] 形 有趣的、
entertain [ˌɛntɚ`ten] 動 使歡樂、entertainment [ˌɛntɚ`tenmənt] 名 娛樂
動詞三態變化 amuse - amused - amused

amputate [`æmpjəˌtet] 動 截肢
▶ To save his life, the doctor decided to amputate his left foot.
為了救他的命，醫生決定將其左腳截肢。
動詞三態變化 amputate - amputated - amputated

analogous [ə`næləgəs] 形 類似的　片 closely analogous 極為相似的

analysis [ə`næləsɪs] 名 分析　片 to make an analysis 作分析　◎ MP3 01-12

analyze [`ænlˌaɪz] 動 分析
▶ Researchers are usually good at analyzing data.
研究人員通常都很擅長分析數據。
動詞三態變化 analyze - analyzed - analyzed

anarchy [`ænɚkɪ] 名 混亂　片 in a state of anarchy 處在混亂狀態

ancestor [`ænsɛstɚ] 名 祖先　反 descendant [dɪ`sɛndənt] 名 子孫
相關衍生字彙 ancient [`enʃənt] 形 古代的、modern [`mɑdɚn] 形 現代的、
grandparents [`grændˌpɛrənts] 名 祖父母、forefather [`forˌfɑðɚ] 名 祖先、
generation [ˌdʒɛnə`reʃən] 名 世代

anchor [`æŋkɚ] 名 錨　片 to drop / cast anchor（船）拋錨停泊

angel [`endʒl̩] 名 天使
片 be on the side of the angels 站在善的／正義的／道德的一邊

anger [`æŋgɚ] 名 憤怒
▶ Albert suddenly felt a lot of anger towards his son's rude behavior.
亞伯特突然對兒子的粗魯行為感到憤怒。

angle [`æŋgl̩] 名 角度　片 an angle of 90 degrees 九十度角

anguish [`æŋgwɪʃ] 名 極度痛苦
▶ Her husband's death caused her great anguish.
她丈夫的死讓她極度痛苦。
相關衍生字彙 pain [pen] 名 痛苦、suffering [`sʌfərɪŋ] 名 苦惱、ache [ek] 名（持續性）疼痛、
hurt [hɝt] 動 傷害

animal [`ænəm]] 名 動物
▶ More and more people pay attention to the issue of animal welfare.
愈來愈多的人注意到動物福祉這個議題。
相關衍生字彙 koala [ko`ɑlə] 名 無尾熊、kangaroo [ˌkæŋgə`ru] 名 袋鼠、camel [`kæm]]
名 駱駝、lion [`laɪən] 名 獅子、tiger [`taɪgɚ] 名 老虎、gorilla [gə`rɪlə] 名 大猩猩、
giraffe [dʒə`ræf] 名 長頸鹿、leopard [`lɛpɚd] 名 美洲豹、panda [`pændə]
名 熊貓、elephant [`ɛləfənt] 名 大象、zebra [`zibrə] 名 斑馬、
monkey [`mʌŋkɪ] 名 猴子、deer [dɪr] 名 鹿、wolf [wulf] 名 狼、bear [bɛr]
名 熊、rhinoceros [raɪ`nɑsərəs] 名 犀牛、hippo [`hɪpo] 名 河馬、horse [hɔrs]
名 馬、sheep [ʃip] 名 綿羊

animate [`ænəˌmet] 動 使活潑，使有生命　片 an animated cartoon 動畫卡通
相關衍生字彙 animated [`ænəˌmetɪd] 形 活生生的，卡通（片）的、animation [ˌænə`meʃən]
名 生氣，活潑，卡通片、vivify [`vɪvəˌfaɪ] 動 （使）有生氣，（使）生動、
enliven [ɪn`laɪvən] 動 使活躍，使快活、invigorate [ɪn`vɪgəˌret]
動 鼓舞，賦予精神
動詞三態變化 animate - animated - animated

animosity [ˌænə`mɑsətɪ] 名 仇恨，敵意　同 hostility [hɑs`tɪlətɪ] 名 敵意，敵視

ankle [`æŋk]] 名 腳踝，踝關節
▶ While he was playing soccer, he fell down and sprained his ankle.
當他踢足球時，他跌倒並扭傷腳踝。
相關衍生字彙 toe [to] 名 腳趾、leg [lɛg] 名 腿、thigh [θaɪ] 名 大腿、finger [`fɪŋgɚ] 名 手指、
arm [ɑrm] 名 手臂、elbow [`ɛlbo] 名 手肘

anniversary [ˌænə`vɝsərɪ] 名 週年紀念　片 wedding anniversary 結婚紀念日

announce [ə`naʊns] 動 宣布
▶ The couple announced their wedding in the newspaper.
這對夫婦在報紙上宣布他們結婚的消息。
動詞三態變化 announce - announced - announced

announcement [ə`naʊnsmənt] 名 公告，宣布
片 to make an announcement 做宣告

annoy [ə`nɔɪ] 動 使惱怒，使煩惱　片 be annoyed with 對～感惱怒
動詞三態變化 annoy - annoyed - annoyed

annoyance [ə`nɔɪəns] 名 煩惱，惱怒
▶ Much to my annoyance, my neighbor's dog often made noise at midnight.
讓我很煩惱的是，鄰居的狗常常在午夜發出噪音。
相關衍生字彙 irritate [`ɪrəˌtet] 動 使煩躁、disturb [dɪs`tɝb] 動 打擾、bother [`bɑðɚ]
動 干擾、calm [kɑm] 動 安撫、comfort [`kʌmfɚt] 動 安慰

annual [`ænjʊəl] 形 一年一次的　片 annual income / salary 年薪

相關衍生字彙 annually [ˈænjʊəlɪ] 副 每年一次、yearly [ˈjɪrlɪ] 形 每年的、perennial [pəˈrɛnɪəl] 形 終年的，長期的

anonymous [əˈnɑnəməs] 形 匿名的
▶ The charity has been supported by an anonymous millionaire.
這個慈善機構一直為一位不具名的富翁所贊助。

anthem [ˈænθəm] 名 聖歌，頌歌　　片 national anthem 國歌　　◎ MP3 01-13

anthropology [ˌænθrəˈpɑlədʒɪ] 名 人類學
▶ Anthropology focuses on the study of the human race, its culture, and society.
人類學主要研究人類及其文化與社會。
相關衍生字彙 anthropological [ˌænθrəpəˈlɑdʒɪk]] 形 人類學的、
anthropologist [ˌænθrəˈpɑlədʒɪst] 名 人類學家

antibiotics [ˌæntɪbaɪˈɑtɪks] 名 抗生素
▶ The patient is taking antibiotics for his infection.
這位病人正服用抗生素治療其傳染病。
相關衍生字彙 antibody [ˈæntɪˌbɑdɪ] 名 抗體

anticipate [ænˈtɪsəˌpet] 動 預期
▶ No one can anticipate how much damage the violent typhoon will do to the small village.
無人能預期強烈颱風會帶給這小村落多大傷害。
相關衍生字彙 expect [ɪkˈspɛkt] 動 期待、foresee [forˈsi] 動 預知、hope [hop] 動 希望、
suppose [səˈpoz] 動 假設、imagine [ɪˈmædʒɪn] 動 想像
動詞三態變化 anticipate - anticipated - anticipated

anticlockwise [ˌæntɪˈklɑkwaɪz] 形 反時鐘方向的
同 counterclockwise [ˌkaʊntɚˈklɑkˌwaɪz] 形 逆時鐘方向的

antidote [ˈæntɪˌdot] 名 解毒劑，解毒藥
▶ Exercise is the best antidote to depression. 運動是憂鬱最好的解藥。

antipathy [ænˈtɪpəθɪ] 名 反感，厭惡
▶ Despite the antipathy between the two countries, they still tried to reach an agreement.
儘管兩國之間有嫌隙，它們仍努力達成協議。
相關衍生字彙 dislike [dɪsˈlaɪk] 動 厭惡、hatred [ˈhetrɪd] 名 厭惡、hate [het] 動 討厭、
hostility [hɑsˈtɪlətɪ] 名 敵意、friendly [ˈfrɛndlɪ] 形 友善的

antique [ænˈtik] 名 古董
▶ The businessman makes a lot of money by collecting and selling antiques.
這名商人藉由收集後轉賣古董而致富。

antiquity [æn`tɪkwətɪ] 名 古代
▶ Socrates is a great man of antiquity. 蘇格拉底是一位古代的偉人。

antonym [`æntə،nɪm] 名 反義字
▶ The antonym of the word "noisy" is "quiet."
「吵雜的」的反義字是「安靜的」。
相關衍生字彙 synonym [`sɪnə،nɪm] 名 同義字、synonymous [sɪ`nɑnəməs] 形 同意義的、
mean [min] 動 意指、meaning [`minɪŋ] 名 意思、definition [،dɛfə`nɪʃən]
名 定義

anxiety [æŋ`zaɪətɪ] 名 焦慮
▶ Most students feel a lot of anxiety before exams.
大部分的學生在考試前都會感到相當焦慮。

anxious [`æŋkʃəs] 形 焦慮的　　**同** worried [`wɝɪd] 形 掛心的

anyhow [`ɛnɪ،haʊ] 副 不論如何　　**同** anyway [`ɛnɪ،we] 副 不論如何

anytime [`ɛnɪ،taɪm] 副 任何時間
▶ When you need help, you can call me anytime.
你需要幫忙時，任何時間都可以打電話給我。
相關衍生字彙 whenever [hwɛn`ɛvɚ] 連 無論什麼時候、invariably [ɪn`vɛrɪəblɪ]
副 不變地，總是、always [`ɔlwez] 副 總是，經常

anywhere [`ɛnɪ،hwɛr] 副 任何地方
▶ Do you plan to go anywhere this summer vacation?
這個暑假你有計劃去哪裡嗎？

apart [ə`pɑrt] 副 分開地　　**片** to take apart 拆開

apartment [ə`pɑrtmənt] 名 公寓
▶ The apartment with three rooms is for sale.
這間三房的公寓正在出售。
相關衍生字彙 house [haʊs] 名 房子、townhouse [`taʊn،haʊs] 名 連棟房屋、
dormitory [`dɔrmə،torɪ] 名 宿舍、home [hom] 名 家、residence [`rɛzədəns]
名 住所

apathy [`æpəθɪ] 名 冷淡
▶ Most students listened to the speech with apathy. Apparently, they were
not interested.
大多數的學生冷漠地聽著演講。顯然地，他們不感興趣。

apologize [ə`pɑlə،dʒaɪz] 動 道歉
▶ The airline apologized to passengers for the delay of the plane.
航空公司為班機延誤向旅客道歉。
動詞三態變化 apologize - apologized - apologized

apology [ə`pɑlədʒ] 名 道歉　　片 to accept an apology 接受道歉

apparatus [ˌæpə`retəs] 名 設備，儀器　　◎ MP3 01-14
同 equipment [ɪ`kwɪpmənt] 名 設備

appall [ə`pɔl] 動 使驚嚇
▶ We were appalled by the accident.
我們都被這意外嚇到。

相關衍生字彙 shock [ʃɑk] 名 驚嚇、dismay [dɪs`me] 名 驚慌、terrify [`tɛrəˌfaɪ] 動 使害怕、startle [`stɑrtl̩] 動 使吃驚、frighten [`fraɪtn̩] 動 使驚恐

動詞三態變化 appall - appalled - appalled

apparel [ə`pærəl] 名 服裝　　同 clothes [kloz] 名 服裝

apparent [ə`pærənt] 形 顯然的
▶ Her happiness and anger are always apparent on the face.
她的喜怒總是很明顯的表現在臉上。

相關衍生字彙 apparently [ə`pærəntlɪ] 副 表面上，似乎

appeal [ə`pil] 動 呼籲，懇求　　片 to appeal to 向～呼籲
動詞三態變化 appeal - appealed - appealed

appear [ə`pɪr] 動 出現
▶ To our surprise, the superstar suddenly appeared at the party.
讓我們驚喜的是，那位超級巨星突然出現在我們的宴會上。

動詞三態變化 appear - appeared - appeared

appearance [ə`pɪrəns] 名 外表
▶ Never judge a person by his or her appearance.
不要用他或她的外表來判斷一個人。

相關衍生字彙 tall [tɔl] 形（身材）高的、short [ʃɔrt] 形 矮的、fat [fæt] 形 肥胖的、thin [θɪn] 形 瘦的、slim [slɪm] 形 苗條的

appendix [ə`pɛndɪks] 名 附錄
▶ There is an appendix at the end of the book. It's worth reading.
這本書後面有附錄，很值得一讀。

appetite [`æpəˌtaɪt] 名 食慾
▶ Exercise can help improve your appetite.
運動會促進你的食慾。

相關衍生字彙 appetizer [`æpəˌtaɪzɚ] 名 開胃小吃、appetizing [`æpəˌtaɪzɪŋ] 形 開胃的

applaud [ə`plɔd] 動 鼓掌，喝采
▶ The speaker was applauded for at least three minutes.
　這位演講者接受至少三分鐘的掌聲。

相關衍生字彙 clap [klæp] 動 拍手、cheer [tʃɪr] 動 歡呼、acclaim [ə`klem] 動 為～喝采、
　　praise [prez] 動 讚美、blame [blem] 動 責怪

動詞三態變化 applaud - applauded - applauded

applause [ə`plɔz] 名 掌聲　　片 a burst of applause 一陣掌聲

applicant [`æpləkənt] 名 申請人
▶ So far, there have been more than one hundred applicants for the job.
　目前為止，已經有超過百人申請這份工作。

application [͵æplə`keʃən] 名 申請　　片 to make an application 提出申請

apply [ə`plaɪ] 動 應用，敷藥，申請
▶ On seeing the job advertisement, I decided to apply at once.
　一看到這工作廣告，我馬上決定申請。

動詞三態變化 apply - applied - applied

appoint [ə`pɔɪnt] 動 指派
▶ Mark was appointed manager of the marketing department.
　馬克被指派擔任行銷部門的經理。

相關衍生字彙 nominate [`nɑmə͵net] 動 提名、designate [`dɛzɪg͵net] 動 指定、
　　assign [ə`saɪn] 動 分派、name [nem] 動 提名，任命

動詞三態變化 appoint - appointed - appointed

appointment [ə`pɔɪntmənt] 名 約定，會面
片 to make an appointment with 和～約見面

appraise [ə`prez] 動 鑑定，評估
▶ The professor will appraise his students' performance at the end of the semester.
　在學期末，教授會評估學生們的表現。

動詞三態變化 appraise - appraised - appraised

appreciate [ə`priʃɪ͵et] 動 感謝，欣賞
▶ I appreciate your help when I was in need.
　當我需要協助時，感謝你的幫忙。

相關衍生字彙 admire [əd`maɪr] 動 讚賞、praise [prez] 動 讚美、treasure [`trɛʒɚ] 動 珍惜、
　　grateful [`gretfəl] 形 感謝的、thankful [`θæŋkfəl] 形 感謝的

動詞三態變化 appreciate - appreciated - appreciated

appreciation [ə͵priʃɪ`eʃən] 名 感激，欣賞
▶ We are surprised at the old man's appreciation of paintings.
　我們很驚訝這位老人對畫作的鑑賞力。

相關衍生字彙 appreciative [əˈpriʃɪ̩etɪv] 形 感謝的，有欣賞力的、appreciator [əˈpriʃɪ̩etɚ] 名 鑑賞者，欣賞者

apprehend [ˌæprɪˈhɛnd] 動 逮捕，理解
▶ According to the latest news, the police have apprehended the murderer.
根據最新消息，警方已經逮捕兇手了。

動詞三態變化 apprehend - apprehended - apprehended

apprehension [ˌæprɪˈhɛnʃən] 名 擔心，掛念，理解
MP3 01-15
同 worry [ˈwɝɪ] 名 擔心

apprehensive [ˌæprɪˈhɛnsɪv] 形 擔心的
▶ I felt apprehensive that you might get lost in the strange city.
我擔心你在陌生的都市裡迷路。

approach [əˈprotʃ] 動 靠近，處理
▶ Be careful! The train is approaching.
小心！火車正在靠近中。

相關衍生字彙 approachable [əˈprotʃəbl̩] 形 可接近的，易親近的

動詞三態變化 approach - approached - approached

appropriate [əˈproprɪ̩et] 形 合適的
▶ I don't think the movie is appropriate for small kids.
我認為這部電影不適合小小孩。

相關衍生字彙 suitable [ˈsutəbl̩] 形 適合的、fitting [ˈfɪtɪŋ] 形 合適的、qualified [ˈkwɑlə̩faɪd] 形 有資格的、proper [ˈprɑpɚ] 形 適當的

approval [əˈpruvl̩] 名 同意，允許
▶ With their parents' approval, they will get married before this fall.
徵得父母同意後，他們將在今年秋天前結婚。

approve [əˈpruv] 動 同意
反 disapprove [ˌdɪsəˈpruv] 動 反對

動詞三態變化 approve - approved - approved

approximate [əˈprɑksəmɪt] 形 大約的
▶ I can't remember the exact time. The approximate time is about five o'clock in the morning.
我不記得正確時間。只記得大約是清晨五點。

相關衍生字彙 approximately [əˈprɑksəmɪtlɪ] 副 大概，近乎

April [ˈeprəl] 名 四月
▶ April rain brings May flowers.
四月雨帶來五月花。

相關衍生字彙 January [ˈdʒænjʊ̩ɛrɪ] 名 一月、February [ˈfɛbrʊ̩ɛrɪ] 名 二月、March [mɑrtʃ] 名 三月、May [me] 名 五月、June [dʒun] 名 六月、July [dʒuˈlaɪ] 名 七月

apron [`eprən] 名 圍裙
▶ Remember to wear an apron while cooking. 煮飯時記得穿圍裙。

apt [æpt] 形 易於～　　⑪ be apt to 傾向於～

aptitude [`æptə‚tjud] 名 天資，才能　　⑪ aptitude test 性向測驗
相關衍生字彙 intelligence [ɪn`tɛlədʒəns] 名 聰明、wit [wɪt] 名 智慧、talent [`tælənt] 名 才華、
skill [`skɪl] 名 技巧、genius [`dʒinjəs] 名 天才、clever [`klɛvɚ] 形 聰明的、
wise [waɪz] 形 有智慧的

aquarium [ə`kwɛrɪəm] 名 水族館
▶ Kids like to watch fishes at the aquarium.
小孩喜歡在水族館看不同種類的魚。
相關衍生字彙 whale [hwel] 名 鯨魚、dolphin [`dɑlfɪn] 名 海豚、otter [`atɚ] 名 水獺、
ray [re] 名 魟魚、shark [`ʃark] 名 鯊魚、jellyfish [`dʒɛlɪ‚fɪʃ] 名 水母、
starfish [`star‚fɪʃ] 名 海星、crab [kræb] 名 螃蟹、shrimp [ʃrɪmp] 名 蝦子、
octopus [`aktəpəs] 名 章魚

arch [artʃ] 名 拱門
▶ Walk straight through the arch, and you can find the beautiful garden.
直走過這座拱門，你就可以找到那個漂亮的花園。

archaeology [‚arkɪ`alədʒɪ] 名 考古學
▶ Mary likes the study of the buildings and objects in the past, so she
decided to major in archaeology.
瑪莉喜歡研究古代的建築物和器物，所以她決定主修考古學。
相關衍生字彙 archaeological [‚arkɪə`ladʒɪkl̩] 形 考古學的、archaeologist [‚arkɪ`alədʒɪst]
名 考古學家

architect [`arkə‚tɛkt] 名 建築師
▶ The designer of the museum is a famous architect.
這座博物館的設計師是一位有名的建築師。

architecture [`arkə‚tɛktʃɚ] 名 建築物（風格）
▶ The Roman architecture in Italy impresses me a lot.
義大利的羅馬建築令我印象深刻。
相關衍生字彙 arena [ə`rinə] 名 競技場、stadium [`stedɪəm] 名 體育場、
gymnasium [dʒɪm`nezɪəm] 名 體育館、auditorium [‚ɔdə`torɪəm] 名 禮堂、
bridge [brɪdʒ] 名 橋、castle [`kæsl̩] 名 城堡

Arctic [`arktɪk] 名 北極 形 北極的　　⑪ the Arctic Circle 北極圈

ardent [`ardənt] 形 熱切的，熱心的
▶ The ardent volunteers helped the poor spend the cold winter.
這些熱心的義工協助窮人們度過寒冬。

arduous [`ardʒʊəs] 形 困苦的，費力的
▶ Climbing the mountain is an arduous journey.
爬這座山會是辛苦的旅程。

相關衍生字彙 hardworking [ˌhard`wɝkɪŋ] 形 辛勤工作的、difficult [`dɪfəˌkəlt] 形 困難的、
hard [hard] 形 辛苦的、laborious [lə`borɪəs] 形 辛苦的

area [`ɛrɪə] 名 地區　　片 area code（電話）區域號碼

argue [`argjʊ] 動 爭論　　片 to argue with 與（人）爭論　　MP3 01-16
動詞三態變化 argue - argued - argued

argument [`argjəmənt] 名 爭辯
▶ The students had an argument about where to have a trip.
學生為了旅遊地點在爭論。

相關衍生字彙 argumentation [ˌargjəmɛn`teʃən] 名 辯論（文）、
argumentative [ˌargjə`mɛntətɪv] 形 爭辯的，好爭論的

arid [`ærɪd] 形 乾燥的　　同 dry [draɪ] 形 乾的

arise [ə`raɪz] 動 升起，產生，出現
▶ Many difficulties arose while she was travelling independently in Africa.
她在非洲自助旅行時出現很多困難。

相關衍生字彙 rise [raɪz] 動 上升、raise [rez] 動 舉高、appear [ə`pɪr] 動 出現、
ascend [ə`sɛnd] 動 升高、mount [maʊnt] 動 登高、climb [klaɪm] 動 爬高
動詞三態變化 arise - arose - arisen

arm [arm] 名 手臂　　片 arm in arm 副 兩人臂挽著臂
相關衍生字彙 armchair [`armˌtʃɛr] 名 扶手椅、armed [armd] 形 武裝的，有把手的、
armful [`armˌfəl] 形（雙臂或單臂）一抱（之量）、arms [armz] 名 武器，戰爭

armor [`armɚ] 名 盔甲
▶ In the past, knights wore suits of armor to protect themselves in battle.
在古代，騎士會穿盔甲在戰場上保護自己。

army [`armɪ] 名 軍隊，陸軍
▶ Her boyfriend is in the army now. 她的男朋友現在在部隊服役。

aroma [ə`romə] 名 香氣
▶ The kitchen is full of the aroma of bread baked by Mom.
廚房充滿媽媽烤麵包的香味。

相關衍生字彙 perfume [`pɝfjum] 名 香水、fragrance [`fregrəns] 名 香氣、odor [`odɚ]
名 氣味，臭氣、scent [sɛnt] 名 氣味、smell [smɛl] 名 味道

arouse [əˋrauz] 動 喚起
▶ The inspiring story aroused many young students' passion.
這則激勵的故事喚起很多年輕學子的熱情。
動詞三態變化 arouse - aroused - aroused

arrange [əˋrendʒ] 動 安排
▶ The secretary helps arrange a meeting on Wednesday afternoon.
祕書幫忙安排於週三下午進行的會議。
動詞三態變化 arrange - arranged - arranged

arrangement [əˋrendʒmənt] 名 安排，佈置
片 make arrangements for 為～做安排

array [əˋre] 名（排列整齊的）陳列
▶ There is an array of magazines on the bookshelf. 書架上有整排的雜誌。

arrest [əˋrɛst] 名 逮捕　片 under arrest 被逮捕
相關衍生字彙 catch [kætʃ] 動 抓住、capture [ˋkæptʃɚ] 動 逮住、stop [stɑp] 動 阻止、
release [rɪˋlis] 動 釋放、free [fri] 動 解放

arrival [əˋraɪvl̩] 名 到達　片 new arrival 新貨上架

arrive [əˋraɪv] 動 到達
▶ Be sure to arrive at the destination by midnight.
半夜十二點前一定要抵達目的地。
動詞三態變化 arrive - arrived - arrived

arrogant [ˋærəgənt] 形 自大的
▶ Kate is such an arrogant girl that she has few friends.
凱特是個自大的女孩，所以沒什麼朋友。
相關衍生字彙 proud [praud] 形 自豪的、selfish [ˋsɛlfɪʃ] 形 自私的、humble [ˋhʌmbl̩]
形 謙虛的、modest [ˋmɑdɪst] 形 謙虛的、shy [ʃaɪ] 形 害羞的

arrow [ˋæro] 名 箭頭
▶ Follow the arrows, and then you can find the train station.
跟著箭頭走，你就可以找到火車站。

art [ɑrt] 名 藝術　片 a bachelor's degree in arts 文學士文憑

artful [ˋɑrtfəl] 形 狡詐的，機靈的
▶ He answered all the questions in an artful way while being interviewed.
面試時，他很機靈地回答所有問題。
相關衍生字彙 cunning [ˋkʌnɪŋ] 形 狡猾的、skillful [ˋskɪlfəl] 形 熟練的、sly [slaɪ] 形 狡猾的、
honest [ˋɑnɪst] 形 誠實的

article [ˋɑrtɪk!] 名 文章，一件物品
▶ There is a long article on the cause of the landslide in the paper today.
今天報紙有一篇長文章談論山崩的原因。

artifact [ˋɑrtɪˎfækt] 名 古文物　　　　　　　　◎ MP3 01-17
▶ Many artifacts were collected by the museum. 這座博物館收集很多古文物。

artificial [ˎɑrtəˋfɪʃəl] 形 人造的　　🄟 artificial intelligence 人工智慧

artist [ˋɑrtɪst] 名 藝術家
▶ Michelangelo, Da Vinci and Raphael are great artists.
米開朗基羅、達文西和拉斐爾都是偉大的藝術家。
相關衍生字彙 artistic [ɑrˋtɪstɪk] 形 藝術的、artistry [ˋɑrtɪstrɪ] 名 藝術性、artless [ˋɑrtlɪs]
形 單純的，自然的、artwork [ˋɑrtˎwɝk] 名 藝術品

ascend [əˋsɛnd] 動 上升，登上　　🄟 to ascend the throne（國王或皇后）登基
動詞三態變化 ascend - ascended - ascended

ascendancy [əˋsɛndənsɪ] 名 優勢
▶ When the mayor loses the election, he will lose his political ascendancy soon.
當這位市長選舉失利後，他將很快地失去政治優勢。
相關衍生字彙 advantage [ədˋvæntɪdʒ] 名 優勢、prestige [prɛsˋtiʒ] 名 聲望、
privilege [ˋprɪvlɪdʒ] 名 特權、power [ˋpauɚ] 名 權力

ash [æʃ] 名 灰燼　　🄟 be burned to ashes 被燒成灰燼

ashamed [əˋʃemd] 形 羞愧的
▶ I felt so ashamed to admit my mistake. 我實在羞愧於承認自己的錯。

ashore [əˋʃor] 副 上岸，朝向陸地去
▶ The strong winds blew the trash and pieces of wood ashore.
強風把垃圾和木塊吹到岸邊。

aside [əˋsaɪd] 副 到一邊　　🄟 to leave something aside 暫不考慮某事

asleep [əˋslip] 形 睡著的　　🄟 to fall asleep 睡著

aspect [ˋæspɛkt] 名 層面，方面
▶ Her parents' accident affects almost every aspect of her life.
他父母親的意外幾乎影響了她生活的每一個層面。

aspire [əˋspaɪr] 動 渴望於
▶ Most people aspire to fame and wealth.
大多數的人都渴望名與利。
相關衍生字彙 ambitious [æmˋbɪʃəs] 形 雄心壯志的、desire [dɪˋzaɪr] 名 慾望、dream [drim]
名 夢想、seek [sik] 動 尋求、pursue [pɚˋsu] 動 追求
動詞三態變化 aspire - aspired - aspired

ass [æs] 名 蠢蛋　　片 to make an ass of oneself 讓自己出糗

---

assassinate [ə`sæsɪnˌet] 動 刺殺
▶ It was said that someone was plotting to assassinate the King.
據說，有人正策劃刺殺國王。
動詞三態變化 assassinate - assassinated - assassinated

---

assassination [əˌsæsə`neʃən] 名 暗殺　　片 a political assassination 政治暗殺
相關衍生字彙 murder [`mɝdɚ] 動 謀殺、kill [kɪl] 動 殺死、massacre [`mæsəkɚ]
動 (種族) 大屠殺、slaughter [`slɔtɚ] 動 屠宰

---

assault [ə`sɔlt] 名 攻擊
▶ They launched an assault on the magazine headquarters.
他們對這間雜誌社總部發動攻擊。

---

assay [ə`se] 動 估計，檢驗
▶ The chemical teacher is teaching the students how to assay the gold.
化學老師正在教學生如何檢驗金子成分。
動詞三態變化 assay - assayed - assayed

---

assemble [ə`sɛmbl̩] 動 招集，聚集，組裝
▶ All the staff were assembled to welcome the foreign visitors.
所有員工都被召集去歡迎外國訪客。
動詞三態變化 assemble - assembled - assembled

---

assembly [ə`sɛmblɪ] 名 集會，裝配
▶ People have the right of assembly. 人民有集會的權力。

---

assent [ə`sɛnt] 名 贊成
▶ Our parents gave their assent to our travelling plan.
父母贊成我們的旅遊計畫。
相關衍生字彙 approve [ə`pruv] 動 贊成、agree [ə`gri] 動 同意、disagree [ˌdɪsə`gri]
動 不同意、permit [pɚ`mɪt] 動 允許、accept [ək`sɛpt] 動 接受

---

assert [ə`sɝt] 動 堅稱　　片 to assert oneself 堅持自己的權利　　⊙ MP3 01-18
動詞三態變化 assert - asserted - asserted

---

assertion [ə`sɝʃən] 名 主張
▶ I can't agree with your assertion that men are braver than women.
我不能苟同你認為男人比女人勇敢的說法。

---

assessment [ə`sɛsmənt] 名 評估
▶ The professor will make an assessment according to the assignment.
教授將會根據作業來做評估。
相關衍生字彙 assess [ə`sɛs] 動 徵 (稅)，評價、judgment [`dʒʌdʒmənt] 名 判決，意見，指責

asset [ˋæsɛt] 名 資產
▶ The excellent player is a great asset to our school team.
這位優秀球員是我們校隊的一大資產。

assiduous [əˋsɪdʒuəs] 形 勤勉的
▶ Mark is such an assiduous student that he has been one of the top students.
馬克是如此勤勉的學生，所以他可以一直名列前茅。
相關衍生字彙 hard-working [͵hɑrdˋwɝkɪŋ] 形 努力工作的、lazy [ˋlezɪ] 形 懶散的、
tireless [ˋtaɪrlɪs] 形 孜孜不倦的、industrious [ɪnˋdʌstrɪəs] 形 勤奮的、
diligent [ˋdɪlədʒənt] 形 勤勉的

assign [əˋsaɪn] 動 指派
▶ Bill was assigned to take charge of the marketing department.
比爾被指派去負責行銷部門。
動詞三態變化 assign - assigned - assigned

assignment [əˋsaɪnmənt] 名 作業，任務
▶ The students complained that they had too many assignments to complete. 學生抱怨他們有太多作業要完成。

assimilate [əˋsɪm͵let] 動 同化，吸收
▶ It's not an easy job to assimilate so much new information.
要吸收這麼多新資訊不是簡單的事。
動詞三態變化 assimilate - assimilated - assimilated

assist [əˋsɪst] 動 協助
▶ We need a designer to assist us with the fashion show.
我們需要一位設計師來協助我們的時裝秀。
動詞三態變化 assist - assisted - assisted

assistance [əˋsɪstəns] 名 協助
▶ We appreciated the engineer for his technical assistance.
我們很感激那位工程師提供技術上的協助。

assistant [əˋsɪstənt] 名 助理，助教　　片 an assistant professor 助理教授
相關衍生字彙 help [hɛlp] 動 幫助、support [səˋport] 動 支持、aid [ed] 動 支援、
service [ˋsɝvɪs] 名 服務、relief [rɪˋlif] 名 救濟

associate [əˋsoʃ͵et] 動 連結，聯繫　　片 to associate A with B 把 A 跟 B 作連結
動詞三態變化 associate - associated - associated

association [ə͵sosɪˋeʃən] 名 協會，聯盟
▶ The football fans decided to set up a football association.
這些足球迷決定成立一個足球協會。

assume [ə`sjum] 動 假設，以為是～
▶ I assumed that you knew Mary because she was your neighbor.
我以為你認識瑪麗，因為她是你的鄰居。
動詞三態變化 assume - assumed - assumed

assumption [ə`sʌmpʃən] 名 假設
▶ The conclusion is made based on the scientist's assumption.
根據那位科學家的假設做了這個結論。

assure [ə`ʃur] 動 擔保，保證
▶ I assure the news that Vicky got divorced is true.
我確定薇琪離婚的消息是真的。
動詞三態變化 assure - assured - assured

assurance [ə`ʃurəns] 名 保證，自信
▶ When facing challenge, never lack your assurance.
面對挑戰，不要缺乏自信。

asthma [`æzmə] 名 氣喘
▶ The little girl has been suffering from asthma.
這位小女孩一直受氣喘之苦。
相關衍生字彙 diabetes [ˌdaɪə`bitiz] 名 糖尿病、obesity [o`bisətɪ] 名 肥胖症、
anorexia [ˌænə`rɛksɪə] 名 厭食症、Alzheimer [`altsˌhaɪmɚ] 名 阿茲海默症

astonish [ə`stanɪʃ] 動 使震驚，使驚訝　　片 be astonished at 對～感到驚訝
相關衍生字彙 astonished [ə`stanɪʃt] 形 驚訝的、astonishing [ə`stanɪʃɪŋ] 形 令人驚訝的
動詞三態變化 astonish - astonished - astonished

astonishment [ə`stanɪʃmənt] 名 驚訝
▶ To our astonishment, the boy can speak four languages.
令我們驚訝的是，這位男孩會講四種語言。

astound [ə`staund] 動 使震驚　　同 surprise [sɚ`praɪz] 動 使驚訝　　◎ MP3 01-19
動詞三態變化 astound - astounded - astounded

astray [ə`stre] 副 迷途
▶ I was led astray by the digital map. 我被電子地圖帶到迷路了。

astrology [ə`stralədʒɪ] 名 占星術
▶ Many girls are interested in astrology, especially when they are falling in love.
很多女孩對占星術感興趣，尤其當她們談戀愛時。
相關衍生字彙 Capricorn [`kæprɪkɔrn] 名 摩羯座、Aquarius [ə`kwɛrɪəs] 名 水瓶座、
Pisces [`pɪsiz] 名 雙魚座、Aries [`ɛriz] 名 白羊座、Taurus [`tɔrəs] 名 金牛座、
Gemini [`dʒɛməˌnaɪ] 名 雙子座、Cancer [`kænsɚ] 名 巨蟹座、Leo [`lio]
名 獅子座、Virgo [`vɝgo] 名 處女座、Libra [`laɪbrə] 名 天秤座、
Scorpio [`skɔrpɪo] 名 天蠍座、Sagittarius [ˌsædʒɪ`tɛrɪəs] 名 射手座

astronaut [ˋæstrəˏnɔt] 名 太空人
▶ Armstrong is the first astronaut to walk on the moon.
阿姆斯壯是踏上月球的第一個太空人。

astronomy [əsˋtrɑnəmɪ] 名 天文學
▶ Mandy has been attracted to stars in the universe. She chose astronomy as her major.
嫚蒂一直著迷宇宙的星星，所以她挑天文學當主修科目。
相關衍生字彙 star [stɑr] 名 星星、moon [mun] 名 月亮、sun [sʌn] 名 太陽、solar [ˋsolɚ] 形 太陽的、lunar [ˋlunɚ] 形 月亮的

athlete [ˋæθlit] 名 運動員　　片 athlete's foot 香港腳

athletic [æθˋlɛtɪk] 形 像運動員的
▶ John is physically strong and athletic looking.
約翰體格強壯，看起來像運動員似的。

atmosphere [ˋætməsˏfɪr] 名 大氣，空氣
▶ The atmosphere of the city is so polluted that the citizens' health has been threatened.
這座城市的空氣污染嚴重以致於市民的健康已經受到威脅。
相關衍生字彙 atmospheric [ˏætməsˋfɛrɪk] 形 大氣的

atom [ˋætəm] 名 原子　　片 atom bomb 原子彈

atomic [əˋtɑmɪk] 形 原子的　　片 atomic energy 原子能
相關衍生字彙 nuclear [ˋnjuklɪɚ] 形 核子的、weapon [ˋwɛpən] 名 武器、submarine [ˋsʌbməˏrin] 名 潛艇、explosion [ɪkˋsploʒən] 名 爆炸

atrocious [əˋtroʃəs] 形 兇暴的　　同 violent [ˋvaɪələnt] 形 猛烈的，兇暴的

attach [əˋtætʃ] 動 使附屬，貼上
▶ Remember to attach your photo to your application form.
記得在申請表上貼上你的照片。
動詞三態變化 attach - attached - attached

attachment [əˋtætʃmənt] 名 附件
▶ I will email you the picture we took in Paris as an attachment.
我會把我們在巴黎拍的照片以附件方式用電子郵件寄給你。

attack [əˋtæk] 動 攻擊
▶ Many postmen are often attacked by dogs.
很多郵差常常被小狗攻擊。
動詞三態變化 attack - attacked - attacked

attain [ə`ten] 動 達到　　片 to attain the goal 達到目標

相關衍生字彙 reach [ritʃ] 動 到達、gain [gen] 動 獲得、fulfill [fʊl`fɪl] 動 成就、realize [`rɪəˌlaɪz] 動 實踐、finish [`fɪnɪʃ] 動 完成

動詞三態變化 attain - attained - attained

attainment [ə`tenmənt] 名 獲得，達到

▶ The attainment of fame and wealth didn't make him satisfied.
名與利的獲得並沒有讓他滿足。

attempt [ə`tɛmpt] 動 試圖

▶ The athlete attempted to break the world record.
這位運動員試圖打破世界紀錄。

動詞三態變化 attempt - attempted - attempted

attend [ə`tɛnd] 動 出席，參加

▶ Hundreds of people attended the lecture last night.
昨晚有數百人來聽此講座。

動詞三態變化 attend - attended - attended

attendance [ə`tɛndəns] 名 出席

▶ The weather was cold that day but the attendance at school was good.
那天天氣很冷，不過學校的出席狀況很好。

attendant [ə`tɛndənt] 名 隨從，隨員

▶ No matter where the Prince goes, he is followed by his attendants.
不論王子走到哪裡，隨從都會跟著他。

相關衍生字彙 absent [`æbsn̩t] 形 缺席的、present [`prɛzn̩t] 形 出席的、follow [`fɑlo] 動 跟隨、trace [tres] 動 追蹤

attention [ə`tɛnʃən] 名 注意力　　◎ MP3 01-20

片 to pay attention to 注意～，專注於～

attentive [ə`tɛntɪv] 形 傾聽的，留意的

▶ The waiter is always very attentive to his guests.
這位服務員總是很關心客人的需求。

attenuate [ə`tɛnjuˌet] 動 變稀薄，變弱

▶ Sunlight can be attenuated by sunglasses.
透過太陽眼鏡會使陽光會變弱。

動詞三態變化 attenuate - attenuated - attenuated

attic [`ætɪk] 名 閣樓

▶ The attic bedroom at the top of the house is the little girl's secret garden.
這屋頂的閣樓房間是這位小女孩的祕密花園。

attire [ə`taɪr] 名 衣服，服裝
▶ Jeans are not appropriate attire for a formal occasion.
牛仔褲對正式場合而言不是合適的服裝。
相關衍生字彙 clothes [kloz] 名 衣物、cloth [klɔθ] 名 布、dress [drɛs] 動 穿衣、
dress [`drɛs] 名 洋裝、skirt [skɜt] 名 裙子、trousers [`traʊzɚz] 名 褲子

---

attitude [`ætətjud] 名 態度
片 to take a positive attitude towards 對〜採取積極態度

---

attorney [ə`tɜnɪ] 名 法定代理人，律師　　同 lawyer [`lɔjɚ] 名 律師

---

attract [ə`trækt] 動 吸引
▶ Men are attracted to charming girls.
男人會被有魅力的女生所吸引。
動詞三態變化 attract - attracted - attracted

---

attraction [ə`trækʃən] 名 吸引力　　片 tourist attraction 觀光勝地

---

attractive [ə`træktɪv] 形 有吸引力的
▶ The job offer is very attractive to me.
這份工作的條件很吸引我。
相關衍生字彙 charming [`tʃɑrmɪŋ] 形 迷人的、beautiful [`bjutəfəl] 形 美麗的、pretty [`prɪtɪ]
形 漂亮的、ugly [`ʌglɪ] 形 醜陋的

---

attribute [ə`trɪbjut] 動 歸因於〜
▶ He attributes the success to his wife's support.
他將成功歸因於太太的支持。
動詞三態變化 attribute - attributed - attributed

---

attrition [ə`trɪʃən] 名 磨損
▶ The long war of attrition makes the country extremely poor.
長期的消耗戰讓這個國家變得極度貧窮。

---

auction [`ɔkʃən] 名 拍賣
▶ They sold all the furniture by auction before moving.
在搬家前，他們拍賣所有的家具。

---

audacious [ɔ`deʃəs] 形 大膽的，無畏的
▶ It was audacious of you to climb such a high mountain.
你真是大膽，敢爬這座高山。
相關衍生字彙 fearless [`fɪrlɪs] 形 無畏的、courageous [kə`redʒəs] 形 有勇氣的、brave [brev]
形 勇敢的、heroic [hɪ`roɪk] 形 英勇的、bold [bold] 形 大膽的

---

audible [`ɔdəbl] 形 聽得到的
▶ The teacher's voice is audible even at the back of the classroom.
老師的聲音就算在教室後面方也聽得到。

audience [`ɔdɪəns] 名 聽眾，觀眾
▶ J.K. Rowling's children's books have a large audience.
J.K. 羅琳的童書擁有廣大的讀者。

audit [`ɔdɪt] 名 審計，查帳
▶ Every company should have an audit at least once a year.
每家公司至少每年一次作帳目審計。

auspicious [ɔ`spɪʃəs] 形 幸運的
▶ What an auspicious year! I won the lottery. 多幸運的一年啊！我中樂透了！

author [`ɔθɚ] 名 作者
▶ The author of the book will make a speech tonight at the bookstore.
這本書的作者今晚將到書店演講。
相關衍生字彙 writer [`raɪtɚ] 名 作家、reporter [rɪ`portɚ] 名 記者、painter [`pentɚ] 名 畫家、singer [`sɪŋɚ] 名 歌手、designer [dɪ`zaɪnɚ] 名 設計師

authority [ə`θɔrətɪ] 名 權威，當局，權力
▶ The professor is an authority on the topic. 這位教授是這個主題的權威。

authorize [`ɔθə,raɪz] 動 授權　　　○ MP3 01-21
▶ While the boss was absent, his secretary was authorized to host the meeting.
當老闆不在時，他的祕書被授權主持這場會議。
動詞三態變化 authorize - authorized - authorized

autobiography [,ɔtəbaɪ`agrəfɪ] 名 自傳
▶ The movie was based on the autobiography of the hero.
這部電影是根據這位英雄的自傳所拍成的。
相關衍生字彙 novel [`nɑvl] 名 小說、story [`storɪ] 名 故事、biography [baɪ`agrəfɪ] 名 傳記、legend [`lɛdʒənd] 名 傳說

automatic [,ɔtə`mætɪk] 形 自動的
▶ In the future, driving may become automatic.
在未來，駕駛可能會變成自動的。
相關衍生字彙 automatically [,ɔtə`mætɪklɪ] 副 自動地，不自覺地

automobile [`ɔtəmə,bɪl] 名 汽車　　同 car [kar] 名 汽車

autonomous [ɔ`tanəməs] 形 自治的　　片 an autonomous region 自治區

augment [ɔg`mɛnt] 動 擴大，增加
▶ After work, he found another part-time job to augment his income.
下班後，他還兼另一份差以增加他的收入。
動詞三態變化 augment - augmented - augmented

August [`ɔgəst] 名 八月
▶ In Taiwan, August is the first month of fall.
在台灣，八月是秋天的第一個月。

相關衍生字彙 September [sɛp`tɛmbɚ] 名 九月、October [ɑk`tobɚ] 名 十月、
November [no`vɛmbɚ] 名 十一月、December [dɪ`sɛmbɚ] 名 十二月

auspices [`ɔspɪsɪz] 名 贊助　　片 under the auspices of somebody 在某人的贊助下

authentic [ɔ`θɛntɪk] 形 真正的
▶ Visitors can eat the authentic Italian food at the restaurant.
遊客可以在這家餐廳品嚐到道地的義大利食物。

autocrat [`ɔtə,kræt] 名 獨裁者
▶ An autocrat always demands his people to totally obey him.
獨裁者總是要求他的人民完全遵從他。

autograph [`ɔtə,græf] 名 簽名
▶ The fans lined up to get the superstar's autograph.
粉絲們排隊要拿這位超級巨星的親筆簽名。

automation [,ɔtə`meʃən] 名 自動化
▶ With the help of the automation, the factory makes more and more money.
有了自動化的助益，工廠愈來愈賺錢。

autumn [`ɔtəm] 名 秋天　　同 fall [fɔl] 名 秋天
相關衍生字彙 season [`sizn̩] 名 季節、spring [sprɪŋ] 名 秋天、summer [`sʌmɚ] 名 夏天、
winter [`wɪntɚ] 名 冬天

avail [ə`vel] 名 幫助，有益　　片 of no avail 完全沒有用的

available [ə`veləbl̩] 形 可用的，有空的
▶ Are you available now? 你現在有空嗎？

avarice [`ævərɪs] 名 貪婪　　同 greed [grid] 名 貪心

avenge [ə`vɛndʒ] 動 報復
▶ The workers decided to avenge themselves on the mean boss.
這些勞工決定對這名吝嗇的老闆進行報復。
動詞三態變化 avenge - avenged - avenged

avenue [`ævə,nju] 名 大道
▶ There are beautiful maple trees along the avenue.
沿著這條大道，有很多漂亮的楓樹。
相關衍生字彙 street [strit] 名 街道、road [rod] 名 道路、lane [len] 名 巷弄、alley [`ælɪ]
名 小巷、path [pæθ] 名 小徑

average [`ævərɪdʒ] 名 平均，一般，中等
▶ The average of 10 and 20 is 15. 十加二十的平均數是十五。

averse [ə`vɝs] 形 嫌惡的，反對的
▶ I am not averse to make friend with him.
　我不排斥跟他做朋友。
相關衍生字彙 aversion [ə`vɝʃən] 名 厭惡，反感

avert [ə`vɝt] 動 預防，避免　　片 to avert conflict 避免衝突　　◎ MP3 01-22
動詞三態變化 avert - averted - averted

aviation [ˌevɪ`eʃən] 名 航空，飛行　　片 aviation security 飛安

avid [`ævɪd] 形 貪婪的，渴望的　　同 eager [`igɚ] 形 渴望的

avoid [ə`vɔɪd] 動 避免
▶ Because of her carefulness, we avoided an accident.
　由於她的細心，我們避開了一個意外事故。
動詞三態變化 avoid - avoided - avoided

avow [ə`vau] 動 公開承認
▶ He avowed that he had made a terrible mistake.
　他公開承認犯了一個很糟的錯誤。
相關衍生字彙 deny [dɪ`naɪ] 動 否認、reject [rɪ`dʒɛkt] 動 拒絕、admit [əd`mɪt] 動 承認、
　　　　　　 confess [kən`fɛs] 動 承認、acknowledge [ək`nɑlɪdʒ] 動 承認
動詞三態變化 avow - avowed - avowed

await [ə`wet] 動 等候　　同 to wait for 等候
動詞三態變化 await - awaited - awaited

awake [ə`wek] 動 喚醒
▶ The noise awoke me early in the morning.
　一大早有噪音吵醒我。
動詞三態變化 awake - awaked / awoke - awaked / awoken

awaken [ə`wekən] 動 醒來，意識到～
▶ His father's death awakened him to the sense of duty.
　他爸爸的去世喚醒了他的責任感。
動詞三態變化 awaken - awakened - awakened

award [ə`wɔrd] 動 頒予，授予
▶ He was awarded a scholarship.
　他獲頒獎學金。
動詞三態變化 award - awarded - awarded

aware [ə`wɛr] 形 察覺的　　片 be aware of 查覺到～

相關衍生字彙 ignorant [`ɪgnərənt] 形 無知的、conscious [`kɑnʃəs] 形 意識到的、
unaware [ʌnə`wɛr] 形 未察覺的、innocent [`ɪnəsn̩t] 形 單純、
awareness [ə`wɛrnɪs] 名 察覺，體認

---

awe [ɔ] 名 敬畏
▶ The boy watched his teacher in awe. 男孩敬畏地看著老師。

---

awesome [`ɔsəm] 形 可怕的，令人敬畏的
▶ I know that there will be an awesome challenge waiting for me.
我知道有個可怕的挑戰正等著我。

---

awful [`ɔful] 形 可怕的
▶ That will be a violent and awful typhoon.
那將是一個猛烈且可怕的颱風。

相關衍生字彙 awfully [`ɔfulɪ] 副 非常地，惡劣地，令人敬畏地

---

awkward [`ɔkwɚd] 形 笨拙的，尷尬的
▶ When speaking of swimming, I become awkward.
談到游泳，我就變得笨拙。

相關衍生字彙 awkwardly [`ɔkwɚdlɪ] 副 笨拙地，困難地，不方便地、
awkwardness [`ɔkwɚdnɪs] 名 笨拙，粗劣，尷尬

MEMO

B

babble ~ bypass

詞性說明

名 名詞	副 副詞	介 介系詞
動 動詞	形 形容詞	連 連接詞
代 代名詞	助 助動詞	

內文圖示說明

片 片語	反 反義字	同 同義字

一網打盡「英語小知識」│月份的縮寫

Jan. 一月	**Feb.** 二月	**Mar.** 三月	**Apr.** 四月
May. 五月	**Jun.** 六月	**Jul.** 七月	**Aug.** 八月
Sep. 九月	**Oct.** 十月	**Nov.** 十一月	**Dec.** 十二月

B babble ~ bypass

MP3 **02-01**

★一網打盡 989 個英文單字 ｜ 一網打盡 195 句英語會話句

babble [ˋbæbl̩] 動 (小嬰兒) 牙牙學語
▶ The baby babbled happily while he was playing with the toys.
小嬰兒邊玩玩具邊開心地說著兒語。

動詞三態變化 babble - babbled - babbled

babysit [ˋbebɪˏsɪt] 動 當臨時保姆
▶ We need a babysitter to babysit our newborn baby.
我們需要一位保姆來照顧新生兒。

相關衍生字彙 crib [krɪb] 名 嬰兒床、cradle [ˋkredl̩] 名 搖籃、diaper [ˋdaɪəpɚ] 名 尿布、
toy [tɔɪ] 名 玩具

動詞三態變化 babysit - babysat - babysat

bachelor [ˋbætʃələ] 名 學士，單身漢　　片 Bachelor of Arts 文學士

backbone [ˋbækˏbon] 名 骨氣，支柱
▶ Tourism is the economic backbone of the small country.
觀光業是這個小國家的經濟支柱。

background [ˋbækˏgraund] 名 背景
▶ The new employee has a background in publishing.
這個新員工有在出版社的背景。

backup [ˋbækˏʌp] 名 備份
▶ Don't forget to make a backup of all the information stored on your computer.
別忘了把你電腦裡的資料做備份。

backward [ˋbækwəd] 形 向後的，落後的　　片 a backward country 落後國家
相關衍生字彙 backer [ˋbækɚ] 名 支援者、backpack [ˋbækˏpæk] 名 背包、
backpacker [ˋbækˏpækɚ] 名 背包客、backyard [ˋbækjɑrd] 名 後院、
backwards [ˋbækwədz] 副 向後

bacteria [bækˋtɪrɪə] 名 細菌
▶ Bacteria have a number of shapes.
細菌有很多形狀。

相關衍生字彙 bactericide [bækˋtɪrəˏsaɪd] 名 殺菌劑、bacteriology [bækˏtɪrɪˋɑlədʒɪ]
名 細菌學、bacteriologist [bækˏtɪrɪˋɑlədʒɪst] 名 細菌學者

badly [ˋbædlɪ] 副 不好地，嚴重地
▶ Luckily, Bill didn't get hurt badly in that accident.
幸運地，比爾沒有在那個意外事故中嚴重受傷。

B

baffle [`bæf l]] 動 使困惑，使受挫折
▶ The doctor was baffled by the patient's strange reaction.
醫生被這位病人的奇怪反應給弄糊塗了。
動詞三態變化 baffle - baffled - baffled

baggage [`bægɪdʒ] 名 行李
▶ If your baggage is too heavy, you will be charged an extra fee by the airline.
如果你的行李過重，航空公司會向你索取額外費用。
相關衍生字彙 suitcase [`sut‚kes] 名 行李箱、trunk [trʌŋk] 名 大行李箱、luggage [`lʌgɪdʒ] 名 行李、bag [bæg] 名 袋子、package [`pækɪdʒ] 名 包裹

bait [bet] 名 誘餌
▶ They use worms as bait while they go fishing. 他們釣魚時都用蟲當誘餌。

bake [bek] 動 烘，烤
▶ Mom baked a cake to celebrate my brother's birthday.
媽媽烤了個蛋糕為弟弟慶生。
相關衍生字彙 baker [`bekɚ] 名 麵包（糕點）師、bakery [`bekərɪ] 名 麵包（糕點）烘坊、broil [brɔɪl] 動 烤，炙、roast [rost] 動 烤，炙，烘
動詞三態變化 bake - baked - baked

balance [`bæləns] 名 平衡，均衡
片 to strike a balance between A and B 在 A 與 B 兩者之間取得平衡

balcony [`bælkənɪ] 名 陽台
▶ The location of the hotel is good. We can see the mountain from the balcony of the room.
飯店的地理位置很好，我們從房間的陽台就可看到山脈。
相關衍生字彙 hedge [hɛdʒ] 名 籬笆、roof [ruf] 名 屋頂、fence [fɛns] 名 圍籬、backyard [`bæk‚jɑrd] 名 後院、courtyard [`kort‚jɑrd] 名 庭院

bald [bɔld] 形 禿頭的
▶ Under the pressure, he became bald soon.
在壓力之下，他很快就變禿頭了。
相關衍生字彙 baldhead [`bɔld‚hɛd] 名 禿頭的人、baldheaded [`bɔld`hɛdɪd] 形 禿頭的、baldish [`bɔldɪʃ] 形 禿頭的，無草木的、baldness [`bɔldnɪs] 名 禿頭，直率，單調

baldly [`bɔldlɪ] 副 光禿禿地，直率地　　片 to put it baldly 坦白說

baleful [`belfəl] 形 邪惡的，有威脅性的
▶ He stared at me with a baleful look. 他用邪惡的表情瞪著我看。

ballet [ˋbæle] 名 芭蕾舞
▶ Since she was a little girl, she has practiced ballet.
從她小的時候，她就一直練習芭蕾舞。

相關衍生字彙 ballerina [ˌbæləˋrinə] 名 女芭蕾舞者、dancer [ˋdænsɚ] 名 舞者、skater [ˋsketɚ] 名 溜冰者、gymnast [ˋdʒɪmnæst] 名 體操選手

---

balk [bɔk] 動 畏怯，猶豫
▶ Common people will balk at such a difficulty.
一般人對這樣的困難都會猶豫。

動詞三態變化 balk - balked - balked

---

balloon [bəˋlun] 名 氣球 ⊙ MP3 02-02
▶ Students decorated the classroom with balloons for the party.
學生為了舞會用氣球裝飾教室。

---

ballot [ˋbælət] 名 選票 片 to cast a ballot 投票
相關衍生字彙 elect [ɪˋlɛkt] 動 選擇、election [ɪˋlɛkʃən] 名 選舉、select [səˋlɛkt] 動 選擇、choice [tʃɔɪs] 名 選擇、option [ˋɑpʃən] 名 選擇權

---

balmy [ˋbɑmɪ] 形 溫和的，宜人的
▶ The weather is so balmy here in spring. 這裡的春天天氣很宜人。

---

ban [bæn] 名 禁止
▶ There is a ban on smoking on campus. 校園是禁止抽菸的。

---

banal [bəˋnɑl] 形 平庸的，陳腐的
▶ Students don't like the teacher's banal teaching.
學生們不喜歡這位老師陳腐的教法。

---

bandage [ˋbændɪdʒ] 名 繃帶
▶ The nurse wrapped a bandage around Lisa's injured finger.
護士幫麗莎受傷的指頭綁上繃帶。

---

banish [ˋbænɪʃ] 動 放逐，消除
▶ You should banish all the negative thoughts from your mind.
你應該摒除心中那些負面的想法。

相關衍生字彙 exile [ˋɛksaɪl] 動 流放、expel [ɪkˋspɛl] 動 驅趕、disappear [ˌdɪsəˋpɪr] 動 消失、rid [rɪd] 動 使免除、clear [klɪr] 動 清除、discard [dɪsˋkɑrd] 動 拋棄

動詞三態變化 banish - banished - banished

---

bankrupt [ˋbæŋkrʌpt] 形 破產的
▶ People said that he went bankrupt after his father died.
據說，他爸爸去世後，他就破產了。

相關衍生字彙 bank [bæŋk] 名 銀行、banker [ˋbæŋkɚ] 名 銀行家、bankruptcy [ˋbæŋkrəptsɪ] 名 破產，倒閉、insolvent [ɪnˋsɑlvənt] 名 破產者 形 破產的，無力償還的

B

banquet [`bæŋkwɪt] 名 盛宴
▶ A banquet was held after their wedding ceremony.
婚禮完後他們還辦了場盛宴。

banter [`bæntɚ] 名 取笑，逗弄
▶ During the coffee break, my colleagues always exchange banter with each other.
喝咖啡休息時，同事都會互相說笑。
相關衍生字彙 laugh [læf] 動 笑、smile [smaɪl] 動 微笑、laughter [`læftɚ] 名 笑聲、joke [dʒok] 名 笑話、tease [tiz] 名 取笑

baptism [`bæptɪzəm] 名 洗禮
▶ The infant will be arranged to accept baptism this Sunday.
這名嬰兒將安排於本周日受洗。

baptize [bæp`taɪz] 動 受洗
▶ When were you baptized a Catholic?
你是何時受洗成為天主教徒的？
動詞三態變化 baptize - baptized - baptized

barbarian [bɑr`bɛrɪən] 名 野蠻人，無教養的人
▶ It's unfair and wrong to treat aboriginals as barbarians.
把原住民當成野蠻人是不公平且錯誤的。

barbarous [`bɑrbərəs] 形 野蠻的，沒教養的
反 civilized [`sɪvəˌlaɪzd] 名 文明的，有教養的
相關衍生字彙 well-educated [wɛl`ɛdʒuˌketɪd] 形 受良好教育的、humanize [`hjumənˌaɪz] 動 使文明、socialize [`soʃəˌlaɪz] 動 使適應社會、education [ˌɛdʒu`keʃən] 名 教育

barber [`bɑrbɚ] 名 理髮師
▶ Father goes to the barber's once a month. 爸爸一個月去理髮店一次。

bare [bɛr] 形 裸的，沒有～的
▶ The house is bare of furniture.
這間屋子幾乎沒有家具。
相關衍生字彙 barely [`bɛrlɪ] 副 僅僅，幾乎沒有，公開地、barefooted [`bɛr`futɪd] 形 赤腳的 副 赤著腳地、barehanded [`bɛr`hændɪd] 形 副 手無寸鐵的（地），空手的（地）、bareheaded [`bɛr`hɛdɪd] 形 光著頭的，不戴帽的 副 光著頭，不戴帽

bargain [`bɑrgɪn] 動 交易，討價還價
▶ For foreign visitors, it's fun to bargain at the night market.
對外國遊客而言，在夜市討價還價很有趣。
動詞三態變化 bargain - bargained - bargained

bark [bɑrk] 動 吠叫，咆哮
▶ The dog is very fierce and always barks at strangers.
這隻狗很兇，常對陌生人吠叫。

相關衍生字彙 yell [jɛl] 動 吼叫、call [kɔl] 動 喊叫、shout [ʃaut] 動 大聲叫、scream [skrim]
動 尖叫、roar [ror] 動 吼叫，呼嘯、bay [be] 動 對～吠叫

動詞三態變化 bark - barked - barked

barley [ˋbɑrlɪ] 名 大麥
▶ The beer was made from barley. 這啤酒是大麥釀成的。

barometer [bəˋrɑmətɚ] 名 氣壓計
▶ A barometer is used to measure air pressure. 氣壓計是用來量大氣的壓力。

barrel [ˋbærəl] 名 木桶　　片 a beer barrel 啤酒桶　　◎ MP3 02-03

barren [ˋbærən] 形 荒蕪的，不孕的
▶ After the war, the land became barren. 戰爭過後，這片土地就變荒蕪了。

barricade [ˋbærəˌked] 名 路障
▶ There was a fire, so the firefighters put barricades to block off the road.
有火災發生，所以消防人員放置路障封鎖此路。

barrier [ˋbærɪr] 名 障礙
▶ It takes time to overcome the language barrier.
克服語言障礙是很費時的。

相關衍生字彙 obstruction [əbˋstrʌkʃən] 名 阻礙、obstacle [ˋɑbstəkl] 名 障礙（物）、
hindrance [ˋhɪndrəns] 名 妨礙

barter [ˋbɑrtɚ] 動 以～作為交換
▶ In the past, the villagers bartered rice for their necessities.
以前，這裡的村民用米去換日常用品。

動詞三態變化 barter - bartered - bartered

base [bes] 動 以～為基礎　　片 be based on 根據～
動詞三態變化 base - based - based

baseball [ˋbesˌbɔl] 名 棒球
▶ After school, kids like to play baseball.
放學後，孩子們喜歡打棒球。

相關衍生字彙 basketball [ˋbæskɪtˌbɔl] 名 籃球、soccer [ˋsɑkɚ] 名 足球、
badminton [ˋbædmɪntən] 名 羽毛球、tennis [ˋtɛnɪs] 名 網球、golf [gɑlf]
名 高爾夫球

basement [ˋbesmənt] 名 地下室
▶ Mark used the basement as his laboratory. 馬克把地下室當成他的實驗室。

B

bash [bæʃ] 動 猛撞，抨擊
▶ Many locals bashed the government for the wrong policy.
很多當地人抨擊政府這項錯誤的政策。
動詞三態變化 bash - bashed - bashed

bashful [`bæʃfəl] 形 害羞的
▶ Her bashful smile is very charming.
她害羞的笑容很迷人。
相關衍生字彙 timid [`tɪmɪd] 形 膽小的、shy [ʃaɪ] 形 害羞的、confident [`kɑnfədənt]
形 有自信的、brave [brev] 形 勇敢的、embarrassed [ɪm`bærəst] 形 尷尬的

basic [`besɪk] 形 基本的　　反 advanced [əd`vænst] 形 進階的

basin [`besn̩] 名 盆子，流域
▶ The Yellow River Basin is very large. 黃河流域很廣。

basis [`besɪs] 名 基礎，根據　　片 on the basis of 根據～
相關衍生字彙 foundation [faun`deʃən] 名 基礎、essential [ɪ`sɛnʃəl] 形 基本的、
necessary [`nɛsəˌsɛrɪ] 形 需要的、necessity [nə`sɛsətɪ] 名 必需品

bask [bæsk] 動 曬太陽
▶ Many monkeys sit on the branches, basking in the sun.
很多猴子坐在樹枝上曬著太陽。
動詞三態變化 bask - basked - basked

bat [bæt] 名 球棒，蝙蝠
▶ The bat was made of steel, which is impossible to break.
這支球棒是鋼製的，不可能折斷。

batter [`bætɚ] 動 連續猛擊，磨損
▶ The news that a policeman was battered to death was shocking.
警察被打死的消息太令人震驚了。
動詞三態變化 batter - battered - battered

bath [bæθ] 名 沐浴　　片 to take a bath 洗澡

bathe [beð] 動 洗澡
▶ The babysitter helped me bathe the baby.
保姆替我幫嬰兒洗澡。
相關衍生字彙 shower [`ʃauɚ] 名 淋浴、bathtub [`bæθˌtʌb] 名 浴缸、bathrobe [`bæθˌrob]
名 浴袍、towel [`tauəl] 名 毛巾、soap [sop] 名 肥皂、bathroom [`bæθˌrum]
名 浴室
動詞三態變化 bathe - bathed - bathed

battery [`bætərɪ] 名 電池
▶ The battery of my flashlight has run down. 我手電筒的電池沒電了。

battle [`bætḷ] 名 戰役，爭鬥
▶ Her only son was killed in battle.
她唯一的兒子在戰場上捐軀。

相關衍生字彙 battlefield [`bætḷ͵fild] 名 戰場、battleship [`bætḷ͵ʃɪp] 名 戰艦、skirmish [`skɝmɪʃ] 名 小規模戰鬥，小衝突、war [wɔr] 名 動 戰爭

beach [bitʃ] 名 沙灘　　　MP3 02-04
▶ The city is famous for its beautiful beach.
這城市以它美麗的沙灘聞名。

相關衍生字彙 seashore [`sɪ͵ʃor] 名 海濱、coast [kost] 名 海岸、waterfront [`wɔtɚ͵frʌnt] 名 濱水區、seaside [`si͵saɪd] 名 海邊

bead [bid] 名 露水，汗珠，淚珠，水滴　　片 beads of sweat 汗珠

beam [bim] 名 光線
▶ The beam from the flashlight is not bright, but dim.
手電筒的光線不亮，反而有點昏暗。

bear [bɛr] 動 忍受，承受　　片 to bear the responsibility 承擔責任
相關衍生字彙 bearable [`bɛrəbḷ] 形 能耐的，忍得住的、bearably [`bɛrəblɪ] 副 能夠忍受地、withstand [wɪð`stænd] 動 抵擋，反抗，禁得起

動詞三態變化 bear - bore - borne

beard [bɪrd] 名 山羊鬍
▶ To make himself look mature, he is growing a beard.
為了讓自己看起來成熟點，他正在留山羊鬍。

相關衍生字彙 moustache [məs`tæʃ] 名 八字鬍、whisker [`hwɪskɚ] 名 頰鬚

beast [bist] 名 野獸
▶ *"Beauty and the Beast"* is a popular fairy tale written by a French novelist.
《美女與野獸》是法國小說家寫的一部很受歡迎的童話故事。

beat [bit] 動 打擊，打敗
▶ It was a pity that he was beaten by his opponent.
很可惜，他被他的對手打敗了。

相關衍生字彙 beating [`bitɪŋ] 名（尤指因處罰而）打，拍打，捶打，打敗、clout [klaʊt] 動（用手）猛擊、pound [paʊnd] 動 搗碎，（連續）猛擊

動詞三態變化 beat - beat - beaten

beautiful [`bjutəfəl] 形 漂亮的
▶ The small town has breathtakingly beautiful scenery.
這小鎮的美景令人屏息。

B

相關衍生字彙 beauty [`bjutɪ] 名 美女、beautifully [`bjutəfəlɪ] 副 美麗地、
beautify [`bjutəˏfaɪ] 動 美化、lovely [`lʌvlɪ] 形 可愛的、beauteous [`bjutɪəs]
形 美麗的

---

because [bɪ`kɔz] 連 因為
▶ Because of air pollution, the locals had no choice but to stay indoors.
因為空氣汙染，當地人只好待在屋內。

---

beckon [`bɛkn̩] 動 招喚，示意
▶ She beckoned to me as if she needed help.
她跟我示意彷彿是需要幫忙。

動詞三態變化 beckon - beckoned - beckoned

---

become [bɪ`kʌm] 動 變成，成為
▶ It's becoming cold. The winter is coming.
天氣變冷了，冬天到了。

動詞三態變化 become - became - become

---

beg [bɛg] 動 請求
▶ I beg your forgiveness.
我請求你的原諒。

相關衍生字彙 beggar [`bɛgɚ] 名 乞丐、poor [pʊr] 形 貧窮的、rich [rɪtʃ] 形 富有的、
homeless [`homlɪs] 形 無家可歸的

動詞三態變化 beg - begged - begged

---

begin [bɪ`gɪn] 動 開始　　同 start [stɑrt] 動 開始
相關衍生字彙 beginner [bɪ`gɪnɚ] 名 初學者，新手、beginning [bɪ`gɪnɪŋ] 名 開始，起源、
commence [kə`mɛns] 動 開始，著手

動詞三態變化 begin - began - begun

---

beguile [bɪ`gaɪl] 動 欺騙，使著迷
▶ The old man was beguiled of all his fortune.
這名老人被騙走全部的財產。

動詞三態變化 beguile - beguiled - beguiled

---

behalf [bɪ`hæf] 名 代表　　片 on behalf of 代表～

---

behave [bɪ`hev] 動 行為，表現
▶ Behave yourself!
請好自為之！

動詞三態變化 behave - behaved - behaved

---

behavior [bɪ`hevjɚ] 名 行為，舉止
▶ The boy's behavior is very rude. 這男孩的舉止很粗魯。

behind [bɪˋhaɪnd] 介 在～後方　　片 to leave something behind 把～遺忘（沒拿）

相關衍生字彙 beneath [bɪˋniθ] 介 在～下方、below [bəˋlo] 介 在～下方、under [ˋʌndɚ] 介 在～下方、over [ˋovɚ] 介 在～上方

---

behold [bɪˋhold] 動 注視，看完
▶ To behold the night scene, we camped in the mountains.
為了看夜景，我們在山上露營。

相關衍生字彙 beholder [bɪˋholdɚ] 名 觀看者，旁觀者、onlooker [ˋɑn͵lukɚ] 名 觀眾，旁觀者

動詞三態變化 behold - beheld - beheld

---

belated [bɪˋletɪd] 形 延期的，太遲的　　片 a belated apology 遲來的道歉

---

belief [bɪˋlif] 名 信念　　◎ MP3 **02-05**
▶ It's my firm belief that all men are born equal.
人人生而平等，是我堅信的信念。

相關衍生字彙 believe [bɪˋliv] 動 相信、trust [trʌst] 動 信任、faith [feθ] 名 信念、promise [ˋprɑmɪs] 名 允諾

---

bellicose [ˋbɛlə͵kos] 形 好戰的
▶ The general was bellicose and insisted on fighting.
這名將軍很好戰，他堅持要打下去。

相關衍生字彙 bellicosity [͵bɛləˋkɑsətɪ] 名 好戰性、belligerency [bəˋlɪdʒərənsɪ] 名 交戰（狀態），敵對態度、defiant [dɪˋfaɪənt] 形 挑戰的，違抗的

---

belong [bəˋlɔŋ] 動 屬於
▶ Both Mary and her boyfriend belong to the science club.
瑪莉跟她的男朋友都是科學社的成員。

相關衍生字彙 belongings [bəˋlɔŋɪŋz] 名 家眷，攜帶物品、sense of belonging 片 歸屬感

動詞三態變化 belong - belonged - belonged

---

beloved [bɪˋlʌvɪd] 形 心愛的
▶ Her beloved dog died last month.
她心愛的小狗在上個月去世了。

相關衍生字彙 dear [dɪr] 形 親愛的、favorite [ˋfevərɪt] 形 最愛的、cherish [ˋtʃɛrɪʃ] 動 珍愛、sweetheart [ˋswit͵hɑrt] 名 心上人

---

below [bəˋlo] 介 在～下方
▶ The school asks all the girls to wear their skirts below the knee.
學校要求女孩們穿的裙子都要長過膝蓋。

---

belt [bɛlt] 名 腰帶，皮帶　　片 to fasten the seat belt 繫好安全帶

---

bench [bɛntʃ] 名 長椅
▶ In early morning, many elderly people sit on the benches chatting in the park.
在清晨，公園裡有很多老人坐在長椅上聊天。

B

bend [bɛnd] 動 彎曲　　片 to bend down 彎下腰來
動詞三態變化 bend - bent - bent

benediction [ˌbɛnəˈdɪkʃən] 名 祝福
▶ He started his travelling with all his friends' benediction.
　帶著朋友的祝福，他出發旅遊去了。
相關衍生字彙 wish [wɪʃ] 名 祝福、blessing [ˈblɛsɪŋ] 名 賜福、hope [hop] 名 希望、
　　　　　　prayer [prɛr] 名 祈禱、grace [ɡres] 名 恩典

benefactor [ˈbɛnəˌfæktɚ] 名 捐助人
▶ With many benefactors' support, the charity can help the sick, the poor and the homeless.
　有了捐助者的支持，這個慈善機構才能幫助那些生病、貧窮及無家可歸的人們。

beneficent [bɪˈnɛfəsənt] 形 行善的，有益的　　片 beneficent bacteria 益菌

beneficial [ˌbɛnəˈfɪʃəl] 形 有益的，有利的
▶ Studying abroad is beneficial to your English ability.
　到國外讀書對你的英文能力有幫助。

benefit [ˈbɛnəfɪt] 名 益處
▶ The new library is a benefit to all of the students.
　這座新的圖書館對所有學生都有好處。
相關衍生字彙 advantage [ədˈvæntɪdʒ] 名 優點、profit [ˈprɑfɪt] 名 利潤、interest [ˈɪntərɪst]
　　　　　　名 利息、earning [ˈɝnɪŋ] 名 收入

benevolent [bəˈnɛvələnt] 形 仁慈的，親切的
▶ The benevolent old man takes care of many stray cats and dogs.
　這位仁慈的老人照顧很多流浪貓狗。

benign [bɪˈnaɪn] 形 良性的　　片 a benign tumor 良性腫瘤

bequeath [bɪˈkwið] 動 把～遺贈給～
▶ The rich man bequeathed the orphanage his fortune in his will.
　這位富翁在遺囑中交代要將全部財產給這所孤兒院。
動詞三態變化 bequeath - bequeathed - bequeathed

beseech [bɪˈsitʃ] 動 哀求
▶ The thief beseeched the policeman to forgive him.
　小偷央求警察原諒他。
相關衍生字彙 ask [æsk] 動 要求、plead [plid] 動 請求、beg 動 [bɛɡ] 懇求、
　　　　　　demand [dɪˈmænd] 動 要求、request [rɪˈkwɛst] 動 要求
動詞三態變化 beseech - beseeched / besought - beseeched / besought

besides [bɪˋsaɪdz] 副 介 除此之外　　同 in addition to 此外

相關衍生字彙 moreover [morˋovɚ] 副 並且，此外、furthermore [ˋfɝðɚˏmor] 副 而且，再者、otherwise [ˋʌðɚˏwaɪz] 副 否則，不然

---

besiege [bɪˋsidʒ] 動 包圍，圍攻

▶ The crowd besieged the TV station to ask for an apology.
群眾包圍電視台要求道歉。

動詞三態變化 besiege - besieged - besieged

---

beset [bɪˋsɛt] 動 使苦惱　　片 be beset with 苦惱於～

動詞三態變化 beset - beset - beset

---

bestow [bɪˋsto] 動 給予，頒贈　　　　　　　　　MP3 02-06

▶ The local government bestowed a certificate of honor citizen upon the foreign doctor.
當地政府頒贈給這位外國醫生一份榮譽市民證書。

相關衍生字彙 award [əˋwɔrd] 動 授予、give [gɪv] 動 給予、receive [rɪˋsiv] 動 接受、gain [gen] 動 獲得、get [gɛt] 動 得到

動詞三態變化 bestow - bestowed - bestowed

---

bet [bɛt] 動 打賭

▶ I bet our team will win the contest.
我打賭我們的隊伍會贏得比賽。

動詞三態變化 bet - bet - bet

---

betray [bɪˋtre] 動 背叛

▶ She felt betrayed by her husband.
她覺得她的老公背叛了她。

動詞三態變化 betray - betrayed - betrayed

---

beverage [ˋbɛvərɪdʒ] 名 飲料

▶ Beverages and food are not allowed in the library.
飲料跟食物都不能帶進圖書館。

相關衍生字彙 liquor [ˋlɪkɚ] 名 酒類、alcohol [ˋælkəˏhɔl] 名 酒，酒精、drink [drɪŋk] 名 飲料、cocktail [ˋkɑkˏtel] 名 雞尾酒

---

beware [bɪˋwɛr] 動 提防，注意　　片 beware of 小心～

動詞三態變化 beware - bewared - bewared

---

bewilder [bɪˋwɪldɚ] 動 使困惑

▶ Visitors are often bewildered by the road signs.
旅客常常被路標搞混。

相關衍生字彙 bewildering [bɪˋwɪldɚ] 形 使人困惑的、bewilderment [bɪˋwɪldɚmənt] 名 迷惑，混亂、bewildered [bɪˋwɪldɚd] 形 困惑的

動詞三態變化 bewilder - bewildered - bewildered

B

beyond [bɪˋjɑnd] 介 超越　　片 beyond description 超出筆墨所能形容

bias [ˋbaɪəs] 名 偏見
▶ We shouldn't have a bias against black people. 我們對黑人不應存有偏見。

Bible [ˋbaɪbl̩] 名 聖經
▶ When going to church on Sunday, don't forget to bring the Bible.
星期天去教堂時，別忘了帶聖經。
相關衍生字彙 Biblical [ˋbɪblɪk l̩] 形 聖經的，出自聖經的

bicycle [ˋbaɪsɪkl̩] 名 腳踏車　　片 by bicycle 騎腳踏車
相關衍生字彙 bus [bʌs] 名 公車、train [tren] 名 火車、subway [ˋsʌbˏwe] 名 地下鐵、
airplane [ˋɛrˏplen] 名 飛機、railroad [ˋrelˏrod] 名 鐵路

bid [bɪd] 動 吩咐，命令
▶ Mom bade Lily to be careful on the way to school.
媽媽吩咐莉莉上學途中要小心。
動詞三態變化 bid - bid / bade - bid / bidden

bigot [ˋbɪgət] 名 偏執的人，固執者
▶ The violent attack was caused by a religious bigot.
這暴力攻擊是一名宗教偏執狂引起的。

bilingual [baɪˋlɪŋgwəl] 形 雙語的
▶ The elementary school is famous for its bilingual curriculum.
這所小學以它的雙語課程而聞名。

bill [bɪl] 名 法案，帳單　　片 to pass a bill 通過法案

billion [ˋbɪljən] 名 十億
▶ The country claims there are 1.6 billion population.
這個國家號稱有十六億人口。
相關衍生字彙 hundred [ˋhʌndrəd] 名 百、thousand [ˋθauzn̩d] 名 千、million [ˋmɪljən]
名 百萬、dozen [ˋdʌzn̩] 名 一打、decade [ˋdɛked] 名 十年

bind [baɪnd] 動 捆，綁，裝訂，束縛
▶ I bound the gift with a beautiful ribbon.
我在禮物上綁了個蝴蝶結。
動詞三態變化 bind - bound - bound

biography [baɪˋɑgrəfɪ] 名 傳記
▶ The reporter plans to write a biography of the mayor.
這位記者打算幫市長寫傳記。

biology [baɪˋɑlədʒɪ] 名 生物學　　片 marine biology 海洋生物學
相關衍生字彙 biotechnology [ˋbaɪotɛkˋnɑlədʒɪ] 名 生物科技、biochemistry [ˋbaɪoˋkɛmɪstrɪ]
名 生物化學、biologist [baɪˋɑlədʒɪst] 名 生物學家

birth [bɝθ] 名 出生，血統
▶ The handsome man has German birth.
　　這位帥哥有德國血統。

相關衍生字彙 birthmark [`bɝθˌmɑrk] 名 胎記，痣、birthplace [`bɝθˌples] 名 出生地、
birthrate [`bɝθˌret] 名 出生率、birthright [`bɝθˌraɪt] 名 與生俱來的權利

---

birthday [`bɝθˌde] 名 生日
▶ I prepared a gift for my daughter's 20th birthday.
　　我替女兒準備了二十歲的生日禮物。

---

bite [baɪt] 動 咬　　片 to bite into the apple 大口咬蘋果　　⊚ MP3 **02-07**
動詞三態變化 bite - bit - bitten

---

bitter [`bɪtɚ] 形 苦的，痛苦的　　片 a bitter lesson 一個慘痛的教訓
相關衍生字彙 bitterly [`bɪtɚlɪ] 副 痛苦地、sweet [swit] 形 甜美的、tasty [`testɪ] 形 美味的、
tasteful [`testfəl] 形 有品味的、flavorful [`flevɚfəl] 形 風味香濃的

---

bizarre [bɪ`zɑr] 形 奇異的　　片 bizarre behavior 怪異行為

---

black [blæk] 名 黑色 形 黑色的
▶ Black is my favorite color.
　　黑色是我最愛的顏色。

相關衍生字彙 blackberry [`blækˌbɛrɪ] 名 黑莓、blackboard [`blækˌbord] 名 黑板、
blacklist [`blækˌlɪst] 名 黑名單、blackhead [`blækˌhɛd] 名 黑頭粉刺

---

blackmail [`blækˌmel] 動 敲詐，勒索
▶ It's illegal to blackmail others.
　　敲詐他人是違法的。

動詞三態變化 blackmail - blackmailed - blackmailed

---

blackout [`blækˌaut] 名 停電
▶ Because of the violent typhoon, we had a blackout for two days.
　　由於強烈颱風，我們停電兩天。

---

blade [bled] 名 刀片　　片 razor blade 刮鬍刀

---

blame [blem] 名 責備
▶ A good leader should take the blame for a mistake.
　　好的領導者要能為錯誤承擔責備。

相關衍生字彙 accuse [ə`kjuz] 動 指控、impeach [ɪm`pitʃ] 動 彈劾、charge [tʃɑrdʒ]
動 指責、praise [prez] 動 讚美

---

blank [blæŋk] 形 空白的　　片 a blank check 空白支票

B

blanket [`blæŋkɪt] 名 毛毯
▶ The weather gets cold. I think you had better prepare a blanket.
天氣變冷了，你最好準備條毯子。

blast [blæst] 名 一陣風，爆炸　　片 a blast of strong wind 一陣強風

blaze [blez] 名 火焰，光輝
▶ It took hours for firefighters to put out the blaze.
消防人員花好幾個小時撲滅這場火。
相關衍生字彙 blazing [`blezɪŋ] 形 熾烈的，鮮明的、flame [flem] 名 火焰，熱情

bleak [blik] 形 嚴峻的，陰冷的
▶ The situation seems bleak. There is little hope to improve the relationship between them.
這情況好像很嚴峻，他們之間的關係沒什麼希望改善。

bleed [blid] 動 流血
▶ He got hurt and was bleeding badly.
他受傷並且流了很多血。
相關衍生字彙 blood [blʌd] 名 血液、fluid [`fluɪd] 名 液體、liquid [`lɪkwɪd] 名 液體、solid [`salɪd] 名 固體
動詞三態變化 bleed - bled - bled

blemish [`blɛmɪʃ] 名 傷疤，瑕疵
▶ There is an ugly blemish on the boy's face. 這位男孩臉上有一道難看的疤。

blend [blɛnd] 動 混合，協調
▶ As we know, oil doesn't blend with water.
誠如我們所知，油跟水是不相融的。
動詞三態變化 blend - blended - blended

bless [blɛs] 動 保佑
▶ May God bless you.
願上帝保佑你。
動詞三態變化 bless - blessed - blessed

blessing [`blɛsɪŋ] 名 賜福
▶ When you feel depressed, please count your blessings.
當你沮喪時，請想想自己擁有的福氣。

blind [blaɪnd] 形 眼盲的，盲目的　　片 to go blind 失明
相關衍生字彙 sight [saɪt] 名 視力、deaf [dɛf] 形 耳聾的、see [si] 動 看見、hear [hɪr] 動 聽到、listen [`lɪsn̩] 動 傾聽

blink [blɪŋk] 動 眨眼

► She blinked her eyes in surprise without saying a word.
她驚訝地眨眼，說不出一句話。

動詞三態變化 blink - blinked - blinked

---

bliss [blɪs] 名 極樂天堂　　片 eternal bliss 天國　　　　◎ MP3 **02-08**

相關衍生字彙 blissful [`blɪsfəl] 形 樂而忘憂的、felicity [fə`lɪsətɪ] 名 幸福、
paradise [`pærə͵daɪs] 名 天堂，極樂，樂園

---

blithe [blaɪð] 形 歡樂的　　同 merry [`mɛrɪ] 形 歡愉的

---

block [blɑk] 名 障礙物　　片 a stumbling block 絆腳石

---

blockade [blɑ`ked] 名 封鎖，障礙物

► The police enforced a blockade around the corner. 警方在街角實施封鎖。

---

blond [blɑnd] 形 金黃色的，金髮碧眼的

► The blond girl catches everyone's attention on campus.
這位金髮碧眼的女孩在校園裡很吸睛。

---

bloody [`blʌdɪ] 形 血淋淋的

► The war was a bloody battle.
這場戰爭是血淋淋的戰役。

相關衍生字彙 bloodless [`blʌdlɪs] 形 無血的，沒精神的、bloodstain [`blʌd͵sten] 名 血跡、
bloodily [`blʌdəlɪ] 副 殘忍地，血腥地

---

bloom [blum] 名 開花　　片 in full bloom（花）盛開

---

blossom [`blɑsəm] 名 花

► In spring, there are blossoms on the cherry trees.
在春天，櫻花樹都開花了。

相關衍生字彙 flower [`flauɚ] 名 花、leaf [lif] 名 葉子、stem [stɛm] 名 莖、trunk [trʌŋk]
名 樹幹、root [rut] 名 樹根

---

blot [blɑt] 名 污點　　片 to leave a blot 留下污點

---

blow [blo] 名 打擊，毆打

► The failure was a fatal blow to him. 那次的失敗對他是致命的一擊。

---

blue [blu] 名 藍色 形 藍色的　　片 out of the blue 出乎意料之外

相關衍生字彙 bluely [`blulɪ] 副 帶藍顏色地、blueness [`blunɪs] 名 藍色，憂鬱、
blue-collar [`blu`kɑlɚ] 形 勞工階級的、blueprint [`blu`prɪnt] 名 藍圖 動 計劃

---

blowout [`blo`aut] 名 爆胎

► Suddenly, our car had a blowout. 突然，我們的車子就爆胎了。

B

blueprint [`blu`prɪnt] 名 藍圖
▶ The government is drawing up a blueprint for the next decade.
政府正為下一個十年草擬藍圖。

bluff [blʌf] 動 虛張聲勢，嚇唬
▶ Don't be afraid! They are just bluffing.
別怕！他們只是虛張聲勢。
相關衍生字彙 threaten [`θrɛtn̩] 動 威脅、warn [wɔrn] 動 警告、admonish [əd`manɪʃ] 動 告誡、menace [`mɛnɪs] 動 威脅
動詞三態變化 bluff - bluffed - bluffed

blunder [`blʌndɚ] 名 大錯誤　片 to commit a blunder 犯大錯

blunt [blʌnt] 形 鈍的，不鋒利的
▶ The knife is blunt, not sharp.
這把刀很鈍，不鋒利。
動詞三態變化 blush - blushed - blushed

blush [blʌʃ] 動 臉紅
▶ He is not good at lying. He blushes readily. 他不善說謊，很容易臉紅。

bluster [`blʌstɚ] 動 咆哮，（風）狂吹
▶ Father was so angry that he blustered for hours.
爸爸很憤怒，所以咆哮數小時。
動詞三態變化 bluster - blustered - blustered

board [bord] 名 板子　片 a bulletin board 佈告欄
相關衍生字彙 blackboard [`blæk͵bord] 名 黑板、boarding [`bordɪŋ] 名 寄膳（宿）、wood [wud] 名 木頭、lumber [`lʌmbɚ] 名 木材、timber [`tɪmbɚ] 名 木料

boast [bost] 動 自吹自擂，誇耀
▶ Don't trust him because he boasts most of the time.
別相信他，因為他大部分的時候都在吹牛。
動詞三態變化 boast - boasted - boasted

boat [bot] 名 小船　片 to row a boat 划船　◎ MP3 **02-09**
相關衍生字彙 ship [ʃɪp] 名 船艦、vessel [`vɛsl̩] 名 船艦、submarine [`sʌbmə͵rin] 名 潛水艇、ferry [`fɛrɪ] 名 渡輪

boil [bɔɪl] 動 沸騰　片 boiling point 沸點
動詞三態變化 boil - boiled - boiled

boisterous [`bɔɪstərəs] 形 狂歡的，喧鬧的
▶ In the kindergarten, kids are always boisterous. 幼稚園裡的孩童總是喧鬧不止。

bold [bold] 形 勇敢的，放肆的，冒失的
▶ May I be so bold as to ask you how much a month you make?
　我可以冒昧的問你一個月賺多少錢嗎？
相關衍生字彙 brave [brev] 形 勇敢的、bravery [`brevərɪ] 名 勇氣、courage [ˏkɝɪdʒ]
　　名 勇氣、courageous [kə`redʒəs] 名 有勇氣的

bolt [bolt] 名 閃電，電光　　片 a bolt out the blue 晴天霹靂

bomb [bam] 名 炸彈
▶ An atomic bomb ended the Second World War.
　一顆原子彈結束二次大戰。
相關衍生字彙 bomber [`bamɚ] 名 轟炸機、missile [`mɪsḷ] 名 飛彈，投射物、
　　torpedo [tɔr`pido] 名 水雷，甩炮、warhead [`wɔrˏhɛd] 名（飛彈等的）彈頭

bombard [bam`bard] 動 轟炸，向～連續提出問題
▶ We were often bombarded with lots of critical questions in class.
　我們在課堂上常常被批判性問題連珠砲似地轟炸。
動詞三態變化 bombard - bombarded - bombarded

bombastic [bam`bæstɪk] 形 誇張的
▶ I don't like our manager's bombastic manner. 我不喜歡經理高調的作風。

bond [band] 名 聯繫，契約，黏貼
▶ We should form a friendly bond with our neighbors.
　我們應該與鄰居建立友好關係。
相關衍生字彙 connection [kə`nɛkʃən] 名 連結、link [lɪŋk] 動 連接、tie [taɪ] 動 聯繫、relation-
　　ship [rɪ`leʃənˏʃɪp] 名 關係

bondage [`bandɪdʒ] 名 束縛，奴役
▶ At that time, many Africans were sold into bondage.
　在當時，很多非洲人被賣為奴。

bone [bon] 名 骨頭
▶ The weather chilled me to the bone. 天氣寒冷刺骨。

bonus [`bonəs] 名 紅利，獎金
▶ At the end of a year, every employee at this company gets an annual
　bonus.
　每年年終，這間公司的每位員工都會拿到年終獎金。

book [buk] 名 書本 動 預訂
▶ The book will be published soon.
　這本書很快就要出版了。

B

相關衍生字彙 bookcase [`buk͵kes] 名 書架、bookkeeper [`buk͵kipə] 名 記帳人員、booklet [`buklɪt] 名 小冊子、bookmark [`buk͵mɑrk] 名 書籤、bookworm [`buk͵wɝm] 名 書呆子、bookstore [`buk͵stor] 名 書店

動詞三態變化 book - booked - booked

boom [bum] 名 繁榮　　片 economic boom 經濟繁榮

boon [bun] 名 恩惠，利益
▶ A smart phone is a boon for getting information.
智慧型手機對獲得資訊真的是很有幫助。

boorish [`burɪʃ] 形 粗俗的　　片 boorish behaviors 粗俗的行為

boost [bust] 名 動 提升，幫助
▶ The prize from the boss is a boost to our morale.
老闆給的獎金對我們的士氣大大提升。

動詞三態變化 boost - boosted - boosted

boot [but] 名 靴子　　片 to polish boots 擦靴子

booth [buθ] 名 亭子　　片 a telephone booth 電話亭

border [`bordə] 名 邊界
▶ It was said that some businessmen smuggled goods across the border.
據說，有生意人越過這邊界走私物品。

相關衍生字彙 boundary [`baundrɪ] 名 分界線、boundless [`baundlɪs] 形 無邊界的、range [rendʒ] 名 範圍、area [`ɛrɪə] 名 區域

born [bɔrn] 形 天生的，出生的　　⊙ MP3 02-10
▶ Is a good leader born or made? 好的領導人是天生還是後天養成的？

borrow [`baro] 動 借出
▶ Local people can borrow books from the public library.
當地人可以從這座公立圖書館借書。

動詞三態變化 borrow - borrowed - borrowed

boredom [`bordəm] 名 厭倦，無聊
▶ The activity was full of boredom. I won't join it again.
這活動很無趣，我不會再參加。

相關衍生字彙 bore [bor] 名 令人厭煩的人、boring [`borɪŋ] 形（事情）無聊的、bored [`bord] 形（人）感到無聊的

bosom [`buzəm] 名 胸部，胸懷
▶ I am lucky. I have been in the bosom of my family.
我很幸運，一直在家庭溫暖的懷抱中。

botanical [bo`tænɪkl̩] 形 植物的
▶ Walking in the botanical garden is relaxing.
在植物園裡散步真是舒服。
相關衍生字彙 botany [`bɑtənɪ] 名 植物學、plant [plænt] 名 植物、garden [`gɑrdn̩]
名 花園、field [fild] 名 原野

bottle [`bɑtl̩] 名 瓶子　　片 a bottle of 一瓶～

bother [`bɑðɚ] 動 打擾，煩惱
▶ Don't bother me while I am studying.
我讀書時請不要打擾我。
動詞三態變化 bother - bothered - bothered

bottom [`bɑtəm] 名 底部　　片 at the bottom of 在～的底部

bough [baʊ] 名 大樹枝
▶ The wind was so strong that the bough was broken.
風大到連大樹枝都被吹斷了。
相關衍生字彙 twig [twɪg] 名 嫩枝、branch [bræntʃ] 名 樹枝、trunk [trʌŋk] 名 樹幹、
root [rut] 名 （植物的）根

bounce [baʊns] 動 彈跳
▶ On hearing the news, he bounced out of the chair.
一聽到這消息，他從椅子上跳了起來。
動詞三態變化 bounce - bounced - bounced

bound [baʊnd] 形 受束縛的，必然的　　片 be bound to 一定會（發生）

bountiful [`baʊntəfəl] 形 充足的，慷慨的
▶ Mom always stores bountiful foods in the refrigerator.
媽媽總在冰箱存放充足的食物。

bounty [`baʊntɪ] 名 賞金，慷慨
▶ The police offer a bounty for catching the thief.
警方提供賞金要抓這個小偷。

bouquet [bu`ke] 名 一束（花），花束
▶ On her birthday, her husband sent a bouquet of flowers to her office.
生日那天，她老公送了一束花到她的辦公室。
相關衍生字彙 box [bɑks] 名 一盒、can [kæn] 名 一罐、roll [rol] 名 （一）捲、bag [bæg]
名 一袋之量

bow [bo] 動 鞠躬，行禮
▶ The little boy bowed politely to his teacher.
小男孩很有禮貌地跟老師鞠躬。
動詞三態變化 bow - bowed - bowed

B

bowel [ˋbauəl] 名 腸子　　🔸 to have loose bowels 拉肚子

boycott [ˋbɔɪ͵kɑt] 動 聯合，抵制，杯葛
▶ Customers were angry and decided to boycott the food company.
消費者很生氣，決定要抵制該食品公司。
動詞三態變化 boycott - boycotted - boycotted

brain [bren] 名 頭腦，腦袋　　🔸 to rack one's brain 絞盡腦汁
相關衍生字彙 brainchild [ˋbren͵tʃaɪld] 名 獨創、brainstorm [ˋbren͵stɔrm] 名 集思廣益、
head [hɛd] 名 頭部

brake [brek] 名 剎車　　🔸 to step on a brake 踩剎車

branch [bræntʃ] 名 樹枝，分店
▶ The headquarters decided to set up a branch in New York.
總公司決定在紐約設立分公司。

brand [brænd] 名 商標，品牌　　　　　　　　　　🔘 MP3 02-11
▶ This is a popular brand but its price is not low.
這是受歡迎的牌子，但是價錢不低。
相關衍生字彙 brander [ˋbrændɚ] 名 打烙印的人或器具、brand-new [ˋbrændˋnu] 形 全新的、
label [ˋlebl̩] 名 標籤，符號、tag [tæg] 名 牌子，貨籤

brandish [ˋbrændɪʃ] 動 揮舞，炫耀
▶ The postman brandished an umbrella to fight back the dog.
郵差揮舞雨傘來嚇退小狗。
動詞三態變化 brandish - brandished - brandished

brawl [brɔl] 名 動 爭吵，打架　　🔵 quarrel [ˋkwɔrəl] 名 動 爭吵
動詞三態變化 brawl - brawled - brawled

breach [britʃ] 名 破壞，違反
▶ The public support the police to arrest the students for committing a breach of peace.
大眾支持警方以違反和平理由逮捕這些學生。
相關衍生字彙 break [brek] 動 破壞、violate [ˋvaɪə͵let] 動 違反、trespass [ˋtrɛspəs] 動 違規、
intrude [ɪnˋtrud] 動 闖入

bread [brɛd] 名 麵包　　🔸 to earn one's daily bread 為自己謀生或餬口

break [brek] 名 動 中斷，休息，破損　　🔸 to take a break 休息一下
相關衍生字彙 breakdown [ˋbrek͵daun] 名 崩潰、breakfast [ˋbrɛkfəst] 名 早餐、
breakout [ˋbrek͵aut] 名 越獄、breakthrough [ˋbrek͵θru] 名 突破
動詞三態變化 break - broke - broken

breast [brɛst] 名 乳房　　🔸 breast cancer 乳癌

breath [brɛθ] 名 呼吸
▶ I tried to relieve my pressure by taking a deep breath.
我試著深呼吸來減緩我的壓力。

breathe [brið] 動 呼吸
▶ The dog is still breathing, which means it is still alive.
小狗仍在呼吸，所以牠還活著。
動詞三態變化 breathe - breathed - breathed

breathless [`brɛθlɪs] 形 喘不過氣的，氣喘吁吁的
▶ Carrying the heavy box makes me breathless. 搬這沉重箱子讓我氣喘吁吁的。

breathtaking [`brɛθ͵tekɪŋ] 形 驚人的，令人喘不過氣的，緊張的
▶ It was a breathtaking moment when the result of the contest was announced.
當比賽結果宣布時，真是緊張的時刻。
相關衍生字彙 nervous [`nɝvəs] 形 緊張不安的、exciting [ɪk`saɪtɪŋ] 形 令人興奮的、upset [ʌp`sɛt] 形 心煩的

breed [brid] 動 繁殖，飼養
▶ Most animals breed in spring.
大部分的動物都在春天繁殖。
動詞三態變化 breed - bred - bred

breeze [briz] 名 微風
▶ Sitting under the tree, I can feel a breeze coming up.
坐在樹下，我可以感受到微風徐徐吹來。

brevity [`brɛvətɪ] 名 簡潔，短促
▶ The professor asked our essays should follow the rule of brevity.
教授要求我們的論文要遵守簡潔的規定。
相關衍生字彙 simple [`sɪmpl] 形 簡單的、easy [`izɪ] 形 容易的、short [ʃɔrt] 形 短的、complexity [kəm`plɛksətɪ] 名 複雜（性）

bribe [braɪb] 名 賄賂
▶ It's wrong to accept a bribe from others.
收受他人賄賂是錯誤的。
相關衍生字彙 briber [`braɪbɚ] 名 行賄者、bribable [`braɪbəbl] 形 能收買的、bribee [͵braɪb`i] 名 受賄者、bribery [`braɪbərɪ] 名 受賄，行賄

brick [brɪk] 名 磚塊　片 to lay bricks 砌磚

bride [braɪd] 名 新娘
▶ The bride is of course the most beautiful one at the wedding ceremony.
新娘當然是婚禮最漂亮的那一個。

B

相關衍生字彙 bridegroom [`braɪdˌgrʊm] 名 新郎、husband [`hʌzbənd] 名 丈夫、
wife [waɪf] 名 太太、spouse [spaʊz] 名 配偶

---

bridge [brɪdʒ] 名 橋梁 動 把～連結起來　片 a suspension bridge 吊橋
動詞三態變化 bridge - bridged - bridged

---

brief [brif] 名 摘要　片 in brief 簡言之
相關衍生字彙 briefly [`briflɪ] 副 簡短地，短暫地、briefness [`brifnɪs] 名 簡單，（時間）短促

---

brighten [`braɪtn̩] 動 明亮，活躍
▶ After rain, the sky brightened up soon.
下雨過後，天空很快就亮起來了。
相關衍生字彙 bright [braɪt] 形 明亮的，開朗的、brightly [`braɪtlɪ] 副 明亮地，爽朗地、
brightness [`braɪtnɪs] 名 明亮，活潑
動詞三態變化 brighten - brightened - brightened

---

brilliant [`brɪljənt] 形 卓越的，聰明的　　　MP3 02-12
▶ It was brilliant of her to speak three foreign languages.
她真是優秀，可以講三種外國語言。

---

brim [brɪm] 名 邊，緣　片 a wide-brimmed hat 寬邊帽

---

bring [brɪŋ] 動 帶來，導致
▶ As the saying goes, "April rain brings May flowers."
誠如諺語所說，「四月雨會帶來五月花」。
相關衍生字彙 carry [`kærɪ] 動 搬運、take [tek] 動 拿走、send [sɛnd] 動 寄送、
deliver [dɪ`lɪvɚ] 動 遞送、convey [kən`ve] 動 傳輸
動詞三態變化 bring - brought - brought

---

brink [brɪŋk] 名 邊緣
▶ The two countries are at the brink of war. 這兩個國家處於戰爭一觸即發的狀態。

---

bristle [`brɪs!] 動 發怒，（毛髮等）直立
▶ He bristled at his son's remarks and behavior.
他對他兒子的言行感到生氣。
動詞三態變化 bristle - bristled - bristled

---

brittle [`brɪt!] 形 易碎的，冷淡的
▶ The elderly's bones are brittle. 老年人的骨頭是易碎的。

broad [brɔd] 形 寬的，概括的，明顯的，各式各樣的
▶ The menu at the restaurant offers a broad choice.
　這家餐廳有各式各樣的菜色可供選擇。

相關衍生字彙 wide [waɪd] 形 寬的、narrow [ˋnæro] 形 窄的、various [ˋvɛrɪəs]
　　　　　形 各式各樣的、spacious [ˋspeʃəs] 形 空間大的、broaden [ˋbrɔdn̩]
　　　　　動 擴大，變寬、broadly [ˋbrɔdlɪ] 副 概括地，明顯地、
　　　　　broad-minded [ˋbrɔdˋmaɪndɪd] 形 心胸開闊的，無偏見的

broadcast [ˋbrɔdˌkæst] 名 廣播　　片 a live broadcast 現場廣播

brochure [broˋʃur] 名 小冊子
▶ Many brochures on vacations are offered by hotels.
　飯店會提供很多度假指南的小冊子。

broil [brɔɪl] 動 烤，曝曬　　同 grill [grɪl] 動（用烤架）烤（魚、肉等）
相關衍生字彙 fry [fraɪ] 動 油煎，油炸、boil [bɔɪl] 動 煮熟、stew [stju] 動 燉，燜、cook [kʊk]
　　　　　動 烹調

動詞三態變化 broil - broiled - broiled

broken-hearted [ˋbrokənˋhartɪd] 形 心碎的，傷心的
▶ When his girlfriend said good bye to him, he was broken-hearted.
　當他女朋友跟他說再見時，他心都碎了。

broker [ˋbrokɚ] 名 經紀人，掮客　　片 an insurance broker 保險經紀人

brood [brud] 動 沉思，籠罩
▶ He brooded his future all night.
　他整夜都在沉思他的未來。

相關衍生字彙 consider [kənˋsɪdɚ] 動 考慮、reflect [rɪˋflɛkt] 動 反思、mediate [ˋmidɪˌet]
　　　　　動 深思、think [θɪŋk] 動 思考、ponder [ˋpandɚ] 動 衡量

動詞三態變化 brood - brooded - brooded

brook [brʊk] 名 小溪，小河
▶ The sound of the babbling brook is so clear at night.
　小溪潺潺的流水聲在夜晚特別清楚。

broom [brum] 名 掃把
▶ I cleaned my bedroom with a broom. 我用掃把清掃我的房間。

broth [brɔθ] 名 湯
▶ Too many cooks spoil the broth.（諺語）廚師多，做壞一鍋湯（人多礙事）。

brotherhood [ˋbrʌðɚˌhud] 名 手足之情
▶ I cherish the brotherhood among my brothers and me.
　我很珍惜兄弟之間的手足之情。

(相關衍生字彙) brother [`brʌðɚ] 名 兄弟、brother-in-law [`brʌðərɪn‚lɔ] 名 姊夫，妹婿、
sister [`sɪstɚ] 名 姊妹、sister-in-law [`sɪstərɪn‚lɔ] 名 嫂嫂，弟妹

brow [braʊ] 名 眉毛　　(片) to winkle one's brow 皺眉

browse [braʊz] 動 瀏覽，翻閱
▶ On weekends, I like going to the bookstore browsing through books.
周末，我喜歡到書店翻閱書籍。
(動詞三態變化) browse - browsed - browsed

bruise [bruz] 名 瘀青
▶ I was lucky enough and only got a few bruises. 我運氣很好，只有瘀青而已。

brush [brʌʃ] 名 刷子 動 刷，擦掉　　(MP3 02-13)
▶ Jack cleaned the dust on his desk with a brush.
傑克用刷子將桌上的灰塵清乾淨。
(相關衍生字彙) paintbrush [`pent‚brʌʃ] 名 畫筆、toothbrush [`tuθ‚brʌʃ] 名 牙刷、
brush-off [`brʌʃ‚ɔf] 名 不理不睬、brushing [`brʌʃɪŋ] 形 疾馳的
(動詞三態變化) brush - brushed - brushed

brusque [brʌsk] 形 直率的，唐突的
▶ He is sometimes a little brusque and uses some rude words, but he is not intended to be.
他有時會直率的用些不當的詞語，但他不是有意的。

brutal [`brutl] 形 殘忍的，苛刻的
▶ Tom feels it is brutal to eat dogs and rabbits. 湯姆覺得吃狗肉跟兔肉太殘忍了。

bubble [`bʌbl] 名 泡泡　　(片) to blow bubbles 吹泡泡

bud [bʌd] 名 花蕾 動 發芽
▶ Lots of flowers in my backyard are in bud.
我後院很多花已經含苞待放了。
(動詞三態變化) bud - budded - budded

Buddhism [`budɪzəm] 名 佛教
▶ Buddhism is a popular religion in Asia.
佛教在亞洲很盛行。
(相關衍生字彙) Islam [`ɪsləm] 名 回教、Christianity [‚krɪstʃɪ`ænətɪ] 名 基督教、
Catholicism [kə`θɑlə‚sɪzəm] 名 天主教

budget [`bʌdʒɪt] 名 預算，經費
▶ Housewives are usually the ones who control the household budget.
家庭主婦通常是控制家庭收支預算的人。

buffer [`bʌfɚ] 名 起緩衝的人（或物），緩衝器　　(片) a buffer zone 緩衝區

build [bɪld] 動 建築，建造
▶ My friends and I build a relationship on trust.
我和朋友的關係建立在信任的基礎上。
相關衍生字彙 building [`bɪldɪŋ] 名 建築物、structure [`strʌktʃɚ] 名 結構、make [mek] 動 製作，建造、construct [kən`strʌkt] 動 建造、develop [dɪ`vɛləp] 動 發展
動詞三態變化 build - built - built

---

bulb [bʌlb] 名 燈泡
▶ Electric bulbs were invented by Edison. 燈泡是愛迪生發明的。

bulge [bʌldʒ] 動 脹，凸起
▶ Men's pockets were often bulging with wallets.
男士們的口袋常因塞有皮夾而鼓鼓的。
動詞三態變化 bulge - bulged - bulged

---

bulk [bʌlk] 名 體積
▶ An elephant has a huge bulk.
大象有龐大的體積。
相關衍生字彙 length [lɛŋθ] 名 長度、width [wɪdθ] 名 寬度、height [haɪt] 名 高度、area [`ɛrɪə] 名 面積，範圍

---

bullet [`bʊlɪt] 名 子彈　　片 a hail of bullets 一陣槍林彈雨

---

bulletin [`bʊlətɪn] 名 公報，公告
▶ The doctor issues a bulletin on the condition of the president's health every year.
醫生每年對總統的健康狀況發布一次報告。

bullish [`bʊlɪʃ] 形 看漲的，樂觀的　　片 bullish market (股票) 多頭市場

bully [`bʊlɪ] 動 霸凌
▶ No kid should be bullied at school.
孩童不應該在學校被霸凌。
動詞三態變化 bully - bullied - bullied

---

bump [bʌmp] 動 碰撞，猛擊
▶ Because of the dim light, the two cars bumped into each other.
由於光線昏暗，兩輛車子互撞。
相關衍生字彙 collide [kə`laɪd] 動 撞擊、hit [hɪt] 動 打擊、clash [klæʃ] 動 撞擊作 (聲)、crush [krʌʃ] 動 壓碎
動詞三態變化 bump - bumped - bumped

---

bundle [`bʌndl̩] 名 捆，包裹，一大筆 (錢)　　片 to make a bundle 賺一大筆錢

buoy [bɔɪ] 名 浮標　　片 a life buoy 救生圈

burden [`bɝdn̩] 名 負擔，噸位

▶ Kids are parents' sweet burden.
　小孩是父母甜蜜的負擔。

相關衍生字彙 load [lod] 名 負荷、responsibility [rɪˌspɑnsə`bɪlətɪ] 名 責任、task [tæsk] 名 任務、job [dʒɑb] 名 工作、duty [`djutɪ] 名 責任

B

bureau [`bjuro] 名（政府機關的）處，局，所，署　　　◎ MP3 02-14
　片 Information Bureau 新聞局

bureaucracy [bju`rɑkrəsɪ] 名 官僚制度

▶ A government with the bureaucracy appears inefficient.
　有官僚制度的政府顯得沒效率。

burgle [`bɝgl̩] 動 撬竊

▶ One of my neighbors was burgled last night.
　有鄰居昨晚家中遭小偷。

相關衍生字彙 steal [stil] 動 偷竊、rob [rɑb] 動 搶劫、take [tek] 動 拿走、burglar [`bɝglɚ] 名 夜盜、thief [θif] 名 小偷、thieve [θiv] 動 偷竊

動詞三態變化 burgle - burgled - burgled

burn [bɝn] 動 燃燒　　片 to burn the midnight oil 熬夜，挑燈夜戰
動詞三態變化 burn - burned / burnt - burned / burnt

burrow [`bɝo] 動 挖掘

▶ Earthworms burrowed into the lawn in our backyard.
　蚯蚓在我家後院草地鑽土。

動詞三態變化 burrow - burrowed - burrowed

burst [bɝst] 動 爆發，突然發生　　片 to burst into tears / laughter 突然大哭／大笑
動詞三態變化 burst - bursted / burst - bursted / burst

bury [`bɛrɪ] 動 掩埋，安葬

▶ To pass the exam, he buried himself in his studying.
　為了通過考試，他埋頭苦讀。

動詞三態變化 bury - buried - buried

bush [buʃ] 名 灌木叢

▶ The gardener trims the bush in our neighborhood every Monday.
　園丁每周一會修剪我們鄰區的灌木叢。

business [`bɪznɪs] 名 生意，商業　　片 to mind your own business 少管閒事

bustle [`bʌsl̩] 名 喧囂 動 催促　　片 hustle and bustle（城市的）熙熙攘攘
相關衍生字彙 busy [`bɪzɪ] 形 忙碌的、noise [nɔɪz] 名 噪音、noisy [`nɔɪzɪ] 形 噪音的、sound [saund] 名 聲音、fuss [fʌs] 名 動 忙亂

動詞三態變化 bustle - bustled - bustled

butterfly [ˋbʌtɚˏflaɪ] 名 蝴蝶
▶ Look! Butterflies are flying from flower to flower.
你看！蝴蝶在花叢中飛來飛去。

---

button [ˋbʌtn̩] 名 鈕扣　　🄗 to sew on a button 縫上鈕扣

---

buy [baɪ] 動 購買
▶ It's cheaper to buy wholesale.
批發買進比較便宜。

(相關衍生字彙) sell [sɛl] 動 販賣、purchase [ˋpɝtʃəs] 動 購買、shop [ʃɑp] 動 採購、
vend [vɛnd] 動 販賣

(動詞三態變化) buy - bought - bought

---

buzz [bʌz] 動 嗡嗡叫
▶ A fly keeps buzzing around my ear.
一隻蒼蠅在我耳邊嗡嗡叫。

(動詞三態變化) buzz - buzzed - buzzed

---

bypass [ˋbaɪˏpæs] 名 旁道 動 繞過
▶ We bypassed to avoid the traffic jam.
我們繞道避開塞車。

(動詞三態變化) bypass - bypassed - bypassed

MEMO

MEMO

詞性說明

名 名詞	副 副詞	介 介系詞
動 動詞	形 形容詞	連 連接詞
代 代名詞	助 助動詞	

內文圖示說明

片 片語　　　　反 反義字　　　　同 同義字

一網打盡「英語小知識」｜星期

Monday
星期一

Tuesday
星期二

Wednesday
星期三

Thursday
星期四

Friday
星期五

Saturday
星期六

Sunday
星期日

C cab ~ cynical

MP3 **03-01**

★一網打盡 1932 個英文單字 ｜ 一網打盡 366 句英語會話句

cab [kæb] 名 計程車　　片 to hail a cab 叫計程車

---

cabin [`kæbɪn] 名 客艙，小屋
▶ The rich man always chooses the first class cabin. 這位有錢人總是坐頭等艙。

---

cabinet [`kæbənɪt] 名 內閣
▶ The new prime minister announced his cabinet.
新的行政院長宣布了他的內閣。

---

cable [`kebḷ] 名 電纜　　片 cable TV 有線電視

---

cafeteria [ˌkæfə`tɪrɪə] 名 自助餐廳
▶ It's cheaper to have meals at the school cafeteria.
在學校自助餐廳用餐比較便宜。
相關衍生字彙 café [kə`fe] 名 小餐館，咖啡館、restaurant [`rɛstərənt] 名 餐廳、hotel [ho`tɛl]
名 飯店、inn [ɪn] 名 小旅館

---

caffeine [`kæfiin] 名 咖啡因
▶ Caffeine in tea and coffee can make people more active.
茶和咖啡中的咖啡因會使人提振精神。

---

cage [kedʒ] 名 籠子
▶ To keep the little bird, Anita bought a beautiful cage.
為了養小鳥，安妮塔買了一個漂亮的鳥籠。

---

cajole [kə`dʒol] 動 勾引，誘騙
▶ His son cajoled him into signing over all his property.
他兒子誘騙他簽字轉讓出所有財產。
動詞三態變化 cajole - cajoled - cajoled

---

cake [kek] 名 蛋糕　　片 a birthday cake 生日蛋糕

---

calamity [kə`læmətɪ] 名 災難
▶ For the couple, their son's death was a serious calamity.
對這對夫婦而言，兒子的死亡是個嚴重的災難。

---

calculate [`kælkjəˌlet] 動 推算，計算
▶ We calculated that it would cost us at least thousands of dollars to spend
the vacation.
這次度假，我們估計要花至少數千美元。
動詞三態變化 calculate - calculated - calculated

C

calculation [ˌkælkjəˈleʃən] 名 計算
▶ The budget is beyond our calculation.
預算超出我們的預估。
相關衍生字彙 calculator [ˈkælkjəˌletɚ] 名 計算機、mathematics [ˌmæθəˈmætɪks] 名 數學、count [kaʊnt] 動 計數、figure [ˈfɪgjɚ] 名 數字

---

calendar [ˈkæləndɚ] 名 日曆 片 the lunar calendar 陰曆

---

calf [kæf] 名 小牛
▶ The cow is in calf.
這隻母牛懷孕了。
相關衍生字彙 cattle [ˈkætl̩] 名 牛群、cow [kaʊ] 名 母牛、bull [bʊl] 名 公牛、ox [ɑks] 名 公牛

---

call [kɔl] 動 呼叫，稱呼，打電話給～ 片 to call at 拜訪
動詞三態變化 call - called - called

---

calligraphy [kəˈlɪgrəfɪ] 名 書法
▶ For Chinese, calligraphy is a kind of art.
對中國人而言，書法是一種藝術。

---

callous [ˈkæləs] 形 麻木不仁的
▶ How callous of him! He left home without saying anything.
好無情！他沒留下一句話就離開家。

---

calm [kɑm] 動 平靜下來 形 鎮靜的 片 to calm down 冷靜下來
相關衍生字彙 calmly [ˈkɑmlɪ] 副 冷靜地、quiet [ˈkwaɪət] 形 安靜的、reason [ˈrizn̩] 動 推理、reasonable [ˈriznəbl̩] 形 講道理的
動詞三態變化 calm - calmed - calmed

---

camera [ˈkæmərə] 名 相機 片 a digital camera 數位相機

---

camp [kæmp] 名 營地 動 露營
▶ This weekend, we plan to go camping near the river.
這周末我們打算在河邊露營。
動詞三態變化 camp - camped - camped

---

campaign [kæmˈpen] 名 活動 ◉ MP3 03-02
▶ Students started a campaign against the rising tuition.
學生們發起抗議學費上漲的活動。

---

campus [ˈkæmpəs] 名 校園
▶ Mary lives in the dorm on campus.
瑪莉住在學校的宿舍。

canal [kə`næl] 名 運河
▶ The canal plays an important role between the two countries.
這條運河在兩國間扮演重要的角色。
相關衍生字彙 river [`rɪvɚ] 名 河流、brook [bruk] 名 小河、stream [strim] 名 小溪流、
waterfall [`wɔtɚˌfɔl] 名 瀑布

cancel [`kænsl̩] 動 取消，廢除
▶ Because of the typhoon, all flights today are cancelled.
由於颱風，今天所有的班機都取消了。
動詞三態變化 cancel - canceled / cancelled - canceled / cancelled

cancer [`kænsɚ] 名 癌症
▶ His father died of lung cancer last month. 他的父親上個月死於肺癌。

candid [`kændɪd] 形 坦率的，公正的
▶ We are good friends and always candid with each other.
我們是好朋友，對彼此都很坦白。
相關衍生字彙 direct [də`rɛkt] 形 直接的、outspoken [aut`spokən] 形 直言不諱的、
honest [`ɑnɪst] 形 誠實的、real [`riəl] 形 真實的

candidate [`kændədet] 名 候選人　　片 to put up a candidate 推舉一位候選人

candle [`kændl̩] 名 蠟燭　　片 to blow out a candle 吹熄蠟燭
相關衍生字彙 candlelight [`kændl̩ˌlaɪt] 名 燭光、candlestick [`kændl̩ˌstɪk] 名 燭台、
lamp [læmp] 名 燈、lamplight [`læmpˌlaɪt] 名 燈光

candy [`kændɪ] 名 糖果
▶ Candy is kids' favorite. 糖果是小孩的最愛。

cane [ken] 名 拐杖，藤條
▶ The old man needs a cane to walk with. 這位老年人走路需要拐杖。

canoe [kə`nu] 名 獨木舟　　片 to paddle one's canoe 自食其力

canon [`kænən] 名 準則　　片 to establish a canon 建立準則

canvas [`kænvəs] 名 帆布
▶ Tents and sails are most made of canvas. 帳篷和船帆多用帆布製成的。

canyon [`kænjən] 名 峽谷
▶ The Grand Canyon in America is a popular tourist attraction.
美國大峽谷是很受歡迎的觀光勝地。

cap [kæp] 名 帽子　　片 a swimming cap 泳帽

C

capable [`kepəbl] 形 有能力的 　　 片 be capable of 有能力做～
相關衍生字彙 able [`ebl] 形 有能力的、capability [ˌkepə`bɪlətɪ] 名 能力、talent [`tælənt] 名 才能、incapable [ɪn`kepəbl] 形 無能的

capacious [kə`peʃəs] 形 容量大的，（心胸等）寬大的
▶ I like the capacious handbag because it can contain more.
我喜歡容量大的手提袋，因為它可以裝比較多。

capacity [kə`pæsətɪ] 名 容量，能力
▶ The new reading room in the library has a seating capacity of 500.
圖書館裡的新閱覽室有五百個位置。

capital [`kæpətl] 名 資金，首都，大寫字母
▶ The capital of Australia is Canberra, not Sydney.
澳洲的首都是坎培拉，不是雪梨。
相關衍生字彙 capitalism [`kæpətlˌɪzəm] 名 資本主義、capitalist [`kæpətlɪst] 名 資本家、capitalize [`kæpətlˌaɪz] 動 供給（資本）、socialism [`soʃəlˌɪzəm] 名 社會主義

caprice [kə`pris] 名 反覆無常，任性
▶ It's hard to get used to the caprices of the weather in fall.
要適應秋天多變的天氣不容易。

capsize [kæp`saɪz] 動 傾覆，弄翻　　 ◎ MP3 **03-03**
▶ When the boat is not balanced, it would capsize easily.
船如果沒有平衡就很容易翻覆。
動詞三態變化 capsize - capsized - capsized

capsule [`kæpsl] 名 膠囊，太空艙
▶ If the medicine is too bitter, you can put it into the capsule.
如果藥太苦，你可以把它裝到膠囊裡。

captain [`kæptɪn] 名 船長，（飛機的）機長
▶ All the passengers were killed in the plane crash, including the captain and the crew.
所有乘客在此墜機事件全喪命，包括機長跟組員。

caption [`kæpʃən] 名 標題，字幕
▶ The caption of the film catches my eye. 這電影的字幕很吸引我。

captivate [`kæptəˌvet] 動 使著迷
▶ The new products captivate consumers successfully.
這項新產品成功的吸引消費者。
相關衍生字彙 attract [ə`trækt] 動 吸引、tempt [tɛmpt] 動 誘惑、fascinate [`fæsnˌet] 動 迷惑、enchant [ɪn`tʃænt] 動 使著迷、charm [tʃɑrm] 動 吸引
動詞三態變化 captivate - captivated - captivated

captive [`kæptɪv] 形 受監禁的，被迷住的
▶ Charged of thief, he was captive for one month.
他被控偷竊，所以被困禁了一個月。

capture [`kæptʃɚ] 動 捕獲，引起（注意）
▶ It's impossible to capture the beauty of the scenery only with a camera.
只用相機很難捕捉這美景。
動詞三態變化 capture - captured - captured

carcass [`karkəs] 名 殘骸，屍體
▶ Wild animals often feed on the rotting carcasses.
野生動物常以腐爛的屍體為食。

card [kard] 名 卡片　　片 a credit card 信用卡
相關衍生字彙 cardboard [`kard‚bord] 名 硬紙板、paper [`pepɚ] 名 紙張、letter [`lɛtɚ]
名 信件、postcard [`post‚kard] 名 明信片、cards [kardz] 名 紙牌

cardiac [`kardɪ‚æk] 形 心臟的　　片 cardiac disease 心臟疾病

cardinal [`kardnəl] 形 基本的　　同 basic [`besɪk] 形 基本的

care [kɛr] 名 照顧，關心　　片 to take care of 照顧
相關衍生字彙 carefree [`kɛr‚fri] 形 自由自在的、careful [`kɛrfəl] 形 小心的、
carefully [`kɛrfəlɪ] 副 小心地、careless [`kɛrlɪs] 形 不小心的

career [kə`rɪr] 名 職業
▶ For a career woman, it's very hard to strike a balance between the work and the housework.
對職業婦女而言，很難在工作跟家務之間取得平衡。

cargo [`kargo] 名 貨物
▶ Hundreds of ships carry cargos by way of the river every day.
每天都有數以百計的船載著貨物經過這條河。

caricature [`kærɪkətʃɚ] 名 漫畫，諷刺畫
▶ The caricature caused the Muslims' protest. 這漫畫引起回教徒的抗議。

carnival [`karnəv!] 名 嘉年華
▶ People enjoy the carnival atmosphere at the festival.
人們享受嘉年華節慶的氣氛。

carol [`kærəl] 名 頌歌　　片 a Christmas carol 聖誕頌歌

carpenter [`karpəntɚ] 名 木匠
▶ We need a carpenter to repair our wooden door.
我們需要一位木匠來修我們的木門。
相關衍生字彙 plumber [`plʌmɚ] 名 水管工人、electrician [‚ɪlɛk`trɪʃən] 名 電工、
painter [`pentɚ] 名 油漆工

carpet [`kɑrpɪt] 名 地毯
▶ It is troublesome to take up the carpet and clean it.
把地毯拿起來清理是一件很麻煩的事。

C

carriage [`kærɪdʒ] 名 四輪馬車，運費　　片 a horse-drawn carriage 馬車

carrier [`kærɪɚ] 名 搬運人，通訊公司　　片 phone carrier 電信業者　　◎ MP3 **03-04**

carry [`kærɪ] 動 搬運，傳達，攜帶
▶ Would you please help me carry the table to the corner of the room?
可以麻煩你幫我把桌子搬到房間的角落嗎？
動詞三態變化 carry - carried - carried

cart [kɑrt] 名 手推車　　片 to put the cart before the horse 本末倒置

cartoon [kɑr`tun] 名 卡通
▶ Kids are always interested in cartoons. 孩子對卡通總是感興趣。

carve [kɑrv] 動 雕刻
▶ He carved a statue for his girlfriend.
他替他的女朋友雕一座雕像。
動詞三態變化 carve - carved - carved

case [kes] 名 盒子，事件，情況　　片 in case 假使～

cash [kæʃ] 名 現金　　片 to pay in cash 付現
相關衍生字彙 check [tʃɛk] 名 支票、credit [`krɛdɪt] 名 信用、loan [lon] 名 貸款、
payment [`pemənt] 名 付款、installment [ɪn`stɔlmənt] 名 分期付款

cashier [kæ`ʃɪr] 名 收銀員
▶ The cashier is very friendly. 這位收銀員很友善。

casino [kə`sino] 名 賭場
▶ The building is a gambling casino, in which you can play card games.
這棟是賭場，你可在裡面玩牌。

cast [kæst] 名 卡司，陣容
▶ The cast of the movie is very popular with the youth.
這部電影的卡司陣容很受年輕人歡迎。

castigate [`kæstə͵get] 動 譴責，矯正，修訂
▶ When the cashier is careless, he or she will be castigated or even fired.
當收銀員粗心時，他或她會被譴責甚至開除。
相關衍生字彙 blame [blem] 動 責備、punish [`pʌnɪʃ] 動 處罰、scold [skold] 動 責罵、
lecture [`lɛktʃɚ] 動 說教
動詞三態變化 castigate - castigated - castigated

castle [`kæsl] 名 城堡
▶ Once upon a time, there was a witch living in the castle.
　很久很久以前，有一個巫婆住在這座城堡裡。

casual [`kæʒʊəl] 形 偶然的，隨意的，非正式的
▶ The boss was not satisfied with her casual attitude.
　老闆對她不嚴謹的態度感到不滿。

cat [kæt] 名 小貓　　片 to rain cats and dogs 下傾盆大雨

catalogue [`kætəlɔg] 名 目錄
▶ There is a mail-order catalogue on their website.
　在他們的網站上有一個郵購目錄。

catastrophe [kə`tæstrəfɪ] 名 大災難，慘敗
▶ The earthquake was a catastrophe for everyone in the mountains.
　這地震對每個山區的人們而言都是場大災難。
相關衍生字彙 flood [flʌd] 名 水災、earthquake [`ɝθ,kwek] 名 地震、tsunami [tsu`nɑmi]
　　　　　　名 海嘯、famine [`fæmɪn] 名 飢荒、typhoon [taɪ`fun] 名 颱風

catch [kætʃ] 動 接住，趕上　　片 to catch up with 趕上（進度，速度～）
動詞三態變化 catch - caught - caught

catchy [`kætʃɪ] 形 動聽的
▶ With a catchy tune, the song has become a hit.
　因為動聽的曲調，這首歌很快就爆紅了。

category [`kætə,gorɪ] 名 種類
▶ There are many categories of books in the library.
　圖書館的書有很多種類。
相關衍生字彙 classify [`klæsə,faɪ] 動 將～分類、classification [,klæsəfə`keʃən] 名 分類、
　　　　　　categorize [`kætəgə,raɪz] 動 分門別類、sort [sɔrt] 動 區分

cater [`ketɚ] 動 承辦（宴會等）的酒席
▶ Mark's wedding reception will be catered by a five-star restaurant.
　馬克的婚宴將由一家五星級餐廳負責承辦。
動詞三態變化 cater - catered - catered

cathedral [kə`θidrəl] 名 大教堂　　　　　　　　　　　　　　MP3 03-05
▶ Every Sunday, many people come to the cathedral for worship.
　每週日，有很多人會到大教堂來做禮拜。

cause [kɔz] 名 原因 動 引起　　同 reason [`rizn] 名 理由
動詞三態變化 cause - caused - caused

caustic [`kɔstɪk] 形 刻薄的，譏諷的
▶ Never make caustic remarks. 千萬不要講刻薄的話。

caution [ˋkɔʃən] 名 小心，謹慎　　片 with caution 小心翼翼地

cautious [ˋkɔʃəs] 形 謹慎的
▶ She is a person you can trust because she is always cautious.
　她值得信任，因為她凡事都很小心謹慎。

cave [kev] 名 山洞
▶ There is a cave in the side of the hill.
　小山丘那裡有個山洞。
相關衍生字彙 cavern [ˋkævɚn] 名（巨大的）洞穴、cavity [ˋkævətɪ] 名 凹洞，蛀洞、hole [hol]
　　　　　名 洞、pit [pɪt] 名 陷阱、hollow [ˋhɑlo] 名 窪地

cease [sis] 動 停止，終止
▶ The experiment on animals has ceased.
　在動物身上做的實驗已經停止。
動詞三態變化 cease - ceased - ceased

ceiling [ˋsilɪŋ] 名 天花板　　片 to hit the ceiling 震怒

celebrate [ˋsɛləˏbret] 動 慶祝
▶ We celebrated joyously my sister's birthday last night.
　昨晚，我們興高采烈地慶祝妹妹的生日。
相關衍生字彙 celebrated [ˋsɛləˏbretɪd] 形 著名的、celebration [ˏsɛləˋbreʃən] 名 慶典、
　　　　　festival [ˋfɛstəvl] 名 節慶、inauguration [ɪnˏɔgjəˋreʃən] 名 就職典禮
動詞三態變化 celebrate - celebrated - celebrated

celebrity [sɪˋlɛbrətɪ] 名 名人，名聲
▶ All national celebrities were invited to attend the meeting.
　全國的名人都獲邀出席此會議。

celestial [sɪˋlɛstʃəl] 形 天空的，神聖的，極佳的
同 heavenly [ˋhɛvənlɪ] 形 天空的，神聖的

cell [sɛl] 名 細胞　　片 a cancer cell 癌細胞

cellar [ˋsɛlɚ] 名 地窖
▶ Father stores lots of bottles of wine in the cellar. 爸爸在地窖裡存放很多酒。

ceremony [ˋsɛrəˏmonɪ] 名 典禮　　片 a graduation ceremony 畢業典禮
相關衍生字彙 ceremonial [ˏsɛrəˋmonɪəl] 形 典禮的、ceremonious [ˏsɛrəˋmonjəs] 形 隆重的、
　　　　　ceremonialist [ˏsɛrəˋmonɪəlɪst] 名 禮法家、ceremonialism [ˏsɛrəˋmonɪəlɪzəm]
　　　　　名 講究禮節

cement [sɪˋmɛnt] 名 水泥
▶ The house was made of cement instead of wood.
　這間房子是用水泥蓋的不是木頭。

cemetery [`sɛmə‚tɛrɪ] 名 公墓，墓地
▶ The general was buried in the cemetery. 這位將軍葬在這個墓園。

censure [`sɛnʃəʳ] 名 指責　　片 a vote of censure 不信任票

census [`sɛnsəs] 名 人口普查
▶ The local government will conduct a census this year.
地方政府今年將實施人口普查。

center [`sɛntəʳ] 名 中心　　片 a day-care center 日間托兒中心
相關衍生字彙 central [`sɛntrəl] 形 中間的，重要的、centerline [`sɛntəʳ‚laın] 名 中線、
middle [`mıdl] 形 中間的、core [kor] 形 核心的

centigrade [`sɛntə‚gred] 名 攝氏
▶ The temperature today will be about 20 degrees centigrade.
今天溫度約攝氏二十度。

certificate [səˋtıfəkıt] 名 證書，執照　　片 a birth certificate 出生證明　 MP3 03-06

century [`sɛntʃʊrɪ] 名 世紀
▶ Queen Victoria passed away at the turn of the century.
維多利亞女王在世紀交替時去世。
相關衍生字彙 centennial [sɛnˋtɛnɪəl] 名 百年紀念、millennium [mıˋlɛnɪəm] 名 千禧年、
decade [`dɛked] 名 十年

cereal [`sırɪəl] 名 麥片
▶ I ate cereal with milk for my breakfast. 我早餐吃麥片配牛奶。

certainty [`sɝtəntɪ] 名 確實，必然
▶ I have no certainty of success. 我沒有成功的把握。
相關衍生字彙 certain [`sɝtən] 形 肯定的、certainly [`sɝtənlı] 副 確定地、uncertain [ʌnˋsɝtn]
形 不確定的、sure [ʃur] 形 確定的

chain [tʃen] 名 鏈條，項圈　　片 a restaurant chain 連鎖餐館

chalk [tʃɔk] 名 粉筆
▶ Our teacher is writing with chalk on the blackboard.
老師用粉筆在黑板上寫字。

chairmanship [`tʃɛrmən‚ʃıp] 名 主席的職位
▶ My chairmanship will last two years.
我的主席任職將持續兩年。
相關衍生字彙 chair [tʃɛr] 名 椅子、chairman [`tʃɛrmən] 名 主席、chairperson [`tʃɛr‚pɝsn]
名 議長，主席、armchair [`arm‚tʃɛr] 名 扶手椅

challenge [`tʃælındʒ] 名 挑戰
▶ It's a difficult job but I will accept the challenge.
這項工作不容易，但是我會接受挑戰。

chamber [`tʃembɚ] 名 房間，會場，議院　　片 the upper chamber（英）上議院

champagne [ʃæm`pen] 名 香檳
▶ I had dinner sipping champagne with my girlfriend.
　 我和女朋友吃晚餐時品嚐香檳。

champion [`tʃæmpɪən] 名 冠軍　　片 world champion 世界冠軍
相關衍生字彙 championship [`tʃæmpɪən͵ʃɪp] 名 冠軍頭銜、winner [`wɪnɚ] 名 獲勝者、
　　victor [`vɪktɚ] 名 勝利者、victorious [vɪk`torɪəs] 形 勝利的

chance [tʃæns] 名 機會
▶ Please give me a chance to explain. 請給我解釋的機會。

change [tʃendʒ] 動 改變，兌換（錢）　　片 to change one's mind 改變心意
動詞三態變化 change - changed - changed

changeable [`tʃendʒəbl] 形 易變的
▶ In spring, the weather is changeable. 在春天，天氣是易變的。

channel [`tʃænl] 名 頻道，海峽
▶ There are more and more television channels. 電視頻道愈來愈多。

chaos [`keas] 名 混亂
▶ The traffic near the downtown area is often in a state of chaos.
　 市區附近的交通常常處在混亂的狀態。
相關衍生字彙 chaotic [ke`ɑtɪk] 形 混亂的、neat [nit] 形 整齊的、messy [`mɛsɪ] 形 凌亂的、
　　tidy [`taɪdɪ] 形 整潔的

chapter [`tʃæptɚ] 名 章節
▶ There are twenty chapters in this textbook. 這本教科書有二十章。

character [`kærɪktɚ] 名 性格，角色，名聲
▶ The scholar is a person of character. 這位學者是一位品格高尚的人。

characteristic [͵kærəktə`rɪstɪk] 名 特色，特徵 形 獨特的
▶ One of her unique characteristics is her nose.
　 她其中一項獨特的特徵就是她的鼻子。

charge [tʃɑrdʒ] 動 指控，索價，充電
▶ He was charged with murder.
　 他被指控謀殺。
動詞三態變化 charge - charged - charged

charity [`tʃærətɪ] 名 慈善　　片 out of charity 出自善意　　◎ MP3 03-07
相關衍生字彙 foundation [faun`deʃən] 名 基金會、volunteer [͵vɑlən`tɪr] 名 志工、
　　kindness [`kaɪndnɪs] 名 善良、fund [fʌnd] 名 基金，專款

charm [tʃɑrm] 名 魅力 動 吸引
▶ Kids are charmed by the puppet show.
孩子們被這木偶戲吸引。
動詞三態變化 charm - charmed - charmed

charming [`tʃɑrmɪŋ] 形 迷人的，有魅力的
同 attractive [ə`træktɪv] 形 有吸引力的

chart [tʃɑrt] 名 圖表
▶ The pie chart shows the proportion of main fatal diseases.
這圓餅圖顯示主要致命疾病的比例。

charter [`tʃɑrtɚ] 名 許可證　　片 charter flight 包機

chase [tʃes] 動 追逐，尋找
▶ Most people spend most of their life chasing after fame.
大多數的人把大部分的生命花在追逐名聲上。
動詞三態變化 chase - chased - chased

chaste [tʃest] 形 正派的，簡樸的
▶ I like to make friends with people chaste in mind.
我喜歡跟思想純正的人做朋友。

chat [tʃæt] 動 聊天，閒談
▶ Weather is the most popular topic people chat about.
天氣是人們最常聊的話題。
相關衍生字彙 chatter [`tʃætɚ] 名 喋喋不休、talk [tɔk] 動 談論、discuss [dɪ`skʌs] 動 討論、
gossip [`gɑsəp] 名 八卦、say [se] 動 訴說
動詞三態變化 chat - chatted - chatted

cheap [tʃip] 形 便宜的，劣質的
▶ It's not cheap to live in New York. 住在紐約的開銷不便宜。

cheat [tʃit] 動 欺騙，詐取　　片 to cheat on the exam 考試作弊
動詞三態變化 cheat - cheated - cheated

check [tʃɛk] 動 檢查，核對　　片 to check in / out （飯店）入住／退房
相關衍生字彙 checklist [`tʃɛkˌlɪst] 名 清單、checkbook [`tʃɛkˌbuk] 名 支票簿、
checkup [`tʃɛkˌʌp] 名 健康檢查
動詞三態變化 check - checked - checked

cheer [tʃɪr] 動 喝采
▶ Cheer up! It's not the end of the world.
振作！又不是世界末日。
動詞三態變化 cheer - cheered - cheered

cheerful [`tʃɪrfəl] 形 興高采烈的
▶ She is always in a cheerful mood. 她總是心情很好。

cheese [tʃiz] 名 乳酪
▶ I put a piece of cheese on my bread. 我在麵包上放了一片乳酪。

chemical [`kɛmɪk!] 形 化學的
▶ Choose natural food instead of food with chemical ingredients.
選擇天然食物來取代含有化學成分的食物。
相關衍生字彙 chemistry [`kɛmɪstrɪ] 名 化學、chemist [`kɛmɪst] 名 化學家、physics [`fɪzɪks] 名 物理學、physical [`fɪzɪk!] 形 物理的，身體的、physicist [`fɪzɪsɪst] 名 物理學家

cherish [`tʃɛrɪʃ] 動 珍愛，撫育
▶ We both cherish the friendship between us.
我們很珍惜兩人之間的友誼。
動詞三態變化 cherish - cherished - cherished

cherry [`tʃɛrɪ] 名 櫻桃　　片 cherry trees 櫻桃樹

chest [tʃɛst] 名 胸腔
▶ Our boss stared at us with his arms across his chest. 老闆雙手抱胸瞪著我們。

chew [tʃu] 動 咀嚼　　片 chewing gum 口香糖
動詞三態變化 chew - chewed - chewed

chicken [`tʃɪkɪn] 名 雞肉　　片 chicken pot 水痘

chief [tʃif] 名 領袖，長官　　片 a police chief 警長　　MP3 03-08

childhood [`tʃaɪld͵hʊd] 名 童年時期
▶ She stayed with her grandparents in her childhood.
她的童年是在爺爺奶奶家渡過的。
相關衍生字彙 childish [`tʃaɪldɪʃ] 形 幼稚的、child [tʃaɪld] 名 小孩、childlike [`tʃaɪld͵laɪk] 形 孩子般的、childcare [`tʃaɪldkɛr] 名 兒童看護、childbirth [`tʃaɪld͵bɝθ] 名 分娩

chill [tʃɪl] 形 冷的 動 感到寒冷
▶ You will be chilled to the bone without wearing a heavy coat.
你不穿厚外套，會覺得寒冷刺骨。
動詞三態變化 chill - chilled - chilled

chilly [`tʃɪlɪ] 形 冷颼颼的　　同 cold [kold] 形 寒冷的

chime [tʃaɪm] 動 和諧，一致
▶ His point of view on the issue chimes with mine.
他對這事件的看法與我相同。
動詞三態變化 chime - chimed - chimed

chimney [ˋtʃɪmnɪ] 名 煙囪
▶ Kids believe that Santa Claus will visit them through the chimney.
　孩子們都相信聖誕老公公會從煙囪進來拜訪他們。

china [ˋtʃaɪnə] 名 瓷器　　片 a set of china 一套瓷器
相關衍生字彙 China [ˋtʃaɪnə] 名 中國、Chinese [ˋtʃaɪˋniz] 名 中國人、Asia [ˋeʃə] 名 亞洲、
　　　　　　Asian [ˋeʃən] 名 亞洲人

chip [tʃɪp] 名 碎片，晶片　　片 potato chips 馬鈴薯片

choice [tʃɔɪs] 名 選擇
▶ Making a correct choice is never an easy job.
　做正確的選擇永遠都不是一件簡單的事。

choke [tʃok] 動 噎住，窒息
▶ The baby choked on a piece of candy.
　小嬰兒被糖果噎住。
動詞三態變化 choke - choked - choked

choose [tʃuz] 動 挑選
▶ I don't know how to choose.
　我不知該如何選擇。
動詞三態變化 choose - chose - chosen

chop [tʃɑp] 動 砍，劈　　片 to chop up 剁碎
相關衍生字彙 chopsticks [ˋtʃɑpˏstɪks] 名 筷子、cut [kʌt] 動 剪，切，割、cleave [kliv] 動 劈開
動詞三態變化 chop - chopped - chopped

chord [kɔrd] 名（樂器的）弦　　片 a minor / major chord 小調／大調和音

chorus [ˋkorəs] 名 合唱團
▶ Mary likes singing, so she joins a chorus.　瑪莉喜歡唱歌，所以她加入合唱團。

chronic [ˋkrɑnɪk] 形 慢性的，長期的
▶ She has suffered a chronic disease.　她一直為慢性疾病所苦。

chronicle [ˋkrɑnɪkl] 名 編年史
▶ There are many historical events recorded in the chronicle.
　這本編年史中記載很多歷史事件。

chubby [ˋtʃʌbɪ] 形 豐滿的，圓胖的
▶ The baby with a chubby face is very cute.
　有著圓嘟嘟的臉的嬰兒真可愛。
相關衍生字彙 fat [fæt] 形 胖的、thin [θɪn] 形 瘦的、round [raʊnd] 形 圓的、thick [θɪk]
　　　　　　形 厚的、plump [plʌmp] 形 胖嘟嘟的

chuckle [`tʃʌkl] 動 咯咯地笑
▶ When she was reading the love letter, she chuckled.
當她讀著情書時，她咯咯地笑著。
動詞三態變化 chuckle - chuckled - chuckled

church [tʃɜtʃ] 名 教堂　　片 to go to church 上教堂做禮拜

cigar [sɪ`gɑr] 名 雪茄　　片 to light up a cigar 點燃雪茄
相關衍生字彙 cigarette [ˌsɪgə`rɛt] 名 香菸、smoke [smok] 名 煙霧、lighter [`laɪtɚ] 名 打火機、smoker [`smokɚ] 名 吸菸者

cinema [`sɪnəmə] 名 電影院　　同 theater [`θɪətɚ] 名 電影院　　MP3 03-09

circle [`sɜkl] 名 圓圈 動 圈出
▶ The teacher asked his students to sit in a circle.
老師要求學生圍成一個圈坐著。
動詞三態變化 circle - circled - circled

circuit [`sɜkɪt] 名 電路，環行
▶ It takes a month for the moon to make a circuit of the earth.
月球繞地球一周需要花一個月的時間。

circular [`sɜkjələ] 名 通知，公告 形 環形的
▶ The school issues a circular a week for the freshmen.
學校一周發一份通知給新生。

circulate [`sɜkjəˌlet] 動 循環，流傳，發行
▶ Taking a hot shower helps the blood circulate well through the body.
洗熱水澡有益體內的血液循環。
相關衍生字彙 circulation [ˌsɜkjə`leʃən] 名 循環，流通、circulatory [`sɜkjələˌtori] 形 循環的、circumference [sɚ`kʌmfərəns] 名 圓周、circulator [`sɜkjəˌletɚ] 名 傳播者
動詞三態變化 circulate - circulated - circulated

circumspect [`sɜkəmˌspɛkt] 形 謹慎小心的　　同 careful [`kɛrfəl] 形 小心的

circumstance [`sɜkəmˌstæns] 名 情況，事件
片 under no circumstance 無論如何

circus [`sɜkəs] 名 馬戲團
▶ Parents promised to take him to the circus on his birthday.
父母答應在他生日那天帶他去看馬戲團。

cite [saɪt] 動 引用，表揚
▶ She cited a part from a famous poem in her article.
她在文章中引用了有名的詩句。
動詞三態變化 cite - cited - cited

citizen [`sɪtəzn̩] 名 公民
▶ The government has the duty to protect its citizens.
政府有責任保護它的公民。
相關衍生字彙 civic [`sɪvɪk] 形 市民的、city [`sɪtɪ] 名 城市、citizenry [`sɪtɪznrɪ] 名（總稱）公民、citizenship [`sɪtəznˌʃɪp] 名 公民身分

---

civil [`sɪvl̩] 形 市民的，世俗的　　片 a civil action 民事訴訟

---

civilization [ˌsɪvlə`zeʃən] 名 文明
▶ Maya is one of the ancient civilizations. 馬雅是古文明之一。

---

claim [klem] 動 聲稱
▶ The factory claimed that they had nothing to do with the water pollution.
這工廠聲稱他們跟水污染無關。
動詞三態變化 claim - claimed - claimed

---

clamor [`klæmɚ] 名 喧囂聲 動 吵鬧
▶ People clamored against wars.
人民大聲疾呼反對戰爭。
動詞三態變化 clamor - clamored - clamored

---

clap [klæp] 動 拍（手），鼓（掌）　　片 to clap one's hands 拍拍手
動詞三態變化 clap - clapped - clapped

---

clasp [klæsp] 動 緊抱，扣住
▶ Before saying goodbye at the airport, she clasped her husband.
在機場道別前，她緊抱她的丈夫。
動詞三態變化 clasp - clasped - clasped

---

classic [`klæsɪk] 形 經典的，最優秀的　　片 a classic novel 經典小說

---

classical [`klæsɪkl̩] 形 古典的　　片 classical music 古典音樂

---

classify [`klæsəˌfaɪ] 動 將～分類
▶ Please help me classify the materials according to their topics.
請幫我把資料根據主題做分類。
相關衍生字彙 classified [`klæsəˌfaɪd] 形 分類的、classification [ˌklæsəfə`keʃən] 名 分類、class [klæs] 名 班級，社會階級、classmate [`klæsˌmet] 名 同班同學、classroom [`klæsˌrum] 名 教室
動詞三態變化 classify - classified - classified

---

cleaner [`klinɚ] 名 清潔工，吸塵器　　片 a vacuum cleaner 吸塵器

---

clearance [`klɪrəns] 名 清掃，清倉大拍賣　　　🔘 MP3 03-10
▶ We bought our new sofa at a clearance sale. 我們在清倉大拍賣中買了新沙發。

clearly [`klɪrlɪ] 副 清楚地
▶ He explained the process slowly and clearly.
他慢慢地、清楚地解釋這整個過程。
相關衍生字彙 clear [klɪr] 動 清除、clean [klin] 動 把～弄乾淨、cleanly [`klɛnlɪ] 副 乾淨地

clench [klɛntʃ] 動 握緊　　片 to clench one's fists 握緊拳頭
動詞三態變化 clench - clenched - clenched

clerk [klɝk] 名 店員，記帳員，職員
▶ You can ask the clerk to wrap the gift for you. 你可以請店員幫你包裝禮物。

clever [`klɛvɚ] 形 聰明的　　同 smart [smɑrt] 形 聰明的

client [`klaɪənt] 名 委託人，顧客
▶ The lawyer has won all his clients' trust. 這位律師贏得所有委託人的信任。

cliff [klɪf] 名 懸崖，峭壁
▶ How exciting it is to climb the cliff! 攀爬這峭壁真的是太刺激了！

climate [`klaɪmɪt] 名 氣候　　片 tropical climate 熱帶氣候
相關衍生字彙 weather [`wɛðɚ] 名 天氣、mild [maɪld] 形 溫和的、warm [wɔrm] 形 溫暖的、
subtropical [sʌb`trɑpɪkl̩] 形 亞熱帶的、arctic [`ɑrktɪk] 形 極地的

climax [`klaɪmæks] 名 頂點，高潮
▶ The election campaign reached a climax last night. 選舉活動昨晚達到最高潮。

climb [klaɪm] 動 攀登　　片 to go mountain climbing 去爬山
動詞三態變化 climb - climbed - climbed

climber [`klaɪmɚ] 名 登山者
▶ He is a good mountain climber. 他是一名登山好手。

cling [klɪŋ] 動 依附，黏著
▶ We shouldn't cling to an old idea.
我們不該固守舊想法。
動詞三態變化 cling - clung - clung

clinic [`klɪnɪk] 名 診所
▶ She and her husband run a clinic and live a happy life.
她和先生經營診所並過著快樂的生活。

clinical [`klɪnɪkl̩] 形 臨床的，客觀的　　片 clinical trials 臨床實驗

clockwise [`klɑk͵waɪz] 形 順時鐘方向的 副 順時鐘方向地
▶ They dance in a clockwise direction.
他們以順時鐘方向跳著舞。
相關衍生字彙 clock [klɑk] 名 時鐘、o'clock [ə`klɑk] 副 ～點鐘、
counterclockwise [͵kaʊntɚ`klɑk͵waɪz] 形 逆時鐘方向的 副 逆時鐘方向地

clone [klon] 名 複製品 動 複製
▶ Can you imagine a world in which humans can be cloned?
你能想像一個可以複製人類的世界嗎？
動詞三態變化 clone - cloned - cloned

---

close [klos] 形 接近的，親密的
▶ Because my husband is very busy, my children are close to me.
因為我先生很忙，所以孩子跟我比較親近。

---

closet [ˋklɑzɪt] 名 衣櫃　　片 to come out of the closet 出櫃（承認是同性戀）

---

closure [ˋkloʒɚ] 名 打烊，結束
▶ Because of the factory closure, Father has been out of employment for months.
因為工廠關閉，爸爸已經失業好幾個月了。

---

cloth [klɔθ] 名 織物，衣料　　片 a piece of cotton cloth 一塊棉布

---

clothe [kloð] 動 給～穿衣服　　　　　　　　　　　　　MP3 03-11
▶ To feed and clothe his children, he works day and night.
為了養育及供給他的小孩衣服穿，他日以繼夜的工作。
相關衍生字彙 clothes [kloz] 名 衣服、clothing [ˋkloðɪŋ] 名 衣物、boutique [buˋtik] 名 精品店、coat [kot] 名 外套、trousers [ˋtrauzɚz] 名 長褲
動詞三態變化 clothe - clothed / clad - clothed / clad

---

cloud [klaud] 名 雲，雲朵
▶ Every cloud has a silver lining.（諺語）總有撥雲見日的一天。

---

cloudy [ˋklaudɪ] 形 多雲的，陰天的
▶ In London, most of the days in winter are cloudy. 在倫敦，冬天大多是陰天。

---

club [klʌb] 名 俱樂部，夜總會
▶ Are you a member of our club? 你是我們俱樂部的會員嗎？

---

clue [klu] 名 線索，情節
▶ The witness provided the police with a clue.
目擊者提供警方一個線索。

---

clumsy [ˋklʌmzɪ] 形 笨拙的，不得體的
▶ I'm clumsy at sports, not to mention swimming.
我對運動很笨拙，更別提游泳了。
相關衍生字彙 awkward [ˋɔkwɚd] 形 笨拙的、stupid [ˋstjupɪd] 形 愚蠢的、foolish [ˋfulɪʃ] 形 傻的、silly [ˋsɪlɪ] 形 糊塗的

---

cluster [ˋklʌstɚ] 名 一串，一群　　片 a cluster of grapes 一串葡萄

C

clutch [klʌtʃ] 動 抓住，攫取
▶ A drowning man would clutch a straw.
（諺語）快淹死的人連稻草都抓（急不暇擇）。
動詞三態變化 clutch - clutched - clutched

coach [kotʃ] 名 教練　　片 a basketball / soccer coach 籃球／足球的教練

coal [kol] 名 煤礦
▶ In that poor country, people burn coal to produce heat.
在那個貧窮的國家，人們燒煤來取暖。

coalesce [ˌkoə`lɛs] 動 聯合，合併
▶ The new country is coalesced by many tribes.
這個新國家是由很多個部落聯合組成的。
動詞三態變化 coalesce - coalesced - coalesced

coarse [kors] 形 粗糙的，粗俗的
▶ It's impolite to use such coarse language. 使用粗俗的言語是很不禮貌的。

coast [kost] 名 海岸
▶ Along the coast, there are many seafood restaurants.
沿著海岸有很多海產店。

coax [koks] 動 勸誘，哄騙
▶ Mom coaxed me to accept the job.
媽媽勸我接受這份工作。
相關衍生字彙 persuade [pɚ`swed] 動 勸說、wheedle [`hwidl] 動 用甜言蜜語欺騙、
advise [əd`vaɪz] 動 勸告，忠告、suggest [sə`dʒɛst] 動 建議，提議
動詞三態變化 coax - coaxed - coaxed

cocktail [`kɑkˌtel] 名 雞尾酒
▶ I know how to mix a cocktail. 我知道如何調雞尾酒。

cocoon [kə`kun] 名 繭　　片 a silkworm cocoon 蠶繭

code [kod] 名 密碼　　片 to break a code 破解密碼

coffee [`kɔfɪ] 名 咖啡
▶ I can't wake up without drinking a cup of coffee in the morning.
早上沒喝咖啡我醒不過來。

coffin [`kɔfɪn] 名 棺木，靈柩
▶ The mummy in the coffin was preserved very well.
這棺木裡的木乃伊保存得很好。

cogitate [`kɑdʒəˌtet] 動 仔細考慮，謀劃
▶ It took me a long time to cogitate on the important subject.
這個重要的主題花了我很長的思考時間。
相關衍生字彙 rethink [ri`θɪŋk] 動 重新考慮、ponder [`pɑndɚ] 動 衡量、reflect [rɪ`flɛkt] 動 思考，反省、deliberate [dɪ`lɪbərɪt] 形 深思熟慮的
動詞三態變化 cogitate - cogitated - cogitated

cognition [kɑg`nɪʃən] 名 認知，知識　　　　　　◎ MP3 03-12
▶ The scholar is studying kids' learning and cognition.
這位學者正在研究孩童的學習與認知。

cohere [ko`hɪr] 動 黏附，協調　　　同 adhere [əd`hɪr] 動 依附
動詞三態變化 cohere - cohered - cohered

coherence [ko`hɪrəns] 名 連貫性
▶ There is something wrong with the coherence of the argument.
這份論證的前後連貫性有問題。

coin [kɔɪn] 名 硬幣
▶ We didn't know how to make a decision, so we tossed a coin.
我們不知道該如何做決定，所以就擲硬幣。

coincide [ˌkɔɪn`saɪd] 動 巧合，重疊
▶ If the typhoon coincides with the high tide, it will result in a terrible flood.
如果颱風遇上漲潮，勢必導致可怕的水災。
相關衍生字彙 coincidence [ko`ɪnsɪdəns] 名 巧合、coincident [ko`ɪnsədənt] 形 巧合的、accidental [ˌæksə`dɛntl] 形 意外的、intentional [ɪn`tɛnʃənl] 形 故意的
動詞三態變化 coincide - coincided - coincided

cold [kold] 名 寒冷，感冒 形 寒冷的，不友善的　　片 to catch a cold 感冒

collaborate [kə`læbəˌret] 動 合作，勾結　　片 to collaborate with... 和～合作
動詞三態變化 collaborate - collaborated - collaborated

collaboration [kəˌlæbə`reʃən] 名 合作，勾結
▶ In the global village, the international collaboration is very important.
在這個地球村，國際合作是很重要的。
相關衍生字彙 cooperate [ko`ɑpəˌret] 動 合作、cooperation [koˌɑpə`reʃən] 名 合作、connect [kə`nɛkt] 動 連結、connection [kə`nɛkʃən] 名 關聯、union [`junjən] 名 結合

collapse [kə`læps] 動 崩塌　　片 mental collapse 精神崩潰
動詞三態變化 collapse - collapsed - collapsed

colleague [`kɑlig] 名 同事　　同 coworker [`koˌwɝkɚ] 名 同事

collection [kəˋlɛkʃən] 名 收集
▶ My brother is interested in stamp collection.
　我弟弟很喜歡集郵。
相關衍生字彙 collect [kəˋlɛkt] 動 收集、collector [kəˋlɛktɚ] 名 收藏家、collective [kəˋlɛktɪv] 名 團體，集體、gather [ˋgæðɚ] 動 招集

C

---

college [ˋkɑlɪdʒ] 名 大專，學院　　片 a community college 社區大學

collide [kəˋlaɪd] 動 碰撞，抵觸
▶ There were two cars colliding with each other at the corner of the road.
　這條路的轉角有兩部車子相撞了。
動詞三態變化 collide - collided - collided

---

collision [kəˋlɪʒən] 名 碰撞，衝突
▶ The sound of the collision was so loud that passersby stopped and watched.
　這撞擊聲如此大，以至於路人都停下來觀看。
相關衍生字彙 bump [bʌmp] 動 碰，撞、clash [klæʃ] 動 砰地相碰撞、push [puʃ] 動 推動，推進、hit [hɪt] 動 碰撞

---

collocation [ˌkɑləˋkeʃən] 名 排列，配置
▶ Our English teacher reminded us to pay attention to the collocation of a verb and a noun.
　英文老師提醒我們要小心動詞跟名詞的搭配。

---

colloquial [kəˋlokwɪəl] 形 口語的，會話的
▶ It's a colloquial word, not suitable in your speech.
　這是個口語用字，不適合用於演講。

---

colony [ˋkɑlənɪ] 名 殖民地
▶ Hong Kong is a former British colony. 香港以前是英國的殖民地。

---

colorful [ˋkʌlɚfəl] 形 多采多姿的，鮮豔的
▶ After retirement, she still lives a colorful life.
　退休後，她仍過著多采多姿的生活。
相關衍生字彙 color [ˋkʌlɚ] 名 色彩、hue [hju] 名 色調、shade [ʃed] 名（色彩的）濃淡、dye [daɪ] 名 染料

---

column [ˋkɑləm] 名 專欄
▶ The novelist is writing a column for a newspaper. 這位小說家正替某報寫專欄。

---

combat [ˋkɑmbæt] 名 格鬥，反對 動 與～戰鬥　　片 hand-to-hand combat 肉搏戰
動詞三態變化 combat - combated / combatted - combated / combatted

combination [ˌkɑmbəˋneʃən] 名 組合，聯盟　　　　　　　◎ MP3 03-13
▶ Chocolate and milk is a delicious combination.
巧克力跟牛奶真是美味的組合。

---

combine [kəmˋbaɪn] 動 結合，聯合
▶ The works of the designer combine creativity and passion.
這位設計師的作品結合了創意與熱情。
動詞三態變化 combine - combined - combined

---

comeback [ˋkʌmˌbæk] 名 恢復，巧妙的反駁
片 to make a comeback 捲土重來
相關衍生字彙 come [kʌm] 動 來、coming [ˋkʌmɪŋ] 形 即將到來的、go [g] 動 去、
arrive [əˋraɪv] 動 到達、run [rʌn] 動 跑、recover [rɪˋkʌvɚ] 動 恢復

---

comedy [ˋkɑmədɪ] 名 喜劇
▶ Compared with tragedy, I prefer comedy. 跟悲劇比起來，我比較喜歡喜劇。

---

comfort [ˋkʌmfɚt] 名 動 安慰，舒適
▶ Travel can offer me lots of spiritual comfort.
旅遊可以帶給我很多精神上的慰藉。
動詞三態變化 comfort - comforted - comforted

---

comfortable [ˋkʌmfɚtəbl̩] 形 舒適的
▶ Sitting on the sofa is quite comfortable.
坐在這沙發真舒服。

---

comic [ˋkɑmɪk] 形 喜劇的，連環漫畫的　　　片 comic books 漫畫書
相關衍生字彙 comical [ˋkɑmɪkl̩] 形 滑稽的、funny [ˋfʌnɪ] 形 好笑的、cozy [ˋkozɪ] 形 舒適的

---

command [kəˋmænd] 動 命令，指揮
▶ The general commanded the soldiers to fire.
將軍命令士兵開火。
動詞三態變化 command - commanded - commanded

---

commemorate [kəˋmɛməˌret] 動 慶祝，紀念
▶ The statue was built to commemorate that battle.
這座雕像用以紀念那次戰役。
動詞三態變化 commemorate - commemorated - commemorated

---

commence [kəˋmɛns] 動 開始，著手
▶ Let's commence our meeting on time!
讓我們準時開始會議吧！
動詞三態變化 commence - commenced - commenced

commencement [kə`mɛnsmənt] 名 開始，畢業典禮
▶ Easter comes at the commencement of spring. 復活節在春天開始時到來。

---

commend [kə`mɛnd] 動 推薦，稱讚
▶ The movie is commended highly.
這部電影被高度推薦。

相關衍生字彙 commendable [kə`mɛndəbl] 形 值得讚揚的、commendation [͵kɑmɛn`deʃən] 名 稱讚、admire [əd`maɪr] 動 讚美、admirable [`ædmərəbl] 形 值得讚美的

動詞三態變化 commend - commended - commended

---

comment [`kɑmɛnt] 名 動 評論，註釋　　片 no comment 不予評論
動詞三態變化 comment - commented - commented

---

commentary [`kɑmən͵tɛrɪ] 名 評論，實況報導
▶ The reporter made a good commentary on baseball games.
這位記者對棒球比賽做很棒的評論。

---

commerce [`kɑmɝs] 名 商業，貿易
▶ With the development of technology, e-commerce becomes more and more important in our daily life.
隨著科技的發達，電子商務在我們日常生活中愈來愈重要。

相關衍生字彙 commercial [kə`mɝʃəl] 形 商業的、business [`bɪznɪs] 名 生意、trade [tred] 名 交易、dealings [`dilɪŋz] 名 買賣

---

commiserate [kə`mɪzə͵ret] 動 憐憫，同情
▶ Her terrible childhood is worth commiserating.
她悲慘的童年值得同情。

動詞三態變化 commiserate - commiserated - commiserated

---

commission [kə`mɪʃən] 名 佣金，回扣
▶ How dare you charge a commission? 你怎敢索取回扣？

---

commit [kə`mɪt] 動 犯（罪），把〜交託給　　片 to commit suicide 自殺
動詞三態變化 commit - committed - committed

---

committee [kə`mɪtɪ] 名 委員會，監護人
▶ The government set up a committee to research new educational policies.
政府成立委員會來研究新的教育政策。

---

commodious [kə`modɪəs] 形 寬敞的　　同 spacious [`speʃəs] 形 寬闊的
相關衍生字彙 space [spes] 名 空間、room [rum] 名 空間、capacious [kə`peʃəs] 形 容量大的、broad [brɔd] 形 遼闊的

---

commodity [kə`mɑdətɪ] 名 商品，日用品　　◎ MP3 03-14
片 farm commodity 農產品

common [`kɑmən] 名 公有地 形 常見的，共同的
▶ The twin brothers have nothing in common. 這兩個雙胞胎兄弟沒有共通點。

commonplace [`kɑmən‚ples] 名 司空見慣的事 形 普通的，平凡的
▶ Smart phones are increasingly commonplace. 智慧型手機已經愈來愈普遍。

commotion [kə`moʃən] 名 騷動
▶ The superstar's arrival caused a commotion in the restaurant.
這位超級巨星的到來引起餐廳裡一陣騷動。
相關衍生字彙 disturbance [dɪs`tɝbəns] 名 擾亂、confusion [kən`fjuʒən] 名 混亂狀況、
disorder [dɪs`ɔrdɚ] 名 無秩序、chaos [`keɑs] 名 混亂

communicate [kə`mjunə‚ket] 動 溝通，傳遞
▶ A good leader should know how to communicate clearly.
好的領導人要能知道如何清楚地溝通。
動詞三態變化 communicate - communicated - communicated

communication [kə‚mjunə`keʃən] 名 溝通，交流
片 mass communication 大眾傳播

community [kə`mjunətɪ] 名 社區
▶ There are many celebrities living in the community. 很多名人住在這個社區。

commute [kə`mjut] 名 動 通勤 動 替代，折合
▶ It's very convenient for me to commute from my place to my office.
從我的住處到辦公室通勤很方便。
動詞三態變化 commute - commuted - commuted

commuter [kə`mjutɚ] 名 通勤族
▶ Every morning, the bus station is crowded with commuters.
每天早上，公車站擠滿通勤族。

compact [`kɑmpækt] 名 契約　片 to make a compact 達成協定

companion [kəm`pænjən] 名 同伴 動 陪伴
▶ How lucky it is to find a life companion!
能找到終身伴侶是很幸運的事！
相關衍生字彙 companionable [kəm`pænjənəbl̩] 形 友善的、companionship
[kəm`pænjən‚ʃɪp] 名 伴侶關係、friend [frɛnd] 名 朋友、mate [met] 名 夥伴
動詞三態變化 companion - companioned - companioned

company [`kʌmpənɪ] 名 公司
▶ John is an engineer at a software company. 約翰是軟體公司的工程師。

comparable [`kɑmpərəbl̩] 形 可比較的
▶ For him, no one can be comparable with his daughter.
對他而言，沒有人可以跟他女兒相比。

相關衍生字彙 comparative [kəmˋpærətɪv]名 比較級、compare [kəmˋpɛr]動 比較、
comparison [kəmˋpærəsn]名 對照、relative [ˋrɛlətɪv]形 相對的

C

compartment [kəmˋpartmənt]名 間隔 動 劃分
▶ I need a refrigerator with a large freezer compartment.
我需要一台有大冷凍庫的冰箱。

動詞三態變化 compartment - compartmented - compartmented

compass [ˋkʌmpəs]名 羅盤
▶ When you go hiking in the mountains, remember to take a compass with you.
當你到山區健行時,記得帶羅盤。

compassion [kəmˋpæʃən]名 同情,憐憫
▶ We helped the homeless out of compassion.
我們是出於同情,去幫助無家可歸的人。

相關衍生字彙 compassionate [kəmˋpæʃnɪt]形 具同情心的、sympathy [ˋsɪmpəθɪ]
名 同情心、pity [ˋpɪtɪ]名 憐憫、mercy [ˋmɝsɪ]名 仁慈

compatible [kəmˋpætəbl]形 相容的
▶ Because I was not compatible with my roommate, I decided to move out.
因為跟室友不合,我決定搬出去。

compel [kəmˋpɛl]動 強迫
▶ It is not reasonable that the girl students were compelled to wear skirts in winter.
女學生冬天被強迫穿裙子是不合理的。

動詞三態變化 compel - compelled - compelled

compensate [ˋkampən‚set]動 補償
▶ All the victims of the fire will be compensated.
所有火災的受害者都將獲得賠償。

相關衍生字彙 compensation [‚kampənˋseʃən]名 補償金、reward [rɪˋwɔrd]名 獎勵、
income [ˋɪn‚kʌm]名 收入、salary [ˋsælərɪ]名 薪水

動詞三態變化 compensate - compensated - compensated

compile [kəmˋpaɪl]動 收集(資料等),匯編
▶ Before writing the novel, the author spent a long time compiling information.
寫這本小說前,作者花很長的時間收集資料。

動詞三態變化 compile - compiled - compiled

complain [kəmˋplen]動 抱怨,控訴
◉ MP3 03-15
▶ Stop complaining! All you need to do is sit and study.
停止抱怨吧!你需要的是坐下並唸書。

動詞三態變化 complain - complained - complained

compete [kəm`pit] 動 競爭，對抗
▶ To win the first place, students compete fiercely.
為了得第一名，學生競爭激烈。
相關衍生字彙 competence [`kampətəns]名 能力、competition [ˌkampə`tɪʃən]名 競爭、
competitive [kəm`pɛtətɪv]形 有競爭性的、competitor [kəm`pɛtətɚ]名 競爭者
動詞三態變化 compete - competed - competed

complete [kəm`plit] 動 完成，結束 形 完整的
▶ Once you complete your homework today, you can watch TV.
你完成今天的作業，就可以看電視。
動詞三態變化 complete - completed - completed

complex [`kamplɛks]名 情結，綜合體 形 複雜的
片 the Electra / Oedipus complex 戀父／戀母情結

complexion [kəm`plɛkʃən]名 膚色　　片 a fair complexion 白皙膚色

complicated [`kampləˌketɪd]形 複雜的，難懂的
▶ The situation seems a little complicated and hard to solve.
這情況似乎有點複雜且難解決。
相關衍生字彙 complicate [`kampləˌket]動 使複雜、complication [ˌkamplə`keʃən]
名 複雜性、simplification [ˌsɪmpləfə`keʃən]名 單純化、simplify [`sɪmpləˌfaɪ]
動 使單純

compliment [`kampləmənt]名 動 恭維，讚美的話
▶ My husband seldom pays me a compliment, but I know he loves me.
我先生很少讚美我，但我知道他是愛我的。

comply [kəm`plaɪ] 動 遵從
▶ You had better comply with your teacher's request.
你最好按照老師的要求。
動詞三態變化 comply - complied - complied

component [kəm`ponənt]名 零件，成分 形 構成的
▶ He makes a lot of money by supplying components for the car factory.
他因供應汽車工廠零件而賺很多錢。

compose [kəm`poz]動 構成，創作　　片 be composed of 由～組成
相關衍生字彙 composer [kəm`pozɚ]名 作曲家、composition [ˌkampə`zɪʃən]名 作品，作文、
produce [prə`djus]動 製作、producer [prə`djusɚ]名 製作人、create [krɪ`et]
動 創造
動詞三態變化 compose - composed - composed

composure [kəm`poʒɚ]名 鎮定，沉著
片 to keep / lose one's composure 保持／失去理智

compound [ˋkɑmpaʊnd] 名 混合物，複合字 形 合成的
▶ His character is a compound of humor and wisdom.
　他的個性是幽默與智慧的結合。

comprehension [ˌkɑmprɪˋhɛnʃən] 名 理解力，包含力
片 beyond comprehension 超出理解力
相關衍生字彙 comprehend [ˌkɑmprɪˋhɛnd] 動 理解、comprehensive [ˌkɑmprɪˋhɛnsɪv]
　　　　　 形 綜合的、understand [ˌʌndɚˋstænd] 動 瞭解、realize [ˋrɪəˌlaɪz] 動 明白

compress [kəmˋprɛs] 動 壓縮，歸納
▶ Remember not to compress the soil in the flower pot so that the plant can grow well.
　記得花盆的土別壓太緊，植物才會長得好。
動詞三態變化 compress - compressed - compressed

comprise [kəmˋpraɪz] 動 包含，由～組成
▶ The USA comprises more than 50 states now.
　美國現在已經包含超過五十個州。
動詞三態變化 comprise - comprised - comprised

compromise [ˋkɑmprəˌmaɪz] 動 妥協，讓步
▶ Don't compromise your value for the sake of money.
　別為了錢而妥協你的價值觀。
動詞三態變化 compromise - compromised - compromised

compulsory [kəmˋpʌlsərɪ] 形 必修的，強制的
▶ Physical education is compulsory at our university.
　我們的大學體育是必修的。

compute [kəmˋpjut] 名 動 計算，估算　　片 to compute correctly 正確地估算
相關衍生字彙 computer [kəmˋpjutɚ] 名 電腦、calculate [ˋkælkjəˌlet] 動 計算、
　　　　　 calculator [ˋkælkjəˌletɚ] 名 計算機、count [kaʊnt] 動 計算、
　　　　　 computing [kəmˋpjutɪŋ] 名 從事電腦工作
動詞三態變化 compute - computed - computed

comrade [ˋkɑmræd] 名 戰友，夥伴
▶ We have cooperated for a long time. He is my old comrade.
　我們合作很久了，他是我的老搭檔。

conceal [kənˋsil] 動 隱藏
▶ You must be concealing something from me.
　你一定對我有所隱瞞。
動詞三態變化 conceal - concealed - concealed

concede [kən`sid] 動（勉強）承認，容許　　　　　　 ⊙ MP3 03-16
▶ I had no choice but to concede my mistake.
我不得不承認錯誤。
動詞三態變化 concede - conceded - conceded

conceit [kən`sit] 名 自滿，個人意見（或想法）
▶ His conceit is the reason why his girlfriend said goodbye to him.
他的自大是他女朋友跟他分手的原因。

conceive [kən`siv] 動 想像，認為　　 同 imagine [ɪ`mædʒɪn] 動 想像
動詞三態變化 conceive - conceived - conceived

concentrate [`kɑnsɛnˌtret] 動 全神貫注
▶ Please concentrate on your study.
請專心讀書。
相關衍生字彙 concentration [ˌkɑnsɛn`treʃən] 名 專心、attention [ə`tɛnʃən] 名 注意力、
focus [`fokəs] 名 焦點、distraction [dɪ`strækʃən] 名 分心
動詞三態變化 concentrate - concentrated - concentrated

conception [kən`sɛpʃən] 名 概念，想法
▶ Regarding globalization, scholars have different conceptions.
關於全球化，學者們有不同的概念。

concern [kən`sɝn] 動 使關心，涉及
▶ Mom's health problem concerns me a lot.
媽媽的健康問題讓我很擔心。
動詞三態變化 concern - concerned - concerned

concerned [kən`sɝnd] 形 關心的，擔心的
片 be concerned about... 對～關心的
相關衍生字彙 concerning [kən`sɝnɪŋ] 介 有關於～、worry [`wɝɪ] 動 擔心、worried [`wɝɪd]
形 擔心的、worrisome [`wɝɪsəm] 形 令人擔心的

concert [`kɑnsɝt] 名 音樂會
▶ The concert was cancelled tonight. 今晚的音樂會被取消了。

concession [kən`sɛʃən] 名 讓步，特許　　 片 to make a concession 做出讓步

conciliate [kən`sɪlɪˌet] 動 安撫，調解
▶ It's not an easy job to conciliate his anger.
很難去安撫他的憤怒。
動詞三態變化 conciliate - conciliated - conciliated

concise [kən`saɪs] 形 簡潔的
▶ Be sure to make your presentation concise and powerful.
務必讓你的報告簡潔有力。

conclusion [kən`kluʒən] 名 結論　　片 to make a conclusion 做結論
相關衍生字彙 conclude [kən`klud] 動 下結論、conclusive [kən`klusɪv] 形 結論性的、decisive [dɪ`saɪsɪv] 形 決定性的，果斷的、decide [dɪ`saɪd] 動 決定

C

concord [`kɑnkɔrd] 名 協調，一致
▶ The two countries have lived in concord. 這兩個國家一直和諧相處。

concrete [`kɑnkrit] 形 具體的，混凝土的　　片 concrete evidence 具體證據

concur [kən`kɝ] 動 同意，同時發生
▶ Health and happiness seldom concur.
健康與幸福很少同時出現。
動詞三態變化 concur - concurred - concurred

condemn [kən`dɛm] 動 譴責，宣告～有罪
▶ Such a terrorist attack should be condemned.
這樣的恐怖攻擊應被譴責。
動詞三態變化 condemn - condemned - condemned

condense [kən`dɛns] 動 壓縮，使凝結　　片 condensed juice 濃縮果汁
動詞三態變化 condense - condensed - condensed

condition [kən`dɪʃən] 名 情況，(健康) 狀況
▶ A good doctor should be concerned about every patient's condition.
一位好的醫生應該關心每位病人的健康狀況。
相關衍生字彙 conditional [kən`dɪʃən] 形 有條件的、situation [ˌsɪtʃu`eʃən] 名 處境、circumstance [`sɝkəmˌstæns] 名 情境、state [stet] 名 狀況

condole [kən`dol] 動 哀悼，同情
▶ I will go to condole the death of my good friend's father.
我將前往弔唁我好友父親的去世。
動詞三態變化 condole - condoled - condoled

condolence [kən`doləns] 名 弔唁，慰問　　片 sincere condolence 誠摯的哀悼

condone [kən`don] 動 寬恕，赦免　　同 forgive [fɚ`gɪv] 動 原諒　　◎ MP3 03-17
動詞三態變化 condone - condoned - condoned

conduct [kən`dʌkt] 動 引導，指揮
▶ The survey is conducted by a professor who is an expert in economics.
這調查是由一位經濟方面的專家教授所指導。
相關衍生字彙 conductor [kən`dʌktɚ] 名 售票員、conductive [kən`dʌktɪv] 形 有傳導力的、conductivity [ˌkɑndʌk`tɪvətɪ] 名 傳導性、conduction [kən`dʌkʃən] 名 傳導，輸送

cone [kon] 名 圓錐形　　片 an ice cream cone 冰淇淋甜筒

confederation [kən͵fɛdəˋreʃən] 名 聯盟，邦聯
▶ Thirteen countries in the southeastern Asia form a new economic confederation.
　東南亞十三個國家組成新的經濟聯盟。

confer [kənˋfɝ] 動 商談
▶ The boss is conferring with the marketing manager.
　老闆正在和行銷經理商談。
動詞三態變化 confer - conferred - conferred

conference [ˋkɑnfərəns] 名 會議　　片 a summit conference 高峰會議
相關衍生字彙 meeting [ˋmitɪŋ] 名 會議、agenda [əˋdʒɛndə] 名 議程、bill [bɪl] 名 議案，法案、minute [ˋmɪnɪt] 名 會議紀錄

confess [kənˋfɛs] 動 承認，坦白
▶ I have to confess these materials are too difficult for me.
　我必須承認這些資料對我而言太困難了。
動詞三態變化 confess - confessed - confessed

confession [kənˋfɛʃən] 名 坦白，供認　　片 to make a confession 認罪

confidence [ˋkɑnfədəns] 名 信心
▶ I have no confidence in finishing the project by myself.
　我對獨立完成此計畫沒信心。
相關衍生字彙 confident [ˋkɑnfədənt] 形 有信心的、certain [ˋsɝtən] 形 確定的、sure [ʃur] 形 確定的、belief [bɪˋlif] 名 信念

confine [kənˋfaɪn] 動 限制
▶ Please confine your discussion to the main idea of the article.
　請你們把討論的重點限制在這篇文章的主題。
動詞三態變化 confine - confined - confined

confirm [kənˋfɝm] 動 確認
▶ Before you go abroad, you have to confirm the flight and hotel.
　在你出國前，要確認班機跟飯店。
動詞三態變化 confirm - confirmed - confirmed

confirmation [͵kɑnfɚˋmeʃən] 名 確認
▶ I have receive an official confirmation. 我已經收到正式的（官方的）確認。

conflict [ˋkɑnflɪkt] 名 衝突　　片 armed conflict 武裝衝突

conform [kənˋfɔrm] 動 遵守，符合
▶ Conform to the traffic rules, or you will be fined.
　遵守交通規則，否則你會被罰款。
動詞三態變化 conform - conformed - conformed

confound [kənˋfaʊnd] 動 混淆　　⑰ confuse [kənˋfjuz] 動 使困惑

動詞三態變化 confound - confounded - confounded

---

confront [kənˋfrʌnt] 動 面臨，遭遇
▶ When he was confronted by so many reporters, he appeared nervous.
當他迎面遇到這麼多記者，他顯得緊張。

相關衍生字彙 confrontation [ˌkɑnfrʌnˋteʃən] 名 對質、encounter [ɪnˋkaʊntɚ] 動 遭遇、
　　　　　　 face [fes] 動 面對、meet [mit] 動 碰面

動詞三態變化 confront - confronted - confronted

---

confusion [kənˋfjuʒən] 名 混亂，困惑
▶ To avoid confusion, the bus system was rearranged.
為了避免混亂，公車系統已被重新安排。

---

congenial [kənˋdʒinjəl] 形 協調的，意氣相投的
▶ I like the congenial working surroundings of my company.
我很喜歡公司的和諧環境。

---

congestion [kənˋdʒɛstʃən] 名 擁塞，稠密
▶ Because of the traffic congestion, I was late today.
因為交通阻塞，我今天遲到了。

---

congratulate [kənˋgrætʃəˌlet] 動 恭賀
▶ We had a party to congratulate on his promotion.
我們舉辦一場派對來恭賀他的晉升。

相關衍生字彙 congratulation [kənˌgrætʃəˋleʃən] 名 祝賀、wish [wɪʃ] 名 願望、hope [hop]
　　　　　　 動 希望、bless [blɛs] 動 祈福

動詞三態變化 congratulate - congratulated - congratulated

---

congress [ˋkɑŋgrəs] 名 立法機關，美國國會　　◉ MP3 03-18
▶ Congress has passed the bill. 美國國會已經通過這項法案。

---

congruent [ˋkɑŋgruənt] 形 全等的，一致的　　⑪ congruent triangles 全等三角形

---

conjunction [kənˋdʒʌŋkʃən] 名 連接詞
▶ The word "because" is a conjunction used to connect two sentences.
「因為」這個字是連接詞，用以連接兩個句子。

---

connect [kəˋnɛkt] 動 連接，結合
▶ I don't know how to connect my computer to the printer.
我不知道如何將電腦連接到印表機。

相關衍生字彙 connection [kəˋnɛkʃən] 名 關聯、join [dʒɔɪn] 動 連結、combine [kəmˋbaɪn]
　　　　　　 動 結合、attach [əˋtætʃ] 動 附加、disconnect [ˌdɪskəˋnɛkt] 動 使分開

動詞三態變化 connect - connected - connected

conquer [ˋkaŋkɚ] 動 征服
▶ Finally, I conquered my fear of swimming in the ocean.
終於，我征服了在大海游泳的恐懼。
動詞三態變化 conquer - conquered - conquered

conqueror [ˋkaŋkərɚ] 名 征服者，勝利者　同 victor [ˋvɪktɚ] 名 勝利者

conquest [ˋkaŋkwɛst] 名 克服　片 to extend one's conquest 擴大征服的版圖

conscience [ˋkanʃəns] 名 良心
▶ The teacher tried to arouse his conscience by telling him a story.
老師藉由一個故事試著喚醒他的良心。

conscientious [ˌkanʃɪˋɛnʃəs] 形 憑良心的，謹慎的，誠實的
▶ She is a conscientious student. She puts lots of effort into her study.
她是個勤奮的學生，很努力的在學習。

conscious [ˋkanʃəs] 形 自覺的　片 be conscious of 意識到

consciousness [ˋkanʃəsnɪs] 名 意識
▶ Jack got hurt in that accident and so far he hasn't recovered consciousness.
傑克在意外中受傷，到現在尚未恢復意識。

consecrate [ˋkansɪˌkret] 動 致力於
▶ She consecrated her life to education.
她終生奉獻給教育。
相關衍生字彙 devote [dɪˋvot] 動 投身於、dedicate [ˋdɛdəˌket] 動 貢獻、contribute [kənˋtrɪbjut] 動 貢獻、sacrifice [ˋsækrəˌfaɪs] 動 犧牲
動詞三態變化 consecrate - consecrated - consecrated

consent [kənˋsɛnt] 名 動 同意，贊成
▶ With parental consent, they will get engaged.
取得父母的同意，他們即將訂婚。
動詞三態變化 consent - consented - consented

consequence [ˋkansəˌkwɛns] 名 結果，後果
▶ If you continue to fool around, you must take the consequences.
如果你繼續游手好閒，你要承擔後果。

consequently [ˋkansəˌkwɛntlɪ] 副 因此　同 as a result 因此
相關衍生字彙 hence [hɛns] 副 因此、therefore [ˋðɛrˌfor] 副 因此、accordingly [əˋkɔrdɪŋlɪ] 副 因此

conservation [ˌkansɚˋveʃən] 名 保存
片 a wildlife conservation area 野生動物保育區

conservative [kən`sɝvətɪv] 形 保守的　　反 liberal [`lɪbərəl] 形 自由的

conserve [kən`sɝv] 動 保護，節省
▶ To conserve electricity, please remember to turn off the light when you are out.
為了省電，外出時請記得關燈。
動詞三態變化 conserve - conserved - conserved

consideration [kənsɪdə`reʃən] 名 考慮，體諒
▶ When I interview a new employee, I take his or her work experience into consideration.
當我面試新人時，我會把他或她的工作經驗納入考慮。
相關衍生字彙 consider [kən`sɪdɚ] 動 考慮、considerable [kən`sɪdərəbl] 形 大量的、considerate [kən`sɪdərɪt] 形 體貼的、considerably [kən`sɪdərəblɪ] 副 非常，相當

consist [kən`sɪst] 動 構成，符合
▶ Our team consists of ten players.
我們的隊伍由十位選手所組成。
動詞三態變化 consist - consisted - consisted

consistent [kən`sɪstənt] 形 一致的　　MP3 03-19
▶ Your actions are not consistent with your words. 你的言行不一。

consolation [ˌkɑnsə`leʃən] 名 安慰，慰藉
▶ All I can do is offer some words of consolation.
我所能做的就是送上幾句安慰的話。

console [kən`sol] 動 安慰，慰問
▶ I consoled Mark on the loss of his beloved dog.
我安慰馬克，因為他失去他心愛的小狗。
相關衍生字彙 comfort [`kʌmfɚt] 動 安慰、cheer [tʃɪr] 動 使振奮、ease [iz] 動 使舒適、torture [`tɔrtʃɚ] 動 折磨
動詞三態變化 console - consoled - consoled

conspicuous [kən`spɪkjuəs] 形 顯著的，炫耀的
▶ The white building appears so conspicuous in the small town.
那棟白色的建築物在小城鎮裡顯得很引人注目。

conspiracy [kən`spɪrəsɪ] 名 陰謀
▶ The six prisoners were charged with conspiracy to escape from jail.
這六名囚犯被控共謀逃獄。

constant [`kɑnstənt] 形 不變的，持續的
▶ To keep the food fresh, we keep the ice box at a constant temperature.
為了保持食物新鮮，我們把冰桶控制在穩定的溫度。

constantly [ˋkɑnstəntlɪ] 副 不斷地，時常地
▶ The little boy constantly makes mistakes. 這個小男孩時常犯錯。

constitution [ˌkɑnstəˋtjuʃən] 名 憲法，（事物的）構造
片 the Constitution of the United States 美國憲法

constrain [kənˋstren] 動 強迫，限制
▶ While listening to the concert, I constrained myself from coughing.
在聽音樂會時，我克制自己不要咳嗽。
動詞三態變化 constrain - constrained - constrained

construction [kənˋstrʌkʃən] 名 建造，結構　　片 under construction 建造中
相關衍生字彙 construct [kənˋstrʌkt] 動 建造、build [bɪld] 動 建設、
manufacture [ˌmænjəˋfæktʃɚ] 動 製造、make [mek] 動 製造

constructive [kənˋstrʌktɪv] 形 建設性的
▶ Please offer constructive suggestions at the meeting.
在會議裡，請提供有建設性的意見。

consult [kənˋsʌlt] 動 商議，請教
▶ Consult your doctor, and then you can take the medicine.
請教醫生，然後才可服用此藥。
動詞三態變化 consult - consulted - consulted

consultant [kənˋsʌltənt] 名 顧問，諮詢師
▶ Professor Hu is the management consultant of our company.
胡教授是我們公司的管理顧問。
相關衍生字彙 consultation [ˌkɑnsəlˋteʃən] 名 磋商、discussion [dɪˋskʌʃən] 名 商討、
debate [dɪˋbet] 動 辯論、argue [ˋɑrgju] 動 爭論

consume [kənˋsjum] 動 消耗，浪費
▶ I consume most of my money in travelling.
我大部分的金錢都花費在旅遊上。
動詞三態變化 consume - consumed - consumed

consumer [kənˋsjumɚ] 名 消費者，用戶
▶ Consumers' advice should be respected. 消費者的意見應該被尊重。

consumption [kənˋsʌmpʃən] 名 消耗　　片 mass consumption 大量消耗

contact [ˋkɑntækt] 名 接觸，聯絡
▶ After graduating from college, I lost contact with him.
大學畢業後，我就跟他失去聯絡了。
相關衍生字彙 touch [tʌtʃ] 動 碰觸、link [lɪŋk] 名 聯繫，關係、combination [ˌkɑmbəˋneʃən]
名 結合、blending [ˋblɛndɪŋ] 名 混合

contagious [kən`tedʒəs] 形 傳染性的
▶ Ebola is a highly contagious disease. 伊波拉是一種高度傳染的疾病。

C

contain [kən`ten] 動 包含
▶ The fruit contains vitamins.
這種水果含有維他命。
動詞三態變化 contain - contained - contained

container [kən`tenɚ] 名 容器
▶ The container is waterproof. 這個容器是防水的。

contaminate [kən`tæmə.net] 動 污染，弄髒　　MP3 03-20
▶ Be careful! Don't let your wound get contaminated.
小心！別讓你的傷口被感染了。
相關衍生字彙 pollute [pə`lut] 動 污染、dirty [`dɝtɪ] 形 髒的、toxic [`taksɪk] 形 有毒的、
deadly [`dɛdlɪ] 形 致命的
動詞三態變化 contaminate - contaminated - contaminated

contemplate [`kantɛm.plet] 動 仔細考慮
▶ I'm contemplating quitting my job.
我正考慮辭掉工作。
動詞三態變化 contemplate - contemplated - contemplated

contemplation [.kantɛm`pleʃən] 名 沉思，凝視
▶ Mom looked out to the window, losing herself in contemplation.
媽媽看著窗外，陷入沉思。

contemporary [kən`tɛmpə.rɛrɪ] 形 當代的，同時代的
▶ Both of them are contemporary writers. 他們倆人是同期的作家。

contempt [kən`tɛmpt] 名 輕視，恥辱
▶ The politician was beneath contempt. 這名政客為人所不齒 。

contend [kən`tɛnd] 動 競爭，辯論
▶ Many players will contend for the championship.
很多選手將爭奪此冠軍頭銜。
動詞三態變化 contend - contended - contended

content [kən`tɛnt] 形 滿足的
▶ I am content with my simple life. 我對我的單純生活感到很滿足。

contented [kən`tɛntɪd] 形 知足的　　片 a contented smile 滿意的微笑
相關衍生字彙 satisfied [`sætɪs.faɪd] 形 滿意的、happy [`hæpɪ] 形 快樂的、glad [glæd]
形 開心的、delighted [dɪ`laɪtɪd] 形 愉快的

contest [ˋkɑntɛst] 名 比賽　　🔘 a speech contest 演講比賽

contestant [kənˋtɛstənt] 名 參加競賽者
▶ All the contestants were asked to follow the rules of the game.
所有參加競賽者都被要求遵守比賽規則。

context [ˋkɑntɛkst] 名 上下文
▶ You can judge the meaning of a word you don't know from its context.
你可以從上下文來判斷一個你不認識的單字的意思。

continent [ˋkɑntənənt] 名 大陸，大洲
▶ Who discovered the Australian continent？
是誰發現澳洲陸地的？
相關衍生字彙 America [əˋmɛrɪkə] 名 美洲、Europe [ˋjurəp] 名 歐洲、Africa [ˋæfrɪkə] 名 非洲、Asia [ˋeʃə] 名 亞洲、Oceania [ˌoʃɪˋænɪə] 名 大洋洲

continental [ˌkɑntəˋnɛntl̩] 形 大陸的　　🔘 continental climate 大陸型氣候

continual [kənˋtɪnjuəl] 形 不間斷的
▶ With the continual noise, I couldn't sleep well. 這連續的噪音讓我睡不好。

continuous [kənˋtɪnjuəs] 形 不斷的，連續的
▶ The continuous heavy rain resulted in the flood.
持續的大雨導致水災。
相關衍生字彙 continue [kənˋtɪnju] 動 繼續、continually [kənˋtɪnjuəlɪ] 副 屢屢地、continuously [kənˋtɪnjuəslɪ] 副 不間斷地

contraband [ˋkɑntrəˌbænd] 形 違禁的　　🔘 smuggled [ˋsmʌg!] 形 走私的

contract [ˋkɑntrækt] 名 契約
▶ If you break the contract, you'll be fined. 如果你違約，你將會被罰款。

contradict [ˌkɑntrəˋdɪkt] 動 反駁，否認
▶ How dare you contradict your boss？
你怎麼敢反駁你的老闆？
動詞三態變化 contradict - contradicted - contradicted

contrary [ˋkɑntrɛrɪ] 名 相反　　🔘 on the contrary 相反地

contrast [ˋkɑnˌtræst] 名 對比
▶ The black and white present a contrast. 黑與白呈現對比。

contribute [kənˋtrɪbjut] 動 捐獻，貢獻　　◉ MP3 03-21
▶ The charity contributed food and water to the earthquake victims.
慈善機構捐很多食物和水給地震災民。
動詞三態變化 contribute - contributed - contributed

contribution [ˌkɑntrəˈbjuʃən] 名 貢獻，資助
🈁 to make an outstanding contribution 做出卓越的貢獻

相關衍生字彙 donate [ˈdonet] 動 捐獻、give [gɪv] 動 給與（某人時間、機會等）、
bestow [bɪˈsto] 動 把～贈與、devote [dɪˈvot] 動 將～奉獻（給）

contrive [kənˈtraɪv] 動 策劃，發明
▶ Would you please contrive a meeting?
你可以幫忙安排個會面嗎？

動詞三態變化 contrive - contrived - contrived

control [kənˈtrol] 名 動 控制，支配
▶ The fire was finally controlled.
大火終於被控制住了。

動詞三態變化 control - controlled - controlled

controversy [ˈkɑntrəˌvɝsɪ] 名 爭論
▶ The new policy has aroused fierce controversy.
這項新的政策已經引起激烈的爭論。

相關衍生字彙 controversial [ˌkɑntrəˈvɝʃəl] 形 有爭議的、controvert [ˈkɑntrəˌvɝt]
動 駁斥、dispute [dɪˈspjut] 動 爭論、quarrel [ˈkwɔrəl] 動 爭吵

convenience [kənˈvinjəns] 名 方便　　🈁 a convenience store 便利商店

convenient [kənˈvinjənt] 形 方便的，合宜的
▶ The public transportation system in Sydney is very convenient.
雪梨的公共交通系統很方便。

conventional [kənˈvɛnʃənl] 形 習慣的，常見的，協定的
🈁 traditional [trəˈdɪʃənl] 形 傳統的

converge [kənˈvɝdʒ] 動 會合，聚集
▶ All the trains converge at the central station.
所有火車都匯集在中央火車站。

動詞三態變化 converge - converged - converged

conversation [ˌkɑnvɚˈseʃən] 名 談話
🈁 to strike up a conversation 開啟一段對話

converse [kənˈvɝs] 動 交談，談話
▶ She is so shy that she never converses with a stranger.
她很害羞，所以她從不跟陌生人交談。

相關衍生字彙 talk [tɔk] 動 談話、speak [spik] 動 說話、say [se] 動 講述、
communicate [kəˈmjunəˌket] 動 傳達

動詞三態變化 converse - conversed - conversed

convert [kən`vɝt] 動 轉變，兌換
▶ They converted an old barn into a greenhouse.
他們把舊穀倉改成溫室。

相關衍生字彙 change [tʃendʒ] 動 改變、exchange [ɪks`tʃendʒ] 動 交換、transfer [træns`fɝ] 動 轉換、alter [`ɔltɚ] 動 改變、differ [`dɪfɚ] 動 相異

動詞三態變化 convert - converted - converted

convey [kən`ve] 動 傳達，搬運
▶ If you see your aunt, please convey my appreciation.
如果你見到你的阿姨，請代為轉達我的謝意。

動詞三態變化 convey - conveyed - conveyed

convict [kən`vɪkt] 動 判決
▶ The judge convicted him of murder.
法官判他謀殺罪。

動詞三態變化 convict - convicted - convicted

conviction [kən`vɪkʃən] 名 定罪，說服力
▶ The young man has no previous conviction. 這位年輕人無前科。

convince [kən`vɪns] 動 說服
▶ His attitude convinced the jury of his innocence.
他的態度使陪審團相信他是無辜的。

相關衍生字彙 persuade [pɚ`swed] 動 說服、assure [ə`ʃur] 動 使確信、guarantee [ˌgærən`ti] 動 保證、promise [`prɑmɪs] 動 允諾

動詞三態變化 convince - convinced - convinced

cooperate [ko`ɑpəˌret] 動 合作，配合
▶ The two countries cooperated with each other to build the tunnel.
這兩個國家合作建造此隧道。

動詞三態變化 cooperate - cooperated - cooperated

cooperation [koˌɑpə`reʃən] 名 合作，協力
▶ Our factory will produce new bicycles in cooperation with a foreign firm.
我們工廠將跟一家外國公司合作生產新的腳踏車。

coordinate [ko`ɔrdn̩et] 動 協調
▶ We need someone to help coordinate the procedures.
我們需要有人幫忙協調整個流程。

動詞三態變化 coordinate - coordinated - coordinated

cope [kop] 動 對付，妥善處理　　片 to cope with 處理
動詞三態變化 cope - coped - coped

copyright [`kɑpɪˌraɪt] 名 版權　　片 to register a copyright 註冊版權　　◎ MP3 03-22

相關衍生字彙 copy [ˋkɑpɪ] 動 複印、copycat [ˋkɑpⳑⳑkæt] 名 模仿者、copywriter [ˋkɑpⳑⳑraɪtɚ] 名 廣告文案撰寫人

cordial [ˋkɔrdʒəl] 形 熱忱的，表心的　　同 friendly [ˋfrɛndlɪ] 形 友善的

core [kor] 名 核心，果核
▶ What the elementary school students learn is the core knowledge.
小學生學的都是核心知識。
相關衍生字彙 cork [kɔrk] 名 軟木塞、corn [kɔrn] 名 玉米、cord [kɔrd] 名 細繩、corps [kɔr] 名 軍團，部隊

corner [ˋkɔrnɚ] 名 角落，街角　　片 around the corner 即將到來

corporal [ˋkɔrpərəl] 形 身體的，私人的　　片 corporal punishment 體罰

corporation [ˌkɔrpəˋreʃən] 名 公司，財團法人
▶ May works in a broadcasting corporation. 梅在一家廣播公司工作。

corpse [kɔrps] 名 屍體，殘骸　　片 to bury a corpse 埋葬屍體

correct [kəˋrɛkt] 形 正確的 動 改正，糾正
▶ It's correct to tell the truth.
說實話是正確的。
相關衍生字彙 wrong [rɔŋ] 形 錯誤的、right [raɪt] 形 正確的、incorrect [ˌɪnkəˋrɛkt] 形 錯誤的、accurate [ˋækjərɪt] 形 精確的
動詞三態變化 correct - corrected - corrected

correction [kəˋrɛkʃən] 名 校正
▶ My teacher made corrections in my English composition.
老師修正我的英文作文。

correspond [ˌkɔrɪˋspɑnd] 動 符合，相應
▶ What the thief said didn't correspond with the witness's words.
小偷說的跟目擊者說的不符。
動詞三態變化 correspond - corresponded - corresponded

correspondence [ˌkɔrəˋspɑndəns] 名 符合，通信
▶ My correspondence with him only lasted one month.
我跟他的通信只維持一周。

correspondent [ˌkɔrɪˋspɑndənt] 名 特派員 形 一致的
▶ Hemingway was a correspondent in war. 海明威曾經是戰地記者。

corridor [ˋkɔrɪdɚ] 名 走廊
▶ The manager's office is at the end of the long corridor.
經理的辦公室在長廊的尾端。

corrode [kə`rod] 動 侵蝕，損害
▶ Iron corrodes easily near the sea.
鐵在海邊很容易腐蝕。
動詞三態變化 corrode - corroded - corroded

corrupt [kə`rʌpt] 動 墮落，腐化 形 貪污的　　片 a corrupt official 貪污的官員
動詞三態變化 corrupt - corrupted - corrupted

corruption [kə`rʌpʃən] 名 賄賂，腐敗
▶ A government corruption will result in a decaying society.
政府的腐敗將使社會退步。

cosmetics [kɑz`mɛtɪks] 名 化妝品
▶ Before going to work, she always puts on cosmetics.
上班前，她都會化妝。
相關衍生字彙 lotion [`loʃən] 名 化妝水、lipstick [`lɪp,stɪk] 名 口紅、toner [`tonɚ] 名 收斂水、cream [krim] 名 乳霜

cosmic [`kɑzmɪk] 形 宇宙的，無限的
▶ My brother gets addicted to the mystery of the cosmic.
我弟弟著迷宇宙的神祕。

cosmos [`kɑzməs] 名 宇宙
▶ I believe that there are other lives somewhere in the cosmos.
我相信宇宙某處有其他的生物。

cost [kɔst] 名 費用 動 花費
▶ The coat cost my husband's one-month salary.
這件外套花掉我老公一個月的薪水。
相關衍生字彙 spend [spɛnd] 動 花費、take [tek] 動 花費、price [praɪs] 名 價錢、value [`vælju] 名 價值
動詞三態變化 cost - cost - cost

costume [`kɑstjum] 名 服裝　　片 an academic costume 大學學士服　　MP3 03-23

cottage [`kɑtɪdʒ] 名 別墅，小屋
▶ My grandma lives in a cottage by herself. 我奶奶獨自一人住在小屋。

cotton [`kɑtn̩] 名 棉花
▶ The quilt was made from cotton. 這件被子是棉花製成的。

couch [kautʃ] 名 沙發　　片 a couch potato 愛看電視的人

cough [kɔf] 名 動 咳嗽
▶ My daughter has a cold and coughs badly.
我的女兒感冒而且咳得很厲害。
動詞三態變化 cough - coughed - coughed

council [ˋkaʊnsḷ] 名 **地方議會**　　片 city council 市議會

counsel [ˋkaʊnsḷ] 動 **商議，勸告**
▶ My job is to counsel students on how to apply to university.
　　我的工作是輔導學生如何申請大學。
動詞三態變化 counsel - counseled / counselled - counseled / counselled

counselor [ˋkaʊnsḷɚ] 名 **顧問**　　片 a marriage counselor 婚姻顧問

count [kaʊnt] 動 **計算，有重要意義**
▶ What counts is your attitude.
　　重要的是你的態度。
相關衍生字彙 countable [ˋkaʊntəbḷ] 形 可數的、countdown [ˋkaʊntˏdaʊn] 名 最後倒數、
　　countless [ˋkaʊntlɪs] 形 數不盡的
動詞三態變化 count - counted - counted

countenance [ˋkaʊntənəns] 名 **臉色** 名動 **贊同**
▶ The boss's angry countenance shocked us.
　　老闆憤怒的表情嚇壞我們了。
動詞三態變化 countenance - countenanced - countenanced

counteract [ˏkaʊntɚˋækt] 動 **中和，抵抗**
▶ Alkalis can counteract acids.
　　鹼可以中和酸性。
動詞三態變化 counteract - counteracted - counteracted

counterfeit [ˋkaʊntɚˏfɪt] 名 **仿製品** 形 **偽造的**
▶ The jewelry she bought at the night market is a counterfeit.
　　她在夜市買的珠寶都是贗品。

country [ˋkʌntrɪ] 名 **國家，鄉下**
▶ a developing / developed country
　　開發中／已開發國家
相關衍生字彙 countryman [ˋkʌntrɪmən] 名 同胞、countryside [ˋkʌntrɪˏsaɪd] 名 鄉間，農村、
　　countrywide [ˏkʌntrɪˋwaɪd] 形 全國性的、county [ˋkaʊntɪ] 名 縣，郡

couple [ˋkʌpḷ] 名 **（一）對，（一）雙**
▶ A newly wedded couple moved to be my neighbor.
　　有一對新婚夫婦搬來當我的鄰居。

courage [ˏkɝɪdʒ] 名 **勇氣**
▶ It takes courageous to say I love you. 說出我愛你是需要勇氣的。

courageous [kəˋredʒəs] 形 **勇敢的**
▶ How courageous of you to stand up for your belief.
　　你真勇敢站出來捍衛自己的信念。

course [kors] 名 課程，路線
▶ Tom spent two years completing his master courses.
　湯姆花了兩年的時間完成他的碩士課程。

court [kort] 名 法院　　片 a juvenile court 少年法庭
相關衍生字彙 judge [dʒʌdʒ] 名 法官、procurator [ˋprɑkjəˌretɚ] 名 檢察官、lawyer [ˋlɔjɚ] 名 律師、warden [ˋwɔrdn̩] 名 典獄長

courteous [ˋkɝtjəs] 形 有禮貌的　　同 polite [pəˋlaɪt] 形 有禮貌的

courtesy [ˋkɝtəsɪ] 名 禮貌
▶ He replied to my letter out of courtesy. 他出於禮貌回信給我。

cousin [ˋkʌzn̩] 名 堂／表兄弟姊妹　　⊙ MP3 03-24
▶ All my family attended my wedding, including my cousins.
　所有的家人都來參加我的婚禮，包括我的堂／表兄弟姊妹。

cover [ˋkʌvɚ] 動 覆蓋，掩飾，報導
▶ The top of the mountain has been covered with snow.
　山頂已經被白雪覆蓋。
相關衍生字彙 coverage [ˋkʌvərɪdʒ] 名 涵蓋範圍、covering [ˋkʌvərɪŋ] 名 覆蓋物、cover-up [ˋkʌvɚˌʌp] 名 掩飾、coverall [ˋkʌvɚˌɔlz] 名（衣褲相連的）工作衣
動詞三態變化 cover - covered - covered

covert [ˋkʌvɚt] 形 隱蔽的
▶ That military base is very covert. 那個軍事基地很隱密。

covet [ˋkʌvɪt] 動 垂涎，貪圖
▶ Don't covet others' fortune.
　不要垂涎他人的財富。
動詞三態變化 covet - coveted - coveted

cowardice [ˋkauɚdɪs] 名 懦弱，膽小
▶ I shouldn't show my cowardice in public. 我不應該公開表現出我的懦弱。

cradle [ˋkredl̩] 名 搖籃，支架　　片 from (the) cradle to (the) grave 終其一生

craft [kræft] 名 手藝，工藝　　片 traditional crafts 傳統手工藝
相關衍生字彙 craftsman [ˋkræftsmən] 名 工匠、craftsmanship [ˋkræftsmənˌʃɪp] 名 技術、skill [ˋskɪl] 名 技術

cranky [ˋkræŋkɪ] 形 暴躁不安的，胡思亂想的
▶ His cranky personality makes him lose all his friends.
　他易怒的個性使他失去所有的朋友。

crash [kræʃ] 名（飛機的）墜落　　片 air crash 墜機事件

C

crawl [krɔl] 動 爬行，蠕動
▶ The baby starts learning how to crawl at about eight month old.
　嬰兒大約八個月大開始學爬。
相關衍生字彙 walk [wɔk] 動 走路、climb [klaɪm] 動 攀登、run [rʌn] 動 跑步、jump [dʒʌmp] 動 跳躍
動詞三態變化 crawl - crawled - crawled

crazy [ˋkrezɪ] 形 瘋狂的
▶ Jim is crazy for music. 吉姆對音樂很狂熱。

cream [krim] 名 奶油膏狀物　　片 ice cream 冰淇淋

create [krɪˋet] 動 創造，設計
▶ God created the world.
　上帝創造世界。
相關衍生字彙 creation [krɪˋeʃən] 名 創造、creative [krɪˋetɪv] 形 有創造力的、creature [ˋkritʃɚ] 名 生物、invent [ɪnˋvɛnt] 動 發明
動詞三態變化 create - created - created

credible [ˋkrɛdəbl̩] 形 可靠的，可信的
▶ The police thought what the witness said was not credible.
　警察認為目擊者說的不可信。

credit [ˋkrɛdɪt] 名 信用，賒帳　　片 a credit card 信用卡

credulous [ˋkrɛdʒuləs] 形 易受騙的
▶ Young people have no working experience so they are credulous.
　年輕人沒有工作經驗，所以容易受騙。

creed [krid] 名 信條，教義　　片 religious creeds 宗教教義

creep [krip] 動 匍匐而行，躡手躡腳地走
▶ I saw a man creeping through the window in the dark.
　我看見一個人在黑暗中爬進窗戶
動詞三態變化 creep - creeped / crept - creeped / crept

cremate [ˋkrimet] 動 火葬
▶ We followed Dad's will to cremate him.
　我們遵照父親的遺囑，進行火葬。
動詞三態變化 cremate - cremated - cremated

crest [krɛst] 名 頂點，(頭盔的) 羽飾　　片 to reach the crest of the hill 抵達山頂

cricket [ˋkrɪkɪt] 名 蟋蟀　　⊙ MP3 **03-25**
▶ Listen! A cricket is singing in the tree. 你聽！蟋蟀在樹上唱歌。

crime [kraɪm] 名 罪行　　片 to commit a crime 犯罪

相關衍生字彙 criminal [ˈkrɪmən]] 名 罪犯、violate [ˈvaɪəˌlet] 動 違反、offender [əˈfɛndəˠ] 名 違法者、unlawful [ʌnˈlɔfəl] 形 不合法的、prisoner [ˈprɪznəˠ] 名 囚犯

---

cripple [ˈkrɪp]] 動 使殘廢
▶ The accident crippled the basketball player.
　這場意外使這位籃球選手殘廢。

動詞三態變化 cripple - crippled - crippled

---

crisis [ˈkraɪsɪs] 名 危機　　片 an energy / economic crisis 能源／經濟危機

---

criterion [kraɪˈtɪrɪən] 名 標準，準則
▶ Our professor announced the criterion of assignment in his outline of the course.
　教授在他的課程大綱裡公布作業的標準。

---

critic [ˈkrɪtɪk] 名 評論家
▶ To be an impartial critic is not easy.
　當一名公正的評論家不容易。

相關衍生字彙 critical [ˈkrɪtɪk]] 形 挑剔的、criticism [ˈkrɪtəˌsɪzəm] 名 批評、criticize [ˈkrɪtɪˌsaɪz] 動 批判、critique [krɪˈtik] 名 評論

---

crop [krɑp] 名 農作物
▶ Coffee is one of the main crops in the poor country.
　咖啡是這個貧窮國家主要的農作物之一。

---

crowd [kraʊd] 名 人群　　片 a huge crowd of people 一大群人

---

cross [krɔs] 名 十字形 動 跨越
▶ Be careful when you are crossing the road!
　跨越馬路時要小心！

相關衍生字彙 cross-examine [ˈkrɔsɪgˈzæmɪn] 動 盤問、crossroads [ˈkrɔsˌrodz] 名 十字路口、crossing [ˈkrɔsɪŋ] 名 渡口

動詞三態變化 cross - crossed - crossed

---

crown [kraʊn] 名 王冠 動 為～加冕
▶ Queen Victoria was crowned in 1837.
　維多利亞女王是在一八三七年加冕成為女王的。

動詞三態變化 crown - crowned - crowned

---

crucial [ˈkruʃəl] 形 決定性的
▶ Her professional knowledge is very crucial to our company.
　她的專業知識對我們公司很重要。

---

crude [krud] 形 粗野的，天然的
▶ How crude of you to say so! 你這樣説話太粗魯了！

C

cruel [ˋkruəl] 形 殘忍的　　片 a cruel blow 殘忍的打擊

相關衍生字彙　cruelty [ˋkruəltɪ] 名 殘忍、kind [kaɪnd] 形 善良的、kindness [ˋkaɪndnɪs] 名 善良、brutal [ˋbrut]] 形 殘酷的

- -

cruise [kruz] 名 動 巡航，航遊

▶ She has saved money for years to take a cruise around the world.
為了航行環遊世界，她存了好幾年的錢。

動詞三態變化　cruise - cruised - cruised

- -

crumble [ˋkrʌmbḷ] 動 崩潰，粉碎

▶ Her son's death made him crumble.
她兒子的死讓她崩潰。

動詞三態變化　crumble - crumbled - crumbled

- -

crush [krʌʃ] 名 迷戀 名 動 壓碎

▶ Mark admitted he had a crush on the girl.
馬克承認戀上這位女孩。

動詞三態變化　crush - crushed - crushed

- -

crutch [krʌtʃ] 名（支在腋下的）拐杖

▶ The doctor advised him to walk on crutches. 醫生建議他用枴杖來走路。

- -

cry [kraɪ] 動 哭泣，叫喊　　片 to cry for joy 喜極而泣

相關衍生字彙　sob [sɑb] 動 啜泣、weep [wip] 動 哭泣、laugh [læf] 動 笑、smile [smaɪl] 動 微笑

動詞三態變化　cry - cried - cried

- -

crystal [ˋkrɪst]] 名 水晶 形 清澈的

▶ The crystal vase was handmade. 這個水晶花瓶是手工製的。

- -

cub [kʌb] 名（熊、獅、虎、狼等的）幼獸，新手

▶ We call a young lion, or bear a cub. 我們稱小獅子或小熊為幼獸。

- -

cube [kjub] 名 立方體　　片 a sugar cube 方糖　　　　　　MP3 **03-26**

cuddle [ˋkʌd]] 動 擁抱，依偎

▶ The baby stopped crying when her mother cuddled her.
媽媽抱小嬰兒時，她就不哭了。

動詞三態變化　cuddle - cuddled - cuddled

- -

cuisine [kwɪˋzin] 名 食譜

▶ Her cuisines on the Internet are very popular. 她放上網路的食譜很受歡迎。

cultivate [`kʌltə‚vet] 動 耕種，養殖
▶ The villagers make a living by cultivating crops.
　村民靠栽種穀物維生。
相關衍生字彙 cultivation [‚kʌltə`veʃən] 名 栽培、cultural [`kʌltʃərəl] 形 文化的、
　　　　culture [`kʌltʃɚ] 名 文化、cultivated [`kʌltə‚vetɪd] 形 栽培的，文雅的
動詞三態變化 cultivate - cultivated - cultivated

cunning [`kʌnɪŋ] 形 狡猾的，熟練的　　同 sly [slaɪ] 形 狡猾的

cure [kjur] 名 治療 動 治癒
▶ Prevention is better than cure.
　（諺語）預防勝於治療。
動詞三態變化 cure - cured - cured

curator [kju`retɚ] 名 館長，監護人
▶ The curator took care of the museum very well. 這位館長把博物館管理得很好。

curiosity [‚kjurɪ`asətɪ] 名 好奇心
▶ Curiosity killed the cat.
　（諺語）好奇心殺死一隻貓。
相關衍生字彙 curious [`kjurɪəs] 形 好奇的、uninterested [ʌn`ɪntərɪstɪd] 形 不感興趣的、
　　　　indifferent [ɪn`dɪfərənt] 形 冷漠的、unconcerned [‚ʌnkən`sɜnd] 形 不關心的

currency [`kɜənsɪ] 名 貨幣　　片 foreign currency 外幣

current [`kɜənt] 名 趨勢 形 當前的，流行的
▶ We have no choice but to swim with the current.
　我們別無選擇，只能順應潮流。

curriculum [kə`rɪkjələm] 名 課程
▶ A good curriculum can help students learn more.
　好的課程可以協助學生學更多。

curse [kɜs] 名 動 詛咒
▶ The witch put a curse on the baby.
　巫婆對小嬰兒施咒語。
動詞三態變化 curse - cursed - cursed

cursory [`kɜsərɪ] 形 粗略的，匆忙的
▶ We will have a cursory exam in class today.
　今天課堂上會有一個簡單的考試。

curtail [kɜ`tel] 動 縮減，省略　　片 to curtail the budget 刪減預算
相關衍生字彙 cut [kʌt] 動 削減、condense [kən`dɛns] 動 濃縮，壓縮、shorten [`ʃɔrtn̩]
　　　　動 縮短、abbreviate [ə`brivɪ‚et] 動 縮寫，使省略
動詞三態變化 curtail - curtailed - curtailed

curtain [`kɝtn̩] 名 簾幕　　片 a curtain call 謝幕

curve [kɝv] 名 曲線 動 彎曲
▶ The road makes many curves in the mountains.
　這條路在山區有很多轉彎處。
動詞三態變化 curve - curved - curved

cushion [`kuʃən] 名 墊子
▶ Put the soft cushion behind your back and you will feel better.
　把軟墊放在背後會讓你舒服點。

custom [`kʌstəm] 名 習俗，慣例
▶ No matter where we go, we should respect the local custom.
　不論我們去哪裡，我們都應尊重當地的習俗。
相關衍生字彙 customary [`kʌstəm‚ɛrɪ] 形 合乎習俗的、habit [`hæbɪt] 名 習慣、
　　tradition [trə`dɪʃən] 名 傳統、folklore [`fok‚lor] 名 民俗

customer [`kʌstəmɚ] 名 顧客
▶ Remember that customers are always right. 記住，顧客永遠是對的。

customs [`kʌstəmz] 名 海關，關稅
▶ It takes some time to pass through customs. 通過海關需要花點時間。

cycle [`saɪkl̩] 名 週期 動 循環　　片 a life cycle 生命／生活週期　　◉ MP3 03-27
動詞三態變化 cycle - cycled - cycled

cyclone [`saɪklon] 名 龍捲風
▶ A cyclone is a tropical storm, just like a typhoon in Taiwan.
　龍捲風是一種熱帶風暴，就如同台灣的颱風。

cynical [`sɪnɪkl̩] 形 憤世嫉俗的，挖苦的
▶ We don't know what makes him so cynical about the society.
　我們不知他為何對社會如此憤世嫉俗。

一網打盡

字母 **D**

daily ~ dynasty

詞性說明

名 名詞	副 副詞	介 介系詞
動 動詞	形 形容詞	連 連接詞
代 代名詞	助 助動詞	

內文圖示說明

片 片語　　反 反義字　　同 同義字

一網打盡「英語小知識」｜星期的縮寫

Mon.
星期一

Tue.
星期二

Wed.
星期三

Thu.
星期四

Fri.
星期五

Sat.
星期六

Sun.
星期日

D daily ~ dynasty

★一網打盡 1296 個英文單字 │ 一網打盡 268 句英語會話句

daily [`delɪ] 副 每日 形 日常的
▶ Jogging is part of my daily routine. 慢跑是我每天例行公事的一部分。

- - -

dainty [`dentɪ] 形 精緻的，美味的
▶ Mom prepared dainty handmade cookies for my birthday.
媽媽為我的生日準備精緻的手工餅乾。

- - -

dairy [`dɛrɪ] 形 乳製品的　　片 dairy products 乳製品

- - -

dam [dæm] 名 水壩
▶ The dam was built for providing water for the area.
這座水壩蓋來提供此區用水。

- - -

damage [`dæmɪdʒ] 名 動 損害　　片 to do damage to 對～造成傷害
相關衍生字彙 harm [hɑrm] 名 傷害、hurt [hɝt] 動 疼痛、injure [`ɪndʒɚ] 動 傷害、heal [hil] 動 治癒、cure [kjur] 動 治療
動詞三態變化 damage - damaged - damaged

- - -

damp [dæmp] 形 潮濕的
▶ It has been damp and cold for days. 天氣已經又濕又冷好幾天了。

- - -

dance [dæns] 動 跳舞
▶ Dancing to the music makes me relaxed.
隨著音樂跳舞讓我覺得放鬆。
動詞三態變化 dance - danced - danced

- - -

danger [`dendʒɚ] 名 危險
▶ Driving on the icy road is a danger.
在結冰的路面上開車是一件危險的事。
相關衍生字彙 dangerous [`dendʒərəs] 形 危險的、risk [rɪsk] 名 危險、risky [`rɪskɪ] 形 危險的、safety [`seftɪ] 名 安全、safe [sef] 形 安全的

- - -

dank [dæŋk] 形 潮濕的，透水的　　同 wet [wɛt] 形 潮濕的

- - -

dare [dɛr] 動 膽敢
▶ I don't dare yell at my boss.
我不敢對著老闆大吼。
動詞三態變化 dare - dared - dared

- - -

daring [`dɛrɪŋ] 形 勇敢的，大膽的
▶ It is daring to walk alone in the forest in the dark.
在黑暗中獨自走在森林裡是很大膽的。

dark [dɑrk] 名 黑夜 形 黑暗的
▶ Before dark, we have to arrive at the next destination.
天黑前，我們得抵達下個目的地。

相關衍生字彙 darken [`dɑrkn̩] 動 變黑暗、darkness [`dɑrknɪs] 名 黑暗、light [laɪt] 動 點亮、
bright [braɪt] 形 明亮的

darling [`dɑrlɪŋ] 名 親愛的（人）
▶ Oh my darling, don't worry about me. 親愛的，別擔心我。

dart [dɑrt] 名 飛鏢
▶ We boys liked to play the game of darts after class.
下課後，我們男孩喜歡玩飛鏢遊戲。

dash [dæʃ] 動 急奔，猛撞
▶ It started to rain so we dashed back home.
因為開始下雨，所以我們趕緊衝回家。

動詞三態變化 dash - dashed - dashed

data [`detə] 名 資料 ，數據
▶ We made a questionnaire to collect data. 我們製作問卷來收集資料。

date [det] 名 日期，約會　　片 to date back 追溯回～（年代或日期）

daughter [`dɔtɚ] 名 女兒
▶ I have a son and a daughter.
我有一兒一女。

相關衍生字彙 son [sʌn] 名 兒子、nephew [`nɛfju] 名 姪子、niece [nis] 名 姪女、
cousin [`kʌzn̩] 名 堂（或表）兄弟、姊妹、grandson [`grænd͵sʌn] 名 孫子、
granddaughter [`græn͵dɔtɚ] 名 孫女

dawdle [`dɔdl̩] 動 閒混，偷懶
▶ Stop dawdling! You are already twenty years old.
別再混了！你已經二十歲了。

動詞三態變化 dawdle - dawdled - dawdled

dawn [dɔn] 名 黎明，曙光
▶ When dawn breaks, you can hear birds singing.
當破曉時刻，你可以聽到許多鳥叫聲。

daydream [`de͵drim] 名 白日夢　　◎ MP3 04-02
▶ He has had a daydream about winning a lottery.
他一直懷有一個中樂透彩的白日夢。

相關衍生字彙 daylight [`de͵laɪt] 名 日光、daytime [`de͵taɪm] 名 白天、evening [`ivnɪŋ]
名 傍晚、night [naɪt] 名 夜晚

dazzle [ˈdæzl̩] 動 使眼花
▶ I was dazzled by the neon light.
這些霓虹燈讓我眼花撩亂。
動詞三態變化 dazzle - dazzled - dazzled

deadline [ˈdɛdˌlaɪn] 名 截止期限
▶ The writer should meet the deadline, or he will be fined.
作家必須在規定的期限內完稿,否則會被罰款。
相關衍生字彙 dead [dɛd] 形 死的、die [daɪ] 動 死亡、deadly [ˈdɛdlɪ] 形 致命的、death [dɛθ] 名 死亡、deadlock [ˈdɛdˌlɑk] 名 僵局

deaf [dɛf] 形 耳聾的
▶ Helen Keller was deaf and blind, but she could speak eight languages..
海倫 · 凱勒又聾又盲,但她會講八種語言。

deal [dil] 名 動 交易
▶ It's a deal!
就這麼說定了!
動詞三態變化 deal - dealt - dealt

debase [dɪˈbes] 動 貶值 　片 to debase the currency 讓貨幣貶值
動詞三態變化 debase - debased - debased

debate [dɪˈbet] 名 動 辯論
▶ Many scholars were invited to debate the new education policy.
很多學者應邀來針對新的教育政策作辯論。
相關衍生字彙 discuss [dɪˈskʌs] 動 討論、dispute [dɪˈspjut] 動 爭論、argue [ˈɑrgju] 動 爭吵、agree [əˈgri] 動 同意、oppose [əˈpoz] 動 反對
動詞三態變化 debate - debated - debated

debris [dəˈbri] 名 殘骸,碎片
▶ The debris of the airplane was scattered in the remote mountains.
飛機殘骸散落在深山裡。

debt [dɛt] 名 負債
▶ To pay off his debt, he works day and night.
為了還清債務,他日以繼夜的工作。

debut [dɪˈbju] 名 初次登台
▶ The little girl made her debut as an actress in a musical.
這位小女孩是在一部歌舞劇中初登場當演員。

decade [ˈdɛked] 名 十年
▶ We have known each other for decades. 我們已經認識數十年了。

decadent [ˋdɛkədn̩t] 形 墮落的，衰落的
▶ There are low moral standards in a decadent society.
在墮落的社會裡，道德水準不會太高。

D

decay [dɪˋke] 動 腐敗，蛀蝕
▶ Candy will make kids' teeth decay easily.
糖果很容易讓小孩的牙齒蛀牙。
動詞三態變化 decay - decayed - decayed

deceit [dɪˋsit] 名 欺騙，奸詐
▶ Her wit exposed the man's deceit.
她的智慧揭穿了這個人的詭計。
相關衍生字彙 deceive [dɪˋsiv] 動 欺騙、trick [trɪk] 動 哄騙、cheat [tʃit] 動 詐取、hoax [hoks] 動 欺騙、fool [ful] 動 愚弄

decelerate [diˋsɛləˌret] 動 減速
▶ At the sight of yellow lights, you have to decelerate your car.
看到黃燈時，你的車子要減速。
動詞三態變化 decelerate - decelerated - decelerated

decency [ˋdisn̩sɪ] 名 合宜，得體
▶ He didn't have the decency to say goodbye. 他連再見都沒說，真不得體。

decision [dɪˋsɪʒən] 名 決定　　片 to make a decision 做決定
相關衍生字彙 decide [dɪˋsaɪd] 動 決定、decisive [dɪˋsaɪsɪv] 形 決定性的、
indecisive [ˌɪndɪˋsaɪsɪv] 形 優柔寡斷的、decisiveness [dɪˋsaɪsɪvnɪs] 名 果斷

decipher [dɪˋsaɪfɚ] 動 解密，辨認
▶ Even her parents couldn't decipher her diary.
甚至她的父母都無法理解她的日記。
動詞三態變化 decipher - deciphered - deciphered

declaration [ˌdɛkləˋreʃən] 名 宣布　　片 to make a declaration 發表聲明

declare [dɪˋklɛr] 動 宣布，聲明
▶ The president declared in public that he supported the proposal.
總統公開宣布他支持此項提案。
動詞三態變化 declare - declared – declared

decline [dɪˋklaɪn] 動 下降，衰退　　◎ MP3 **04-03**
▶ The number of the students studying at the school keeps declining.
在這所學校就讀的學生數持續下降。
相關衍生字彙 fall [fɔl] 動 降落、decrease [dɪˋkris] 動 減少、weaken [ˋwikən] 動 變弱、
progress [ˋprɑˋgrɛs] 動 進步、improve [ɪmˋpruv] 動 改善
動詞三態變化 decline - declined - declined

decompose [ˌdikəm`poz] 動 分解，腐爛
▶ The bird corpse decomposed easily in the sun.
這隻小鳥的屍體在太陽下很容易腐爛。
動詞三態變化 decompose - decomposed - decomposed

decorate [`dɛkəˌret] 動 裝飾
▶ The room was decorated with beautiful curtains.
房間用漂亮的布簾來裝飾。
動詞三態變化 decorate - decorated- decorated

decoration [ˌdɛkə`reʃən] 名 裝潢，裝飾品
▶ The palace was amazingly in good of decoration. 這皇宮的裝潢美得令人驚嘆。

decorous [`dɛkərəs] 形 有禮貌的　　同 polite [pə`laɪt] 形 有禮貌的

decrease [dɪ`kris] 動 減少，減小
▶ The rate of crime keeps decreasing.
犯罪率持續下降。
動詞三態變化 decrease – decreased – decreased

decree [dɪ`kri] 名 動 命令，判決
▶ The principal mailed a letter to every student and decreed to say no to racism.
校長寫信給每位學生並且頒佈禁止種族歧視的命令。
動詞三態變化 decree - decreed – decreed

dedicate [`dɛdəˌket] 動 致力，奉獻
▶ The volunteer dedicated her life to the poor.
這位義工奉獻她的一生給貧困者。
相關衍生字彙 dedication [ˌdɛdə`keʃən] 名 貢獻、contribution [ˌkɑntrə`bjuʃən] 名 捐獻、devotion [dɪ`voʃən] 名 奉獻
動詞三態變化 dedicate - dedicated- dedicated

deduction [dɪ`dʌkʃən] 名 扣除
▶ I make a deduction from my salary for my insurance every month.
我每個月從薪水中扣除保險費。

deed [did] 名 行為　　片 a brave deed 勇敢的行為

deem [dim] 動 視為，認為
▶ Most men deem that it is their duty to make money to support their family.
大部分的男人認為賺錢養家是他們的責任。
動詞三態變化 deem - deemed - deemed

deep [dip] 形 深的，濃的
▶ The river is too deep for kids to swim in.
這條河流太深不適合孩子游泳。
相關衍生字彙 shallow [ˋʃælo] 形 淺的、depth [dɛpθ] 名 深度、bottom [ˋbɑtəm] 名 底部、
bottomless [ˋbɑtəmlɪs] 形 深不見底的

D

defame [dɪˋfem] 動 毀謗
▶ The report in the magazine defamed the rich man.
雜誌中的報導毀謗了這名有錢人。
動詞三態變化 defame - defamed - defamed

default [dɪˋfɔlt] 名 違約 動 不履行 名動 棄權
▶ He didn't mean to default on his debt.
他不是故意拖欠他的債務的。
動詞三態變化 default - defaulted – defaulted

defeat [dɪˋfit] 名動 擊敗，戰勝
▶ Our team defeated the opponent and entered the final.
我們的隊伍擊敗了對手進入決賽。
動詞三態變化 defeat - defeated - defeated

defect [dɪˋfɛkt] 名 缺點   片 a birth defect 天生的缺陷

defend [dɪˋfɛnd] 動 保禦，為～辯護
▶ The duty of soldiers is to defend our homeland.
士兵的責任是保衛我們的國土。
相關衍生字彙 defense [dɪˋfɛns] 名 防護、defendant [dɪˋfɛndənt] 名（法律）被告、
self-defense [ˏsɛlfdɪˋfɛns] 名 自我防衛、defensive [dɪˋfɛnsɪv] 形 保護的
動詞三態變化 defend - defended - defended

defer [dɪˋfɝ] 動 推遲，延期
▶ I decided to defer my plan to study abroad.
我決定延後出國讀書的計畫。
動詞三態變化 defer - deferred – deferred

deference [ˋdɛfərəns] 名 服從，尊敬   片 blind deference 盲從

defiance [dɪˋfaɪəns] 名 藐視，反抗
▶ Such a violent demonstration is defiance towards the police.
這樣的暴力示威是對警方的藐視。

deficiency [dɪˋfɪʃənsɪ] 名 缺乏，虧損，缺陷   ◎ MP3 04-04
▶ Girls often have an iron deficiency.
女孩們常有缺鐵的現象。
相關衍生字彙 deficient [dɪˋfɪʃənt] 形 不足的、enough [əˋnʌf] 名 足夠的、rich [rɪtʃ]
形 豐富的、insufficient [ˏɪnsəˋfɪʃənt] 形 不足的

define [dɪˋfaɪn] 動 解釋，給～下定義
▶ It's hard to define the word "beauty."
「美麗」這個字很難下定義。

動詞三態變化 define- defined - defined

---

definite [ˋdɛfənɪt] 形 明確的，肯定的
▶ I am definite about my job. 我對我的工作絕不含糊。

---

definition [͵dɛfəˋnɪʃən] 名 定義
▶ You can find the definition of a new word in the dictionary.
你可以在字典裡找到生字的定義。

---

deform [dɪˋfɔrm] 動 使變形，變醜陋
▶ Age will make us deformed.
年老會讓我們變醜。

動詞三態變化 deform - deformed - deformed

---

defraud [dɪˋfrɔd] 動 欺騙，詐取
▶ The bad guy defrauded them of all their savings.
這個壞蛋騙走他們全部的存款。

動詞三態變化 defraud - defrauded - defrauded

---

deft [dɛft] 形 靈巧的，熟練的
▶ He is old but his movements are still very deft.
雖然他年紀大了，不過他的動作仍很靈巧。

---

defy [dɪˋfaɪ] 動 公然反抗，蔑視
▶ Students shouldn't defy teachers.
學生不該公然反抗老師。

動詞三態變化 defy - defied - defied

---

degrade [dɪˋgred] 動 降低，降級
▶ Telling a lie will degrade yourself.
說謊會使你沒格調。

動詞三態變化 degrade - degraded - degraded

---

degree [dɪˋgri] 名 度數，程度，學位
▶ To earn a master's degree at Harvard is my dream.
在哈佛拿到碩士學位是我的夢想。

---

dejected [dɪˋdʒɛktɪd] 形 情緒低落的，氣餒的
▶ When he was informed he failed the exam, he appeared dejected.
當他被告知考試被當時，他顯得情緒低落。

---

delay [dɪˋle] 動 耽擱，延誤
▶ All the planes this morning were delayed.
今天早上的班機全部延誤起飛。

D

動詞三態變化 delay - delayed - delayed

---

delegation [ˌdɛlə`geʃən] 名 代表團，委任，授權
▶ A delegation from Japan will visit our school. 有一個日本代表團將拜訪我們學校。

delete [dɪ`lit] 動 刪除
▶ Please delete the spam.
請刪除這些垃圾郵件。
動詞三態變化 delete - deleted - deleted

---

deliberate [dɪ`lɪbərɪt] 形 深思熟慮的　　片 a deliberate decision 深思熟慮的決定
相關衍生字彙 thoughtful [`θɔtfəl] 形 深思的、considerate [kən`sɪdərɪt] 形 考慮周到的、
ponder [`pandə] 動 仔細衡量、think [θɪŋk] 動 思考

---

delicacy [`dɛləkəsɪ] 名 柔軟，美味
▶ I admire the delicacy of your skin. 我很羨慕你柔嫩的肌膚。

---

delicate [`dɛləkət] 形 精美的，易碎的
▶ Be careful! The vase is delicate. 小心！這個花瓶是易碎的。

---

delicious [dɪ`lɪʃəs] 形 美味的
▶ My wife always cooks delicious meals for me. 我老婆總是替我準備美味的佳餚。

---

delight [dɪ`laɪt] 名 愉快 動 使高興　　片 with delight 興高采烈地
相關衍生字彙 delighted [dɪ`laɪtɪd] 形 高興的、delightful [dɪ`laɪtfəl] 形 令人高興的、
pleased [plizd] 形 高興的、glad [glæd] 形 樂意的、happy [`hæpɪ] 形 快樂的
動詞三態變化 delight - delighted - delighted

---

deliver [dɪ`lɪvə] 動 投遞，發表
▶ Postmen deliver letters door to door.
郵差挨家挨戶的投遞信件。
動詞三態變化 deliver - delivered - delivered

---

delivery [dɪ`lɪvərɪ] 名 投遞，交付　　◎ MP3 **04-05**
▶ In the small town, there is only a delivery a week. 這個小鎮一周只送一次信件。

---

delirious [dɪ`lɪrɪəs] 形 胡言亂語的
▶ You must be out of your mind. You are delirious now.
你一定瘋了，你正在胡言亂語。

---

delude [dɪ`lud] 動 哄騙
▶ He deluded the girl into falling in love with him.
他哄騙女孩愛上他。
動詞三態變化 delude - deluded - deluded

demand [dɪˋmænd] 名 動 要求，需求
▶ Our boss demands us to reach his high standard.
老闆要求我們達到他的高標準。
相關衍生字彙 ask [æsk] 動 要求、inquire [ɪnˋkwaɪr] 動 詢問、request [rɪˋkwɛst] 動 要求、
beg [bɛg] 動 哀求，請求
動詞三態變化 demand - demanded - demanded

democracy [dɪˋmɑkrəsɪ] 名 民主
▶ We should cherish the democracy we own in Taiwan.
我們應該珍惜台灣所擁有的民主。

democratic [ˌdɛməˋkrætɪk] 形 民主的　　片 a democratic country 民主國家

demolish [dɪˋmɑlɪʃ] 動 毀壞，推翻，撤銷
▶ The earthquake demolished lots of houses in the mountains.
這次地震毀掉許多山區的房子。
動詞三態變化 demolish - demolished - demolished

demonstrate [ˋdɛmənˌstret] 動 示範，論證
▶ The salesman is demonstrating how to operate the machine.
銷售員正在示範如何操作此機器。
動詞三態變化 demonstrate - demonstrated - demonstrated

demonstration [ˌdɛmənˋstreʃən] 名 示威，證明
片 a mass demonstration 群眾示威抗議
相關衍生字彙 protest [prəˋtɛst] 動 抗議、object [əbˋdʒɛkt] 動 反對、dispute [dɪˋspjut]
動 爭論、oppose [əˋpoz] 動 反對、disagree [ˌdɪsəˋgri] 動 不同意

demote [dɪˋmot] 動 降級
▶ The manager was demoted to a clerk because of the mistake.
這位經理因為犯錯被降級為成職員。
動詞三態變化 demote - demoted - demoted

demure [dɪˋmjur] 形 端莊的，嚴肅的
▶ I was impressed by her demure attitude. 我對她端莊的態度很有印象。

denial [dɪˋnaɪəl] 名 否認，拒絕
▶ The athlete issued a denial of taking drugs. 這位運動員否認嗑藥。

denote [dɪˋnot] 動 表示，指稱
▶ In Japan, the color red denotes something unlucky.
在日本，紅色代表不吉利的事情。
相關衍生字彙 mean [min] 動 表示～的意思、indicate [ˋɪndəˌket] 動 指示、illustrate [ˋɪləstret]
動 說明、demonstrate [ˋdɛmənˌstret] 動 證明、show [ʃo] 動 顯示
動詞三態變化 denote - denoted - denoted

denounce [dɪ`naʊns] 動 譴責，告發
▶ The new school rule has been denounced.
這條新校規一直被批評。
動詞三態變化 denounce - denounced - denounced

D

density [`dɛnsətɪ] 名 密度
▶ The population density is very high in the big city. 大都市的人口密度很高。

dentist [`dɛntɪst] 名 牙醫
▶ Most kids are afraid of going to the dentist's.
大部分的孩子都害怕看牙醫。
相關衍生字彙 veterinarian [ˌvɛtərə`nɛrɪən] 名 獸醫、surgeon [`sɝdʒən] 名 外科醫生、
physician [fɪ`zɪʃən] 名 內科醫生、doctor [`dɑktɚ] 名 醫生

deny [dɪ`naɪ] 動 否認　　片 there's no denying that... 不可否認的～
動詞三態變化 deny - denied - denied

depart [dɪ`pɑrt] 動 離開，去世
▶ I will depart for Paris tomorrow.
明天我將要前往巴黎。
動詞三態變化 depart - departed - departed

department [dɪ`pɑrtmənt] 名 部門　　片 a department store 百貨公司

departure [dɪ`pɑrtʃɚ] 名 啟程，背離，偏差
▶ When is the departure time of your plane? 你的班機幾點起飛？

depend [dɪ`pɛnd] 動 依賴　　◎ MP3 **04-06**
▶ You should solve the problem yourself instead of depending on others.
你應該自己解決問題而不是依賴他人。
動詞三態變化 depend - depended - depended

dependable [dɪ`pɛndəbl] 形 可信任的
片 a dependable friend 可靠的朋友

dependent [dɪ`pɛndənt] 形 依賴的，隸屬的
▶ Your success will be dependent on how hard you work.
你的成功端看你有多認真工作。
相關衍生字彙 independent [ˌɪndɪ`pɛndənt] 形 獨立的、self-reliant [`sɛlfrɪ`laɪənt]
形 自力更生的、reliant [rɪ`laɪənt] 形 依賴的、trust [trʌst] 名 動 信任

deplete [dɪ`plit] 動 耗盡～的資源
▶ We are depleting the Earth's natural resources.
我們正在耗盡地球的天然資源。
動詞三態變化 deplete - depleted – depleted

deplorable [dɪˋplorəb!] 形 可悲的，糟糕的
▶ Drug abuse is deplorable behavior. 毒品濫用是可悲的行為。

deplore [dɪˋplor] 動 悲悼，譴責
▶ I deeply deplore the passing of time.
我深深哀嘆時間的逝去。
相關衍生字彙 regret [rɪˋgrɛt] 動 懊悔、lament [ləˋmɛnt] 動 悲嘆、sorry [ˋsɑrɪ] 形 難過的、miserable [ˋmɪzərəb!] 形 悲慘的、woeful [ˋwofəl] 形 悲傷的
動詞三態變化 deplore - deplored - deplored

deport [dɪˋport] 動 驅逐（出境），放逐
▶ The illegal immigrants will be deported soon.
這些非法移民將很快地被驅逐出境。
動詞三態變化 deport - deported - deported

deposit [dɪˋpɑzɪt] 名 存款 動 寄存，放置
▶ You can deposit the salary in a bank.
你可以把薪水存入銀行。
動詞三態變化 deposit - deposited - deposited

deploy [dɪˋplɔɪ] 名 部署 動 展開　　🔑 to deploy troops 佈署軍隊
動詞三態變化 deploy - deployed - deployed

depose [dɪˋpoz] 動 罷免
▶ Because of the scandal, the mayor was deposed.
因為這則醜聞，該市長被罷免了。
動詞三態變化 depose - deposed - deposed

depreciate [dɪˋpriʃɪˏet] 動 貶值，輕視
▶ The value of our house depreciated after the earthquake happened.
地震發生後，我們的房價就貶值了。
相關衍生字彙 value [ˋvælju] 名 價值、importance [ɪmˋportṇs] 名 重要性、worth [wɝθ] 名 價值、merit [ˋmɛrɪt] 名 長處、quality [ˋkwɑlətɪ] 名 品質
動詞三態變化 depreciate - depreciated - depreciated

depress [dɪˋprɛs] 動 壓制，使沮喪
▶ My son's terrible grades depressed me.
兒子糟糕的成績讓我很沮喪。
動詞三態變化 depress - depressed - depressed

depression [dɪˋprɛʃən] 名 意氣消沉，不景氣
▶ He has suffered from depression for a long time. 他長期受憂鬱所苦。

D

deprive [dɪˋpraɪv] 動 剝奪
▶ No one can deprive people of their freedom of speech.
沒有人可以剝奪人們的言論自由。

動詞三態變化 deprive - deprived - deprived

deputy [ˋdɛpjətɪ] 名 代理人 形 代理的
▶ While I am abroad, you can talk to my deputy.
當我人在國外時，你可以跟我的代理人洽談。

derive [dɪˋraɪv] 動 起源，取得
▶ Many English words derive from Latin words.
很多英文字起源於拉丁文字。

相關衍生字彙 origin [ˋɔrədʒɪn] 名 起源、originate [əˋrɪdʒəˏnet] 動 發源、appear [əˋpɪr]
動 出現、disappear [ˏdɪsəˋpɪr] 動 消失

動詞三態變化 derive - derived - derived

descend [dɪˋsɛnd] 動 下降，沿～向下
▶ Over the hill, the road begins to descend to the lake.
越過山丘後，這條路就會往下通到湖邊。

動詞三態變化 descend - descended - descended

descendant [dɪˋsɛndənt] 名 後裔　　⊗ ancestor [ˋænsɛstə] 名 祖先

descent [dɪˋsɛnt] 名 下降，血統，衰落　　⊕ direct descent 直系血統

describe [dɪˋskraɪb] 動 描述
▶ My son described the exciting experience vividly to me.
我兒子生動地描述那個刺激的經驗給我聽。

動詞三態變化 describe - described - described

description [dɪˋskrɪpʃən] 名 描寫，敘述　　◎ MP3 **04-07**
▶ The beauty of the lake is beyond description.
這座湖泊的美景超出我所能描述的。

相關衍生字彙 portray [porˋtre] 動 把～描繪成、depict [dɪˋpɪkt] 動 描寫、delineate [dɪˋlɪnˏet]
動 畫～的輪廓、picture [ˋpɪktʃə] 動（生動地）描繪

desert [ˋdɛzət] 名 沙漠 [dɪˋzɜt] 動 拋棄
▶ Sahara is the biggest desert in the world.
撒哈拉是世界上最大的沙漠。

動詞三態變化 desert - deserted - deserted

deserve [dɪˋzɜv] 動 應變，該得
▶ You study so hard. You deserve a holiday.
你這麼認真唸書應該放個假。

動詞三態變化 deserve - deserved - deserved

design [dɪˋzaɪn] 動 設計
▶ She is very creative and like to design things.
她很有創意，而且喜歡設計東西。
相關衍生字彙 designer [dɪˋzaɪnɚ] 名 設計師、sketch [skɛtʃ] 動 素描、draw [drɔ] 動 繪畫、paint [pent] 動 繪畫、picture [ˋpɪktʃɚ] 名 圖畫
動詞三態變化 design - designed - designed

designate [ˋdɛzɪgˌnet] 動 指派，表明
▶ In this country, the King has power to designate his successor.
在這個國家，國王有權力指派他的繼承者。
動詞三態變化 designate - designated - designated

desirable [dɪˋzaɪrəbl̩] 形 值得嚮往的，令人滿意的
▶ The top university is a desirable school. 這所頂尖大學是值得嚮往的學校。

desire [dɪˋzaɪr] 名 動 渴望
▶ I have a strong desire to travel all the places in Europe.
我非常渴望玩遍歐洲各地。
相關衍生字彙 desirous [dɪˋzaɪrəs] 形 渴望的、wish [wɪʃ] 動 希望、want [wɑnt] 動 想要、lust [lʌst] 動 渴望、covet [ˋkʌvɪt] 動 垂涎
動詞三態變化 desire - desired - desired

desist [dɪˋzɪst] 動 停止，打消念頭
▶ The heavy rain is expected to desist this evening.
豪雨預估今晚會停止。
動詞三態變化 desist - desisted - desisted

desk [dɛsk] 名 桌子　🖈 an office desk 辦公桌

desolate [ˋdɛslɪt] 形 荒蕪的
▶ Only the elderly live in the desolate village.
只剩老年人居住在這荒涼的村落。
相關衍生字彙 desolation [ˌdɛslˋeʃən] 名 荒蕪、empty [ˋɛmptɪ] 形 空的、vacant [ˋvekənt] 形 空缺的、solitary [ˋsɑləˌtɛrɪ] 形 單獨的

despair [dɪˋspɛr] 名 絕望
▶ When my girlfriend said goodbye to me, I was totally in the mood of despair.
當女朋友跟我分手時，我完全陷入絕望的情緒裡。

desperate [ˋdɛspərɪt] 形 絕望的，危急的
▶ The tsunami survivors are facing a desperate situation.
海嘯倖存者正面臨絕望的情境。

despise [dɪˋspaɪz] 動 鄙視
▶ I despise those who are selfish.
我鄙視那些自私的人。
相關衍生字彙 hate [het] 動 憎恨、scorn [skɔrn] 名 動 輕蔑，藐視、admire [ədˋmaɪr] 動 欽佩，欣賞、respect [rɪˋspɛkt] 名 動 尊敬、appreciate [əˋpriʃɪˏet] 動 賞識，感激
動詞三態變化 despise - despised - despised

D

despite [dɪˋspaɪt] 介 儘管，任憑
▶ We still enjoyed our vacation despite the rain.
儘管下雨，我們仍享受這次的假期。

despoil [dɪˋspɔɪl] 動 掠奪，剝奪　　同 rob [rɑb] 動 搶奪
動詞三態變化 despoil - despoiled - despoiled

dessert [dɪˋzɝt] 名 餐後甜點
▶ Apple pie is my favorite dessert.
蘋果派是我最愛的餐後甜點。
相關衍生字彙 cake [kek] 名 蛋糕、tart [tɑrt] 名 水果餡餅、biscuit [ˋbɪskɪt] 名 小餅乾、pudding [ˋpʊdɪŋ] 名 布丁

destination [ˏdɛstəˋneʃən] 名 目的地，終點
▶ It took five hours for us to arrive at our destination.
我們花了五小時才到達目的地。

destined [ˋdɛstɪnd] 形 (場所) 預定的，命中注定的
▶ The girl is destined to be his wife. 這位女孩注定做他的老婆。

destiny [ˋdɛstənɪ] 名 命運
▶ I want to control my own destiny. 我要掌握自己的命運。

destroy [dɪˋstrɔɪ] 動 破壞，消滅
▶ The landslide completely destroyed the landscape.
山崩完全破壞了景色。
動詞三態變化 destroy - destroyed - destroyed

destruction [dɪˋstrʌkʃən] 名 破壞，毀滅　　MP3 **04-08**
▶ The destruction of the rainforest will lead to serious result.
雨林的破壞將導致嚴重的後果。

destructive [dɪˋstrʌktɪv] 形 破壞性的，毀滅性的
▶ The typhoon will have destructive power.
這個颱風將會有破壞性的強度。
相關衍生字彙 harmful [ˋharmfəl] 形 有害的、harm [harm] 動 傷害、damage [ˋdæmɪdʒ] 動 損害、hurt [hɝt] 動 疼痛、injure [ˋɪndʒɚ] 動 受傷

detail [`ditel] 名 細節
▶ I still don't know the precise details of the accident.
　我仍不知道此意外事故的詳細細節。

---

detain [dɪ`ten] 動 拘留，使耽擱
▶ The suspect has been detained.
　這名嫌疑犯已經被扣押。
動詞三態變化 detain - detained - detained

---

detect [dɪ`tɛkt] 動 察覺，發現
▶ I didn't detect his anger while I was talking to him.
　跟他談話的過程，我沒有察覺到他的憤怒。
相關衍生字彙 detective [dɪ`tɛktɪv] 名 偵探、discover [dɪs`kʌvɚ] 動 發現、find [faɪnd]
　　　　　動 發現、uncover [ʌn`kʌvɚ] 動 揭露
動詞三態變化 detect - detected - detected

---

deter [dɪ`tɝ] 動 威懾住，使斷念
▶ The cold weather deterred me from hiking outside.
　寒冷的天氣讓我斷了想外出健行的念頭。
動詞三態變化 deter - deterred - deterred

---

deteriorate [dɪ`tɪrɪəˌret] 動 退化，惡化
▶ Her father's condition deteriorated, so she worried so much.
　她爸爸的狀況惡化，所以她很擔心。

---

determine [dɪ`tɝmɪn] 動 決定
▶ What you eat will determine your health.
　你吃的東西會決定你的健康。
動詞三態變化 determine - determined - determined

---

determination [dɪˌtɝmə`neʃən] 名 決心　　　同 decision [dɪ`sɪʒən] 名 決定
動詞三態變化 deteriorate - deteriorated - deteriorated

---

detest [dɪ`tɛst] 動 厭惡
▶ I detest any kind of racial discrimination.
　我厭惡任何形式的種族歧視。
相關衍生字彙 hate [het] 動 討厭、dislike [dɪs`laɪk] 動 不喜歡、admire [əd`maɪr] 動 欣賞、
　　　　　adore [ə`dor] 動 崇拜
動詞三態變化 detest - detested - detested

---

detrimental [dɛtrə`mɛntl] 形 有害的，不利的　　　同 harmful [`hɑrmfəl] 形 有害的

---

devastate [`dɛvəsˌtet] 動 破壞，使荒蕪
▶ The chemical factory completely devastates the ecosystem of the river.
　這間化學工廠徹底破壞河流的生態。

動詞三態變化 devastate - devastated - devastated

develop [dɪˋvɛləp] 動 發展，開發

▶ They intend to develop the area into a big shopping mall.
他們打算把這區開發成大型的購物商場。

相關衍生字彙 development [dɪˋvɛləpmənt] 名 發展、developing [dɪˋvɛləpɪŋ] 形 開發中的、developed [dɪˋvɛləpt] 形 已開發的、undeveloped [ˌʌndɪˋvɛləpt] 形 未開發的

動詞三態變化 develop - developed - developed

deviate [ˋdivɪˌet] 動 脫離，越軌

▶ She never deviates her moral standard.
她從不偏離她的道德標準。

動詞三態變化 deviate - deviated - deviated

device [dɪˋvaɪs] 名 設備，裝置　　片 an electronic device 電子裝置

devil [ˋdɛvl̩] 名 惡魔

▶ Smiling makes a baby an angle while crying makes it a devil.
微笑讓嬰兒像天使，而哭泣讓嬰兒像惡魔。

devise [dɪˋvaɪz] 動 設計，發明

▶ The scientist devised a new way to improve humans' memory.
科學家發明一種幫助人類改善記憶的新方法。

相關衍生字彙 design [dɪˋzaɪn] 動 設計、plan [plæn] 名動 計畫、invent [ɪnˋvɛnt] 動 發明，創造、discover [dɪsˋkʌvɚ] 動 發現、originate [əˋrɪdʒəˌnet] 動 發源，創始

動詞三態變化 devise - devised - devised

devoid [dɪˋvɔɪd] 形 缺乏的

▶ When we moved to the new house, we found it devoid of everything.
當我們搬到新房子時，發現什麼都缺。

devote [dɪˋvot] 動 把〜奉獻（給）

▶ He devoted all his time to studying.
他把所有的時間投注在學習上。

動詞三態變化 devote - devoted - devoted

devour [dɪˋvaur] 動 狼吞虎嚥地吃

▶ The hungry boy devoured all the food his mom prepared for him.
這位飢餓的男孩狼吞虎嚥地吃媽媽幫他準備的食物。

相關衍生字彙 swallow [ˋswɑlo] 動 吞嚥、eat [it] 動 吃、consume [kənˋsjum] 動 消耗、nibble [ˋnɪbl̩] 動 一點一點地咬（或吃）

動詞三態變化 devour - devoured - devoured

devout [dɪˋvaut] 形 虔誠的，衷心的　　MP3 04-09

▶ My parents are very devout. They go to church every Sunday morning.
我的父母很虔誠，每周日早上都到教堂做禮拜。

dew [dju] 名 露水　　片 beads of dew 露珠

diagnose [`daɪəgnoz] 動 診斷
▶ He was diagnosed as having a heart disease.
他被診斷出有心臟病。
動詞三態變化 diagnose - diagnosed - diagnosed

diagram [`daɪəˏgræm] 名 圖表
▶ The diagram shows how they recycle the waste water.
這張圖表顯示他們是如何回收廢水再利用的。

dial [`daɪəl] 動 撥打
▶ You can dial this telephone number direct.
可以直接撥這個電話號碼。
動詞三態變化 dial - dialed - dialed

dialect [`daɪəlɛkt] 名 方言
▶ We won't use a dialect in the official document.
我們不會在正式公文中使用方言。

dialogue [`daɪəˏlɔg] 名 對話，交談
▶ I'm sorry to interrupt your dialogue. 很抱歉打斷你們的對話。

diamond [`daɪəmənd] 名 鑽石　　片 a diamond ring 鑽戒
相關衍生字彙 gold [gold] 名 金、silver [`sɪlvɚ] 名 銀、copper [`kɑpɚ] 名 銅、bronze [brɑnz] 名 青銅、tin [tɪn] 名 錫、iron [`aɪɚn] 名 鐵

diary [`daɪərɪ] 名 日記　　片 to keep a diary 寫日記

dictate [`dɪktet] 動 口述，命令
▶ Before he went abroad, the boss dictated his secretary about many important things.
在他出國前，老闆口述祕書做很多重要的事。
動詞三態變化 dictate - dictated - dictated

dictation [dɪk`teʃən] 名 聽寫
▶ In class, the teacher asked us to take dictation. 課堂上，老師要求我們做聽寫。

dictator [`dɪkˏtetɚ] 名 獨裁者
▶ Hitler was a brutal dictator. 希特勒是個殘忍的獨裁者。

dictionary [`dɪkʃənˏɛrɪ] 名 字典
片 to look up in the dictionary 查字典

diffident [`dɪfədənt] 形 懦怯的，缺乏自信的
▶ You shouldn't be so diffident about your ability.
你不該對自己的能力沒信心。

D

相關衍生字彙 confident [ˈkɑnfədənt] 形 有信心的、shy [ʃaɪ] 形 羞怯的、bashful [ˈbæʃfəl] 形 害羞的、timid [ˈtɪmɪd] 形 膽小的

---

die [daɪ] 動 死亡，枯萎
▶ My grandfather died of a heart attack.
我爺爺死於心臟病發作。
動詞三態變化 die - died - died

---

diet [ˈdaɪət] 名 飲食　　片 to go on a diet 減肥節食

---

differ [ˈdɪfɚ] 動 不同，相異
▶ They are twins, but they differ in appearance.
他們是雙胞胎，可是外表不同。
相關衍生字彙 difference [ˈdɪfərəns] 名 差異性、different [ˈdɪfərənt] 形 不同的、differentiate [ˌdɪfəˈrɛnʃˌet] 動 使不同、same [sem] 形 相同的
動詞三態變化 differ - differed - differed

---

difficult [ˈdɪfəˌkəlt] 形 困難的
▶ It's a difficult problem to solve. 這是個很難解決的問題。

---

difficulty [ˈdɪfəˌkʌltɪ] 名 困境，艱難
▶ I have difficulty getting used to a new environment. 我在適應新環境上有困難。

---

diffuse [dɪˈfjuz] 動 傳播，擴散
▶ The Internet is a convenient means of diffusing information.
網路是傳播訊息的方便管道。
動詞三態變化 diffuse - diffused - diffused

---

dig [dɪg] 動 挖掘　　片 to dig for gold 挖金礦　　◎ MP3 **04-10**
動詞三態變化 dig - dug - dug

---

digest [daɪˈdʒɛst] 動 消化（食物），融會貫通
▶ Taking a walk after meals can help digest.
餐後散步可以有助消化。
相關衍生字彙 digestion [dəˈdʒɛstʃən] 名 消化、appetite [ˈæpəˌtaɪt] 名 食慾、absorb [əbˈsɔrb] 動 吸收、eat [it] 動 吃、drink [drɪŋk] 動 喝
動詞三態變化 digest - digested - digested

---

digital [ˈdɪdʒɪt]] 形 數位的　　片 a digital age 數位時代

---

dignity [ˈdɪgnətɪ] 名 尊嚴　　片 to die with dignity 有尊嚴地死去

---

dilemma [dəˈlɛmə] 名 進退兩難
▶ I face the dilemma of studying abroad or marrying him.
我面臨兩難的狀況，出國讀書還是嫁給他。

diligent [ˈdɪlədʒənt] 形 勤勉的　　🔘 a diligent student 用功的學生

dim [dɪm] 形 暗淡的，模糊的
▶ Reading in the dim light will hurt your eyesight.
　在昏暗的燈光下看書有損你的視力。
相關衍生字彙 faint [fent] 形 暗淡的、pale [pel] 形 蒼白的、clear [klɪr] 形 清楚的、
　　　　　　bright [braɪt] 形 明亮的

dimension [dɪˈmɛnʃən] 名 尺寸，面積
▶ I have no idea about the dimensions of the room. 我對這個房間的大小沒概念。

diminish [dəˈmɪnɪʃ] 動 縮減，使貶低
▶ The high living expenses in the big city diminish greatly my savings.
　大都市的高生活費大大耗損我的存款。
動詞三態變化 diminish - diminished - diminished

dine [daɪn] 動 用餐
▶ I prefer to dine at home.
　我寧願在家吃飯。
相關衍生字彙 dinner [ˈdɪnɚ] 名 晚餐、breakfast [ˈbrɛkfəst] 名 早餐、lunch [lʌntʃ] 名 午餐、
　　　　　　supper [ˈsʌpɚ] 名 晚餐、brunch [brʌntʃ] 名 早午餐
動詞三態變化 dine - dined - dined

dioxide [daɪˈɑksaɪd] 名 二氧化物　　🔘 carbon dioxide 二氧化碳

dip [dɪp] 動 浸洗，舀取
▶ She dipped her fingers into the bathtub to test the temperature of the water.
　她把手指浸入浴缸來測量水溫。
動詞三態變化 dip - dipped - dipped

diploma [dɪˈplomə] 名 文憑　　🔘 a high-school diploma 中學文憑

diplomacy [dɪˈploməsɪ] 名 外交　　🔘 international diplomacy 國際外交
相關衍生字彙 diplomat [ˈdɪpləmæt] 名 外交官、diplomatic [ˌdɪpləˈmætɪk] 形 外交的、
　　　　　　internal [ɪnˈtɝnl] 形 內部的、domestic [dəˈmɛstɪk] 形 國內的

direct [dəˈrɛkt] 動 指揮 形 直接的
▶ This is a direct train to Taipei.
　這是直達台北的火車。
動詞三態變化 direct - directed - directed

direction [dəˈrɛkʃən] 名 方向
▶ Please show me the directions to the museum. 請告訴我去博物館的方向。

director [dəˈrɛktɚ] 名 導演，主任，董事　　🔘 a film director 電影導演

dirty [ˋdɝtɪ] 形 髒的　　反 clean [klin] 形 乾淨的

disable [dɪsˋebḷ] 動 使傷殘
▶ How poor she is! She was disabled in that accident.
她好可憐！她因那場意外而傷殘。
動詞三態變化 disable - disabled - disabled

disadvantage [ˌdɪsədˋvæntɪdʒ] 名 缺點，弱勢
反 advantage [ədˋvæntɪdʒ] 名 優點
相關衍生字彙 advantage [ədˋvæntɪdʒ] 名 優點、drawback [ˋdrɔˌbæk] 名 缺點、handicap [ˋhændɪˌkæp] 名 不利條件、weakness [ˋwiknɪs] 名 弱點

disagree [ˌdɪsəˋgri] 動 不同意　　　　　　　　MP3 04-11
▶ I disagree with the decision made at the meeting.
我不同意會議上所做的決定。
動詞三態變化 disagree - disagreed - disagreed

disappear [ˌdɪsəˋpɪr] 動 消失，滅絕
▶ I couldn't find my cell phone. It disappeared!
我找不到手機，它消失無蹤了！
動詞三態變化 disappear - disappeared - disappeared

disappoint [ˌdɪsəˋpɔɪnt] 動 使失望，挫敗
▶ The superstar never disappoints his fans.
這名超級巨星從不讓粉絲失望。
動詞三態變化 disappoint - disappointed - disappointed

disappointment [ˌdɪsəˋpɔɪntmənt] 名 失望，沮喪
片 to one's disappointment 令人失望的是～

disapproval [ˌdɪsəˋpruvḷ] 名 不贊成
▶ My parents didn't say anything, but I could sense their disapproval of my plan.
雖然父母沒有多說什麼，但我可以感受到他們不贊成我的計畫。

disapprove [ˌdɪsəˋpruv] 動 不同意
▶ I strongly disapprove of smoking on campus.
我強烈反對在校園裡吸菸。
相關衍生字彙 agree [əˋgri] 動 同意、disagree [ˌdɪsəˋgri] 動 不同意、accept [əkˋsɛpt] 動 接受、refuse [rɪˋfjuz] 動 拒絕
動詞三態變化 disapprove - disapproved - disapproved

disarm [dɪsˋɑrm] 動 解除～的武裝
▶ To disarm the bomb is a dangerous task.
拆卸炸彈是危險的工作。
動詞三態變化 disarm - disarmed - disarmed

disarray [ˌdɪsəˋre] 名 無秩序 動 使混亂　　片 in a state of disarray 處在混亂狀態
[動詞三態變化] disarray - disarrayed – disarrayed

---

disaster [dɪˋzæstɚ] 名 災難
▶ The 311 tsunami in Japan is a great disaster.
日本三一一海嘯真的是個大災難。
[相關衍生字彙] disastrous [dɪzˋæstrəs] 形 災難的、flood [flʌd] 名 洪水、
earthquake [ˋɝθˌkwek] 名 地震、drought [draʊt] 名 乾旱

---

disband [dɪsˋbænd] 動 解散，遣散
▶ The pop band disbanded last month.
這個流行樂團上個月解散了。
[動詞三態變化] disband - disbanded - disbanded

---

discard [dɪsˋkɑrd] 動 丟棄，摒棄
▶ Some used furniture was discarded at the corner of the street.
一些舊家具被丟棄在街角。
[動詞三態變化] discard - discarded - discarded

---

discern [dɪˋzɝn] 動 察覺到，分辨
▶ It's too dark to discern the direction.
太暗很難分辨方向。
[動詞三態變化] discern - discerned - discerned

---

discharge [dɪsˋtʃɑrdʒ] 動 排出，卸貨
▶ Lots of waste water was discharged into the river during the night.
夜晚時，大量的廢水被排放到河流中。
[動詞三態變化] discharge - discharged - discharged

---

discipline [ˋdɪsəplɪn] 名 紀律 動 使有紀律，訓練
▶ There should be good discipline in the army.
軍隊中應該要有良好的紀律。
[相關衍生字彙] self-discipline [ˌsɛlfˋdɪsəplɪn] 名 自律、rule [rul] 名 規則、
regulation [ˌrɛgjəˋleʃən] 名 規則、management [ˋmænɪdʒmənt] 名 管理
[動詞三態變化] discipline - disciplined - disciplined

---

disclose [dɪsˋkloz] 動 揭發，透露
▶ The police disclosed that the murderer was arrested.
警方透露那位謀殺犯已經被逮捕。
[動詞三態變化] disclose - disclosed - disclosed

---

discomfort [dɪsˋkʌmfɚt] 名 不適，不舒服
▶ After taking the medicine, I felt a little discomfort.
吃完藥後，我覺得有點不舒服。

D

discontent [dɪskən`tɛnt] 名 不滿足 形 不滿的
▶ There is widespread discontent about the new traffic rule.
　有關新的交通規則，普遍有不滿的聲音。

discord [`dɪskɔrd] 名 不和，爭吵，喧鬧
▶ The discord between the couple finally resulted in their divorce.
　夫妻間的不合終究會導致離婚。
[相關衍生字彙] conflict [`kɑnflɪkt] 名 衝突、fight [faɪt] 動 打架、quarrel [`kwɔrəl] 名 爭吵、argument [`ɑrgjəmənt] 名 爭論

discount [`dɪskaunt] 名 折扣
▶ They offer a twenty percent discount for the members of the club.
　他們提供社團會員打八折的折扣。

discourage [dɪs`kɝɪdʒ] 動 使沮喪　　反 encourage [ɪn`kɝɪdʒ] 動 鼓勵
[動詞三態變化] discourage - discouraged - discouraged

discourse [`dɪskɔrs] 名 演講，交談　　◎ MP3 **04-12**
▶ We will have a discourse on the global warming this afternoon.
　今天下午我們有一場關於全球暖化的演講。

discover [dɪs`kʌvɚ] 動 發現，找到
▶ Scientists have discovered how to cure the disease.
　科學家已經發現如何治療該疾病的方法。
[相關衍生字彙] discovery [dɪs`kʌvərɪ] 名 發現、invent [ɪn`vɛnt] 動 發明、invention [ɪn`vɛnʃən] 名 發明、inventor [ɪn`vɛntɚ] 名 發明家、find [faɪnd] 動 找到，發現
[動詞三態變化] discover - discovered - discovered

discreet [dɪ`skrit] 形 謹慎的，考慮周到的
▶ My secretary is very discreet. She is a good assistant.
　我的祕書很謹慎，是個好幫手。

discrimination [dɪ͵skrɪmə`neʃən] 名 歧視　　片 racial discrimination 種族歧視

discussion [dɪ`skʌʃən] 名 討論　　片 under discussion 討論中
[相關衍生字彙] discuss [dɪ`skʌs] 動 討論、talk [tɔk] 動 談論、consider [kən`sɪdɚ] 動 考慮、consult [kən`sʌlt] 動 請教

disdain [dɪs`den] 名 動 鄙視
▶ I regard the cheating on the exam with disdain.
　我瞧不起考試作弊。
[動詞三態變化] disdain - disdained - disdained

disease [dɪ`ziz] 名 疾病
▶ Ebola is a fatal disease. 伊波拉是一種致命的疾病。

disgorge [dɪsˋgɔrdʒ] 動 吐出，被迫交出
▶ The baby disgorged the milk he drank. He must be sick.
　小嬰兒把喝的牛奶吐出來，他一定是生病了。
動詞三態變化 disgorge - disgorged- disgorged

disgrace [dɪsˋgres] 名 恥辱，丟臉
▶ If you cheat, you will bring disgrace on our team.
　如果你作弊，將會為我們的隊伍帶來恥辱。
相關衍生字彙 honor [ˋɑnɚ] 名 榮耀、shame [ʃem] 動 使丟臉、humiliate [hjuˋmɪlɪˏet] 動 羞辱、insult [ˋɪnsʌlt] 動 侮辱

disguise [dɪsˋgaɪz] 動 偽裝
▶ To attend the Halloween party, I disguised myself as a witch.
　為了參加萬聖節派對，我把自己打扮成巫婆。
動詞三態變化 disguise - disguised - disguised

disgusting [dɪsˋgʌstɪŋ] 形 令人作嘔的，可憎的
▶ It's disgusting that there is so much trash left in the park.
　公園裡有這麼多垃圾真噁心。

dish [dɪʃ] 名 菜餚，餐具　　片 to do the dishes 洗碗盤

dishearten [dɪsˋhɑrtn̩] 動 使沮喪，使氣餒　　同 discourage [dɪsˋkɝɪdʒ] 動 使沮喪
動詞三態變化 dishearten - disheartened - disheartened

disinfect [ˏdɪsɪnˋfɛkt] 動 消毒
▶ Our school disinfect the toilets once a week.
　我們學校一周消毒一次廁所。
動詞三態變化 disinfect - disinfected - disinfected

disintegrate [dɪsˋɪntəgret] 動 碎裂，瓦解，崩潰
▶ The great empire disintegrated into many small kingdoms.
　這個大帝國後來分裂成很多小王國。
動詞三態變化 disintegrate - disintegrated - disintegrated

dislocate [ˋdɪsləˏket] 動 移位，使脫臼
▶ After the ball game, he found his knee was dislocated.
　球賽結束後，他發現他的膝蓋脫臼了。
動詞三態變化 dislocate - dislocated - dislocated

dismal [ˋdɪzml̩] 形 憂鬱的，陰暗的
▶ The old woman lives by herself in a dismal little room.
　老婦人獨自一人住在陰暗的小房間。

D

dismay [dɪsˋme] 名 驚慌，氣餒
▶ To my dismay, my laptop and cellphone were stolen.
讓我驚慌的是，我的手提電腦跟手機都被偷了。

相關衍生字彙 calm [kɑm] 名 平靜、confusion [kənˋfjuʒən] 名 混亂、surprise [sɚˋpraɪz] 動 使驚嚇、frightened [ˋfraɪtn̩d] 形 受驚的

dismiss [dɪsˋmɪs] 動 解雇，解散
▶ The teacher said, "Class dismissed."
老師說：「下課」。

動詞三態變化 dismiss - dismissed - dismissed

dismount [dɪsˋmaʊnt] 名 動 下馬，下車
▶ A lady dismounted from the horse cart.
一位女士從馬車上下來。

動詞三態變化 dismount - dismounted - dismounted

dispatch [dɪˋspætʃ] 名 動 派遣，發送 名 新聞稿 ⊙ MP3 04-13
▶ Please dispatch an experienced worker to help me.
請派有經驗的員工來幫我。

動詞三態變化 dispatch - dispatched - dispatched

dispel [dɪˋspɛl] 動 驅散，消除
▶ To dispel my son's fear, I kept the light on.
為了讓兒子不害怕，我一直開著燈。

動詞三態變化 dispel - dispelled - dispelled

dispense [dɪˋspɛns] 動 分配，免除
▶ The volunteers help dispense clean clothes to the victims.
志工協助分配乾淨的衣物給災民。

動詞三態變化 dispense - dispensed - dispensed

disperse [dɪˋspɚs] 動 驅散，傳播
▶ The police used gas to disperse the crowds.
警方用瓦斯來驅散群眾。

動詞三態變化 disperse - dispersed - dispersed

displace [dɪsˋples] 動 離開，取代
▶ The local government planned to displace the habitants in this area.
當地政府打算遷移此區的居民。

動詞三態變化 displace - displaced - displaced

display [dɪˋsple] 名 動 陳列，展出
▶ Mom displayed the photos from our childhood on the wall in the living room.
媽媽把我們小時候的照片展示在客廳的牆面上。

動詞三態變化 display - displayed - displayed

displease [dɪs`pliz] 動 得罪，觸怒
▶ I don't want to do anything to displease my parents, who cherish me so much.
父母很疼我，我不想做任何讓他們不高興的事。

相關衍生字彙 irritate [`ɪrə‚tet] 動 激怒、anger [`æŋgɚ] 名 憤怒、pleasant [`plɛzənt] 形 愉悅的、flatter [`flætɚ] 動 奉承，諂媚

動詞三態變化 displease - displeased - displeased

---

disposal [dɪ`spozl] 名 處理，配置，轉讓　　片 at one's disposal 任憑某人使用或處理

---

dispose [dɪ`spoz] 動 處置
▶ It took me a lot of time to dispose of the old furniture before I migrated to America.
移居美國之前，我花了蠻多時間在處理我的舊家具。

動詞三態變化 dispose - disposed - disposed

---

disposition [‚dɪspə`zɪʃən] 名 意向，性格，處理，贈予
▶ I am of a nervous disposition. 我是那種容易緊張的個性。

---

dispute [dɪ`spjut] 名 動 爭論，爭執　　片 to stir up a dispute 挑起爭端
動詞三態變化 dispute - disputed - disputed

---

disregard [‚dɪsrɪ`gɑrd] 名 動 漠視
▶ As a leader, how could you disregard your employees' opinion?
身為領導人，你怎麼能忽視員工的意見呢？

相關衍生字彙 ignore [ɪg`nor] 動 忽略、neglect [nɪg`lɛkt] 動 疏忽、mind [maɪnd] 動 在意、overlook [‚ovɚ`luk] 動 忽略

動詞三態變化 disregard - disregarded - disregarded

---

dissemble [dɪ`sɛmbl] 動 掩飾，假裝
▶ If you feel sad, then cry. You don't have to dissemble your feelings.
如果你覺得悲傷就大哭，不必掩飾你的情緒。

動詞三態變化 dissemble - dissembled- dissembled

---

dissent [dɪ`sɛnt] 名 動 不同意，異議
▶ He dissented from the suggestion by standing up and going out of the meeting room.
他不同意此建議便起身離開會議室。

動詞三態變化 dissent - dissented - dissented

---

dissolve [dɪ`zɑlv] 動 溶解，驅散
▶ Salt dissolves in water.
鹽巴可溶解於水。

動詞三態變化 dissolve - dissolved - dissolved

distance [ˋdɪstəns] 名 距離
▶ My school is within walking distance of my place.
學校離我住處是走路就可以到的距離。

---

distinct [dɪˋstɪŋkt] 形 有區別的，清楚的
▶ The flower gives off a distinct smell.
這朵花散發出特殊的味道。

相關衍生字彙 special [ˋspɛʃəl] 形 特別的、different [ˋdɪfərənt] 形 不同的、vague [veg]
形 模糊的、clear [klɪr] 形 清楚的

---

distinction [dɪˋstɪŋkʃən] 名 差別，對比
▶ There's a clear distinction between the styles of the two designers.
這兩位設計師的風格有明顯的差別。

---

distinguish [dɪˋstɪŋgwɪʃ] 動 區別，辨別
▶ How do you distinguish the twin sisters?
你是怎麼辨別這對雙胞胎姊妹的？

動詞三態變化 distinguish - distinguished - distinguished

---

distinguished [dɪˋstɪŋgwɪʃt] 形 著名的，高貴的
▶ Ang Lee is a distinguished director. 李安是一位著名的導演。

相關衍生字彙 famous [ˋfeməs] 形 著名的、outstanding [ˋautˋstændɪŋ] 形 傑出的、
noble [ˋnobḷ] 形 高貴的、noted [ˋnotɪd] 形 有名的、renowned [rɪˋnaund]
形 有名的

---

distort [dɪsˋtɔrt] 動 扭曲，曲解　　　○ MP3 04-14
▶ What he said was totally distorted by reporters.
他所說的話完全被記者曲解了。

動詞三態變化 distort - distorted - distorted

---

distract [dɪˋstrækt] 動 分散，使分心
▶ Listening to music will distract me from my studies.
聽音樂會讓我無法專心讀書。

動詞三態變化 distract - distracted - distracted

---

distraction [dɪˋstrækʃən] 名 分心
▶ The terrible noise drove me to distraction. 那可怕的噪音讓我分心。

---

distress [dɪˋstrɛs] 名 苦惱
▶ Her son's behavior did cause her distress.
她兒子的行為的確讓她很苦惱。

相關衍生字彙 annoy [əˋnɔɪ] 動 使苦惱、trouble [ˋtrʌbḷ] 動 使麻煩、bother [ˋbɑðɚ] 動 干擾、
worry [ˋwɝɪ] 動 擔心

distribute [dɪˋstrɪbjut] 動 分配，散布
▶ The teacher distributed the test papers to every student.
老師把考卷分發給每位學生。

動詞三態變化 distribute - distributed - distributed

distribution [ˌdɪstrəˋbjuʃən] 名 分配，銷售量
▶ The graph shows the distribution of global food supply.
這張圖表顯示出全球糧食分配的狀況。

district [ˋdɪstrɪkt] 名 行政區，地區
▶ Washington, the District of Columbia (Washington, D. C.) is the capital of the United States.
華盛頓特區是美國首府。

disturb [dɪsˋtɝb] 動 打擾，妨礙
▶ Don't disturb me this weekend because I will have an exam next Monday.
因為下周有考試，所以這個周末別吵我。

動詞三態變化 disturb - disturbed - disturbed

disturbance [dɪsˋtɝbəns] 名 騷擾，干擾   片 to cause a disturbance 引起騷動

dive [daɪv] 名 動 潛水，跳水
▶ The weather today is very suitable for us to dive off the coast into the ocean.
今天的天氣很適合我們離開岸邊跳入海裡去。

動詞三態變化 dive - dived – dove

diverge [daɪˋvɝdʒ] 動 分叉，離題
▶ Though you and I are good friends, our goals in life diverge.
雖然我們倆是好朋友，可是人生目標是不同的。

相關衍生字彙 diverse [daɪˋvɝs] 形 不同的、differ [ˋdɪfɚ] 動 與～不同、unlike [ʌnˋlaɪk] 介 不像、contrast [ˋkɑnˌtræst] 動 對比

動詞三態變化 diverge - diverged - diverged

diversion [daɪˋvɝʒən] 名 消遣，轉移
▶ Watching movies is my diversion on weekends. 看電影是我周末的消遣。

diversity [daɪˋvɝsətɪ] 名 差異，多樣性   片 a wide diversity of choice 多元的選擇

divert [daɪˋvɝt] 動 轉向，使改道
▶ Because of the typhoon, our flight had no choice but to divert to the nearest airport.
因為颱風，我們的班機只好轉向到最近的機場。

動詞三態變化 divert - diverted - diverted

divide [də`vaɪd] 動 劃分，分配
▶ The fence divides my garden from my neighbor's.
這個籬笆劃分了鄰居跟我的花園。
動詞三態變化 divide - divided - divided

divine [də`vaɪn] 形 神聖的，天賜的
▶ To err is human, to forgive divine.（諺語）犯錯是人性，原諒是神性。
相關衍生字彙 holy [`holɪ] 形 神聖的、heavenly [`hɛvənlɪ] 形 天國的、sacred [`sekrɪd] 形 神聖的、religious [rɪ`lɪdʒəs] 形 宗教的

division [də`vɪʒən] 名 分開區域，部門　　片 cell division 細胞分裂

divorce [də`vors] 名 動 離婚
▶ It's a pity that their marriage ends up with a divorce.
很遺憾，他們的婚姻以離婚收場。
動詞三態變化 divorce - divorced - divorced

dizzy [`dɪzɪ] 形 頭暈目眩的
▶ The cold medicine made me dizzy. 這種感冒藥讓我暈眩。

dock [dɑk] 名 碼頭，船塢
▶ There are many workers working on the dock.
碼頭有很多工人在工作。
相關衍生字彙 port [port] 名 港口、haven [`hevən] 名 避風港、harbor [`hɑrbɚ] 名 港口

doctrine [`dɑktrɪn] 名 教義，信條　　片 Christian doctrine 基督教教義　　◎ MP3 04-15

doctor [`dɑktɚ] 名 醫生
▶ An apple a day keeps the doctor away.（諺語）一天一顆蘋果醫生遠離我。

document [`dɑkjəmənt] 名 文件
▶ One of a secretary's tasks is to file the documents.
祕書的工作之一是把文件歸檔。

documentary [ˌdɑkjə`mɛntərɪ] 形 文件的，記錄的
片 a documentary film 紀錄片

dodge [dɑdʒ] 動 閃避
▶ Something fell down from the top of the building. Luckily, I dodged.
有東西從建築物上方掉落，很幸運地，我躲開了。
相關衍生字彙 escape [ə`skep] 動 逃離、run [rʌn] 動 奔跑、runaway [`rʌnəˌwe] 名 逃跑、avoid [ə`vɔɪd] 動 避免
動詞三態變化 dodge - dodged - dodged

dog [dɔg] 名 小狗　　片 a dog's life 悲慘的生活

doll [dɑl] 名 洋娃娃
▶ Barbie is the most popular toy doll. 芭比娃娃是最受歡迎的玩具洋娃娃。

dollar [ˋdɑlə] 名 美元，一元紙幣　　片 the rising / falling dollar 上升／下跌的美元

domain [doˋmen] 名 領土，區域　　片 in the domain of 在～領域裡

domestic [dəˋmɛstɪk] 形 國內的　　片 a domestic flight 國內班機

dominate [ˋdɑmə،net] 動 支配，統治
▶ He is such a powerful manager that he always dominates every meeting.
　他是如此強勢的主管，總是掌握每一場會議。

相關衍生字彙　control [kənˋtrol] 動 控制、command [kəˋmænd] 動 命令、order [ˋɔrdə]
動 命令、master [ˋmæstə] 動 掌握

動詞三態變化　dominate - dominated - dominated

donation [doˋneʃən] 名 捐贈
▶ We appreciate your regular donation of money.
　我們很感謝你固定的捐款。

doom [dum] 名 厄運 動 注定，判決
▶ The project was doomed to failure without your support.
　沒有你的支持，這項計畫注定要失敗。

動詞三態變化　doom - doomed - doomed

door [dor] 名 門　　片 from door to door 挨家挨戶地

dormant [ˋdɔrmənt] 形 潛伏的，靜止的　　片 a dormant volcano 休火山

相關衍生字彙　active [ˋæktɪv] 形 活潑的、sleeping [ˋslipɪŋ] 形 睡著的、awake [əˋwek]
形 醒著的、dead [dɛd] 形 死亡的

dormitory [ˋdɔrmə،torɪ] 名 學生宿舍
▶ The university offers enough dormitories for all the freshmen.
　這所大學提供足夠的宿舍給新生。

dosage [ˋdosɪdʒ] 名（藥的）劑量
▶ The dosage is one pill a day before going to bed. 劑量為一天一顆於睡前服用。

doubt [daʊt] 名 動 懷疑
▶ I have no doubt about your ability.
　我對你的能力毫無疑問。

相關衍生字彙　doubtful [ˋdaʊtfəl] 形 疑惑的、suspect [səˋspɛkt] 動 懷疑、trust [trʌst] 動 信任、
suspicious [səˋspɪʃəs] 形 懷疑的

動詞三態變化　doubt - doubted - doubted

dot [dɑt] 名 小圓點
▶ Don't forget to put a dot at the end of the sentence.
別忘了在句子最後加上一個小圓點（句號）。

double [ˋdʌbl̩] 形 兩倍的
▶ We get double pay for working overtime.
我們下班後的加班費，老闆給我們雙倍薪資。

download [ˋdaʊn͵lod] 動 下載　　片 to download software 下載軟體　　◎ MP3 **04-16**
相關衍生字彙 downpour [ˋdaʊn͵por] 名 大雨、downstairs [͵daʊnˋstɛrz] 副 下樓、
downtown [͵daʊnˋtaʊn] 名 市區、downward [ˋdaʊnwɚd] 副 向下地
動詞三態變化 download - downloaded - downloaded

doze [doz] 動 打瞌睡
▶ I felt so tired that I dozed in class.
我太累了，所以在課堂上打瞌睡。
動詞三態變化 doze - dozed - dozed

dozen [ˋdʌzn̩] 名 一打　　片 dozens of 很多的～

draft [dræft] 名 動 起草
▶ The outline is only a draft.
這個大綱只是草案。
相關衍生字彙 draw [drɔ] 動 繪畫，拖，拉、drawing [ˋdrɔɪŋ] 名 圖畫
動詞三態變化 draft - drafted - drafted

drag [dræg] 動 拖曳
▶ Dragging the chair will make noise.
拖椅子會製造噪音。
動詞三態變化 drag - dragged - dragged

drain [dren] 名 排水管
▶ The kitchen drain is easily blocked. 廚房的水管很容易堵塞。

drama [ˋdrɑmə] 名 戲劇
▶ She majored in drama at college.
她大學主修戲劇。
相關衍生字彙 dramatic [drəˋmætɪk] 形 戲劇性的、theater [ˋθɪətɚ] 名 劇院、movie [ˋmuvɪ]
名 電影、film [fɪlm] 名 影片

drastic [ˋdræstɪk] 形 激烈的，嚴厲的　　片 drastic measures 嚴厲措施

drawback [ˋdrɔ͵bæk] 名 缺點，障礙，撤銷
▶ One of the drawbacks of living in the big city is the air pollution.
住在大都市的缺點之一就是空氣污染。

drawer [`drɔɚ] 名 抽屜
▶ She locked her diary in the drawer. 她把日記鎖在抽屜裡。

dread [drɛd] 動 懼怕，擔心
▶ I dread swimming in the ocean.
我很怕在海裡游泳。
相關衍生字彙 dreadful [`drɛdfəl] 形 可怕的、awful [`ɔful] 形 嚇人的、terrible [`tɛrəbl]
形 可怕的、horrible [`hɔrəbl] 形 令人毛骨悚然的
動詞三態變化 dread - dreaded - dreaded

dream [drim] 名 夢想　　片 to make a dream come true 夢想成真

dreary [`drɪərɪ] 形 沉悶的
▶ What a dreary movie! It made me feel sleepy. 好沉悶的電影，讓我覺得想睡。

drench [drɛntʃ] 動 浸濕
▶ A sudden rain drenched me to the skin yesterday.
昨天突如其來的大雨讓我濕透了。
動詞三態變化 drench - drenched - drenched

dress [drɛs] 動 給～穿衣
▶ She dressed herself fashionably for the party.
她為參加派對打扮時髦。
相關衍生字彙 dressing [`drɛsɪŋ] 名 穿衣、dresser [`drɛsɚ] 名 衣櫥、dressy [`drɛsɪ]
形 講究穿著的、dress [drɛs] 名 洋裝
動詞三態變化 dress - dressed - dressed

drift [drɪft] 動 漂流　　片 to drift with the tide 隨波逐流
動詞三態變化 drift - drifted - drifted

drill [drɪl] 動 在～上鑽孔
▶ They tried to drill for clean water.
他們試著鑽探乾淨的水源。
動詞三態變化 drill - drilled - drilled

drink [drɪŋk] 動 飲用，喝酒
▶ After exercising, don't forget to drink plenty of water.
運動後，別忘了喝大量的水。
動詞三態變化 drink - drank - drunk

drizzle [`drɪzl] 動 下毛毛雨
▶ It has been drizzling for days.
已經下了好幾天的毛毛雨。
動詞三態變化 drizzle - drizzled - drizzled

drive [draɪv] 動 駕駛
▶ My son drives to work every day.
　我兒子每天開車上班。
相關衍生字彙 driver [`draɪvɚ] 名 司機、ride [raɪd] 動 搭乘、driveway [`draɪvˌwe] 名 私人車道、
　　　rider [`raɪdɚ] 名 騎乘的人
動詞三態變化 drive - drove - driven

droop [drup] 動 低垂，枯萎　　　　　　　　　　　　　MP3 **04-17**
▶ Because of the hot weather, flowers in the garden all drooped.
　天氣太熱，花園的花都枯萎了。
動詞三態變化 droop - drooped - drooped

drop [drɑp] 動 滴下，落下　　　片 to drop somebody a line 寫短信給某人
動詞三態變化 drop - dropped - dropped

drought [draʊt] 名 乾旱
▶ There is no rain for a long time. It may result in drought.
　很久沒下雨了，有可能會導致乾旱。

drown [draʊn] 動 溺水
▶ A drowning man will clutch at a straw.
　（諺語）快溺死的人連稻草都抓（狗急跳牆）。
動詞三態變化 drown - drowned - drowned

drowsy [`draʊzɪ] 形 昏昏欲睡的，懶散的
▶ On such a drowsy summer afternoon, I don't want to work.
　在這樣令人昏昏欲睡的夏日午後，我不想工作。
相關衍生字彙 sleepy [`slipɪ] 形 想睡的、lazy [`lezɪ] 形 懶散的、tired [taɪrd] 形 疲倦的、
　　　dozy [`dozɪ] 形 想睡的

drug [drʌg] 名 藥品，毒品　　　片 drug abuse 藥物濫用

drum [drʌm] 名 鼓 動 咚咚地敲，灌輸
▶ Parents should drum the good value into their kids at an early age.
　父母應在孩子小的時候，灌輸他們好的價值觀。
動詞三態變化 drum - drummed - drummed

dubious [`djubɪəs] 形 半信半疑的　　　片 dubious behavior 可疑的舉止

due [dju] 形 到期的
▶ The assignment will be due next Monday. 這份作業的繳交期限是下周一。

dull [dʌl] 形 模糊的，愚鈍的
▶ All work and no play makes Jack a dull boy.
（諺語）只工作不玩耍會使聰明的孩子也變傻。
相關衍生字彙 brilliant [`brɪljənt] 形 優秀的、stupid [`stjupɪd] 形 愚笨的、fool [ful] 名 傻瓜、
silly [`sɪlɪ] 形 傻傻的

---

dump [dʌmp] 動 傾倒，拋售　　片 to dump the garbage 倒垃圾
動詞三態變化 dump - dumped - dumped

---

duplicate [`djuplə͵ket] 動 複印 [`djuplə͵kɪt] 形 複製的，副本的
▶ Before the meeting, please duplicate the file for everyone.
會議開始前，請複印這份資料給每個人。
動詞三態變化 duplicate - duplicated - duplicated

---

dust [dʌst] 名 灰塵
▶ The floor was covered in dust. 地板都是灰塵。

---

duty [`djutɪ] 名 責任
▶ It's parents' duty to educate their kids. 教育小孩是父母的責任。

---

dwell [dwɛl] 動 居住，思索
▶ My aunt has dwelled in Paris for years.
我姑姑在巴黎定居好幾年了。
相關衍生字彙 live [lɪv] 動 居住、stay [ste] 動 待在、inhabit [ɪn`hæbɪt] 動 棲息、
occupy [`ɑkjə͵paɪ] 動 佔據
動詞三態變化 dwell - dwelt - dwelled

---

dye [daɪ] 名 染料 動 染色
▶ Mom dyed her hair black.
媽媽把頭髮染黑。
動詞三態變化 dye - dyed - dyed

---

dynamite [`daɪnə͵maɪt] 名 炸藥
▶ Dynamite was invented by Alfred Nobel. 炸藥是阿佛雷德 ‧ 諾貝爾發明的。

---

dynasty [`daɪnəstɪ] 名 朝代
▶ The Qing dynasty lasted longer than two hundred years.
清朝維持長達兩百多年。

MEMO

一網打盡

E

字母

eager ~ eye

詞性說明

名 名詞　　副 副詞　　介 介系詞

動 動詞　　形 形容詞　　連 連接詞

代 代名詞　　助 助動詞

內文圖示說明

片 片語　　反 反義字　　同 同義字

一網打盡「英語小知識」┃星座介紹┃ ─────────────

Capricorn
摩羯座

Aquarius
水瓶座

Pisces
雙魚座

Aries
牡羊座

Taurus
金牛座

Gemini
雙子座

E eager ~ eye

MP3 **05-01**

★一網打盡 975 個英文單字 ｜ 一網打盡 197 句英語會話句

eager [`igɚ] 形 熱切的，渴望的
▶ I'm so eager to meet you.
　我是如此渴望認識你。

相關衍生字彙 eagerly [`igɚlɪ] 副 熱切地，渴望地、eagerness [`igɚnɪs] 名 渴望，熱心，熱切、desirous [dɪ`zaɪrəs] 形 渴望的，想要的、enthusiastic [ɪn͵θjuzɪ`æstɪk] 形 熱情的，熱烈的

---

eagle [`ig!] 名 老鷹
▶ Eagles' sight is very good, and they can see very well.
　老鷹的視力很好，牠們可以看得很清楚。

---

early [`ɝlɪ] 形 提早的 副 在開始階段　片 to get up early 早起

---

earn [ɝn] 動 賺得，贏得
▶ Don't ask others how much they earn!
　別問別人賺多少錢！

動詞三態變化 earn - earned - earned

---

earnest [`ɝnɪst] 形 誠摯的　片 in earnest 認真地

相關衍生字彙 earnestly [`ɝnɪstlɪ] 副 認真地，誠摯地、earnestness [`ɝnɪstnɪs] 名 認真，誠摯、sincere [sɪn`sɪr] 形 衷心的，真誠的，忠實的、devoted [dɪ`votɪd] 形 虔誠的，摯愛的

---

earphone [`ɪr͵fon] 名 耳機
▶ He is exercising with earphones. 他戴著耳機運動。

---

ease [iz] 名 舒適 動 減緩　片 with ease 輕鬆地

相關衍生字彙 easily [`izɪlɪ] 副 簡單地、easy [`izɪ] 形 簡單的、easygoing [`izɪ͵goɪŋ] 形 隨和的

動詞三態變化 ease - eased - eased

---

earth [ɝθ] 名 地球，泥土
▶ The Earth goes around the Sun.
　地球繞著太陽轉。

相關衍生字彙 earthy [`ɝθɪ] 形 土質的，粗俗的、earthly [`ɝθlɪ] 形 地球的，世俗的、earth science 片 地球科學、earthborn [`ɝθ͵bɔrn] 形 地中長出的，凡人的、earthbound [`ɝθ͵baund] 形 局限於土地的，向地球移動的、earthen [`ɝθən] 形 土製的，地球上的、earthenware [`ɝθən͵wɛr] 名 陶器，土器

---

earthquake [`ɝθ͵kwek] 名 地震
▶ In 1999, a violent earthquake hit the central Taiwan.
　一九九九年有一個強烈的地震襲擊中台灣。

earthworm [ˋɝθˏwɝm] 名 蚯蚓
▶ After rain, many earthworms move through the earth in the garden.
　下過雨後，蚯蚓在花園的泥土鑽動。

east [ist] 名 東方 形 東方的
▶ The sun rises in the east.
　太陽由東方升起。
相關衍生字彙 eastern [ˋistən] 形 東方的、eastbound [ˋistˏbaund] 形 向東行的、Easter [ˋistə] 名 復活節、west [wɛst] 名 西方、western [ˋwɛstən] 形 西方的

ebb [ɛb] 名 動 衰退，退潮　　⑪ at a low ebb 處於低潮階段
動詞三態變化 ebb - ebbed - ebbed

eat [it] 動 吃，喝
▶ He didn't feel good, so he didn't feel like eating.
　他不舒服，所以不想吃東西。
動詞三態變化 eat - ate - eaten

eccentric [ɪkˋsɛntrɪk] 形 古怪的
▶ The old man is eccentric in his habits, so he has no friends.
　這位老人很古怪，所以沒有朋友。
相關衍生字彙 eccentricity [ˏɛksɛnˋtrɪsətɪ] 名 古怪，怪癖、strange [strendʒ] 形 奇怪的、unusual [ʌnˋjuʒuəl] 形 不尋常的

echo [ˋɛko] 名 回音
▶ In the valley, you can hear the echo of your scream.
　在山谷，你可以聽到你大叫的回音。

eclipse [ɪˋklɪps] 名 蝕　　⑪ the moon eclipse 月蝕

ecological [ˏɛkəˋladʒɪkəl] 形 生態的
▶ Pollution often leads to ecological disaster.
　污染常引起生態浩劫。
相關衍生字彙 ecology [ɪˋkalədʒɪ] 名 生態、ecologist [ɪˋkalədʒɪst] 名 生態學家、biology [baɪˋalədʒɪ] 名 生物學、biological [ˏbaɪəˋladʒɪkl̩] 形 生物的

economic [ˏikəˋnamɪk] 形 經濟的
▶ The country has a good economic state. 這個國家有很好的經濟狀況。

economical [ˏikəˋnamɪkl̩] 形 節約的，經濟的
▶ Please show me the most economical way of using the air conditioner.
　請告訴我使用此空調最節約的方式。

economy [ɪˋkanəmɪ] 名 經濟，節省　　⑪ the global economy 全球經濟

ecstasy [`ɛkstəsɪ] 名 入迷，狂喜，出神　　　　　　　　　　 ⊙ MP3 **05-02**
▶ On hearing the good news, we were all in ecstasy.
一聽到這個消息，我們都欣喜若狂。

相關衍生字彙 ecstatic [ɛk`stætɪk] 形 狂喜的、happy [`hæpɪ] 形 開心的、excited [ɪk`saɪtɪd] 形 興奮的、joy [dʒɔɪ] 名 歡樂

---

edge [ɛdʒ] 名 邊，緣，刀口
▶ Too much pressure makes him teeter on the edge of madness.
太多的壓力讓他處在快要發瘋的邊緣。

---

edible [`ɛdəbl̩] 形 食用的
▶ The mushroom is poisonous, not edible. 這朵磨菇有毒，不能食用。

---

edify [`ɛdə͵faɪ] 動 教化，訓誨
▶ It takes time to edify the prisoners.
要教化這些犯人需要時間。

動詞三態變化 edify - edified - edified

---

edit [`ɛdɪt] 動 編輯，校訂
▶ The publisher helped the writer edit his novel.
出版社幫作家編輯他的小說。

相關衍生字彙 edition [ɪ`dɪʃən] 名 編輯、editor [`ɛdɪtɚ] 名 編輯，主筆、editorial [͵ɛdə`tɔrɪəl] 名 社論 形 編輯上的、critic [`krɪtɪk] 名 評論家

動詞三態變化 edit - edited - edited

---

educate [`ɛdʒə͵ket] 動 教育，培養
▶ It costs more and more to educate a child.
教育一個孩子成本愈來愈高。

相關衍生字彙 education [͵ɛdʒʊ`keʃən] 名 教育，educational [͵ɛdʒʊ`keʃənl̩] 形 教育的，educator [`ɛdʒʊ͵ketɚ] 名 教育家、educated [`ɛdʒʊ͵ketɪd] 形 受過教育的

動詞三態變化 educate - educated - educated

---

effect [ɪ`fɛkt] 名 效果，作用 動 招致　　 ⊕ to come into effect 生效
動詞三態變化 effect - effected - effected

---

effective [ɪ`fɛktɪv] 形 有效的，生效的
▶ The medicine is effective for toothache. 這種藥對牙痛有效。

---

efficiency [ɪ`fɪʃənsɪ] 名 效率
▶ The efficiency of the company is impressive. 這間公司的效率很令人印象深刻。

---

efficient [ɪ`fɪʃənt] 形 效率高的，有效的
▶ Mom is very efficient in doing the housework. 媽媽做家事效率超高的。

effort [ˋɛfɚt] 名 努力　　片 to make an effort 努力地做～

相關衍生字彙 effortless [ˋɛfɚtlɪs] 形 不出力的，容易的、effortlessly [ˋɛfɚtlɪslɪ] 副 輕鬆地，毫不費勁地、endeavor [ɪnˋdɛvɚ] 名 努力 動 力圖、exertion [ɪgˋzɝʃən] 名 努力，費力，（能力，權力等的）運用

---

egg [ɛg] 名 雞蛋　　片 to lay an egg 下蛋，生蛋

相關衍生字彙 eggplant [ˋɛgˏplænt] 名 茄子、eggshell [ˋɛgˏʃɛl] 名 蛋殼、yolk [jok] 名 蛋黃

---

ego [ˋigo] 名 自我意識　　片 an enormous ego 強烈的自我意識

相關衍生字彙 egoism [ˋigoˏɪzəm] 名 利己主義，自負，自大、egoist [ˋigoɪst] 名 自我中心者，自負的人、ego ideal 片 自我理想、ego massage 片 自我鼓勵、ego tripping 片 自以為是、egocentric [ˏigoˋsɛntrɪk] 名 自我中心主義者 形 自我中心的、egocentricity [ˏigosɛnˋtrɪsɪtɪ] 名 自我中心、ego-dystonic 片 與自我相衝突的

Egypt [ˋidʒɪpt] 名 埃及

▶ The Pyramids in Egypt are one of the wonders in the world.
　埃及的金字塔是世界奇景之一。

相關衍生字彙 Egyptian [ɪˋdʒɪpʃən] 名 埃及人，古代埃及語 形 埃及的、Egyptianism [ɪˋdʒɪpʃəˏnɪzəm] 名 埃及之特徵、Egyptologist [ˏidʒɪpˋtalədʒɪst] 名 埃及古物學者、Egyptology [ˏidʒɪpˋtalədʒɪ] 名 埃及古物學

---

eighth [etθ] 名 第八 形 第八個的

▶ His birthday is on the eighth of July.
　他的生日是七月八日。

相關衍生字彙 eight [et] 名 八 形 八的、eighteen [ˋeˋtin] 名 十八 形 十八的、eighty [ˋetɪ] 名 八十 形 八十的、eightieth [ˋetɪɪθ] 名 第八十 形 第八十的

---

either [ˋiðɚ] 代 (兩者之中) 任一的

▶ Either of my parents will join the activity. 我父母會有一人來參加活動。 ·

---

eject [ɪˋdʒɛkt] 動 驅逐，噴射

▶ The owner of the restaurant ejected the noisy teenagers.
　餐廳的老闆把吵鬧的青少年趕出去。

動詞三態變化 eject - ejected - ejected

---

elaborate [ɪˋlæbəret] 動 詳細闡述，精心製作 形 詳盡的，精巧的

▶ The boy elaborated on his reasons for being late.
　男孩詳細描述遲到的原因。

相關衍生字彙 elaborately [ɪˋlæbərɪtlɪ] 副 精心地，精巧地、elaboration [ɪˏlæbəˋreʃən] 名 精巧，精心製作，詳細闡述、elaborate on / upon 片 詳細說明、elaborative [ɪˋlæbəˏretɪv] 形 仔細的，煞費苦心的、elaborator [ɪˋlæbəˏretɚ] 名 精心製作者

動詞三態變化 elaborate - elaborated - elaborated

E

elastic [ɪ`læstɪk] 名 橡皮圈 形 有彈性的，靈活的
▶ The socks were made of elastic material.
這雙襪子的材質很有彈性。
相關衍生字彙 elastic band 片 橡皮筋，橡皮圈、elasticity [ˌɪlæs`tɪsətɪ]
名 彈性，靈活性，伸縮性、elastically [ɪ`læstɪklɪ] 副 有彈性地，伸縮自如地、
elasticated [ɪ`læstɪketɪd] 形 (織物中) 織入橡皮筋的，有鬆緊性的、
elasticize [ɪ`læstə͵saɪz] 動 (加橡皮筋) 使具伸縮性

---

elbow [`ɛlbo] 名 手肘 動 用手肘推   片 to elbow one's way 用手肘推開人群往前
相關衍生字彙 elbowroom [`ɛlbo͵rum] 名 足夠的空間、wrist [rɪst] 名 手腕、finger [`fɪŋgɚ]
名 手指、arm [ɑrm] 名 手臂
動詞三態變化 elbow - elbowed- elbowed

---

elder [`ɛldɚ] 名 長者 形 年齡較大的   ◉ MP3 **05-03**
▶ Sometimes, the advice of elders is helpful. 有時候，長者的忠告是很有幫助的。

elect [ɪ`lɛkt] 動 選舉
▶ He was elected as the chairman of our company.
他被選為我們公司的董事長。
動詞三態變化 elect - elected - elected

---

election [ɪ`lɛkʃən] 名 選舉，當選   片 an election campaign 選舉活動
相關衍生字彙 elective [ɪ`lɛktɪv] 形 選舉的，選修的、elector [ɪ`lɛktɚ]
名 選舉人，(美) 總統選舉人、electorate [ɪ`lɛktərɪt] 名 (總稱) (全體) 選民、
election day 片 (美國) 選舉日，大選日、electioneer [ˌɪlɛkʃən`ɪr]
名 積極競選的人 動 積極參加競選、electioneering [ˌɪlɛkʃən`ɪrɪŋ] 名 競選活動
形 競選活動的、electively [ɪ`lɛktɪvlɪ] 副 選舉地，可選地，可任意選舉地、
electoral [ɪ`lɛktərəl] 形 選舉的，選舉人的

---

electric [ɪ`lɛktrɪk] 形 電的，電動的   片 an electric light 電燈
相關衍生字彙 electricity [ˌɪlɛk`trɪsətɪ] 名 電、electrician [ˌɪlɛk`trɪʃən] 名 電工、
electronic [ɪlɛk`trɑnɪk] 形 電子的、electronics [ɪlɛk`trɑnɪks] 名 電子學

---

elegant [`ɛləgənt] 形 優美的
▶ His wife is an elegant woman.
他的老婆是一位優雅的女人。
相關衍生字彙 elegantly [`ɛləgəntlɪ] 副 優美地，雅緻地，高雅地、graceful [`gresfəl]
形 優美的，典雅的，得體的、glorious [`glorɪəs] 形 光榮的，壯麗的，極好的

---

element [`ɛləmənt] 名 元素，成分    ◉ component [kəm`ponənt] 名 構成要素

elemental [ˌɛlə`mɛntl̩] 形 基本的，自然力的
▶ Food and water are the elemental needs of life. 食物跟水是生活基本所需。

elementary [ˌɛlə`mɛntərɪ] 形 基礎的，初級的   片 an elementary school 小學

相關衍生字彙 elementary particle 片 基本粒子，元質點、elementary school 片 小學、
fundamental [ˌfʌndəˋmɛnt]] 形 基礎的，原始的、essential [ɪˋsɛnʃəl]
形 必要的，實質的，精華的

elephant [ˋɛləfənt] 名 大象
▶ Elephants are the biggest animals in the zoo. 大象是動物園裡最大的動物。

E

elevate [ˋɛləˌvet] 動 提升，舉起，振奮
▶ With his professional skills, he was elevated to a higher rank soon.
因擁有專業技術，他很快就被提升到較高的位階。

相關衍生字彙 elevation [ˌɛləˋveʃən] 名 海拔，提升、elevator [ˋɛləˌvetɚ] 名 電梯、
elevated [ˋɛləˌvetɪd] 形 高層的

動詞三態變化 elevate - elevated - elevated

elicit [ɪˋlɪsɪt] 動 引起，誘出
▶ The politician knows how to elicit the support of the public.
這位政治人物懂得如何引發大眾的支持。

動詞三態變化 elicit - elicited - elicited

eligible [ˋɛlɪdʒəbl̩] 形 合格的，適當的
▶ In Taiwan, people over 20 years old are eligible to vote.
台灣要年滿二十歲以上才能投票。

相關衍生字彙 qualified [ˋkwɑləˌfaɪd] 形 具備必要條件的，合格的、desirable [dɪˋzaɪrəbl̩]
名 合意的人（或事物）形 值得嚮往的，令人滿意的、suitable [ˋsutəbl̩]
形 適當的，合適的

eliminate [ɪˋlɪməˌnet] 動 淘汰，排除
▶ It's a pity that she was eliminated in the speech contest.
很可惜，她在演講比賽中被淘汰。

相關衍生字彙 elimination [ɪˌlɪməˋneʃən] 名 排除，淘汰、eliminator [ɪˋlɪməˌnetɚ]
名 排除器，整流器，交流接收器、exclude [ɪkˋsklud] 動 拒絕接納，不包括，逐出、
get rid of 片 擺脫

動詞三態變化 eliminate - eliminated - eliminated

eloquence [ˋɛləkwəns] 名（流利的）口才
▶ The writer is known for his eloquence. 這位作家以他的口才聞名。

eloquent [ˋɛləkwənt] 形 雄辯的，有說服力的
▶ He is young but very eloquent. 他年輕但口才很好。

elusive [ɪˋlusɪv] 形 難以理解的，逃避的
▶ The new theory is very elusive.
這個新的理論很難懂。

相關衍生字彙 elusively [ɪˋlusɪvlɪ] 副 巧妙逃避地，容易忘記地、evasive [ɪˋvesɪv]
形 逃避的，難以捉住的、elusory [ɪˋlusərɪ] 形 巧妙地逃避的、fleeting [ˋflitɪŋ]
形 轉瞬間的，短暫的

emancipation [ɪˌmænsəˈpeʃən] 名 解放　片 black emancipation 黑人解放

相關衍生字彙 emancipate [ɪˈmænsəˌpet] 動 解放，使不受束縛、
emancipated [ɪˈmænsəˌpetɪd] 形 被解放的、
emancipationist [ɪˌmænsəˈpeʃənɪst] 名 解放主義者，解放論者、
emancipative [ɪˈmænsəˌpetɪv] 形 有助於解放的、emancipator [ɪˈmænsəˌpetɚ]
名 解放者、emancipatory [ɪˈmænsəpəˌtɔrɪ] 形 解放的

---

embargo [ɪmˈbargo] 名 動 禁運，禁止

▶ The government enforced an embargo on imports of cigarettes.
當時政府強制禁止香菸進口。

動詞三態變化 embargo - embargoed - embargoed

---

embark [ɪmˈbark] 動 上船（或飛機），從事，著手

▶ He migrated to America last year and embarked on a new career.
他去年移民到美國並開始新職業。

動詞三態變化 embark - embarked - embarked

---

embarrass [ɪmˈbærəs] 動 使不好意思

▶ What you said at the meeting embarrassed him.
你會議裡說的話讓他很尷尬。

相關衍生字彙 embarrassing [ɪmˈbærəsɪŋ] 形（事物）尷尬的、
embarrassment [ɪmˈbærəsmənt] 名 尷尬、embarrassed [ɪmˈbærəst]
形（人物）感到尷尬的

動詞三態變化 embarrass - embarrassed - embarrassed

---

embassy [ˈɛmbəsɪ] 名 大使館　　　　　　　　　　MP3 05-04

▶ When you get into trouble abroad, you can turn to the Embassy for help.
當你在國外遇到麻煩時，你可以跟大使館求助。

---

embed [ɪmˈbɛd] 動 栽種，把～嵌進

▶ The professor suggested we embed the academic theory into our
practical experience.
教授建議我們把學術理論放入實際的經驗裡。

動詞三態變化 embed - embedded - embedded

---

emblem [ˈɛmbləm] 名 動 象徵 名 標誌

▶ A plum blossom is an emblem of Taiwan.
梅花是台灣的一個象徵。

相關衍生字彙 sign [saɪn] 名 符號，標誌、symbol [ˈsɪmbl] 名 象徵，記號、token [ˈtokən]
名 標記、symptom [ˈsɪmptəm] 名 症狀，徵兆、mark [mark] 名 痕跡，標記

動詞三態變化 emblem - emblemed - emblemed

---

embody [ɪmˈbadɪ] 動 使具體化，包含

▶ The good teacher embodies the role model.
這位好老師具體化了典範。

相關衍生字彙 embodiment [ɪm`badɪmənt] 名 具體化、comprise [kəm`praɪz] 動 包含，構成、
incorporate [ɪn`kɔrpəˌret] 動 包含，使併入，使具體化

動詞三態變化 embody - embodied - embodied

embrace [ɪm`bres] 動 擁抱
▶ She leant over to embrace her son.
她彎下腰來擁抱兒子。

動詞三態變化 embrace - embraced - embraced

E

embroider [ɪm`brɔɪdə] 動 刺繡
▶ My daughter embroidered a butterfly on my scarf.
女兒在我圍巾上繡一隻蝴蝶。

相關衍生字彙 embroidery [ɪm`brɔɪdərɪ] 名 刺繡品，潤飾、embroidery hoop
片（刺繡用的）繃圈，圓形繡架

動詞三態變化 embroider - embroidered - embroidered

embryo [`ɛmbrɪo] 名 胚胎，初期　　片 in embryo 未完成，未成熟

相關衍生字彙 embryoctony [ɛmbrɪ`aktənɪ] 名 墮胎、embryogenesis [ɛmbrɪo`dʒɛnəsɪs]
名 胚胎形成、embryogenic [`ɛmbrɪo`dʒɛnɪk] 形 胚胎發生（形成）的、
embryologist [ɛmbrɪ`alədʒəst] 名 胚胎學者、embryology [ɛmbrɪ`alədʒɪ]
名 胚胎學、embryonic [ɛmbrɪ`anɪk] 形 胎兒的，初期的

emerge [ɪ`mɝdʒ] 動 浮現，暴露
▶ The facts finally emerged after investigation.
調查後，事實終於浮上檯面。

相關衍生字彙 emergent [ɪ`mɝdʒənt] 形 意外的，緊急的、emergence [ɪ`mɝdʒəns]
名 出現，浮現

動詞三態變化 emerge - emerged- emerged

emergency [ɪ`mɝdʒənsɪ] 名 緊急情況　　片 an emergency exit 緊急出口

emigrate [`ɛməˌgret] 動 移居外國
▶ All his family emigrated to America about five years ago.
大約五年前，他們全家移民到美國。

相關衍生字彙 emigrant [`ɛməgrənt] 名 移民、immigrate [`ɪməˌgret] 動 遷入、
immigrant [`ɪməgrənt] 名（外來）移民

動詞三態變化 emigrate - emigrated - emigrated

eminent [`ɛmənənt] 形 卓越的，傑出的
▶ Edison is an eminent scientist.
愛迪生是一位卓越的科學家。

相關衍生字彙 eminently [`ɛmənəntlɪ] 副 突出地，極好地、eminence [`ɛmənəns]
名（地位、成就等的）卓越，著名、eminent domain
片（國家對私人產業之）徵用權，支配權、distinguished [dɪ`stɪŋgwɪʃt]
形 卓越的，高貴的、outstanding [`aut`stændɪŋ] 形 凸出的，傑出的

emission [ɪˋmɪʃən] 名 發射，散發，發行
▶ Car emissions are one of the sources of air pollution.
汽車排放氣體是空氣污染的來源之一。

---

emotion [ɪˋmoʃən] 名 情緒，感情
▶ A good leader controls emotions very well.
好的領導人情緒會控管得宜。

相關衍生字彙 emotional [ɪˋmoʃənl̩] 形 情緒的、feeling [ˋfilɪŋ] 名 感情、passion [ˋpæʃən] 名 熱情、love [lʌv] 名 愛情

---

empathy [ˋɛmpəθɪ] 名 移情作用
▶ A true friend will have empathy with you. 一個真正的好朋友會十分瞭解你。

---

emperor [ˋɛmpərɚ] 名 皇帝   反 empress [ˋɛmprɪs] 名 女皇

---

emphasis [ˋɛmfəsɪs] 名 強調
▶ More and more schools put emphasis on the importance of reading.
愈來愈多學校強調閱讀的重要性。

---

emphasize [ˋɛmfəˌsaɪz] 動 強調，著重
▶ Our boss emphasizes that everyone should come on time.
我們老闆強調上班要準時。

動詞三態變化 emphasize - emphasized - emphasized

---

empire [ˋɛmpaɪr] 名 帝國，大企業
▶ His ambition is to build an empire.
他的企圖心是建立一個帝國。

相關衍生字彙 realm [rɛlm] 名 王國，領土、dominion [dəˋmɪnjən] 名 統治，管轄、kingdom [ˋkɪŋdəm] 名 王國

---

employment [ɪmˋplɔɪmənt] 名 雇用   片 out of employment 失業

相關衍生字彙 employ [ɪmˋplɔɪ] 動 雇用、employee [ˌɛmplɔɪˋi] 名 員工、employer [ɪmˋplɔɪɚ] 名 雇主、employable [ɪmˋplɔɪəbl̩] 形 適宜雇用的

---

empower [ɪmˋpauɚ] 動 授權
▶ A good manager should know how to empower people.
一個好的管理者應該知道如何下放權力。

動詞三態變化 empower - empowered - empowered

---

empty [ˋɛmptɪ] 形 空的，未佔用的   ◎ MP3 05-05
▶ That is an empty house. No one lives there.
那是棟空房子，沒人住那裡。

相關衍生字彙 empty-handed [ˋɛmptɪˋhændɪd] 形副 空手的（地），一無所有的（地）、emptiness [ˋɛmptɪnɪs] 名 空虛，無意義，空曠、empty of 片 缺乏、empty spam 片 清空垃圾郵件、empty-headed [ˋɛmptɪˋhɛdɪd] 形 傻的，沒腦筋的

enable [ɪn`ebl̩] 動 使能夠
▶ Smart phones enable us to get information anytime and anywhere.
智慧型手機讓我們可以隨時隨地獲得資訊。
動詞三態變化 enable - enabled - enabled

enchant [ɪn`tʃænt] 動 使陶醉，使入迷
▶ Her fans are all deeply enchanted by her voice.
她的粉絲深深為她的聲音所著迷。
動詞三態變化 enchant - enchanted - enchanted

enchanting [ɪn`tʃæntɪŋ] 形 迷人的　　同 charming [`tʃɑrmɪŋ] 形 有魅力的

encircle [ɪn`sɝkl̩] 動 包圍，環繞
▶ The castle is encircled by a river.
這座城堡為一條河流所環繞。
相關衍生字彙 surround [sə`raʊnd] 動 包圍、enclose [ɪn`kloz] 動 圍住、open [`opən] 動 開放、circle [`sɝkl̩] 動 圈出
動詞三態變化 encircle - encircled - encircled

enclose [ɪn`kloz] 動 把～封入，附上，圍住
▶ Please remember to enclose a picture with your application form.
請記得隨你的申請表格附上一張照片。
動詞三態變化 enclose - enclosed - enclosed

encounter [ɪn`kaʊntɚ] 動 遭遇，遇到
▶ When I encounter difficulties, I always consult my teacher.
遇到困難時，我都會請教我的老師。
動詞三態變化 encounter - encountered - encountered

encourage [ɪn`kɝɪdʒ] 動 鼓勵
▶ I was encouraged by his touching story and decided to be brave.
我受到他感人故事的鼓勵，決定要勇敢。
相關衍生字彙 discourage [dɪs`kɝɪdʒ] 動 挫折、encouragement [ɪn`kɝɪdʒmənt] 名 鼓勵、inspire [ɪn`spaɪr] 動 激勵、provoke [prə`vok] 動 激起
動詞三態變化 encourage - encouraged - encouraged

encyclopedia [ɪn͵saɪklə`pidɪə] 名 百科全書
▶ Wiki is the free encyclopedia online. 維基是網路上的免費百科全書。

endangered [ɪn`dendʒɚd] 形 瀕臨絕種的
▶ Pandas are endangered animals. 熊貓是瀕臨絕種的動物。

endear [ɪnˋdɪr] 動 使受喜愛

▶ She endears herself to her classmates with friendly manners.
她友善的舉止讓她受到同學的喜愛。

相關衍生字彙 endearing [ɪnˋdɪrɪŋ] 形 可愛的，惹人喜愛的、endearment [ɪnˋdɪrmənt]
名 親愛的表示，愛意、endear to 片 使受喜愛，使被愛慕、endearingly [ɪnˋdɪrɪŋlɪ]
副 討人喜歡地，引人愛慕地

動詞三態變化 endear - endeared - endeared

endeavor [ɪnˋdɛvɚ] 名 動 努力

▶ Scientists are endeavoring to solve the problem.
科學家正努力解決這個問題。

動詞三態變化 endeavor - endeavored - endeavored

ending [ˋɛndɪŋ] 名 結尾，結局

▶ Not all the fairy tales have a happy ending.
並非所有的童話故事都有幸福的結尾。

相關衍生字彙 end [ɛnd] 動 結束、begin [bɪˋgɪn] 動 開始、start [stɑrt] 動 開始、
conclusion [kənˋkluʒən] 名 結論、finish [ˋfɪnɪʃ] 動 完成

endless [ˋɛndlɪs] 形 無盡的，不斷的

▶ His father gave him an endless supply of money.
他爸爸不斷的給他金錢上的供應。

相關衍生字彙 endlessly [ˋɛndləslɪ] 副 無窮地，繼續地、continuous [kənˋtɪnjuəs]
形 連續的，不斷的、ceaseless [ˋsislɪs] 形 不停的，不間斷的、incessant [ɪnˋsɛsn̩t]
形 連續的、uninterrupted [ˌʌnɪntəˋrʌptɪd] 形 不間斷的、
everlasting [ˌɛvɚˋlæstɪŋ] 形 永遠的，持久的

endorse [ɪnˋdɔrs] 動 背書，認可

▶ The advertisement was endorsed by a popular superstar.
這個廣告是由一位受歡迎的巨星所背書的。

相關衍生字彙 endorsee [ɪnˌdɔrˋsi] 名 原收款人自己背書以讓渡的對象、
endorsement [ɪnˋdɔrsmənt] 名 背書，簽署，贊同、endorser [ɪnˋdɔrsɚ]
名 背書人，轉讓人、endorsor [ɛnˋdɔrsɚ] 名 背書人

動詞三態變化 endorse - endorsed - endorsed

endow [ɪnˋdaʊ] 動 捐贈，資助

▶ The hospital has been endowed by a kindhearted millionaire.
這間醫院一直由一位善心富翁資助。

相關衍生字彙 endowment [ɪnˋdaʊmənt] 名（基金，財產等的）捐贈、endowed with
片 天生具有、bequeath [bɪˋkwið] 動（立遺囑）把～遺贈給、
contribute [kənˋtrɪbjut] 動 捐（款），捐助，貢獻

動詞三態變化 endow - endowed - endowed

endurance [ɪnˋdjurəns] 名 忍耐   片 beyond endurance 超出能忍耐的程度

E

相關衍生字彙 endure [ɪn`dʒur] 動 忍受、bear [bɛr] 動 承擔、persist [pə·`sɪst] 動 堅持、last [læst] 動 持續

---

enemy [`ɛnəmɪ] 名 敵人
▶ I treat you as a friend instead of an enemy.
我視你如朋友，而非敵人。

相關衍生字彙 opponent [ə`ponənt] 名 對手，敵手、adversary [`ædvə·ˌsɛrɪ] 名 敵手，敵人、antagonist [æn`tægənɪst] 名 對手，反對者

---

energetic [ˌɛnə·`dʒɛtɪk] 形 精力旺盛的
▶ Most teenagers are energetic and creative. 多數的青少年是有活力且具創意的。

---

energy [`ɛnə·dʒɪ] 名 活力，能量
▶ Eating breakfast can give you more energy. 吃早餐可以帶給你更多能量。

---

enforce [ɪn`fors] 動 強制，執行
⊙ MP3 05-06
▶ The new traffic rule will be enforced from July first.
這條新的交通規則將從七月一日執行。

相關衍生字彙 enforcement [ɪn`forsmənt] 名 實施，執行、enforceable [ɪn`forsəbl] 形 可實施的，可加強的、enforced [ɪn`forst] 形 實施的，強制執行的、compel [kəm`pɛl] 動 強迫，使不得不、oblige [ə`blaɪdʒ] 動 迫使，施恩於

動詞三態變化 enforce - enforced - enforced

---

engaged [ɪn`gedʒd] 形 從事～的，訂婚的
▶ Mark will be engaged to Vicky next week.
馬克將在下周和薇琪訂婚。

相關衍生字彙 engagement [ɪn`gedʒmənt] 名 訂婚、marry [`mærɪ] 動 結婚、wedding [`wɛdɪŋ] 名 婚禮、marriage [`mærɪdʒ] 名 婚姻

---

engrave [ɪn`grev] 動 雕刻，將～銘記
▶ Her husband's name was engraved on the ring.
她將先生的名字刻在戒指上。

動詞三態變化 engrave - engraved - engraved

---

engrossed [ɪn`grost] 形 全神貫注的
▶ The speech was so touching that students were engrossed in listening.
這場演講很精彩，學生都全神貫注的聽講。

相關衍生字彙 spellbound [`spɛl.baund] 形 入迷的，出神的、absorbed [əb`sorbd] 形 專心一意的，被吸收的、pensive [`pɛnsɪv] 形 沉思的，悲傷的、abstracted [æb`stræktɪd] 形 出神的，發呆的

---

engine [`ɛndʒən] 名 引擎，發動機
▶ There is something wrong with my car engine.
我車子的引擎有點問題。

相關衍生字彙 engineer [ˌɛndʒə`nɪr] 名 工程師、engineering [ˌɛndʒə`nɪrɪŋ] 名 工程學、machine [mə`ʃin] 名 機器、machinery [mə`ʃinərɪ] 名 機械

enhance [ɪn`hæns] 動 增高，提高

▶ The successful interview enhanced the mayor's reputation.
這次成功的訪談讓市長的聲望大增。

動詞三態變化 enhance - enhanced - enhanced

enlighten [ɪn`laɪtn̩] 動 啟發，教導

▶ A good cartoon can enlighten children.
好的卡通可以啟發小孩。

相關衍生字彙 enlightened [ɪn`laɪtn̩d] 形 開明的，有知識的、enlightenment [ɪn`laɪtn̩mənt] 名 啟蒙，教化、disillusion [ˌdɪsɪ`luʒən] 名 醒悟 動 使不再抱幻想

動詞三態變化 enlighten - enlightened - enlightened

enjoy [ɪn`dʒɔɪ] 動 享受，喜愛

▶ After retirement, I enjoy my life by traveling.
退休後，我透過旅遊來享受人生。

相關衍生字彙 enjoyable [ɪn`dʒɔɪəbl] 形 使人快樂的、like [laɪk] 動 喜歡、enjoyment [ɪn`dʒɔɪmənt] 名 樂趣、joy [dʒɔɪ] 名 歡樂

動詞三態變化 enjoy - enjoyed - enjoyed

enlarge [ɪn`lardʒ] 動 放大（照片），擴大

▶ The textbook was enlarged for the student with eyesight problem.
教科書要放大給視力有問題的學生。

動詞三態變化 enlarge - enlarged - enlarged

enlargement [ɪn`lardʒmənt] 名 擴大，增建，（書的）增訂

▶ The boss announced the enlargement of the marketing department.
老闆宣布擴大行銷部門。

enmity [`ɛnmətɪ] 名 敵意，不和

▶ I don't know why she always shows enmity towards me.
我不知道為何她總是對我有敵意。

相關衍生字彙 hostility [hɑs`tɪlətɪ] 名 敵意，戰爭、antipathy [æn`tɪpəθɪ] 名 反感，厭惡、rancor [`ræŋkɚ] 名 仇恨，激烈的憎惡、loathing [`loðɪŋ] 名 嫌惡，強烈的反感 形 有強烈反感的

enormous [ɪ`nɔrməs] 形 龐大的，兇暴的

▶ After his father passed away, he was given an enormous fortune.
他父親去世後，他獲得一大筆財產。

enough [ə`nʌf] 形 足夠的

▶ Stop! I've heard enough your complaint.
停！我已經聽夠你的抱怨了。

相關衍生字彙 plenty [`plɛntɪ] 形 足夠的、sufficient [sə`fɪʃənt] 形 充分的、ample [`æmpl] 形 大量的、abundant [ə`bʌndənt] 形 豐富的、rich [rɪtʃ] 形 富有的

enrich [ɪnˋrɪtʃ] 動 使富裕，使豐富

▶ Painting enriches my life.
畫畫豐富了我的生活。

相關衍生字彙 enrichment [ɪnˋrɪtʃmənt]名 致富，豐富、aggrandize [əˋgrænˏdaɪz] 動 加大，強化，誇張

動詞三態變化 enrich - enriched - enriched

enroll [ɪnˋrol] 動 註冊，登記，入學，捲起

▶ If you like the course, you can enroll online.
如果你喜歡這個課程，可以上網登記。

相關衍生字彙 enrollment [ɪnˋrolmənt]名 登記，入會，入伍、enrollee [ɪnroˋli] 名 入學者，入伍者、register [ˋrɛdʒɪstɚ]名 動 登記，註冊、sign up 片 註冊，簽約，報名登記

動詞三態變化 enroll - enrolled - enrolled

ensue [ɛnˋsu] 動 接踵而來

▶ No one knows what will ensue from the protest movement.
沒人知道這抗議行動過後會發生什麼事。

動詞三態變化 ensue - ensued - ensued

ensure [ɪnˋʃur] 動 擔保，保證　　片 to ensure safety 確認安全性

相關衍生字彙 assure [əˋʃur] 動 擔保，使確信、guarantee [ˏgærənˋti]名 保證書 動 保證，擔保、make certain 片 確定，確信

動詞三態變化 ensure - ensured - ensured

entail [ɪnˋtel] 動 必需，使承擔

▶ All kinds of investment entail some risk.
所有投資都有些許的風險。

動詞三態變化 entail - entailed – entailed

entangle [ɪnˋtæŋgl] 動 纏住，連累

▶ The poor dolphin died because it got entangled with the nets and choked.
可憐的海豚因為被網子纏住窒息而死。

動詞三態變化 entangle - entangled - entangled

enter [ˋɛntɚ] 動 進入，參加

▶ I am used to entering my garage by the side door.
我習慣從側門進入我的車庫。

動詞三態變化 enter - entered - entered

enterprise [`ɛntɚ͵praɪz]名 事業，冒險精神　　　　　　　◎MP3 **05-07**
▶ My son showed a lot of enterprise in applying for the admission.
　兒子在申請入學許可上展現無比的進取心。

相關衍生字彙　enterprising [`ɛntɚ͵praɪzɪŋ]形 有事業心的、entrepreneur [͵ɑntrəprə`nɝ]
　　　　　　　名 企業家、ambition [æm`bɪʃən]名 企圖心、desire [dɪ`zaɪr]名動 渴望

---

entertain [͵ɛntɚ`ten]動 款待，使歡樂
▶ To entertain kids, we prepared a lot of balloons.
　為了讓孩子們開心，我們準備了很多氣球。

動詞三態變化　entertain - entertained - entertained

---

entertainment [͵ɛntɚ`tenmənt]名 娛樂
▶ TV programs should provide entertainment and education as well.
　電視節目應提供娛樂與教育。

相關衍生字彙　amusement [ə`mjuzmənt]名 樂趣，消遣、divertissement [dɪ`vɝtɪsmənt]
　　　　　　　名 兩幕間之餘興表演，消遣、distraction [dɪ`strækʃən]名 分心，消遣，散心、
　　　　　　　pastime [`pæs͵taɪm]名 消遣，娛樂、recreation [͵rɛkrɪ`eʃn]
　　　　　　　名 娛樂，（身心的）休養、enjoyment [ɪn`dʒɔɪmənt]名 樂趣，享受

---

enthusiasm [ɪn`θjuzɪ͵æzəm]名 熱忱，熱心
▶ You should not lose your enthusiasm for learning.
　你不該失去學習的熱忱。

相關衍生字彙　enthusiastic [ɪn͵θjuzɪ`æstɪk]形 有熱忱的、passion [`pæʃən]名 熱情、
　　　　　　　passionate [`pæʃənɪt]形 熱情的、craze [krez]名 狂熱

---

entire [ɪn`taɪr]形 全部的，完全的
▶ I spent my entire holiday reading and sleeping.
　我整個假期不是閱讀就是睡覺。

相關衍生字彙　entirely [ɪn`taɪrlɪ]副 完全地，徹底地、entirety [ɪn`taɪrtɪ]名 全部，全體、
　　　　　　　plenary [`plinərɪ]形 完全的，絕對的、unabridged [͵ʌnə`brɪdʒd]
　　　　　　　形 未刪節的，完整的

---

entitle [ɪn`taɪt!]動 給～權力（或資格）
▶ The coupon entitles you a free cup of coffee.
　這張優待券可以讓你享有一杯免費的咖啡。

動詞三態變化　entitle - entitled - entitled

---

entrance [`ɛntrəns]名 入口，入學許可
▶ Entrance to the big company can make me more experienced.
　進入這間大公司工作有助於我學習更多經驗。

---

entreat [ɪn`trit]動 懇求，請求
▶ I have to entreat my son to eat some vegetables almost every meal.
　我幾乎每餐都得求兒子吃點蔬菜。

E

相關衍生字彙 ask [æsk] 動 詢問，要求、plead [plid] 動 辯護、beg [bɛg] 動 懇求、appeal [ə`pil] 動 呼籲

動詞三態變化 entreat - entreated - entreated

entrust [ɪn`trʌst] 動 信託，託管

▶ I entrusted my pet dog to my best friend while I went travelling.
我出門旅遊時，把我的寵物小狗託給我最好的朋友照顧。

動詞三態變化 entrust - entrusted - entrusted

envelop [`ɛnvə͵ləp] 動 包住，裹住

▶ It was cold so the woman enveloped her baby in a heavy blanket.
天氣太冷，婦人把嬰兒裹進厚毛毯裡。

動詞三態變化 envelop - enveloped - enveloped

envelope [`ɛnvə͵lop] 名 信封　片 a red envelope（中國習俗）紅包

envious [`ɛnvɪəs] 形 嫉妒的，羨慕的

▶ We are very envious of your achievement.
我們都很羨慕你的成就。

相關衍生字彙 envious of 片 嫉妒，羨慕、enviously [`ɛnvɪəslɪ] 副 嫉妒地，羨慕地、begrudging [bɪ`grʌdʒɪŋ] 形 勉強的，不情願的，嫉妒的、green-eyed [`grin͵aɪd] 形 嫉妒的、covetous [`kʌvɪtəs] 形 垂涎的，貪圖的、resentful [rɪ`zɛntfəl] 形 忿恨的，怨恨的

environment [ɪn`vaɪrənmənt] 名 環境

▶ It's everyone's duty to protect the environment from pollution.
保護環境不受污染是每個人的責任。

相關衍生字彙 environmental [ɪn͵vaɪrən`mɛntl̩] 形 環境的、environmentalism [ɪn͵vaɪrən`mɛntl̩ɪzəm] 名 環境保護論、environmentalist [ɪn͵vaɪrən`mɛntl̩ɪst] 名 環保人士

envy [`ɛnvɪ] 名 動 嫉妒，羨慕

▶ Don't envy those who are wealthy.
不要嫉妒那些有錢人。

動詞三態變化 envy - envied - envied

epic [`ɛpɪk] 名 史詩

▶ The Iliad is an ancient Greek epic poem. 伊里亞德是古希臘的史詩。

epidemic [͵ɛpɪ`dɛmɪk] 名 流行病 形 傳染的

▶ An epidemic breaks out in that area. 那個區域爆發流行病。

episode [`ɛpə͵sod] 名（連續劇的）一齣

▶ The last episode of the drama moved its audience to tears.
那齣戲劇的最後一集讓觀眾感動的哭了。

epoch [ˋɛpək] 名 時代　　🅟 to mark an epoch 開啟新紀元

equal [ˋikwəl] 形 相等的，勝任的
▶ All people are born equal.
　人人生而平等。

相關衍生字彙　equality [iˋkwɑlətɪ] 名 平等、equally [ˋikwəlɪ] 副 平等地、fair [fɛr] 形 公平的、
　　　　　　　unfair [ʌnˋfɛr] 形 不公平的、equilibrium [͵ikwəˋlɪbrɪəm] 名 均衡、
　　　　　　　equivalent [ɪˋkwɪvələnt] 形 相等的

equator [ɪˋkwetɚ] 名 赤道
▶ Equator is an imaginary line drawn around the middle of the Earth.
　赤道是一條畫在地球中間的假想線。

相關衍生字彙　equatorial [͵ɛkwəˋtorɪəl] 形 赤道的，酷熱的、equator anti-cyclone
　　　　　　　片 赤道反氣旋、Equatorial Guinea 片 赤道幾內亞

equip [ɪˋkwɪp] 動 配備，使有資格　　　　　　　　　　🎧 MP3 **05-08**
▶ To equip a new lab will cost a lot.
　為一間新的實驗室配置所有設備要花很多錢。

動詞三態變化　equip - equipped - equipped

equipment [ɪˋkwɪpmən] 名 設備　　🅟 kitchen equipment 廚房設備

era [ˋɪrə] 名 時代　　🅟 the cold war era 冷戰時代

eradicate [ɪˋrædɪ͵ket] 動 根除，消滅
▶ With the new medicine, the disease has now been eradicated.
　有了新的藥，這種疾病現在已經被根除了。

動詞三態變化　eradicate - eradicated - eradicated

erase [ɪˋres] 動 擦掉，清除
▶ It's hard to erase such terrible memories.
　很難抹去如此可怕的回憶。

動詞三態變化　erase - erased - erased

eraser [ɪˋresɚ] 名 橡皮擦
▶ Pens, rulers, and erasers are all stationery. 筆、尺和橡皮擦都是文具。

erect [ɪˋrɛkt] 動 樹立，設立 形 直立的
▶ The statue was erected there long time ago.
　那座雕像很久以前就被豎立在那裡了。

相關衍生字彙　erectly [ɪˋrɛktlɪ] 副 直立地，垂直地、erectile [ɪˋrɛktɪl] 形 可使直立的、
　　　　　　　upright [ˋʌp͵raɪt] 形 挺直的，直立的、vertical [ˋvɝtɪkl] 形 垂直的，立式的

動詞三態變化　erect - erected - erected

erosion [ɪˋroʒən] 名 腐蝕，侵蝕　　🅟 wind erosion 風蝕作用
相關衍生字彙　erosive [ɪˋrosɪv] 形 腐蝕（性）的

errand [ˋɛrənd] 名 差事，任務，使命　　片 to run errands 跑腿辦事

error [ˋɛrɚ] 名 錯誤，過失　　片 to make an error 犯錯
相關衍生字彙 err [ɝ] 動 犯錯、erroneous [ɪˋronɪəs] 形 錯誤的、mistake [mɪˋstek] 名 錯誤、
defect [dɪˋfɛkt] 名 缺點、mistaken [mɪˋstekən] 形 錯誤的

erupt [ɪˋrʌpt] 動 爆發，噴發
▶ Experts forecast that the volcano will erupt soon.
　　專家預估火山即將爆發。
動詞三態變化 erupt - erupted - erupted

eruption [ɪˋrʌpʃən] 名（火山）爆發，（熔岩的）噴出
片 a volcanic eruption 火山爆發
相關衍生字彙 eruptive [ɪˋrʌptɪv] 形 噴出的，爆發的、explosion [ɪkˋsploʒən] 名 爆發，擴張、
cataclysm [ˋkætəˌklɪzəm] 名 地殼之劇烈變動、detonation [ˌdɛtəˋneʃən]
名 爆炸（聲），引爆

escalator [ˋɛskəˌletɚ] 名 手扶梯
▶ It's dangerous for kids to play on the escalator.
　　小孩在手扶梯上玩耍很危險。
相關衍生字彙 escalate [ˋɛskəˌlet] 動 使逐步上升（增強或擴大）、escalatory [ˌɛskəˋletərɪ]
形 使增加的、moving staircase 片 電梯、elevator [ˋɛləˌvetɚ] 名 電梯，升降機

escape [əˋskep] 名 動 逃跑，漏出
▶ It was reported that one prisoner escaped from jail last night.
　　據報導，有一名囚犯昨晚逃獄。
動詞三態變化 escape - escaped - escaped

escort [ˋɛskɔrt] 名 護花使者 名 動 護送
▶ No matter where the pretty girl goes, an escort follows her.
　　這位漂亮的女孩不論走到哪裡，都有護花使者跟隨著。
動詞三態變化 escort - escorted - escorted

especially [əˋspɛʃəlɪ] 副 尤其是
▶ I like movies, especially comedy. 我喜歡電影，尤其是喜劇。

essay [ˋɛse] 名 散文，論文
▶ We are asked to write an essay on globalization.
　　我們被要求寫一篇有關全球化的論文。
相關衍生字彙 paper [ˋpepɚ] 名 論文，報告、composition [ˌkɑmpəˋzɪʃən] 名 作文、
article [ˋɑrtɪkl] 名 文章，論文、thesis [ˋθisɪs] 名 畢業（或學位）論文

essence [ˋɛsns] 名 本質，要素　　片 in essence 本質上

essential [ɪ`sɛnʃəl] 形 必要的，基本的
▶ Financial support from your family is very essential if you want to study abroad.
如果你想出國讀書，家裡財務上的支援是很重要的。
相關衍生字彙 essentially [ɪ`sɛnʃəlɪ] 副 實質上，本來、essential oil 片 香精油、essentiality [ɪˌsɛnʃɪ`ælətɪ] 名 必要性，實質性、essentialize [ə`sɛnʃəˌlaɪz] 動 扼要地表示，使精錬

establish [ə`stæblɪʃ] 動 創辦，設立
▶ These theories were established in the 13th century.
這些理論都是十三世紀時建立的。
動詞三態變化 establish - established - established

establishment [ɪs`tæblɪʃmənt] 名 建立的機構　　MP3 05-09
片 an educational establishment 教育機構
相關衍生字彙 institution [ˌɪnstə`tjuʃən] 名 機構、bureau [`bjuro] 名 事務處、office [`ɔfɪs] 名 政府機關，營業處、authority [ə`θɔrətɪ] 名 官方，當局

estate [ɪs`tet] 名 財產，遺產
▶ She has no child, so she left her estate to her nephew.
她沒有小孩，所以她把財產留給姪子。

esteem [ɪs`tim] 名 動 尊敬
▶ The statesman was held in high esteem.
這位政治家極受尊重。
動詞三態變化 esteem - esteemed - esteemed

estimate [`ɛstəˌmet] 名 動 估計，評斷
▶ They estimate that the typhoon will bring a heavy rain.
他們預估這次颱風將帶來豪雨。
相關衍生字彙 estimation [ˌɛstə`meʃən] 名 評價，預算，尊敬，estimator [`ɛstəˌmetɚ] 名 評價者、estimative [`ɛstəˌmetɪv] 形 有估計能力的，估計的、evaluate [ɪ`væljuˌet] 動 對～評價，為～鑑定
動詞三態變化 estimate - estimated - estimated

eternal [ɪ`tɜnḷ] 形 永恆的，不朽的
▶ I hope our friendship will be eternal.
希望我們的友誼可以長存。
相關衍生字彙 eternity [ɪ`tɜnətɪ] 名 永恆、forever [fɚ`ɛvɚ] 副 永遠地、lasting [`læstɪŋ] 形 持久的、everlasting [ˌɛvɚ`læstɪŋ] 形 不朽的

ethic [`ɛθɪk] 名 倫理標準 形 倫理的　　片 professional ethic 職業道德
相關衍生字彙 ethical [`ɛθɪkḷ] 形 倫理的，道德的、ethics [`ɛθɪks] 名 倫理學，道德標準、ethical film 片 倫理片、ethically [`ɛθɪklɪ] 副 倫理（學）上，道德上、ethicize [`ɛθɪˌsaɪz] 動 使合乎倫理

etiquette [`ɛtɪkɛt] 名 禮儀
▶ Lady first is one of the etiquettes.
女士優先是禮儀之一。
相關衍生字彙 formality [fɔr`mælətɪ] 名 拘泥形式，禮節、decorum [dɪ`korəm]
名 端莊，禮儀、decency [`disn̩sɪ] 名 合宜，得體

E

evacuate [ɪ`vækjuˌet] 動 撤離，排空（腸或胃）
▶ Before the typhoon came, all the villagers had been evacuated.
颱風來之前，村民已經被撤離。
相關衍生字彙 evacuation [ɪˌvækju`eʃən] 名 撤空，排泄、evacuee [ɪˌvækju`i] 名 被疏散者、
evacuative [ɪˌvækju`etɪv] 形 撤離的，疏散的、evacuator [ɪ`vækjuˌetɚ]
名 撤退者，（醫）排出器
動詞三態變化 evacuate - evacuated - evacuated

evaluate [ɪ`væljuˌet] 動 評估，評價
▶ He was evaluated as unfit for a soccer player.
他被評估不適合當足球選手。
動詞三態變化 evaluate - evaluated - evaluated

evaluation [ɪˌvælju`eʃən] 名 評估　　片 a fair evaluation 公正的評估

evaporate [ɪ`væpəˌret] 動 蒸發，消失
▶ The sun soon evaporated the water in the pond.
太陽很快就蒸發了池塘裡的水。
相關衍生字彙 evaporation [ɪˌvæpə`reʃn̩] 名 蒸發，消失、evaporative [ɪ`væpəˌretɪv]
形 成為爭氣的，蒸發的、evaporator [ɪ`væpəˌretɚ] 名 蒸發器，脫水器
動詞三態變化 evaporate - evaporated - evaporated

evening [`ivnɪŋ] 名 傍晚
▶ I hope you two enjoy the evening.
希望你們倆有個愉快的晚上。
相關衍生字彙 morning [`mɔrnɪŋ] 名 早上、afternoon [`æftɚ`nun] 名 下午、noon [nun]
名 中午、night [naɪt] 名 夜晚

eventual [ɪ`vɛntʃuəl] 形 最後的　　片 the eventual judgment 最終的判斷

eventually [ɪ`vɛntʃuəlɪ] 副 最後，終於
▶ Years later, he eventually succeeded. 幾年過後，他終於成功了。

evidence [`ɛvədəns] 名 證據
▶ The police are looking for evidence. 警方正在尋找證據。

evident [ˋɛvədənt] 形 明顯的，明白的
▶ Her love for you is so evident. How can you not know?
　她對你的愛如此明顯，你怎麼會不知道？
相關衍生字彙 evidently [ˋɛvədntlɪ] 副 顯然地、obvious [ˋɑbvɪəs] 形 明顯的、clear [klɪr]
　　　　形 清楚的、apparent [əˋpærənt] 形 明顯的

evil [ˋivl̩] 名 罪惡 形 邪惡的
▶ Money is the root of evil.
　金錢是罪惡的根源。
相關衍生字彙 evilly [ˋivl̩ɪ] 副 邪惡地、evil-minded [ˋivl̩ˋmaɪndɪd] 形 惡意的，心毒的、
　　　　evil-eyed [ˋivl̩ˋaɪd] 形 惡毒眼光的、evil winds 片 歪風、evildoer [ˋivl̩ˋduɚ]
　　　　名 做壞事的人、evildoing [ˋivl̩ˋduɪŋ] 名 惡行，做壞事、evilness [ˋivəlnəs]
　　　　名 不幸，邪惡，有害

evoke [ɪˋvok] 動 喚起
▶ The old picture evokes the memory of my first love.
　這張舊照片喚起我初戀的回憶。
動詞三態變化 evoke - evoked - evoked

evolution [͵ɛvəˋluʃən] 名 進化，發展　　　片 the theory of evolution 進化論
相關衍生字彙 evolutionary [͵ɛvəˋluʃən͵ɛrɪ] 形 進化的，發展的、
　　　　evolutionism [͵ɛvəˋluʃənɪzəm] 名 進化論、evolutional [͵ɛvəˋluʃən̩]
　　　　形 發展的，進化的、evolutionary biologist 片 進化生物學家、
　　　　evolutionist [͵ɛvəˋluʃənɪst] 名 進化論者 形 進化（論）的

exactly [ɪgˋzæktlɪ] 副 準確地，恰好地
▶ Please tell me what exactly happened. 請告訴我真正發生的事。

exaggerate [ɪgˋzædʒə͵ret] 動 誇大　　　◎ MP3 05-10
▶ The newspaper exaggerated the fact.
　報紙誇大了事實。
動詞三態變化 exaggerate - exaggerated - exaggerated

exaggeration [ɪg͵zædʒəˋreʃən] 名 誇張
▶ It would be no exaggeration to say that your daughter is the most beautiful
　baby I've ever seen.
　妳女兒是我看過最漂亮的嬰兒，這麼說一點都不誇張。

exalt [ɪgˋzɔlt] 動 提拔，高舉，讚揚
▶ He was exalted to take charge of the new department.
　他被擢升去管理新的部門。
相關衍生字彙 exaltation [͵ɛgzɔlˋteʃən] 名 提拔，欣喜，exalted [ɪgˋzɔltɪd]
　　　　形（地位）高貴的，欣喜的、exaltedly [ɪgˋzɔltədlɪ] 副 得意忘形地、
　　　　dignify [ˋdɪgnə͵faɪ] 動 使有尊嚴，使高貴
動詞三態變化 exalt - exalted - exalted

examination [ɪɡ͵zæmə`neʃən] 名 考試，檢查
🔵 a midterm / final examination 期中／期末考

examine [ɪɡ`zæmɪn] 動 檢驗，測驗
▶ My car needs examining carefully.
　我的車子需要仔細檢查。
動詞三態變化 examine - examined - examined

example [ɪɡ`zæmpl̩] 名 例子　　🔵 to set a good example 樹立典範

excavate [`ɛkskə͵vet] 動 挖掘
▶ The workers are excavating a tunnel.
　工人正在挖隧道。
動詞三態變化 excavate - excavated - excavated

exceed [ɪk`sid] 動 超過，勝過
▶ The cost exceeds my budget.
　這價錢超過我的預算。
相關衍生字彙 excess [ɪk`sɛs] 名 過分、excessive [ɪk`sɛsɪv] 形 過度的、
　　　　　　excessiveness [ɪk`sɛsɪvnɛs] 名 過度，極端
動詞三態變化 exceed - exceeded - exceeded

excel [ɪk`sɛl] 動 優於，勝過
▶ Bill excelled in math when he was an elementary school student.
　比爾念小學時數學很優秀。
動詞三態變化 excel - excelled - excelled

excellent [`ɛkslənt] 形 優秀的，極好的
▶ The food at this restaurant is excellent.
　這間餐廳的食物很棒。
相關衍生字彙 excellence [`ɛksləns] 名 優秀，傑出、excellently [`ɛksləntlɪ]
　　　　　　副 優異地，極好地、excellent company 片 先進企業

exception [ɪk`sɛpʃən] 名 例外　　🔵 no exception 沒有例外
相關衍生字彙 exceptional [ɪk`sɛpʃənl̩] 形 例外的，特殊的，優秀的、
　　　　　　exceptionable [ɪk`sɛpʃənəbl̩] 形 不可反對的，例外的、
　　　　　　exceptionably [ɪk`sɛpʃənəblɪ] 副 可以反對地、exceptionally [ɪk`sɛpʃənəlɪ]
　　　　　　副 例外地，異常地

exchange [ɪks`tʃendʒ] 名 動 交換，兌換
▶ At the Christmas party, we exchanged gifts.
　聖誕派對上我們交換禮物。
動詞三態變化 exchange - exchanged - exchanged

E

excite [ɪkˈsaɪt] 動 使興奮
▶ Rowing a canoe excited me a lot.
划獨木舟讓我覺得好興奮。

相關衍生字彙 excited [ɪkˈsaɪtɪd] 形 興奮的、excitement [ɪkˈsaɪtmənt] 名 興奮、
exciting [ɪkˈsaɪtɪŋ] 形 令人興奮的

動詞三態變化 excite - excited - excited

exclaim [ɪksˈklem] 動 呼喊，尖叫
▶ She exclaimed excitedly on receiving the admission of Harvard University.
收到哈佛大學的入學通知，她興奮地尖叫。

相關衍生字彙 exclamation [ˌɛksкləˈmeʃən] 名 驚叫，感歎（句）、exclamation mark
片 感歎號、exclamation point 片 驚嘆號、exclamatory [ɪkˈsklæmə͵torɪ]
形 叫喊的，感歎的

動詞三態變化 exclaim - exclaimed - exclaimed

exclude [ɪkˈsklud] 動 把～排除在外
▶ People over 60 years old are excluded from the dangerous activity.
六十歲以上的人不能參加此危險活動。

動詞三態變化 exclude - excluded - excluded

exclusive [ɪkˈsklusɪv] 形 除外的，獨家的，排外的
▶ Some medicines are mutually exclusive. 有些藥物是互相排斥的。

excursion [ɪkˈskɝʒən] 名 遠足，短途旅行　片 to go on an excursion 做短程旅遊

excuse [ɪkˈskjuz] 名 藉口 動 原諒
▶ You had better have a good excuse for being late again today.
你最好有好的藉口說明今天又遲到的原因。

動詞三態變化 excuse - excused- excused

execution [ˌɛksɪˈkjuʃən] 名 執行，死刑
▶ A new ISIS video showed their execution of an American reporter.
一部新的短片說明 ISIS 已經處死一名美國記者。

executive [ɪgˈzɛkjutɪv] 名 管理者　片 CEO = Chief Executive Officer 執行長

exempt [ɪgˈzɛmpt] 動 免除，豁免　　　　　　　　　　　MP3 05-11
▶ The new tax policy will exempt those small companies.
這項新的稅制將排除小公司。

動詞三態變化 exempt - exempted - exempted

exercise [ˈɛksɚ͵saɪz] 名 習題 動 運動
▶ Exercising in the morning is part of my routine life.
早晨運動是我規律生活的一部分。

動詞三態變化 exercise - exercised - exercised

exert [ɪgˋzɝt] 動 用（力），盡（力）　片 to exert oneself 盡心盡力
動詞三態變化 exert - exerted - exerted

exhale [ɛksˋhel] 動 呼氣　反 inhale [ɪnˋhel] 動 吸氣
動詞三態變化 exhale - exhaled - exhaled

exhaust [ɪgˋzɔst] 動 用完，耗盡

E

▶ Too many assignments and exams will exhaust children's energy.
太多的作業跟考試會耗盡孩子們的精力。

相關衍生字彙 exhausted [ɪgˋzɔstɪd] 形 精疲力竭的、exhaustive [ɪgˋzɔstɪv] 形 徹底的、
exhausting [ɪgˋzɔstɪŋ] 形 使人精疲力竭的

動詞三態變化 exhaust - exhausted - exhausted

exhaustion [ɪgˋzɔstʃən] 名 精疲力竭　片 heat exhaustion 中暑，熱衰竭

exhibit [ɪgˋzɪbɪt] 動 陳列，展示

▶ The artist's works are often exhibited at the gallery.
這位藝術家的作品常常在美術館展出。

動詞三態變化 exhibit - exhibited - exhibited

exhibition [ˌɛksəˋbɪʃən] 名 展覽　片 an art exhibition 美術展

exhort [ɪgˋzɔrt] 動 規勸，告誡

▶ Our teacher always exhorts us to study harder.
老師總是規勸我們再用功點。

相關衍生字彙 exhortation [ˌɛgzɔrˋteʃən] 名 規勸，告誡、exhortative [ɪgˋzɔrtətɪv]
形 高興的，令人興奮的、exhortatory [ɪgˋzɔrtəˌtɔrɪ] 形 勸誡的，告誡的

動詞三態變化 exhort - exhorted - exhorted

exile [ˋɛksaɪl] 名 動 流放

▶ The King was exiled after the war.
戰爭過後，這名國王被流放。

動詞三態變化 exile - exiled - exiled

exist [ɪgˋzɪst] 動 存在，生活

▶ Many people believe that UFOs exist.
很多人都相信幽浮的存在。

動詞三態變化 exist - existed - existed

existence [ɪgˋzɪstəns] 名 存在，生存

▶ Do you believe in the existence of ghosts?
你相信鬼魂的存在嗎？

相關衍生字彙 existent [ɪgˋzɪstənt] 形 存在的，實有的、existing [ɪgˋzɪstɪŋ]
形 現存的，現行的、existential [ˌɛgzɪsˋtenʃəl] 形 （有關）存在的，存在主義的、
existentialism [ˌɛgzɪsˋtenʃəlɪzm] 名 存在主義、existentialist [ˌɛgzɪsˋtenʃəlɪst]
名 存在主義者 形 存在主義的

exit [`ɛksɪt] 名 出口 動 出去　　片 an emergency exit 緊急出口
動詞三態變化 exit - exited - exited

---

exotic [ɛg`zɑtɪk] 形 異國的，外來的
▶ I enjoyed exotic food while I was travelling in Italy.
在義大利旅遊時，我很享受異國美食。
相關衍生字彙 exotic species 片 外來物種、exotica [ɪg`zɑtɪkə] 名 異族事物，新奇事物、
exoticism [ɛg`zɑtəsɪzəm] 名 外國風味，異國情調、exotism [ɪg`zɑtɪzəm]
名 異國情趣，外來語（物）

---

expand [ɪk`spænd] 動 展開，擴大
▶ We decided to expand our business in Europe.
我們決定擴展歐洲的業務。
相關衍生字彙 expanse [ɪk`spæns] 名 廣闊的區域、expansion [ɪk`spænʃən] 名 擴展、
expansive [ɪk`spænsɪv] 形 擴張的
動詞三態變化 expand - expanded - expanded

---

expect [ɪk`spɛkt] 動 期待，預期
▶ I expect your coming so much.
我多麼期待你的到來。
動詞三態變化 expect - expected - expected

---

expectation [ˌɛkspɛk`teʃən] 名 期待　　片 to live up to the expectation 符合期待

---

expedition [ˌɛkspɪ`dɪʃən] 名 遠征，探險，考察
▶ The tour guide arranged a shopping expedition on the last day of our trip.
導遊在我們旅遊的最後一天安排了一個購物行程。

---

expel [ɪk`spɛl] 動 驅逐，排出
▶ If you continue to violate school rules, you will be expelled.
如果你繼續違反校規，將會被退學。
動詞三態變化 expel - expelled - expelled

---

expend [ɪk`spɛnd] 動 消費，花費
▶ I expend much effort on learning foreign languages.
我花很多力氣在學外國語言。
動詞三態變化 expend - expended - expended

---

expenditure [ɪk`spɛndɪtʃɚ] 名 經費，支出　　◉ MP3 05-12
片 to cut expenditure 刪減經費

---

expense [ɪk`spɛns] 名 費用
▶ The living expense in New York is very high.
紐約的生活費很高。
相關衍生字彙 expensive [ɪk`spɛnsɪv] 形 昂貴的、cheap [tʃip] 形 便宜的、costly [`kɔstlɪ]
形 貴重的、luxurious [lʌg`ʒʊrɪəs] 形 奢華的

experience [ɪkˋspɪrɪəns] 名 經驗 動 經歷
▶ We will take your work experience into consideration.
我們會將你的工作經驗納入考慮。

動詞三態變化 experience - experienced - experienced

experiment [ɪkˋspɛrəmənt] 名 實驗
▶ Are you for or against the experiment on animals?
你贊成或反對拿動物做實驗？

E

experimental [ɪkˏspɛrəˋmɛntl] 形 實驗性的
片 at the experimental stage 實驗階段

expert [ˋɛkspɝt] 名 專家
▶ He is an expert at gardening. 他是一位園藝專家。

相關衍生字彙 professional [prəˋfɛʃən] 形 職業性的、amateur [ˋæməˏtʃur] 名 業餘從事者、
specialist [ˋspɛʃəlɪst] 名 專家、master [ˋmæstɚ] 名 大師，能手

expire [ɪkˋspaɪr] 動 屆期，吐氣
▶ My credit card will expire next month.
我的信用卡下個月到期。

動詞三態變化 expire - expired - expired

explain [ɪkˋsplen] 動 解釋，說明
▶ If there is any misunderstanding, you had better explain it.
如果有任何誤會，你應該要解釋。

相關衍生字彙 explanation [ˏɛkspləˋneʃən] 名 解釋、explanatory [ɪksˋplænəˏtorɪ] 形 解釋的、
misunderstand [ˋmɪsʌndɚˋstænd] 動 誤會、misinterpret [ˋmɪsɪnˋtɝprɪt]
動 誤解

動詞三態變化 explain - explained - explained

explode [ɪkˋsplod] 動 爆炸
▶ A bomb exploded at the railway station; many people were killed.
車站因炸彈爆炸造成很多人死亡。

動詞三態變化 explode - exploded - exploded

exploit [ˋɛksplɔɪt] 名 功績 動 剝削
▶ Factories should not exploit their workers.
工廠不應該剝削工人。

動詞三態變化 exploit - exploited - exploited

explore [ɪkˋsplor] 動 探索   片 to explore the world 探索世界

相關衍生字彙 explorer [ɪkˋsplorɚ] 名 探險家、research [rɪˋsɝtʃ] 動 研究、
investigate [ɪnˋvɛstəˏget] 動 調查、search [sɝtʃ] 動 搜尋

動詞三態變化 explore - explored - explored

export [ɪks`port] 動 輸出　　反 import [ɪm`port] 動 輸入
動詞三態變化 export - exported - exported

expose [ɪk`spoz] 動 暴露，揭發
▶ Don't expose your children to violence of the video games.
不要讓你的孩子接觸暴力的電玩遊戲。
動詞三態變化 expose - exposed - exposed

exposure [ɪk`spoʒɚ] 名 暴曬，揭露
▶ Limit your exposure to the sun, or you will get sunburned.
別曬太久的太陽，否則會曬傷。

express [ɪk`sprɛs] 名 快遞 動 表達
▶ She is shy and doesn't know how to express her feelings.
她很害羞，不知如何表達情感。
相關衍生字彙 expression [ɪk`sprɛʃən] 名 表達、expressive [ɪk`sprɛsɪv] 形 表情豐富的、
tell [tɛl] 動 說明、show [ʃo] 動 展現
動詞三態變化 express - expressed - expressed

expunge [ɪk`spʌndʒ] 動 除去，刪去
▶ Because of getting hurt badly, the coach had no choice but to expunge his name from the team.
因為受傷嚴重，教練只好將他從隊上除名。
動詞三態變化 expunge - expunged - expunged

exquisite [`ɛkskwɪzɪt] 形 精美的
▶ The china is so exquisite. 這瓷器好精美。

extension [ɪk`stɛnʃən] 名 延期，分機
▶ He asked his professor to give an extension of the assignment deadline.
他要求教授讓他延期繳交作業。

extensive [ɪk`stɛnsɪv] 形 寬闊的，大量的　　片 extensive discussion 廣泛的討論

extent [ɪk`stɛnt] 名 程度，寬度，長度
片 to some extent 就某個程度而言

exterior [ɪk`stɪrɪɚ] 名 表面 形 外部的　　MP3 05-13
▶ The exterior of the house looks old. 這屋子的外觀看起來很舊。

exterminate [ɪk`stɝmə,net] 動 根絕，消滅
▶ Cockroaches and ants are hard to exterminate.
很難杜絕蟑螂跟螞蟻。
動詞三態變化 exterminate - exterminated - exterminated

external [ɪk`stɝnəl] 名 外觀 形 外部的　　片 the external appearance 外表

相關衍生字彙 inside [`ɪn`saɪd] 介 在～之內、outside [`aʊt`saɪd] 介 在～外面、inner [`ɪnɚ] 形 內部的、outer [`aʊtɚ] 形 外部的

extinction [ɪk`stɪŋkʃən] 名 熄滅，撲滅，滅絕

▶ Some wild animals are facing the risk of extinction.
有些野生動物正面臨滅絕的危機。

相關衍生字彙 extinctive [ɪk`stɪŋktɪv] 形 消滅的

E

extinguish [ɪk`stɪŋgwɪʃ] 動 熄滅，破滅   片 to extinguish a fire 滅火

相關衍生字彙 extinguishable [ɛk`stɪŋgwɪʃəbl̩] 形 可熄滅的，可滅絕的、
extinguisher [ɪk`stɪŋgwɪʃɚ] 名 熄滅者，滅火器、
extinguishment [ɪk`stɪŋgwɪʃmənt] 名 熄滅，滅絕，失效

動詞三態變化 extinguish - extinguished - extinguished

extort [ɪk`stɔrt] 動 敲詐，侵佔   片 to extort money from somebody 跟某人敲詐金錢

相關衍生字彙 extortion [ɪk`stɔrʃən] 名 敲詐，勒索、extortionary [ɪk`stɔrʃɪnˌɛrɪ]
形 勒索的，敲詐性的、extortionate [ɪk`stɔrʃənɪt] 形 勒索的，強求的、
extortioner [ɪk`stɔrʃənɚ] 名 敲詐者，勒索者、extortionist [ɪk`stɔrʃənɪst]
名 敲詐者，強奪者

動詞三態變化 extort - extorted - extorted

extra [`ɛkstrə] 形 額外的

▶ To prepare for the exam, he has been studying an extra one hour a day.
為了準備考試，他每天多唸一個小時的書。

extracurricular [ˌɛkstrəkə`rɪkjələ] 形 課外的

片 an extracurricular activity 課外活動

extract [ɪk`strækt] 動 提煉，榨取

▶ The oil is extracted from peanuts.
這種油是從花生所提煉出來的。

相關衍生字彙 extraction [ɪk`strækʃən] 名 抽出，拔出，榨出、extractive [ɪk`stræktɪv]
形 拔出的，精萃的、extractable [ɪk`stræktəbl̩] 形 可抽出的，可摘錄的，可榨取的

動詞三態變化 extract - extracted - extracted

extraordinary [ɪk`strɔrdn̩ˌɛrɪ] 形 異常的，特別的

▶ It takes extraordinary willpower to complete the project.
要完成此計畫，需要過人的意志力。

相關衍生字彙 unusual [ʌn`juʒʊəl] 形 不尋常的、outstanding [`aʊt`stændɪŋ] 形 與眾不同的、
common [`kɑmən] 形 一般的

extravagant [ɪk`strævəgənt] 形 奢侈的，放肆的

▶ Taking a taxi to school every day is too extravagant.
天天搭計程車去上學太奢侈了。

extravagance [ɪk`strævəgəns] 名 奢侈，浪費
▶ His wife's extravagance destroyed their marriage.
他太太的奢侈毀掉他們的婚姻。

相關衍生字彙 extravagancy [ɪk`strævəgənsɪ] 名 浪費，放縱，奢侈品、
prodigality [͵prɑdɪ`gælətɪ] 名 浪費，極度慷慨、lavishness [`lævɪʃnɪs]
名 大方，浪費，豐富、profligacy [`prɑfləgəsɪ] 名 放蕩，浪費、
wastefulness [`westfəlnɪs] 名 浪費，揮霍無度

---

extreme [ɪk`strim] 形 極端的，盡頭的
▶ I can't stand the extreme heat this summer.
我無法忍受今年夏天的酷熱。

相關衍生字彙 extremely [ɪk`strimlɪ] 副 極端地，極其，非常、extremism [ɪk`strimɪzm̩]
名 極端性，極端主義、extremist [ɪk`strimɪst] 名 激進主義者、
extremity [ɪk`strɛmətɪ] 名 末端，極端，手足、extreme sport 片 極限運動、
extremeness [ɪk`strimnɪs] 名 極端，極度

---

extrovert [`ɛkstrovɜt] 名 個性外向的人
▶ He is an extrovert, energetic and outgoing.
他是個外向、活力十足且好交際的人。

---

exult [ɪg`zʌlt] 動 歡欣鼓舞
▶ All the teammates exulted over their championship the whole night.
隊友整夜狂歡慶祝他們得冠軍。

動詞三態變化 exult - exulted - exulted

---

eye [aɪ] 名 眼睛　　片 catch one's eye 引起某人注意

相關衍生字彙 eyeball [`aɪ͵bɔl] 名 眼球、eyebrow [`aɪ͵braʊ] 名 眉毛、eyelash [`aɪ͵læʃ]
名 睫毛、eyelid [`aɪ͵lɪd] 名 眼皮、eyesight [`aɪ͵saɪt] 名 視力、eyesore [`aɪ͵sɔr]
名 看上去不順眼的東西

MEMO

F

fable ~ future

一網打盡「英語小知識」| 星座介紹 II ────────────────

Cancer
巨蟹座

Leo
獅子座

Virgo
處女座

Libra
天秤座

Scorpio
天蠍座

Sagittarius
射手座

F fable ~ future

fable [ˋfebḷ] 名 寓言，傳說

▶ Most kids are familiar with the fable of the tortoise and the hare.
大部分的孩子都很熟悉龜兔賽跑的寓言故事。

相關衍生字彙 fabled [ˋfebḷd] 形 寓言中的，虛構的、fabliau [ˋfæblɪo]
名 中世紀英法的故事詩、legend [ˋlɛdʒənd] 名 傳說，傳奇故事、myth [mɪθ]
名 神話、fairy tale 片 神話故事，童話

fabric [ˋfæbrɪk] 名 織品，布料

▶ The skirt is made of cotton fabrics.
這件裙子是棉布做的。

相關衍生字彙 fabric conditioner 片 織物柔軟劑、fabric sample 片 布料樣本、fabric softener
片 衣物柔軟精、textile [ˋtɛkstaɪl] 名 紡織品 形 紡織的

fabricate [ˋfæbrɪˏket] 動 組裝，製造，杜撰　　片 to fabricate an excuse 編造藉口

相關衍生字彙 fabrication [ˏfæbrɪˋkeʃən] 名 製造，構造物、fabricative [ˋfæbrəˏketɪv]
形 建造的、fabricator [ˋfæbrɪˏketɚ] 名 製作者，裝配工、construct [kənˋstrʌkt]
動 建造，創立（學說等）、assemble [əˋsɛmbḷ] 動 集合，配裝

動詞三態變化 fabricate - fabricated - fabricated

fabulous [ˋfæbjələs] 形 難以置信的，極好的

▶ The location of the apartment is fabulous.
這間公寓的地理位置非常好。

相關衍生字彙 fabulously [ˋfæbjələslɪ] 副 難以置信地、unbelievable [ˏʌnbɪˋlivəbḷ]
形 令人難以置信的、remarkable [rɪˋmɑrkəbḷ] 形 值得注意的，非凡的、
notable [ˋnotəbḷ] 形 值得注意的，顯要的、marvelous [ˋmɑrvələs] 形 不可思議的

face [fes] 名 臉 動 面臨　　片 to make a face 做鬼臉

相關衍生字彙 facecloth [ˋfesˏklɔθ] 名 洗臉毛巾、faceless [ˋfeslɪs] 形 無個性的、
facelift [ˋfeslɪft] 名 整容

動詞三態變化 face - faced - faced

facility [fəˋsɪlətɪ] 名 設施，能力

▶ The hotel offers many facilities to its customers.
這家飯店提供很多設施給房客。

fact [fækt] 名 事實　　片 as a matter of fact 事實上

相關衍生字彙 fact of life 片 生活中的殘酷現實、fact sheet 片 內容概要說明書、
fact-finder [ˋfæktˏfaɪndɚ] 名 實情調查者、fact-finding [ˋfæktˏfaɪndɪŋ]
名 實情調查，調解、in fact 片 事實上

factor [`fæktɚ] 名 **因素**
▶ Price is a major factor to attract me.
價錢是吸引我的主要因素。
相關衍生字彙 element [`ɛləmənt] 名 元素、part [part] 名 一部分、ingredient [ɪn`gridɪənt]
名 （混合物的）組成部分、component [kəm`ponənt] 名 零件，成分

---

factory [`fæktərɪ] 名 **工廠**
▶ There are many car factories along the river.
沿著河流有很多汽車工廠。
相關衍生字彙 factory farm 片 工廠化的農場、factory farming
片 （牲畜，家禽的）大規模室內飼養、factory floor 片 （全體）工廠工人，職員、
factory ship 片 有加工設備的漁船

F

---

faculty [`fækl̩tɪ] 名 **（學校的）教職員**
▶ He is the dean of the Faculty of Education. 他是教育學院的院長。

---

fade [fed] 動 **凋謝，（顏色）褪色**　　片 to fade away 逐漸凋零，逐漸褪色
相關衍生字彙 fade out 片 （電影，電視畫面）漸隱，淡出、fadeaway [`fedə,we] 名 消退、
fade-in [`fed,ɪn] 名 （電影，電視）漸顯，淡入、fadeless [`fedlɪs]
形 不褪色的，不凋落的、fadeproof [`fed,pruf] 形 不褪（色）的、fading [`fedɪŋ]
名 褪色，凋謝
動詞三態變化 fade - faded - faded

Fahrenheit [`færən,haɪt] 名 **華氏（溫度）**
反 Celsius / Centigrade [`sɛlsɪəs] / [`sɛntə,gred] 名 攝氏（溫度）

---

fail [fel] 動 **失敗**
▶ She failed in her attempt to win the championship. 她沒能贏得冠軍頭銜。

---

failure [`feljɚ] 名 **不及格**
▶ Failure is the mother of success.
（諺語）失敗為成功之母。
相關衍生字彙 succeed [sək`sid] 動 成功、successful [sək`sɛsfəl] 形 成功的、
success [sək`sɛs] 名 成功、achievement [ə`tʃivmənt] 名 成就

---

faint [fent] 形 **頭暈的**
▶ I need to eat something or I will feel faint with hunger.
我需要吃點東西，否則我會因飢餓而暈眩。
相關衍生字彙 faintest [`fentɪst] 形 （用於否定句、加強語氣）一點也（不）的，極小的、
faintheart [`fent`hart] 名 不果斷的人，膽小者、fainthearted [`fent`hartɪd]
形 懦弱的，無精神的、fainting [`fentɪŋ] 名 昏暈、faintingly [`fentɪŋlɪ]
副 似將暈厥地、faintish [`fentɪʃ] 形 較弱的，略為模糊的、faintly [`fentlɪ]
副 微弱地，模糊地，懦弱地、faintness [`fentnɪs] 名 虛弱，暈眩

fair [fɛr] 形 公平的　　反 unfair [ʌn`fɛr] 形 不公平的

相關衍生字彙 fair and square 片 誠實地，不偏不倚地、fair ball 片 界內球、fair enough 片 有道理、fair play 片 公平競爭、fair price 片 公平價格、fair shake 片 公平待遇、fair trade 片 互惠貿易、fair-trade agreement 片 互惠貿易協定、fairish [`fɛrɪʃ] 形 還好的、fair-minded [`fɛr`maɪndɪd] 形 公正的、fairness [`fɛrnɪs] 名 公正，公平、fair-spoken [`fɛr`spokən] 形 懇切的，花言巧語的、fair-weather [`fɛrˌwɛðɚ] 形 晴天的

fairly [`fɛrlɪ] 副 公平地，相當地
▶ I am fairly sure that it will rain this afternoon. 我蠻確定下午會下雨。

fairy [`fɛrɪ] 名 仙女　　片 fairy tale 童話故事

faith [feθ] 名 信念，信仰，信任
▶ I have great faith in the new CEO. 我對新的執行長很有信心。

faithful [`feθfəl] 形 忠誠的
▶ Dogs are faithful animals.
小狗是忠心的動物。

相關衍生字彙 loyal [`lɔɪəl] 形 忠誠的、faithless [`feθlɪs] 形 不忠實的、disloyal [dɪs`lɔɪəl] 形 不忠誠的、unfaithful [ʌn`feθfəl] 形 不忠實的

fake [fek] 動 偽造，佯裝 形 假的，冒充的　　◎ MP3 06-02
▶ The painting is fake, not real.
這幅畫是假的，不是真的。

動詞三態變化 fake - faked - faked

fall [fɔl] 名 動 落下，跌倒
▶ Betty fell off her bicycle and got hurt.
貝蒂從腳踏車上跌下來且受傷了。

動詞三態變化 fall - fell - fallen

fallacy [`fæləsɪ] 名 謬論
▶ It is a fallacy that men are better leaders than women.
男人比女人適合做領導人這是個謬論。

false [fɔls] 形 不正確的，偽造的　　反 true [tru] 形 真實的

相關衍生字彙 falsehood [`fɔlsˌhud] 名 虛假、wrong [rɔŋ] 形 錯誤的、correct [kə`rɛkt] 形 正確的、incorrect [ˌɪnkə`rɛkt] 形 錯誤的、right [raɪt] 形 對的

falter [`fɔltɚ] 動 搖晃，蹣跚，結巴地說話
▶ He faltered in his determination.
他的決心動搖了。

動詞三態變化 falter - faltered - faltered

fame [fem] 名 名聲
▶ Fame and fortune are the things many people hope for.
名與利是很多人渴望的東西。

famed [femd] 形 有名的，著名的　　⑩ famous [`feməs] 形 有名的

familiar [fə`mɪljɚ] 形 熟悉的
片 be familiar with somebody / something 熟悉人／物

familiarity [fəˌmɪlɪ`ærətɪ] 名 熟悉，親近
▶ Familiarity breeds contempt.
（諺語）親密易生侮慢之心。

相關衍生字彙 family [`fæməlɪ] 名 家庭，家人、close [klos] 形 親密的、strange [strendʒ] 形 陌生的、understanding [ˌʌndɚ`stændɪŋ] 名 理解

famine [`fæmɪn] 名 飢荒
▶ Famine often results from crop failure. 飢荒常常是為穀物的欠收。

fan [fæn] 名 電扇，粉絲
▶ To get the tickets to the concert, many fans lined up for hours.
為了買演唱會的票，很多粉絲排隊排好幾個小時。

fanatic [fə`nætɪk] 名 狂熱者
▶ My son is a soccer fanatic.
我兒子是足球狂。

相關衍生字彙 fanatical [fə`nætək!] 形 狂熱的，入迷的、fanatically [fə`nætɪk!ɪ] 副 狂熱地、fanaticism [fə`nætəˌsɪzəm] 名 狂熱，著迷、fanaticize [fə`nætəˌsaɪz] 動 使狂熱

fancy [`fænsɪ] 名 迷戀
▶ I was arranged to have a blind date, but the man didn't take my fancy.
我被安排相親，但是該男士並不吸引我。

相關衍生字彙 fantastic [fæn`tæstɪk] 形 極好的、fantasy [`fæntəsɪ] 名 幻想、imagination [ɪˌmædʒə`neʃən] 名 想像、imagine [ɪ`mædʒɪn] 動 幻想

far [fɑr] 形 遙遠的
▶ How far is it from your place to the station? 從你的住處到車站有多遠？

faraway [`fɑrə`we] 形 遙遠的，遠方的
▶ I wish I could travel to faraway unknown places.
我希望可以到遙遠不知名的地方去旅行。

fare [fɛr] 名 票價，費用
▶ Which is cheaper, bus fares or train fares? 公車和火車的票價，哪一種比較便宜？

farewell [`fɛr`wɛl] 名 告別　　片 a farewell party 惜別餐會
相關衍生字彙 farewell ceremony 片 告別儀式、farewell party 片 告別會，歡送會、farewell present 片 餞別禮物、farewell speech 片 告別演說

farmer [`farmɚ] 名 農夫
▶ He chose to be a farmer taking care of a farm.
他選擇當農夫去照顧農田。

相關衍生字彙 farmland [`farm‚lænd] 名 農田、farmhouse [‚farm‚haus] 名 農舍、farming [`farmɪŋ] 名 農業、agriculture [`ægrɪ‚kʌltʃɚ] 名 農業

fascinating [`fæsn‚etɪŋ] 形 迷人的
▶ The main actress in the film is very fascinating.
這部電影的女主角很迷人。

相關衍生字彙 fascinatingly [`fæsn‚etɪŋlɪ] 副 迷人地、fascinator [`fæsn‚etɚ] 名 迷人的人（或東西）、fascinate [`fæsn‚et] 動 迷住，有吸引力

fascination [‚fæsn`eʃən] 名 魅力，迷戀
▶ Since childhood, he has had a fascination with stamp collection.
他從小時候就很著迷集郵。

fashion [`fæʃən] 名 時尚
MP3 06-03
▶ Her dream is to become a fashion designer.
她的夢想是成為一位時尚設計師。

相關衍生字彙 fashionable [`fæʃənəbl] 形 流行的、old-fashioned [`old`fæʃənd] 形 舊式的、new-fashioned [`nju`fæʃənd] 形 時髦的

fasten [`fæsn̩] 動 繫緊，全神貫注　　片 to fasten the seatbelt 繫安全帶
動詞三態變化 fasten - fastened - fastened

fat [fæt] 名 油脂 形 肥胖的　　反 slender [`slɛndɚ] 形 苗條的

fatal [`fetl̩] 形 致命的，決定性的
▶ The poor clerk made a fatal mistake and was fired.
這名職員犯了致命的錯誤而被開除。

相關衍生字彙 fatalism [`fetl̩‚ɪzəm] 名 宿命論、fatalist [`fetl̩ɪst] 名 宿命論者、fatalistic [‚fetl̩`ɪstɪk] 形 宿命論的、fatality [fə`tælətɪ] 名 （因意外事故的）死亡，宿命，（疾病等）致命、fatally [`fetl̩ɪ] 副 致命地，宿命地、fatalness [`fetl̩nɪs] 名 危險性，致命性

fate [fet] 名 命運
▶ No one can decide your fate, but yourself.
沒有人可以決定你的命運，除了你自己。

相關衍生字彙 fated [`fetɪd] 形 命運已定的、fateful [`fetfəl] 形 重大的，命中註定的

fatigue [fə`tig] 名 動 疲勞
▶ The car accident was caused by the driver's fatigue.
這場車禍是駕駛疲勞所引起的。

相關衍生字彙 fatigued [fə`tigd]形 疲憊的、tired [taɪrd]形 疲勞的、exhausted [ɪg`zɔstɪd]
形 精疲力竭的

動詞三態變化 fatigue - fatigued - fatigued

fault [fɔlt]名 缺點，錯誤
▶ It's not my fault.
這不是我的錯。

相關衍生字彙 faultfinder [`fɔlt͵faɪndɚ]名 吹毛求疵者，故障探測器、
faultfinding [`fɔlt͵faɪndɪŋ]名 挑剔，吹毛求疵 形 愛挑剔的、faultful [`fɔltfəl]
形 毛病很多的、faultily [`fɔltɪlɪ]副 有缺點地，不完美地、faultiness [`fɔltɪnɪs]
名 有缺點，不完美、faultless [`fɔltlɪs]形 無缺點的，完美無缺的、
faultlessly [`fɔltlɪslɪ]副 完美地，無可挑剔地、faulty [`fɔltɪ]
形 有缺點的，不完美的

favor [`fevɚ]名 恩惠 動 擁護　片 to do somebody a favor 幫（某人）一個忙
動詞三態變化 favor - favored - favored

favorable [`fevərəbl]形 贊成的，順利的
▶ The chairman said, " I need your favorable response."
主席說：「我需要你們贊成的回應」。

favorite [`fevərɪt]形 特別喜歡的
▶ The color black is my favorite. 黑色是我的最愛。

fear [fɪr]名 動 害怕，恐懼
▶ The little boy hid himself under the desk, trembling with fear.
小男孩躲在書桌底下，害怕地發抖。

相關衍生字彙 fearful [`fɪrfəl]形 可怕的、fearless [`fɪrlɪs]形 大膽無懼的、fearsome [`fɪrsəm]
形 可怕的、dreadful [`drɛdfəl]形 令人恐懼的

動詞三態變化 fear - feared - feared

feasible [`fizəbl]形 可行的，合理的
▶ I don't think your project is feasible. 我不認為你的計畫可行。

feast [fist]名 盛宴，節目
▶ I dressed up to attend my friend's wedding feast.
我盛裝去參加朋友的婚宴。

相關衍生字彙 feast on 片 盡情欣賞（或享受）、feastful [`fistfəl]形 祝宴的，過節的、
feast-or-famine [`fistɚ`fæmɪn]形 不是極好就是極差的

feat [fit]名 功績，業績　片 a heroic feat 英雄事蹟

feather [ˋfɛðɚ] 名 羽毛

▶ Birds of a feather flock together.
（諺語）物以類聚。

相關衍生字彙 feather plane 片 輕型飛機、feathered [ˋfɛðɚd] 形 有羽毛的，有翅膀的、featheriness [ˋfɛðərɪnɪs] 名 羽毛狀，輕柔、feathering [ˋfɛðərɪŋ] 名（總稱）羽毛，羽狀物、featherlike [ˋfɛðɚˏlaɪk] 形 輕如鴻毛的、featherstitch [ˋfɛðɚˏstɪtʃ] 名 刺繡之羽狀針法 動 以羽狀針法刺繡、feather-veined [ˋfɛðɚˏvend] 形（指樹葉）有羽狀葉脈的、featherweight [ˋfɛðɚˏwet] 名（拳擊）次輕量級選手 形 極輕的、feathery [ˋfɛðərɪ] 形 有羽毛的，輕軟的

feature [fitʃɚ] 名 特色，特徵

▶ The town's main feature is its hot spring.
這小鎮的特色是溫泉。

相關衍生字彙 featured [ˋfitʃɚd] 形 作為號召的，有～面貌的、feature-length [ˋfitʃɚˏlɛŋθ] 形 長篇的、featureless [ˋfitʃɚlɪs] 形 無特色的，平凡的

February [ˋfɛbruˏɛrɪ] 名 二月

▶ It's still cold in February in Taiwan. 在台灣，二月仍然寒冷。

federal [ˋfɛdərəl] 形 聯邦政府的　　片 the federal government 聯邦政府

相關衍生字彙 federalism [ˋfɛdərəˏlɪzəm] 名 聯邦主義、federalist [ˋfɛdərəlɪst] 名 聯邦主義者、federalization [ˏfɛdərəlɪˋzeʃən] 名 同盟，聯邦（化）、federalize [ˋfɛdərəˏlaɪz] 動 使成聯邦、federally [ˋfɛdərəlɪ] 副 聯盟地，聯邦地、federate [ˋfɛdərɪt] 動 結成同盟 形 同盟的，聯邦的、federated [ˋfɛdəˏretɪd] 形 聯邦的，結成同盟的、federation [ˏfɛdəˋreʃən] 名 聯邦政府，聯邦制度、federative [ˋfɛdəˏretɪv] 形 聯邦的，聯合的、federatively [ˋfɛdəˏretɪvlɪ] 副 聯盟地，聯邦地

feeble [fibḷ] 形 虛弱的，無力的

▶ The old man appeared very feeble after the operation.
手術後，這位老人顯得非常虛弱。

相關衍生字彙 week [wik] 形 虛弱的、strong [strɔŋ] 形 強壯的、helpless [ˋhɛlplɪs] 形 無助的、powerful [ˋpauɚfəl] 形 強而有力的

feed [fid] 動 餵（養），飼（養）　　片 to feed on 以～為食

動詞三態變化 feed - fed - fed

feedback [ˋfidˏbæk] 名 回饋

MP3 06-04

▶ We need to know the feedback from the market about our new product.
我們需要知道新產品的市場反應。

相關衍生字彙 feedback control 片 反饋控制、feedback form 片 回饋格式、feedback inhibition 片 反饋抑制、feedback mechanism 片 反饋機制

feel [fil] 動 觸摸，感覺
▶ How do you feel about the movie?
這部電影你覺得如何？
動詞三態變化 feel - felt - felt

feeling [`filɪŋ] 名 感覺，氣氛
▶ It was so cold that I lost feeling in my fingers. 太冷了，所以我的手指失去了感覺。

feign [fen] 動 假裝，捏造
▶ When the teacher tells us boring jokes, we feign interest.
當老師講著無聊的笑話時，我們都佯裝感興趣。
動詞三態變化 feign - feigned - feigned

fellow [`fɛlo] 名 夥伴，同事
▶ Mark is a good fellow. We have known each other more for than 30 years.
馬克是個好夥伴，我們認識超過三十年。
相關衍生字彙 fellowship [`fɛloˌʃɪp] 名 夥伴關係、friendship [`frɛndʃɪp] 名 友誼、
partner [`pɑrtnɚ] 名 夥伴、mate [met] 名 同伴

female [`fimel] 名 女人 形 女（性）的　　反 male [mel] 名 男子 形 男性的

feminine [`fɛmənɪn] 形 女性的，嬌柔的
▶ He is a man who likes to wear feminine clothes.
他是喜歡穿女性化服裝的男人。
相關衍生字彙 femininely [`fɛmənɪnlɪ] 副 女人似地、femininity [ˌfɛmə`nɪnətɪ]
名 女子氣質，嬌柔、feminisation [ˌfɛmənaɪ`zeʃən] 名 女性化、
feminism [`fɛmənɪzəm] 名 爭取女權運動，男女平等主義者、
feminist [`fɛmənɪst] 名 男女平等主義者 形 主張男女平等的、
feminity [fɛ`mɪnətɪ] 名 婦女特質，溫柔、feminize [`fɛməˌnaɪz]
動 （使）女性化

fence [fɛns] 名 柵欄，籬笆　　片 to sit on the fence 中立觀望
相關衍生字彙 fenceless [`fɛnslɪs] 形 沒有圍牆的，不設防的、fence-sitter [`fɛnsˌsɪtɚ]
名 猶豫不決者，中立者、fence-sitting [`fɛnsˌsɪtɪŋ] 名 猶豫不決，中立、
fence-straddler [`fɛnsˌstrædlɚ] 名 兩面討好者、fencer [`fɛnsɚ]
名 劍術家，籬笆匠

ferment [`fɝmɛnt] 名 酵素 動 發酵，醞釀
▶ The first step in making wine is to learn how to ferment.
製酒的第一步得先學會發酵。
動詞三態變化 ferment - fermented - fermented

ferry [`fɛrɪ] 名 渡輪　　片 to take a ferry 搭渡輪

相關衍生字彙 ferry pier 片 渡輪碼頭、ferryboat [`fɛrɪˌbot] 名 渡船、ferryman [`fɛrɪmən] 名 渡船夫，渡船業者

---

fertile [`fɝtl] 形 肥沃的，豐富的

▶ The farm is very fertile and always produces good crops.
這塊農田很肥沃，總是可以種出好的農產品。

相關衍生字彙 fertileness [`fɝtlnɪs] 名 生產力，人口出生率、fertility [fɝ`tɪlətɪ] 名（土地的）肥沃，繁殖力、fertilizer [`fɝtlˌaɪzɚ] 名 肥料、fertilization [ˌfɝtlə`zeʃən] 名 施肥，肥沃、fertilize [`fɝtlˌaɪz] 動 使肥沃，施肥

---

fervent [`fɝvənt] 形 熱情的，強烈的

▶ The candidate expressed thanks to his fervent supporters.
候選人感謝他的熱情支持者。

---

festival [`fɛstəvl] 名 節慶

▶ Of all the festivals, I like Christmas most.
所有節慶中，我最愛聖誕節。

相關衍生字彙 festive [`fɛstɪv] 形 節日的，歡樂的、festive season 片 節期（常指耶誕節這段時間）、festiveness [`fɛstɪvnɪs] 名 歡慶、festivity [fɛs`tɪvətɪ] 名 歡慶，慶典

---

fetch [fɛtʃ] 動 去拿～給

▶ He trains his dog to fetch newspapers for him.
他訓練狗幫他拿報紙。

動詞三態變化 fetch - fetched - fetched

---

feudal [`fjudl] 形 封建的　　片 the feudal system 封建制度

相關衍生字彙 feudalism [`fjudlˌɪzəm] 名 封建制度、feudalist [`fjudlɪst] 名 封建主義者、feudalistic [ˌfjudl`ɪstɪk] 形 封建制度的，封建主義的、feudality [fju`dælətɪ] 名 封建制，封建領地、feudalize [`fjudlˌaɪz] 動 使實行封建制度、feudally [`fjudlɪ] 副 以封建方式

---

fever [`fivɚ] 名 發燒

▶ He got a cold and had a fever.
他感冒而且發燒了。

相關衍生字彙 sneeze [sniz] 動 打噴嚏、sore throat 片 喉嚨痛、running nose 片 流鼻水、cough [kɔf] 名動 咳嗽

---

fiction [`fɪkʃən] 名 小說，虛構的事

▶ The movie is based on a science-fiction novel.
這部電影是根據科幻小說所翻拍的。

相關衍生字彙 fictional [`fɪkʃənl] 形 虛構的，小說的、fictionalize [`fɪkʃənˌaɪz] 動 使小說化，把～編成小說、fictionally [`fɪkʃənlɪ] 副 杜撰地，編造地、fictioneer [ˌfɪkʃə`nɪr] 名（尤指粗製濫造的）小說家、fictioneering [ˌfɪkʃə`nɪrɪŋ]

名（尤指粗製濫造的）小說寫作、fictionist [`fɪkʃənɪst] 名 小說家，創作家、
fictionize [`fɪkʃənaɪz] 動 使小說化，把～編成小說、fictitious [fɪk`tɪʃəs]
形 虛構的，假裝的

---

fickle [`fɪk!] 形 易變的，無常的
▶ The noise outside made me fickle. 外頭的噪音讓我很浮躁。

---

fiddle [`fɪd!] 名 小提琴　　片 to play the fiddle 拉小提琴

相關衍生字彙 fiddleback [`fɪd!,bæk] 名 形似小提琴背的東西 形 形似小提琴的、fiddler [`fɪdlɚ]
名 小提琴手，遊手好閒的人、fiddlestick [`fɪd!,stɪk] 名 提琴弓，（複數）胡說

---

fidelity [fɪ`dɛlətɪ] 名 忠貞
▶ Fidelity plays an important role in a marriage.
忠貞在婚姻裡扮演重要的角色。

相關衍生字彙 loyalty [`lɔɪəltɪ] 名 忠誠、faithfulness [`feθfəlnɪs] 名 忠貞，忠誠、
allegiance [ə`lidʒəns] 名（對國家、事業、個人等的）忠誠，忠貞、fealty [`fiəltɪ]
名（對領主之）效忠，忠誠

---

fidget [`fɪdʒɪt] 名 動 坐立不安，煩燥　　◎ MP3 06-05
▶ Kids in the kindergarten often fidget.
幼稚園的孩子常常坐不住。

動詞三態變化 fidget - fidgeted - fidgeted

---

field [fild] 名 原野，運動場
▶ The teacher said we would have a field trip in the middle of the semester.
老師說期中會有一次校外教學。

相關衍生字彙 field event 片 田賽項目、field hockey 片 路上曲棍球、field hospital 片 戰地醫院、
field investigation 片 田野調查，實地研究、field mouse 片 田鼠、field of force
片 力場、field of honor 片 戰場、field of vision 片 視野、field survey
片 現場調查，實地考察、fielder [`fildɚ] 名（棒球等）外野手、
field-test [`fild,tɛst] 動 對（新產品等）作實地試驗、fieldwork [`fild,wɝk]
名 實地考察工作、fieldworker [`fildwɚkɚ] 名 實地考察工作者

---

fierce [fɪrs] 形 兇猛的，猛烈的
▶ The competition is very fierce.
競爭非常激烈。

相關衍生字彙 violent [`vaɪələnt] 形 暴力的、savage [`sævɪdʒ] 形 兇猛的、cruel [`kruəl]
形 殘忍的、barbarous [`barbərəs] 形 野蠻的

---

fiery [`faɪərɪ] 形 熱烈的，燃燒般的
▶ The fiery sunset is so beautiful.
火紅的夕陽好美。

相關衍生字彙 burning [`bɝnɪŋ] 形 燃燒的，火熱的，緊急的、flaming [`flemɪŋ]
形 灼熱的，火焰般的，激昂的、feverish [`fivərɪʃ] 形 發熱的，狂熱的、
fervent [`fɝvənt] 形 熱烈的，強烈的

fight [faɪt] 名 動 打架，搏鬥
▶ Stop fighting! The teacher is coming!
別再打了！老師來了！

相關衍生字彙 fight it out 片 爭鬥到底、fight off 片 擊退、fight shy of 片 設法避開、
fightable [`faɪtəbl] 形 適合戰鬥的，有戰鬥力的、fightback [`faɪt͵bæk]
名 回擊，反擊、fighter [`faɪtɚ] 名 戰士，戰鬥機、fighting [`faɪtɪŋ] 名 戰鬥，搏鬥
形 戰鬥的，好戰的、fighting drunk 片 酗酒鬧事、fighting game 片 格鬥遊戲

動詞三態變化 fight - fought - fought

---

figurative [`fɪgjərətɪv] 形 象徵的，比喻的 　　片 a figurative sense 象徵的意義

---

figure [`fɪgjɚ] 名 體形，人物，數字
▶ Women always hope to have a lovely figure. 女人總希望有漂亮的體態。

---

filial [`fɪljəl] 形 孝順的，子女的
▶ In Chinese tradition, filial piety is emphasized.
在中國的傳統裡，孝道是備受重視的。

相關衍生字彙 filial piety 片 孝道、filially [`fɪljəlɪ] 副 子女似地，孝順地

---

fill [fɪl] 動 填滿，堵塞 　　片 be filled with 充滿 ～

動詞三態變化 fill - filled - filled

---

film [fɪlm] 名 影片 　　片 the film industry 電影工業

相關衍生字彙 film club 片 電影俱樂部、film cutter 片 剪輯師、film distribution company
片 電影發行公司、film festival 片 電影節、film library 片 電影資料館、film shooting
片 電影拍攝、film society 片 電影協會、film star 片 電影明星、film studio
片 電影製片廠、film trailer 片 電影預告片、film type 片 電影類型、
filmdom [`fɪlmdəm] 名 電影界、filmic [`fɪlmɪk] 形 有薄膜的，電影的、
filmmaker [`fɪlm͵mekɚ] 名 產生影片製作人及導演等、
filmmaking [`fɪlm͵mekɪŋ] 名 電影製作、filmstrip [`fɪlm͵strɪp] 名 幻燈片

---

filter [`fɪltɚ] 名 濾器 動 過濾
▶ The water filter can help make our drinking water clean.
濾水器有助淨化我們的飲用水。

---

final [`faɪnl̩] 名 決賽 形 最後的
▶ We already got through to the final.
我們已經進入決賽了。

相關衍生字彙 finally [`faɪnl̩ɪ] 副 後來、finalize [`faɪnl̩͵aɪz] 動 結束，完成、begin [bɪ`gɪn]
動 開始、beginning [bɪ`gɪnɪŋ] 名 開端

動詞三態變化 filter - -filtered - filtered

---

finance [faɪ`næns] 名 財政，金融
▶ The finance department takes charge of the budget of our company.
財政部門負責處理公司的預算。

financial [faɪˋnænʃəl] 形 財務的，金融的　　片 financial crisis 財政危機

find [faɪnd] 動 找到，發現
▶ I can't find my cellphone. What should I do?
　我找不到我的手機，該怎麼辦？
動詞三態變化 find - found - found

finger [ˋfɪŋɡɚ] 名 手指　　片 index finger 食指
相關衍生字彙 finger food 片 手抓小食品，手指食物、fingerboard [ˋfɪŋɡɚˏbord]
名（提琴等的）指板，（鋼琴等的）鍵盤、fingerbreadth [ˋfɪŋɡɚˏbrɛdθ] 名 指寬、
fingered [ˋfɪŋɡɚd] 形 有指的，指狀的、fingering [ˋfɪŋɡərɪŋ]
名 用指撥弄，手指彈奏、fingernail [ˋfɪŋɡɚˏnel] 名 手指甲、
fingerprint [ˋfɪŋɡɚˏprɪnt] 名 指紋，特徵、fingerstall [ˋfɪŋɡɚˏstɔl]
名（用以保護受傷手指的）指套、fingertip [ˋfɪŋɡɚˏtɪp] 名 指尖

finish [ˋfɪnɪʃ] 動 完成，結束
▶ As long as you finish your homework, you can watch TV.
　只要你完成作業，就可以看電視。
動詞三態變化 finish - finished - finished

finite [ˋfaɪnaɪt] 形 有限的　　同 limit [ˋlɪmɪt] 名 動 限制

fire [faɪr] 名 火　　片 to put out the fire 滅火
相關衍生字彙 fireplace [ˋfaɪrˏples] 名 火爐、firecracker [ˋfaɪrˏkrækɚ] 名 鞭炮、
firefighter [ˋfaɪrˏfaɪtɚ] 名 消防員、fireproof [ˋfaɪrˋpruf] 形 防火的、
firework [ˋfaɪrˏwɝk] 名 煙火

firm [fɝm] 形 牢固的，結實的，堅定的
▶ My goal in life is so firm that I won't give it up easily.
　我人生的目標如此堅定，我不會輕易放棄的。

first [fɝst] 名 第一名 形 第一的 副 首先　　片 first aid 急救　　◎ MP3 06-06

fishery [ˋfɪʃərɪ] 名 水產業
▶ Most of the residents in the area live on the fishery.
　這個區域的居民多靠水產業為生。
相關衍生字彙 fish [fɪʃ] 名 魚、fisherman [ˋfɪʃɚmən] 名 漁夫、fishnet [ˋfɪʃˏnɛt] 名 漁網、
fishy [ˋfɪʃɪ] 形 似魚的，可疑的

fission [ˋfɪʃən] 名 分裂　　片 nuclear fission 核子分裂

fist [fɪst] 名 拳頭　　片 to clench the fist 握緊拳頭

fit [fɪt] 動（衣服）合身 形 適合的，相稱的
▶ The mini skirt fits you so perfectly.
　這件迷你裙太適合你了。
動詞三態變化 fit - fit - fit

F

fitness [`fɪtnɪs] 名 適合，健康
▶ I improved my fitness by exercising in the morning.
我藉著早上運動，來改善健康狀況。
相關衍生字彙 health [hɛlθ] 名 健康、suit [sut] 動 適合、suitable [`sutəb|] 形 合適的、
unfit [ʌn`fɪt] 形 不合適的

fix [fɪks] 動 修理
▶ I didn't know how to fix my bicycle.
我不知如何修理我的腳踏車。
動詞三態變化 fix - fixed - fixed

flame [flem] 名 火焰 動 燃燒
▶ Suddenly, the car burst into flames.
突然間，那台車子就燒了起來。
動詞三態變化 flame - flamed - flamed

flap [flæp] 名 動 拍打 名 混亂　　🔸 a political flap 政治混亂
動詞三態變化 flap - flapped - flapped

flash [flæʃ] 名 動 閃光　　🔸 flash light 閃光燈
動詞三態變化 flash - flashed - flashed

flat [flæt] 形 平坦的，單調的
▶ The surface of the old desk is not flat. 這張舊書桌的表面不平坦。

flatter [`flætɚ] 動 諂媚，奉承
▶ You don't have to flatter me. I won't lend you any money.
不要巴結我，我不會借你錢的。
相關衍生字彙 flatterer [`flætərɚ] 名 奉承者、flattery [`flætərɪ] 名 奉承、please [pliz]
動 取悅、praise [prez] 動 讚美
動詞三態變化 flatter - flattered - flattered

flaunt [flɔnt] 動 炫耀，誇示
▶ He was born in a rich family, but he never flaunts his wealth.
他家境富裕，但從不炫耀。
動詞三態變化 flaunt - flaunted - flaunted

flavor [`flevɚ] 名 味道，香料
▶ I don't like the food with artificial flavor. 我不喜歡添加人工風味的食物。

flee [fli] 動 逃離，消失
▶ People said that the criminal fled to the mountains.
人們說那名罪犯逃入山區了。
動詞三態變化 flee- fled - fled

flesh [flɛʃ] 名 肌肉，果肉　　片 flesh and blood 血肉之軀

flexible [`flɛksəbl] 形 彈性的，柔性的
▶ I am finding a job with flexible working hours. 我在找一份有彈性工時的工作。

flicker [`flɪkɚ] 名 動 閃爍，搖曳
▶ The light of the candle keeps flickering.
　燭光一直閃爍。
動詞三態變化 flicker - flickered - flickered

F

flight [flaɪt] 名 飛行，班次
▶ My flight to Sydney was delayed.
　我前往雪梨的班機延誤了。
相關衍生字彙 fly [flaɪ] 動 飛行、airplane [`ɛr͵plen] 名 飛機、hover [`hʌvɚ] 動 盤旋、
　　　　　　helicopter [`hɛlɪkɑptɚ] 名 直升機

flinch [flɪntʃ] 動 畏懼，退縮
▶ I flinched telling him the bad news.
　我畏縮不敢告訴他這個壞消息。
動詞三態變化 flinch - flinched - flinched

fling [flɪŋ] 動 扔，擲　　　　　　　　　　　　　　　　　　　　 ⊙ MP3 06-07
▶ He flung the dear John letter into the fireplace.
　他把女朋友給他的分手信丟到火爐裡。
動詞三態變化 fling - flung - flung

flippant [`flɪpənt] 形 輕率的，無禮的
▶ I don't like the girl's flippant attitude. 我不喜歡那個女孩的輕率態度。

float [flot] 動 漂浮
▶ A bottle with a letter inside floated along the river.
　有信紙在裡頭的瓶子沿著河流漂浮。
動詞三態變化 float - floated - floated

flock [flɑk] 名（飛禽、牲畜等的）群　　片 a flock of sheep / goats 羊群
相關衍生字彙 herd [hɝd] 名（大型野獸）群、flock [flɑk] 名（鳥禽）群、swarm [swɔrm]
　　　　　　名（昆蟲）群

flood [flʌd] 名 洪水，水災
▶ The heavy rain caused a flood. 豪雨引發水災。

floor [flor] 名 地板，（樓房的）層
▶ I mop the floor every day. 我每天擦地板。

flout [flaʊt] 動 嘲笑，藐視
▶ Many drivers flout the traffic rule and run a red light.
很多駕駛會藐視交通規則而闖紅燈。
動詞三態變化 flout - flouted - flouted

---

flour [flaʊr] 名 麵粉
▶ To make a cake, you need flour, eggs and sugar.
要做蛋糕，你得準備麵粉、雞蛋跟糖。

---

flourish [`flɝɪʃ] 動 繁茂，揮舞
▶ The plants are flourishing with enough sunshine.
植物有足夠的陽光就會長得很茂盛。
相關衍生字彙 grow [gro] 動 成長、develop [dɪ`vɛləp] 動 發展、thrive [θraɪv] 動 繁榮，興旺
動詞三態變化 flourish - flourished - flourished

---

flow [flo] 動 流動，淹沒
▶ The river flows into the ocean.
這條河流流入大海。
動詞三態變化 flow - flowed - flowed

---

flower [`flaʊɚ] 名 花朵　　片 a bouquet of flowers 一束花
相關衍生字彙 bud [bʌd] 名 花苞、petal [`pɛtl] 名 花瓣、rose [roz] 名 玫瑰、lily [`lɪlɪ] 名 百合、
jasmine [`dʒæsmɪn] 名 茉莉

---

flu [flu] 名 流行性感冒
▶ Jack was absent today because he caught flu.
傑克今天缺席因為他得了流行性感冒。

---

fluctuation [ˌflʌktʃu`eʃən] 名 變動，波動
▶ There are often huge fluctuations in temperature in spring.
春天的溫度常有很大的變化。

---

fluency [`fluənsɪ] 名 流暢
▶ She has fluency in at least two foreign languages.
她至少能流暢的說兩種外語。

---

fluent [`fluənt] 形 流暢的，流利的
▶ She is fluent in English.
她的英文很流利。
相關衍生字彙 eloquent [`ɛləkwənt] 形 有說服力的、well-spoken [`wɛl`spokən] 形 善於辭令的、
expressive [ɪk`sprɛsɪv] 形 表情豐富的、fluently [`fluəntlɪ] 副 流利地

---

fluid [`fluɪd] 名 流質，液體 形 流體的
▶ I am not hungry, but I think I should drink some fluid.
我不餓，但我想我應該喝點流質的東西。

flunk [flʌŋk] 名 動（在考試中）失敗，不及格
▶ I am sorry to tell you that you flunked your exam.
很抱歉要告訴你，你沒通過考試。
動詞三態變化 flunk - flunked - flunked

flush [flʌʃ] 動 用水沖洗，臉紅
▶ Remember to flush the toilet after using it.
上完廁所要記得沖水。
動詞三態變化 flush - flushed - flushed

flutter [ˋflʌtɚ] 動 拍翅，飄揚
▶ The bird fluttered its wings and flew away.
小鳥拍拍翅膀飛走了。
動詞三態變化 flutter - fluttered - fluttered

foam [fom] 名 泡沫　　片 shaving foam 刮鬍泡

focus [ˋfokəs] 名 焦點 動 使聚焦　　MP3 06-08
▶ Please focus your attention on the class. 請把注意力集中在課堂上。

foe [fo] 名 敵人，危害物　　同 enemy [ˋɛnəmɪ] 名 敵人

foot [fut] 名 腳 動 步行
▶ This is the first time I set my foot on foreign soil.
這是我第一次踏上外國的土地。
相關衍生字彙 football [ˋfut‚bɔl] 名 美式足球、footstep [ˋfut‚stɛp] 名 步伐、footprint [ˋfut‚prɪnt] 名 足跡、foothold [ˋfut‚hold] 名 立足點
動詞三態變化 foot - footed - footed

fog [fɑg] 名 霧氣
▶ Driving in the heavy fog is very dangerous. 在濃霧中開車是很危險的。

fold [fold] 動 摺疊，交叉
▶ He folded the newspaper and put it on the shelf.
他把報紙摺好放在架子上。
動詞三態變化 fold - folded - folded

foment [foˋmɛnt] 動 煽動，激起
▶ The issue fomented racial tension.
這事件挑起種族間的緊張感。
動詞三態變化 foment - fomented - fomented

folk [fok] 名 親屬 形 民間的　　片 folk songs 民謠

follow [`falo] 動 跟隨，追逐
▶ No matter where I go, my dog follows me.
不論我走到哪，我的小狗都會跟著我。
相關衍生字彙 follower [`falowɚ] 名 追隨者、follow-up [`falo͵ʌp] 名 後續行動、following [`falowɪŋ] 形 下述的
動詞三態變化 follow - followed - followed

fond [fɑnd] 形 喜愛的　　片 be fond of 喜歡～

fondly [`fɑndlɪ] 副 深情地，天真地
▶ Grandma smiled fondly at the newborn baby. 奶奶深情對著新生嬰兒微笑。

food [fud] 名 食物　　片 frozen food 冷凍食品

fool [ful] 名 傻瓜　　片 to make a fool of 愚弄～
相關衍生字彙 foolish [`fulɪʃ] 形 傻的、foolproof [`ful͵pruf] 形 防呆的，極簡單的、silly [`sɪlɪ] 形 愚蠢的、idiot [`ɪdɪət] 名 白癡、idiotic [͵ɪdɪ`ɑtɪk] 形 笨的

forbear [fɔr`bɛr] 動 克制，忍耐
▶ I could not forbear from laughing.
我忍不住笑出來。
動詞三態變化 forbear - forbore - forborne

forbid [fɚ`bɪd] 動 禁止，防礙
▶ Teenagers are forbidden to purchase cigarettes.
青少年被禁止買菸。
動詞三態變化 forbid - forbade / forbad - forbidden / forbid

force [fors] 名 力量 動 迫使　　片 air force 空軍
動詞三態變化 force - forced - forced

forceful [`forsfəl] 形 強而有力的，有說服力的
▶ Sometimes, remarks are more forceful than actions.
有時候，言論比行動來的強而有力。

forecast [`for͵kæst] 動 預測 名 預報
▶ Heavy rain has been forecast for tomorrow.
明天預測會下大雨。
動詞三態變化 forecast - forecast / forecasted - forecast / forecasted

forehead [`for͵hɛd] 名 額頭
▶ I kissed the kid on his forehead. 我在這孩子的額頭上親了一下。

foreign [`fɔrɪn] 形 外國的，陌生的　　片 a foreign language 外國語言
相關衍生字彙 foreigner [`fɔrɪnɚ] 名 外國人、abroad [ə`brɔd] 副 在國外、domestic [də`mɛstɪk] 形 國內的、international [͵ɪntɚ`næʃən!] 形 國際的

foremost [`for͵most] 形 最先的，最重要的
▶ The National Palace Museum is the foremost museum in Taiwan.
　故宮是台灣最重要的博物館。

foresee [for`si] 動 預見，預知　◎ MP3 06-09
▶ We can foresee the difficulties in the future, but we are not afraid.
　我們可預知未來的難處，但是我們不怕。
動詞三態變化 foresee - foresaw - foreseen

foresight [`for͵saɪt] 名 遠見
▶ Our boss has had the foresight to explore the new market.
　我們老闆一直都很有遠見地去擴展新市場。
相關衍生字彙 foreshadow [for`ʃædo] 名 預兆、foreseeable [for`siəbl] 形 可預期的、
　foreleg [`for͵lɛg] 名（昆蟲）前腳、foreman [`formən] 名 領班、
　foretell [for`tɛl] 動 預言

forest [`fɔrɪst] 名 森林　片 tropical rain forest 熱帶雨林

forever [fə`ɛvɚ] 副 永遠
▶ I will love you forever. 我將永遠愛你。

forfeit [`fɔr͵fɪt] 動 喪失
▶ These criminals have forfeited the right to vote.
　這些罪犯喪失投票權利。
動詞三態變化 forfeit - forfeited - forfeited

forget [fɚ`gɛt] 動 忘記
▶ I am sorry, I completely forgot the appointment.
　很抱歉，我完全忘記我們有約。
相關衍生字彙 forgetful [fɚ`gɛtfəl] 形 健忘的、forgettable [fɚ`gɛtəbl] 形 易被忘記的、
　unforgettable [͵ʌnfɚ`gɛtəbl] 形 無法忘記的
動詞三態變化 forget - forgot - forgotten

forgive [fɚ`gɪv] 動 原諒
▶ Please forgive my carelessness.
　請原諒我的粗心。
動詞三態變化 forgive - forgave - forgiven

forgo [fɔr`go] 動 拋棄，對～斷念
▶ Because of the financial problem, I have to forgo the dream of studying abroad.
　因為財務上的問題，我只好放棄出國讀書的夢想。
動詞三態變化 forgo - forwent - forgone

F

fork [fɔrk] 名 叉子
▶ When you eat steak, you need a knife and a fork.
當你吃牛排時，你需要刀子和叉子。

formal [`fɔrml̩] 形 正式的，有條理的
▶ He made a formal announcement about his retirement.
他針對退休一事做了正式的宣布。

相關衍生字彙 formality [fɔr`mælətɪ] 名 正式、formally [`fɔrml̩ɪ] 形 正式地、formalize [`fɔrml̩͵aɪz] 動 使正式、casual [`kæʒʊəl] 形 隨意的

formation [fɔr`meʃən] 名 形成，構成
▶ The cloud formations can tell us something about the sign of weather.
雲層多少可以告訴我們一點天氣的徵兆。

former [`fɔrmɚ] 形 前者的，從前的   片 the former president 前任總統

formidable [`fɔrmɪdəbl̩] 形 棘手的，令人畏懼的
▶ We need an expert to help deal with the formidable task.
我們需要一位專家來協助處理這個棘手的工作。

formula [`fɔrmjələ] 名 慣例，配方，公式
▶ There is no special formula for good grades. You need to study hard.
想要好成績，沒有特殊方法，你必須要認真用功。

forsake [fɚ`sek] 動 拋棄，革除
▶ For her family, she decided to forsake her job.
為了家人，她決定拋棄工作。

相關衍生字彙 stop [stɑp] 動 停止、leave [liv] 動 留下、quit [kwɪt] 動 放棄、cease [sis] 動 終止、halt [hɔlt] 動 停止

動詞三態變化 forsake - forsook - forsaken

fort [fort] 名 要塞，保壘
▶ The ancient military fort is preserved very well.
這個古代的軍事要塞被保存得很好。

forthwith [forθ`wɪθ] 副 立即，馬上    同 immediately [ɪ`midɪɪtlɪ] 副 即刻，馬上

forthcoming [͵forθ`kʌmɪŋ] 形 即將到來的
▶ The forthcoming election makes the society a little unstable.
這場即將到來的選舉讓社會有點動蕩。

fortify [`fortə͵faɪ] 動 增強
▶ I fortify myself with a hearty breakfast.
我以豐盛的早餐來增強體力。

相關衍生字彙 strengthen [`strɛŋθən] 動 增強，鞏固、reinforce [͵riɪn`fɔrs] 動 加強、intensify [ɪn`tɛnsə͵faɪ] 動 增強、weaken [`wikən] 動 削弱

動詞三態變化 fortify - fortified - fortified

fortnight [`fɔrt͵naɪt] 名 兩周，十四天
▶ Every employee can take three days off once a fortnight.
員工可以兩周休三天。

fortress [`fɔrtrɪs] 名 要塞，保壘　　同 fort [fort] 名 要塞，保壘　　◎ MP3 06-10

fortunate [`fɔrtʃənɪt] 形 幸運的，僥倖的
▶ How fortunate I am! I didn't get hurt in the accident.
多幸運啊！我在意外事件中沒有受傷。
相關衍生字彙 fortunately [`fɔrtʃənɪtlɪ] 副 幸運地、fortune [`fɔrtʃən] 名 財富、
fortune-teller [`fɔrtʃən͵tɛlɚ] 名 算命師

forum [`forəm] 名 討論會，論壇
▶ There is a forum on globalization this afternoon.
今天下午有場針對全球化的研討會。

forward [`fɔrwɚd] 副 向前，今後 形 前面的　　片 to look forward to 期待

fossil [`fɑsḷ] 名 化石，頑固不化的人
▶ He is a fossil and not willing to accept new ideas.
他是個老頑固，不肯接受新觀念。

foster [`fɔstɚ] 動 養育，培養
▶ To foster a child is not an easy job.
養育一個孩子，不是一件簡單的事。
動詞三態變化 foster - fostered - fostered

foul [faʊl] 形 骯髒的，邪惡的，（天氣）惡劣的
▶ The small zoo seems foul. 這座小動物園好像髒髒的。

found [faʊnd] 動 建立，創辦
▶ The foundation was founded by a successful scientist.
這個基金會是由一位成功的科學家所建立的。
相關衍生字彙 foundation [faʊn`deʃən] 名 基礎、founder [`faʊndɚ] 名 建立者、
founding [`faʊndɪŋ] 形 創辦的、well-founded [`wɛl`faʊndɪd] 形 理由充足的
動詞三態變化 found - founded - founded

fountain [`faʊntɪn] 名 噴泉
▶ Many visitors make a wish by throwing a coin into the fountain.
很多遊客將硬幣投入噴泉來許願。

fowl [faʊl] 名 家禽
▶ Chickens and ducks are fowls. 雞和鴨都是禽類。

fraction [`frækʃən] 名 片段，小部分，分數　　片 a small fraction of 一小部分

fracture [`fræktʃɚ] 名 動 斷裂 名 骨折
片 a simple / compound fracture 單純性／複雜性骨折
動詞三態變化 fracture - fractured - fractured

fragile [`frædʒəl] 形 易碎的
▶ The china vase is very fragile. 那個瓷器花瓶非常易碎。

fragment [`frægmənt] 名 碎片
▶ The earthquake made the glass of the window broken into fragments.
地震讓窗戶玻璃破成碎片。

fragrance [`fregrəns] 名 芬芳，香味
▶ The room is full of the fragrance of roses.
屋內滿是玫瑰芬芳味道。
相關衍生字彙 fragrantly [`fregrəntlɪ] 副 芬芳地、fragrant [`fregrənt] 形 芳香的、
perfumed [pɚ`fjumd] 形 芬芳的、odor [`odɚ] 名 氣味

frail [frel] 形 身體虛弱的，意志薄弱的
▶ What we saw was a frail old man sitting by the door.
我們看見的是一位虛弱的老人坐在門邊。

frame [frem] 名 骨架，框架，結構　　片 a painting frame 畫框

framework [`frem͵wɝk] 名 架構，組織
▶ The framework of the novel is based on the writer's childhood.
這本小說的架構是以作者的童年為基礎。

frank [fræŋk] 形 坦白的，真誠的
▶ To be perfectly frank with you, the dress doesn't fit you.
跟你說實話，這件洋裝不適合你。

frantic [`fræntɪk] 形 發狂似的
▶ On hearing her son was hurt, she was frantic with worry.
一聽到她兒子受傷，她擔心得快抓狂了。

fraternal [frə`tɝnl] 形 兄弟的，友好的　　◉ MP3 06-11
▶ How could he betray the fraternal love?
他怎能背叛兄弟之情呢？
相關衍生字彙 fraternity [frə`tɝnətɪ] 名 手足之情、fraternize [`frætɚ͵naɪz] 動 親如兄弟、
brother [`brʌðɚ] 名 兄弟、brotherhood [`brʌðɚ͵hud] 名 兄弟關係

fraud [frɔd] 名 欺騙，詭計
▶ He was charged with election fraud. 他被控選舉舞弊。

freckle [`frɛkl̩] 名 雀斑
▶ She has been annoyed with the freckles on the face.
她一直為臉上的雀斑而苦惱。

freedom [`fridəm] 名 自由　　片 freedom of speech 言論自由

freelance [`fri`læns] 名 自由作家
▶ I prefer to be a freelance, working from home.
我情願在家當自由作家。
相關衍生字彙 free [fri] 形 自由的、freehand [`fri͵hænd] 形 徒手畫的、freely [`frilɪ] 副 自由自在地、freestyle [`fri͵staɪl] 名（游泳）自由式

freeze [friz] 動 冷凍，凝固
▶ Put on your coat, or you will freeze to death.
穿上外套，不然你會凍死。
動詞三態變化 freeze - froze - frozen

freight [fret] 名 貨物，運費
▶ The ship only carries freight. 這艘船只載貨物。

frequency [`frikwənsɪ] 名 頻率，次數
▶ The frequency of terrorist attacks keeps increasing.
恐怖攻擊的頻率不斷地增加。
相關衍生字彙 frequent [`frikwənt] 形 頻繁的、frequently [`frikwəntlɪ] 副 頻繁地、rare [rɛr] 形 鮮少的、often [`ɔfən] 副 經常

fret [frɛt] 動 煩躁，侵蝕
▶ I fret all day long because the weather is so terrible.
天氣很糟，讓我整天都覺得煩躁。
動詞三態變化 fret - fretted - fretted

friction [`frɪkʃən] 名 摩擦，爭執
▶ When you rub two stones together, the friction produces fire.
當你摩擦兩塊石頭，會產生火花。

fridge [frɪdʒ] 名 冰箱
▶ Remember to keep the food in the fridge, or it will spoil soon.
記得把食物放回冰箱，否則容易壞掉。

fresh [frɛʃ] 形 新鮮的，新穎的　　片 fresh water 淡水
相關衍生字彙 freshman [`frɛʃmən] 名 大一新鮮人、freshwater [`frɛʃ͵wɔtɚ] 形 淡水的、freshen [`frɛʃən] 動 變得新鮮、refresh [rɪ`frɛʃ] 動 使清涼

friendly [`frɛndlɪ] 形 友善的　　片 environmentally friendly 對環境無害的

friendship [`frɛndʃɪp] 名 友誼
▶ The friendship between us is invaluable. 我們之間的友誼無價。

fright [fraɪt] 名 驚嚇，恐怖　　片 stage fright 怯場
相關衍生字彙 frighten [`fraɪtn̩] 動 驚恐、frightened [`fraɪtn̩d] 形 受驚的、scared [skɛrd] 形 吃驚的、panic [`pænɪk] 形 恐慌的

fringe [frɪndʒ] 名 邊緣，（頭髮的）瀏海
▶ My parents are living in the northern fringe of our town.
我父母目前住在我們城鎮的北邊。

---

frontier [frʌnˋtɪr] 名 國境，邊疆，領域　　🄟 the frontier of science 科學領域

---

frost [frɑst] 名 霜，嚴寒
▶ Frost did damage to our tea trees.
霜對我們的茶樹造成傷害。

相關衍生字彙 frostbite [ˋfrɔst͵baɪt] 名 凍傷、frosty [ˋfrɔstɪ] 形 霜凍的、ice [aɪs] 名 冰、icy [ˋaɪsɪ] 形 冰冷的、snow [sno] 名 雪、snowy [ˋsnoɪ] 形 下雪的

---

frugal [ˋfrugl̩] 形 節約的，廉價的　　🄟 to live a frugal life 過著節儉的生活

---

fruitful [ˋfrutfəl] 形 多產的，肥沃的　　🄐 fruitless [ˋfrutlɪs] 形 無效果的

---

frustrate [ˋfrʌs͵tret] 動 挫敗，阻撓　　⊙ MP3 **06-12**
▶ Your severe criticism did frustrate me.
你嚴苛的批評真的讓我很受挫。

相關衍生字彙 frustration [͵frʌsˋtreʃən] 名 挫折、frustrated [ˋfrʌstretɪd] 形 感到挫折的、frustrating [ˋfrʌstretɪŋ] 形 令人挫折的、discouragement [dɪsˋkɝɪdʒmənt] 名 沮喪

動詞三態變化 frustrate - frustrated - frustrated

---

fry [fraɪ] 動 油炸
▶ I fried an egg as my breakfast.
我煎蛋當早餐。

動詞三態變化 fry - fried - fried

---

fuel [ˋfjuəl] 名 燃料　　🄟 to add fuel to the fire 火上加油

---

fulfill [fulˋfɪl] 動 執行，滿足，實現
▶ He finally fulfilled his ambition to sail around the world.
他終於實現他的抱負，完成航行世界。

動詞三態變化 fulfill - fulfilled - fulfilled

---

fulfillment [fulˋfɪlmənt] 名 履行，實現，滿足（感）
▶ I found fulfillment in my career. 我在我的工作上找到滿足。

---

full [ful] 形 充滿的，吃飽的　　🄟 be full of 充滿

---

fume [fjum] 名 煙霧
▶ The fumes from cooking in the kitchen may cause lung cancer.
廚房烹煮產生的油煙有可能會造成肺癌。

相關衍生字彙 smoke [smok] 名 菸、mist [mɪst] 名 薄霧、fog [fɑg] 名 霧、haze [hez] 名 霧霾

---

fun [fʌn] 名 娛樂，樂趣　　🄟 make fun of 嘲弄

function [`fʌŋkʃən] 名 功能，職責
▶ The function of the machine is to test your blood pressure precisely.
這台機器的功能是能精準測量你的血壓。

fund [fʌnd] 名 資金，專款，（銀行）存款
▶ The hospital set up a fund to help the poor patients.
醫院設立專款來幫助窮困的病人。

fundamental [ˌfʌndə`mɛnt!] 形 基礎的，十分重要的
▶ You have to make fundamental changes if you want to improve your health.
想改善你的健康，你要做點基本改變。

相關衍生字彙 basic [`besɪk] 形 基本的、essential [ɪ`sɛnʃəl] 形 必要的、necessary [`nɛsəˌsɛrɪ] 形 必需的、primary [`praɪˌmɛrɪ] 首要的，主要的、elementary [ˌɛlə`mɛntərɪ] 形 基本的

funeral [`fjunərəl] 名 喪葬
▶ When will Uncle Joe's funeral be held? 喬叔叔的喪禮何時舉行？

fungus [`fʌŋgəs] 名 菌類植物
▶ Funguses, such as mushrooms, are good for your health.
菌類植物，像是香菇，對你的健康有益。

funnel [`fʌn!] 名 漏斗，（輪船、火車頭等的）煙囪
▶ You can use a funnel to help pour water into the bottle.
你可以用漏斗來幫你把水導入瓶子內。

funny [`fʌnɪ] 形 有趣的，滑稽的
▶ He is good at telling funny jokes. 他擅長說有趣的笑話。

fur [fɝ] 名 （獸類的）軟毛　　片 a fur coat 毛皮大衣

furious [`fjuərɪəs] 形 暴烈的，狂怒的
▶ The storm was so furious that the public transportation system was affected.
這場暴風雨很猛烈，所以大眾運輸系統受到了影響。

furnish [`fɝnɪʃ] 動 供應，裝備
片 to furnish somebody with something 供應某人某物

相關衍生字彙 provide [prə`vaɪd] 動 提供、supply [sə`plaɪ] 動 供應、give [gɪv] 動 給予、offer [`ɔfɚ] 動 供給

動詞三態變化 furnish - furnished - furnished

furniture [`fɝnɪtʃɚ] 名 家具
▶ We bought second-hand furniture because it was cheaper.
我們買二手家具，因為比較便宜。

further [ˋfɝðɚ] 形 更遠的 副 進一步地
▶ With the rain, we didn't go any further with the construction.
因為下雨，所以建設的進度一直沒有再往前進展。

furthermore [ˋfɝðɚˋmor] 副 再者，而且，此外　　　◎ MP3 **06-13**
▶ Reading can kill time. Furthermore, it can increase my knowledge.
閱讀可以消磨時間，此外，它還可以增長知識。

furtive [ˋfɝtɪv] 形 鬼鬼祟祟的，佼猾的
▶ There is something furtive about the new neighbor's behavior.
新鄰居的行為有點鬼鬼祟祟的。

fuss [fʌs] 名 動 忙亂，大驚小怪
▶ Don't make a fuss about such a mistake.
不要為了一個錯誤而大驚小怪的。
動詞三態變化 fuss - fussed - fussed

future [ˋfjutʃɚ] 名 未來，前途
▶ The teacher encourages us to make a plan for the future.
老師鼓勵我們要替未來做規劃。

MEMO

MEMO

G

gaiety ~ gymnastics

Rat
鼠

Ox
牛

Tiger
虎

Rabbit
兔

Dragon
龍

Snake
蛇

G gaiety ~ gateway

★一網打盡 315 個英文單字 ｜ 一網打盡 109 句英語會話句

gaiety [`geətɪ] 名 興高采烈
▶ We all enjoyed the gaiety of the party. 我們都很喜歡派對的歡樂氣氛。

---

gain [gen] 名 動 獲得，增加，得益
▶ I was so glad to gain admission to Harvard University.
我真高興能獲得哈佛大學的入學許可。
動詞三態變化 gain - gained - gained

---

galaxy [`gæləksɪ] 名 銀河　　● the Milky Way 銀河

---

gale [gel] 名 強風
▶ All the trees along the seashore were blown down in the gales.
所有沿岸的樹都被強風吹倒了。
相關衍生字彙 wind [wɪnd] 名 風、breeze [briz] 名 微風、windy [`wɪndɪ] 形 多風的、
storm [stɔrm] 名 暴風雨、windstorm [`wɪnd͵stɔrm] 名 暴風、gust [gʌst]
名 一陣強風

---

gallant [`gælənt] 形 華麗的，英勇的
▶ It was gallant of him to save the drowning boy. 他救起快溺斃的孩子，真英勇。

---

gallery [`gælərɪ] 名 畫廊，美術館
▶ There are many beautiful works of art in the gallery.
這個畫廊有好多漂亮的藝術品。

---

gallop [`gæləp] 動 疾馳
▶ We saw him riding a horse and galloping away.
我們看到他騎著馬疾馳而去。
動詞三態變化 gallop - galloped - galloped

---

gamble [`gæmbl] 名 動 賭博，打賭
▶ His divorce resulted from gambling.
他的離婚起因於賭博。
動詞三態變化 gamble - gambled - gambled

---

game [gem] 名 遊戲，競賽　　● to lose / win a game 輸了／贏得 比賽

---

gang [gæŋ] 名 幫派 動 結夥
▶ He joined a gang. 他加入幫派。

---

gangster [`gæŋstɚ] 名 流氓，歹徒
▶ The gangsters often bully kids.
這群流氓常常霸凌小孩。
相關衍生字彙 mobster [`mɑbstɚ] 名 暴徒、racketeer [͵rækɪt`ɪr] 名 詐騙者、fraud [frɔd]
名 欺騙（行為），騙子、rascal [`ræskl̩] 名 流氓，惡棍

gap [gæp] 名 缺口，間隔，隔閡　　片 the generation gap 代溝

gape [gep] 名 動 目瞪口呆
▶ He gaped at the snake on his table.
　他目瞪口呆地看著桌上的蛇。
動詞三態變化 gape - gaped - gaped

garage [gə`raʒ] 名 車庫　　片 a garage sale 二手拍賣會

garbage [`gɑrbɪdʒ] 名 垃圾
▶ I always take out the garbage after dinner.
　我總是在晚餐後倒垃圾。
相關衍生字彙 trash [træʃ] 名 垃圾、rubbish [`rʌbɪʃ] 名 廢棄物、waste [west] 名 廢（棄）物、
litter [`lɪtɚ] 名 垃圾

garden [`gɑrdn̩] 名 花園
▶ Papa waters our garden early in the morning. 爸爸於清晨在花園澆水。

garland [`gɑrlənd] 名 花環，花冠
▶ We welcome our guests with garlands. 我們用花環歡迎我們的客人。

garment [`gɑrmənt] 名 服裝
▶ At the shopping mall, you can shop for all kinds of garments.
　在這個購物廣場，你可以買到各式各樣的衣服。
相關衍生字彙 suit [sut] 名（一套）衣服，西裝、dress [drɛs] 名 洋裝、gown [gaʊn] 名 女禮服、
uniform [`junəˌfɔrm] 名 制服、jacket [`dʒækɪt] 名 夾克、
windbreaker [`wɪndˌbrekɚ] 名 防風上衣的一種

garrison [`gærɪsn̩] 名 要塞，駐防地 動 駐防
▶ The small town has been a garrison because of its location.
　因為地理位置，這個小鎮一直是個要塞。

gas [gæs] 名 瓦斯　　片 natural gas 天然氣

gash [gæʃ] 名 深長的痂（或傷口）名 動 劃開　　◎ MP3 07-02
▶ He fell down and got a gash on the leg. 他跌倒且大腿上有一道深長的傷口。

gasoline [`gæsəˌlin] 名 汽油　　片 lead-free gasoline 無鉛汽油

gasp [gæsp] 動 倒抽一口氣，喘氣
▶ When he found his lost bicycle, he gasped in surprise.
　當他找到腳踏車時，他驚訝地倒抽一口氣。
動詞三態變化 gasp - gasped - gasped

gateway [ˈgetˏwe] 名 入口處，通道
▶ You can park your car at the gateway in front of my house.
你可以把車子停在我家的入口通道上。

相關衍生字彙 gate [get] 名 大門、gatekeeper [ˈgetˏkipɚ] 名 大門警衛、
gatehouse [ˈgetˏhaus] 名 警衛室、gatecrash [ˈgetˏkræʃ] 動 擅自入場

gather [ˈgæðɚ] 動 聚集、收集
▶ I spent hours gathering information.
我花很多時間在收集資訊。

動詞三態變化 gather - gathered - gathered

gaze [gez] 動 凝視
▶ I stood in front the painting gazing at it for a long time.
我站在這幅畫前凝視了很久。

動詞三態變化 gaze - gazed - gazed

gear [gɪr] 名 齒輪工具，設備
▶ The gear of golf is very heavy. 高爾夫球具很重。

gender [ˈdʒɛndɚ] 名 性別
▶ It's a pity that gender discrimination still exists.
遺憾的是性別歧視仍存在。

general [ˈdʒɛnərəl] 名 將軍 形 一般的，首席的　　片 generally speaking 一般說來
相關衍生字彙 generalize [ˈdʒɛnərəlˏaɪz] 動 推斷、generally [ˈdʒɛnərəlɪ] 副 一般地、
common [ˈkɑmən] 形 一般的、special [ˈspɛʃəl] 形 特別的

generate [ˈdʒɛnəˏret] 動 產生，引起，生育
▶ The invention of computers generates some new jobs.
電腦的發明產生一些新的工作。

動詞三態變化 generate - generated - generated

generation [ˏdʒɛnəˈreʃən] 名 世代
▶ The young generation is familiar with the digital world.
年輕的世代對數位世界很熟悉。

generosity [ˏdʒɛnəˈrɑsətɪ] 名 慷慨
▶ His generosity makes himself popular with his friends.
他的慷慨讓他很受朋友的歡迎。

相關衍生字彙 generous [ˈdʒɛnərəs] 形 慷慨的、ungenerous [ʌnˈdʒɛnərəs] 形 吝嗇的、
stingy [ˈstɪndʒɪ] 形 小氣的、miserly [ˈmaɪzɚlɪ] 形 貪婪的

genesis [ˈdʒɛnəsɪs] 名 起源　　同 origin [ˈɔrədʒɪn] 名 起源

genial [`dʒinjəl] 形 友好的，適宜的
▶ The teacher is not only experienced but also genial.
　老師不僅有經驗而且還很親切。

genius [`dʒinjəs] 名 天才
▶ You must be a genius to solve such a difficult problem.
　你一定是個天才，能解決如此困難的問題。

genteel [dʒɛn`til] 形 有教養的
▶ My grandmother is a genteel lady. 我奶奶是位優雅的女士。

gentle [`dʒɛntl] 形 溫和的
▶ He always wears a gentle smile on his face.
　他總是臉上掛著溫和的笑容。
相關衍生字彙 gentleman [`dʒɛntlmən] 名 紳士、gently [`dʒɛntlɪ] 副 溫和地、tender [`tɛndɚ] 形 溫柔的、serious [`sɪrɪəs] 形 嚴肅的

genuine [`dʒɛnjuɪn] 形 真正的，純血統的
▶ The price of a genuine drawing is much higher than you can imagine.
　真跡畫作的價錢，比你想像的高很多。

germ [dʒɝm] 名 細菌，微生物
▶ Cockroaches spread germs. 蟑螂會傳播細菌。

geography [`dʒɪ`agrəfɪ] 名 地勢，地理學
▶ While studying in university, his major is geography.
　他在大學的主修是地理。
相關衍生字彙 geographic [dʒɪə`græfɪk] 形 地理學的、geographer [dʒɪ`agrəfɚ] 名 地理學家、geology [dʒɪ`alədʒɪ] 名 地質學、geometry [dʒɪ`amətrɪ] 名 幾何學

germinate [`dʒɝmə͵net] 動 發芽，成長　　ⓞ MP3 07-03
▶ The seed only germinate in spring.
　這種子只在春天發芽。
動詞三態變化 germinate - germinated - germinated

gesture [`dʒɛstʃɚ] 名 手勢，姿勢　　片 to make a gesture 做手勢

ghastly [`gæstlɪ] 形 可怕的，極壞的
▶ I don't want to read the ghastly details of the murder in the newspaper.
　我不想讀報紙裡命案的可怕細節。
相關衍生字彙 terrible [`tɛrəbl] 形 可怕的，極糟糕的、horrible [`hɔrəbl] 形 可怕的、awful [`ɔful] 形 嚇人的、dread [drɛd] 形 令人畏懼的

ghost [gost] 名 鬼
▶ I don't believe in ghosts. 我不相信有鬼。

giant [`dʒaɪənt] 名 巨人
▶ McDonald's one of the fast-food giants. 麥當勞是速食業的巨人之一。

---

gift [gɪft] 名 禮物　　片 a birthday gift 生日禮物

---

gigantic [dʒaɪ`gæntɪk] 形 巨人的，龐大的
▶ The little boy has gigantic strength. 小男孩有著巨人般的力氣。

---

giggle [`gɪgl̩] 名 動 咯咯地笑　　片 a silly giggle 傻笑
動詞三態變化 giggle - giggled - giggled

---

gimmick [`gɪmɪk] 名 花招，竅門
▶ "Buy one, get one free" is an advertising gimmick.
「買一送一」是一種廣告噱頭。

---

girl [gɝl] 名 女孩　　反 boy [bɔɪ] 名 男孩
相關衍生字彙 girlfriend [`gɝl̩frɛnd] 名 女朋友、girlhood [`gɝlhʊd] 名 女孩時期、
girlish [`gɝlɪʃ] 形 女孩的、boyfriend [`bɔɪfrɛnd] 名 男朋友、boyish [`bɔɪʃ]
形 男孩的、boyhood [`bɔɪhʊd] 名 男孩時期

---

girth [gɝθ] 名 周長
▶ The old tree in the national park must be more than three meters in girth.
國家公園裡的這棵老樹圍長一定超過三公尺。

---

give [gɪv] 動 給　　片 to give up 放棄
動詞三態變化 give - gave - given

---

given [`gɪvən] 介 考慮到
▶ Given the location, the price of the house is reasonable.
如果把地理位置考慮進來，這房子的價錢算合理。

---

glacial [`gleʃəl] 形 冰河的，冷淡的　　片 a glacial period 冰河時期

---

glacier [`gleʃɚ] 名 冰河
▶ With the global warming, glaciers in the world are disappearing.
隨著全球暖化，世上的冰河正在消失中。

---

glad [glæd] 形 高興的，樂意的
▶ I am so glad to meet you.
真高興見到你。
相關衍生字彙 happy [`hæpɪ] 形 （感到）高興的、pleased [plizd] 形 高興的、joyous [`dʒɔɪəs]
形 快樂的、merry [`mɛrɪ] 形 愉快的、joyful [`dʒɔɪfəl] 形 充滿喜悅的

---

glamour [`glæmɚ] 名 魅力 動 迷惑
▶ Few boys can resist the glamour of the pretty girl.
鮮少男孩可以抵抗這位美女的魅力。
動詞三態變化 glamour - glamoured - glamoured

glance [glæns] 名 瞥見
▶ I understood what you meant at a glance. 我看一眼就知道你的意思了。

glare [glɛr] 名 怒視 動 顯眼
▶ Our boss glared at us without telling us the reasons.
老闆沒告訴我們原因就怒視我們。

相關衍生字彙 stare [stɛr] 動 凝視、gaze [gez] 動 凝視，注視、look [luk] 動 觀看、
watch [wɑtʃ] 動 觀看

動詞三態變化 glare - glared - glared

glass [glæs] 名 玻璃，眼鏡　　片 a pair of glasses 一副眼鏡

G

gleam [glim] 名 微光，閃爍　　◎ MP3 07-04
▶ I saw a faint gleam in her room. 我看見她房裡有微光。

glee [gli] 名 歡樂，重唱曲
▶ We danced and sang songs with glee. 我們歡樂地唱歌跳舞。

glide [glaɪd] 名 動 滑行，滑翔
▶ We saw a glider gliding above the hill.
我們看到一架滑翔機飛過山丘上方。

動詞三態變化 glide - glided - glided

glimpse [glɪmps] 名 動 瞥見　　片 to catch a glimpse of 瞥見
動詞三態變化 glimpse - glimpsed - glimpsed

glitter [ˋɡlɪtɚ] 動 閃爍
▶ All is not gold that glitters.
（諺語）發光的東西未必是金。

動詞三態變化 glitter - glittered - glittered

global [ˋglobl] 形 全世界的　　片 global warming 全球暖化
相關衍生字彙 globe [glob] 名 球體、earth [ɝθ] 名 地球、world [wɝld] 名 世界、
continent [ˋkɑntənənt] 名 大陸、universe [ˋjunəˏvɝs] 名 宇宙

glove [glʌv] 名 手套
▶ If you feel cold, remember to wear a scarf, a hat and a pair of gloves.
如果你覺得冷，記得圍圍巾、戴帽子和手套。

gloom [glum] 名 黑暗，憂鬱的心情 動 使陰沈
▶ The writer's novels are often full of gloom.
這位作家的小說常充滿著黑暗。

動詞三態變化 gloom - gloomed - gloomed

glorify [`glorə͵faɪ] 動 讚美，美化
▶ The holiday is set aside to glorify the country's father.
這個節日是用以頌揚該國國父。

相關衍生字彙 glorious [`glorɪəs] 形 榮耀的、glory [`glorɪ] 名 榮譽、honor [`ɑnɚ] 動 榮耀、respect [rɪ`spɛkt] 動 尊敬

動詞三態變化 glorify - glorified - glorified

glow [glo] 名 灼熱 動 發光
▶ His face glows with confidence.
他的臉散發著自信的光芒。

動詞三態變化 glow - glowed - glowed

gnaw [nɔ] 動 咬，啃
▶ Look! Your dog is gnawing the toy bone.
瞧！你的狗狗正在咬那根玩具骨頭。

動詞三態變化 gnaw - gnawed - gnawed

goal [gol] 名 目標，終點　　片 to achieve / reach a goal 達到目的

gold [gold] 名 金色 形 金色的　　片 a gold ring 金戒指
相關衍生字彙 golden [`goldn] 形 金色的、goldfish [`gold͵fɪʃ] 名 金魚、goldsmith [`gold͵smɪθ] 名 金匠、goldmine [`goldmaɪn] 名 金礦

goose [gus] 名 鵝
▶ In general, geese are larger than ducks. 一般說來，鵝比鴨子大。

gorge [gɔrdʒ] 名 峽谷 動 狼吞虎嚥
▶ If you keep gorging yourself on chocolate, you will gain weight.
你再繼續大吃巧克力，你會變胖。

動詞三態變化 gorge - gorged - gorged

gorgeous [`gɔrdʒəs] 形 華麗的，燦爛的
▶ What a gorgeous mountain! 多麼壯麗的山景！

gorilla [gə`rɪlə] 名 大猩猩
▶ According to research, gorillas are very clever. 根據研究，大猩猩很聰明。

goodness [`gudnɪs] 名 善良，仁慈
▶ Mother Teresa's goodness is admired by people all over the world.
德雷莎修女的善良是普世讚美的。

相關衍生字彙 goodwill [`gud`wɪl] 名 善意、good-hearted [`gud`hɑrtɪd] 形 仁慈的、good-looking [`gud`lukɪŋ] 形 好看的、goodly [`gudlɪ] 形 討人喜歡的

gospel [`gɑspḷ] 名 福音，教義　　片 to preach the gospel 傳播福音

gossip [`gɑsəp] 名 流言蜚語 動 閒聊
▶ I don't like to gossip about others' private lives.
我不喜歡八卦別人的私生活。
動詞三態變化 gossip - gossiped - gossiped

Gothic [`gɑθɪk] 形 哥德式的　片 Gothic architecture 哥德式建築　◎ MP3 **07-05**

govern [`gʌvɚn] 動 管理，統治，支配
▶ Do you know which party is governing the country?
你知道哪一個政黨在治理這個國家嗎？
相關衍生字彙 government [`gʌvɚnmənt] 名 政府、governor [`gʌvɚnɚ] 名 管理者、
manage [`mænɪdʒ] 動 管理、rule [rul] 動 統治
動詞三態變化 govern - governed - governed

G

gown [gaʊn] 名 (婦女穿的) 長禮服，長袍
▶ The pretty woman in a black gown is Mark's wife.
穿著黑色長禮服的美麗婦人是馬克的太太。

grab [græb] 名 動 抓取，攫取
▶ I grabbed the kid's arm to stop him from rolling down the stairs.
我抓住孩子的手臂，以免他滾下樓梯。
動詞三態變化 grab - grabbed - grabbed

gracious [`greʃəs] 形 親切的，優美的
▶ I can't forget her gracious smile.
我忘不了她親切的笑容。
相關衍生字彙 grace [gres] 名 優雅、graceful [`gresfəl] 形 優雅的、elegant [`ɛləgənt]
形 優美的、tasteful [`testfəl] 形 有品味的

grade [gred] 名 成績，等級，階段
▶ Mary studies very hard and always gets good grades.
瑪莉很用功並總是拿到好成績。

gradually [`grædʒʊəlɪ] 副 漸漸地
▶ Gradually, I realized what true love is. 漸漸地，我瞭解什麼是真愛。

graduate [`grædʒʊ͵et] 動 畢業
▶ You must be proud of your son, who will graduate from the Harvard
University.
你一定很以兒子為榮，他馬上就要從哈佛畢業了。
動詞三態變化 graduate - graduated - graduated

graduation [͵grædʒʊ`eʃən] 名 畢業　片 a graduation ceremony 畢業典禮

grain [gren] 名 穀類
▶ Don't waste any grain of rice. 不要浪費任何米粒。

grammatical [grə`mætɪkḷ] 形 文法的
▶ My English teacher helps correct the grammatical errors in my composition.
　我的英文老師幫忙更正我作文裡的文法錯誤。

- -

grandeur [`grændʒɚ] 名 宏偉，壯觀
▶ I was touched by the grandeur of the great architecture.
　這偉大建築物的雄偉感動了我。
　相關衍生字彙 grand [grænd] 形 雄偉的、grandiose [`grændɪos] 形 宏偉的、
　　　　　　magnificent [mæg`nɪfəsənt] 形 壯麗的、gorgeous [`gɔrdʒəs] 形 華麗的

- -

granite [`grænɪt] 名 花崗岩
▶ The statue is made of granite. 這座雕像是花崗岩雕成的。

- -

grant [grænt] 名 補助金，獎學金 名 動 同意，給予
　片 to take somebody / something for granted 把某人／某物視為理所當然
　動詞三態變化 grant - granted - granted

- -

grape [grep] 名 葡萄　　片 a bunch of grape 一串葡萄

- -

grass [græs] 名 草地
▶ There is a vast expanse of green grass in back of my house.
　我家後面有一大片的綠草地。
　相關衍生字彙 grasshopper [`græs͵hɑpɚ] 名 蚱蜢、grassland [`græs͵lænd] 名 草原、
　　　　　　lawn [lɔn] 名 草坪、grassy [`græsɪ] 形 長滿草的

- -

graph [græf] 名 曲線圖
▶ The graph shows clearly the number of both genders in the workplace over the last five years.
　這張圖表清楚顯現過去五年職場上的性別數字。

- -

grasp [græsp] 名 動 抓牢，緊握
▶ He suddenly grasped me by the arm.
　他突然抓住我的手臂。
　動詞三態變化 grasp - grasped - grasped

- -

grateful [`gretfəl] 形 感激的
▶ I am so grateful for your goodness.
　我非常感謝你的善意。
　相關衍生字彙 gratify [`grætə͵faɪ] 動 使滿意、gratitude [`grætə͵tjud] 名 感謝、
　　　　　　appreciate [ə`priʃɪ͵et] 動 感激、thankful [`θæŋkfəl] 形 感謝的

- -

gratuitous [grə`tjuətəs] 形 無端的，無償的
▶ There are too many gratuitous dirty words in that movie.
　那部電影裡面有很多不必要的髒話。

grave [grev] 名 墓穴　　　　　　　　　　　　　　🎧 MP3 07-06
▶ It's one of our traditions to visit our ancestors' graves once a year.
一年去掃祖先的墓一次，是我們的傳統之一。

gravity [`grævətɪ] 名 地心引力，重力　　🄟 the law of gravity 萬有引力定律

gray [gre] 名 灰色 形 灰色的　　🄟 gray hair 白頭髮

grease [gris] 名 油脂
▶ I made my boots shiny with grease. 我用點油脂讓靴子油亮。

great [gret] 形 非常的，極好的，巨大的　　🄟 a great deal of 很多～
相關衍生字彙 greatly [`gretlɪ] 副 極大地、greater [`gretɚ] 名 偉人、greatness [`gretnɪs]
名 偉大、big [bɪg] 形 大的、many [`mɛnɪ] 形 多的

greed [grid] 名 貪婪
▶ The greed for money is the root of ruin. 貪圖錢財是毀滅的根源。

greet [grit] 動 招呼，問候
▶ When we met at the airport, we greeted each other with a hug.
當我們在機場相遇時，我們彼此擁抱問候。
動詞三態變化 greet - greeted - greeted

greeting [`gritɪŋ] 名 問候，賀詞
▶ He gave me Christmas greetings by sending me a card.
他寄卡片給我，捎來聖誕節的問候。

green [grin] 名 綠色 形 綠色的　　🄟 a green hand 生手
相關衍生字彙 greenhouse [`grin,haʊs] 名 溫室、greenback [`grin,bæk] 名 美鈔、
greenish [`grinɪʃ] 形 淺綠色的、greenery [`grinərɪ] 名 綠色植物

gregarious [grɪ`gɛrɪəs] 形 群居性的，合群的
▶ I am a gregarious person, liking to be with friends.
我是個群居的人，喜歡跟朋友在一起。

grief [grif] 名 悲傷，不幸
▶ The grief of losing my pet dog makes me depressed.
失去寵物狗的悲傷讓我沮喪。
相關衍生字彙 sadness [`sædnɪs] 名 悲傷、sorrow [`saro] 名 悲哀、misery [`mɪzərɪ]
名 痛苦，不幸，悲慘、agony [`ægənɪ] 名 極度痛苦、distress [dɪ`strɛs]
名 悲痛，憂傷、pain [pen] 名 痛苦，疼痛

grill [grɪl] 動（用烤架）烤
▶ I ordered grilled fish as my dinner.
我點了烤魚當晚餐。
動詞三態變化 grill - grilled - grilled

G

grim [grɪm] 形 殘忍的，令人生畏的，糟糕的
▶ If you continue to play computer games, your future will become grim.
如果你繼續這樣玩電動下去，你的前途就堪慮了。

grin [grɪn] 動 露齒而笑
▶ The stranger grinned at me.
那個陌生人對我露齒笑著。
動詞三態變化 grin - grinned - grinned

grind [graɪnd] 動 磨碎，壓榨　　片 to grind coffee 研磨咖啡豆
動詞三態變化 grind - ground - ground

grip [grɪp] 名 緊握，握住　　片 to lose one's grip 掌握不住，無法掌握
相關衍生字彙 hold [hold] 動 握著，抓住、seize [siz] 動 抓住，逮捕、grasp [græsp]
動 抓牢，緊握、clutch [klʌtʃ] 動 抓住，攫取

gripe [graɪp] 動 發牢騷，絞痛　　同 complain [kəm`plen] 動 抱怨
動詞三態變化 gripe - griped - griped

grocery [`grosərɪ] 名 食品雜貨，食品雜貨店
▶ I always shop for the grocery I need on Sunday morning.
我總是在周日早上採購所需的食品雜貨。

grope [grop] 動 摸索，探索
▶ I groped for my car keys in the darkness.
我在黑暗中摸尋我的車鑰匙。
動詞三態變化 grope - groped - groped

gross [gros] 名 總額 形 總的
▶ To buy the house, I spent all my gross income this year.
為了買房子，我花掉今年收入總額。

grotesque [gro`tɛsk] 形 怪誕的，可笑的　　　　　MP3 07-07
▶ The green hat on his head looks very grotesque.
他頭上的綠帽子看起來很好笑。

ground [graʊnd] 名 地面
▶ It snowed the whole night and the ground was covered with snow.
雪下了一夜，地面都被白雪給覆蓋了。
相關衍生字彙 floor [flor] 名 地板，地面、earth [ɝθ] 名 地球，地面、dirt [dɝt] 名 泥，土、
story [`storɪ] 名（建築物的）層，樓

grouchy [`graʊtʃɪ] 形 不平的，愛抱怨的
▶ That is a grouchy experience. 那是一個不愉快的經驗。

group [grup] 名 集體　　片 a group of 一群～

grown-up [ˋgronˏʌp] 名 成人
▶ Since you are a grown-up, you have to take the responsibility.
既然你是成年人了，就要為自己負責。

相關衍生字彙 grow [gro] 動 成長、growth [groθ] 名 成長、adult [əˋdʌlt] 名 成年人、
grown [gron] 形 成熟的

grudge [grʌdʒ] 名 動 忌妒，怨恨
▶ I didn't have a grudge against you.
我對你沒有怨恨。

動詞三態變化 grudge - grudged - grudged

G

grumble [ˋgrʌmbḷ] 名 怨言 動 發牢騷
▶ I am tired of your constant grumbling.
我厭倦你的不斷他抱怨。

動詞三態變化 grumble - grumbled - grumbled

guarantee [ˏgærənˋti] 名 保證書 動 擔保
▶ He guaranteed me no more cheating.
他跟我保證不再欺騙。

動詞三態變化 guarantee - guaranteed - guaranteed

guard [gɑrd] 名 管理員 動 保衛　　 片 a security guard 警衛
動詞三態變化 guard - guarded - guarded

guardian [ˋgɑrdɪən] 名 監護人
▶ Since her parents died, her uncle has been her legal guardian.
她父母去世後，叔叔是她的法定監護人。

guess [gɛs] 名 動 猜測，推測
▶ Don't guess my age, please.
請不要猜我的年齡。

動詞三態變化 guess - guessed - guessed

guest [gɛst] 名 賓客
▶ The hotel offers all the guests free breakfast. 飯店提供所有客人免費的早餐。

guide [gaɪd] 名 導遊 動 指導
▶ How kind of you to guide me to the train station!
你人真好，還指引我怎麼到火車站！

相關衍生字彙 guidance [ˋgaɪdns] 名 指導、guideline [ˋgaɪdˏlaɪn] 名 準則、
guidebook [ˋgaɪdˏbuk] 名 旅遊指南

動詞三態變化 guide - guided - guided

guilty [ˋgɪltɪ] 形 有罪的，內疚的
▶ I feel so guilty about breaking your vase. 打破你的花瓶我覺得好內疚。

guise [gaɪz] 名 外觀，偽裝
▶ The policeman entered the bar in the guise of a drug dealer.
警察佯裝是販毒者進入酒吧。

guitar [gɪ`tɑr] 名 吉他　　片 to play the guitar 彈吉他
相關衍生字彙 flute [flut] 名 長笛、saxophone [`sæksə͵fon] 名 薩克斯風、trumpet [`trʌmpɪt]
名 喇叭，小號、violin [͵vaɪə`lɪn] 名 小提琴、cello [`tʃɛlo] 名 大提琴、
drum [drʌm] 名 鼓

gulf [gʌlf] 名 海灣
▶ There will be a firework display along the gulf. 沿著海灣將施放煙火。

gullible [`gʌləbl] 形 易受騙的
▶ Comparatively speaking, housewives are gullible.
相較而言，家庭主婦較容易受騙。

gulp [gʌlp] 動 狼吞虎嚥，大口地飲
▶ Take your time! Don't gulp your breakfast.
慢慢來！你的早餐別吃太大口。
動詞三態變化 gulp - gulped - gulped

gum [gʌm] 名 樹脂　　片 chewing gum 口香糖

gun [gʌn] 名 槍　　　　　　　　　　　　　　　　MP3 07-08
▶ Every policeman is equipped with a gun. 每位警察都配戴槍枝。

gust [gʌst] 名 一陣強風
▶ All the trees along the road were felled by a gust of wind.
路旁的樹都被強風吹倒了。

gym [dʒɪm] 名 健身房，體育館
▶ Kate goes to the gym once a week. 凱特一周去一次健身房。

gymnasium [dʒɪm`nezɪəm] 名 體育館
▶ A class of students are having their physical education in the gymnasium.
有一班的學生正在體育館裡上體育課。

gymnastics [dʒɪm`næstɪks] 名 體操
片 a women's gymnastics team 女子體操隊

MEMO

一網打盡

H

habit ~ hysteria

詞性說明

名 名詞	副 副詞	介 介系詞
動 動詞	形 形容詞	連 連接詞
代 代名詞	助 助動詞	

內文圖示說明

片 片語	反 反義字	同 同義字

一網打盡「英語小知識」│生肖介紹 II ────────────

Horse
馬

Goat
羊

Monkey
猴

Rooster
雞

Dog
狗

Pig
豬

H habit ~ hysteria

★一網打盡 337 個英文單字 ｜ 一網打盡 101 句英語會話句

habit [`hæbɪt] 名 習慣
▶ I make a habit of getting up early. 我養成早起的習慣。

habitat [`hæbə͵tæt] 名 棲息地，產地　　片 a natural habitat 天然棲息地

habitual [hə`bɪtʃʊəl] 形 習慣的　　片 a habitual thief 慣竊

hackneyed [`hæknɪd] 形 陳腐的，平庸的
▶ The plot of the novel is hackneyed, not creative.
這小說的情節很平庸，沒有創新。

相關衍生字彙 cliché [kli`ʃe] 名 陳腔濫調、innovation [͵ɪnə`veʃən] 名 創新、creative [krɪ`etɪv]
形 有創意的、old [old] 形 舊的、new [nju] 形 新的

haggard [`hægə˞d] 形 憔悴的
▶ Being sick, she looks a little haggard. 因為生病，她看起來有點憔悴。

haggle [`hægl̩] 動 討價還價，爭論不休
▶ At the night market, you can haggle over the price of things.
在夜市，你可以討價還價。

動詞三態變化 haggle - haggled - haggled

hail [hel] 動 招呼，為～喝采　　片 to hail a taxi 叫計程車
動詞三態變化 hail - hailed - hailed

hair [hɛr] 名 頭髮，毛髮
▶ You had better have your hair cut before your interview.
面試前，你最好剪一下頭髮。

halfway [`hæf`we] 形 中途的 副 在中途
▶ The student fell asleep halfway through the class.
這學生上課上到一半就睡著了。

相關衍生字彙 half-brother [`hæf͵brʌðə˞] 名 同父異母（或同母異父）的兄弟、half-moon
[`hæf`mun] 名 半月、half-breed [`hæf͵brid] 名 混血兒、halftone [`hæf͵ton]
名（音樂）半音

hall [hɔl] 名 大廳　　片 city hall 市政廳

Halloween [͵hælo`in] 名 萬聖節
▶ Halloween is a happy time for kids to play trick or treat games.
萬聖節是小孩的快樂時光，可以玩不給糖就搗蛋的遊戲。

halt [hɔlt] 名 動 停止，終止
▶ All the activities came to a halt because of the storm.
因為暴風雨，所有的活動都停止了。

動詞三態變化 halt - halted - halted

hamburger [`hæmbɝgɚ] 名 漢堡

▶ I ate a hamburger for lunch.
我吃漢堡當午餐。

相關衍生字彙 ham [hæm] 名 火腿、salad [`sæləd] 名 沙拉、cola [`kolə] 名 可樂、fries [fraɪz] 名 薯條

handicapped [`hændɪ͵kæpt] 形 殘障的　　片 the handicapped 殘障人士

handle [`hændḷ] 名 把手 動 處理

▶ I don't think I can handle the task alone.
我不認為我可以單獨處理這項任務。

動詞三態變化 handle - handled - handled

hand [hænd] 名 手　　片 the hour / minute hand 時針／分針

相關衍生字彙 handbook [`hænd͵bʊk] 名 手冊、handcuff [`hænd͵kʌf] 名 手銬、handful [`hændfəl] 名 一把、handkerchief [`hæŋkɚ͵tʃɪf] 名 手帕、handwriting [`hænd͵raɪtɪŋ] 名 筆跡、handsome [`hænsəm] 形 瀟灑的，帥氣的、handy [`hændɪ] 形 方便的、handshake [`hænd͵ʃek] 名 握手

hang [hæŋ] 動 懸掛　　片 to hang out 在外閒蕩

動詞三態變化 hang - hanged / hung - hanged / hung

haphazard [͵hæp`hæzɚd] 形 隨意的，無計畫的

▶ How can you handle the important files in such a haphazard manner?
你怎麼能這麼雜亂地處理這些重要檔案呢？

happen [`hæpən] 動（偶然）發生

▶ What happened to your computer?
你的電腦怎麼了？

動詞三態變化 happen - happened - happened

happiness [`hæpɪnɪs] 名 幸福，快樂　　片 to seek happiness 追求幸福

相關衍生字彙 happily [`hæpɪlɪ] 副 開心地、happy [`hæpɪ] 形 快樂的、cheerful [`tʃɪrfəl] 形 興高采烈的、glad [glæd] 形 高興的

harbor [`harbɚ] 名 港灣，海港　　片 a fishing harbor 漁港　　○ MP3 08-02

harden [`hardṇ] 動 變硬

▶ The clay hardens soon in the sun.
在太陽下，黏土很快就變硬了。

動詞三態變化 harden - hardened - hardened

hardship [`hardʃɪp] 名 艱難，困苦
▶ He overcame his financial hardship by working day and night.
他日以繼夜的工作克服了他在財務上的困難。

相關衍生字彙 hard [hard] 形 困難的、hardly [`hardlɪ] 副 幾乎不、hardy [`hardɪ] 形 吃苦耐勞的、hardworking [ˌhard`wɜkɪŋ] 形 努力工作的、hardware [`hard͵wɛr] 名 五金器具

harm [harm] 名 動 傷害，損害　　片 to do harm to 對～造成傷害
動詞三態變化 harm - harmed - harmed

harmful [`harmfəl] 形 有害的
▶ Air pollution is harmful to our health. 空氣污染對身體是有害的。

harmonious [har`monɪəs] 形 和諧的
▶ The relationship among all my colleagues is harmonious.
我們同事間的關係很和樂。

harmony [`harmənɪ] 名 和睦，融洽
▶ They sang in harmony and won the praise. 他們唱得好和諧，贏得讚美。

haste [hest] 名 急忙，迅速
▶ More haste, less speed.
（諺語）欲速則不達。

相關衍生字彙 hasten [`hesn̩] 動 加速，催促、hastily [`hestɪlɪ] 副 匆忙地、hasty [`hestɪ] 形 匆忙的、quick [kwɪk] 形 快速的、hurry [`hɜɪ] 動 趕緊

harsh [harʃ] 形 苛刻的，惡劣的
▶ Never be too harsh with children. 千萬不要對孩子太嚴苛。

harvest [`harvɪst] 名 動 收穫
▶ The farmers feel so happy because they have a good harvest this year.
農夫很開心，因為今年大豐收。

動詞三態變化 harvest - harvested - harvested

hatch [hætʃ] 名 動 孵化，策劃
▶ Don't count your chickens before they are hatched.
（諺語）勿打如意算盤。

動詞三態變化 hatch - hatched - hatched

haughty [`hotɪ] 形 傲慢的，自大的
▶ I dislike her haughty manner. 我不喜歡她傲慢的態度。

hatred [`hetrɪd] 名 憎恨，敵意
▶ Don't stir up hatred.
不要挑起仇恨。

相關衍生字彙 hate [het] 動 討厭、hateful [`hetfəl] 形 討厭的、dislike [dɪs`laɪk] 動 不喜歡、despise [dɪ`spaɪz] 動 鄙視

haul [hɔl] 名 動 拖，拉，搬運
▶ The broken boat was hauled out of the lake.
　壞掉的船已經從湖裡被拉出來了。
動詞三態變化 haul - hauled - hauled

haunt [hɔnt] 動 縈繞在～心頭
▶ I am often haunted by the terrible memories.
　那些可怕的回憶經常纏繞著我。
動詞三態變化 haunt - haunted - haunted

havoc [`hævək] 名 浩劫
▶ The 7.9 earthquake wreaked havoc in Nepal.
　這場規模七點九的地震對尼泊爾是場浩劫。

H

hay [he] 名 乾草
▶ Make hay while the sun shines. （諺語）打鐵趁熱。

hazard [`hæzəd] 名 危險
▶ A firefighter's job is full of hazards. 消防員的工作充滿危險。

haze [hez] 名 薄霧
▶ Many cities in China were trapped in a severe haze.
　中國很多城市受困於嚴重的霾害。

headline [`hɛd͵laɪn] 名 標題，頭條新聞　片 the front-page headline 頭版頭條新聞
相關衍生字彙 head [hɛd] 名 頭部、headache [`hɛd͵ek] 名 頭痛、headquarters
　　　　　　 [`hɛd`kwɔrtəz] 名 總部、headlong [`hɛd͵lɔŋ] 副 頭向前地、
　　　　　　 headway [`hɛd͵we] 名 進展

heal [hil] 動 治療，癒合　　　　　　　　　　　　　　　　MP3 08-03
▶ My wound already healed, so I will go back to school soon.
　我的傷口已痊癒，很快就能重返校園。
動詞三態變化 heal - healed - healed

heap [hip] 名 （一）堆，許多 動 堆積
▶ I have a whole heap of work to do by this weekend.
　這周末以前，我有一堆工作要做。
動詞三態變化 heap - heaped - heaped

hear [hɪr] 動 聽見，聽說
▶ When we get older, we may not hear very well.
　當我們年紀漸長，我們可能就無法聽得很清楚。
動詞三態變化 hear - heard - heard

hearing [`hɪrɪŋ] 名 聽力，聽覺　片 impared hearing 聽力受損

health [hɛlθ] 名 健康

相關衍生字彙 healthcare [ˋhɛlθˌkɛr] 名 醫療保健、healthful [ˋhɛlθfəl] 形 有益健康的、
healthy [ˋhɛlθɪ] 形 健康的、sound [saund] 形 健全的

hearsay [ˋhɪrˌse] 名 謠傳 形 傳聞的
▶ The news about his love affair is hearsay. 有關他戀情的消息都是傳聞。

heaven [ˋhɛvən] 名 天堂　　片 for heaven's sake 看在上帝的份上

heart [hɑrt] 名 心臟，內心　　片 from the bottom of one's heart 由衷地
相關衍生字彙 heartbreaking [ˋhɑrtˌbrekɪŋ] 形 (事物) 令人心碎的、heartbroken
[ˋhɑrtˌbrokən] 形 悲傷的、heartily [ˋhɑrtɪlɪ] 副 衷心地、hearty [ˋhɑrtɪ]
形 熱情友好的

heat [hit] 名 熱度，高溫 動 把～加熱
▶ The heat of the summer here is unbearable.
這裡夏天的高溫難以忍受。
動詞三態變化 heat - heated - heated

heavy [ˋhɛvɪ] 形 重的，多的
▶ He is a heavy hitter in politics. 在政治方面，他是一位舉足輕重的人。

hedge [hɛdʒ] 名 防備措施　　片 a safe hedge 安全措施

heed [hid] 名 動 注意，留心
▶ As a student, you should heed the advice of your teacher.
身為學生，你應留意老師給你的忠告。
動詞三態變化 heed - heeded - heeded

heel [hil] 名 腳後跟　　片 high heels 高跟鞋

height [haɪt] 名 高度，海拔
▶ The height of Taipei 101 is more than 1,440 feet.
台北一〇一的高度是一千四百四十多英尺。
相關衍生字彙 altitude [ˋæltəˌtjud] 名 高度，海拔、depth [dɛpθ] 名 深度、stature [ˋstætʃɚ]
名 身高，身材、width [wɪdθ] 名 寬度、extent [ɪkˋstɛnt] 名 廣度，範圍

heir [ɛr] 名 繼承人　　反 heiress [ˋɛrɪs] 名 女繼承人

hell [hɛl] 名 地獄　　反 heaven [ˋhɛvən] 名 天堂

helmet [ˋhɛlmɪt] 名 頭盔，安全帽
▶ In Taiwan, motorcyclists are required to wear helmets while they are riding.
在台灣，摩托車騎士騎車時一定要戴安全帽。

helpful [`hɛlpfəl] 形 有益的，有幫助的
▶ Your suggestion is very helpful.
你的建議很有幫助。
相關衍生字彙 helpless [`hɛlplɪs] 形 無助的、help [hɛlp] 動 幫忙、aid [ed] 名 支援、
assistance [ə`sɪstəns] 名 幫忙

---

hemisphere [`hɛməsˏfɪr] 名 (地球的) 半球
片 the northern / southern hemisphere 北／南半球

---

hen [hɛn] 名 母雞　　反 cock [kɑk] 名 公雞

---

hence [hɛns] 副 因此　　同 therefore [`ðɛrˏfor] 副 因此　　　MP3 08-04

henceforth [ˏhɛs`forθ] 副 今後
▶ Henceforth, my life would be more meaningful.
今後，我的人生會更有意義。

hereditary [hə`rɛdəˏtɛrɪ] 形 世襲的，遺傳的
▶ The noble title is hereditary. 這貴族的頭銜是世襲的。

heredity [hə`rɛdətɪ] 名 遺傳
▶ Heredity plays an important role in a person's health.
遺傳在一個人的健康上扮演重要的角色。
相關衍生字彙 inherit [ɪn`hɛrɪt] 動 繼承（傳統，遺產等）、descend [dɪ`sɛnd]
動 傳下來，來自於、transmit [træns`mɪt] 動 傳達，傳送、gene [dʒin] 名 基因、
genetics [dʒə`nɛtɪks] 名 遺傳學

---

heritage [`hɛrətɪdʒ] 名 遺產
▶ It's a pity that the cultural heritage was totally destroyed in the earthquake.
遺憾的是文化遺產在地震中全被摧毀。

---

hero [`hɪro] 名 英雄　　反 heroine [`hɛroˏɪn] 名 女英雄

hesitate [`hɛzəˏtet] 動 猶豫，躊躇
▶ Don't hesitate, or you will lose the opportunity.
別猶豫，不然會失去機會。
相關衍生字彙 hesitant [`hɛzətənt] 形 猶豫的、hesitation [ˏhɛzə`teʃən] 名 猶豫、
decisive [dɪ`saɪsɪv] 形 果斷的、uncertain [ʌn`sɝtn̩] 形 不確定的
動詞三態變化 hesitate - hesitated - hesitated

---

hibernate [`haɪbɚˏnet] 動 冬眠
▶ Polar bears hibernate in winter.
北極熊會冬眠。
動詞三態變化 hibernate - hibernated - hibernated

---

hideous [`hɪdɪəs] 形 駭人聽聞的
▶ The news of the murder was hideous. 命案的新聞真是駭人聽聞。

highlight [ˋhaɪˏlaɪt] 動 用強光照射，強調
▶ My teacher highlighted my spelling mistakes in red.
老師用紅筆標出我的拼字錯誤。
相關衍生字彙 highway [ˋhaɪˏwe] 名 公路、high-class [ˋhaɪˋklæs] 形 高級的、
highland [ˋhaɪlənd] 名 高地、high-spirited [ˋhaɪˋspɪrɪtɪd] 形 亢奮的
動詞三態變化 highlight - highlighted - highlighted

hijack [ˋhaɪˏdʒæk] 動 劫持
▶ It was reported the airplane might be hijacked by terrorists.
據報導，飛機有可能被恐怖分子劫持了。
動詞三態變化 hijack - hijacked - hijacked

hike [haɪk] 動 健行
▶ Hiking in the mountains make me refreshed.
在山中健行，讓我神清氣爽。
動詞三態變化 hike - hiked - hiked

hilarious [hɪˋlɛrɪəs] 形 極可笑的，熱鬧的
▶ The cartoon is hilarious. No wonder kids like it.
這部卡通超好笑，難怪孩子們會喜歡。

hill [hɪl] 名 山丘　　🄟 over the hill 人老珠黃
相關衍生字彙 hilltop [ˋhɪlˏtɑp] 名 山頂、hillside [ˋhɪlˏsaɪd] 名 山腰，山坡、hilly [ˋhɪlɪ]
形 多山丘的、hillock [ˋhɪlək] 名 山丘

hinder [ˋhɪndɚ] 動 阻礙，妨礙
▶ Her timidity hindered her progress.
她的膽小阻礙了進步。
動詞三態變化 hinder - hindered - hindered

hindrance [ˋhɪndrəns] 名 障礙
▶ The lack of English skill is a hindrance at work.
缺乏英文技能是工作上的阻礙。

hint [hɪnt] 名 動 暗示 動 示意
▶ I don't know the answer. Please give me a hint.
我不知道答案，請給我一個提示。
動詞三態變化 hint - hinted - hinted

historic [hɪsˋtɔrɪk] 形 歷史上著名的
▶ A historic war happened in this area. 這個地方曾發生過歷史上有名的戰爭。

historical [hɪsˋtɔrɪkl̩] 形 歷史的，史學的
▶ Many important historical documents are stored in the library.
很多重要的歷史文件保存在這間圖書館裡。

history [`hɪstərɪ]名 歷史　　片 to make history 創造歷史

相關衍生字彙 historian [hɪs`torɪən]名 歷史學家、geography [`dʒɪ`ɑgrəfɪ]名 地理學、linguistics [lɪŋ`gwɪstɪks]名 語言學、literature [`lɪtərətʃɚ]名 文學、museology [ˌmjuzɪ`alədʒɪ]名 博物館學

---

hit [hɪt]動 打擊，碰撞　　　　　　　　　　　　　⊙ MP3 08-05

▶ He jumped high and hit his head on the ceiling.
　他跳很高，頭撞到了天花板。

動詞三態變化 hit - hit - hit

---

hitchhike [`hɪtʃˌhaɪk]動 搭便車

▶ Girls had better not hitchhike by themselves.
　女孩子最好別自己搭便車。

動詞三態變化 hitchhike - hitchhiked - hitchhiked

---

hive [haɪv]名 蜂巢

▶ The hive is so big that there must be hundreds of bees living inside.
　這蜂巢這麼大，一定有上百隻蜜蜂住在裡頭。

相關衍生字彙 queen [`kwin]名（蜜蜂、螞蟻等的）后、drone [dron]名 雄蜂、worker bees 片 工蜂、nectar [`nɛktɚ]名 花蜜、honey [`hʌnɪ]名 蜂蜜

---

hoarse [hors]形 沙啞的

▶ She got a hoarse voice because of a cold. 她感冒，所以聲音沙啞了。

---

hoax [hoks]名 騙局 動 愚弄　　片 to play a hoax on smebody 愚弄某人

動詞三態變化 hoax - hoaxed - hoaxed

---

hobble [`habl]名 動 跛行 動 蹣跚

▶ The old man hobbled with a stick.
　老人拄著拐杖蹣跚的走著。

動詞三態變化 hobble - hobbled - hobbled

---

hobby [`habɪ]名 嗜好

▶ Photography is one of my hobbies. 攝影是我的嗜好之一。

---

hoist [hɔɪst]動 吊起，升起　　片 to hoist a flag 升起旗子

動詞三態變化 hoist - hoisted - hoisted

---

hold [hold]動 握著，持有，舉行

▶ The couple took a walk holding hands.
　這對夫妻手牽著手散步。

相關衍生字彙 holder [`holdɚ]名 持有者、holdout [`holdˌaut]名 抵抗、holding [`holdɪŋ]名 把持，支持、holdup [`holdˌʌp]名 阻塞

動詞三態變化 hold - held - held

---

hole [hol]名 洞　　片 to dig a hole 挖洞

holiday [ˋhɑlə͵de] 名 假期
▶ We spent our holiday in Hawaii. 我們去夏威夷度假。

hollow [ˋhɑlo] 名 洞穴 形 中空的
▶ Having worked hard for days, you have hollow cheeks.
這幾天拼命的工作，你的臉頰都凹陷了。

holy [ˋholɪ] 形 神聖的　　片 a holy task 神聖的工作

homage [ˋhɑmɪdʒ] 名 尊敬，崇敬
▶ We pay homage to the brave firefighters. 我們向英勇的打火弟兄致敬。

homesick [ˋhom͵sɪk] 形 思鄉的
▶ Having studied abroad for a year, I feel more and more homesick.
留學了一年，我愈來愈想家了。
相關衍生字彙 homework [ˋhom͵wɝk] 名 作業、homely [ˋhomlɪ] 形 家庭的、
homeland [ˋhom͵lænd] 名 國土、homeless [ˋhomlɪs] 形 無家可歸的

honest [ˋɑnɪst] 形 誠實的　　片 to be honest 說實話

honesty [ˋɑnɪstɪ] 名 誠實
▶ Honesty is the best policy. （諺語）誠實為上策。

honeymoon [ˋhʌnɪ͵mun] 名 蜜月
▶ Paris is a good place for a honeymoon.
巴黎是度蜜月的好地方。
相關衍生字彙 honey [ˋhʌnɪ] 名 蜂蜜、honeydew [ˋhʌnɪ͵dju] 名 甘露、bee [bi] 名 蜜蜂、
beehive [ˋbihaɪv] 名 蜂窩

honor [ˋɑnɚ] 名 榮耀
▶ May I have the honor of your company? 我有這榮幸邀你同行嗎？

honorable [ˋɑnərəbl] 形 光榮的
▶ It's not honorable to cheat on the exam. 考試作弊是不光榮的。

hook [huk] 名 鉤子　　　　　　　　　　　　　　　　MP3 08-06
▶ I took off my coat and hung it on the hook. 我脫掉外套並將它掛在鉤子上。

hope [hop] 名 希望　　片 to arouse / inspire hope 燃起希望
相關衍生字彙 hopeful [ˋhopfəl] 形 有希望的、hopeless [ˋhoplɪs] 形 沒希望的、wish [wɪʃ]
名 願望、dream [drim] 名 願望

horizon [həˋraɪzn̩] 名 地平線　　片 to broaden somebody's horizon 擴展視野

horizontal [͵harəˋzɑntl̩] 形 水平的　　反 vertical [ˋvɝtɪkl̩] 形 垂直的

horn [hɔrn] 名 角　　片 to blow a horn 吹號角

horrible [ˋhɔrəbl] 形 糟糕的
▶ It's horrible that Mark was fired last week. 糟糕的是，馬克上周被開除了。

horror [ˋhɔrɚ] 名 恐怖　🅟 to cry out in horror 驚恐地喊叫

horse [hɔrs] 名 馬匹　🅟 to eat like a horse 食量很大
相關衍生字彙 horseback [ˋhɔrsˏbæk] 名 馬背、horseshoe [ˋhɔrsˏʃu] 名 馬蹄、
horsepower [ˋhɔrsˏpauɚ] 名 馬力、horsetail [ˋhɔrsˏtel] 名 馬尾

hospitable [ˋhɑspɪtəbl] 形 好客的
▶ Generally speaking, people in Taiwan are very hospitable.
一般説來，台灣人民很好客。

hospital [ˋhɑspɪtl] 名 醫院
▶ She works in a hospital as a nurse. 她在醫院當護士。

hospitality [ˏhɑspɪˋtælətɪ] 名 好客，熱情招待
▶ My homestay parents showed me great hospitality.
我寄宿家庭的父母對我很殷勤招待。

host [host] 名 主人 動 主持
▶ Which country will host the next Olympic Games?
哪個國家將主辦下屆奧運？
動詞三態變化 host - hosted - hosted

hostage [ˋhɑstɪdʒ] 名 人質
▶ The robber seized a kid as a hostage. 搶匪劫持一個孩子當人質。

hostile [ˋhɑstɪl] 形 懷有敵意的
▶ It seems that you are hostile to me. 你似乎對我有敵意。

hostility [hɑsˋtɪlətɪ] 名 敵意
▶ North Korea shows hostility to South Korea. 北韓一直對南韓有敵意。

hotel [hoˋtɛl] 名 飯店　🅟 a five-star hotel 五星級飯店

household [ˋhausˏhold] 名 家庭 形 為人所熟知的
▶ He is a household figure.
他是個家喻戶曉的人物。
相關衍生字彙 house [haus] 名 房子、housekeeper [ˋhausˏkipɚ] 名 管家、
housework [ˋhausˏwɝk] 名 家事、housemaid [ˋhausˏmed] 名 女僕、
houseplant [ˋhausˏplænt] 名 室內植物、housing [ˋhauzɪŋ] 名 住房

hover [ˋhʌvɚ] 動 徘徊，盤旋
▶ An eagle is hovering in the sky.
一隻老鷹在天空中盤旋。
動詞三態變化 hover - hovered - hovered

however [haʊ`ɛvɚ] 副 然而
▶ I felt tired. However, I had to host another meeting.
　我很疲憊。然而，我還有另一個會議要主持。

howl [haʊl] 動 怒吼，嚎啕大哭
▶ The night was so silent that we could hear a wolf howling in the distance.
　夜晚非常安靜，我們都可聽得到遠處的狼嚎。
相關衍生字彙 cry [kraɪ] 動 哭，叫喊、yell [jɛl] 動 叫喊，吼叫（聲）、shout [ʃaʊt] 名 動 呼喊、bawl [bɔl] 動 大喊，大叫、sob [sɑb] 動 啜泣、weep [wip] 動 哭泣，流淚
動詞三態變化 howl - howled - howled

hug [hʌg] 名 動 擁抱　　　　　　　　　　　　　🔊 MP3 08-07
▶ Before my daughter goes to school, I always give her a hug.
　女兒上學前，我都會給她一個擁抱。
動詞三態變化 hug - hug - hug

huge [hjudʒ] 形 巨大的，大量的
▶ Their house is as huge as a castle. 他們的房子就像城堡一樣大。

humanity [hju`mænətɪ] 名 人性
▶ The cruelty of wars is against humanity.
　戰爭的殘忍違反人性。
相關衍生字彙 human [`hjumən] 名 人類、humane [hju`men] 形 人道的，仁慈的、humankind [`hjumən͵kaɪnd] 名 人類、humanism [`hjumən͵ɪzəm] 名 人文主義

humble [`hʌmbl] 形 謙虛的，簡樸的
▶ To our surprise, the rich man lives a humble life.
　讓我們驚訝的是，這位富翁過著簡樸的生活。

humid [`hjumɪd] 形 潮濕的
▶ The summer in Taiwan is very hot and humid. 台灣的夏天又熱又潮濕。

humiliate [hju`mɪlɪ͵et] 動 羞辱，使丟臉
▶ They humiliated the poor boy by laughing at his ragged clothes.
　他們嘲笑那個貧困男孩的破衣服來羞辱他。
動詞三態變化 humiliate - humiliated - humiliated

humility [hju`mɪlətɪ] 名 謙卑
▶ We respect our boss because he always shows humility.
　我們很尊敬老闆，因為他很謙卑。

hungry [`hʌŋgrɪ] 形 飢餓的
▶ After work, we all feel tired and hungry.
　下班後，我們都會覺得又累又餓。
相關衍生字彙 hunger [`hʌŋgɚ] 名 飢餓、starved [stɑrvd] 形 挨餓的、starvation [star`veʃən] 名 飢餓、food [fud] 名 食物

humor [`hjumɚ] 名 幽默　　片 a sense of humor 幽默感

humorous [`hjumərəs] 形 幽默的，詼諧的
▶ He is very humorous and makes his friends happy.
　他非常幽默，常讓他的朋友開心。

hundred [`hʌndrəd] 名 一百 形 很多的　　片 hundreds of 數以百計的

hunt [hʌnt] 動 打獵，追捕
▶ Cats hunt for mice.
　小貓獵捕老鼠。

相關衍生字彙 hunter [`hʌntɚ] 名 獵人、job-hunter [`dʒɑbhʌnt] 名 求職者、hunting [`hʌntɪŋ]
名 獵殺、prey [pre] 名 獵物、game [gem] 名 獵物

動詞三態變化 hunt - hunted - hunted

hurdle [`hɝdl] 名 跨欄賽跑 動 跨（欄）　　片 high / low hurdles 高／低欄

hurl [hɝl] 名 動 猛力投擲　　片 to hurl insults at somebody 狠狠地侮辱某人
動詞三態變化 hurl - hurled - hurled

hurry [`hɝɪ] 名 急忙 動 趕緊
▶ Hurry up, or we will late.
　快點，不然我們會遲到。

動詞三態變化 hurry - hurried - hurried

hurt [hɝt] 名 創傷 動 使受傷
▶ He was badly hurt in that car accident.
　他在車禍裡受重傷。

動詞三態變化 hurt - hurt - hurt

husband [`hʌzbənd] 名 丈夫　　反 wife [waɪf] 名 老婆
相關衍生字彙 spouse [spaʊz] 名 配偶、partner [`pɑrtnɚ] 名 夥伴，拍檔、
girlfriend [`gɝl͵frɛnd] 名 女朋友、boyfriend [`bɔɪ͵frɛnd] 名 男朋友、
fiancee [͵fiən`se] 名 未婚妻、fiance [͵fiən`se] 名 未婚夫

hush [hʌʃ] 名 沉默 動 使安靜
▶ There was a hush in the classroom when the electricity was out.
　當停電時，教室裡突然很安靜。

相關衍生字彙 silent [`saɪlənt] 形 安靜的、silence [`saɪləns] 名 寂靜、noisy [`nɔɪzɪ] 形 吵雜的、
noise [nɔɪz] 名 噪音

動詞三態變化 hush - hushed - hushed

hustle [`hʌsl̩] 名 忙碌 動 催促　　片 hustle and bustle（城市）熙熙攘攘
動詞三態變化 hustle - hustled - hustled

H

hybrid [`haɪbrɪd] 名 混血兒
▶ A mule is a hybrid of a horse and a donkey. 騾子是馬跟驢的混血品種。

hygiene [`haɪdʒin] 名 衛生　　　　　　　　　　　　　　　　◎ MP3 **08-08**
▶ The disease resulted from poor hygiene.
這個疾病起因於很差的衛生情況。

相關衍生字彙 sanitation [ˌsænəˈteʃən] 名 環境衛生、sanitary [`sænəˌtɛrɪ] 形 衛生的、
clean [klin] 形 乾淨的、hygienic [ˌhaɪdʒɪˈɛnɪk] 形 衛生（學）的，保健的

hypocrisy [hɪˈpɑkrəsɪ] 名 虛偽
▶ I got sick of hypocrisy. 我厭惡虛偽。

hypothesis [haɪˈpɑθəsɪs] 名 假說，前提
▶ These are meaningless hypotheses. 這些都是無意義的假設。

hysteria [hɪsˈtɪrɪə] 名 歇斯底里
▶ The angry girl is almost close to hysteria. 那位憤怒的女孩幾乎是歇斯底里。

MEMO

MEMO

I

ice ~ ivy

詞性說明

名 名詞	副 副詞	介 介系詞
動 動詞	形 形容詞	連 連接詞
代 代名詞	助 助動詞	

內文圖示說明

片 片語	反 反義字	同 同義字

一網打盡「英語小知識」│「詢問」他人有沒有空時 ───────

想詢問或邀約他人，可以委婉地詢問對方：

Do you have a minute?
你有空嗎？

Got a minute?
你有空嗎？

Are you busy?
你現在有空嗎？

Can I talk to you for a second?
我可以和你談一會嗎？

May I interrupt you for a couple of seconds?
我可以打擾你一會嗎？

I ice ～ ivy

ice [aɪs] 名 冰 動 冷卻
▶ I would like my juice with some ice, please.
請給我加冰塊的果汁。
相關衍生字彙 iceberg [ˋaɪsˏbɝg] 名 冰山、ice-cold [ˋaɪsˏkold] 形 冰冷的、icebox [ˋaɪsˏbɑks] 名 冰箱、Iceland [ˋaɪslənd] 名（國家）冰島、icy [ˋaɪsɪ] 形 多冰的，冰冷的
動詞三態變化 ice - iced - iced

idea [aɪˋdiə] 名 點子，想法
▶ That's a good idea. 那真是個好主意。

ideal [aɪˋdiəl] 形 理想的，完美的
▶ The girl is ideal for being your wife.
那女孩當你的老婆太理想了。
相關衍生字彙 idealism [aɪˋdiəˏlɪzəm] 名 理想主義、idealize [aɪˋdiəˏaɪz] 動 使理想化、perfect [ˋpɝfɪkt] 形 完美的、flawless [ˋflɔlɪs] 形 無瑕疵的

identical [aɪˋdɛntɪkl̩] 形 相同的
▶ The twin brothers are identical to each other. 這對雙胞胎兄弟長得完全一樣。

identify [aɪˋdɛntəˏfaɪ] 動 認同
▶ I can't identify with the role of the stepmother in the film.
我無法認同影片裡繼母那個角色。
動詞三態變化 identify - identified - identified

identity [aɪˋdɛntətɪ] 名 身分
▶ Do you have any ID card to prove your identity?
你有任何證件能證明你的身分嗎？

idiom [ˋɪdɪəm] 名 慣用語，成語
▶ Every language has its idioms. 每一種語言都有它的慣用語。

idle [ˋaɪdl̩] 形 懶散的，閒置的
▶ My car has stood idle for months. 我的車子已經閒置好幾個月了。

idol [ˋaɪdl̩] 名 偶像
▶ Most teenagers worship idols.
大部分的青少年都會崇拜偶像。
相關衍生字彙 idolize [ˋaɪdl̩ˏaɪz] 動 偶像化、model [ˋmɑdl̩] 名 典範、mentor [ˋmɛntɚ] 名 良師益友

ignite [ɪgˋnaɪt] 動 點燃　　片 to ignite a storm of protest 點燃抗議風暴
動詞三態變化 ignite - ignited - ignited

ignoble [ɪgˋnobḷ] 形 卑鄙的　　反 noble [ˋnobḷ] 形 高貴的

---

ignorance [ˋɪgnərəns] 名 無知
▶ Meaningless words will show your ignorance.
無意義的話語會顯露你的無知。

相關衍生字彙 ignorant [ˋɪgnərənt] 形 無知的、ignore [ɪgˋnor] 動 忽視、
educated [ˋɛdʒʊˌketɪd] 形 有知識的、foolish [ˋfulɪʃ] 形 愚蠢的

---

illegal [ɪˋligḷ] 形 不合法的
▶ It's illegal to sell alcohol to teenagers. 賣酒給青少年是違法的。

---

illegible [ɪˋlɛdʒəbḷ] 形 難以辨認的
▶ The boy's writing is so illegible that I can't understand.
這男孩的字跡難以辨識，我無法瞭解其意思。

---

illiterate [ɪˋlɪtərɪt] 形 不識字的
▶ A high percentage of the elderly in that small town are illiterate.
小鎮的老人很高比例不識字。

---

ill [ɪl] 形 生病的
▶ If you feel ill, you can take a rest.
如果你不舒服，你可以休息一下。

相關衍生字彙 illness [ˋɪlnɪs] 名 疾病、ill-equipped [ˋɪlɪˋkwɪpt] 形 設備不良的、
ill-bred [ˋɪlˋbrɛd] 形 粗魯的，沒教養的、ill-fated [ˋɪlˋfetɪd] 形 不幸的

---

illuminate [ɪˋluməˌnet] 動 照亮
▶ The lobby was illuminated with colorful lights to celebrate Christmas.
用彩色燈飾點亮大廳來慶祝聖誕節。

動詞三態變化 illuminate - illuminated - illuminated

---

illusion [ɪˋljuʒən] 名 幻覺
▶ I often have illusion about my ability to fly. 我常有幻覺我會飛。

---

illustrate [ˋɪləstret] 動 闡明
▶ The professor illustrated his theory with many examples.
教授用很多例子闡明他的理論。

相關衍生字彙 illustration [ˌɪlʌsˋtreʃən] 名 實例，說明、illustrator [ˋɪləsˌtretɚ] 名 插畫家、
cartoonist [kɑrˋtunɪst] 名 漫畫家、novelist [ˋnɑvḷɪst] 名 小說家

動詞三態變化 illustrate - illustrated - illustrated

---

illustrious [ɪˋlʌstrɪə] 形 著名的
▶ He graduated from an illustrious university. 他畢業於著名的大學。

---

image [ˋɪmɪdʒ] 名 像，形象　　　　　　　　　　　 MP3 09-02
▶ The advertisement is to improve the image of the politician.
這則廣告是用來提升該政治人物的形象。

I

imaginary [ɪˋmædʒəˌnɛrɪ] 形 虛構的，想像的

▶ The novel is set in an imaginary planet.
這小說是以一個虛構星球做背景。

相關衍生字彙 imaginable [ɪˋmædʒɪnəbl] 形 可以想像的、imagination [ɪˌmædʒəˋneʃən] 名 想像力、imaginative [ɪˋmædʒəˌnetɪv] 形 有想像力的、imagine [ɪˋmædʒɪn] 動 想像

imbue [ɪmˋbju] 動 灌輸，使充滿

▶ The song is imbued with animals' voices.
這首歌有好多動物的聲音。

動詞三態變化 imbue - imbued - imbued

imitate [ˋɪməˌtet] 動 模仿

▶ Papa imitated a dog's barking to make my sister laugh.
爸爸模仿狗吠逗妹妹笑。

動詞三態變化 imitate - imitated - imitated

imitation [ˌɪməˋteʃən] 名 模仿　　片 to do a imitation of 模仿～

immature [ˌɪməˋtjur] 形 不成熟的　　反 mature [məˋtjur] 形 成熟的

immediate [ɪˋmidɪɪt] 形 立刻的

▶ You don't have to make an immediate response.
你不必立刻反應。

相關衍生字彙 immediately [ɪˋmidɪɪtlɪ] 副 立刻，馬上、instantly [ˋɪnstəntlɪ] 副 立刻，馬上、promptly [ˋprɑmptlɪ] 副 立刻、soon [sun] 副 很快地

immemorial [ˌɪməˋmorɪəl] 形 遠古的　　片 from time immemorial 自古以來

immense [ɪˋmɛns] 形 巨大的

▶ It's hard to imagine his immense wealth. 很難想像他的龐大財富。

immerse [ɪˋmɝs] 動 使深陷於

▶ His father was immersed in gambling.
他爸爸沉溺於賭博。

相關衍生字彙 dip [dɪp] 動 浸泡、sink [sɪŋk] 動（船等）下沉、submerge [səbˋmɝdʒ] 動 把～浸入水中，淹沒、emerge [ɪˋmɝdʒ] 動 浮現，出現

動詞三態變化 immerse - immersed - immersed

immigrant [ˋɪməgrənt] 名（移入）移民

反 emigration [ˌɛməˋgreʃən] 名（移出）移民

immigration [ˌɪməˋgreʃən] 名（移入）移民

反 migration [maɪˋgreʃən] 名（移出）移民

immoral [ɪˋmɔrəl] 形 不道德的

▶ Cheating is immoral behavior. 欺騙是不道德的行為。

immortal [ɪ`mɔrtl] 形 不朽的　🔑 an immortal soul 不朽的靈魂

---

immortalize [ɪ`mɔrtl͵aɪz] 動 使不朽
▶ An excellent actor can immortalize a role in a movie.
好演員能讓電影角色不朽。

動詞三態變化 immortalize - immortalized - immortalized

---

immune [ɪ`mjun] 形 免疫的　🔑 the immune system 免疫系統

---

impact [`ɪmpækt] 名 衝擊 動 對～產生影響
▶ The policy will make an impact on education.
這個政策將對教育造成很大的衝擊。

相關衍生字彙 influence [`ɪnfluəns] 名 影響，作用、affect [ə`fɛkt] 動 影響、effect [ɪ`fɛkt] 名 結果，效果、attack [ə`tæk] 動 抨擊、change [tʃendʒ] 名 變化 動 (使) 改變

動詞三態變化 impact - impacted - impacted

---

impairment [ɪm`pɛrmənt] 名 損傷
▶ The poor girl suffers from hearing impairment. 這個可憐的女孩聽力受損。

---

impart [ɪm`pɑrt] 動 傳授，傳達
▶ I feel so sorry to impart the bad news.
很遺憾我得傳達這個壞消息。

動詞三態變化 impart - imparted - imparted

---

impartial [ɪm`pɑrʃəl] 形 公正的，無偏見的
▶ A judge should be impartial.
法官必須公正。

相關衍生字彙 fair [fɛr] 形 公平的、unfair [ʌn`fɛr] 形 不公平的、neutral [`njutrəl] 形 中立的、justice [`dʒʌstɪs] 名 正義，公平

---

impasse [`ɪmpæs] 名 僵局　　　　　　　　　　🔘 MP3 **09-03**
▶ The relationship between them reached an impasse.
他們之間的關係陷入僵局

---

impassive [ɪm`pæsɪv] 形 無感情的，冷淡的
▶ Mark's face is so impassive, showing no emotion.
馬克的臉完全冷淡，沒有任何感情。

---

impassioned [ɪm`pæʃənd] 形 慷慨激昂的
▶ Dr. King's speech was so impassioned. 金恩博士的演講是如此慷慨激昂。

---

impatient [ɪm`peʃənt] 形 沒耐心的
▶ A good teacher shouldn't be impatient with students.
好老師不應對學生沒耐心。

impede [ɪmˋpid] 動 阻礙
▶ No difficulty can impede his decision.
　沒有困難可以阻礙他的決定。
相關衍生字彙 hinder [ˋhɪndɚ] 動 妨礙、obstruct [əbˋstrʌkt] 動 阻塞、block [blɑk] 動 阻擋、
　　　　　stop [stɑp] 名 動 停止，中止
動詞三態變化 impede - impeded - impeded

----

impending [ɪmˋpɛndɪŋ] 形 逼近的，即將發生的
片 an impending storm 即將來臨的暴風雨

imperative [ɪmˋpɛrətɪv] 形 必要的，命令式的
▶ The mayor said it was imperative that all the victims be taken good care of.
　市長說所有的災民都要受到妥善照顧。

----

imperil [ɪmˋpɛrɪl] 動 使陷於危險
▶ The snowstorm will imperil the lives of the climbers.
　暴風雪將危及登山者的生命。
動詞三態變化 imperil - imperiled - imperiled

----

implement [ˋɪmpləmənt] 名 工具　　片 agricultural implements 農具
相關衍生字彙 tool [tul] 名 工具、instrument [ˋɪnstrəmənt] 名 器具，儀器、utensil [juˋtɛnsl]
　　　　　名 器皿，用具、apparatus [͵æpəˋretəs] 名 設備，裝置、gear [gɪr] 名 工具，設備

----

implicate [ˋɪmplɪ͵ket] 動 使牽連
▶ Without evidence, we shouldn't implicate the mayor in the scandal.
　沒有證據，我們不能把市長扯進醜聞裡。
動詞三態變化 implicate - implicated - implicated

----

implicit [ɪmˋplɪsɪt] 形 暗示的　　片 implicit consent 默許

implore [ɪmˋplor] 動 哀求
▶ She implored her parents to support her studying abroad.
　她哀求父母支持她出國留學。
動詞三態變化 implore - implored - implored

----

imply [ɪmˋplaɪ] 動 暗示，意味著
▶ He implied that the truth was very cruel.
　他暗示事實很殘酷。
動詞三態變化 imply - implied - implied

----

impolite [͵ɪmpəˋlaɪt] 形 沒禮貌的
▶ It's impolite to interrupt others' conversation. 打斷別人談話是不禮貌的。

----

import [ɪmˋport] 動 進口　　反 export [ɪksˋport] 動 出口
動詞三態變化 import - imported - imported

importance [ɪmˋpɔrtn̩s] 名 重要性
▶ The doctor stresses the importance of exercise.
醫生強調運動的重要性。

相關衍生字彙 important [ɪmˋpɔrtn̩t] 形 重要的、significant [sɪgˋnɪfəkənt] 形 重要的、significance [sɪgˋnɪfəkəns] 名 重要性

impose [ɪmˋpoz] 動 強加於
▶ I won't impose my values on my friends.
我不會把我的價值觀強加給朋友。

動詞三態變化 impose - imposed - imposed

imposing [ɪmˋpozɪŋ] 形 壯觀的
▶ The building is so imposing that it draws many visitors.
這棟建築物如此壯觀，所以吸引很多旅客。

impossible [ɪmˋpasəbl̩] 形 不可能的　片 an impossible mission 不可能的任務

impractical [ɪmˋpræktɪkl̩] 形 不實際的　反 practical [ˋpræktɪkl̩] 形 實際的

impress [ɪmˋprɛs] 動 使留下深刻印象　　◎ MP3 09-04
▶ We were so impressed with the girl's talents.
我們對這女孩的才華都印象深刻。

相關衍生字彙 impression [ɪmˋprɛʃən] 名 印象、impressive [ɪmˋprɛsɪv] 形 印象深刻的、impressionist [ɪmˋprɛʃənɪst] 名 印象派畫家、impressionism [ɪmˋprɛʃənˏɪzəm] 名 印象派

動詞三態變化 impress - impressed - impressed

imprint [ɪmˋprɪnt] 動 蓋印章
▶ The paper should be imprinted with the mayor's seal.
這份文件需要蓋上市長的印章。

動詞三態變化 imprint - imprinted - imprinted

imprison [ɪmˋprɪzn̩] 動 監禁
▶ The criminal has been imprisoned for decades.
這個犯人已經被關幾十年了。

動詞三態變化 imprison - imprisoned - imprisoned

impromptu [ɪmˋpramptju] 形 即席的，即興的
片 an impromptu speech 即席演講

improper [ɪmˋprapɚ] 形 不合適的，不適當的
▶ It's improper to wear a pair of slippers to attend a meeting.
穿拖鞋出席會議是不適當的。

improve [ɪm`pruv] 動 改善
▶ To improve his English, he studies English at least two hours a day.
為了提升英文程度，他每天至少唸兩小時英文。
相關衍生字彙 improvement [ɪm`pruvmənt] 名 改善、better [`bɛtɚ] 形 更好的、worse [wɝs]
形 更糟的、improved [ɪm`pruvd] 形 改善過的，改良的
動詞三態變化 improve - improved - improved

imprudent [ɪm`prudn̩t] 形 輕率的
▶ Never be an imprudent boy. 決不要做個輕率的孩子。

impudent [`ɪmpjədn̩t] 形 放肆的　　片 impudent remarks 放肆的言論

impulse [`ɪmpʌls] 名 衝動　　片 a sudden impulse 一時的衝動

impulsive [ɪm`pʌlsɪv] 形 衝動的
▶ Think twice! Never be impulsive!
再三思考！千萬不要衝動！
相關衍生字彙 calm [kɑm] 形 鎮靜的、tranquil [`træŋkwɪl] 形 平靜的、peaceful [`pisfəl]
形 平靜的、serene [sə`rin] 形 安詳的，寧靜的

inaccessible [ˌɪnæk`sɛsəbl̩] 形 難以接近的
片 an inaccessible person 難以接近的人

inactive [ɪn`æktɪv] 形 不活躍的　　反 active [`æktɪv] 形 活躍的

inappropriate [ˌɪnə`propriɪt] 形 不適合的　　同 improper [ɪm`prapɚ] 形 不適合的

inauguration [ɪnˌɔgjə`reʃən] 名 就職典禮
▶ Many important persons were invited to attend the inauguration.
很多重要人物都被邀請出席此就職典禮。

incapable [ɪn`kepəbl̩] 形 沒能力的　　同 unable [ʌn`eb!] 形 沒能力的

incarnation [ˌɪnkar`neʃən] 名 化身
▶ The baby must be the incarnation of an angel. 這嬰兒必定是天使的化身。

incense [`ɪnsɛns] 名 香（祭祀用）　　片 to burn incense 燒香

incentive [ɪn`sɛntɪv] 名 動力，激勵
▶ Good salary can provide an incentive to work harder.
好的薪水是認真工作的動力。
相關衍生字彙 encouragement [ɪn`kɝɪdʒmənt] 名 鼓勵、stimulus [`stɪmjələs] 名 刺激、
motive [`motɪv] 名 動機、motivate [`motəˌvet] 動 刺激，激發、
inspire [ɪn`spaɪr] 動 鼓舞

incessant [ɪn`sɛsn̩t] 形 持續不斷的
▶ The incessant rain caused a flood. 不間斷的雨水引發洪水。

incident [`ɪnsədṇt] 名 意外　　片 an unfortunate incident 不幸的意外

incisive [ɪn`saɪsɪv] 形 一針見血的，切中要害的　　◎ MP3 **09-05**
▶ Your point of view was incisive. 你的意見真是一針見血。

inclination [ˌɪnklə`neʃən] 名 傾向，愛好
▶ Most girls have an inclination for dancing. 大多數的女孩都喜歡跳舞。

incline [ɪn`klaɪn] 動 喜愛，傾向
▶ I incline to believe that you love me.
我傾向於相信你是愛我的。
動詞三態變化 incline - inclined - inclined

include [ɪn`klud] 動 包含，包括
▶ The tuition includes student insurance.
這學費包含學生的保險。
動詞三態變化 include - included - included

inclusive [ɪn`klusɪv] 形 包括的　　片 be inclusive of 包含～

incoherent [ˌɪnko`hɪrənt] 形 語無倫次的
▶ He became incoherent after he got drunk. 他喝醉後就語無倫次。

income [`ɪnˌkʌm] 名 收入
▶ Those who are on low incomes need more help. 那些低收入者需要多點幫忙。

incomparable [ɪn`kɑmpərəbl] 形 無與倫比的
▶ Her incomparable beauty is beyond description.
她無與倫比的美貌是言語無法形容的。

inconsistent [ˌɪnkən`sɪstənt] 形 前後矛盾的，不一致的
▶ Why are the two answers to the same question inconsistent?
為什麼同一個問題的兩個答案是不一致的？

inconvenience [ˌɪnkən`vinjəns] 名 不便
反 convenience [kən`vinjəns] 名 方便，方便性

incorporate [ɪn`kɔrpəˌret] 動 使合併，包含
▶ The designer incorporated many factors into her final work of art.
設計師在最後的藝術作品中加進許多元素。
動詞三態變化 incorporate - incorporated - incorporated

increase [`ɪnkris] 名 增加，增強 [ɪn`kris] 動 增大，增長
反 decrease [`dikris] 名 減少 [dɪ`kris] 動 減小
相關衍生字彙 extend [ɪk`stɛnd] 動 擴展、expand [ɪk`spænd] 動 展開、enlarge [ɪn`lɑrdʒ]
動 擴大、grow [gro] 動 成長，增加、stretch [strɛtʃ] 動 延伸
動詞三態變化 increase - increased - increased

incredible [ɪnˋkrɛdəbḷ] 形 難以置信的
▶ It is incredible that they got married so soon. 他們的閃婚實在令人難以置信。

incur [ɪnˋkɝ] 動 招致
▶ The report incurred the protest of the women.
這篇報導招惹婦女的抗議。
動詞三態變化 incur - incurred - incurred

indebted [ɪnˋdɛtɪd] 形 感激的
▶ I am indebted to the old couple for their help. 我很感激這對老夫婦的幫忙。

indecisive [ˌɪndɪˋsaɪsɪv] 形 不果斷的
▶ An indecisive manager can't be a good leader.
一個不果斷的管理者決不會是好的領導人。
相關衍生字彙 indecisively [ˌɪndɪˋsaɪsɪvlɪ] 副 優柔寡斷地、decisive [dɪˋsaɪsɪv] 形 決定性的、
decisively [dɪˋsaɪsɪvlɪ] 副 果斷地、determined [dɪˋtɝmɪnd] 形 已下決心的

indeed [ɪnˋdid] 副 真正地，實在
▶ I feel indeed proud to have a good daughter like you.
我能有像你這樣乖的女兒，真的感到驕傲。

indefinite [ɪnˋdɛfənɪt] 形 不明確的
▶ The number of the students who got hurt in the accident is still indefinite.
意外事故中受傷的學生人數仍未明確。

indelible [ɪnˋdɛləbḷ] 形 難以去除的
▶ For me, the nightmare is very indelible. 對我而言，這噩夢很難抹去。

independence [ˌɪndɪˋpɛndəns] 名 獨立　　　　MP3 09-06
片 Independence Day（美國）獨立紀念日

independent [ˌɪndɪˋpɛndənt] 形 獨立的
▶ Since I was 18 years old, I have been independent of my parents.
從我十八歲以來，我就不依賴父母了。

indicate [ˋɪndəˌket] 動 表示，表明
▶ He indicated to his secretary that he didn't want to meet anyone this afternoon.
他向他的祕書表示，下午他不見任何人。
動詞三態變化 indicate - indicated - indicated

indifferent [ɪnˋdɪfərənt] 形 漠不關心的
▶ He is indifferent to his future.
他對未來漠不關心。
相關衍生字彙 indifference [ɪnˋdɪfərəns] 名 冷淡、concerned [kənˋsɝnd] 形 關心的、
interested [ˋɪntərɪstɪd] 形 感興趣的、care [kɛr] 動 在乎

indigenous [ɪnˋdɪdʒɪnəs] 形 土著的　🔵 indigenous people 原住民

indignant [ɪnˋdɪgnənt] 形 憤慨的
▶ He became very indignant when he knew he was cheated.
當他知道被騙時變得很憤慨。

indignity [ɪnˋdɪgnətɪ] 名 侮辱
▶ You don't have to suffer that kind of indignity. 你不必受那種侮辱。

indirect [͵ɪndəˋrɛkt] 形 間接的　🔵 direct [dəˋrɛkt] 形 直接的

indiscriminate [͵ɪndɪˋskrɪmənɪt] 形 無差別的，任意的
▶ The indiscriminate use of fertilizers will do damage to the land.
農藥的亂用將對土地造成傷害。

indispensable [͵ɪndɪsˋpɛnsəbl̩] 形 不可或缺的
▶ A good dictionary is indispensable when you are learning a language.
學語言時，一本好字典是不可或缺的。

individual [͵ɪndəˋvɪdʒʊəl] 形 個人的
▶ We will prepare for individual needs.
我們將為每個人的需求作準備。
相關衍生字彙 individuality [͵ɪndə͵vɪdʒʊˋælətɪ] 名 個人，個體、personal [ˋpɝsn̩l̩] 形 個人的、
individualism [ɪndəˋvɪdʒʊəl͵ɪzəm] 名 個人主義

induce [ɪnˋdjus] 動 引誘
▶ Nothing can induce me to gamble.
我不會被引誘去賭博。
動詞三態變化 induce - induced - induced

indulge [ɪnˋdʌldʒ] 動 沉迷
▶ The student indulges in playing video games.
這位學生沉迷於玩電玩。
動詞三態變化 indulge - indulged - indulged

indulgent [ɪnˋdʌldʒənt] 形 寬容的
▶ The teacher was indulgent towards his students' mistakes.
老師對學生的錯誤寬容以待。

industrial [ɪnˋdʌstrɪəl] 形 工業的　🔵 an industrial nation 工業國家
相關衍生字彙 industrialize [ɪnˋdʌstrɪəl͵aɪz] 動 工業化、industry [ˋɪndəstrɪ] 名 工業、
business [ˋbɪznɪs] 名 商業、economy [ɪˋkɑnəmɪ] 名 經濟

industrious [ɪnˋdʌstrɪəs] 形 勤奮的，勤勞的
▶ He is an industrious worker. 他是位勤奮的員工。

inevitable [ɪnˋɛvətəbl] 形 不可避免的
▶ Sometimes, making a mistake is inevitable. 有時候，犯錯是不可避免的。

infallible [ɪnˋfæləbl] 形 絕對可靠的
▶ Is the news infallible? 這消息可靠嗎？

infamous [ˋɪnfəməs] 形 惡名昭彰的
▶ He is infamous for his dirty words. 他因為愛講髒話而惡名昭彰。

infancy [ˋɪnfənsɪ] 名 嬰兒期　　片 in one's infancy 在初期
相關衍生字彙 infant [ˋɪnfənt] 名 嬰兒、baby [ˋbebɪ] 名 嬰兒、embryo [ˋɛmbrɪo] 名 胚胎

infect [ɪnˋfɛkt] 動（疾病或電腦病毒的）感染，傳染　　MP3 09-07
▶ My laptop was infected by a computer virus.
我的手提電腦被病毒入侵。
動詞三態變化 infect - infected - infected

infection [ɪnˋfɛkʃən] 名 影響，感染　　片 to spread an infection 傳播疾病

infer [ɪnˋfɝ] 動 推斷，猜想
▶ Can you infer a conclusion from his letter?
你可以從他的信中推出結論嗎？
動詞三態變化 infer - inferred - inferred

inference [ˋɪnfərəns] 名 推論　　片 to draw an inference 推出結論

inferior [ɪnˋfɪrɪɚ] 形 較差的，低等的　　反 superior [səˋpɪrɪɚ] 形 優秀的，上等的

inferiority [ɪnfɪrɪˋɑrətɪ] 名 劣等　　反 an inferiority complex 自卑感
相關衍生字彙 worse [wɝs] 形 更壞的、superior [səˋpɪrɪɚ]
形（在品質等方面）較好的，優秀的，上等的、better [ˋbɛtɚ] 形 較佳的，更好的

infinite [ˋɪnfənɪt] 形 無限的
▶ The professor explained the difficult theory with infinite patience.
教授以無限的耐心解釋此困難的理論。

inflame [ɪnˋflem] 動 使燃燒，激起　　片 to inflame passion 點燃熱情
動詞三態變化 inflame - inflamed - inflamed

inflation [ɪnˋfleʃən] 名 通貨膨脹　　片 to control inflation 控制通貨膨脹

influence [ˋɪnfluəns] 名 影響，影響力
▶ A good movie can influence teenagers' values.
一部好電影可以影響青少年的價值觀。

influential [ˌɪnfluˋɛnʃəl] 形 有影響力的
▶ The newspaper is very influential. 報紙是非常有影響力的。

influenza [ˌɪnfluˈɛnzə] 名 流行性感冒　　回 flu [flu] 名 流行性感冒

inform [ɪnˈfɔrm] 動 通知
▶ We were informed about the good news.
　我們被通知了這個好消息。
動詞三態變化 inform - informed - informed

informal [ɪnˈfɔrml] 形 不拘禮節的，非正式的
▶ There will be an informal meeting between the two parties.
　這兩個黨將有一個非正式的會議。

information [ˌɪnfɚˈmeʃən] 名 資訊，消息
▶ You can get further information in the museum.
　你可以在博物館獲得更進一步的資訊。
相關衍生字彙 informative [ɪnˈfɔrmətɪv] 形 增進知識的、informed [ɪnˈfɔrmd] 形 見聞廣的、
　　　　　 informer [ɪnˈfɔrmɚ] 名 告密者

ingenious [ɪnˈdʒinjəs] 形 機靈的　　回 clever [ˈklɛvɚ] 形 聰慧的

ingenuity [ˌɪndʒəˈnuətɪ] 名 心靈手巧，獨創性
▶ Use your ingenuity well, and you must achieve a lot.
　善用你的獨創性，你一定可以很有成就。

ingredient [ɪnˈgridɪənt] 名 成分
▶ If you don't know the ingredients of the medicine, don't take it.
　如果你不知道藥的成分，別吃。

inhabit [ɪnˈhæbɪt] 動 居住於
▶ The area in the mountains is inhabited by aborigines.
　山的那區是原住民居住的地方。
動詞三態變化 inhabit - inhabited - inhabited

inhale [ɪnˈhel] 動 吸入　　反 exhale [ɛksˈhel] 動 吐出
動詞三態變化 inhale - inhaled - inhaled

inherit [ɪnˈhɛrɪt] 動 繼承　　　　　　　　　　　　　　　　　⊙ MP3 09-08
▶ His son inherited all his fortune.
　他兒子繼承他所有的財產。
相關衍生字彙 inherent [ɪnˈhɪrənt] 形 與生俱來的、inheritance [ɪnˈhɛrɪtəns] 名 繼承、
　　　　　 inheritor [ɪnˈhɛrɪtɚ] 名 繼承人、will [wɪl] 名 遺囑
動詞三態變化 inherit - inherited - inherited

inhuman [ɪnˈhjumən] 形 不人道的　　片 inhuman treatment 不人道的對待

initial [ɪˈnɪʃəl] 形 最初的
▶ The draft is the designer's initial idea. 這張草圖是設計師最初的想法。

initiative [ɪˋnɪʃətɪv] 名 主動的行動　🟠 on your own initiative 自動自發地

injection [ɪnˋdʒɛkʃən] 名 注射
▶ The nurse gave me an injection. 護士幫我打針。

injure [ˋɪndʒɚ] 動 受傷
▶ Luckily, no one got injured in the accident.
　很幸運地，沒有人在那場意外中受傷。
相關衍生字彙　injurious [ɪnˋdʒʊrɪəs] 形 有害的、injury [ˋɪndʒərɪ] 名 受傷、hurt [hɝt] 動 受傷、
　　　　　　　wound [wund] 名 傷口
動詞三態變化　injure - injured - injured

injustice [ɪnˋdʒʌstɪs] 名 不公平　🟢 unfairness [ʌnˋfɛrnɪs] 名 不公平

ink [ɪŋk] 名 墨水
▶ Be careful! The ink is not dry. 小心！墨水還沒乾。

inland [ˋɪnlənd] 形 內地的，內陸的　🟠 an inland sea 內陸海

inner [ˋɪnɚ] 形 內部的
▶ Music can give me a sense of inner peace. 音樂可以帶給我內心的平靜。

innocence [ˋɪnəsn̩s] 名 無罪，無知，天真無邪
▶ No one believes her innocence.
　沒有人相信她是無辜的。
相關衍生字彙　innocent [ˋɪnəsn̩t] 形 無罪的、guilt [gɪlt] 名 罪惡、guilty [ˋgɪltɪ] 形 有罪的、
　　　　　　　crime [kraɪm] 名 罪刑

innovative [ˋɪnoˏvetɪv] 形 創新的
▶ Our company needs someone innovative to offer new ideas.
　我們公司需要有人很創新，能提供新點子。

innovation [ˏɪnəˋveʃən] 名 革新，創新
▶ In computer technology, there are always surprising innovations.
　電腦科技永遠有令人驚喜的創新。

input [ˋɪnˏput] 動 輸入
▶ Please input your password.
　請輸入密碼。
動詞三態變化　input - input / inputted - input / inputted

inquire [ɪnˋkwaɪr] 動 詢問
▶ You can inquire anything at the information desk.
　你可以在服務台詢問任何事。
動詞三態變化　inquire - inquired - inquired

inquiry [ɪnˋkwaɪrɪ] 名 詢問　🟠 to make inquiries 詢問，打聽

相關衍生字彙 ask [æsk] 動 詢問、require [rɪ`kwaɪr] 動 需要、inquiring [ɪn`kwaɪrɪŋ] 形 愛追根究底的、requirement [rɪ`kwaɪrmənt] 名 要求，必需品

insane [ɪn`sen] 形 瘋狂的，愚蠢的
▶ This summer vacation, I want to do something insane.
這個暑假，我要做點瘋狂的事。

inscribe [ɪn`skraɪb] 動 刻，雕
▶ The wall of the temple was inscribed with the names of donators.
廟的牆面刻著捐贈者的名字。

動詞三態變化 inscribe - inscribed - inscribed

insect [`ɪnsɛkt] 名 昆蟲
▶ Bees are one of the insects. 蜜蜂是昆蟲的一種。

insist [ɪn`sɪst] 動 堅持　　片 to insist on 堅持～
相關衍生字彙 insistence [ɪn`sɪstəns] 名 堅持、insistent [ɪn`sɪstənt] 形 堅持的、abandon [ə`bændən] 動 放棄、forgo [fɔr`go] 動 放棄

動詞三態變化 insist - insisted - insisted

insecure [ˌɪnsɪ`kjʊr] 形 不安全的　　◎ MP3 09-09
▶ Because the door was broken, I felt insecure. 因為門壞了，讓我沒有安全感。

insensitive [ɪn`sɛnsətɪv] 形 感覺遲鈍的　　反 sensitive [`sɛnsətɪv] 形 敏感的

insert [ɪn`sɝt] 動 插入，嵌入
▶ Please insert your credit card and input your pin number.
請插入你的信用卡並輸入個人識別碼。

動詞三態變化 insert - inserted - inserted

insight [`ɪnˌsaɪt] 名 洞察力
▶ As a scientist, he has professional insights. 身為科學家，他很有專業的洞察力。

insomnia [ɪn`samnɪə] 名 失眠
▶ Mark has suffered from insomnia for years. 馬克多年來受失眠所苦。

inspect [ɪn`spɛkt] 動 檢查
▶ I asked the technician to inspect my car carefully.
我要求技師仔細檢查我的車子。

相關衍生字彙 inspection [ɪn`spɛkʃən] 名 檢查、inspector [ɪn`spɛktɚ] 名 檢查人員、examine [ɪg`zæmɪn] 動 檢查、check [tʃɛk] 動 檢查

動詞三態變化 inspect - inspected - inspected

inspiration [ˌɪnspə`reʃən] 名 靈感，鼓舞
▶ To seek inspiration, the writer spent one year travelling.
為尋找靈感，作家花了一年旅遊。

inspire [ɪnˈspaɪr] 動 鼓舞

▶ A good leader always inspires his followers instead of punishing them.

好的領導人會不斷激勵員工，而不是處罰他們。

動詞三態變化 inspire - inspired - inspired

---

install [ɪnˈstɔl] 動 安裝　　片 to install the software 安裝軟體

動詞三態變化 install - installed - installed

---

instance [ˈɪnstəns] 名 例子　　片 for instance 例如

---

instant [ˈɪnstənt] 名 頃刻 形 立即的

▶ At that instant, I realized I fell in love with her.

在那一刻，我知道我愛上她了。

相關衍生字彙 instantaneous [ˌɪnstənˈtenɪəs] 形 即時的、instantly [ˈɪnstəntlɪ] 副 立即，馬上、
moment [ˈmomənt] 名 片刻、immediately [ɪˈmidɪɪtlɪ] 副 立刻

---

instead [ɪnˈstɛd] 副 反而

▶ My boss didn't fire me; instead, he gave me another opportunity.

老闆沒有開除我，反而給我另一個機會。

---

instinct [ˈɪnstɪŋkt] 名 本能，直覺　　片 by instinct 憑直覺

---

institute [ˈɪnstətjut] 名 學院，研究所

片 the Massachusetts Institute of Technology 麻省理工學院

---

institution [ˌɪnstəˈtjuʃən] 名 機構，團體　　片 an educational institution 教育機構

---

instruction [ɪnˈstrʌkʃən] 名 指示

▶ I followed the instructions to operate the washing machine.

我按照說明操作洗衣機。

相關衍生字彙 instructive [ɪnˈstrʌktɪv] 形 指示的、instruct [ɪnˈstrʌkt] 動 指示，指導、direct
[dəˈrɛkt] 動 指導、teach [titʃ] 動 教導、instructor [ɪnˈstrʌktɚ] 名 指導者

---

instrument [ˈɪnstrəmənt] 名 器具，樂器　　片 musical instrument 樂器

---

insulate [ˈɪnsəˌlet] 動 使孤立，使絕緣

▶ You can insulate your room from the noise by closing all the windows.

你可以把窗戶都關起來以隔絕噪音。

動詞三態變化 insulate - insulated - insulated

---

insult [ˈɪnsʌlt] 動 侮辱

▶ Your criticism is an insult to me.

你的批評對我是一種侮辱。

相關衍生字彙 humiliate [hjuˈmɪlɪˌet] 動 羞辱、embarrass [ɪmˈbærəs] 動 使不好意思、
disgrace [dɪsˈgres] 動 使丟臉、dishonor [dɪsˈɑnɚ] 名 動 侮辱

動詞三態變化 insult - insulted - insulted

insurance [ɪnˋʃʊrəns] 名 保險
▶ Our factory takes out extra fire insurance. 我們工廠投保額外的火險。

intact [ɪnˋtækt] 形 完整無缺的   ⊙ MP3 **09-10**
▶ The car is old, but it remains intact. 這部車子很舊了,但是仍維持完好無損。

intellect [ˋɪntḷˌɛkt] 名 智力
▶ He is a doctor of superior intellect. 他是個智力極優的醫生。

intellectual [ˌɪntḷˋɛktʃʊəl] 形 智力的
▶ Watching the cartoon takes nothing intellectual.
看這種卡通不太需要耗費腦力。
相關衍生字彙 intelligence [ɪnˋtɛlədʒəns] 名 聰明、intelligent [ɪnˋtɛlədʒənt] 形 聰明的、
clever [ˋklɛvɚ] 形 聰明的、wise [waɪz] 形 聰明的、wisdom [ˋwɪzdəm] 名 智慧

integrate [ˋɪntəˌgret] 動 使合併,使成為一體
▶ It's not an easy job for me to integrate into a new culture.
我不容易融入新文化。
動詞三態變化 integrate - integrated - integrated

integrity [ɪnˋtɛgrətɪ] 名 正直
▶ Our professor is a man of integrity. 我們教授是個正直的人。

intend [ɪnˋtɛnd] 動 打算
▶ I intend to go to Paris next year.
我打算明年去巴黎。
動詞三態變化 intend - intended - intended

intense [ɪnˋtɛns] 形 強烈的   片 intense heat / cold 酷熱／酷寒
相關衍生字彙 intensity [ɪnˋtɛnsətɪ] 名 強度、intensive [ɪnˋtɛnsɪv] 形 密集的、strong [strɔŋ]
形 強烈的、extremely [ɪkˋstrimlɪ] 副 極端地

intention [ɪnˋtɛnʃən] 名 意圖
▶ I have no intention of cheating you. 我無意欺騙你。

interact [ˌɪntəˋrækt] 動 互動
▶ The game is designed to encourage kids to interact with each other.
這個遊戲是設計來鼓勵孩子們互動的。
動詞三態變化 interact - interacted - interacted

interaction [ˌɪntəˋrækʃən] 名 互動,相互影響
▶ There is interaction between the human beings and the environment.
人跟環境是會互相影響的。

intercept [ˌɪntɚˋsɛpt] 動 攔截
▶ The police intercepted a truck of smuggled goods.
　警方攔截一台走私的卡車。
動詞三態變化 intercept - intercepted - intercepted

interchange [ˌɪntɚˋtʃendʒ] 名動 交換 動 輪流進行
▶ The workshop was held for the interchange of different experiences.
　這個研討會是用以交流不同的經驗。
動詞三態變化 interchange - interchanged - interchanged

interested [ˋɪntərɪstɪd] 形 感興趣的　　片 be interested in（人）對～感興趣
相關衍生字彙 interest [ˋɪntərɪst] 動 使～感興趣、interesting [ˋɪntərɪstɪŋ] 形 有趣的、
　　interestingly [ˋɪntrəstɪŋlɪ] 副 有趣地

interfere [ˌɪntɚˋfɪr] 動 衝突，干預
▶ The noise you made interfered with my concentration.
　你製造的噪音干擾了我的專心。
動詞三態變化 interfere - interfered - interfered

interference [ˌɪntɚˋfɪrəns] 名 干涉，干擾　　片 electronic interference 電子干擾

interior [ɪnˋtɪrɪɚ] 名 內部　　片 the Department of the Interior 內政部

intermediate [ˌɪntɚˋmidɪət] 形 中間的
▶ The levels of the language test can be divided into basic, intermediate and advanced.
　這語言測驗的等級可分為基礎、中級、進階。

intermission [ˌɪntɚˋmɪʃən] 名 間歇，中斷
▶ There is a short intermission during the process of the meeting.
　會議的過程會有一個短暫的中場休息。

internal [ɪnˋtɝnḷ] 形 內部的　　片 internal affairs 內政事務

international [ˌɪntɚˋnæʃənḷ] 形 國際的　　片 an international call 國際電話
相關衍生字彙 internationalization [ˌɪntɚˌnæʃənḷɪˋzeʃən] 名 國際化、
　　internationalize [ˌɪntɚˋnæʃənḷˌaɪz] 動 使國際化、
　　internationalism [ˌɪntɚˋnæʃənḷˌɪzəm] 名 國際主義

Internet [ˋɪntɚˌnɛt] 名 網際網路　　　　　　　　　　MP3 09-11
▶ With the Internet, it becomes very convenient to get information.
　有了網際網路，找資料變得很方便。

interpret [ɪnˋtɝprɪt] 動 詮釋，作口譯
▶ The interpreter interpreted the statement very well.
　這位口譯人員詮釋此敘述很清楚。
動詞三態變化 interpret - interpreted - interpreted

interpretation [ɪnˌtɝprɪˈteʃən] 名 詮釋
▶ I still feel confused about the interpretation of the theory.
我對這個理論的詮釋仍然感到困惑。

相關衍生字彙 interpreter [ɪnˈtɝprɪtɚ] 名 口譯員、explain [ɪkˈsplen] 動 解釋，說明、translate [trænsˈlet] 動 翻譯、translator [trænsˈletɚ] 名 譯者

---

interrupt [ˌɪntəˈrʌpt] 動 打斷
▶ I'm sorry to interrupt your meeting.
很抱歉，打斷你們的會議。

動詞三態變化 interrupt - interrupted - interrupted

---

intersection [ˌɪntɚˈsɛkʃən] 名 十字路口
▶ Go straight ahead, and turn right at the second intersection.
直走，然後在第二個十字路口右轉。

---

interval [ˈɪntɚvl̩] 名 間隔，距離　　　🔑 a regular interval 每隔一段時間

---

intervene [ˌɪntɚˈvin] 動 介入，調停
▶ The lawyer intervened between the two persons.
律師在兩人之間調解。

動詞三態變化 intervene - intervened - intervened

---

interview [ˈɪntɚˌvju] 動 面試
▶ Our boss is busy interviewing new employees.
我們老闆正忙著面試新員工。

動詞三態變化 interview - interviewed - interviewed

---

intimacy [ˈɪntəməsɪ] 名 親密，熟悉
▶ Intimacy between professors and students is not allowed.
教授跟學生之間不允許有親密關係。

---

intimate [ˈɪntəmɪt] 形 親密的　　　🔑 intimate relationship 親密關係

---

intimidate [ɪnˈtɪməˌdet] 動 威嚇，脅迫
▶ The employee was intimidated into keeping the fault a secret.
這個員工被威脅保密此錯誤。

相關衍生字彙 threaten [ˈθrɛtn̩] 動 威脅，恐嚇、menace [ˈmɛnɪs] 名 動 恐嚇，威脅、frighten [ˈfraɪtn̩] 動 使害怕、terrify [ˈtɛrəˌfaɪ] 動 使恐怖

動詞三態變化 intimidate - intimidated - intimidated

---

intolerable [ɪnˈtɑlərəbl̩] 形 不能忍受的
▶ The pollution of the river is already intolerable.
這河流的污染已經無法忍受的。

---

intolerant [ɪnˈtɑlərənt] 形 難耐的
▶ I am intolerant of the messy environment. 我不能忍受髒亂的環境。

intonation [ˌɪntoˈneʃən] 名 語調
▶ Your intonation sounds like an Italian. 你的語調聽起來像義大利人

intoxicate [ɪnˈtɑksəˌket] 動 使喝醉　　同 drunk [drʌŋk] 形 喝醉（酒）的
相關衍生字彙 intoxication [ɪnˌtɑksəˈkeʃən] 名 醉酒，中毒、alcohol [ˈælkəˌhɔl] 名 酒精，含酒精飲料、liquor [ˈlɪkɚ] 名 酒、whisky [ˈhwɪskɪ] 名 威士忌酒、beer [bɪr] 名 啤酒

動詞三態變化 intoxicate - intoxicated - intoxicated

intricate [ˈɪntrəkɪt] 形 錯綜複雜的
▶ The details of the case is very intricate. 這案件的細節非常錯綜複雜。

introduce [ˌɪntrəˈdjus] 動 介紹，引見
▶ Allow me to introduce my sister to you.
讓我介紹我妹妹給你認識。

動詞三態變化 introduce - introduced - introduced

introduction [ˌɪntrəˈdʌkʃən] 名 介紹，採用
片 to make a self-introduction 做自我介紹

intrude [ɪnˈtrud] 動 侵入，打擾
▶ A thief intruded into their garden last night.
昨夜有小偷侵入他們的花園。

動詞三態變化 intrude - intruded - intruded

intuition [ˌɪntjuˈɪʃən] 名 直覺
▶ I often make a decision by intuition. 我常憑直覺做決定。

invade [ɪnˈved] 動 侵略，擁入　　　　　　　　MP3 09-12
▶ I hate to find my privacy invaded.
我痛恨隱私被侵犯。

相關衍生字彙 invasion [ɪnˈveʒən] 名 入侵、invader [ɪnˈvedɚ] 名 入侵者、force [fɔrs] 名 武力、army [ˈɑrmɪ] 名 軍隊、attack [əˈtæk] 動 攻擊

動詞三態變化 invade - invaded - invaded

invalid [ɪnˈvælɪd] 形 無效的
▶ Your passport will be invalid next month. 你的護照下個月將過期無效。

invaluable [ɪnˈvæljəb!] 形 無價的
▶ Work experience is invaluable. 工作經驗是無價的。

invent [ɪnˈvɛnt] 動 發明，創造
▶ Edison invented the light bulb.
愛迪生發明燈泡。

動詞三態變化 invent - invented - invented

invention [ɪnˋvɛnʃən] 名 發明
▶ Necessity is the mother of invention.（諺語）需求為發明之母。

invest [ɪnˋvɛst] 動 投資
▶ Don't invest all your money in the stock market.
　不要把全部的錢都投資在股市。
相關衍生字彙 investor [ɪnˋvɛstɚ] 名 投資者、investment [ɪnˋvɛstmənt] 名 投資、
　　　　　 capital [ˋkæpətl̩] 名 資金、stock [stɑk] 名 股票
動詞三態變化 invest - invested - invested

investigate [ɪnˋvɛstəˏget] 動 調查
▶ The police are investigating the case.
　警方正在調查此案件。
動詞三態變化 investigate - investigated - investigated

invisible [ɪnˋvɪzəbl̩] 形 看不見的
▶ Viruses are invisible to the naked eye. 病毒用肉眼是看不到的。

invite [ɪnˋvaɪt] 動 邀請
▶ All my relatives were invited to attend my wedding.
　我所有的親戚都受邀參加我的婚禮。
相關衍生字彙 invitation [ˏɪnvəˋteʃən] 名 邀請、ask [æsk] 動 邀請、request [rɪˋkwɛst]
　　　　　 動 邀請、invitee [ˏɪnvaɪˋti] 名 被邀請者
動詞三態變化 invite - invited - invited

invoke [ɪnˋvok] 動 祈求，訴諸（法律），喚起
▶ The local drama is performed to invoke gods for peace.
　這當地戲曲的表演是用以祈求神保佑平安。
動詞三態變化 invoke - invoked - invoked

involve [ɪnˋvɑlv] 動 使捲入，連累
▶ I don't want to get involved in their argument.
　我不想捲入他們的爭論。
動詞三態變化 involve - involved - involved

iron [ˋaɪɚn] 名 熨斗，鐵，鐵質 動 燙，熨　　片 to iron a shirt 燙襯衫
動詞三態變化 iron - ironed - ironed

ironic [aɪˋrɑnɪk] 形 諷刺的　　片 ironic remarks 諷刺的言論

irony [ˋaɪrənɪ] 名 諷刺
▶ The irony is that the school rule will punish hardworking students.
　諷刺的是這校規會處罰到認真的學生。

irrational [ɪˋræʃənl̩] 形 無理性的　　反 rational [ˋræʃənl̩] 形 理性的

irregular [ɪ`rɛgjələ˙] 形 不規則的　　　反 regular [`rɛgjələ˙] 形 規則的

irritate [`ɪrə͵tet] 動 使煩躁
▶ The humid and hot weather irritates me.
潮濕又熱的天氣讓我煩躁。

相關衍生字彙 irresponsible [͵ɪrɪ`spɑnsəbḷ] 形 無責任感的、irresistible [͵ɪrɪ`zɪstəbḷ]
形 不可抵抗的、irrelevant [ɪ`rɛləvənt] 形 無關係的、irritable [`ɪrətəbḷ] 形 易怒的

動詞三態變化 irritate - irritated - irritated

island [`aɪlənd] 名 島嶼
▶ Taiwan is an island country. 台灣是個島國。

isolate [`aɪsḷ͵et] 動 使孤立
▶ The village is isolated in the mountains.
這個村落孤立在山區。

動詞三態變化 isolate - isolated - isolated

issue [`ɪʃju] 名 問題，發行物 動 發布，核發
▶ The government will issue the good news.
政府即將發布這個好消息。

動詞三態變化 issue - issued - issued

item [`aɪtəm] 名 項目，一則，一項　　　◎ MP3 09-13
▶ There are many items on the shopping list. 購物清單上有很多要買的品項。

itinerary [aɪ`tɪnə͵rɛrɪ] 名 行程
▶ Before starting off, I always plan an itinerary.
動身出發前，我都會擬定行程計畫。

ivory [`aɪvərɪ] 名 象牙 形 象牙色的
▶ There is a ban on hunting for ivory. 有禁令不可獵取象牙。

ivy [`aɪvɪ] 名 常春藤　　　片 the Ivy League（美國）常春藤名校

MEMO

一網打盡

字母 J

jacket ~ juvenile

一網打盡「英語小知識」｜關於「期待」的其他用語 ──────────

I look forward to your reply. 我期待你的回覆。

I look forward to hearing from you soon. 我期待很快聽到你的消息。

I look forward to working with you on this project.
我期待與你一起執行這個專案。

J jacket ~ juvenile

★一網打盡 194 個英文單字 ｜ 一網打盡 30 句英語會話句

jacket [`dʒækɪt] 名 夾克
▶ The black jacket is a gift from his wife.
這件黑色夾克是他太太給他的禮物。

相關衍生字彙 coat [kot] 名 外套，大衣、coatee [ˌkot`i] 名（女人，軍人等的）緊身短上衣、blazer [`blezɚ] 名 色彩鮮艷的運動上衣，發光體、windbreaker [`wɪndˌbrekɚ] 名 防風上衣的一種

jackpot [`dʒækˌpat] 名 累積獎金
▶ How I wish I could win the jackpot! 多希望我可以贏得獎金！

jail [dʒel] 名 監牢　　片 to be released from jail 從監獄中獲釋

相關衍生字彙 prison [`prɪzn] 名 監獄、imprison [ɪm`prɪzn] 動 監禁、confine [kən`faɪn] 動 禁閉、sentence [`sɛntəns] 動 宣判，判決

jam [dʒæm] 名 堵塞　　片 a traffic jam 交通阻塞

January [`dʒænjuˌɛrɪ] 名 一月
▶ January is the first month of the year. 一月是一年的第一個月。

jargon [`dʒɑrgən] 名 術語
▶ The military jargon confused me.
軍事用語令我困惑。

相關衍生字彙 slang [slæŋ] 名 俚語，行話、vocabulary [və`kæbjəˌlɛrɪ] 名 字彙，單字集、dialect [`daɪəlɛkt] 名 方言

jasmine [`dʒæsmɪn] 名 茉莉花
▶ The jasmine smells sweet. 茉莉花聞起來有甜甜的香味。

jaunt [dʒɔnt] 名 遠足
▶ The teacher is planning a jaunt for us.
老師正為我們安排遠足。

相關衍生字彙 journey [`dʒɜnɪ] 名 動 旅行、excursion [ɪk`skɜʒən] 名 遠足，遊覽團、outing [`autɪŋ] 名 遠足，郊遊，體育比賽

jaw [dʒɔ] 名 下頷，下巴　　片 upper / lower jaw 上／下顎

相關衍生字彙 jawbone [`dʒɔˌbon] 名 頷骨、maxilla [mæk`sɪlə] 名 上頷（骨）、mandible [`mændəbl] 名（哺乳動物、魚的）頷，下顎骨、jowl [dʒaul] 名 大顎，頷骨，面頰

jazz [dʒæz] 名 爵士　　片 jazz music 爵士樂

相關衍生字彙 disco [`dɪsko] 名 小舞廳、rock [rak] 名 搖滾、folk [fok] 名 民謠、tango [`tæŋgo] 名 探戈、waltz [wɔlts] 名 華爾滋舞

jealous [ˋdʒɛləs] 形 嫉妒的
▶ Never be jealous of others' fortune.
不要嫉妒別人的財富。
相關衍生字彙 jealously [ˋdʒɛləslɪ] 副 妒忌地，謹慎地、jealousness [ˋdʒɛləsnɪs]
名 猜忌，吃醋、jealous of 片 妒忌、envious [ˋɛnvɪəs] 形 嫉妒的，羨慕的、
covetous [ˋkʌvɪtəs] 形 垂涎的，貪圖的，渴望的、desirous of 片 想得到

jealousy [ˋdʒɛləsɪ] 名 猜忌，警惕
▶ You should deal with your jealousy. 你應該要好好處理你忌妒的情緒。

jeer [dʒɪr] 動 嘲弄　　片 to jeer at 嘲弄
相關衍生字彙 taunt [tɔnt] 名 動 辱罵，嘲笑，奚落、scoff [skɔf] 名 動 嘲笑、mock [mɑk]
名 動 嘲弄、make fun of 片 取笑，嘲弄
動詞三態變化 jeer - jeered - jeered

jelly [ˋdʒɛlɪ] 名 果凍，果醬
▶ A strawberry jelly is my daughter's favorite.
草莓果凍是我女兒的最愛。
相關衍生字彙 jam [dʒæm] 名 果醬、conserve [ˋkɑnsɝv] 名 蜜餞，果醬、
marmalade [ˋmɑrml͵ed] 名（帶碎果皮的）橘子（或檸檬）果醬、
gelatin [ˋdʒɛlətn̩] 名 明膠，動物膠、gelatinoid [dʒəˋlætə͵nɔɪd] 名 膠樣物質
形 膠樣的、blancmange [bləˋmɑnʒ] 名 牛奶凍

jellyfish [ˋdʒɛlɪ͵fɪʃ] 名 水母　　▶ Are jellyfish poisonous? 水母有毒嗎？

jest [dʒɛst] 名 笑話，俏皮話
▶ He said it in jest. He didn't really mean you were ugly.
他開玩笑的，不是真的說你很醜。

jet [dʒɛt] 名 噴射機
▶ That millionaire owns a private jet.
那位百萬富翁擁有一架私人噴射機。
相關衍生字彙 jet aircraft 片 噴射機、jet boat 片 噴射艇、jet engine 片 噴射（機）引擎、
jet fighter 片 噴射戰鬥機、jet foil 片 噴氣水翼船、jet propulsion 片 噴射推進、
jetliner [ˋdʒɛt͵laɪnɚ] 名 噴射客機、turbojet [ˋtɝbo͵dʒɛt]
名 渦輪噴射引擎（飛機）、ramjet [ˋræmdʒɛt] 名 噴射推進引擎

jewel [ˋdʒuəl] 名 寶石
▶ Her ring was set with a valuable jewel.
她的戒指鑲有一枚價值不斐的寶石。
相關衍生字彙 jeweler [ˋdʒuəlɚ] 名 珠寶商、jewelry [ˋdʒuəlrɪ] 名 珠寶、pearl [pɝl] 名 珍珠、
treasure [ˋtrɛʒɚ] 名 寶藏

J

job [dʒɑb] 名 工作　　片 a part-time job 兼職工作

相關衍生字彙 job-hunt [`dʒɑbhʌnt] 動 找工作、job alert system 片 就業預警機制、job center 片 就業服務中心、job creation 片 創造就業機會、job description 片 工作說明，職務說明、jobless [`dʒɑblɪs] 形 失業的、joblessness [`dʒɑblɪsnɪs] 名 失業、job expo 片 就業博覽會、job opening 片 徵才、job satisfaction 片 工作滿意度、job scheduling 片 作業調度、job seeker 片 求職者

---

join [dʒɔɪn] 動 參加
▶ I will join my friends for dinner after work.
下班後我會跟朋友一起吃飯。

動詞三態變化 join - joined - joined

---

joint [dʒɔɪnt] 名 接合點，關節　　片 a knee joint 膝關節　　　　　　　　◎ MP3 10-02

相關衍生字彙 jointly [`dʒɔɪntlɪ] 副 共同地，聯合地、junction [`dʒʌŋkʃən] 名 接合，連接，交叉點、juncture [`dʒʌŋktʃɚ] 名 連接點，緊要關頭、jointer [`dʒɔɪntɚ] 名 接合人（或物）、intersection [ˌɪntɚ`sɛkʃən] 名 橫斷，交叉，十字路口、union [`junjən] 名 結合，聯邦，學生自治會

---

joke [dʒok] 名 笑話　　片 to crack a joke 説笑話

相關衍生字彙 joker [`dʒokɚ] 名 愛開玩笑的人、jokey [`dʒokɪ] 形 愛開玩笑的、jolly [`dʒɑlɪ] 形 快活的

---

journal [`dʒɝn!] 名 期刊，雜誌
▶ His theory was published in a medical journal.
他的理論被發表在醫學期刊上。

相關衍生字彙 diary [`daɪərɪ] 名 日記，日誌、chronicle [`krɑnɪk!] 名 編年史，記事、newspaper [`njuzˌpepɚ] 名 報紙、magazine [ˌmægə`zin] 名 雜誌，期刊

---

journey [`dʒɝnɪ] 名 旅程
▶ Life is often compared to a journey. 人生常常被比喻成旅程。

---

joy [dʒɔɪ] 名 歡樂 動 高興
▶ Their marriage is full of joy.
他們的婚姻充滿歡樂。

動詞三態變化 joy - joyed - joyed

---

joyful [`dʒɔɪfəl] 形 開心的　　同 happy [`hæpɪ] 形 快樂的

相關衍生字彙 joyfully [`dʒɔɪfəlɪ] 副 喜悅地，高興地、joyfulness [`dʒɔɪfəlnɪs] 名 高興，快樂、joyless [`dʒɔɪlɪs] 形 不高興的、joyous [`dʒɔɪəs] 形 快樂的，高興的、joyously [`dʒɔɪəslɪ] 副 快樂地，高興地、cheerful [`tʃɪrfəl] 形 興高采烈的，樂意的、blissful [`blɪsfəl] 形 樂而忘憂的、jovial [`dʒovɪəl] 形 愉快的，天性快活的、gleeful [`glifəl] 形 歡欣的

---

journalist [`dʒɝnəlɪst] 名 新聞從業人員
▶ Being a journalist is her career plan.
成為新聞從業人員是她的生涯規劃。

相關衍生字彙 journalism [`dʒɜnḷɪzm] 名 新聞業、news [njuz] 名 消息，新聞、newspaper [`njuzˌpepɚ] 名 報紙、reporter [rɪ`portɚ] 名 記者

jubilant [`dʒubḷənt] 形 令人喜悅的
▶ The championship made every teammate jubilant.
　冠軍頭銜讓隊友都很高興。
相關衍生字彙 jubilantly [`dʒubələntlɪ] 副 歡欣地，喜氣洋洋地、rejoicing [rɪ`dʒɔɪsɪŋ] 名 欣喜，高興，慶祝、triumphant [traɪ`ʌmfənt] 形 勝利的，（因勝利而）喜悅的、overjoyed [ˌovɚ`dʒɔɪd] 形 狂喜的、delighted [dɪ`laɪtɪd] 形 高興的，快樂的

judge [dʒʌdʒ] 動 判斷
▶ Never judge others by their appearance.
　不要用外表來判斷別人。
動詞三態變化 judge - judged - judged

judgment [`dʒʌdʒmənt] 名 判斷　　片 in one's judgment 根據某人的判斷

judicial [dʒu`dɪʃəl] 形 司法的，法官的
片 to take judicial proceedings 採取法律程序
相關衍生字彙 judicial review 片 司法審查、judiciary [dʒu`dɪʃɛrɪ] 名 司法部，司法制度 形 司法的，法官的、judicially [dʒu`dɪʃəlɪ] 副 名斷地，公正地、objective [əb`dʒɛktɪv] 形 客觀的，如實的

judicious [dʒu`dɪʃəs] 形 有見識的，明斷的
▶ To make judicious use of the information can help us learn a lot.
　善用資訊可以幫助我們學到很多東西。

juice [dʒus] 名 果汁　　片 apple juice 蘋果汁
相關衍生字彙 latex [`letɛks] 名 乳汁，乳膠、serum [`sɪrəm] 名 漿液，血清，樹液、soup [sup] 名 湯、nectar [`nɛktɚ] 名 花蜜，甘露、beverage [`bɛvərɪdʒ] 名 飲料

juicy [`dʒusɪ] 形 多汁的
▶ I enjoy eating juicy fruit. 我喜歡吃多汁的水果。

July [dʒu`laɪ] 名 七月
▶ In Taiwan, the weather in July is very hot. 在台灣，七月的天氣非常熱。

jumble [`dʒʌmbḷ] 名 雜亂的一堆 動 使混亂
▶ All the books were jumbled on his desk.
　他桌上的書亂七八糟的。
相關衍生字彙 messy [`mɛsɪ] 形 混亂的、order [`ɔrdɚ] 名 次序，整齊、disorder [dɪs`ɔrdɚ] 名 混亂，無秩序、tangle [`tæŋgḷ] 動 使糾結、complicate [`kɑmpləˌket] 動 使複雜化、knot [nɑt] 動 把～打結

jumbo [ˋdʒʌmbo] 形 特大（號）的　　片 a jumbo-sized bed 特大號的床

相關衍生字彙 enormous [ɪˋnɔrməs] 形 巨大的，兇暴的、immense [ɪˋmɛns] 形 廣大的，極妙的、colossal [kəˋlɑsl] 形 巨大的，少有的，驚人的、gigantic [dʒaɪˋgæntɪk] 形 巨人的，龐大的、mammoth [ˋmæməθ] 名 毛象 形 巨大的，龐大的、tremendous [trɪˋmɛndəs] 形 極大的，驚人的

jump [dʒʌmp] 動 跳躍

▶ Look! The kids are jumping up and down happily.
瞧！孩子們開心地跳上跳下。

相關衍生字彙 jumping [ˋdʒʌmpɪŋ] 形 跳躍的、jumpy [ˋdʒʌmpɪ] 形 跳動的，神經質的、jump ball 片 跳球、jump hook 片 鉤手跳投、jump shot 片 跳投

動詞三態變化 jump - jumped - jumped

June [dʒun] 名 六月

▶ Most schools hold their graduation ceremonies in June.
大部分的學校在六月舉辦畢業典禮。

jungle [ˋdʒʌŋgl] 名 （熱帶）叢林

▶ Many wild animals are living in the tropical jungle.
很多野生動物住在這座熱帶叢林。

相關衍生字彙 forest [ˋfɔrɪst] 名 森林、timberland [ˋtɪmbɚˋlænd] 名 森林，林地、wildwood [ˋwaɪldˋwud] 名 原始叢林、rain forest 片 雨林

junior [ˋdʒunjɚ] 形 晚輩的，年紀較輕的　　片 a junior high school 國中　◎MP3 **10-03**

jury [ˋdʒʊrɪ] 名 陪審團

▶ He was invited to be one of the members of the jury.
他被邀請擔任陪審團成員之一。

justice [ˋdʒʌstɪs] 名 公平，正義　　反 injustice [ɪnˋdʒʌstɪs] 名 不公平

justify [ˋdʒʌstəˋfaɪ] 動 為～辯護，開釋

▶ Before I take actions, I have to make sure the measures are justified.
採取行動之前，我得確認這些措施是合理的。

相關衍生字彙 justly [ˋdʒʌstlɪ] 副 公正地，應得地、justifiable [ˋdʒʌstəˋfaɪəbl] 形 可辯護的、justifiably [ˋdʒʌstəˋfaɪəblɪ] 副 有正當理由地、justification [ˋdʒʌstəfəˋkeʃən] 名 辯護，正當的理由，藉口

動詞三態變化 justify - justified - justified

juvenile [ˋdʒuvənl] 名 青少年 形 未成熟的　　片 a juvenile court 少年法庭

相關衍生字彙 young [jʌŋ] 形 年輕的、adult [əˋdʌlt] 形 成年的、mature [məˋtjur] 形 成熟的、adolescent [ˋædlˋɛsnt] 形 青春期的

MEMO

字母 K

keen ~ koala

詞性說明

名 名詞	副 副詞	介 介系詞
動 動詞	形 形容詞	連 連接詞
代 代名詞	助 助動詞	

內文圖示說明

片 片語	反 反義字	同 同義字

遇到需要他人協助的時候，不妨試試下列的說法：

Could you please...?　　　Would you...?

Can you...?　　　　　　　Could I possibly...?

Would you mind...?

K keen ~ koala

★一網打盡 130 個英文單字 ｜ 一網打盡 18 句英語會話句

keen [kin] 形 熱衷的，渴望的
▶ I am so keen to make money as soon as possible.
我是如此渴望盡快地賺錢。

相關衍生字彙 keenly [ˋkinlɪ] 副 敏銳地，強烈地、keenness [ˋkinlnɪs] 名 熱心，敏銳，強烈、keen on 片 喜愛，熱衷於、keen-edged [ˋkinˋɛdʒd] 形 銳利的、keen-eyed [ˋkinˋaɪd] 形 眼光銳利的

keep [kip] 動 保持，飼養，記（日記，帳簿）　片 to keep on + Ving 繼續做〜
相關衍生字彙 keeper [ˋkipɚ] 名 飼養者，保管人，守衛、keep-fit [kipˋfɪt] 名 健身活動、keepsake [ˋkipˌsek] 名 紀念品
動詞三態變化 keep - kept - kept

ken [kɛn] 名 視野　片 beyond one's ken 超乎某人理解範圍
相關衍生字彙 perception [pɚˋsɛpʃən] 名 感知，察覺，看法

key [ki] 名 鑰匙，關鍵
▶ The key to success is hard work.
成功的關鍵是努力。

相關衍生字彙 keyboard [ˋkiˌbord] 名 鍵盤、keynote [ˋkiˌnot] 名 主音，基調、keystone [ˋkiˌston] 名 基本原則、keycard [ˋkiˌkɑrd] 名 門卡

kick [kɪk] 動 踢　片 to kick a ball 踢球
動詞三態變化 kick - kicked - kicked

kidnap [ˋkɪdnæp] 動 綁架，劫持
▶ Their daughter was kidnapped from the backyard.
他們的女兒在後院被綁架。

相關衍生字彙 kidnapper [ˋkɪdnæpɚ] 名 綁票者、abduct [æbˋdʌkt] 動 誘拐，劫持、highjack [ˋhaɪdʒæk] 名 劫持事件 動 搶奪（運輸中的貨物），劫持
動詞三態變化 kidnap - kidnapped - kidnapped

kidney [ˋkɪdnɪ] 名 腎臟
▶ The kidneys are important organs.
腎臟是很重要的器官。

相關衍生字彙 kidney bean 片 菜豆、kidney machine 片 人工腎、kidney stone 片 腎結石

kill [kɪl] 動 殺死，抵銷
▶ All the passengers were killed in the air crash.
此次墜機，所有乘客皆喪生。

相關衍生字彙 killer [`kɪlɚ] 名 殺手、killing [`kɪlɪŋ] 名 謀殺 形 致命的、kill off 片 殺光，滅絕、kill oneself 片 自殺、kill time 片 消磨時間、killable [`kɪləbl̩] 形 能殺的、killed [kɪld] 形 被殺死的，（疫苗等）不再有傳染力的

動詞三態變化 kill - killed - killed

kind [kaɪnd] 名 種類 形 親切的

▶ What kind of job do you like best?
你最喜歡哪種工作？

相關衍生字彙 kindhearted [`kaɪnd`hɑrtɪd] 形 好心的、kind [kaɪnd] 形 親切的、kindness [`kaɪndnɪs] 名 仁慈、kindly [`kaɪndlɪ] 形 和藹的

kindergarten [`kɪndɚ͵gɑrtn̩] 名 幼稚園

▶ She works as a teacher at a kindergarten. 她在幼稚園當老師。

kindle [`kɪndl̩] 動 點燃，照亮　　片 to kindle a fire 點火

動詞三態變化 kindle - kindled - kindled

kindred [`kɪndrɪd] 名 血緣，親屬　　片 kindred spirit 志趣相投的人

king [kɪŋ] 名 國王　　反 queen [`kwin] 名 女王

相關衍生字彙 kingly [`kɪŋlɪ] 形 國王的，高貴的、kingmaker [`kɪŋ͵mekɚ] 名 擁立國王者、ruler [`rulɚ] 名 統治者，管理者、sovereign [`sɑvrɪn] 名 君主，元首、monarch [`mɑnɚk] 名 君主，最高統治者、potentate [`potn͵tet] 名 君主，統治者

kingdom [`kɪŋdəm] 名 王國

▶ The king ruled his kingdom very well and was popular with his people.
這位國王將他的王國治理得很好而且受人們愛戴。

相關衍生字彙 country [`kʌntrɪ] 名 國家，國土、nation [`neʃən] 名 國家，民族、state [stet] 名 國家、empire [`ɛmpaɪr] 名 帝國、realm [rɛlm] 名 王國，領土、territory [`tɛrə͵torɪ] 名 領土，版圖

kinky [`kɪŋkɪ] 形 扭結的，怪癖的　　片 kinky behavior 變態行為

相關衍生字彙 kinkily [`kɪŋkəlɪ] 副 糾結地，捲毛地、curly [`kɝlɪ] 形 蜷曲的

kiss [kɪs] 動 親吻

▶ Every night, I kiss my children good night.
每晚我都會親吻我的孩子道晚安。

動詞三態變化 kiss - kissed - kissed

kitchen [`kɪtʃɪn] 名 廚房

▶ Mom is busy cooking in the kitchen.
媽媽在廚房裡忙著煮飯。

相關衍生字彙 cookroom [`kuk͵rum] 名 廚房、cookhouse [`kuk͵haus] 名 野外燒煮處，船上的廚房、cookery [`kukərɪ] 名 烹調、scullery [`skʌlərɪ] 名 炊具放存室，廚房的洗物槽、pantry [`pæntrɪ] 名 餐具室，食品儲藏室

K

kite [kaɪt] 名 風箏　　片 to fly a kite 放風箏

---

knack [næk] 名 本領
▶ Our manager has a knack for remembering names.
我們經理有記住名字的本領。

相關衍生字彙 skill [`skɪl] 名 技能、talent [`tælənt] 名 天資、aptitude [`æptəˌtjud] 名 天資，才能、gift [gɪft] 名 天賦，才能、ability [ə`bɪlətɪ] 名 能力

---

knead [nid] 動 揉（麵團、黏土），捏製，按摩
▶ I kneaded my grandmother's back.
我幫奶奶按摩背部。

動詞三態變化 knead - kneaded - kneaded

---

knee [ni] 名 膝蓋　　　　　　　　　　　　　◎ MP3 **11-02**
▶ She was on her knees cleaning the floor.
她跪著清理地板。

相關衍生字彙 kneecap [`niˌkæp] 名 膝蓋骨、knee-deep [`ni`dip] 形 深及膝的、knee breeches 片 長及膝部的短褲、knee mail 片 （跪地）祈禱、kneecapping [`niˌkæpɪŋ] 名 用槍擊穿膝蓋（或腿部）、kneed [nid] 形 有節的，有膝一般的關節的、knee-high [`ni`haɪ] 形 高及膝的

---

kneel [nil] 動 跪（下）　　片 to kneel down 跪下來

動詞三態變化 kneel - kneeled / knelt - kneeled / knelt

---

knife [naɪf] 名 刀子　　片 a steak knife 牛排刀

相關衍生字彙 knife-edge [`naɪfˌɛdʒ] 名 刀刃，銳利物、knife-edged [`naɪfˌɛdʒd] 形 鋒利的、knifeman [`naɪfmən] 名 持刀行兇者、knifing [`naɪfɪŋ] 名 持刀行兇

---

knight [naɪt] 名 騎士　　片 a white knight 救星

相關衍生字彙 horseman [`hɔrsmən] 名 騎馬者，馬術師、fighter [`faɪtɚ] 名 鬥士、warrior [`wɔrɪɚ] 名 戰士、soldier [`soldʒɚ] 名 士兵、cavalryman [`kævlrɪmən] 名 騎兵、equestrian [ɪ`kwɛstrɪən] 名 騎馬者 形 騎術的、fighter [`faɪtɚ] 名 戰士，鬥士、warrior [`wɔrɪɚ] 名 武士，勇士、knight-errant [`naɪt`ɛrənt] 名 有俠義心的人，（中世紀）遊俠騎士

---

knit [nɪt] 動 編織，接合
▶ Alice knitted a scarf for her boyfriend.
愛麗絲織了一條圍巾給男朋友。

相關衍生字彙 knitting [`nɪtɪŋ] 名 編織，針織、knitwear [`nɪtˌwɛr] 名 （總稱）針織衣物、knitter [`nɪtɚ] 名 編織者，編織機器、knitting needle 片 手工編織用的針、unknit [ʌn`nɪt] 動 拆散（編織物），解開，平整

動詞三態變化 knit - knitted / knit - knitted / knit

knock [nɑk] 動 敲，擊，打

▶ I heard someone knocking on the door.
我聽到有人敲門。

相關衍生字彙 knockout [`nɑk͵aut] 名（拳擊）擊倒，淘汰賽 形 擊倒對手的、punch [pʌntʃ]
動 用拳猛擊、pound [paund] 動 搗碎，（連續）猛擊、hammer [`hæmɚ] 名 鐵鎚
形 捶打

動詞三態變化 knock - knocked - knocked

---

knot [nɑt] 名（繩子的）結 動 打結

▶ The teacher is teaching the kids how to tie a knot.
老師正在教小朋友如何打結。

相關衍生字彙 slipknot [`slɪp͵nɑt] 名 活結、knotty [`nɑtɪ] 形 多結的的、aglet [`æglɪt] 名 釦鏈

動詞三態變化 knot - knotted - knotted

---

knowledge [`nɑlɪdʒ] 名 知識

▶ Knowledge is power.
（諺語）知識就是力量。

相關衍生字彙 know [no] 動 知道，認識、know-how [`no͵hau] 名 技術、
knowledgeable [`nɑlɪdʒəb!] 形 有知識的、well-known [`wɛl`non] 形 知名的

---

koala [ko`ɑlə] 名 無尾熊

▶ A koala is an Australian animal. 無尾熊是澳洲的動物。

K

MEMO

一網打盡

字母 **L**

label ~ lyric

詞性說明

名 名詞	副 副詞	介 介系詞
動 動詞	形 形容詞	連 連接詞
代 代名詞	助 助動詞	

內文圖示說明

片 片語　　反 反義字　　同 同義字

一網打盡「英語小知識」│如何用正式英文來溝通 II ───────

需要他人協助的時候，不妨試試下列的說法：

Yes, of course.

Yes, that's fine.

Certainly.

Absolutely.

By all means.

L label ~ lyric

★一網打盡 480 個英文單字 ｜ 一網打盡 95 句英語會話句　　　　　　　　　　○ MP3 **12-01**

label [ˋlebḷ] 名 商標，品牌
▶ Coach is a designer label and very popular in America.
　Coach 是個設計師品牌，在美國很受歡迎。

---

labor [ˋlebɚ] 名 勞力，陣痛　　片 in labor（婦女）分娩

---

laboratory [ˋlæbrəˌtorɪ] 名 實驗室　　片 a chemical laboratory 化學實驗室

---

laborer [ˋlebərɚ] 名 勞工　　片 a foreign laborer 外籍勞工

---

laborious [ləˋborɪəs] 形 費力的，牽強的
▶ Working at the factory is a laborious task.
　在工廠工作是很費力的工作。

相關衍生字彙 laboriously [ləˋborɪəslɪ] 副 費力地，艱苦地、labor-saving [ˋlebɚˌsevɪŋ] 形 省力的、labour camp 片 勞動營、labour exchange 片 職業介紹所、painful [ˋpenfəl] 形 疼痛的，困難的，辛勤的、tiresome [ˋtaɪrsəm] 形 令人厭倦的，煩人的、strenuous [ˋstrɛnjuəs] 形 費勁的，激烈的，緊張的、arduous [ˋardʒuəs] 形 艱鉅的，努力的，陡峭的、exhausting [ɪgˋzɔstɪŋ] 形 使耗盡的，使人精疲力竭的

---

lace [les] 名 花邊，蕾絲
▶ The skirt with pink lace makes you look cute.
　有粉紅色花邊的裙子讓妳顯得可愛。

---

lack [læk] 名 欠缺 動 不足
▶ Lack of sleep for days makes me tired.
　連日缺乏睡眠讓我好累。

動詞三態變化 lack - lacked - lacked

---

ladder [ˋlædɚ] 名 梯子
▶ The clerk used a ladder to reach for the book on the top shelf.
　店員用梯子去拿架子最上層的書。

---

lady [ˋledɪ] 名 女士　　反 gentleman [ˋdʒɛntḷmən] 名 紳士

相關衍生字彙 ladybird [ˋledɪˌbɝd] 名 瓢蟲、ladyship [ˋledɪˌʃɪp] 名 貴婦身分、lady-killer [ˋledɪˌkɪlɚ] 名 師奶殺手、ladylike [ˋledɪˌlaɪk] 形 嫻淑高貴的

---

lag [læg] 名 動 落後 動 延遲
▶ If you don't want to lag behind, study harder.
　如果你不想落後，就用功點。

動詞三態變化 lag - lagged - lagged

lake [lek] 名 湖泊
▶ They camped at the lake last weekend.
他們上個周末在湖邊露營。

相關衍生字彙 lakeside [`lek͵saɪd] 名 湖邊、lakefront [`lek͵frʌnt] 名 面臨湖水之處，湖邊、lakeport [`lek͵port] 名 湖畔港埠、pond [pɑnd] 名 池塘、tarn [tɑrn] 名 冰斗湖、lakelet [`leklɪt] 名 小湖、loch [lɑk] 名 湖，海灣

lamb [læm] 名 小羊　　片 as gentle as a lamb 非常溫馴
相關衍生字彙 sheep [ʃip] 名 綿羊、goat [got] 名 山羊、mutton [`mʌtn̩] 名 羊肉

lame [lem] 形 跛腳的
▶ The poor dog went lame. 可憐的狗腳跛了。

lament [lə`mɛnt] 名 動 痛哭，哀悼
▶ The little boy lamented over the death of his goldfish.
小男孩因為他死去的金魚痛哭。

動詞三態變化 lament - lamented - lamented

lamp [læmp] 名 燈　　片 a desk lamp 桌燈
相關衍生字彙 lamplight [`læmp͵laɪt] 名 燈光、lamppost [`læmp͵post] 名 街燈柱、lampshade [`læmp͵ʃed] 名 燈罩、lamp post 片 燈柱、lampion [`læmpɪən] 名 彩色燈，裝飾用燈、illuminant [ɪ`ljumənənt] 名 光源，發光體 形 發光的、luminant [`lumɪnənt] 名 發光體 形 發光的、lantern [`læntɚn] 名 燈籠

L

landscape [`lænd͵skep] 名 （陸上的）風景
▶ The town is famous for its beautiful landscape.
這小鎮以美麗的風景聞名。

相關衍生字彙 land [lænd] 名 土地、landlady [`lænd͵ledɪ] 名 女房東、landlord [`lænd͵lɔrd] 名 房東、landowner [`lænd͵onɚ] 名 地主

lane [len] 名 小路，巷弄
▶ His house is located in the narrow lane. 他的房子坐落在窄小的巷弄內。

language [`læŋgwɪdʒ] 名 語言
▶ Learning a foreign language takes time. 學外國語言需要花時間。

languid [`læŋgwɪd] 形 倦怠的，遲緩的
▶ She spoke in a languid voice.
她有氣無力地說話。

相關衍生字彙 languish [`læŋgwɪʃ] 動 變得無生氣，（植物等）凋萎、languidly [`læŋgwɪdlɪ] 副 疲倦地，陰沉地，不感興趣地、languish for 片 苦思、languisher [`læŋgwɪʃɚ] 名 衰弱，憔悴，煩惱、languishing [`læŋgwɪʃɪŋ] 形 漸漸衰弱的，懶洋洋的，拖延的、feeble [fib] 形 虛弱的，無力的，薄弱的、debilitated [dɪ`bɪlə͵tetɪd] 形 疲憊不堪的，操勞過度的、listless [`lɪstlɪs] 形 無精打采的，倦怠的

lantern [`læntɚn] 名 燈籠
▶ Lanterns have been replaced by electric lights. 燈籠已經被電燈取代了。

lapse [læps] 名 失誤，間隔 動 (時間) 流逝　　　　 MP3 12-02
▶ Sorry, it's my memory lapse.
抱歉，是我記錯了。
動詞三態變化 lapse - lapsed - lapsed

large [lɑrdʒ] 形 多數的，大規模的　　 片 by and large 總體而言
相關衍生字彙 largely [`lɑrdʒlɪ] 副 大量地，大部分、largeness [`lɑrdʒnɪs] 名 巨大、
large-scale [`lɑrdʒ`skel] 形 大規模的、large intestine 片 大腸、
large number of 片 大量的，眾多的、large-handed [`lɑrdʒ`hændɪd]
形 手大的，慷慨的、largehearted [`lɑrdʒ`hɑrtɪd] 形 度量寬大的、
large-minded [`lɑrdʒ`maɪndɪd] 形 心胸開闊的

lark [lɑrk] 名 雲雀
▶ She sings as beautifully as a lark. 她唱歌唱得如雲雀般優美。

lash [læʃ] 名 鞭子 名 動 鞭打
▶ The poor laborers were lashed by their employer.
可憐的勞工被雇主鞭打。
動詞三態變化 lash - lashed - lashed

last [læst] 形 僅剩的 副 最後地　　 片 last but not least 最後但同樣重要的是
相關衍生字彙 late [let] 形 遲的、lately [`letlɪ] 副 最近、later [`letɚ] 副 待會、latter [`lætɚ]
形 後者的、latest [`letɪst] 形 最新的

latch [lætʃ] 名 門閂
▶ Remember to leave the door on the latch. 記得把門閂上。

latent [`letn̩t] 形 潛伏的，隱性的
▶ The boy has the latent artistic talents. 這男孩有潛在的藝術天分。

latitude [`lætə‚tjud] 名 緯度　　 反 longitude [`lɑndʒə`tjud] 名 經度

laugh [læf] 名 笑聲 動 嘲笑　　 片 to laugh at 嘲笑
相關衍生字彙 laughter [`læftɚ] 名 笑聲、smile [smaɪl] 動 微笑、cry [kraɪ] 動 哭泣、
giggle [`gɪgl̩] 動 咯咯地笑、sob [sɑb] 動 啜泣
動詞三態變化 laugh - laughed - laughed

launch [lɔntʃ] 動 開始，發射，出版
▶ The new car will be launched soon.
新車很快就要推出了。
動詞三態變化 launch - launched - launched

laundry [`lɔndrɪ] 名 洗衣店　　 片 to do the laundry 洗衣服

相關衍生字彙 laundry basket 片 洗衣籃、laundry detergent 片 洗衣精、
laundryman [`lɔndrɪmən] 名 洗衣男工,(洗衣店中)取送衣服的人、
laundrywoman [`lɔndrɪˌwumən] 名 洗燙衣服的女工、washing [`wɑʃɪŋ]
名 洗滌(劑)、launderette [ˌlɔndə`rɛt] 名 自助洗衣店、dry cleaner 片 洗衣店

lava [`lɑvə] 名 熔岩
▶ Lava is hot liquid rock erupted from a volcano. 熔岩是從火山噴出的高溫岩漿。

lavish [`lævɪʃ] 動 揮霍 形 浪費的
▶ His lavish spending keeps him from saving money.
他奢侈的花費讓他存不了錢。

動詞三態變化 lavish - lavished - lavished

law [lɔ] 名 法律,規則,法學
▶ Mother warns us never to be against the law.
媽媽要我們別違法。

相關衍生字彙 lawyer [`lɔjɚ] 名 律師、lawsuit [`lɔˌsut] 名 訴訟、lawful [`lɔfəl] 形 合法的、
lawmaker [`lɔˌmekɚ] 名 立法者

lawn [lɔn] 名 草地　　片 to mow the lawn 割草

lay [le] 動 放置
▶ Lay aside your cellphone and focus your mind on the course.
請拿開你的手機,專心課程。

相關衍生字彙 layer [`leɚ] 名 階層,地層、layman [`lemən] 名 俗人,門外漢、lay a finger on
片 碰觸

動詞三態變化 lay - laid - laid

layout [`leˌaut] 名 版面編排
▶ The layout of the book is very beautiful.
這本書的編排很漂亮。

相關衍生字彙 layoff [`leˌɔf] 名 解雇、layover [`leˌovɚ] 名 中途停留、layer [`leɚ] 名 層

lazy [`lezɪ] 形 懶散的　　片 a lazy Susan 大桌上的轉盤

leader [`lidɚ] 名 領導者
▶ Few people deny that Jobs is a born leader.
大家應同意賈伯斯是個天生領導者。

相關衍生字彙 lead [lid] 動 領導、leadership [`lidɚ ʃɪp] 名 領導能力、leading [`lidɪŋ]
形 領導的、management [`mænɪdʒmənt] 名 管理

leaf [lif] 名 葉子　　片 falling leaves 落葉

L

leak [lik] 名 裂縫 動 使滲漏
MP3 12-03
▶ It seems oil is leaking out of your car.
你的車子好像在漏油。
動詞三態變化 leak - leaked - leaked

lean [lin] 動 傾身，倚靠
▶ If you feel tired, you can lean your head back.
如果覺得累，你可以把頭往後靠。
動詞三態變化 lean - leaned - leaned

leap [lip] 動 跳
▶ Look before you leap.
（諺語）三思而後行。
動詞三態變化 leap - leaped - leaped

learn [lɜn] 動 學習
▶ It's never too late to learn.
（諺語）活到老學到老。
相關衍生字彙 learned [`lɜnɪd] 形 有學問的、learning [`lɜnɪŋ] 名 學習、study [`stʌdɪ]
動 學習、read [rid] 動 閱讀
動詞三態變化 learn - learned / learnt - learned / learnt

least [list] 名 最小，最少　　片 at least 至少

leather [`lɛðɚ] 名 皮革
▶ A leather coat can keep you warm. 皮衣可以保暖。

leave [liv] 動 離開（某處），把～交給
▶ Hurry up! The train will leave in ten minutes.
趕快！火車再十分鐘就要離開了。
動詞三態變化 leave - left - left

lecture [`lɛktʃɚ] 名 演講 名動 授課
▶ All the students were asked to listen to the lecture.
所有的學生被要求去聽這場演講。
動詞三態變化 lecture - lectured - lectured

left [lɛft] 形 左方的　　反 right [raɪt] 形 右方的
相關衍生字彙 left-handed [`lɛft`hædɪd] 形 左撇的，笨拙的、left-wing [`lɛft.wɪŋ] 形 左派的、
left field 片 左外野、left fielder 片 左外野手、left luggage 片 行李寄放、
sinister [`sɪnɪstɚ] 形 惡意的，不祥的，左邊的

leg [lɛg] 名 腿
▶ A lady sat by the window, crossing her legs.
有位女士坐在窗邊，雙腿交叉著。

相關衍生字彙 thigh [θaɪ] 名 大腿、calf [kæf] 名 小腿、limb [lɪm] 名 四肢、foot [fʊt] 名 腳，足、sole [sol] 名 腳底、knee [ni] 名 膝蓋

legacy [ˋlɛgəsɪ] 名 遺產，遺贈
▶ After he died, he handed down a legacy. 他死後，留下大筆的遺產。

legal [ˋligl] 形 合法的　　反 illegal [ɪˋligl] 形 不合法的

legend [ˋlɛdʒənd] 名 傳奇
▶ The movie was adapted from a legend.
這部電影改編自一個傳奇故事。

相關衍生字彙 legendary [ˋlɛdʒəndˏɛrɪ] 形 傳奇的、legendarily [ˋlɛdʒəndˏɛrəlɪ] 副 傳奇性地、legendize [ˋlɛdʒənˏdaɪz] 動 使傳奇化、legendry [ˋlɛdʒəndrɪ] 名 傳說之集稱、fiction [ˋfɪkʃən] 名（總稱）小說，捏造、myth [mɪθ] 名 神話，虛構的人（或事物）、folklore [ˋfokˏlor] 名 民間傳說，民俗

legible [ˋlɛdʒəbl] 形 易讀的，易辨識的　　反 illegible [ɪˋlɛdʒəbl] 形 難讀的

legislative [ˋlɛdʒɪsˏletɪv] 形 立法的　　片 the Legislative Yuan 立法院
相關衍生字彙 legislation [ˏlɛdʒɪsˋleʃən] 名 立法，法律、legislator [ˋlɛdʒɪsˏletɚ] 名 立法者，立法委員、legislate [ˋlɛdʒɪsˏlet] 動 立法，制定（或通過）法律、legislative decree 片 法令、legislatively [ˋlɛdʒɪsˏletɪvlɪ] 副 以立法方式、legislatorial [ˏlɛdʒɪsləˋtorɪəl] 形 立法者的，立法機構的、legislatorship [ˋlɛdʒɪsˏletɚʃɪp] 名 立法者，立法委員、legislature [ˋlɛdʒɪsˏletʃɚ] 名 立法機關

legitimate [lɪˋdʒɪtəmɪt] 形 合法的
▶ Is it legitimate to set up a party without application?
沒有申請就設立一個黨，合法嗎？

leisure [ˋliʒɚ] 名 閒暇 形 空閒的
▶ I enjoy listening to music at leisure.
有空時我喜歡聽音樂。
相關衍生字彙 free [fri] 形 空閒的、busy [ˋbɪzɪ] 形 忙碌的、liberty [ˋlɪbɚtɪ] 名 自由、unrestrained [ˏʌnrɪˋstrend] 形 無拘束的

lemon [ˋlɛmən] 名 檸檬
▶ I like to put a slice of lemon in my hot tea.
我喜歡在熱茶裡放一片檸檬。
相關衍生字彙 lemonade [ˏlɛmənˋed] 名 檸檬水、lemon curd 片 檸檬酪、lemon drop 片 檸檬味的水果糖、lemon grass 片 檸檬香茅、lemon juice 片 檸檬汁、lemon squeezer 片 檸檬榨汁器、lemon yellow 片 檸檬黃，淡黃色、lemony [ˋlɛmənɪ] 形 有檸檬味的，檸檬色的

lend [lɛnd] 動 把～借給　　反 borrow [ˋbaro] 動 借入
動詞三態變化 lend - lent - lent

length [lɛŋθ] 名 （距離、尺寸的）長度
▶ Please tell me the length and width of the desk.
　請告訴我桌子的長與寬。
相關衍生字彙 lengthen [`lɛŋθən] 動 增長、long [lɔŋ] 形 長的、wide [waɪd] 形 寬的、
　　width [wɪdθ] 名 寬度、high [haɪ] 形 高的、height [haɪt] 名 高度

---

lenient [`linjənt] 形 仁慈的，寬大的　　　　　MP3 **12-04**
▶ A judge should not be too lenient or too cruel. 法官不能太仁慈也不能太殘忍。

leopard [`lɛpɚd] 名 美洲豹
▶ A leopard can't change its spots. （諺語）本性難改。

less [lɛs] 形 較少的
▶ Eat less chocolate, or you will get fatter and fatter.
　少吃點巧克力，不然你會愈來愈胖。
相關衍生字彙 lessen [`lɛsn] 動 減少、lesson [`lɛsn] 名 課程、little [`lɪt!] 形 少的、few [fju]
　　形 少的、fewer [`fjuɚ] 形 較少的

lest [lɛst] 連 惟恐，免得
▶ We dared not tell him the truth, lest he would faint.
　我們不敢告訴他事實，以免他昏倒。

lethal [`liθəl] 形 致命的　　片 lethal weapons 致命的武器

letter [`lɛtɚ] 名 信件　　片 a dear John letter 分手信件

level [`lɛvl] 名 水平面，程度，級別
▶ Students at the low level need more practice. 程度較低的學生需要多加練習。

liable [`laɪəbl̩] 形 有義務的
▶ Parents are liable if their young kids are against the law.
　小孩違法父母有責任的。
相關衍生字彙 liability [ˌlaɪə`bɪlətɪ] 名 傾向，責任，義務、liable to 片 易於，可能、
　　responsible [rɪ`spansəbl] 形 承擔責任的，有責任感的、
　　accountable [ə`kauntəbl] 形 可說明的，應負責任的、answerable [`ænsərəbl]
　　形 有責任的，可答覆的

libel [`laɪbl̩] 名 動 誹謗
▶ The magazine was sued for libel.
　這本雜誌被控誹謗。
動詞三態變化 libel - libeled - libeled

liberal [`lɪbərəl] 形 自由的，開明的
▶ We are proud of our liberal society.
　我們以我們自由的社會為榮。
相關衍生字彙 liberate [`lɪbəˌret] 動 解放、liberty [`lɪbɚtɪ] 名 自由、free [fri] 形 自由的、
　　freedom [`fridəm] 名 自由

library [`laɪˌbrɛrɪ] 名 圖書館　　片 a public library 公立圖書館

相關衍生字彙 librarian [laɪ`brɛrɪən] 名 圖書館員，圖書館館長、bibliotheca [ˌbɪblɪə`θikə] 名 圖書室、bibliothecary [ˌbɪblɪ`αθəˌkɛrɪ] 名 圖書管理員、reading room 片 閱覽室

---

license [`laɪsn̩s] 名 執照

▶ You can't drive without a driver's license. 沒有駕照不能開車。

---

lie [laɪ] 名 謊話 動 撒謊　　片 to tell a lie 說謊話

相關衍生字彙 liar [`laɪɚ] 名 說謊者、honest [`αnɪst] 形 誠實的、honesty [`αnɪstɪ] 名 誠實、trustworthy [`trʌstˌwɝðɪ] 形 值得信賴的

動詞三態變化 lie - lay - lain

---

life [laɪf] 名 生命，人生

▶ How I wish to live a happy life!
多希望能過著幸福的人生！

相關衍生字彙 lifetime [`laɪfˌtaɪm] 名 一生、lifeboat [`laɪfˌbot] 名 救生艇、lifeguard [`laɪfˌgɑrd] 名 救生員、lifelong [`laɪfˌlɔŋ] 形 終生的、live [lɪv] 動 活著、lively [`laɪvlɪ] 形 活潑的、liver [`lɪvɚ] 名 肝臟

---

lift [lɪft] 動 舉起，提高

▶ Thank you for lifting the box for me.
謝謝你幫我把箱子抬起來。

動詞三態變化 lift - lifted - lifted

---

light [laɪt] 名 光線 動 點燃　　片 to turn on / off the light 開／關燈

動詞三態變化 light - lighted / lit - lighted / lit

---

lighten [`laɪtn̩] 動 照亮　　反 darken [`dɑrkn̩] 動 使變暗

相關衍生字彙 lighthouse [`laɪtˌhaʊs] 名 燈塔、lightly [`laɪtlɪ] 副 輕輕地、lightning [`laɪtnɪŋ] 名 閃電

動詞三態變化 lighten - lightened - lightened

---

lily [`lɪlɪ] 名 百合花

▶ Of all the flowers, I like lilies the best. 所有的花裡，我最喜歡百合。

---

limb [lɪm] 名 四肢　　片 an artificial limb 義肢

---

likewise [`laɪkˌwaɪz] 副 同樣地

▶ Please clean the windows, and likewise the ones in the kitchen.
請擦乾淨這些窗戶，還有廚房的也要擦乾淨。

相關衍生字彙 like [laɪk] 動 喜歡、likely [`laɪklɪ] 形 很可能的、likeness [`laɪknɪs] 名 相似

L

limitation [ˌlɪməˈteʃən] 名 限制
▶ With the budget limitation, it's impossible for us to buy a larger house.
因為有預算上的限制，我們不可能買更大的房子。

相關衍生字彙 limit [ˈlɪmɪt] 動 界線，限度，範圍、limited [ˈlɪmɪtɪd] 形 有限的，不多的、
constraint [kənˈstrent] 名 約束，強迫，抑制

line [laɪn] 名 線條，（詩、文的）一行　片 to read between the lines 體會言外之意

liner [ˈlaɪnɚ] 名 班機，眼線筆　片 a luxury liner 豪華客輪

linger [ˈlɪŋgɚ] 動 拖延，徘徊
▶ The terrible smell lingered in the car for days.
難聞的味道在車內停留好幾天。

動詞三態變化 linger - lingered - lingered

link [lɪŋk] 名 環節 動 連接
▶ With Wi-Fi, I can make a link to the Internet.
有無線網路，我就可以連上網。

動詞三態變化 link - linked - linked

lion [ˈlaɪən] 名 獅子
▶ Lions are the king of animals. 獅子是萬獸之王。

lip [lɪp] 名 嘴唇
▶ He kissed her on the lips. 他親吻她的唇。

liquid [ˈlɪkwɪd] 名 液體　反 solid [ˈsɑlɪd] 名 固體

liquor [ˈlɪkɚ] 名 含酒精飲料
▶ Drinking too much liquor does harm to your health. 喝太多烈酒會傷身。

list [lɪst] 名 名冊，目錄　片 to make a list 列清單

listen [ˈlɪsṇ] 動 傾聽　片 to listen to music 聽音樂
動詞三態變化 listen - listened - listened

literally [ˈlɪtərəlɪ] 副 逐字地
▶ I have read your letter literally. 我已經逐字地讀過你的信了。

literature [ˈlɪtərətʃɚ] 名 文學
▶ Shakespeare plays an important role in British literature.
莎士比亞在英國文學中扮演重要的角色。

相關衍生字彙 literary [ˈlɪtəˌrɛrɪ] 形 文學的、literate [ˈlɪtərɪt] 形 能讀能寫的、
science [ˈsaɪəns] 名 科學、scientific [ˌsaɪənˈtɪfɪk] 形 科學的

litter [ˈlɪtɚ] 名 廢棄物 動 亂丟（雜物）　片 No littering! 禁止亂丟垃圾！
動詞三態變化 litter - littered - littered

livestock [ˈlaɪv͵stak] 名 家畜
▶ Pigs and sheep are livestock. 豬跟羊都是家畜。

load [lod] 名 動 裝載　　片 to be loaded with 裝載（東西）
相關衍生字彙 overload [͵ovɚˈlod] 動 超載、unload [ʌnˈlod] 動 卸貨、loading [ˈlodɪŋ] 名 負荷
動詞三態變化 load - loaded - loaded

loaf [lof] 名（一條）麵包　　片 a loaf of bread 一條麵包

loan [lon] 名 貸款
▶ She got a loan to finish her studies. 她貸款完成學業。

loath [loθ] 形 不願意的　　同 unwilling [ʌnˈwɪlɪŋ] 形 不願意的

loathe [loð] 動 厭惡，憎恨　　同 hate [het] 動 厭惡
動詞三態變化 loathe - loathed - loathed

lobby [ˈlabɪ] 名 大廳　　◉ MP3 **12-06**
▶ The lobby is a non-smoking zone. 大廳是非吸菸區。

local [ˈlokl̩] 形 當地的
▶ Remember to respect the local culture.
　請尊重當地的文化。
相關衍生字彙 locate [loˈket] 動 找出、location [loˈkeʃən] 名 地理位置、region [ˈridʒən]
　　　　名 地區、regional [ˈridʒənl̩] 形 區域的、localize [ˈlokl̩͵aɪz] 動 使具地方色彩

lock [lak] 名 鎖 動 鎖上
▶ The secretary locked all the files in her drawer.
　祕書把檔案鎖在抽屜裡。
動詞三態變化 lock - locked - locked

lodge [ladʒ] 動 寄宿
▶ I lodged with my uncle when I first came to America.
　我剛到美國時，寄住在叔叔家。
動詞三態變化 lodge - lodged - lodged

lodging [ˈladʒɪŋ] 名 旅社
▶ Living in lodgings costs less than staying in the hotel. 住民宿比待在飯店便宜。

lofty [ˈlɔftɪ] 形 高聳的　　片 a lofty mountain 高聳的山

log [lɔg] 名 圓木　　片 to split a log 劈木頭

logic [ˈladʒɪk] 名 邏輯
▶ There is no logic in the new policy. 這項新政策實在沒有邏輯。

logical [`lɑdʒɪkl] 形 合邏輯的
▶ His suggestion is very logical and acceptable. 他的建議很合邏輯，可接受。

---

lonesome [`lonsəm] 形 寂寞的，荒涼的
▶ Are you lonesome tonight?
你今晚寂寞嗎？
相關衍生字彙 lonely [`lonlɪ] 形 寂寞的、alone [ə`lon] 形 單獨的

---

long [lɔŋ] 形 長久的 動 渴望
▶ People all longed for peace.
人們都渴望和平。
相關衍生字彙 long-distance [`lɔŋ`dɪstəns] 形 長途的，長距離的、longevity [lɑn`dʒɛvətɪ] 名 長壽、longhaired [`lɔŋ`hɛrd] 形 長髮的、longing [`lɔŋɪŋ] 名 渴望，熱望 形 渴望的
動詞三態變化 long - longed - longed

---

longitude [`lɑndʒə`tjud] 名 經度　　反 latitude [`lætə‚tjud] 名 緯度

---

look [luk] 動 觀看，注意　　片 to look forward to 期盼
動詞三態變化 look - looked - looked

---

lookout [`luk`aut] 名 守望，警戒
片 to be on the lookout for something / sombody 尋找

---

loop [lup] 名 環狀物
▶ The teacher asked her students to make a loop. 老師要學生繞成一圈。

---

loophole [`lup‚hol] 名（法律等的）漏洞　　片 a loophole in the law 法律的漏洞

---

loose [lus] 形 鬆散的，不拘謹的
▶ The nails in the windows seem loose.
窗戶的釘子好像鬆了。
相關衍生字彙 loosely [`luslɪ] 副 不嚴謹地、loosen [`lusn̩] 動 解開、tighten [`taɪtn̩] 動 弄緊、tight [taɪt] 形 緊的

---

loot [lut] 名 贓物 動 搶劫
▶ The police finally found the stolen loot.
警方終於找到被偷的贓物。
動詞三態變化 loot - looted - looted

---

lord [lɔrd] 名 貴族，巨擘
▶ His father is a media lord. 他爸爸是媒體大亨。

---

lost [lɔst] 形 遺失的，輸掉的
▶ Kids get lost easily while their mothers are shopping in the department store.
當媽媽在百貨公司逛街時，孩子最容易走失。

相關衍生字彙 lose [luz] 動 遺失、loss [lɔs] 名 損失、gain [gen] 名 動 獲得、get [tʃ ɡɛt] 動 獲得

lot [lɑt] 名 多數　　**片** a lot of / lots of 很多的　　◎ MP3 **12-07**

lottery [`lɑtərɪ] 名 彩券
▶ Everyone at the party has a chance of winning the lottery.
　派對上的每個人都有機會贏得彩金。

loudly [`laʊdlɪ] 副 高聲地
▶ They were talking so loudly that I could hear in the next room.
　他們説話很大聲，我在隔壁房間都聽得到。

lounge [laʊndʒ] 名 休息室 動 閒蕩
▶ You can take a rest in the lounge before the meeting begins.
　會議開始前，你可以在休息室休息。
動詞三態變化 lounge - lounged - lounged

lousy [`laʊzɪ] 形 討厭的，不潔的
▶ The service the hotel offered was lousy. 這間飯店的服務很差。

love [lʌv] 名 愛情 動 愛好，喜歡
▶ I will love you forever.
　我將永遠愛你。
相關衍生字彙 lovely [`lʌvlɪ] 形 可愛的，秀美動人的、lover [`lʌvɚ] 名 戀人，情人、love affair
　　　　 片 戀愛關係，風流事、love apple 片 番茄、loveless [`lʌvlɪs]
　　　　 形 無愛情的，得不到愛的、affection [ə`fɛkʃən] 名 情愛，鍾愛、
　　　　 adoration [ˌædə`reʃən] 名 崇拜，敬愛
動詞三態變化 love - loved - loved

low [lo] 形 低的，不足的　　反 high [haɪ] 形 高的

loyal [`lɔɪəl] 形 忠誠的
▶ Dogs are always loyal to their owners.
　小狗對主人很忠心。
相關衍生字彙 loyalty [`lɔɪəltɪ] 名 忠誠、disloyal [dɪs`lɔɪəl] 形 不忠誠的、betray [bɪ`tre]
　　　　 動 背叛、loyalist [`lɔɪəlɪst] 名 忠誠的人

lubricate [`lubrɪˌket] 動 使潤滑
▶ An engine should be lubricated with oil.
　引擎需要油來潤滑。
動詞三態變化 lubricate - lubricated - lubricated

luggage [`lʌɡɪdʒ] 名 行李
▶ When you are traveling, don't take heavy luggage. 旅行時，不要帶重的行李。

lucky [`lʌkɪ] 形 幸運的
▶ I am so lucky to get acquainted with you.
很幸運可以認識你。
相關衍生字彙 luck [lʌk] 名 運氣、luckily [`lʌkɪlɪ] 副 幸運地、fortunate [`fɔrtʃənɪt] 形 幸運的、unlucky [ʌn`lʌkɪ] 形 不幸的

- - -

lull [lʌl] 動 使入睡，使緩和
▶ The tender music lulled the baby to sleep.
柔和的音樂讓嬰兒睡著了。
相關衍生字彙 lullaby [`lʌlə‚baɪ] 名 搖籃曲、quell [kwɛl] 動 鎮壓，消除，減輕、alleviate [ə`livɪ‚et] 動 減輕，緩和
動詞三態變化 lull - lulled - lulled

- - -

lumber [`lʌmbɚ] 名 木材
▶ The lumber is prepared for building a bridge.
這些木材是準備用來蓋一座橋。
相關衍生字彙 wood [wʊd] 名 木頭、timber [`tɪmbɚ] 名 木材、log [lɔg] 名 圓木，原木、firewood [`faɪr‚wʊd] 名 木柴，柴火

- - -

luminous [`lumənəs] 形 發光的，清楚的
▶ Look! The roof of the house is luminous with sunlight.
瞧！屋頂被陽光照得發亮。

lump [lʌmp] 名 團，塊 片 a lump of clay 一團黏土

lunar [`lunɚ] 形 陰曆的，蒼白的 片 lunar calendar 農曆

lunatic [`lunə‚tɪk] 名 瘋子 形 瘋狂的
▶ He suddenly screamed like a lunatic. 他突然大叫，像個瘋子一樣。

luncheon [`lʌntʃən] 名（正式的）午餐會
▶ The boss has a luncheon with his managers regularly.
老闆會定期跟他的主管們吃午餐。
相關衍生字彙 lunch [lʌntʃ] 名 午餐、brunch [brʌntʃ] 名 早午餐、supper [`sʌpɚ] 名 晚餐、banquet [`bæŋkwɪt] 名 宴會、feast [fist] 名 盛宴

lung [lʌŋ] 名 肺部 片 lung cancer 肺癌

lure [lur] 名 魅力，誘惑物
▶ Few people can resist the lure of money. 鮮少有人能抵抗金錢的誘惑。

lurk [lɝk] 動 潛伏，埋伏 ◉ MP3 12-08
▶ Some enemies were lurking in the forest.
有敵軍潛伏在森林裡。
動詞三態變化 lurk - lurked - lurked

luster [`lʌstɚ] 名 光澤，榮耀 動 發光
▶ Good shampoo can help restore the luster to your hair.
好的洗髮精有助於恢復你頭髮的光澤。

---

luxury [`lʌkʃərɪ] 名 奢侈
▶ He is not rich, but lives in luxury.
他不富有，但卻過著奢侈的生活。

相關衍生字彙 luxuriant [lʌg`ʒʊrɪənt] 形 濃密的、luxurious [lʌg`ʒʊrɪəs] 形 奢侈的、
humble [`hʌmbl] 形 簡樸的、poor [pʊr] 形 貧窮的

---

lyrics [`lɪrɪks] 名 歌詞
▶ The lyrics of the song are poetic. 這首歌的歌詞像詩一般。

MEMO

L

一網打盡「英語小知識」｜表示「贊成」的說法

I agree with your opinion. 我贊成你的意見。

I couldn't agree more. 我完全贊同。

I agree with you on all points. 你的見解我全都認同。

That's my idea, too. 我的想法也是那樣。

That's exactly how I see it. 我的看法就是那樣。

machine ~ mythology

★一網打盡 583 個英文單字 ｜ 一網打盡 170 句英語會話句　　◎ MP3 **13-01**

machine [mə`ʃin] 名 機器　片 a vending machine 自動販賣機
相關衍生字彙 machinery [mə`ʃinəri] 名 機器、mechanic [mə`kænɪk] 名 技師、
mechanical [mə`kænɪkl] 形 機械的、mechanism [`mɛkə،nɪzəm] 名 機制

mad [mæd] 形 瘋狂的，魯莽的
▶ Under the pressure, I will be going mad. 在這樣的壓力底下，我會瘋掉。

madness [`mædnɪs] 名 瘋狂，愚蠢
▶ A war is stupid madness. 戰爭是愚蠢的瘋狂行為。

magazine [،mægə`zin] 名 雜誌
▶ *Esquire* is a men's magazine.《君子時代》是男性雜誌。

magic [`mædʒɪk] 名 魔術　片 to perform magic 表演魔術
相關衍生字彙 magical [`mædʒɪkl] 形 神奇的、magician [mə`dʒɪʃən] 名 魔術師、
witchcraft [`wɪtʃ،kræft] 名 巫術、witch [wɪtʃ] 名 巫婆

magistrate [`mædʒɪs،tret] 名 地方行政官
▶ Her husband is a civil magistrate in the government.
她老公是政府機構裡的一名文職官員。

magnificent [mæg`nɪfəsənt] 形 壯麗的，極好的
▶ The magnificent view is so impressive. 壯麗的景色真令人印象深刻。

magnet [`mægnɪt] 名 磁鐵
▶ A magnet is able to attract iron.
磁鐵能吸鐵。
相關衍生字彙 magnetic [mæg`nɛtɪk] 形 有磁性的、magnetism [`mægnə،tɪzəm]
名 磁性，魅力、magnetize [`mægnə،taɪz] 動 使具磁性

magnify [`mægnə،faɪ] 動 放大，誇大
▶ The accident magnified the racial conflict.
這個意外事件加深了種族衝突。
動詞三態變化 magnify - magnified - magnified

magnitude [`mægnə،tjud] 名 巨大，重要
▶ Don't ignore the magnitude of the problem. 不要忽視這個問題的重要性。

maid [med] 名 女僕，少女
▶ The apartment building offers daily maid service.
這棟公寓提供每天的家居清潔服務。

mailman [`mel͵mæn] 名 郵差　　同 postman [`postmən] 名 郵差
相關衍生字彙　mailbox [`mel͵bɑks] 名 郵筒、mail [mel] 名 郵件、post office 名 郵局、post [post] 名 郵政

maim [mem] 名 傷殘 動 使殘廢
▶ Many people were maimed in the war.
很多人在戰爭中受重傷。
動詞三態變化　maim - maimed - maimed

main [men] 形 主要的，盡力的
▶ The main idea of the article is about technology. 這篇文章的主旨是科技

mainland [`menlənd] 名 大陸 形 本土的　　片 Mainland China 中國大陸

maintain [men`ten] 動 維持，保養，主張
▶ Despite graduating from university for years, we have maintained a close friendship.
儘管大學畢業很多年，我們仍是好朋友。
動詞三態變化　maintain - maintained - maintained

maintenance [`mentənəns] 名 保持，維修，堅持
▶ Cars need regular maintenance. 汽車需要定期保養。

majestic [mə`dʒɛstɪk] 形 雄偉的，崇高的
▶ The majestic scenery takes all the visitors' breath away.
這雄偉的景色讓旅客震懾。
相關衍生字彙　majesty [`mædʒɪstɪ] 名 雄偉，崇高、great [gret] 形 偉大的、gorgeous [`gɔrdʒəs] 形 華麗的、magnificent [mæg`nɪfəsənt] 形 壯麗的

major [`medʒɚ] 動 主修 形 較多的
▶ He majored in leadership and management at Cambridge.
他在劍橋主修領導與管理。
動詞三態變化　major - majored - majored

majority [mə`dʒɔrətɪ] 名 多數　　反 minority [maɪ`nɔrətɪ] 名 少數

make [mek] 動 製作，成為，使成功　　片 to make up 和解，補償　　MP3 13-02
相關衍生字彙　makeshift [`mek͵ʃɪft] 名 臨時代用品、make-believe [`mekbə͵liv] 名 假裝、makeover [`mekovɚ] 名 美容、maker [`mekɚ] 名 製造者
動詞三態變化　make - made - made

malady [`mælədɪ] 名 疾病，腐敗　　同 disease [dɪ`ziz] 名 疾病

male [mel] 形 男性的　　反 female [`fimel] 形 女性的

malice [`mælɪs] 名 惡意，怨恨
▶ There is no malice in what I said. 我之前說的話完全沒有惡意。

malicious [məˋlɪʃəs] 形 惡意的
▶ The rumor is too malicious. 這個謠言太惡毒。

malnutrition [ˌmælnjuˋtrɪʃən] 名 營養失調
▶ Most of the refugees are suffering from malnutrition, especially women and kids.
大部分的難民都營養不良，尤其是婦女跟小孩。

mammal [ˋmæml] 名 哺乳動物
▶ The whale is a mammal, not a fish. 鯨魚是哺乳動物，不是魚。

man [mæn] 名 男人　　　反 woman [ˋwʊmən] 名 女人

manage [ˋmænɪdʒ] 動 管理，控制
▶ He is a person with lots of experience of managing workers.
他是一個很有管理工人經驗的人。
相關衍生字彙 management [ˋmænɪdʒmənt] 名 管理、manager [ˋmænɪdʒɚ] 名 經理、
lead [lid] 動 領導、leader [ˋlidɚ] 名 領導、leadership [ˋlidɚʃɪp] 名 領導能力
動詞三態變化 manage - managed - managed

maneuver [məˋnuvɚ] 名 軍事演習　　　片 to perform maneuver 進行軍事演習

mangle [ˋmæŋgl] 動 損毀
▶ What a terrible accident! The bicycle became a pile of mangled metal.
好可怕的車禍！那腳踏車變成一堆廢鐵。
動詞三態變化 mangle - mangled - mangled

mania [ˋmenɪə] 名 狂熱，瘋狂
▶ He has a mania for toy collection. 他有收集玩具的癖好。

manifold [ˋmænəˌfold] 形 各式各樣的
▶ Despite her manifold disadvantages, her husband loves her so much.
儘管她很多缺點，她老公還是很愛她。

manipulate [məˋnɪpjəˌlet] 動 操作，控制
▶ The politician is very good at manipulating the media.
這位政客很會操控媒體。
相關衍生字彙 operate [ˋɑpəˌret] 動 操作，經營、handle [ˋhændl] 動 操縱、govern [ˋgʌvɚn]
動 管理，統治、control [kənˋtrol] 動 控制，支配
動詞三態變化 manipulate - manipulated - manipulated

mankind [mænˋkaɪnd] 名 人類　　　片 the good of mankind 人類福祉

manly [ˋmænlɪ] 形 有男子氣概的
▶ Fighting is not a manly manner. 打架不是有男子氣概的行為。

manner [ˋmænɚ] 名 舉止，態度
▶ Because of her friendly manner, she is popular with peers.
因為她很友善，所以很受同儕歡迎。

---

mansion [ˋmænʃən] 名 大廈，官邸
▶ Only rich men can afford to live in the mansion.
只有有錢人住得起這棟宅第。

相關衍生字彙 apartment [əˋpɑrtmənt] 名 公寓、palace [ˋpælɪs] 名 皇宮、villa [ˋvɪlə] 名 別墅、castle [ˋkæsl̩] 名 城堡、suite [swit] 名 套房

---

manual [ˋmænjuəl] 名 手冊 形 手工的
▶ Many manual jobs are replaced by machines. 很多手工工作已經被機器取代。

---

manufacture [͵mænjəˋfæktʃɚ] 名 製造業 動 加工
▶ His company is famous for manufacturing car parts.
他的公司以製造汽車零件而聞名。

相關衍生字彙 manufacturer [͵mænjəˋfæktʃərɚ] 名 製造商、produce [prəˋdjus] 動 製造、production [prəˋdʌkʃən] 名 生產、product [ˋprɑdəkt] 名 產品

動詞三態變化 manufacture - manufactured - manufactured

---

manuscript [ˋmænjə͵skrɪpt] 名 手稿　　　　　　　◎ MP3 13-03
▶ The writer spent months finishing his manuscript.
作家花了好幾個月完成他的手稿。

M

---

map [mæp] 名 地圖 動 繪製地圖
▶ There is a map of the world on the wall of my room.
我房間牆上有一張世界地圖。

動詞三態變化 map - mapped - mapped

---

marathon [ˋmærə͵θɑn] 名 馬拉松
▶ It's not easy to run a marathon. 跑馬拉松不是件容易的事。

---

marble [ˋmɑrbl̩] 名 大理石
▶ The statue is made of marble. 這雕像是大理石做的。

March [mɑrtʃ] 名 三月
▶ They plan to go to Japan in March. 他們打算三月去日本。

---

march [mɑrtʃ] 名 遊行示威，進行曲　　　片 a wedding march 結婚進行曲

---

margin [ˋmɑrdʒɪn] 名 邊緣，頁邊空白
▶ I used to write some ideas in the margin.
我以前習慣在書的頁邊空白處寫下想法。

---

marine [məˋrin] 形 海洋的　　　片 marine life 海洋生物

---

mariner [ˋmærənɚ] 名 船員，水手　　　同 sailor [ˋselɚ] 名 船員

mark [mɑrk] 名 記號 動 標明
▶ There are some dirty marks on my car. It's time to wash it.
我車上有很多髒的印子，該洗車了。
動詞三態變化 mark - marked - marked

---

market [`mɑrkɪt] 名 市場　片 a stock market 股票市場

---

marketing [`mɑrkɪtɪŋ] 名 行銷學
▶ Marketing is the key to success of a company. 行銷是公司成功的關鍵。

---

marriage [`mærɪdʒ] 名 婚姻　片 a happy marriage 幸福的婚姻
相關衍生字彙 married [`mærɪd] 形 已婚的、marry [`mærɪ] 動 結婚、engaged [ɪn`gedʒd]
形 訂婚的、divorced [də`vɔrst] 形 離婚的

---

marsh [mɑrʃ] 名 沼澤，濕地
▶ There is a marsh near the lake. 湖邊有一塊溼地。

---

martyr [`mɑrtɚ] 名 烈士，殉難者
▶ Dr. King is a martyr to racial discrimination. 金恩博士是種族歧視的烈士。

---

marvel [`mɑrvl] 名 令人驚奇的事物 動 感到驚訝
▶ It's a marvel that I won the first place. 讓我驚訝的是，我居然贏得第一名。

---

marvelous [`mɑrvələs] 形 非凡的，不可思議的
▶ The work of art is marvelous. 這件藝術品真是不可思議。

---

masculine [`mæskjəlɪn] 形 男子氣概的　同 manly [`mænlɪ] 形 有男子氣概的

---

mask [mæsk] 名 面具　片 an oxygen mask 氧氣罩

Mass [mæs] 名 彌撒
▶ The Pope will attend the Mass in person. 教宗將親自出席此彌撒。

---

massacre [`mæsəkɚ] 名 大屠殺　　　　　　MP3 13-04
▶ The massacre was ordered by Hitler. 這個大屠殺是希特勒下令的。

---

massive [`mæsɪv] 形 大量的，巨大的　片 on a massive scale 大規模地

---

master [`mæstɚ] 名 大師 動 控制 形 精通的
▶ He is a master of fashion.
他是時尚大師。
相關衍生字彙 masterpiece [`mæstɚ͵pis] 名 傑作、mastery [`mæstərɪ] 名 精通、
masterful [`mæstɚfəl] 形 熟練的、mastermind [`mæstɚmaɪnd]
名 才華洋溢的人，策畫者
動詞三態變化 master - mastered - mastered

match [mætʃ] 名 比賽 動 和～相配
▶ The colors of your shirt and skirt match very well.
　你襯衫跟裙子的顏色搭配得很好。
動詞三態變化 match - matched - matched

---

mate [met] 名 夥伴，配偶（或夫妻）
▶ Alice is not only my sister but also my best mate.
　愛麗絲不僅是我的妹妹也是我最好的夥伴。

---

material [mə`tɪrɪəl] 名 材料 形 物質的
▶ Stone is one of the building materials.
　石頭是建築材料之一。
相關衍生字彙 materialism [mə`tɪrɪəlɪzəm] 名 唯物論、materialist [mə`tɪrɪəlɪst] 名 唯物論者、
materialistic [mə,tɪrɪəl`ɪstɪk] 形 唯物論的

---

maternal [mə`tɜnl] 形 母親的　　反 paternal [pə`tɜnl] 形 父親般的

---

mathematics [,mæθə`mætɪks] 名 數學
▶ My son is especially interested in mathematics.
　我兒子對數學特別感興趣。
相關衍生字彙 mathematician [,mæθəmə`tɪʃən] 名 數學家、mathematical [,mæθə`mætɪkl]
形 數學的、arithmetic [ə`rɪθmətɪk] 名 算數、arithmetical [,ærɪθ`mɛtɪkl]
形 算數的

M

matter [`mætɚ] 名 事情 動 要緊
▶ It doesn't matter.
　那不重要。
動詞三態變化 matter - mattered - mattered

---

mattress [`mætrɪs] 名 床墊
▶ The mattress makes my bed comfortable. 這床墊讓我的床很舒服。

---

mature [mə`tjur] 形 成熟的，穩重的
▶ Although he is only ten years old, he is very mature.
　雖然他只有十歲，卻非常成熟。
相關衍生字彙 maturity [mə`tjurətɪ] 名 成熟、young [jʌŋ] 形 年輕的、innocent [`ɪnəsṇt]
形 涉世未深的、immature [,ɪmə`tjur] 形 不成熟的

---

maxim [`mæksɪm] 名 座右銘，格言　　片 moral maxims 道德準則

---

maximum [`mæksəməm] 名 最大值　　反 minimum [`mɪnəməm] 名 最小值

May [me] 名 五月
▶ April showers bring May flowers.（諺語）四月陣雨帶來五月花。

maybe [`mebɪ] 副 可能
▶ Maybe I am wrong.
　也許我錯了。
相關衍生字彙 may [me] 助 可能、can [kæn] 助 能夠、might [maɪt] 助 可能、could [kʊd]
　　　　　　助 能夠

mayor [`meɚ] 名 市長
▶ The new mayor promises he will govern the city well.
　新市長允諾他一定會好好管理市政。

maze [mez] 名 迷宮
▶ Many children are running around in the maze. 好多孩子在迷宮裡跑來跑去。

meadow [`mɛdo] 名 牧草地
▶ A herd of sheep are roaming in the meadow. 草地上有羊群漫步著。

meal [mil] 名 一餐
▶ How many meals a day do you eat? 你一天吃幾餐？

mean [min] 動 意指 形 吝嗇的
▶ What do you mean by that?
　你說的是什麼意思？
相關衍生字彙 meaning [`minɪŋ] 名 意義、meaningful [`minɪŋfəl] 形 有意義的、
　　　　　　meaningless [`minɪŋlɪs] 形 沒有意義的、meanness [`minnɪs] 名 卑賤
動詞三態變化 mean - meant - meant

means [minz] 名 方法　　片 by all means 務必　　　　MP3 **13-05**

meantime [`min͵taɪm] 名 其間
▶ I need to study from eight to nine o'clock. In the meantime, please turn
　down the TV.
　我八點到九點要念書，請把電視關小聲。

meanwhile [`min͵hwaɪl] 副 其間，同時
▶ Carl has a long vacation. Meanwhile, he will stay in Italy.
　卡爾有個長假，其間他將待在義大利。

measure [`mɛʒɚ] 動 測量
▶ The doctor reminds my father to measure his blood pressure.
　醫生提醒我爸爸要量血壓。
相關衍生字彙 measurement [`mɛʒɚmənt] 名 測量、survey [`sɝve] 名 調查、
　　　　　　estimate [`ɛstə͵met] 動 評估、assessment [ə`sɛsmənt] 名 評估
動詞三態變化 measure - measured - measured

medal [`mɛdl̩] 名 獎章
▶ He was awarded a medal for his excellent design. 他因傑出的設計獲頒獎章。

meddle [ˋmɛdl̩] 動 干涉
▶ You had better not meddle in others' problems.
你最好不要干涉別人的問題。
動詞三態變化 meddle - meddled - meddled

media [ˋmidɪə] 名 媒體
▶ CNN is an international media outlet.　CNN 是一家國際媒體。

mediate [ˋmidɪˌet] 動 調解
▶ The judge tried to mediate between the two sides.
法官嘗試調解雙方。
動詞三態變化 mediate - mediated - mediated

medical [ˋmɛdɪkl̩] 形 醫學的，醫療的
▶ Doctors and nurses are all medical workers. 醫生和護士都是醫療工作人員。

medicine [ˋmɛdəsn̩] 名 醫學，內服藥　　片 to take medicine 吃藥

medieval [ˌmɪdɪˋivəl] 形 中世紀的
▶ I like the medieval castles in Italy. 我喜歡義大利的中古世紀城堡。

mediocre [ˋmidɪˌokɚ] 形 中等的，平凡的
▶ The plot of the movie is mediocre, not creative at all.
這部電影的情節不怎麼樣，一點都不創新。

M

meditate [ˋmɛdəˌtet] 動 沉思
▶ I'm used to meditating for a few minutes before going to work.
我習慣上班前冥想幾分鐘。
相關衍生字彙 meditation [ˌmɛdəˋteʃən] 名 沉思、think [θɪŋk] 動 思考、thought [θɔt]
名 思想、consider [kənˋsɪdɚ] 動 考慮
動詞三態變化 meditate - meditated - meditated

medium [ˋmidɪəm] 形 中等的　　片 medium height（身高）中等高度

meek [mik] 形 溫馴的
▶ My cat is very meek. 我的貓咪很溫馴。

meet [mit] 動 遇見，符合
▶ When and where will we meet?
我們將在何時何地見面？
相關衍生字彙 meeting [ˋmitɪŋ] 名 會議、encounter [ɪnˋkauntɚ] 動 遇見、see [si] 動 看、
look [luk] 動 注視
動詞三態變化 meet - met - met

melancholy [ˋmɛlənˌkɑlɪ] 名 憂鬱 形 令人沮喪的
▶ She has suffered from melancholy for years. 多年來她受憂鬱情緒所苦。

mellow [`mɛlo] 形 （聲音）圓潤的，（水果）成熟的
▶ The singer has a mellow voice. 這位歌手有著圓潤悅耳的嗓音。

melody [`mɛlədɪ] 名 旋律　　片 to hum a melody 哼唱旋律

melt [mɛlt] 名 動 融化
▶ The chocolate only melts in your mouth, not in your hands.
　這種巧克力只溶你口，不溶你手。
動詞三態變化 melt - melted - melted

member [`mɛmbɚ] 名 會員　　◉ MP3 **13-06**
▶ I am not a member of the club.
　我不是該社團的會員。
相關衍生字彙 membership [`mɛmbɚˌʃɪp] 名 會員身分、friendship [`frɛndʃɪp] 名 友誼、
　scholarship [`skalɚˌʃɪp] 名 獎學金

memoir [`mɛmwɑr] 名 回憶錄
▶ The ex-president's memoir will be published next year.
　前總統的回憶錄明年將出版。

menace [`mɛnɪs] 名 動 威脅，恐嚇
▶ The serious air pollution is a menace to everyone in the city.
　這嚴重的空氣污染對都市裡的每個人都是威脅。
動詞三態變化 menace - menaced - menaced

mend [mɛnd] 名 動 修理，使恢復健康　　片 on the mend 在康復中
動詞三態變化 mend - mended - mended

memory [`mɛmərɪ] 名 回憶　　片 unforgettable memories 難忘的回憶
相關衍生字彙 memorable [`mɛmərəbl̩] 形 值得懷念的、memorandum [ˌmɛməˈrændəm]
　名 備忘錄、memorial [məˈmorɪəl] 名 紀念碑、memorize [`mɛməˌraɪz] 動 熟記

mental [`mɛntl̩] 形 精神的，心理的
▶ Mom's physical and mental health was in good condition.
　媽媽的身心健康狀況都很好。

mention [`mɛnʃən] 動 提及　　片 not to mention 更不必說
動詞三態變化 mention - mentioned - mentioned

menu [`mɛnju] 名 菜單
▶ Here is our latest menu. 這是我們最新的菜單。

merchandise [`mɝtʃənˌdaɪz] 名 商品，貨物
▶ I want to make sure of the quality of the merchandise.
　我要確定這商品的品質。

相關衍生字彙 merchant [ˋmɝtʃənt] 名 商人、business [ˋbɪznɪs] 名 生意、trade [tred] 名 貿易、businessman [ˋbɪznɪsmən] 名 商人

mercury [ˋmɝkjərɪ] 名 水銀　　片 mercury poisoning 水銀中毒

mercy [ˋmɝsɪ] 名 慈悲，憐憫
▶ Mother Teresa shows her mercy, helping the sick, the poor and the homeless.
德雷莎修女展現她的慈悲，幫助了病人、窮人和無家可歸的人。

merge [mɝdʒ] 動 合併，同化
▶ We decided to merge the two companies.
我們決定合併這兩家公司。
動詞三態變化 merge - merged - merged

merit [ˋmɛrɪt] 名 長處，優點
▶ She is a pianist of merit. 她是很優秀的鋼琴家。

merry [ˋmɛrɪ] 形 歡樂的　　片 in a merry mood 快樂的心情
相關衍生字彙 merrily [ˋmɛrɪlɪ] 副 歡樂地、merry-go-round [ˋmɛrɪgoˏraʊnd] 名 旋轉木馬、joyful [ˋdʒɔɪfəl] 形 高興的

mess [mɛs] 名 雜亂　　片 in a mess 一團亂

message [ˋmɛsɪdʒ] 名 訊息
▶ Our boss is not in. Do you want to leave a message?
我們老闆不在，你要不要留言？

metal [ˋmɛtl̩] 名 金屬
▶ Metal rusts easily when it is humid. 潮濕時，金屬很容易生鏽。

metaphor [ˋmɛtəfɚ] 名 暗喻　　反 simile [ˋsɪməˏlɪ] 名 明喻

method [ˋmɛθəd] 名 方法
▶ What is the best method for learning a language?
學習語言的最佳方法是什麼？
相關衍生字彙 methodical [məˋθɑdɪkəl] 形 講究方法的、methodology [ˏmɛθədˋɑlədʒɪ] 名 方法論、methodism [ˋmɛθədˏɪzəm] 名 墨守成規

metropolis [məˋtrɑplɪs] 名 大都會
▶ It's not easy to make a living in the metropolis. 在大都會生存不容易。

microbe [ˋmaɪkrob] 名 微生物，細菌　　MP3 13-07
▶ Microbe is too small to see with the naked eye.
微生物太小，以致於肉眼看不到。
相關衍生字彙 microscopic [ˋmaɪkrəˋskɑpɪk] 形 微小的、microscope [ˋmaɪkrəˏskop] 名 顯微鏡、bacteria [bækˋtɪrɪə] 名（複數）細菌、virus [ˋvaɪrəs] 名 病毒

M

middle [`mɪd!] 名 中央 形 中等的　　片 in the middle of 在～的中間
相關衍生字彙 midnight [`mɪd.naɪt] 名 午夜、midsummer [`mɪd.sʌmɚ] 名 仲夏、
middle-aged [`mɪd!.edʒd] 形 中年的、midpoint [`mɪd.pɔɪnt] 名 中點、
midway [`mɪd`we] 副 在中途

---

mighty [`maɪtɪ] 形 強大的　　片 a mighty country 強大的國家

---

migrate [`maɪ.gret] 動 遷移
▶ Birds migrate south before winter.
　鳥類會在冬天之前南遷。
動詞三態變化 migrate - migrated - migrated

---

mild [maɪld] 形 溫和的
▶ Even in winter, the weather is mild here. 即使在冬天，這裡的天氣一樣溫和。

---

milestone [`maɪl.ston] 名 里程碑
▶ Graduating from university is a real milestone in my life.
　從大學畢業是我人生真正的里程碑。
相關衍生字彙 mile [maɪl] 名 英里、mileage [`maɪlɪdʒ] 名 里程數、meter [`mitɚ] 名 公尺

---

military [`mɪlə.tɛrɪ] 形 軍事的　　片 military force 軍力

---

milk [mɪlk] 名 牛奶
▶ Babies feed on milk. 嬰兒以牛奶為主食。

---

milky [`mɪlkɪ] 形 乳白色的，溫順的　　片 the Milky Way 銀河

---

millennium [mɪ`lɛnɪəm] 名 千禧年
▶ The year 2000 AD is the millennium. 西元兩千年是千禧年。

---

millionaire [.mɪljən`ɛr] 名 百萬富翁
▶ Everyone hopes to become a millionaire.
　人人都想成為百萬富翁。
相關衍生字彙 million [`mɪljən] 名 百萬、thousand [`θaʊzṇd] 名 千、hundred [`hʌndrəd]
名 百

---

mimic [`mɪmɪk] 動 模仿
▶ Parrots can mimic people's speaking.
　鸚鵡會模仿人類說話。
動詞三態變化 mimic - mimicked - mimicked

---

mind [maɪnd] 動 介意，注意，留心
▶ Would you mind opening the door for me?
　你可以幫我開個門嗎？
動詞三態變化 mind - minded - minded

---

mine [maɪn] 名 礦坑　　片 a coal mine 煤礦

mineral [`mɪnərəl] 名 礦物　　片 vitamins and minerals 維他命跟礦物質

mingle [`mɪŋg!] 動 使混合
▶ You can try to mingle the two flavors.
你可以嘗試混合這兩種味道。
動詞三態變化 mingle - mingled - mingled

minimize [`mɪnə‚maɪz] 動 低估，小看
▶ We should try our best to minimize the impact.
我們應盡力減少此衝擊。
相關衍生字彙 miniature [`mɪnɪətʃɚ] 名 縮小版、minimum [`mɪnəməm] 名 最小值、
maximum [`mæksəməm] 名 最大值、maximize [`mæksə‚maɪz] 動 達到最大值
動詞三態變化 minimize - minimized - minimized

minister [`mɪnɪstɚ] 名 部長　　片 a prime minister 總理，行政院長

ministry [`mɪnɪstrɪ] 名 部門
片 the Ministry of Defense / Education 國防部 / 教育部

minority [maɪ`nɔrətɪ] 名 少數　　反 majority [mə`dʒɔrətɪ] 名 多數

minute [`mɪnɪt] 名 片刻　　　　　　　　　　　　　　　MP3 13-08
▶ She finally arrived at the last minute. 最後一刻她終於抵達。

M

miracle [`mɪrək!] 名 奇蹟
▶ It was a miracle that the baby survived the earthquake.
嬰兒在地震中存活真是奇蹟。
相關衍生字彙 miraculous [mɪ`rækjələs] 形 不可思議的、unexpected [‚ʌnɪk`spɛktɪd]
形 非預期的、accidental [‚æksə`dɛnt!] 形 意外的

mirage [mə`rɑʒ] 名 海市蜃樓，妄想
▶ A mirage actually doesn't exist. 海市蜃樓事實上並不存在。

mire [maɪr] 名 污泥，困境
▶ Mark found himself in the mire. 馬克發現自己陷在困境裡。

mirror [`mɪrɚ] 名 鏡子　　片 to look at oneself in the mirror 照鏡子

miscellaneous [‚mɪsɪ`lenjəs] 形 混雜的，五花八門的
▶ There are miscellaneous items in the grocery store.
雜貨店裡有各式各樣的東西。

mischief [`mɪstʃɪf] 名 惡作劇，頑皮
▶ Let your boy play with the toys, or he may get into mischief.
讓你兒子玩玩具，不然他會調皮搗蛋。
相關衍生字彙 mischievous [`mɪstʃɪvəs] 形 調皮搗蛋的、naughty [`nɔtɪ] 形 頑皮的、
well-mannered [`wɛl`mænɚd] 形 有禮貌的

miser [`maɪzɚ] 名 守財奴
▶ The old man is a miser. 這位老人是個守財奴。

miserable [`mɪzərəbl] 形 不幸的，悽慘的
▶ I never feel miserable about my failure. 我對自己的失敗絕不感到悲哀。

misery [`mɪzərɪ] 名 痛苦悲慘　　🕭 in the depths of misery 陷在深深痛苦中

misfortune [mɪs`fɔrtʃən] 名 不幸
▶ She had the misfortune to lose her son in the accident.
她很不幸，在意外中失去兒子。

相關衍生字彙 tragedy [`trædʒədɪ] 名 慘案、disaster [dɪ`zæstɚ] 名 災難、
catastrophe [kə`tæstrəfɪ] 名 大災難、calamity [kə`læmətɪ] 名 災難、
casualty [`kæʒjuəltɪ] 名 意外事故

misgiving [mɪs`gɪvɪŋ] 名 擔憂，疑慮
▶ Young men often have misgiving about their future.
年輕人常對他們的前途感到疑慮。

mislead [mɪs`lid] 動 把～引入歧途
▶ A good leader never misleads his followers.
好的領導人不會誤導下屬。

動詞三態變化 mislead - misled - misled

miss [mɪs] 動 想念，錯過
▶ I miss you so much.
我很想念你。

動詞三態變化 miss - missed - missed

missile [`mɪsl̩] 名 導彈　　🕭 to launch a missile 發射飛彈

missing [`mɪsɪŋ] 形 失蹤的，缺席的　　🟰 lost [lɔst] 形 遺失的

mission [`mɪʃən] 名 任務
▶ He is carrying out an impossible mission.
他正在執行一個不可能的任務。

相關衍生字彙 duty [`djutɪ] 名 職責、chore [tʃor] 名 家庭雜務、task [tæsk] 名 工作，任務、
errand [`ɛrənd] 名 差事、business [`bɪznɪs] 名 職責，本分、work [wɝk] 名 工作

missionary [`mɪʃənˌɛrɪ] 名 傳教士　　🕭 a foreign missionary 外國傳教士

mist [mɪst] 名 薄霧
▶ The top of the hill is covered in mist. 山丘頂端被薄霧覆蓋。

mistake [mɪ`stek] 名 錯誤 動 誤解　　🕭 to make a mistake 犯錯
動詞三態變化 mistake - mistook - mistaken

misunderstand [`mɪsʌndɚ`stænd] 動 誤會，曲解　　◎ MP3 13-09
▶ I think I misunderstood your meaning.
我想我當時誤會你的意思。

動詞三態變化 misunderstand - misunderstood - misunderstood

mitigate [`mɪtə,get] 動 減輕，使緩和
▶ The teacher decided to mitigate the student's punishment.
老師決定對這名學生從輕處罰。

動詞三態變化 mitigate - mitigated - mitigated

mitt [mɪt] 名 連指手套　　片 a catcher's mitt 捕手的手套

mix [mɪks] 動 混合
▶ It's impossible to mix oil and water.
油跟水不可能混在一起。

相關衍生字彙 separate [`sɛpə,ret] 動 分開、stir [stɝ] 動 攪拌、blend [blɛnd] 動 使混合、
combine [kəm`baɪn] 動 結合

動詞三態變化 mix - mixed - mixed

mixture [`mɪkstʃɚ] 名 混合物
▶ The dressing is a mixture of Western and Eastern styles.
這件洋裝融合了東西方的風格。

moan [mon] 動 呻吟
▶ The patient moaned with pain.
病人痛苦地呻吟。

動詞三態變化 moan - moaned - moaned

mob [mɑb] 名 暴民
▶ Many policemen were hurt in the mob violence.
這次的暴民暴力中有很多警察受傷。

mobile [`mobɪl] 形 移動式的　　片 a mobile phone / a cellphone 手機
相關衍生字彙 mobilize [`mobḷ,aɪz] 動 動員、mobility [mo`bɪlətɪ] 名 流動性、
mobilization [,mobḷə`zeʃən] 名 動員

mock [mɑk] 動 嘲笑　　同 to laugh at 嘲笑
動詞三態變化 mock - mocked - mocked

mockery [`mɑkərɪ] 名 嘲笑，徒勞無功　　片 to make a mockery of 使成為徒勞

mode [mod] 名 方式，形式
▶ Taking a bus is the most convenient mode. 搭公車是最方便的方式。

M

model [`mɑdḷ] 名 模型，模特兒
▶ Since college, she has worked as a fashion model.
自從念大學開始，她就擔任服裝模特兒。

modern [`mɑdɚn] 形 現代化的
▶ We are proud of the modern airport. 我們都以此現代化的機場為榮。

modest [`mɑdɪst] 形 謙虛的
▶ She is always modest about her excellent performance.
她總是對自己傑出的表現很謙虛。
相關衍生字彙 modesty [`mɑdɪstɪ] 名 謙虛、humble [`hʌmbḷ] 形 謙虛的、shy [ʃaɪ] 形 害羞的、arrogant [`ærəgənt] 形 自大的，傲慢的

modify [`mɑdəˏfaɪ] 動 修改，減輕
▶ You had better modify your wrong behavior.
你最好改變你錯誤的行為。
動詞三態變化 modify - modified - modified

moist [mɔɪst] 形 潮濕的，多雨的
▶ Keep the soil moist; then the flower will last for days.
保持土壤濕潤，花就可以持續好幾天。

moment [`momənt] 名 時機，時刻   片 a critical moment 關鍵時刻

momentary [`momənˏtɛrɪ] 形 瞬間的
▶ Sometimes, a momentary hesitation will make you lose a good opportunity.
有時候，瞬間的猶豫會讓你失去一個好機會。

monarch [`mɑnɚk] 名 君王
▶ The monarch is notorious for his cruelty.   這君王以他的殘酷而惡名昭彰。

Monday [`mʌnde] 名 星期一
片 Monday blue 憂鬱的星期一（指一周第一天的上班日很痛苦）

monetary [`mʌnəˏtɛrɪ] 形 金融的，貨幣的   ◎ MP3 13-10
▶ The monetary unit of the USA is dollar. 美國的金錢單位是美元。

monitor [`mɑnətɚ] 名 螢幕 動 監控
▶ All the workers in the factory are monitored closely.
這間工廠的員工都被嚴密監視。
動詞三態變化 monitor - monitored - monitored

monkey [`mʌŋkɪ] 名 猴子   片 to make a monkey of somebody 愚弄某人

monologue [ˋmɑnḷͺɔg] 名 獨白
▶ The monologue of the actor in the movie is very touching.
電影中男主角的獨白很感人。

monopoly [məˋnɑpḷɪ] 名 壟斷，獨佔
▶ Education should not be the monopoly of the privileged.
教育不該被特權壟斷。

monotonous [məˋnɑtənəs] 形 單調的，無聊的
▶ The song is monotonous. 這首歌曲太單調。

monster [ˋmɑnstɚ] 名 怪獸
▶ It has been said that there is a monster living in the river.
一直都有傳說，有隻怪獸住在河裡。
〔相關衍生字彙〕monstrous [ˋmɑnstrəs] 形 怪異的、strange [strendʒ] 形 奇怪的、
　　　　　　 unusual [ʌnˋjuʒuəl] 形 不尋常的、weird [wɪrd] 形 古怪的

month [mʌnθ] 名 月份
▶ There are twelve months in a year. 一年有十二個月。

monument [ˋmɑnjəmənt] 名 紀念碑
▶ The government set up a monument to the hero. 政府為這位英雄造了紀念碑。

mood [mud] 名 心境
▶ I'm in no mood for your complaint. 我沒心情聽你抱怨。

moonlight [ˋmunͺlaɪt] 名 月光
▶ We had a BBQ in the soft moonlight.
我們在柔和的月光下烤肉。
〔相關衍生字彙〕moon [mun] 名 月亮、moonbeam [ˋmunͺbim] 名 一道月光、
　　　　　　 moonless [ˋmunlɪs] 形 沒有月光的、moonshine [ˋmunͺʃaɪn] 名 月光

moor [mʊr] 動 停泊，繫住　　　片 to moor a boat 停泊船隻
〔動詞三態變化〕moor - moored - moored

morale [məˋræl] 名 士氣，道德
▶ The good bonus excited the team's morale. 優渥的獎金激勵了團隊士氣。

moral [ˋmɔrəl] 形 道德的
▶ It's my moral obligation to tell the truth. 說實話是我的道德責任。

morbid [ˋmɔrbɪd] 形 病態的，可怖的
▶ It's morbid to think about negative things all the time.
總是想到負面的事情是病態的。

moreover [morˋovɚ] 副 並且，此外
▶ You hand in your homework late. Moreover, there are many mistakes in it.
你遲交作業。此外，裡面有很多錯誤。

M

mortal [`mɔrtl̩] 形 致死的　　　反 immortal [ɪ`mɔrtl̩] 形 不朽的
相關衍生字彙 mortality [mɔr`tælətɪ] 名 死亡率、die [daɪ] 動 死亡、death [dɛθ] 名 死亡、
immortality [ˌɪmɔr`tælətɪ] 名 不朽

---

mortgage [`mɔrgɪdʒ] 名 抵押借款
▶ You had better pay off the mortgage as soon as possible.
你最好儘快還清貸款。

---

mosque [mɑsk] 名 清真寺
▶ The mosque is a place for Islamic religion. 清真寺是屬於回教。

---

moth [mɔθ] 名 蛾
▶ A moth is different from a butterfly. 蛾不同於蝴蝶。

---

mother [`mʌðɚ] 名 母親　　片 Mothers' Day 母親節　　◎ MP3 **13-11**
相關衍生字彙 motherboard [`mʌðɚˌbɔrd] 名 主機板、motherland [`mʌðɚˌlænd] 名 祖國、
motherhood [`mʌðɚˌhud] 名 母親身份、mother-in-law [`mʌðərɪnˌlɔ]
名 岳母，婆婆

---

motion [`moʃən] 名 動作，提議
▶ He made a motion at the end of the meeting. 會議後段，他提出動議。

---

motionless [`moʃənlɪs] 形 不動的，靜止的
▶ Why does your dog lie motionless on the sofa? Is it sick?
為什麼你的小狗在沙發上躺著不動？牠生病了嗎？

---

motivate [`motəˌvet] 動 刺激，激發
▶ A good teacher knows how to motivate students.
一位好的老師知道如何激發學生。
動詞三態變化 motivate - motivated - motivated

---

motivation [ˌmotə`veʃən] 名 激勵，動力
▶ What is your motivation to learn painting? 你學繪畫的動機是什麼？

---

motive [`motɪv] 名 動機 動 激起
▶ Nobody knows the motive for his leaving home.
沒人知道他離家的原因。
動詞三態變化 motive - motived - motived

---

motor [`motɚ] 名 馬達
▶ There is something wrong with the motor of my car. 我汽車的馬達有問題。

---

motto [`mɑto] 名 座右銘，格言　　片 a school motto 校訓

---

mountain [`mauntn̩] 名 山脈　　片 to make a mountain out of a molehill 小題大作
相關衍生字彙 mound [maund] 名 土墩、mount [maunt] 動 騎上，跨上 (馬或單車)、
mountaineer [ˌmauntə`nɪr] 名 登山者、mountainous [`mauntənəs] 形 多山的

mourning [`mornɪŋ] 名 哀悼　　片 national mourning 全國性哀悼

---

mouth [maʊθ] 名 嘴巴
▶ Don't speak with food in your mouth. 嘴裡有食物時不要說話。

---

mouthful [`maʊθfəl] 名 一口
▶ He was sick. He only ate a few mouthfuls of rice. 他生病了，只吃了幾口白飯。

---

move [muv] 動 移動，遷移，採取行動
▶ After retirement, he moved to the village.
　退休後，他搬到村子裡。
動詞三態變化 move - moved - moved

---

movement [`muvmənt] 名 活動，動作
片 the labor / a peace / the women's movement 勞工／和平／婦女運動
相關衍生字彙 campaign [kæm`pen] 名 競選運動、motion [`moʃən] 名（會議上的）動議、
　　　　　　 activity [æk`tɪvətɪ] 名 活動、action [`ækʃən] 名 行動

---

movie [`muvɪ] 名 電影
▶ Every Sunday night, I go to the movies. 每個周日晚上，我都會去看電影。

---

muddle [`mʌdl̩] 名 混亂狀態 動 使糊塗
▶ Don't get into a muddle about the students' names.
　別把學生的名字搞混了。
動詞三態變化 muddle - muddled - muddled

---

muddy [`mʌdɪ] 形 泥濘的，模糊的
▶ It's difficult to walk on the muddy road. 在泥濘的路上很難行走。

---

multiple [`mʌltəpl̩] 形 多樣的，複合的
▶ It's not an easy job for you to get multiple achievements.
　能有多種成就，你真是不簡單。

---

multiply [`mʌltəplaɪ] 動 使相乘，增加
▶ If you multiply five by two, you get ten.
　五乘二得十。
相關衍生字彙 add [æd] 動 加、subtract [səb`trækt] 動 減、divide [də`vaɪd] 動 除
動詞三態變化 multiply - multiplied - multiplied

---

murder [`mɝdɚ] 名 動 謀殺
▶ The young man was charged with murder.
　這名年輕人被控謀殺。
動詞三態變化 murder - murdered - murdered

M

murmur [`mɝmɚ] 名 低語聲 動 咕噥

MP3 13-12

▶ Why are you murmuring?
你為何一直嘀咕？

動詞三態變化 murmur - murmured - murmured

muscle [`mʌsl] 名 肌肉

▶ He exercises every day to build his muscles. 他每天運動鍛鍊肌肉。

muscular [`mʌskjələ] 形 肌肉的，健壯的

▶ The man was very muscular. 這位男士肌肉發達。

muse [mjuz] 動 沉思，冥想

▶ I often muse about my future.
我常沉思自己的未來。

動詞三態變化 muse - mused - mused

museum [mju`zɪəm] 名 博物館

▶ It's free to visit the museum every Saturday afternoon.
每周六下午，博物館可以免費參觀。

mushroom [`mʌʃrum] 名 蘑菇

▶ Some wild mushrooms are poisonous. 有些野菇是有毒的。

music [`mjuzɪk] 名 音樂　　片 classical music 古典音樂

musical [`mjuzɪkl] 形 音樂的　　片 a musical instrument 樂器

相關衍生字彙 musician [mju`zɪʃən] 名 音樂家、song [sɔŋ] 名 歌曲、melody [`mɛlədɪ] 名 旋律、tone [ton] 名 音色

musty [`mʌstɪ] 形 陳腐的，發霉的

▶ There is a musty smell in the room. 房間有發霉的味道。

mute [mjut] 形 沉默的，靜音的

▶ No matter what the teacher asked, the boy stood mute.
不論老師問什麼，男孩就是站著不說話。

mutiny [`mjutṇɪ] 名 叛亂 動 反叛

▶ Regarding the news of mutiny, it was proved a rumor.
有關叛變的消息，後來證明只是謠言。

相關衍生字彙 riot [`raɪət] 名 暴亂、revolt [rɪ`volt] 名 動 反叛，起義、revolution [ˌrɛvə`luʃən] 名 革命、rebel [`rɛbl] 名 反叛者

動詞三態變化 mutiny - mutinied - mutinied

mutter [`mʌtɚ] 名 抱怨 動 低聲嘀咕

▶ I encourage you to speak up instead of muttering.
我鼓勵你大聲說出來，不要小聲低語。

動詞三態變化 mutter - muttered - muttered

mutual [`mjutʃʊəl] 形 互相的，共同的　　片 mutual respect 互相尊重

mysterious [mɪs`tɪrɪəs] 形 神祕的
▶ Her private life has remained very mysterious.
她的私生活一直都很神祕。
相關衍生字彙 mystery [`mɪstərɪ] 名 神祕、myth [mɪθ] 名 迷思、secret [`sikrɪt] 名 祕密、
hidden [`hɪdn̩] 形 隱藏的

mythology [mɪ`θɑlədʒɪ] 名 神話
▶ Greek and Roman mythologies are the foundation of the Western literature.
希臘羅馬神話是西方文學的基礎。

MEMO

M

一網打盡

字母 N

nail ~ nurture

詞性說明

名 名詞　　　　副 副詞　　　　介 介系詞

動 動詞　　　　形 形容詞　　　連 連接詞

代 代名詞　　　助 助動詞

內文圖示說明

片 片語　　　反 反義字　　　同 同義字

一網打盡「英語小知識」｜表達「驚訝」的用語 I ─────────

Astounded!
太神奇了！

Incredible!
不敢相信！

Fancy that!
不會吧！

It can't be!
不可能啦！

nail ~ nurture

★一網打盡 247 個英文單字 ｜ 一網打盡 60 句英語會話句　　　　　　○ MP3 **14-01**

nail [nel] 名 指甲，釘子
▶ Please help me hammer a nail. 請幫我釘個釘子。

---

naïve [nɑˋiv] 形 天真的
▶ What a naïve girl! 真是個天真的女孩！

---

naked [ˋnekɪd] 形 裸體的，無覆蓋的　　片 the naked eye 裸視，肉眼

---

name [nem] 名 名字 動 命名　　片 last name / first name 姓／名
動詞三態變化 name - named - named

---

namely [ˋnemlɪ] 副 那就是　　同 that is to say 那就是説

---

nap [næp] 名 午睡 動 打盹
▶ Taking a nap can help students stay focused in the afternoon.
小睡片刻有助於學生下午保持專心。
動詞三態變化 nap - napped - napped

---

narcotic [nɑrˋkɑtɪk] 名 麻醉劑 形 有麻醉作用的
▶ It's illegal to sell narcotic drugs.
販賣麻醉劑是違法的。
相關衍生字彙 narcotize [ˋnɑrkəˌtaɪz] 動 麻醉，使昏迷、soporific [ˌsopəˋrɪfɪk] 名 催眠劑
形 催眠的，想睡的、hypnotic [hɪpˋnɑtɪk] 名 安眠藥 形 催眠的、
anesthetic [ˌænəsˋθɛtɪk] 名 麻醉劑 形 麻醉的、painkilling [ˋpenkɪlɪŋ]
形 止痛的、depressant [dɪˋprɛsn̩t] 名 鎮靜劑 形 有鎮靜作用的、
downer [ˋdaʊnɚ] 名 鎮定劑，掃興的人（或事）

---

narrate [næˋret] 動 敘述
▶ Essays should be narrated in an academic way.
論文須以學術方式論述。
相關衍生字彙 narration [næˋreʃən] 名 敘述、narrative [ˋnærətɪv] 形 敘事的、
narrator [næˋretɚ] 名 敘述者
動詞三態變化 narrate - narrated - narrated

---

narrow [ˋnæro] 形 狹窄的　　反 wide [waɪd] 形 寬廣的
相關衍生字彙 narrowness [ˋnæronɪs] 名 狹窄，狹小、narrowly [ˋnæroli]
副 勉強地，狹窄地，嚴密地、narrow-minded [ˋnæroˋmaɪndɪd] 形 胸襟狹窄的、
cramped [ˋkræmpt] 形 狹窄的，難認的、restricted [rɪˋstrɪktɪd] 形 受限制的

---

nasty [ˋnæstɪ] 形 齷齪的，卑鄙的
▶ How do you know so many nasty things about him?
你怎麼知道這麼多他的齷齪事？

nationality [ˌnæʃəˈnælətɪ] 名 國籍，民族性
▶ Your nationality will be shown on your passport.
你的國籍會秀在護照上。

相關衍生字彙 nation [ˈneʃən] 名 國家、national [ˈnæʃənḷ] 形 國家的、
nationalism [ˈnæʃənḷˌɪzəm] 名 國家主義、nationalist [ˈnæʃənḷɪst]
名 國家主義、naturalization [ˌnætʃərələˈzeʃən]
名（外國人的）歸化，（動植物的）移植、naturalize [ˈnætʃərəˌlaɪz]
動 加入國籍，接收（外國僑民等）入籍

native [ˈnetɪv] 形 天生的，自然的
▶ English is her native language. 英文是她的母語。

naughty [ˈnɔtɪ] 形 頑皮的　　同 mischief [ˈmɪstʃɪf] 名 頑皮

nausea [ˈnɔʃɪə] 名 暈船，作嘔
▶ Nausea will make you vomit.
噁心的感覺會讓你吐。

相關衍生字彙 nauseate [ˈnɔsɪet] 動 作嘔，厭惡、nauseous [ˈnɔʃɪəs] 形 令人作嘔的

naval [ˈnevḷ] 形 海軍的　　片 a naval officer 海軍軍官

natural [ˈnætʃərəl] 形 天然的
▶ I prefer natural foods to artificial ones.
我喜歡天然食品勝於人工食品。

相關衍生字彙 naturally [ˈnætʃərəlɪ] 副 天然地、nature [ˈnetʃɚ] 名 大自然、
naturalist [ˈnætʃərəlɪst] 名 博物學家、naturalism [ˈnætʃərəlɪzəm] 名 自然主義

N

navigate [ˈnævəˌget] 動 駕駛，操縱
▶ The special equipment can help sailors to navigate ships.
這些特別裝置可以幫助水手操縱船隻。

動詞三態變化 navigate - navigated - navigated

navigation [ˌnævəˈgeʃən] 名 航海，航空，航行
▶ Navigation on the narrow river is very dangerous.
航行在這狹窄的河道很危險。

navy [ˈnevɪ] 名 海軍
▶ My brother is serving in the Navy.
我弟弟正服役於海軍。

相關衍生字彙 air force 片 空軍、army [ˈɑrmɪ] 名 陸軍、submarine [ˈsʌbməˌrin]
名 潛水艇、soldier [ˈsoldʒɚ] 名 士兵

nearly [ˈnɪrlɪ] 副 幾乎　　同 almost [ˈɔlˌmost] 副 幾乎

neat [nit] 形 整齊的

◉ MP3 **14-02**

▶ My room is always neat.

我的房間總是很整齊。

相關衍生字彙 neatly [`nitlɪ] 副 整潔地，靈巧地、neatness [`nitnɪs] 名 整潔，乾淨、orderly [`ɔrdɚlɪ] 形 有條理的，愛整潔的、shipshape [`ʃɪpˌʃep] 形 整齊的 副 整潔地、tidy [`taɪdɪ] 形 整潔的，井然的

---

necessary [`nɛsəˌsɛrɪ] 形 需要的

▶ If necessary, I can help you.

如果需要的話，我可以幫你。

相關衍生字彙 necessitate [nɪ`sɛsəˌtet] 動 使成需要、necessity [nə`sɛsətɪ] 名 必需品、need [nid] 動 需要、needless [`nidlɪs] 形 不需要的

---

neck [nɛk] 名 脖子，衣領

▶ The neck of your shirt is dirty. 你襯衫的領子髒了。

---

needle [`nidl̩] 名 針　　片 a needle and thread 針與線

---

negative [`nɛgətɪv] 形 否定的，負面的　　反 positive [`pɑzətɪv] 形 正面的

---

neglect [nɪg`lɛkt] 名 動 忽略，疏忽

▶ Don't neglect a small mistake.

不要忽視一個小錯誤。

相關衍生字彙 negligence [`nɛglɪdʒəns] 名 疏忽，粗心、negligent [`nɛglɪdʒənt] 形 粗心的、negligible [`nɛglɪdʒəbl̩] 形 可忽略的，無關緊要的

動詞三態變化 neglect - neglected - neglected

---

negotiate [nɪ`goʃɪˌet] 動 談判，協商

▶ The government refused to negotiate with those terrorists.

政府拒絕與恐怖分子協商。

動詞三態變化 negotiate - negotiated - negotiated

---

negotiation [nɪˌgoʃɪ`eʃən] 名 協商

▶ After negotiation, they finally reached an agreement.

協商後，他們終於達成協議了。

---

neighbor [`nebɚ] 名 鄰居

▶ Luckily, we have a good relationship with our neighbors.

很幸運地，我們跟鄰居的關係很好。

相關衍生字彙 neighborhood [`nebɚˌhud] 名 鄰近，相鄰、neighboring [`nebərɪŋ] 形 鄰近的、acquaintance [ə`kwentəns] 名（與人）相識，瞭解

---

neither [`niðɚ] 代 兩者都不

▶ Neither of his parents attended his graduation ceremony.

他的父母都沒有參加他的畢業典禮。

nephew [ˋnɛfju] 名 姪子　　反 niece [nis] 名 姪女

nerve [nɝv] 名 神經　　片 to get on somebody's nerves 讓某人惱怒

nervous [ˋnɝvəs] 形 緊張的
▶ I am very nervous about my presentation next week.
我很緊張我下周的報告。
相關衍生字彙 nervously [ˋnɝvəslɪ] 副 神經質地，焦急地、nervousness [ˋnɝvəsnɪs]
名 神經質，焦躁、restless [ˋrɛstlɪs] 形 焦躁不安的，受打擾的、
disturbed [dɪˋstɝbd] 形 心亂的，心理不正常的、flustered [ˋflʌstɚd]
形 激動不安的，慌張的、strained [ˋstrend] 形 緊張的，牽強附會的、
jittery [ˋdʒɪtərɪ] 形 緊張不安的、high-strung [ˋhaɪˋstrʌŋ]
形 十分敏感的，神經緊張的

nest [nɛst] 名 巢穴
▶ The bird lays her eggs in the nest.
鳥兒在鳥巢裡下蛋。
相關衍生字彙 hotbed [ˋhɑtˌbɛd] 名（培育植物的）溫床、roost [rust] 名 鳥巢，棲息處、
pen [pɛn] 名（關禽，畜的）欄，圈、hive [haɪv] 名 蜂巢

net [nɛt] 名 網子　　片 a fishing net 漁網

neutral [ˋnjutrəl] 形 中立的
▶ The small country always remains neutral. 這個小國一直保持中立。

never [ˋnɛvɚ] 副 從不
▶ Never give up easily. 決不要輕言放棄。

nevertheless [ˌnɛvɚðəˋlɛs] 副 然而　　同 however [hauˋɛvɚ] 副 然而

new [nju] 形 新穎的　　反 old [old] 形 舊的

newly [ˋnjulɪ] 副 最近，最新
▶ They are a newly wedded couple. 他們是新婚夫婦。

newspaper [ˋnjuzˌpepɚ] 名 報紙　　　　　　　　　　MP3 **14-03**
▶ Printed newspapers are gradually replaced by online ones.
印刷的報紙已逐漸被電子報取代。
相關衍生字彙 news [njuz] 名 新聞、newsagent [ˋnjuzˌedʒnt] 名 書報亭、
newsstand [ˋnjuzˌstænd] 名 報攤、newsworthy [ˋnjuzˌwɝðɪ] 形 有新聞價值的

next [ˋnɛkst] 形 緊鄰的 副 接下來
▶ There is a school next to my apartment. 我的公寓旁有一間學校。

nibble [ˋnɪbl̩] 動 一點點地咬（或吃）
▶ The small fish is nibbling the waterweed.
小魚正小口吃著水草。
動詞三態變化 nibble - nibbled - nibbled

N

nightmare [`naɪtˌmɛr] 名 惡夢
▶ The terrible part-time job is a nightmare for the young man.
那份可怕的兼差工作對這個年輕人而言是場噩夢。

相關衍生字彙 night [naɪt] 名 夜晚、nightgown [`naɪtˌgaʊn] 名 睡袍、nightclub [`naɪtˌklʌb] 名 夜總會、nightingale [`naɪtɪŋˌgel] 名 夜鶯

- - -

nice [naɪs] 形 美好的，愉快的
▶ Nice to meet you.
很高興見到你。

相關衍生字彙 nicely [`naɪslɪ] 副 出色地，恰好地，謹慎地、niceness [`naɪsnɪs] 名 美好，舒適，精密，講究、affectionate [ə`fɛkʃənɪt] 形 溫柔親切的、gracious [`greʃəs] 形 和藹的，仁慈的，優美的、flavorful [`flevɚfəl] 形 有風味的，充滿～味道

- - -

nickname [`nɪkˌnem] 名 綽號 動 取綽號
▶ I don't like my nickname. Please stop calling me by that.
我不喜歡我的綽號，請不要那樣叫我。

動詞三態變化 nickname - nicknamed - nicknamed

- - -

ninth [naɪnθ] 名 第九（個）形 第九的
▶ The first semester will star on the ninth of September.
第一學期將於九月九日開始。

相關衍生字彙 nine [naɪn] 名 九 形 九的、nineteen [`naɪn`tin] 名 十九 形 十九的、ninety [`naɪntɪ] 名 九十 形 九十的

- - -

noble [`nobl] 形 高尚的　　片 a single noble 單身貴族
相關衍生字彙 nobleness [`noblnɪs] 名 高貴，崇高、nobly [`noblɪ] 副 高貴地，勇敢地，貴族出生地、nobility [no`bɪlətɪ] 名 貴族（階層），崇高，高貴的地位、nobleman [`noblmən] 名 貴族、noble-minded [`noblˈmaɪndɪd] 形 高尚的、lofty [`lɔftɪ] 形 高聳的，高尚的，地位高的、grandiose [`grændɪos] 形 宏偉的，浮誇的、stately [`stetlɪ] 形 莊重的，堂皇的、aristocratic [ˌærɪstə`krætɪk] 形 貴族的，勢利的、dignified [`dɪgnəˌfaɪd] 形 有尊嚴的，高貴的

- - -

nobody [`nobadɪ] 名 小人物 代 沒有人
▶ I regard myself as a nobody. 我視自己為一個沒沒無聞的人。

nod [nad] 動 點頭　　片 a nodding acquaintance 點頭之交
動詞三態變化 nod - nodded - nodded

noisy [`nɔɪzɪ] 形 噪音的
▶ It's hard to stay focused in such a noisy environment.
在吵雜的環境中很難專心。

相關衍生字彙 noise [nɔɪz] 名 噪音、sound [saʊnd] 名 聲音、voice [vɔɪs] 名 聲音、silent [`saɪlənt] 形 安靜的、quiet [`kwaɪət] 形 安靜的

nominate [`nɑməˌnet] 動 提名
▶ Who will be nominated for the presidency?
  誰將被提名為下屆總統候選人？

相關衍生字彙 nomination [ˌnɑmə`neʃən] 名 任命，提名、nominee [ˌnɑmə`ni] 名 被提名人、election [ɪ`lɛkʃən] 名 選舉、vote [vot] 動 投票

動詞三態變化 nominate - nominated - nominated

nonsense [`nɑnsɛns] 名 胡說
▶ Don't speak nonsense!
  不要胡說八道！

相關衍生字彙 nonsensical [nɑn`sɛnsɪkl̩] 形 荒謬的，愚蠢的、nonsensically [ˌnɑn`sɛnsɪkəlɪ] 副 可笑地，愚笨地、foolishness [`fulɪʃnɪs] 名 愚蠢，愚笨、ridiculousness [rɪ`dɪkjələsnɪs] 名 滑稽，荒謬、absurdity [əb`sɝdətɪ] 名 荒誕，荒謬、stupidity [stju`pɪdətɪ] 名 愚蠢，愚笨、rubbish [`rʌbɪʃ] 名 垃圾，廢物、poppycock [`pɑpɪˌkɑk] 名 胡說，廢話

nook [nuk] 名 角落，隱蔽處
▶ I design a cozy nook in my room. 我在房間裡設計了一個舒適的角落。

normal [`nɔrml̩] 形 正常的　　反 abnormal [æb`nɔrml̩] 形 不正常的

norm [nɔrm] 名 基準，規範
▶ You can set a norm for your students to follow.
  你可以設立一個標準來讓學生遵守。

north [nɔrθ] 名 北方 形 北方的 副 向北方
▶ The town is to the north of Taipei.
  這個小鎮在台北的北邊。

相關衍生字彙 northern [`nɔrðɚn] 形 北方的、south [sauθ] 名 南方、southern [`sʌðɚn] 形 南方的

nose [noz] 名 鼻子　　片 to turn up one's nose at 對～嗤之以鼻
相關衍生字彙 nosebleed [`nozˌblid] 名 流鼻血、nostril [`nɑstrɪl] 名 鼻孔、olfactory [ɑl`fæktərɪ] 名 嗅覺器官 形 嗅覺的

notable [`notəbl̩] 形 值得注意的，顯著的
▶ Her first performance already shows a notable achievement.
  她的第一場演出已經展現很棒的成就。

note [not] 名 筆記，紀錄
▶ You can take notes in class.
  上課你可以作筆記。

相關衍生字彙 notebook [`notˌbuk] 名 筆記本、noted [`notɪd] 形 著名的、noteworthy [`notˌwɝðɪ] 形 值得注意的

N

nothing [ˈnʌθɪŋ] 名 微不足道的事（或人）副 一點也不 代 沒什麼　　⊙ MP3 **14-04**
▶ There is nothing wrong with your cellphone. 你的手機沒問題。

notion [ˈnoʃən] 名 想法，概念
▶ My daughter has a notion to study abroad. 我女兒有出國念書的打算。

notice [ˈnotɪs] 名 公告 動 注意到
▶ Did you notice that anyone came into my room?
你有注意到有人進入我的房間嗎？

相關衍生字彙 notification [ˌnotəfəˈkeʃən] 名 通知，通告、notify [ˈnotəˌfaɪ] 動 通知、
attention [əˈtɛnʃən] 名 注意力、inform [ɪnˈfɔrm] 動 通知

動詞三態變化 notice - noticed - noticed

notorious [noˈtorɪəs] 形 惡名昭彰的
▶ The company is notorious for its poor quality.
這家公司以品質差而惡名昭彰。

相關衍生字彙 notoriety [ˌnotəˈraɪətɪ] 名 惡名昭彰、notoriously [noˈtorɪəslɪ] 副 聲名狼藉地、
infamous [ˈɪnfəməs] 形 臭名昭著的，罪大惡極的、renowned [rɪˈnaʊnd]
形 有名的，有聲譽的、flagrant [ˈfleɡrənt] 形 公然的，罪惡昭彰的、
dishonorable [dɪsˈɑnərəbl] 形 不名譽的，可恥的、well-known [ˈwɛlˈnon]
形 出名的，眾所周知的

nourish [ˈnɝɪʃ] 動 滋養，培育
▶ Babies need milk to nourish them.
嬰兒需要牛奶來餵養他們。

動詞三態變化 nourish - nourished - nourished

nourishment [ˈnɝɪʃmənt] 名 營養
▶ We can get nourishment from good fresh food.
我們從好的新鮮的食物可以獲得營養。

novel [ˈnɑvl] 名 小說 形 新奇的
▶ The director made the novel into a film.
導演把這部小說拍成電影。

相關衍生字彙 novelist [ˈnɑvlɪst] 名 小說家、novelize [ˈnɑvlˌaɪz] 動 使成小說、
novelette [ˌnɑvlˈɛt] 名 短篇（中篇）小說、novelistic [ˌnɑvlˈɪstɪk]
形（長篇）小說的、novella [noˈvɛlə] 名 短篇故事，中篇小說

novelty [ˈnɑvltɪ] 名 新奇，新穎
▶ Kids are attracted by the novelty of the toys. 孩子被玩具的新鮮感所吸引。

November [noˈvɛmbɚ] 名 十一月
▶ The weather in November is mild in Taiwan. 在台灣，十一月的天氣是溫和的。

novice [ˈnɑvɪs] 名 新手，初學者
▶ Speaking of painting, I am a complete novice. 說到畫畫，我完全是生手。

noxious [`nɑkʃəs] 形 有害的，討厭的　　回 harmful [`hɑrmfəl] 形 有害的

nowadays [`nauə,dez] 副 現今，時下
▶ Nowadays, more and more women are not willing to get married.
現今，愈來愈多女人不願意結婚。
相關衍生字彙 present [`prɛznt] 形 現在的，當前的、current [`kɜənt] 形 現行的、
modern [`mɑdən] 形 近代的、contemporary [kən`tɛmpə,rɛrɪ] 形 當代的

nuclear [`njuklɪə] 形 核能的　　片 a nuclear power plant 核能電廠

nucleus [`njuklɪəs] 名 核心　　片 the nucleus of the power 權力的核心

nude [njud] 名 裸體 形 無裝飾的
▶ Someone is swimming in the nude over there. 有人在那邊裸泳。

nuisance [`njusn̩s] 名 討厭的人（或事物）
▶ It was a nuisance for me to have a mosquito flying around in my room.
我很討厭有蚊子在我房裡飛來飛去。

numb [nʌm] 形 麻木的，發楞的
▶ My fingers were numb with cold. 我的手指因寒冷而僵掉了。

number [`nʌmbə] 名 數字
▶ The number of newborn babies is decreasing.
新生兒的數字在下降中。
相關衍生字彙 numberless [`nʌmbəlɪs] 形 數不盡的、numerous [`njumərəs] 形 許多的、
sum [sʌm] 名 總數、total [`totl̩] 名 總數

N

nun [nʌn] 名 修女，尼姑　　反 monk [mʌŋk] 名 修道士，僧侶

nurse [nɜs] 名 護士
▶ It takes patience to be a nurse. 當護士需要耐心。

nursery [`nɜsərɪ] 名 育兒室，托兒所　　片 a day nursery 日間托兒所　　◎ MP3 **14-05**

nut [nʌt] 名 堅果　　片 a hard / tough nut to crack 棘手的問題，難對付的人

nutrition [nju`trɪʃən] 名 營養
▶ Because of poor nutrition, the boy is shorter than his peers.
因為營養不良，所以這個男孩比同儕還要矮小。
相關衍生字彙 nutritional [nju`trɪʃən!] 形 營養的，滋養的、nutritionist [nju`trɪʃənɪst]
名 營養學家、nutritious [nju`trɪʃəs] 形 有營養的、nourishment [`nɜɪʃmənt]
名 營養品，滋養

nurture [`nɜtʃə] 名 動 養育，培育
▶ To nurture her children, she decided to quit her job.
為了養育小孩，她決定辭去工作。
動詞三態變化 nurture - nurtured - nurtured

字母 O

oasis ~ oxygen

詞性說明

名 名詞	副 副詞	介 介系詞
動 動詞	形 形容詞	連 連接詞
代 代名詞	助 助動詞	

內文圖示說明

片 片語　　反 反義字　　同 同義字

一網打盡「英語小知識」| 表達「驚訝」的用語 II

How amazing! 太厲害了！

Oh my gosh, this is wild! 天啊！這什麼怪東西啊！

Wow, how awesome is this? 哇，這也太棒了！

O oasis ~ oxygen

★一網打盡 325 個英文單字 ｜ 一網打盡 93 句英語會話句　　　　　　　◎ MP3 **15-01**

oasis [o`esɪs] 名 **綠洲**
▶ In a desert, an oasis is the only place where there is water.
　在沙漠裡，綠洲是唯一有水的地方。

---

obedience [ə`bidjəns] 名 **順從，服從**
▶ For soldiers, obedience is very important.
　對軍人而言，服從很重要。

相關衍生字彙 acquiescence [͵ækwɪ`ɛsəns] 名 默認，默從、compliance [kəm`plaɪəns]
　　　　　　名 承諾，順從，屈從、obedient [ə`bidjənt] 形 服從的，恭順的、
　　　　　　obediently [ə`bidɪəntlɪ] 副 服從地，忠順地、submission [sʌb`mɪʃən]
　　　　　　名 歸順，提交（物），屈從、submissiveness [səb`mɪsɪvnɪs] 名 柔順，服從、
　　　　　　reverence [`rɛvərəns] 名 動 敬愛，威望，敬禮

---

obeisance [o`besn̩s] 名 **敬禮，尊敬**

---

obey [ə`be] 動 **遵守，聽從**
▶ If you don't obey the traffic rules, you will be fined.
　如果你沒有遵守交通規則，你會被罰款。

相關衍生字彙 obedient [ə`bidjənt] 形 順從的、disobey [͵dɪsə`be] 動 不遵守、
　　　　　　violate [`vaɪə͵let] 動 違反、follow [`fɑlo] 動 遵從

動詞三態變化 obey - obeyed - obeyed

---

object [`ɑbdʒɪkt] 名 **物體**　　🅗 UFO = Unidentified Flying Object 不明飛行物，幽浮

---

objection [əb`dʒɛkʃən] 名 **反對，異議**
▶ I have no objection.
　我不反對。

相關衍生字彙 objectionable [əb`dʒɛkʃənəbl̩] 形 令人不愉快的、complaint [kəm`plent]
　　　　　　名 抱怨，抗議、disapproval [͵dɪsə`pruvl̩] 名 不贊成，不准許、dissent [dɪ`sɛnt]
　　　　　　名 動 不同意、criticism [`krɪtə͵sɪzəm] 名 批評，苛求

---

objective [əb`dʒɛktɪv] 名 **目標** 形 **客觀的**
▶ I think your opinion is objective enough.
　我想你的意見夠客觀了。

相關衍生字彙 objectively [əb`dʒɛktɪvlɪ] 副 客觀地、objectivism [əb`dʒɛktəvɪzəm]
　　　　　　名 客觀主義，客觀性、objectivity [͵ɑbdʒɛk`tɪvətɪ] 名 客觀（性）、
　　　　　　purpose [`pɝpəs] 名 目的，意圖、intention [ɪn`tɛnʃən] 名 意向，目的、
　　　　　　animus [`ænəməs] 名 敵意，主導精神、aspiration [͵æspə`reʃən]
　　　　　　名 志向，抱負、implication [͵ɪmplɪ`keʃən] 名 涉及，含意、scheme [skim]
　　　　　　名 方案，體制 動 計劃，密謀

obligation [ˌɑblə`geʃən] 名 義務，責任

▶ Parents have the obligation to educate their children.
父母有責任教育他們的孩子。

相關衍生字彙 obligatory [ə`blɪgəˌtorɪ] 形 有義務的，必修的、responsibility [rɪˌspɑnsə`bɪlətɪ] 名 責任（感）、burden [`bɝdn̩] 名 重擔，職位、accountability [əˌkaʊntə`bɪlətɪ] 名 負有責任，可說明性、liability [ˌlaɪə`bɪlətɪ] 名 傾向，責任，義務

oblige [ə`blaɪdʒ] 動 迫使

▶ The law obliges all the factories to emphasize the welfare of their workers.
法律迫使所有工廠要重視員工的福利。

相關衍生字彙 require [rɪ`kwaɪr] 動 要求、force [fors] 動 強迫，迫使、demand [dɪ`mænd] 名 動 要求、obligate [`ɑbləˌget] 動 使負義務、compel [kəm`pɛl] 動 強迫

動詞三態變化 oblige - obliged - obliged

oblique [əb`lik] 名 斜線 形 拐彎抹角的

▶ What he said is not direct but a little oblique.
他所說的並不直接，有點閃爍其詞。

oblivious [ə`blɪvɪəs] 形 不注意的，忘卻的

▶ I was oblivious to what was happening outside. 我沒注意外面發生什麼事。

obscure [əb`skjur] 形 模糊的，偏僻的

▶ The new policy is obscure for many people.
對很多人而言，這項新政策很模糊。

相關衍生字彙 obscurely [əb`skjurlɪ] 副 費解地，隱匿地、indistinct [ˌɪndɪ`stɪŋkt] 形 模糊的，未明確限定的，不分開的、unclear [ʌn`klɪr] 形 不清楚的，含糊不清的、indefinite [ɪn`dɛfənɪt] 形 未定的，不明確的，無限期的、vague [veg] 形（形狀等）模糊不清的，（想法等）不明確的、shadowy [`ʃædəwɪ] 形 多蔭的，朦朧的，虛無的、blurred [blɝd] 形 難辨別的、fuzzy [`fʌzɪ] 形 有絨毛的，模糊不清的

O

observe [əb`zɝv] 動 觀察

▶ By observing their parents, children learn how to interact with others.
藉由觀察父母，孩子學會與人互動。

相關衍生字彙 observance [əb`zɝvəns] 名 遵守，觀察、observation [ˌɑbzɝ`veʃən] 名 觀察、observatory [əb`zɝvəˌtorɪ] 名 天文台

動詞三態變化 observe - observed - observed

obsolete [`ɑbsəˌlit] 形 廢棄的，淘汰的

▶ Typewriters became obsolete when computers got popular.
電腦普及後，打字機就被淘汰了。

obstacle [`ɑbstəkl̩] 名 障礙（物），妨礙

▶ The biggest obstacle to their love is their parents' objection.
他們愛情的最大障礙是父母的反對。

obstinate [ˋɑbstənɪt] 形 頑固的　　片 as obstinate as a mule 跟驢一樣固執

obstruct [əbˋstrʌkt] 動 阻塞，阻擾
▶ The car accident obstructed the road for hours.
　車禍讓道路阻塞好幾個小時。

相關衍生字彙 obstruction [əbˋstrʌkʃən] 名 妨礙，障礙、obstructive [əbˋstrʌktɪv] 名 障礙物
　　　　　　形 妨礙的，堵塞的、obstructor [əbˋstrʌktɚ] 名 阻礙者，妨礙物、block [blɑk]
　　　　　　動 堵住，阻擋，限制、hinder [ˋhɪndɚ] 動 妨礙，阻礙、clog [klɑg] 名 障礙物
　　　　　　動 塞滿，阻礙

動詞三態變化 obstruct - obstructed - obstructed

obtain [əbˋten] 動 獲得，得到
▶ Before we get married, we should obain our parents' permission.
　結婚前，我們得徵求父母的同意。

相關衍生字彙 obtainable [əbˋtenəb!] 形 能得到的、unobtainable [ˌʌnəbˋtenəb!]
　　　　　　形 難獲得的、obtainment [əbˋtenmənt] 名 獲得，得到、acquire [əˋkwaɪr]
　　　　　　動 取得，養成、procure [proˋkjur] 動（努力）取得，導致，達成

動詞三態變化 obtain - obtained - obtained

obvious [ˋɑbvɪəs] 形 明顯的，平淡無奇的
▶ It's obvious that Mark doesn't like you.
　很明顯的，馬克並不喜歡你。

相關衍生字彙 obviously [ˋɑbvɪəslɪ] 副 明顯地、apparent [əˋpærənt] 形 明顯的、
　　　　　　apparently [əˋpærəntlɪ] 副 顯然地、clear [klɪr] 形 清楚的

occasion [əˋkeʒən] 名 場合，時機
▶ You should dress yourself according to the occasion. 你要根據場合來穿衣服。

occasionally [əˋkeʒən!ɪ] 副 偶爾　　　　　　　　MP3 **15-02**
▶ After graduating, I met him occasionally at the market.
　畢業後，我偶爾在市場遇見他。

occupation [ˌɑkjəˋpeʃən] 名 職業
▶ She is a nurse by occupation.
　她的職業是護士。

相關衍生字彙 occupational [ˌɑkjəˋpeʃən!] 形 職業的，佔領的、occupational disease
　　　　　　片 職業病、occupational hazard 片 職業傷害

occupy [ˋɑkjəˌpaɪ] 動 佔據，佔用
▶ All the seats in the library were occupied.
　圖書館的位置全被佔滿。

動詞三態變化 occupy - occupied - occupied

occur [əˋkɝ] 動 發生
▶ A good idea occurred to me.
　我突然想到一個好主意。

動詞三態變化 occur - occurred - occurred

occurrence [ə`kɝəns] 名 發生，事件
▶ Fighting is a frequent occurrence among the teenagers.
打架是青少年間常見的事。

相關衍生字彙 event [ɪ`vɛnt] 名 事件、incident [`ɪnsədṇt] 名 事件、accident [`æksədənt] 名 意外事件、happening [`hæpənɪŋ] 名 事件、affair [ə`fɛr] 名 事件，風流韻事

ocean [`oʃən] 名 海洋　　片 the Pacific Ocean 太平洋

October [ak`tobɚ] 名 十月
▶ October tenth is our national birthday. 十月十日是我們的國慶日。

odd [ad] 形 奇數的，奇特的
▶ Her grandfather is an odd man.
她的爺爺是個古怪的人。

相關衍生字彙 oddity [`adətɪ] 名 奇特，古怪、oddly [`adlɪ] 副 奇怪地，古怪地、oddness [`adnɪs] 名 奇怪，古怪、unusual [ʌn`juʒuəl] 形 奇特的，獨特的、mysterious [mɪs`tɪrɪəs] 形 神祕的，詭祕的、queer [kwɪr] 形 奇怪的，古怪的

odds [ads] 名 機會，可能性
▶ All the odds were against our team. 所有情勢都對我們的隊伍不利。

odor [`odɚ] 名 氣味，名聲
▶ The classroom is full of the odor of sweet. 教室充滿汗臭味。

offend [ə`fɛnd] 動 冒犯
▶ I didn't mean to offend you.
我無意冒犯你。

相關衍生字彙 offense [ə`fɛns] 名 過錯、offensive [ə`fɛnsɪv] 形 冒犯的、polite [pə`laɪt] 形 有禮貌的、defensive [dɪ`fɛnsɪv] 形 保護的

動詞三態變化 offend - offended - offended

offer [`ɔfɚ] 動 給予，提供
▶ I was offered a job in the hospital.
我在醫院找到一份工作。

相關衍生字彙 offering [`ɔfərɪŋ] 名 供奉，捐獻物，祭品、offertory [`ɔfɚˌtorɪ] 名 奉獻祈禱與詩歌，奉獻金

動詞三態變化 offer - offered - offered

office [`ɔfɪs] 名 辦公室　　片 a post office 郵局

officer [`ɔfəsɚ] 名 軍官，公務員
片 an army / a naval / an air-force officer 陸／海／空 軍官

O

official [ə`fɪʃəl] 名 官員 形 官方的
▶ My father is a civil service official. 我爸爸是公務員。

offspring [`ɔf.sprɪŋ] 名 後代，子女
▶ They didn't have any offspring. 他們沒有任何子女。

old-fashioned [`old`fæʃənd] 形 舊式的，過時的
▶ Her hair style is too old-fashioned. 她的髮型很過時。

olive [`ɑlɪv] 名 橄欖　　片 olive oil 橄欖油

omen [`omən] 名 預兆 動 預告
▶ I see the dream as an omen of success.
　我視此夢為成功的兆頭。
相關衍生字彙 sign [saɪn] 名 前兆、indication [.ɪndə`keʃən] 名 徵兆、warning [`wɔrnɪŋ]
　　　　　 名 前兆，警告、admonition [.ædmə`nɪʃən] 名 告誡、advice [əd`vaɪs] 名 忠告
動詞三態變化 omen - omened - omened

omission [o`mɪʃən] 名 省略，刪除，疏忽
▶ Please correct the omission in your assignment. 請更正你作業裡的疏漏。

omit [o`mɪt] 動 遺漏，忘記　　　　　　　　　　　　　⊙ MP3 **15-03**
▶ I omitted to leave a message to him.
　我忘了留訊息給他。
動詞三態變化 omit - omitted - omitted

once [wʌns] 副 一次，曾經　　片 once in a while 偶而

opening [`opənɪŋ] 名 開幕
▶ The new department store will have a formal opening tomorrow.
　這家新的百貨公司明天將有正式的開幕。
相關衍生字彙 open [`opən] 動 打開、openly [`opənlɪ] 副 公開地、opener [`opənɚ] 名 開罐器

opera [`ɑpərə] 名 歌劇
▶ I went to the opera last night. 昨晚，我去聽了一場歌劇。

operate [`ɑpə.ret] 動 操作，動手術
▶ The surgeon operated on his heart.
　醫生幫他做心臟手術。
相關衍生字彙 operative [`ɑpərətɪv] 形 操作的，有效的、operator [`ɑpə.retɚ]
　　　　　 名 操作者，接線生，司機
動詞三態變化 operate - operated - operated

operation [.ɑpə`reʃən] 名 操作，經營，手術　　片 to perform an operation 動手術

opinion [ə`pɪnjən] 名 意見
▶ In my opinion, he will win the game. 根據我的看法，他將贏得比賽。

opponent [ə`ponənt] 名 對手
▶ To beat his opponent in chess, he practices day and night.
為擊敗棋賽對手，他日以繼夜的練習。

opportunity [ˌɑpɚ`tjunətɪ] 名 機會
▶ Grab the opportunity! Don't give it up! 抓住機會！別放棄！

oppose [ə`poz] 動 反對，妨礙
▶ Mom opposed my part-time job.
媽媽反對我去打工。
相關衍生字彙 opposite [`ɑpəzɪt] 形 相反的、opposition [ˌɑpə`zɪʃən] 名 反對、agree [ə`gri]
動 贊成、contrary [`kɑntrɛrɪ] 形 相反的
動詞三態變化 oppose - opposed - opposed

oppression [ə`prɛʃən] 名 壓迫，壓抑　　片 under oppression 在壓迫之下
相關衍生字彙 oppress [ə`prɛs] 動 壓迫，壓制、oppressive [ə`prɛsɪv]
形 壓制的，暴虐的，沉重的、persecution [ˌpɝsɪ`kjuʃən] 名 迫害，困擾、
despotism [`dɛspət͵ɪzəm] 名 專制政治，暴政、tyranny [`tɪrənɪ]
名 專制，暴虐，苛刻、compulsion [kəm`pʌlʃən] 名（被）強迫，強制力

optical [`ɑptɪk]] 形 視覺的　　片 optical art 視覺藝術

optimistic [ˌɑptə`mɪstɪk] 形 樂觀的
▶ He is optimistic that he will pass the exam.
他對通過考試很樂觀。
相關衍生字彙 optimism [`ɑptəmɪzəm] 名 樂觀、pessimism [`pɛsəmɪzəm] 名 悲觀、
pessimistic [ˌpɛsə`mɪstɪk] 形 悲觀的

option [`ɑpʃən] 名 選擇
▶ Life is full of options.
人生充滿選擇。
相關衍生字彙 optional [`ɑpʃən]] 名 選修科目 形 隨意的，非必須的、choice [tʃɔɪs] 名 選擇、
substitute [`sʌbstə͵tjut] 名 代替人（或物），代用品、equivalent [ɪ`kwɪvələnt]
名 相等物，同義字

oral [`orəl] 形 口頭的，口述的
▶ Every student in the department should pass the oral test.
系上的每個學生都得通過口試。

orange [`ɔrɪndʒ] 名 柳橙　　片 orange juice 柳橙汁

oratory [`ɔrətorɪ] 名 雄辯術　　片 campaign oratory 競選演講
相關衍生字彙 orator [`ɔrətɚ] 名 演說者、oratorical [ˌɔrə`tɔrɪk]] 形 雄辯的 演說的，雄辯術的、
eloquence [`ɛləkwəns] 名 雄辯，（流利的）口才

O

351

orbit [`ɔrbɪt] 名 運行軌道
▶ NASA will put a new satellite into the orbit.
美國太空總署將把新的衛星送入軌道。

orchard [`ɔrtʃəd] 名 果園
▶ I plan to run an orchard after retirement. 退休後，我打算經營果園。

orchestra [`ɔrkɪstrə] 名 管弦樂隊　　片 a chamber orchestra 室內管絃樂隊

ordain [ɔr`den] 動 命令，委任　　　　　　　　　　　　　　　MP3 15-04
▶ He was ordained as a grand justice.
他被委任為大法官。

相關衍生字彙 order [`ɔrdə] 動 命令，指示、instruct [ɪn`strʌkt] 動 指示、
command [kə`mænd] 動 命令、bid [bɪd] 動 命令，吩咐、advise [əd`vaɪz]
動 勸告

動詞三態變化 ordain - ordained - ordained

ordeal [ɔr`diəl] 名 折磨，嚴峻考驗　　片 to go through an ordeal 經歷折磨

order [`ɔrdə] 名 順序，命令 動 指揮，定購
▶ Everything in her room is in good order.
她房間裡的每樣東西都井然有序。

相關衍生字彙 orderly [`ɔrdəlɪ] 形 整齊的，有條理的、arrangement [ə`rendʒmənt]
名 安排，約定、condition [kən`dɪʃən] 名 情況，條件、disposition [ˌdɪspə`zɪʃən]
名 性格，配置，清除、formation [fɔr`meʃən] 名 構成，隊形

動詞三態變化 order - ordered - ordered

ordinary [`ɔrdṇˌɛrɪ] 形 普通的，平凡的
▶ The house is very ordinary, nothing special.
這間房子很普通，沒有什麼特別的。

相關衍生字彙 ordinarily [`ɔrdṇˌɛrɪlɪ] 副 通常地，一般地、usual [`juʒʊəl]
形 通常的，平常的、common [`kɑmən] 形 普通的，共有的，粗鄙的、
normal [`nɔrml] 形 正常的，身心健全的、regular [`rɛgjələ]
形 有規律的，定期的，一般的、mediocre [`midɪˌokə] 形 中等的，平凡的、
customary 形 習慣上的，合乎習俗的

organ [`ɔrgən] 名 器官　　片 organ transplantation 器官移植

organic [ɔr`gænɪk] 形 有機的
▶ Organic vegetables are more expensive.
有機蔬菜比較貴。

相關衍生字彙 organism [`ɔrgənˌɪzəm] 名 生物，有機體、organically [ɔr`gænɪkəlɪ]
副 有機耕作地，施有機肥地、organic chemistry 片 有機化學、organic content
片 有機物含量、organic cotton 片 有機棉、organic solvent extraction
片 有機溶劑抽取法

organization [ˌɔrgənəˋzeʃən] 名 組織，機構
▶ Our boss hopes we can become a learning organization.
老闆希望我們成為學習型組織。

相關衍生字彙 organize [ˋɔrgəˌnaɪz] 動 組織，始有條理、organized [ˋɔrgənˌaɪzd] 形 有組織的，參加工會的、organizer [ˋɔrgəˌnaɪzɚ] 名 組織者、organizational [ˌɔrgənaɪˋzeʃənəl] 形 組織（上）的，編制（中）的

oriental [ˌɔrɪˋɛntl̩] 形 東方的
▶ Many Westerners are attracted deeply to the oriental culture.
很多西方人深深被東方文化所吸引。

originality [əˌrɪdʒəˋnælətɪ] 名 創造力，獨創性
▶ The artist is famous for his originality.
這位藝術家以他的獨創性所著稱。

相關衍生字彙 original [əˋrɪdʒən!] 形 原創的，原本的、originally [əˋrɪdʒənlɪ] 副 原本地、originate [əˋrɪdʒəˌnet] 動 發源於、origin [ˋɔrədʒɪn] 名 起源

ornament [ˋɔrnəmənt] 名 裝飾品
▶ She uses lots of pink ornaments in her room.
她房間用了很多粉紅色的裝飾品。

相關衍生字彙 ornamental [ˌɔrnəˋmɛnt!] 名 裝飾品 形 裝飾的、ornamentation [ˌɔrnəmɛnˋteʃən] 名 裝飾，（總稱）裝飾品、ornamentally [ˌɔrnəˋmɛntl̩ɪ] 副 裝飾地、decoration [ˌdɛkəˋreʃən] 名 裝飾，裝飾品、adornment [əˋdɔrnmənt] 名 裝飾品，裝飾法

orphan [ˋɔrfən] 名 孤兒
▶ About 20 orphans live in the orphanage.
大約二十名孤兒住在這個孤兒院。

相關衍生字彙 orphanage [ˋɔrfənɪdʒ] 名 孤兒院，孤兒身分、orphanhood [ˋɔrfənˌhud] 名 孤兒、foundling [ˋfaʊndlɪŋ] 名 棄兒，棄嬰

O

orthodox [ˋɔrθəˌdɑks] 形 正統的，傳統的　　⬤ traditional [trəˋdɪʃən!] 形 傳統的

otherwise [ˋʌðɚˌwaɪz] 副 否則
▶ You had better take notes; otherwise, you will forget what the teacher says.
你最好做筆記，否則會忘記老師說什麼。

ought [ɔt] 助 應該
▶ We all ought to love the country of our own. 我們都應該要愛自己的國家。

outbreak [ˋaʊtˌbrek] 名 爆發，暴動
▶ The outbreak of Ebola will lead to a disaster. 伊波拉的爆發將引發一場災難。

outburst [`aut͵bɝst] 名 (情感、力量等的)爆發，(火山的)噴發
▶ His carelessness provoked an outburst of anger from the manager.
他的粗心引發經理的憤怒。

------

outcome [`aut͵kʌm] 名 結果
▶ It's hard to predict the outcome of the election. 很難預測選舉的結果。

------

outdo [͵aut`du] 動 勝過，超越
▶ He always gets good grades and outdoes the others in the class.
他的好成績總是勝過班上其他人。

相關衍生字彙 surpass [sɚ`pæs] 動 勝過，優於、excel [ɪk`sɛl] 動 勝過、defeat [dɪ`fit]
名 動 戰勝，擊敗、beat [bit] 動 打敗，勝過、win [wɪn] 名 動 獲勝，成功

動詞三態變化 outdo - outdid - outdone

------

outdoor [`aut͵dor] 形 戶外的　　🖐 outdoor activities 戶外活動

------

outdoors [`aut`dorz] 副 戶外地
▶ When the weather is good, I like to go picnicking outdoors.
天氣好時，我喜歡到戶外野餐。

------

outfit [`aut͵fɪt] 名 全套裝備　　　　　　　　　　🔊 MP3 **15-05**
▶ I wore a witch outfit for the Halloween party.
我穿了巫婆的裝扮去萬聖節派對。

------

outlet [`aut͵lɛt] 名 銷路，商店
▶ You can buy anything at the retail outlet. 你可以在這個零售商店買到任何東西。

------

outline [`aut͵laɪn] 名 大綱
▶ The teacher asked us to hand in the outline of our final report.
老師要求我們交期末報告的大綱。

------

outlive [aut`lɪv] 動 比～活得久
▶ She outlived her husband by ten years.
她比她先生多活了十年。

動詞三態變化 outlive - outlived - outlived

------

outlook [`aut͵luk] 名 觀點，看法
▶ I always have a positive outlook on my future.
我一直對前途抱持正面的看法。

相關衍生字彙 view [vju] 名 觀點，看法、opinion [ə`pɪnjən] 名 意見，見解、thought [θɔt]
名 思維，見解、conception [kən`sɛpʃən] 名 概念，想法、
impression [ɪm`prɛʃən] 名 印象，感想、idea [aɪ`diə] 名 主意，構想、
notion [`noʃən] 名 概念，想法

------

output [`aut͵put] 名 產量
▶ The output of the factory fell by 5% last month.
這間工廠上個月的產量下跌百分之五。

outrage [`aut͵redʒ] 名 憤怒
▶ The public express their outrage with a demonstration.
大眾用示威活動來表達憤怒。
相關衍生字彙 outrageous [aut`redʒəs] 形 可惡的、evil [`iv]] 形 邪惡的、wicked [`wɪkɪd] 形 邪惡的、anger [`æŋgɚ] 名 憤怒

outright [`aut`raɪt] 副 全部地
▶ The violent TV programs should be banned outright.
暴力的電視節目應該全面禁止。

outset [`aut͵sɛt] 名 最初，開端
▶ From the very outset, I didn't like the person. 從一開始，我就不喜歡這個人。

outside [`aut`saɪd] 名 外面 形 外部的　反 inside [`ɪn`saɪd] 名 內部 形 內部的
相關衍生字彙 outsider [`aut`saɪdɚ] 名 門外漢，局外人、outside broadcast 片 實況轉播、outside lane 片 外（車）道、outside-the-box 形 創造性的，大破傳統的、periphery [pə`rɪfərɪ] 名 周圍，圓周、surface [`sɝfɪs] 名 表面，外觀

outskirt [`aut͵skɝt] 名 郊區
▶ A museum will be set up on the outskirts of Taipei.
有一間博物館將設在台北的郊區。

outstanding [`aut`stændɪŋ] 形 傑出的
片 an outstanding performance 傑出的表現
相關衍生字彙 excellent [`ɛksḷənt] 形 傑出的、commonplace [`kɑmən͵ples] 形 平凡的、distinguished [dɪ`stɪŋgwɪʃt] 形 卓越的、striking [`straɪkɪŋ] 形 顯著的，突出的、noticeable [`notɪsəb]] 形 顯而易見的、eminent [`ɛmənənt] 形 卓越的

outweigh [aut`we] 動 比～更重要
▶ I think the disadvantages of the project outweigh the advantages of it.
我認為此計畫的缺點比優點多。
動詞三態變化 outweigh - outweighed - outweighed

oven [`ʌvən] 名 烤箱
▶ The cookies in the oven are for your dessert. 烤箱裡的餅乾讓妳當點心。

overall [`ovɚ͵ɔl] 形 全部的，全面的
▶ The overall situation is bad for the development of baseball.
全部的條件都不利於棒球的發展。

overcoat [`ovɚ͵kot] 名 外套，大衣
▶ It's cold. You need to take an overcoat. 太冷了，你要帶件外套。

overeat [`ovɚ`it] 動 吃得過飽
▶ Overeating is harmful to your health.
吃太飽對健康有害。
動詞三態變化 overeat - overate - overeaten

O

overflow [ˌovɚ`flo] 動 滿（或多）得溢出

▶ The heavy rain made the river overflow.
大雨讓河川氾濫了。

動詞三態變化 overflow - overflowed - overflowed

overhear [ˌovɚ`hɪr] 動 無意中聽到

▶ I happened to overhear a secret between them.
我碰巧聽到他們的一個祕密。

動詞三態變化 overhear - overheard - overheard

overlap [ˌovɚ`læp] 動 部分重疊

▶ Our tasks overlap.
我們的任務有部分重疊。

動詞三態變化 overlap - overlapped - overlapped

overlook [ˌovɚ`luk] 動 眺望

MP3 **15-06**

▶ Our house overlooked the valley.
從我們的房子能眺望山谷。

動詞三態變化 overlook - overlooked - overlooked

overnight [`ovɚ`naɪt] 副 一夜之間，突然

▶ People want to get rich overnight. 人們想一夜致富。

overseas [`ovɚ`siz] 副 海外

▶ My son is studying overseas. 我兒子正在海外讀書。

oversee [`ovɚ`si] 動 監視，管理，眺望

▶ The clerk was assigned to oversee the change of the marketing.
這位職員被指派監督市場行銷的變化。

動詞三態變化 oversee - oversaw - overseen

oversleep [`ovɚ`slip] 動 睡過頭

▶ I overslept this morning, so I was late.
我今天早上睡過頭，所以遲到了。

動詞三態變化 oversleep - overslept - overslept

overthrow [ˌovɚ`θro] 動 推翻，廢除

▶ The autocratic government was overthrown.
那個獨裁政府被推翻了。

相關衍生字彙 overpower [ˌovɚ`pauɚ] 動 制伏，擊敗、conquer [`kɑŋkɚ] 動 攻克，戰勝、
overcome [ˌovɚ`kʌm] 動 克服，戰勝、overwhelm [ˌovɚ`hwɛlm]
動 征服，壓倒、overtake [ˌovɚ`tek] 動 超過，趕上

動詞三態變化 overthrow - overthrew - overthrown

overturn [ˌovɚˋtɝn] 動 翻轉，顛覆，傾覆
▶ The car hit the fence and overturned.
車子撞到圍牆翻覆了。
動詞三態變化 overturn - overturned - overturned

overwhelm [ˌovɚˋhwɛlm] 動 壓倒，淹沒，征服
▶ I was almost overwhelmed by the pressure.
我幾乎要被壓力壓垮了。
動詞三態變化 overwhelm - overwhelmed - overwhelmed

overwork [ˋovɚˋwɝk] 動 工作過度
▶ I overworked myself and felt tired to death.
我工作過度覺得快要累死了。
動詞三態變化 overwork - overworked / overwrought - overworked / overwrought

owe [o] 動 欠（債），應該把～歸功於
▶ You didn't owe me anything.
你沒欠我任何東西。
動詞三態變化 owe - owed - owed

owing [ˋoɪŋ] 形 欠著的，未付的　　片 owing to 由於，因為

owl [aul] 名 貓頭鷹
▶ An owl has large eyes. 貓頭鷹有著大眼睛。

own [on] 形 自己的 動 擁有，承認
▶ We finally own our house and a car.
我們終於擁有房子跟車子了。
相關衍生字彙 owner [ˋonɚ] 名 擁有人、ownership [ˋonɚˌʃɪp] 名 所有權、
state-owned [ˋstetˌond] 形 國家擁有的、family-owned [ˋfæməlɪˌond] 形 家族的
動詞三態變化 own - owned - owned

oxygen [ˋɑksədʒən] 名 氧氣
▶ Without water, oxygen and food, we can't live.
沒有水、氧氣與食物，我們沒辦法生存。
相關衍生字彙 oxygen mask 片 氧氣面罩、oxygenate [ˋɑksədʒənˌet]
動 為～充氧，使與氧化合、oxygen scavenger 片 氧氣清除劑（例單寧酸等）、
oxygen tent 片（急救輸氧用的）氧氣罩、oxygenase 名 氧化酵素

一網打盡「英語小知識」│「表達意見」時 ────────

想表達自己的意見，可以用：

In my opinion... 我的意見是～

I think / believe that... 我覺得／相信～

The point is that... 我的觀點是～

As far as I'm concerned... 就我而言～。

P pace ~ puzzle

★一網打盡 986 個英文單字 │ 一網打盡 253 句英語會話句   ◎ MP3 **16-01**

pace [pes] 名 步伐
▶ I walked faster to keep pace with him. 為了跟上他的步伐，我加快腳步。

pacify [`pæsə͵faɪ] 動 撫慰，使平靜
▶ She pacified her baby with music.
她用音樂安撫她的寶寶。

動詞三態變化 pacify - pacified - pacified

package [`pækɪdʒ] 名 包裹
▶ There is a package delivered for you.
有一個包裹是送來給你的。

相關衍生字彙 pack [pæk] 動 包裝、packet [`pækɪt] 名 小包、packed [pækt] 形 塞滿的

paddle [`pædl̩] 動 用槳划   片 to paddle one's own canoe 自立更生
動詞三態變化 paddle - paddled - paddled

page [pedʒ] 名 頁數
▶ Please turn to page 10. 請翻到第十頁。

pail [pel] 名 提桶，一桶的量   同 bucket [`bʌkɪt] 名 桶子

painful [`penfəl] 形 疼痛的
▶ I don't want to recall the painful memories.
我不想再憶起那痛苦的回憶。

相關衍生字彙 painkiller [`pen͵kɪlɚ] 名 止痛藥、painless [penlɪs] 形 不痛的、ache [ek]
名 疼痛、pain [pen] 名 痛苦、pang [pæŋ] 名 一陣劇痛

painstaking [`penz͵tekɪŋ] 形 不辭辛勞的
▶ It took them years of painstaking experiments to find the answer.
他們花了數年不辭辛勞的實驗才找到答案。

pair [pɛr] 名 一雙   片 a pair of shoes 一雙鞋

paint [pent] 名 油漆，塗料 動 繪畫
▶ I plan to paint my room blue.
我打算把我的房間漆成藍色。

相關衍生字彙 painting [`pentɪŋ] 名 繪畫、painter [`pentɚ] 名 畫家、picture [`pɪktʃɚ]
名 照片、portrait [`portret] 名 肖像

動詞三態變化 paint - painted - painted

pajamas [pə`dʒæməs] 名 睡衣
▶ It's not polite to greet guests in your pajamas. 穿睡衣見客人是不禮貌的。

pal [pæl] 名 伙伴，好友　　片 a pen pal 筆友

palace [ˋpælɪs] 名 皇宮，宮殿　　片 the National Palace Museum 故宮博物院

pale [pel] 形 蒼白的，（顏色）淡的
▶ Why are you looking so pale today? 你今天看起來怎麼這麼蒼白？

palm [pɑm] 名 手掌
▶ She knows how to read the palm. 她會看手相。

pamphlet [ˋpæmflɪt] 名 小冊子
▶ The pamphlet can help you understand more about the museum.
這本小冊子有助你更加瞭解此博物館。
相關衍生字彙 booklet [ˋbʊklɪt] 名 小冊子、brochure [broˋʃʊr] 名 小冊子、folder [ˋfoldɚ]
名 摺頁說明書、leaflet [ˋliflɪt] 名 傳單

pancake [ˋpænˏkek] 名 煎餅　　片 as flat as a pancake 非常平坦的

panda [ˋpændə] 名 貓熊
▶ Pandas are endangered animals. 貓熊是瀕臨絕種的動物。

pane [pen] 名 窗玻璃片，窗格　　片 window pane 窗玻璃

panel [ˋpænl] 名 專家小組　　片 panel discussion 小組會談

panic [ˋpænɪk] 名 驚慌 形 恐慌的　　　　　　　MP3 16-02
▶ The disease has caused a panic in the area. 這種疾病已經在該區引起恐慌。

panorama [ˏpænəˋræmə] 名 全景
▶ From the top of the tower, you can enjoy a panorama of the town.
從塔的頂端，你就可以看到小鎮的全景。

P

pants [pænts] 名 褲子　　片 a pair of pants 一件褲子

paper [ˋpepɚ] 名 紙張，論文　　片 a sheet / piece of paper 一張紙
相關衍生字彙 paperwork [ˋpepɚˏwɝk] 名 文書工作、paperback [ˋpepɚˏbæk]
名 平裝本、paperweight [ˋpepɚˏwet] 名 書鎮、papery [ˋpepərɪ] 形 紙狀的

parachute [ˋpærəˏʃut] 名 降落傘　　片 to make a parachute jump 跳傘

parade [pəˋred] 名 遊行
▶ Many people took part in the victory parade. 很多人參加勝利遊行。

paradise [ˋpærəˏdaɪs] 名 天堂
▶ Hong Kong has been said to be a shopping paradise.
香港一直以來都被認為是購物天堂。

paradox [`pærəˌdɑks] 名 自相矛盾的議論
▶ It's a paradox that such good friends like us can't work together.
像我們這樣的好朋友卻無法一起工作，實在是很矛盾的事。

paragraph [`pærəˌgræf] 名 段落
▶ The teacher asked us "what is the main idea of the first paragraph?"
老師問我們：「第一段的主旨是什麼？」

parallel [`pærəˌlɛl] 名 平行線 形 同方向的
▶ The two roads run parallel with each other. 這兩條路互相平行。

paralysis [pə`ræləsɪs] 名 麻痺，癱瘓
▶ The coldness of the weather causes paralysis easily.
寒冷的天氣容易引起中風。

paraphrase [`pærəˌfrez] 名 動 釋義 名 改述
▶ We practice paraphrasing an article in the composition class.
上作文課時，我們練習改寫文章。
動詞三態變化 paraphrase - paraphrased - paraphrased

parcel [`pɑrsl] 名 包裹
▶ I went to the post office to mail a parcel.
我到郵局寄包裹。
相關衍生字彙 package [`pækɪdʒ] 名 包裹、pack [pæk] 動 打包、registered [`rɛdʒɪstɚd] 形 已掛號的、ordinary mail 片 平信、special delivery 片 限時專送

pardon [`pɑrdn] 名 動 原諒，饒恕
▶ Please pardon me for my carelessness.
請原諒我的粗心。
動詞三態變化 pardon - pardoned - pardoned

parent [`pɛrənt] 名 雙親
▶ All the parents will be invited to attend the meeting at school.
所有的家長都將被邀請來學校參加此會議。

parental [pə`rɛntl] 形 父母親的
▶ It's up to the parental decision. 這全憑父母親的決定。

park [pɑrk] 名 公園 動 停車
▶ There is no parking here.
這裡禁止停車。
動詞三態變化 park - parked - parked

parliament [`pɑrləmənt] 名 議會，國會　　片 a house of parliament 議會大廈

parrot [`pærət] 名 鸚鵡
▶ The parrot copies the human voice very well. 這隻鸚鵡學人講話講得很好。

partial [`par ʃəl] 形 部份的，偏袒的　　反 impartial [ɪm`par ʃəl] 形 公平的

相關衍生字彙 part [part] 名 部分、partake [par`tek] 動 分享、partiality [‚par ʃɪ`ælətɪ] 名 偏袒、fair [fɛr] 形 公平的、unfair [ʌn`fɛr] 形 不公平的

---

participate [par`tɪsə‚pet] 動 參加　　◎ MP3 **16-03**
▶ I seldom participated in parties while studying at university.
在大學唸書時，我很少參加派對。

動詞三態變化 participate - participated - participated

---

particle [`partɪk!] 名 微粒，顆粒　　片 a dust particle 灰塵

---

particularly [pɚ`tɪk jələˑlɪ] 副 特別，尤其
▶ Speaking of travelling, I prefer Europe, particularly Italy.
談到旅遊，我偏愛歐洲，特別是義大利。

---

partner [`partnɚ] 名 伙伴，拍檔
▶ We are partners, not lovers.
我們是夥伴，不是戀人。

相關衍生字彙 partnership [`partnɚ‚ʃɪp] 名 夥伴關係、friendship [`frɛndʃɪp] 名 友誼、mate [met] 名 夥伴、companion [kəm`pæn jən] 名 夥伴

---

party [`partɪ] 名 黨派，聚會
▶ There are two major parties in Taiwan at present. 台灣目前有兩大黨派。

---

pass [pæs] 名 通行證 動 通過　　片 to pass down 傳下來

動詞三態變化 pass - passed - passed

---

passenger [`pæsṇdʒɚ] 名 乘客
▶ Buses carry many passengers every day.
公車每天載很多旅客。

相關衍生字彙 passage [`pæsɪdʒ] 名 通道、passageway [`pæsɪdʒ‚we] 名 走廊、commuter [kə`m jutɚ] 名 通勤者、pedestrian [pə`dɛstrɪən] 名 行人

---

passion [`pæ ʃən] 名 熱情　　片 to stir up passion 激發熱情

---

passionate [`pæ ʃənɪt] 形 熱情的
▶ It's hard to say no to your passionate invitation. 很難拒絕你熱情的邀約。

---

passive [`pæsɪv] 形 被動的，消極的　　反 active [`æktɪv] 形 主動的

---

passport [`pæs‚port] 名 護照
▶ Before you go abroad, remember to apply for a passport.
出國前，記得申請護照。

---

password [`pæs‚wɝd] 名 密碼
▶ Please key in your password. 請輸入你的密碼。

P

past [pæst] 名 昔日 形 過去的
▶ How can I forget the sweet past? 我要怎樣忘記甜蜜的過往？

pastime [`pæs͵taɪm] 名 消遣，娛樂
▶ Swimming is my favorite pastime.
游泳是我最愛的消遣活動。
相關衍生字彙 recreation [͵rɛkrɪ`eʃən] 名 消遣，娛樂、entertainment [͵ɛntɚ`tenmənt]
名 餘興、amusement [ə`mjuzmənt] 名 娛樂活動、relaxation [͵rilæks`eʃən]
名 放鬆，消遣

pat [pæt] 名 動 輕拍
▶ He comforted me by patting on my shoulder.
他拍拍我的肩膀安慰我。
動詞三態變化 pat - patted - patted

patent [`pætṇt] 名 專利權　　㊀ to apply for a patent 申請專利

path [pæθ] 名 路徑
▶ I believe that is a path to success. 我相信那是通往成功的路徑。

pathetic [pə`θɛtɪk] 形 可憐的，可悲的
▶ It's pathetic that he failed so many times. 他失敗這麼多次，真可憐。

patience [`peʃəns] 名 耐心，毅力
▶ It takes patience to master a skill. 要精通一樣技術需要耐心。

patient [`peʃənt] 名 病人 形 有耐心的
▶ She is a cardiac patient. 她是一位心臟病患者。

patriot [`petrɪət] 名 愛國者　　◉ MP3 16-04
▶ We love our country. We are all patriots.
我們很愛自己的國家，我們都是愛國者。
相關衍生字彙 patriotic [͵petrɪ`ɑtɪk] 形 愛國的、patriotism [`petrɪət͵ɪzəm] 名 愛國主義、
betray [bɪ`tre] 動 背叛、betrayer [bɪ`treɚ] 名 背叛者

patrol [pə`trol] 名 動 巡邏
▶ The police make regular patrols in the city.
警方在市區定期巡邏。
動詞三態變化 patrol - patrolled - patrolled

patron [`petrən] 名 主顧，贊助者
▶ The man is a regular patron of the café. 這個人是那間咖啡店的老主顧。

pattern [`pætɚn] 名 花樣，形態　　㊀ a behavior pattern 行為模式

pause [pɔz] 名 動 暫停，中斷
▶ She kept talking without pause.
　她一直說話都沒停過。
動詞三態變化 pause - paused - paused

---

pavement [ˋpevmənt] 名 人行道　　同 sidewalk [ˋsaɪdˏwɔk] 名（英）人行道

pay [pe] 動 支付　　片 to pay off 付清
動詞三態變化 pay - paid - paid

payment [ˋpemənt] 名 支付，付款
▶ They asked for payment on receipt of the products.
　他們要求收到貨品再付錢。
相關衍生字彙 payoff [ˋpeˏɔf] 名 償清、paycheck [ˋpeˏtʃɛk] 名 薪資、payable [ˋpeəbl̩]
形 可支付的、payday [ˋpeˏde] 名 發薪日

---

peace [pis] 名 和平　　片 to negotiate peace with 進行和談

peaceful [ˋpisfəl] 形 平靜的
▶ I desire to live a peaceful life. 我渴望過著平靜的生活。

peasant [ˋpɛzn̩t] 名 農夫　　同 farmer [ˋfɑrmɚ] 名 農夫

peck [pɛk] 動 啄食
▶ Chickens are pecking at grains.
　小雞啄著穀物。
動詞三態變化 peck - pecked - pecked

---

peculiarity [pɪˏkjulɪˋærətɪ] 名 奇特，古怪
▶ The fashion designer is famous for her peculiarity.
　這位服裝設計師以她的獨特性而聞名。
相關衍生字彙 peculiar [pɪˋkjuljɚ] 形 獨特的、peculiarly [pɪˋkjuljɚlɪ] 副 獨特地、
　　unusually [ʌnˋjuʒʊəlɪ] 副 不尋常地、creative [krɪˋetɪv] 形 有創意的

---

pedal [ˋpɛdl̩] 名 踏板　　片 a brake pedal 煞車踏板

peel [pil] 動 剝落
▶ You are a good brother to peel the orange for your sister.
　你真是個好哥哥，幫妹妹剝柳丁。
動詞三態變化 peel - peeled - peeled

---

peep [pip] 動 偷看　　片 peeping Tom 偷窺狂
動詞三態變化 peep - peeped - peeped

---

peer [pɪr] 名 同儕
▶ Don't leave behind your peers. 別落後你的同儕。

P

penalty [`pɛn!tɪ] 名 處罰　　🅟 death penalty 死刑

相關衍生字彙 punishment [`pʌnɪʃmənt] 名 懲罰、imprisonment [ɪm`prɪznmənt] 名 監禁、condemnation [ˌkɑndɛm`neʃən] 名 譴責、discipline [`dɪsəplɪn] 動 紀律，懲戒

---

pendulum [`pɛndʒələm] 名 鐘擺
▶ I was so bored that I watched the pendulum swinging.
　我無聊到看著鐘擺擺動。

---

penetrate [`pɛnəˌtret] 動 滲透入，進入
▶ It's difficult to penetrate the overseas markets.
　要進入海外市場很困難。

動詞三態變化 penetrate - penetrated - penetrated

---

penitent [`pɛnətənt] 形 悔罪的　　◎ MP3 **16-05**
▶ He said sorry to me with a penitent attitude. 他以懺悔的態度跟我說抱歉。

---

penny [`pɛnɪ] 名 一分硬幣
▶ A penny saved is a penny earned.（諺語）積少成多。

---

pension [`pɛnʃən] 名 撫恤金，退休金
▶ He is living on his pension. 他靠退休金度日。

---

pepper [`pɛpɚ] 名 胡椒（粉）
▶ Black pepper can add a favor to your soup. 黑胡椒可增添湯的味道。

---

perceive [pɚ`siv] 動 察覺
▶ I perceived the environment is a little dangerous.
　我察覺到這個環境有點危險。

相關衍生字彙 observe [əb`zɝv] 動 觀察、feel [fil] 動 感覺、detect [dɪ`tɛkt] 動 察覺、discover [dɪs`kʌvɚ] 動 發現、sense [sɛns] 動 意識到

動詞三態變化 perceive - perceived - perceived

---

percent [pɚ`sɛnt] 名 百分之一

---

percentage [pɚ`sɛntɪdʒ] 名 百分比
▶ The percentage of the near-sighted students in Taiwan is high.
　台灣近視的學生比例很高。

---

perch [pɝtʃ] 動 棲息
▶ A mother bird with her babies perches in the tree.
　一隻母鳥跟她的小鳥棲息在樹上。

動詞三態變化 perch - perched - perched

---

perfect [`pɝfɪkt] 形 完美的
▶ Practice makes perfect.
　（諺語）熟能生巧。

相關衍生字彙 perfection [pɚˋfɛkʃən] 名 完美、perfectly [ˋpɝfɪktlɪ] 副 完美地、ideal [aɪˋdiəl] 形 理想的、intact [ɪnˋtækt] 形 完整的

perform [pɚˋfɔrm] 動 表演
▶ The girl performed so brilliantly.
這位女孩表演得真出色。
動詞三態變化 perform - performed - performed

performance [pɚˋfɔrməns] 名 表演
▶ Her performance is very impressive. 她的表演真令人印象深刻。

perfume [ˋpɝfjum] 名 香水　　片 to spray on perfume 噴香水

perhaps [pɚˋhæps] 副 也許　　同 maybe [ˋmebɪ] 副 也許

peril [ˋpɛrəl] 名 危險
▶ The typhoon was so strong that the villagers' lives were in peril.
颱風很強,村民們的生命面臨危險。
相關衍生字彙 perilous [ˋpɛrələs] 形 危險的、danger [ˋdendʒɚ] 名 危險、dangerous [ˋdendʒərəs] 形 危險的、risky [ˋrɪskɪ] 形 危險的

period [ˋpɪrɪəd] 名 期間
▶ That is only a transitional period. 那只是個過渡時期。

periodical [ˌpɪrɪˋadɪkl] 名 期刊
▶ You can consult the periodicals in the library. 你可以參閱圖書館裡的期刊。

perish [ˋpɛrɪʃ] 動 消滅,死亡　　片 to perish in battle 陣亡
動詞三態變化 perish - perished - perished

permanent [ˋpɝmənənt] 形 永久的,固定性的
▶ I hope to look for a permanent job. 我希望找一份固定的工作。

permission [pɚˋmɪʃən] 名 許可
▶ Without permission, nobody can enter the lab.
未經允許,誰都不能進入此實驗室。

permit [pɚˋmɪt] 名 許可證
▶ With a work permit, you can do a part-time job.
有了工作證,你可以找兼差工作。

perpendicular [ˌpɝpənˋdɪkjələ] 形 垂直的　　● MP3 16-06
反 horizontal [ˌharəˋzant!] 形 水平的

P

perplex [pɚ`plɛks] 動 使困惑
▶ The difficult math problem made the students perplexed.
這困難的數學問題讓學生很困惑。

相關衍生字彙 perplexity [pɚ`plɛksɪtɪ] 名 困惑、confuse [kən`fjuz] 動 使困惑、
confusing [kən`fjuzɪŋ] 形 讓人感到困惑的

動詞三態變化 perplex - perplexed - perplexed

persecute [`pɝsɪ.kjut] 動 迫害
▶ No one should be persecuted only because of his race.
沒有人可以因為種族而被迫害。

動詞三態變化 persecute - persecuted - persecuted

perseverance [.pɝsə`vɪrəns] 名 堅忍不拔，毅力
▶ Trust me. I will display perseverance to overcome any difficulty.
放心，我一定會展現毅力克服困難。

persevere [.pɝsə`vɪr] 動 堅持
▶ If you can persevere, you will succeed.
只要你能堅持，就會成功。

相關衍生字彙 persist [pɚ`sɪst] 動 堅持、persistent [pɚ`sɪstənt] 形 堅持的、
persistence [pɚ`sɪstəns] 名 堅毅不撓

動詞三態變化 persevere - persevered - persevered

personality [.pɝsn̩`ælətɪ] 名 個性　　片 multiple personality disorder 多重人格障礙
相關衍生字彙 personal [`pɝsn̩l] 形 個人的、personally [`pɝsn̩lɪ] 副 個人地、
personnel [.pɝsn̩`ɛl] 名 人事、personalize [`pɝsnəl.aɪz] 動 使個人化

perspective [pɚ`spɛktɪv] 名 角度，觀點，看法
▶ We should view the education reform from a new perspective.
我們應用新的角度來看此教育改革。

perspire [pɚ`spaɪr] 動 出汗
▶ Standing in such hot weather, I began to perspire soon.
站在這麼熱的天氣裡，我很快就開始流汗了。

動詞三態變化 perspire - perspired - perspired

persuade [pɚ`swed] 動 勸說
▶ I persuaded her not to invest all her money in the stock market.
我勸她別把錢全放在股市。

動詞三態變化 persuade - persuaded - persuaded

persuasion [pɚ`sweʒən] 名 說服
▶ With a bit of persuasion, he will lend you some money.
遊說一下，他一定會借你一點錢。

相關衍生字彙 inducement [ɪnˋdjusmənt] 名 勸誘、temptation [tɛmpˋteʃən] 名 引誘、allurement [əˋlurmənt] 名 誘惑、seduction [sɪˋdʌkʃən] 名 魅力，吸引、advise [ədˋvaɪz] 動 勸告

pertain [pɚˋten] 動 與～有關
▶ The clues pertain to the murder.
這些線索跟此命案有關。
動詞三態變化 pertain - pertained - pertained

perverse [pɚˋvɝs] 形 違反常理的
▶ It's a perverse logic. 那是違反常理的邏輯。

pessimistic [ˌpɛsəˋmɪstɪk] 形 悲觀的　　　反 optimistic [ˌɑptəˋmɪstɪk] 形 樂觀的

pester [ˋpɛstɚ] 動 糾纏
▶ He pestered me for borrowing my notebook.
他纏著我要跟我借筆記。
動詞三態變化 pester - pestered - pestered

pet [pɛt] 名 寵物　　片 to keep a pet 養寵物

petal [ˋpɛtl] 名 花瓣
▶ The flower has many beautiful petals. 這朵花有很多美麗的花瓣。

petition [pəˋtɪʃən] 名 請願書
▶ More than ten thousand people signed the petition. 超過萬人簽署此請願書。

petroleum [pəˋtroliəm] 名 石油
▶ The small country is rich in petroleum. 這個小國家富藏石油。

phantom [ˋfæntəm] 名 鬼魅　　片 the Phantom of the Opera（歌劇名）歌劇魅影

pharmacy [ˋfɑrməsɪ] 名 藥房
▶ You can get the medicine at the pharmacy.
你可以在這間藥房買到藥。
相關衍生字彙 pharmacist [ˋfɑrməsɪst] 名 藥師、doctor [ˋdɑktɚ] 名 醫生、dentist [ˋdɛntɪst] 名 牙醫

phase [fez] 名 階段　　　　　　　　　　　　　　　MP3 16-07
▶ After graduating from school, you will go through another phase.
畢業後，你將經歷另一個階段。

phenomenon [fəˋnɑməˌnɑn] 名 現象　　片 a natural phenomenon 自然現象

philosophy [fəˋlɑsəfɪ] 名 哲學　　片 the philosophy of life 人生觀

photography [fə`tɑgrəfɪ] 名 攝影術
▶ I like the photography in the movie.
我喜歡這部電影裡的攝影技術。
相關衍生字彙 photo [`foto] 名 照片、photograph [`fotə,græf] 名 照片、
photographer [fə`tɑgrəfɚ] 名 攝影師、photographic [,fotə`græfɪk]
形 攝影的

physical [`fɪzɪk]] 形 身體的　片 physical education 體育

physician [fɪ`zɪʃən] 名 內科醫生　反 surgeon [`sɝdʒən] 名 外科醫生

physics [`fɪzɪks] 名 物理
▶ Physics and chemistry are two of the subjects. 物理與化學是兩門科目。

piano [pɪ`æno] 名 鋼琴
▶ My daughter plays the piano every day. 我女兒每天彈鋼琴。

pick [pɪk] 動 拾起　片 to pick up 開車接載～
動詞三態變化 pick - picked - picked

picnic [`pɪknɪk] 名 野餐　片 to go on a picnic 去野餐

picturesque [,pɪktʃə`rɛsk] 形 如畫一般的
▶ The scenery of the mountain is picturesque.
這山景如畫。
相關衍生字彙 picture [`pɪktʃɚ] 名 畫、pictorial [pɪk`torɪəl] 形 圖畫的、draw [drɔ] 動 畫畫、
paint [pent] 動 繪畫，上油漆

pie [paɪ] 名 派　片 an apple pie 蘋果派

piecemeal [`pis,mil] 副 一點一點地 形 零碎的
▶ Why do you always do everything piecemeal? 為何你總是一點一點的做事情？

piety [`paɪətɪ] 名 虔誠
▶ We show our piety by going to church every Sunday.
我們每周日上教堂表達我們的虔誠。

pigeon [`pɪdʒɪn] 名 鴿子
▶ He raises many pigeons in the top of his house. 他在屋頂養很多鴿子。

pile [paɪl] 名 堆
▶ A pile of books was put in the corner of the classroom.
教室的角落堆了一堆書。

pill [pɪl] 名 藥丸　片 a sleeping pill 安眠藥

pillar [`pɪlɚ] 名 柱子
▶ There are many pillars supporting the house.
這房子有很多柱子支撐。

pillow [`pɪlo] 名 枕頭
▶ I like to rest my head on the pillow to take a rest.
我喜歡把頭靠在枕頭上休息一下。
相關衍生字彙 quilt [kwɪlt] 名 被（子）、sheet [ʃit] 名 床單、blanket [`blæŋkɪt] 名 毛毯、
mattress [`mætrɪs] 名 床墊、bed [bɛd] 名 床、bedding [`bɛdɪŋ]
名 寢具（指床單、被褥、床墊、床等）

pilot [`paɪlət] 名 飛行員　　片 an airline pilot 航空公司機師

pin [pɪn] 名 別針　　片 a safety pin 安全別針　　◎ MP3 16-08

pink [pɪŋk] 名 粉紅色
▶ Pink is girls' favorite color. 粉紅色是女孩的最愛。

pinnacle [`pɪnəkl] 名 頂峰
片 to reach the pinnacle of the career 到達事業的巔峰

pioneer [ˌpaɪə`nɪr] 名 先驅者
▶ The pioneer of the car industry is Ford. 汽車工業的先驅者是福特。

pious [`paɪəs] 形 虔誠的
▶ Mom is a pious Buddhist. 媽媽是虔誠的佛教徒。

piracy [`paɪrəsɪ] 名 盜版　　片 music / software piracy 音樂／軟體盜版

pitch [pɪtʃ] 動 搭（帳篷），紮（營）
▶ Before it gets too dark, we have to pitch a tent.
天黑前，我們得先搭帳篷。
動詞三態變化 pitch - pitched - pitched

pity [`pɪtɪ] 名 動 憐憫，同情
▶ It's a pity that you choose to give up.
很可惜，你選擇放棄。
動詞三態變化 pity - pitied - pitied

place [ples] 名 地方　　片 to take the place of 取代

placid [`plæsɪd] 形 平靜的
▶ Grandfather enjoys the placid country life. 爺爺喜歡平靜的鄉間生活。

plague [pleg] 名 瘟疫
▶ A plague of rats spread in the poor country. 鼠疫在那個貧窮國家蔓延。

P

plain [plen] 形 簡樸的　🅟 plain English 簡單明瞭的英文
[相關衍生字彙] plainly [`plenlɪ] 副 清楚地、plainspoken [`plen`spokən] 形 直言的、plaintive [`plentɪv] 形 悲傷的、simple [`sɪmpl̩] 形 簡單的

---

plan [plæn] 名 動 計畫　🅟 to make a plan 擬訂計畫
[動詞三態變化] plan - planned - planned

---

plane [plen] 名 飛機　🅘 airplane [`ɛr͵plen] 名 飛機

---

planet [`plænɪt] 名 行星
▶ The Earth is a planet. 地球是行星。

---

plant [plænt] 名 植物　🅟 a house plant 室內植物
[相關衍生字彙] plantation [plæn`teʃən] 名 農園、farm [fɑrm] 名 農場、transplantation [͵trænsplæn`teʃən] 名 移植、botanical [bo`tænɪk l̩] 形 植物的

---

plastic [`plæstɪk] 形 塑膠的　🅟 plastic money / credit card 信用卡

---

plate [plet] 名 盤子
▶ There is nothing left on the plate. 盤子裡已經沒有東西了。

---

platform [`plæt͵fɔrm] 名 月台
▶ There are twenty–five platforms at the train station.
這個火車站有二十五個月台。

---

plausible [`plɔzəbl̩] 形 貌似合理的
▶ What you said seems a plausible explanation. 你說的好像是有道理的解釋。

---

play [ple] 動 玩耍　　　🅜 MP3 **16-09**
▶ Many kids are playing in the park.
很多孩子在公園裡玩耍。
[相關衍生字彙] playground [`ple͵graund] 名 操場、player [`pleɚ] 名 選手、playboy [`ple͵bɔɪ] 名 花花公子、playful [`plefəl] 形 愛玩耍的
[動詞三態變化] play - played - played

---

plea [pli] 名 懇求　🅟 to put forward a plea 提出申訴

---

plead [plid] 動 懇求
▶ He keeps pleading for forgiveness.
他一直請求原諒。
[動詞三態變化] plead - pleaded - pleaded

---

pleasure [`plɛʒɚ] 名 榮幸
▶ It's my pleasure.
我的榮幸。
[相關衍生字彙] pleasant [`plɛzənt] 形 令人愉快的、please [pliz] 動 取悅、pleased [plizd] 形 高興的

pledge [plɛdʒ] 名 誓言　🔹 to make a pledge 發誓

---

plentiful [`plɛntɪfəl] 形 豐富的
▶ There are plentiful fruits in Taiwan. 台灣的水果種類很多。

---

plenty [`plɛntɪ] 名 大量，充足　🔹 plenty of 多量的

---

plot [plɑt] 名 情節
▶ The plot of the film is very complicated. 這部電影的情節很複雜。

---

pluck [plʌk] 動 拔（毛）
▶ He helped his mother pluck feathers from the chicken.
他幫忙媽媽把雞毛拔乾淨。
動詞三態變化 pluck - plucked - plucked

---

plug [plʌg] 名 插頭　🔹 an electrical plug 電器插頭

---

plunder [`plʌndɚ] 動 掠奪
▶ During the war, many treasures were plundered.
戰爭期間，很多寶物被掠奪。
相關衍生字彙 rob [rɑb] 動 搶劫、thieve [θiv] 動 偷竊、steal [stil] 動 竊取、pillage [`pɪlɪdʒ] 名 動 搶劫，掠奪
動詞三態變化 plunder - plundered - plundered

---

plunge [plʌndʒ] 名 跳水
▶ The swimmer made a plunge into the swimming pool.
這位游泳者跳水進入游泳池。

---

plus [plʌs] 名 加號，有利
▶ Your work experience will be a plus in applying for a top university.
申請頂尖大學時，你的工作經驗可以加分。

---

ply [plaɪ] 動 往返於
▶ The shuttle plies between the airport and the train station.
接駁車往返於機場跟火車站之間。
動詞三態變化 ply - plied - plied

---

pocket [`pɑkɪt] 名 口袋　🔹 pocket money 零用錢

---

poetic [po`ɛtɪk] 形 充滿詩意的
相關衍生字彙 poet [`poɪt] 名 詩人、poem [`poɪm] 名 詩、poetry [`poɪtrɪ] 名（總稱）詩

---

point [pɔɪnt] 名 地點，觀點　🔹 point of view 觀點

---

poison [`pɔɪzn̩] 名 毒，毒藥
▶ The medicine is a fatal poison. 這種藥物是致命的毒藥。

P

poisonous [`pɔɪznəs] 形 有毒的
▶ Many chemicals are poisonous. 很多化學製品是有毒的。

poke [pok] 動 戳
▶ Be careful! Your umbrella will poke others.
小心！你的雨傘會戳到別人。
動詞三態變化 poke - poked - poked

polar [`polɚ] 形 極地的　　片 polar bear 北極熊　　◎ MP3 **16-10**

polite [pə`laɪt] 形 有禮貌的
▶ Be polite to the elderly.
對長輩要有禮貌。
相關衍生字彙 politely [pə`laɪtlɪ] 副 有禮地、politeness [pə`laɪtnɪs] 名 禮貌、courtesy [`kɝtəsɪ] 名 禮貌、well-mannered [`wɛl`mænɚd] 形 有禮貌的

police [pə`lis] 名 警方
▶ The police are looking for the missing boy. 警方正在尋找失踪的男孩。

policy [`pɑləsɪ] 名 政策　　片 a foreign policy 外交政策

polish [`pɑlɪʃ] 動 擦亮
▶ I polish the furniture every two weeks.
我每兩周會擦拭一次家具。
動詞三態變化 polish - polished - polished

politics [`pɑlətɪks] 名 政治
▶ He is interested in politics, so he plans to be a politician in the future.
他對政治感興趣，所以他未來打算進入政壇。
相關衍生字彙 political [pə`lɪtɪkl] 形 政治的、politician [ˌpɑlə`tɪʃən] 名 政治人物、politic [`pɑləˌtɪk] 形 精明的

pollute [pə`lut] 動 污染
▶ The factories along the river pollute the water so much.
沿著河流的工廠嚴重污染水質。
動詞三態變化 pollute - polluted - polluted

pollution [pə`luʃən] 名 污染
片 noise / water / air / environmental pollution 噪音／水／空氣／環境污染

ponder [`pɑndɚ] 動 衡量，仔細考慮
▶ I need some time to ponder over the problem.
我需要點時間思考這個問題。
動詞三態變化 ponder - pondered - pondered

ponderous [`pɑndərəs] 形 冗長的，沉悶的
▶ Students all felt bored about the ponderous speech.
學生對此冗長的演講感到無聊。

---

pool [pul] 名 池子　　🅟 a swimming pool 游泳池

---

poor [pur] 形 貧乏的
▶ The country is poor in natural resources. 這個國家缺乏天然資源。

---

popular [`pɑpjələ] 形 受歡迎的
▶ The girl is very popular with her peers.
這位女孩很受同儕歡迎。
相關衍生字彙 popularity [ˌpɑpjə`lærətɪ] 名 流行，普及、populated [`pɑpjəˌletɪd]
形 有人居住的、population [ˌpɑpjə`leʃən] 名 人口

---

pose [poz] 名 姿勢
▶ Please hold the pose for one minute. 請保持此姿勢一分鐘。

---

position [pə`zɪʃən] 名 立場，態度
▶ Regarding my children's education, I always take a firm position.
關於我小孩的教育，我一直有堅定的立場。

---

positive [`pɑzətɪv] 形 肯定的，正面的　　反 negative [`nɛɡətɪv] 形 否定的，負面的

---

possess [pə`zɛs] 動 擁有
▶ The couple didn't possess any house.
這對夫妻沒有擁有任何房子。
動詞三態變化 possess - possessed - possessed

---

possessions [pə`zɛʃnz] 名 所有物，財產　　🅟 personal possessions 個人財產

---

possibility [ˌpɑsə`bɪlətɪ] 名 可能性　　反 impossibility [ɪmˌpɑsə`bɪlətɪ] 名 不可能性

---

possible [`pɑsəbl] 形 可能的
▶ Is it possible to cure his disease? 有可能治療他的疾病嗎？

---

post [post] 名 郵政　　🅟 the post office 郵局　　🅒 MP3 **16-11**
相關衍生字彙 postage [`postɪdʒ] 名 郵資、postal [`postl] 形 郵政的、postcard [`postˌkɑrd]
名 明信片、postmaster [`postˌmæstə] 名 郵政局長、postmark [`postˌmɑrk]
名 郵戳

---

postgraduate [post`ɡrædʒuɪt] 名 研究生
▶ She is a postgraduate of Harvard. 她是哈佛的研究生。

---

postpone [post`pon] 動 延後
▶ I plan to postpone our wedding.
我打算延後我們的婚禮。
動詞三態變化 postpone - postponed - postponed

P

postscript [`post͵skrɪpt] 名 附言
▶ I added a postscript at the end of the letter. 我在信件的最後加上附言。

posture [`pastʃɚ] 名 姿勢
▶ Pay attention to your sitting posture. 注意你的坐姿。

potato [pə`teto] 名 馬鈴薯　　片 potato chips 馬鈴薯片，洋芋片

potent [`potn̩t] 形 強而有力的　　片 a potent symbol 強而有力的象徵
相關衍生字彙 potently [`potəntlɪ] 副 強而有力地、powerful [`pauɚfəl] 形 強而有力的、forceful [`forsfəl] 形 強而有力的、effective [ɪ`fɛktɪv] 形 有效的

potential [pə`tɛnʃəl] 名 潛力
▶ A good school should help students develop their potential.
好學校要能協助學生發展潛能。

poultry [`poltrɪ] 名 家禽
▶ Chickens are poultry. 雞是家禽類。

pounce [pauns] 動 猛撲
▶ The cat pounced on the mouse.
小貓撲向老鼠。
動詞三態變化 pounce - pounced - pounced

pour [por] 動 灌入
▶ I poured some milk into the coffee.
我把一些牛奶倒進咖啡裡。
動詞三態變化 pour - poured - poured

poverty [`pɑvɚtɪ] 名 貧窮
▶ The government has the duty to solve the problem of poverty.
政府有義務解決貧窮的問題。

powder [`paudɚ] 名 粉末　　片 milk powder 奶粉

power [`pauɚ] 名 權力
▶ Knowledge is power.（諺語）知識就是力量。

practical [`præktɪkl̩] 形 實際的
▶ He is a practical person. You can consult him.
他是個很實際的人，你可以請教他。
相關衍生字彙 practice [`præktɪs] 動 練習、practicable [`præktɪkəbl̩] 形 可行的、train [tren] 動 訓練、practitioner [præk`tɪʃənɚ] 名 開業醫生

praise [prez] 名 動 讚美
▶ Her performance earned praise.
他的表現贏得讚美。

動詞三態變化 praise - praised - praised

pray [pre] 動 祈禱
▶ I pray devoutly for your happiness.
我虔誠地為你的幸福祈禱。

動詞三態變化 pray - prayed - prayed

preach [pritʃ] 動 傳教，說教
▶ Please stop preaching at me.
請停止對我說教。

動詞三態變化 preach - preached - preached

precaution [prɪˋkɔʃən] 名 謹慎，預防措施
▶ You had better take an umbrella as a precaution. 你最好帶把傘以防下雨。

precedent [ˋprɛsədənt] 名 先例　　🅟 to create a precedent 開先例

precious [ˋprɛʃəs] 形 珍貴的　　　　　　　◎ MP3 16-12
▶ I cherish the precious friendship between you and me.
我很珍惜你我之間的珍貴友誼。

相關衍生字彙 costly [ˋkɔstlɪ] 形 貴的、valuable [ˋvæljuəbḷ] 形 珍貴的、
expensive [ɪkˋspɛnsɪv] 形 貴的、priceless [ˋpraɪslɪs] 形 無價的

precisely [prɪˋsaɪslɪ] 副 準確地
▶ The boy is young, but he is able to describe the plot precisely.
男孩雖然年紀小，可是他可以準確地描述情節。

相關衍生字彙 precision [prɪˋsɪʒən] 名 精確、precise [prɪˋsaɪs] 形 精確的、accurate [ˋækjərɪt]
形 準確的、exact [ɪgˋzækt] 形 確切的、correct [kəˋrɛkt] 形 正確的

predecessor [ˋprɛdɪˏsɛsɚ] 名 前輩
▶ I respect the predecessor very much. 我很尊重這位前輩。

predicament [ˏprɪˋdɪkəmənt] 名 困境
▶ Please help me out of my financial predicament. 請幫我脫離財務困境。

predict [prɪˋdɪkt] 動 預告
▶ At present, it's impossible to predict an earthquake.
目前，仍無法預測地震。

動詞三態變化 predict - predicted - predicted

preface [ˋprɛfɪs] 名 序言
▶ The writer wrote a touching preface. 作者寫了一篇感人的序。

prefer [prɪˋfɝ] 動 較喜歡　　🅟 prefer to A rather than B 較喜歡 A 勝於 B

P

動詞三態變化 prefer - preferred - preferred

preference [ˋprɛfərəns] 名 偏好
▶ The girl shows her preference in music. 這位女孩展現對音樂的偏好。

pregnant [ˋprɛgnənt] 形 懷孕的
▶ She is three months pregnant. 她懷孕三個月了。

prejudice [ˋprɛdʒədɪs] 名 偏見
▶ Some people have prejudice against homosexuals. 有些人對同性戀有偏見。

prelude [ˋprɛljud] 名 序曲
▶ I enjoy the prelude of the musical composition. 我喜歡這首樂曲的序曲。

premature [͵priməˋtjur] 形 早熟的，過早的
▶ Sunburns cause premature aging of skin. 曬傷會造成皮膚提早老化。

premise [ˋprɛmɪs] 名 前提   片 the major premise 大前提

preparation [͵prɛpəˋreʃən] 名 準備
▶ I am making preparations for my essay.
我正在為我的論文做準備。

相關衍生字彙 preparatory [prɪˋpærə͵torɪ] 形 準備的、prepare [prɪˋpɛr] 動 準備、
prepared [prɪˋpɛrd] 形 有準備的、ready [ˋrɛdɪ] 形 準備好的

prescribe [prɪˋskraɪb] 動 開藥方
▶ The doctor prescribed a remedy for my father.
醫生替我爸爸開治療藥方。

動詞三態變化 prescribe - prescribed - prescribed

prescription [prɪˋskrɪpʃən] 名 處方，藥方
▶ I went to the pharmacy to fill my prescription. 我到藥房配我處方籤的藥。

presence [ˋprɛzn̩s] 名 出席   片 in someone's presence 當～的面

present [ˋprɛzn̩t] 形 出席的
▶ All my friends were present at my birthday party.
所有朋友都出席我的生日派對。

preserve [prɪˋzɝv] 動 保存
▶ We should try our best to preserve the environment.
我們要盡力保護環境。

相關衍生字彙 preservation [͵prɛzɚˋveʃən] 名 保存，維護、preservative [prɪˋzɝvətɪv]
名 防腐劑、preserve [prɪˋzɝv] 名 保護區、preserves [prɪˋzɝvz] 名 蜜餞

動詞三態變化 preserve - preserved - preserved

preside [prɪˋzaɪd] 動 主持
▶ The professor presided the important seminar.
教授主持了這場重要的研討會。
動詞三態變化 preside - presided - presided

presidency [ˋprɛzədənsɪ] 名 總統職位 ◉ MP3 **16-13**
▶ He was elected to the presidency. 他被選為總統。

president [ˋprɛzədənt] 名 總統
▶ We should encourage women to run for the presidency.
我們應該鼓勵婦女出來競選總統。

press [prɛs] 名 新聞界 ﾋ press conference 記者招待會
相關衍生字彙 press [prɛs] 動 按壓、press-up [ˋprɛsˏʌp] 名 伏地挺身、
journalism [ˋdʒɜnḷˏɪzm] 名 新聞業、reporter [rɪˋportɚ] 名 記者、
journalist [ˋdʒɜnəlɪst] 名 新聞從業人員

pressure [ˋprɛʃɚ] 名 壓力 ﾋ high blood pressure 高血壓

prestige [prɛsˋtiʒ] 名 聲望
▶ The scandal damaged his prestige. 醜聞重創他的聲望。

presume [prɪˋzum] 動 假設
▶ We can presume that the boy got hurt in the mountains.
我們可以假設男孩在山區受傷了。
動詞三態變化 presume - presumed - presumed

presumption [prɪˋzʌmpʃən] 名 假設
▶ That is only a presumption. We need more evidence.
那只是一個假設，我們需要更多證據。

pretend [prɪˋtɛnd] 動 假裝
▶ All I can do is pretend nothing happened.
我所能做的就是裝作什麼事都沒發生。
動詞三態變化 pretend - pretended - pretended

pretense [prɪˋtɛns] 名 虛偽，假裝
▶ I continue a pretense of nothing. 我繼續假裝沒事。

pretty [ˋprɪtɪ] 形 漂亮的 ⊜ beautiful [ˋbjutəfəl] 形 美麗的

prevail [prɪˋvel] 動 勝過
▶ I believe that kindness will prevail evil.
我相信善良會勝過邪惡。
動詞三態變化 prevail - prevailed - prevailed

P

prevailing [prɪˋvelɪŋ] 形 主要的
▶ White is the prevailing color of my house. 白色是我房子的主要顏色。

prevent [prɪˋvɛnt] 動 預防
▶ Experts are trying to prevent the disease from spreading.
專家試圖預防此疾病的擴散。

動詞三態變化 prevent - prevented - prevented

prevention [prɪˋvɛnʃən] 名 預防
▶ Prevention is better than cure.（諺語）預防勝於治療。

previous [ˋprivɪəs] 形 先前的
▶ The previous documents were lost. 先前的文件不見了。

prey [pre] 名 獵物
▶ The tiger is looking for its prey. 老虎正在找尋牠的獵物。

price [praɪs] 名 價錢
▶ The price of oil keeps going up and down. 油價持續浮動。

pride [praɪd] 名 驕傲
▶ He takes pride in himself.
他很自豪。

相關衍生字彙 proud [praʊd] 形 驕傲的、humble [ˋhʌmbḷ] 形 謙遜的、modesty [ˋmɑdɪstɪ]
名 謙虛

primary [ˋpraɪmɛrɪ] 形 主要的，初級的，初等的　　片 a primary school 小學

prime [praɪm] 形 主要的，最初的　　片 Prime Minister 首相，行政院長

primitive [ˋprɪmətɪv] 形 原始的　　MP3 16-14
▶ The homeless man lives a primitive life by the river.
這個流浪漢在河邊過著原始生活。

prince [prɪns] 名 王子　　反 princess [ˋprɪnsɪs] 名 公主

principal [ˋprɪnsəpḷ] 名 校長
▶ The principal of the senior high school is an artist.
這間高中的校長是一位藝術家。

principle [ˋprɪnsəpḷ] 名 原則
▶ I will offer you some principles to follow. 我將提供你一些原則去遵守。

print [prɪnt] 動 列印
▶ There are two documents waiting to print.
有兩份文件等著列印。

相關衍生字彙 printer [`prɪntɚ] 名 列表機、computer [kəm`pjutɚ] 名 電腦、laptop [`læptɑp] 名 手提電腦、mouse [maʊs] 名 滑鼠

動詞三態變化 print - printed - printed

priority [praɪ`ɔrətɪ] 名 優先
▶ I arrange my schedule according to priority. 我按照優先順序來安排我的工作表。

prison [`prɪzn̩] 名 監獄　同 jail [dʒel] 名 監獄

prisoner [`prɪznɚ] 名 犯人　片 a political prisoner 政治犯

privacy [`praɪvəsɪ] 名 隱私
▶ Everyone's privacy should be respected. 每個人的隱私都應當被尊重。

private [`praɪvɪt] 形 私人的
▶ I worked at a private high school. 我以前在私立中學工作。

privilege [`prɪvl̩ɪdʒ] 名 特權，優待
▶ It's a great privilege to enter the office. 能進入這辦公室是相當的榮幸。

prize [praɪz] 名 獎金
▶ I was so lucky to win the prize.
我好幸運可以贏得獎金。

相關衍生字彙 reward [rɪ`wɔrd] 名 賞金、cash [kæʃ] 名 現金、award [ə`wɔrd] 名 獎學金、compensation [ˌkɑmpən`seʃən] 名 補償金、commission [kə`mɪʃən] 名 佣金、scholarship [`skɑlɚˌʃɪp] 名 獎學金

probability [ˌprɑbə`bɪlətɪ] 名 可能性
▶ Smoking will increase the probability of cancer. 抽菸會增加癌症的可能性。

P

probable [`prɑbəbl̩] 形 可能的
▶ It's probable that I won't arrive till tomorrow afternoon.
我有可能要到明天下午才會抵達。

probe [prob] 動 調查，刺探
▶ The boss tried to probe into our private life.
老闆在刺探我們的私生活。

動詞三態變化 probe - probed - probed

problem [`prɑbləm] 名 問題　片 to solve the problem 解決問題

procedure [prə`sidʒɚ] 名 程序
▶ Please follow the procedures to operate the machine.
請依照此程序操作機器。

proceed [prə`sid] 動 著手進行
▶ He sat down and proceeded to tell us the process.
他坐下來開始告訴我們過程。
相關衍生字彙 process [`prɑsɛs] 名 過程、procession [prə`sɛʃən] 名 行列、
continue [kən`tɪnju] 動 繼續、start [stɑrt] 動 開始、begin [bɪ`gɪn] 動 開始
動詞三態變化 proceed - proceeded - proceeded

proclamation [ˌprɑklə`meʃən] 名 聲明　片 to issue a proclamation 發表聲明

procure [pro`kjur] 動 設法取得
▶ My friend procured the book for me.
我朋友幫我取得這本書。
動詞三態變化 procure - procured - procured

prod [prɑd] 動 刺激，促使　◎ MP3 **16-15**
▶ I was prodded to buy a new coat.
我被慫恿買件新大衣。
動詞三態變化 prod - prodded - prodded

prodigy [`prɑdədʒɪ] 名 天才
▶ I have to tell you that your son is a child prodigy.
我必須告訴你，你的兒子是個天才兒童。

produce [prə`djus] 動 生產
▶ Italy produces olive oil for export.
義大利生產橄欖油來出口。
相關衍生字彙 product [`prɑdəkt] 名 產品、production [prə`dʌkʃən] 名 生產、
productive [prə`dʌktɪv] 形 生產的、producer [prə`djusɚ] 名 製作人
動詞三態變化 produce - produced - produced

profane [prə`fen] 形 褻瀆的，不敬的
▶ His profane language makes himself unpopular.
他不敬的語言讓他不受歡迎。

proficient [prə`fɪʃənt] 形 熟練的
▶ She is very proficient in English. 她的英文很熟練。

professional [prə`fɛʃən!] 形 專業的
▶ His professional skills helped a lot of people.
他的專業技術幫過很多人。
相關衍生字彙 profession [prə`fɛʃən] 名 專業、professor [prə`fɛsɚ] 名 教授、
professionally [prə`fɛʃənəlɪ] 副 專業地

profit [`prɑfɪt] 名 利潤　片 to make a profit 賺取利潤

profitable [`prɑfɪtəbl]形 有盈利的
▶ It's profitable to sell the new products. 這項新產品非常有利可圖。

profound [prə`faund]形 深層的　🄟 profound influence 深層的影響

profuse [prə`fjus]形 充沛的，十分慷慨的
🄘 generous [`dʒɛnərəs]形 慷慨的

program [`progræm]名 節目　🄟 a TV program 電視節目

progress [`prɑgrɛs]名 進步
▶ The company keeps making progress.
這間公司不斷在進展。
相關衍生字彙 progressive [prə`grɛsɪv]形 進步的、progression [prə`grɛʃən]名 進展，級數、
advance [əd`væns]動 前進、advanced [əd`vænst]形 先進的

prohibit [prə`hɪbɪt]動 禁止
▶ During the period of time, all the kids are prohibited from going out.
這段時間，孩子們將禁止外出。
動詞三態變化 prohibit - prohibited - prohibited

prohibition [ˌproə`bɪʃən]名 禁止
▶ There is a prohibition against swimming here. 這裡禁止游泳。

project [`prɑdʒɛkt]名 計畫
▶ Many engineers joined the project. 很多工程師參與此計畫。

prolong [prə`lɔŋ]動 延長
▶ I decided to prolong my vacation.
我決定延長我的假期。
動詞三態變化 prolong - prolonged - prolonged

prominent [`prɑmənənt]形 突起的　🄟 a prominent nose 高鼻子

promise [`prɑmɪs]動 允諾
▶ He promised me never to smoke again.
他允諾我不再抽菸。
動詞三態變化 promise - promised - promised

promote [prə`mot]動 促進，升等
▶ The clerk was promoted to be a manager soon.
小職員很快被升為經理。
動詞三態變化 promote - promoted - promoted

P

promotion [prə`moʃən] 名 推動
▶ He takes charge of the promotion of new products.
他負責新產品的促銷。

相關衍生字彙 improvement [ɪm`pruvmənt] 名 改善、advancement [əd`vænsmənt]
名 進展、progress [prə`grɛs] 動 進步、proceed [prə`sid] 動 進行

prompt [prɑmpt] 形 快速的　◎ MP3 16-16
▶ They are prompt to respond to my complaint. 他們迅速回應我的申訴抱怨。

prone [pron] 形 易於
▶ He is prone to give up everything easily. 他很容易放棄每件事。

pronounce [prə`nauns] 動 發音
▶ The boy can pronounce every word clearly.
這男孩可以發音發得很清楚。

動詞三態變化 pronounce - pronounced - pronounced

pronunciation [prə͵nʌnsɪ`eʃən] 名 發音
▶ The best way to improve your pronunciation is to listen carfully to native speakers.
改善發音的最佳方法是仔細聽母語人士説話。

proof [pruf] 名 證據，證明
▶ Please provide your documentary proof.
請提供你的文件證明。

相關衍生字彙 fact [fækt] 名 事實、evidence [`ɛvədəns] 名 證據、guarantee [͵gærən`ti]
名 保證、promise [`prɑmɪs] 名 承諾、clue [klu] 名（解決疑案、問題等的）線索

proofread [`pruf͵rid] 動 校正
▶ Please help me proofread my draft.
請協助我校正我的草稿。

動詞三態變化 proofread - proofread - proofread

propel [prə`pɛl] 動 驅使
▶ He must be propelled by evil.
他一定被惡魔驅使了。

動詞三態變化 propel - propelled - propelled

proper [`prɑpɚ] 形 適合的
▶ It's not proper to cry in public. 在大眾面前哭不適合。

property [`prɑpɚtɪ] 名 資產
▶ Who will inherit the rich man's property? 誰將繼承這位富翁的資產？

prophecy [`prɑfəsɪ] 名 預言　🔒 to make a prophecy 作出預言

相關衍生字彙 prophesy [`prɑfə͵saɪ]動 預言、prophet [`prɑfɪt]名 預言家、predict [prɪ`dɪkt]
動 預言、foresee [for`si]動 預知、foretell [for`tɛl]動 預知

proportion [prə`porʃən]名 比例
▶ The tax will be in proportion to how much you earn. 稅金將與你的收入成比例。

proposal [prə`pozl]名 建議
▶ Someone made a proposal at the meeting. 有人在會議中提出建議。

prose [proz]名 散文
▶ The female writer is good at proses. 這位女作家擅長散文。

prosecute [`prɑsɪ͵kjut]動 起訴
▶ The man was prosecuted for murder.
此人因謀殺而被起訴。
相關衍生字彙 prosecution [͵prɑsɪ`kjuʃən]名 起訴、sue [su]動 控告、charge [tʃɑrdʒ]
動 控告、judge [dʒʌdʒ]名 法官
動詞三態變化 prosecute - prosecuted - prosecuted

prospect [`prɑspɛkt]名 前景
▶ She hopes her college degree can help her career prospects.
她希望她的大學文憑能有助於職場前景。

prosper [`prɑspɚ]動 繁榮
▶ The manufacturers prospered at that time.
在當時，許多廠商都很興旺。
相關衍生字彙 prosperity [prɑs`pɛrətɪ]名 繁榮、prosperous [`prɑspərəs]形 繁榮的、
successful [sək`sɛsfəl]形 成功的
動詞三態變化 prosper - prospered - prospered

protection [prə`tɛkʃən]名 保護
▶ Kids grow up under parents' protection. 孩子在父母的保護下長大。

protest [prə`tɛst]動 抗議
▶ Hundreds of people were protesting against the new policy.
數百位人民在抗議新政策。
動詞三態變化 protest - protested - protested

prototype [`protə͵taɪp]名 原型
▶ This is a prototype of a space shuttle. 這是太空梭的原型。

proud [praʊd]形 驕傲的　　片 be proud of 以～為榮
相關衍生字彙 haughty [`hɔtɪ]形 高傲的、arrogant [`ærəgənt]形 傲慢的、boastful [`bostfəl]
形 自誇的、humble [`hʌmbḷ]形 謙遜的、modest [`mɑdɪst]形 謙虛的

P

prove [pruv] 動 證實　　　　　　　　　　　　　　　　🔘 MP3 **16-17**
▶ I proved to be a good wife.
　我證明了我是個好太太。
動詞三態變化 prove - proved - proved

---

proverb [ˋpravɜb] 名 諺語
▶ As the proverb goes, "Failure is the mother of success."
　誠如諺語所説:「失敗為成功之母」。

---

provide [prəˋvaɪd] 動 提供
▶ The library provides books and a comfortable environment for citizens.
　這座圖書館提供市民書籍及舒適的環境。
動詞三態變化 provide - provided - provided

---

province [ˋpravɪns] 名 省分　　　🔵 inland provinces 內地省分

---

provision [prəˋvɪʒən] 名 供應
▶ The provision of clean water and food is the first step.
　第一步驟是提供乾淨的水與食物。

---

provocative [prəˋvakətɪv] 形 挑釁的
▶ Your words and actions are highly provocative.
　你的言論跟行為均具有高度的挑釁意味。

---

provoke [prəˋvok] 動 激起，激怒
▶ He was provoked to fight.
　他被激怒而打架。
相關衍生字彙 annoy [əˋnɔɪ] 動 惹惱、anger [ˋæŋgɚ] 動 使發怒、irritate [ˋɪrəˌtet] 動 使惱怒、
　arouse [əˋrauz] 動 喚起，激發
動詞三態變化 provoke - provoked - provoked

---

proximity [prakˋsɪmətɪ] 名 鄰近　　　🔵 in the proximity of 在～的附近

---

prudent [ˋprudn̩t] 形 謹慎的
▶ When you sign a contract, you had better be prudent.
　簽契約書時，最好要謹慎一些。

---

pry [praɪ] 動 窺探
▶ Paparazzi's job is to pry others' lives.
　狗仔隊的工作就是去窺探他人的生活。
動詞三態變化 pry - pried - pried

---

pseudonym [ˋsudn̩ˌɪm] 名 假名，筆名
▶ This name is the writer's pseudonym, not real one.
　這個名字是作家的筆名，非真名。

psychology [saɪˋkɑlədʒɪ] 名 心理學
▶ Psychology is an interesting science.
心理學是門有趣的科學。

相關衍生字彙 psychologist [saɪˋkɑlədʒɪst] 名 心理學家、psychic [ˋsaɪkɪk] 形 精神上的、
psyche [ˋsaɪkɪ] 名 心靈、psychiatry [saɪˋkaɪətrɪ] 名 精神病學、
psychiatrist [saɪˋkaɪətrɪst] 名 精神病學家

public [ˋpʌblɪk] 名 大眾　　片 in public 公開地

publication [͵pʌblɪˋkeʃən] 名 發表
▶ Her new novel starts publication. 她的新小說開始出版。

publicity [pʌbˋlɪsətɪ] 名 宣傳
▶ The advertising agency will launch a publicity campaign soom.
廣告公司很快會開始進行宣傳活動。

publish [ˋpʌblɪʃ] 動 出版
▶ The magazine will be published at the end of this month.
雜誌將於這個月底出版。

動詞三態變化 publish - published - published

pull [pʊl] 動 拉　　反 push [pʊʃ] 動 推
動詞三態變化 pull - pulled - pulled

pulse [pʌls] 名 脈搏
▶ Exercise will quicken your pulse. 運動會使你的脈搏加快。

punch [pʌntʃ] 名（一）拳
▶ He gave the thief a punch in the face. 他揍了小偷的臉一拳。

punctual [ˋpʌŋktʃuəl] 形 準時的
▶ I am always punctual at work. 我上班總是準時到。

puncture [ˋpʌŋktʃɚ] 名 穿刺　　◎ MP3 16-18
▶ The tire of my bicycle had a puncture. 我腳踏車的輪胎被刺了一個洞。

punish [ˋpʌnɪʃ] 動 處罰
▶ The naughty boy was punished for making a mistake.
這頑皮的男孩因為犯錯而被處罰。

動詞三態變化 punish - punished - punished

punishment [ˋpʌnɪʃmənt] 名 處罰　　片 severe punishment 嚴厲的處罰

P

pupil [`pjupl] 名 學生
▶ There are about two hundred pupils in the primary school.
這間小學大約有兩百名學生。
相關衍生字彙 apprentice [ə`prɛntɪs] 名 學徒、student [`stjudn̩t] 名 學生、trainer [`trenɚ]
名 訓練員、learner [lɝnɚ] 名 初學者

---

puppet [`pʌpɪt] 名 木偶　　片 a puppet show 木偶戲，布袋戲

---

purchase [`pɝtʃəs] 動 購買
▶ You should purchase the ticket to the game in advance.
你要事先買好比賽的票。
動詞三態變化 purchase - purchased - purchased

---

pure [pjur] 形 純的
▶ Pure apple juice is my favorite.
純蘋果汁是我的最愛。
相關衍生字彙 purify [`pjurə‚faɪ] 動 使純化、purity [`pjurətɪ] 名 純潔、purely [`pjurlɪ]
副 純粹地、purge [pɝdʒ] 動 肅清

---

purple [`pɝpl] 名 紫色 形 紫色的
片 to be born to the purple 生於望族，生於帝王之家

---

purport [`pɝport] 動 聲稱
▶ He purported to receive a letter from the mayor.
他聲稱收到市長的來信。
動詞三態變化 purport - purported - purported

---

purpose [`pɝpəs] 名 目的　　片 on purpose 故意地

---

purse [pɝs] 名 手提包
▶ Girls like to put all the stuff into the purse. 女孩喜歡把所有東西都放到包包裡。

---

pursue [pɚ`su] 動 追求
▶ I devote my life to pursuing my dream.
我投入人生追求夢想。
動詞三態變化 pursue - pursued - pursued

---

pursuit [pɚ`sut] 名 追求　　片 in pursuit of 追求

---

push [puʃ] 動 推
▶ The bus was so crowded that we needed to push into it.
公車太擠，我們得往裡面推。
動詞三態變化 push - pushed - pushed

---

put [put] 動 放置　　片 to put off 延遲
動詞三態變化 put - put - put

puzzle [ˋpʌzl̩] 名 **難題，迷惑**
▶ The whole thing is a puzzle to us. 對我們而言，整件事情是個難題。

| MEMO |

一網打盡 ——————

字母 **Q**

quake ~ quote

詞性說明

名 名詞	副 副詞	介 介系詞
動 動詞	形 形容詞	連 連接詞
代 代名詞	助 助動詞	

內文圖示說明

片 片語　　　反 反義字　　　同 同義字

一網打盡「英語小知識」｜誠心誠意的「道歉」

該如何道歉成為一門藝術，除了「I'm sorry.（對不起。）」，不妨學學：

I'm terrible sorry. 非常抱歉。

I didn't mean it, please forgive me. 我不是故意的，請原諒我。

Can you forgive me? Please give me a second chance.

可以原諒我嗎？再給我個機會。

I apologize for the things I said earlier, please don't take offense.

我為今天說的話道歉，請不要生氣了。

Q quake ~ quote

★一網打盡 99 個英文單字 ｜ 一網打盡 15 句英語會話句　　　　　◎ MP3 **17-01**

quake [kwek] 動 顫抖，哆嗦
▶ John made a mistake and quaked with fear.
　約翰犯了錯，害怕得發抖。
相關衍生字彙 tremble [`trɛmbl] 動 發抖，震顫，擔憂、vibrate [`vaɪbret] 動 顫動，震動、
　　　　　　quiver [`kwɪvɚ] 名 動 顫抖 動 發抖，抖動（翅膀等）、shudder [`ʃʌdɚ]
　　　　　　名 動 發抖，戰慄，震動、shiver [`ʃɪvɚ] 名 顫抖 動 打顫
動詞三態變化 quake - quaked - quaked

qualification [ˌkwɑləfəˈkeʃən] 名 資格
▶ If you want to be a teacher, you should have a teaching qualification.
　如果你想要當老師，你得擁有教師資格。
相關衍生字彙 qualified [`kwɑləˌfaɪd] 形 有資格的、qualify [`kwɑləˌfaɪ] 動 使具有資格、
　　　　　　equip [ɪ`kwɪp] 動 使具備、disqualify [dɪs`kwɑləˌfaɪ] 動 取消～的資格

quality [`kwɑlətɪ] 名 品質
▶ Quality is more important than quantity.
　質比量重要。
相關衍生字彙 quality assurance 片 品質保證、quality control 片 品質控制，品管、
　　　　　　quality management 片 品質管理、quality time 片 珍貴時光

qualm [kwɔm] 名 疑慮
▶ I had no qualms about telling you the truth.
　我對於告訴你實情沒有任何疑慮。
相關衍生字彙 qualmish [`kwɑmɪʃ] 形 疑慮的，不安的、skepticism [`skɛptəsɪzəm]
　　　　　　名 懷疑論，懷疑的態度、misgiving [mɪs`gɪvɪŋ] 名 擔憂，疑慮、
　　　　　　anxiety [æŋ`zaɪətɪ] 名 焦慮，掛念

quandary [`kwɑndərɪ] 名 為難，窘境　　　片 in a quandary 左右為難
相關衍生字彙 dilemma [də`lɛmə] 名 進退兩難、perplexity [pɚ`plɛksɪtɪ] 名 困惑，茫然、
　　　　　　embarrassment [ɪm`bærəsmənt] 名 難堪、uneasiness [ʌn`izɪnɪs]
　　　　　　名 侷促，不安、uncomfortableness [ʌn`kʌmfɚtəbl̩nɪs] 名 不舒適

quantity [`kwɑntətɪ] 名 數量　　　片 a large / small quantity of 大量的／少量的
相關衍生字彙 amount [ə`maʊnt] 名 總額，數量、multitude [`mʌltəˌtjud]
　　　　　　名 許多，大眾、sum [sʌm] 名 總數，總計、quantity surveyor 片 估算師、
　　　　　　quantization [ˌkwɑntɪ`zeʃən] 名 量子化

quarantine [`kwɔrənˌtin] 名 隔離檢疫
▶ All the food should be in quarantine at customs.
　所有的食物都需在海關做隔離檢疫。

quarrel [`kwɔrəl] 名 動 爭吵
▶ They had a quarrel about their son's grades.
他們為了兒子的成績而爭吵。
相關衍生字彙 quarrelsome [`kwɔrəlsəm] 形 喜歡爭吵的、argue [`ɑrgju] 動 爭論、argument [`ɑrgjəmənt] 名 爭論、fight [faɪt] 動 吵架
動詞三態變化 quarrel - quarreled - quarreled

quarter [`kwɔrtɚ] 名 四分之一
▶ I divided the cake into quarters. 我把蛋糕分成四份。

quaver [`kwevɚ] 動 顫抖
▶ Her voice was quavering with cold.
因為寒冷，她的聲音在顫抖。
動詞三態變化 quaver - quavered - quavered

queasy [`kwizɪ] 形 不安的
▶ Her son didn't call her and she began to feel queasy.
她兒子沒打電話給她，讓她覺得不安。
相關衍生字彙 queasily [`kwizɪlɪ] 副 令人噁心地，難消化地、queasiness [`kwizɪnɪs] 名 噁心

queen [`kwin] 名 女王，王后　　反 king [kɪŋ] 名 國王
相關衍生字彙 queenly [`kwinlɪ] 形 副（似）女王的（地）、queen-size [`kwin͵saɪz]
形 大號的、queen bee 片 蜂王、queen consort 片 王后、queen mother
片 皇太后、queen regnant 片 執政的王后、queendom [`kwindəm]
名 女王統治、queenliness [`kwinlɪnɪs] 名 像女王，適合當女王、Queen's Bench
片 英國高等法院、Queen's Counsel 片 英國王室法律顧問、queenship [`kwinʃɪp]
名 女王（或皇后）的地位或身分

quell [kwɛl] 動 鎮壓
▶ The police were ordered to quell the unrest.
警方奉命鎮壓動亂。
動詞三態變化 quell - quelled - quelled

quench [kwɛntʃ] 動 滿足，撲滅，解（渴）　　片 to quench the thirst 解渴
相關衍生字彙 quenchable [`kwɛntʃəbl] 形 可熄滅的，可以壓制的、quencher [`kwɛntʃɚ]
名 抑制者，熄滅的人（或物）、quenchless [`kwɛntʃlɪs] 形 難壓制的，難熄滅的
動詞三態變化 quench - quenched - quenched

question [`kwɛstʃən] 名 問題　　片 to answer the question 回答問題
相關衍生字彙 question mark 片 問號、question tag 片 附加問句、
questionable [`kwɛstʃənəbl] 形 可疑的，不確定的、
questionably [`kwɛstʃənəblɪ] 副 可疑地，不清楚地、
questionary [`kwɛstʃən͵ɛrɪ] 名 調查表，問卷 形 質問的、
questioner [`kwɛstʃənɚ] 名 發問者，質問者、questioningly [`kwɛstʃənɪŋlɪ]
副 詢問地，探詢地、questionless [`kwɛstʃənlɪs] 形 無疑的，不發問的

Q

questionnaire [ˌkwɛstʃənˈɛr] 名 問卷，調查表
▶ They designed a questionnaire to do a survey. 他們設計問卷來做普查。

quick [kwɪk] 形 快速的
▶ I had a quick breakfast and rushed to work.
我迅速的吃完早餐，趕去上班。
相關衍生字彙 quickly [ˈkwɪklɪ] 副 迅速地、fast [fæst] 形 速度快的、speedy [ˈspidɪ] 形 快的、
rapid [ˈræpɪd] 形 動作快的、swift [swɪft] 形 快速的、hasty [ˈhestɪ] 形 勿忙的

quicken [ˈkwɪkən] 動 加速
▶ Exercise can quicken your heart rate.
運動可以讓心跳加快。
動詞三態變化 quicken - quickened - quickened

quietly [ˈkwaɪətlɪ] 副 安靜地
▶ He walked away quietly.
他安靜地走開。
相關衍生字彙 quiet [ˈkwaɪət] 形 安靜的、silent [ˈsaɪlənt] 形 沉默的、silently [ˈsaɪləntlɪ]
副 沉默地、noisy [ˈnɔɪzɪ] 形 吵的

quit [kwɪt] 動 辭去，停止　　片 to quit the job 辭職
動詞三態變化 quit - quit / quitted - quit / quitted

quotation [kwoˈteʃən] 名 引用，引文　　片 quotation marks 引號　　◉ MP3 17-02

quote [kwot] 動 引用
▶ She quoted a poem to end her speech.
她引用一首詩作為演講的結尾。
動詞三態變化 quote - quoted - quoted

MEMO

一網打盡

字母 R

racial ~ rust

一網打盡「英語小知識」｜拒絕他人的「邀請」

想要拒絕他人的邀請，卻又不知道該如何開口時，不妨利用下方的句子，
委婉地拒絕吧！

I'm afraid I can't. 恐怕我不能來。

I have things to do. 我有事情要做。

I'm kind of busy. Maybe later. 我有點忙，也許晚點再說。

I can't come over right now. 我不能馬上過來。

R racial ~ rust

racial [`reʃəl] 形 種族的　　片 racial discrimination 種族歧視
相關衍生字彙 race [res] 名 賽跑，種族、racism [`resɪzəm] 名 種族主義、racist [`resɪst] 名 種族主義者、racetrack [`restræk] 名 跑道

---

racket [`rækɪt] 名 球拍　　片 a tennis racket 網球拍

---

radar [`redɑr] 名 雷達
▶ The ships can track each other on radar. 船隻可以彼此用雷達追蹤。

---

radiant [`redjənt] 形 容光煥發的
▶ She looks radiant with joy. 她看起來喜氣洋洋。

---

radiation [ˌredɪˋeʃən] 名 輻射
▶ A large amount of radiation will do harm to health. 大量輻射對健康有害。

---

radio [`redɪo] 名 收音機　　片 to listen to the radio 聽收音機

---

rage [redʒ] 名 狂怒
▶ His words provoked the boss's rage.
他的言語激怒了老闆。
相關衍生字彙 anger [`æŋɡɚ] 名 生氣、fury [`fjurɪ] 名 暴怒、passion [`pæʃən] 名 忿怒、violence [`vaɪələns] 名 猛烈

---

ragged [`rægɪd] 形 衣衫襤褸的
▶ The homeless man was wearing ragged clothes. 流浪漢穿著破衣服。

---

raid [red] 名 動 突襲，襲擊　　片 an air raid 空襲
動詞三態變化 raid - raided - raided

---

railroad [`relˌrod] 名 鐵路　　同 railway [`relˌwe] 名 鐵路

---

rain [ren] 動 下雨
▶ It rained cats and dogs.
下著傾盆大雨。
相關衍生字彙 rainbow [`renˌbo] 名 彩虹、raincoat [`renˌkot] 名 雨衣、raindrop [`renˌdrɑp] 名 雨滴、rainy [`renɪ] 形 下雨的、rainfall [`renˌfɔl] 名 降雨量
動詞三態變化 rain - rained - rained

---

raise [rez] 動 增加，提高
▶ We all hope our boss can raise our salary.
我們都希望老闆給我們加薪。
動詞三態變化 raise - raised - raised

raisin [`rezṇ] 名 葡萄乾
▶ I like to add some raisins to my milk. 我喜歡在牛奶裡加一些葡萄乾。

rally [`rælɪ] 名 集會
▶ Students are organizing a peace rally. 學生正在組織一個和平集會。

random [`rændəm] 形 隨機的，任意的
▶ These are all random samples. 這些都是隨機取樣的樣品。

range [rendʒ] 名 山脈
▶ There is a mountain range in the middle of Taiwan. 台灣的中央有一座山脈。

rank [ræŋk] 名 等級，級別
▶ His mother is a professor who teaches at a university of the first rank.
他母親是一名教授，在一所頂尖的大學教書。

ransom [`rænsəm] 名 贖金
▶ They demanded a ransom for the kidnapped boy.
他們要求為被綁架的男孩付贖金。

rapid [`ræpɪd] 形 快速的
▶ The world is full of rapid change. 這世界充滿快速的改變。

rapture [`ræptʃɚ] 名 欣喜若狂　　片 with rapture 欣喜若狂地
相關衍生字彙 delight [dɪ`laɪt] 名 欣喜、ecstasy [`ɛkstəsɪ] 名 狂喜、glee [gli] 名 歡欣、
joy [dʒɔɪ] 名 歡樂、happiness [`hæpɪnɪs] 名 快樂

rare [rɛr] 形 罕見的　　片 a rare disease 罕見疾病　　◎ MP3 **18-02**

rarely [`rɛrlɪ] 副 很少
▶ I rarely have time to watch a movie. 我很少有空看電影。

rate [ret] 名 比率，速度　　片 a birth / death rate 出生率／死亡率

R

rather [`ræðɚ] 副 寧願
▶ I would rather exercise than play the computer games.
我寧願運動也不要打電玩。

rational [`ræʃən!] 形 合理的，有理性的
▶ It's rational that students should focus on studying.
學生要專心讀書，這是合理的。

ravage [`rævɪdʒ] 動 使荒蕪
▶ After the earthquake, the village was ravaged.
地震後，村落變得荒蕪。
相關衍生字彙 destroy [dɪ`strɔɪ] 動 破壞、damage [`dæmɪdʒ] 名 動 損害、ruin [`rʊɪn]
動 毀壞、harm [hɑrm] 名 動 傷害，危害、spoil [spɔɪl] 動 損壞
動詞三態變化 ravage - ravaged - ravaged

rave [rev] 動 熱烈討論
▶ They are raving about the issue.
她們正熱烈討論此議題。
動詞三態變化 rave - raved - raved

raw [rɔ] 形 生的
▶ The Japanese enjoy eating raw fish. 日本人喜歡吃生魚片。

ray [re] 名 光線　 片 a ray of sunshine 一道陽光

reach [ritʃ] 動 觸及　 片 to reach a conclusion 得出結論
動詞三態變化 reach - reached - reached

react [rɪˋækt] 動 反應
▶ You don't have to react so angrily to their criticism.
對他們的批評，你不必如此憤怒地反應。
動詞三態變化 react - reacted - reacted

reaction [rɪˋækʃən] 名 反應
▶ The issue caused a chain reaction. 這議題引發連鎖反應。

read [rid] 動 閱讀
▶ She likes to read to her children.
她喜歡讀書給孩子聽。
動詞三態變化 read - read - read

ready [ˋrɛdɪ] 形 準備好的
▶ Are you ready to take the challenge? 你準備好接受挑戰了嗎？

reality [riˋælətɪ] 名 事實
▶ Let's face reality together.
讓我們一起面對現實。
相關衍生字彙 real [ˋriəl] 形 真的、realize [ˋrɪəˌlaɪz] 動 瞭解、realization [ˌrɪələˋzeʃən] 名 領悟、really [ˋrɪəlɪ] 副 真正地

reap [rip] 動 收穫
▶ You reap what you have sown.
種瓜得瓜，種豆得豆。
動詞三態變化 reap - reaped - reaped

reason [ˋrizn̩] 名 原因
▶ Please give me a reason why you were late.
請給我一個理由，說明你為何遲到。

reasonable [`riznəbl̩] 形 合理的
▶ The price is very reasonable.
這價錢很合理。
相關衍生字彙 logical [`lɑdʒɪkl̩] 形 合理的，合邏輯的、sensible [`sɛnsəbl̩] 形 合情理的、
rational [`ræʃənl̩] 形 理性的、unreasonable [ʌn`riznəbl̩] 形 不合理的

reassure [͵riə`ʃur] 動 使放心，向～再保證
▶ I reassured you of my support.
我再次保證支持你。
動詞三態變化 reassure - reassured - reassured

rebel [rɪ`bɛl] 動 造反，反叛
▶ The people rebelled against the new government.
人民反叛此新政府。
動詞三態變化 rebel - rebelled - rebelled

rebound [rɪ`baund] 動 彈回　　　　　　　　　　　○ MP3 **18-03**
▶ The ball rebounded from the ground.
球從地面彈回。
動詞三態變化 rebound - rebounded - rebounded

rebuke [rɪ`bjuk] 動 指責
▶ The boss rebuked those who were often late.
老闆指責那些常遲到的人。
動詞三態變化 rebuke - rebuked - rebuked

recall [rɪ`kɔl] 動 回想起，回憶起
▶ I recall you as a handsome boy.
我記得你是個帥氣的男孩。
相關衍生字彙 recollect [͵rɛkə`lɛkt] 動 回憶、remember [rɪ`mɛmbɚ] 動 記得，回憶起、
review [rɪ`vju] 動 回顧，回憶、remind [rɪ`maɪnd] 動 提醒，使想起、
memorize [`mɛmə͵raɪz] 動 記住
動詞三態變化 recall - recalled - recalled

receipt [rɪ`sit] 名 收據
▶ Here is the receipt for your book. 這是你的書的收據。

receive [rɪ`siv] 動 收到
▶ I have already received the gift from you.
我收到你寄來的禮物。
動詞三態變化 receive - received - received

recently [`risn̩tlɪ] 副 最近地
▶ Recently, I especially miss you. 最近，我特別想念你。

R

reception [rɪ`sɛpʃən] 名 招待會，接待
▶ The mayor gave a reception for the foreign friends.
市長辦招待會歡迎外國友人。

recession [rɪ`sɛʃən] 名 蕭條，經濟衰退
▶ An economic recession will lead to a high rate of unemployment.
經濟蕭條會引起高失業率。

recipe [`rɛsəpɪ] 名 食譜
▶ I cook according to the recipe.
我按照食譜烹調。

相關衍生字彙 menu [`mɛnju] 名 菜單、formula [`fɔrmjələ] 名 處方、ingredient [ɪn`gridɪənt] 名（烹調的）原料、appetizer [`æpə͵taɪzɚ] 名 開胃小吃、dressing [`drɛsɪŋ] 名（拌沙拉等用的）調料

recipient [rɪ`sɪpɪənt] 名 接受者，領受者
▶ You are a worthy recipient. 你是當之無愧的得主。

recital [rɪ`saɪtl̩] 名 獨奏會
▶ The recital at the beginning of the program was excellent.
節目一開始的獨奏會相當精采。

recite [ri`saɪt] 動 背誦
▶ When I was young, I recited many beautiful poems.
我小時候背誦過很多優美的詩。

動詞三態變化 recite - recited - recited

reckless [`rɛklɪs] 形 冒失的　　反 careful [`kɛrfəl] 形 小心的

reckon [`rɛkən] 動 指望，盼望
▶ I reckon on you to fix my laptop.
我指望你幫我修理筆記型電腦。

動詞三態變化 reckon - reckoned - reckoned

recognition [͵rɛkəg`nɪʃən] 名 認出，承認　　片 beyond recognition 無法辨認

recognize [`rɛkəg͵naɪz] 動 辨認，認可
▶ We haven't seen each other for thirty years, but I still can recognize you.
我們三十年沒見，我仍可認出你。

相關衍生字彙 acknowledge [ək`nɑlɪdʒ] 動 承認、confess [kən`fɛs] 動 供認，坦白、admit [əd`mɪt] 動 承認、realize [`rɪə͵laɪz] 動 瞭解，領悟、comprehend [͵kɑmprɪ`hɛnd] 動 理解，領會

動詞三態變化 recognize - recognized - recognized

recollect [ˌrɛkə`lɛkt] 動 回憶，記起
▶ Can you recollect our childhood?
　你想得起我們的童年嗎？
動詞三態變化 recollect - recollected - recollected

---

recollection [ˌrɛkə`lɛkʃən] 名 回憶　　同 memory [`mɛmərɪ] 名 回憶

---

recommend [ˌrɛkə`mɛnd] 動 推薦
▶ He recommended a good book.
　他推薦了一本好書。
動詞三態變化 recommend - recommended - recommended

---

recommendation [ˌrɛkəmɛn`deʃən] 名 推薦
片 a recommendation letter 推薦函

---

recompense [`rɛkəmˌpɛns] 動 報酬，賠償　　◉ MP3 18-04
▶ We decided to recompense her for her loss.
　我們決定賠償她的損失。
動詞三態變化 recompense - recompensed - recompensed

---

reconcile [`rɛkənsaɪl] 動 使一致，使順從
▶ I don't want to reconcile myself to the so-called fate.
　我不想聽由所謂的命運。
動詞三態變化 reconcile - reconciled - reconciled

---

reconstruct [ˌrikən`strʌkt] 動 重建
▶ All the houses here were reconstructed after the earthquake.
　這裡所有的房子都是地震後重建的。
動詞三態變化 reconstruct - reconstructed - reconstructed

---

reconstruction [ˌrikən`strʌkʃən] 名 重建
片 post-war reconstruction 戰後重建

---

record [`rɛkɚd] 名 紀錄　　片 to break a record 打破紀錄

---

recourse [rɪ`kors] 名 求助，依靠
▶ We hope to solve the problem without recourse to the law.
　我們希望能不要求助法律，就能解決此問題 。

---

recovery [rɪ`kʌvərɪ] 名 恢復
▶ The patient made a quick recovery with the help of the doctor.
　在醫生協助下病人恢復得很快。
相關衍生字彙 recover [rɪ`kʌvɚ] 動 恢復、discover [dɪs`kʌvɚ] 動 發現、
　　　　　　discovery [dɪs`kʌvərɪ] 名 發現、cover [`kʌvɚ] 動 覆蓋

---

recreation [ˌrɛkrɪ`eʃən] 名 消遣，娛樂
▶ Riding a bicycle is one of my recreations. 騎腳踏車是我的消遣之一。

R

recruit [rɪ`krut] 動 招募
▶ The club is recruiting new members.
社團正在招募新社員。
動詞三態變化 recruit - recruited - recruited

recur [rɪ`kɝ] 動 重新憶起，再現
▶ The old idea recurs to me.
那個舊點子重新浮現在我腦海。
動詞三態變化 recur - recurred - recurred

recycle [ri`saɪkl] 動 回收利用
▶ We should help recycle the old stuff.
我們應協助回收舊東西。
動詞三態變化 recycle - recycled - recycled

redeem [rɪ`dim] 動 贖回
▶ To redeem his car, he worked hard to save money.
為贖回他的車，他努力工作存錢。
動詞三態變化 redeem - redeemed - redeemed

reduce [rɪ`djus] 動 減少
▶ The plane is reducing its speed.
飛機正在減速。
相關衍生字彙 reduction [rɪ`dʌkʃən] 名 減少、decrease [dɪ`kris] 動 減少、increase [ɪn`kris] 動 增加、add [æd] 動 加上、plus [plʌs] 名 加號
動詞三態變化 reduce - reduced - reduced

reference [`rɛfərəns] 名 參考
▶ Here is some information for your reference. 這裡有些資訊供你參考。

refill [ri`fɪl] 名 動 再填滿
▶ My car needs a gas refill.
我的車子要加油了。
動詞三態變化 refill - refilled - refilled

refine [rɪ`faɪn] 動 提煉，使精煉
▶ I need some time to refine the plan.
我需要一點時間讓這項計畫更精煉。
動詞三態變化 refine - refined - refined

reflect [rɪ`flɛkt] 動 反省，深思
▶ It's worthwhile for everyone to reflect on his past.
反省一下自己的過往是很值得的事。
動詞三態變化 reflect - reflected - reflected

reflection [rɪˋflɛkʃən] 名 反省，深思
▶ On reflection, I decided to admit the mistake. 經反省後，我決定承認錯誤。

reform [ˌrɪˋfɔrm] 名 動 改革
▶ It's time to reform education.
該是改革教育的時候。
動詞三態變化 reform - reformed - reformed

reformation [ˌrɛfɚˋmeʃən] 名 改革　片 education reformation 教育改革

refresh [rɪˋfrɛʃ] 動 使恢復精力　◎ MP3 18-05
▶ He often refreshes himself by drinking beer.
他常藉著喝啤酒來提神。
動詞三態變化 refresh - refreshed - refreshed

refuge [ˋrɛfjudʒ] 名 避難所
▶ The woman turned to a refuge for help.
這名婦人向避難所求救。
相關衍生字彙 refugee [ˌrɛfjuˋdʒi] 名 難民、shelter [ˋʃɛltɚ] 名 避難處、victim [ˋvɪktɪm] 名 受害者、helpless [ˋhɛlplɪs] 形 無助的、flee [fli] 動 逃走

refund [ˋrɪˌfʌnd] 名 退費
▶ If you are not satisfied with the product, you can demand a refund within seven days.
如果你不滿意產品，七天內可要求退費。

refuse [rɪˋfjuz] 動 拒絕
▶ I refused to lend him more money.
我拒絕借他更多錢。
動詞三態變化 refuse - refused - refused

regard [rɪˋgɑrd] 動 視為
▶ I regard you as my best friend.
我視你為最好的朋友。
動詞三態變化 regard - regarded - regarded

regarding [rɪˋgɑrdɪŋ] 介 關於，至於
▶ Regarding the topic of the meeting, let's discuss it later.
關於會議的主題，我們待會再討論。

regime [rɪˋʒim] 名 政體，政權
▶ The corrupt regime was finally overthrown.
這腐敗的政府終於被推翻了。
相關衍生字彙 government [ˋgʌvɚnmənt] 名 政府、administration [ədˌmɪnəˋstreʃən] 名 行政、ruler [ˋrulɚ] 名 統治者，管理者、party [ˋpɑrtɪ] 名 政黨，黨派、dominion [dəˋmɪnjən] 名 統治，管轄

R

region [ˋridʒən] 名 區域
▶ No people live in the mountainous region. 沒有人住在這山區。

register [ˋrɛdʒɪstɚ] 動 登記　　片 registered mail 掛號郵件
動詞三態變化 register - registered - registered

regret [rɪˋgrɛt] 動 後悔，遺憾
▶ I regret having to say goodbye to you.
　我很遺憾得跟你分手。
動詞三態變化 regret - regretted - regretted

regular [ˋrɛgjələ] 形 規律的　　片 to live a regular life 過著規律的生活
相關衍生字彙 regularly [ˋrɛgjələlɪ] 副 規律地、regulate [ˋrɛgjəˏlet] 動 使規律、
　　regulation [ˏrɛgjəˋleʃən] 名 規則、steady [ˋstɛdɪ] 形 穩定的

rehearsal [rɪˋhɝsl] 名 彩排
▶ This is the last rehearsal; every actor is very nervous.
　這是最後的彩排，演員都很緊張。

reign [ren] 動 統治
▶ Queen Victoria reigned over Britain for more than 50 years.
　維多利亞女王統治英國超過五十年。
動詞三態變化 reign - reigned - reigned

reject [rɪˋdʒɛkt] 動 拒絕　　同 refuse [rɪˋfjuz] 動 拒絕
動詞三態變化 reject - rejected - rejected

rejoice [rɪˋdʒɔɪs] 動 欣喜
▶ Everyone rejoiced at the news that the princess was born .
　大家都好開心小公主的誕生。
動詞三態變化 rejoice - rejoiced - rejoiced

relapse [rɪˋlæps] 名 舊病復發
▶ She has been suffering a relapse. 她的舊疾一直復發。

relate [rɪˋlet] 動 有關聯
▶ Your failure is related to your attitude.
　你的失敗與你的態度有關。
相關衍生字彙 relation [rɪˋleʃən] 名 關係、relationship [rɪˋleʃənˏʃɪp] 名 關係、
　　relative [ˋrɛlətɪv] 形 相關的，相對的、relatively [ˋrɛlətɪvlɪ] 副 相對地、
　　relativity [ˏrɛləˋtɪvətɪ] 名 相關性，相對性、relevant [ˋrɛləvənt] 形 有關的
動詞三態變化 relate - related - related

relax [rɪˋlæks] 動 放鬆
▶ During the afternoon, I always relax with a cup of coffee.
　在下午，我都會喝杯咖啡來放鬆一下。

動詞三態變化 relax - relaxed - relaxed

relay [rɪ`le] 名 接替　　片 a relay race 大隊接力賽

release [rɪ`lis] 名 動 釋放
▶ He was released from prison last month.
他上個月出獄。
動詞三態變化 release - released - released

reliable [rɪ`laɪəbḷ] 形 可靠的　　反 unreliable [ˌʌnrɪ`laɪəbḷ] 形 不可靠的　　◎ MP3 **18-06**
相關衍生字彙 reliance [rɪ`laɪəns] 名 依賴、reliant [rɪ`laɪənt] 形 依賴的、depend [dɪ`pɛnd]
動 依賴、dependent [dɪ`pɛndənt] 形 依賴的、rely [rɪ`laɪ] 動 依賴

relic [`rɛlɪk] 名 遺跡
▶ Here are some relics from the Stone Age. 這些是石器時代的遺跡。

relief [rɪ`lif] 名 寬慰
▶ What a relief! The exam is over! 真輕鬆！考試已經結束了！

religious [rɪ`lɪdʒəs] 形 宗教的
▶ He is deeply religious.
他對宗教很虔誠。
相關衍生字彙 religion [rɪ`lɪdʒən] 名 宗教、Buddhism [`budɪzəm] 名 佛教、
Christianity [ˌkrɪstʃɪ`ænətɪ] 名 基督教、Catholicism [kə`θɑləˌsɪzəm]
名 天主教、Islam [`ɪsləm] 名 回教

reluctant [rɪ`lʌktənt] 形 不情願的
▶ I was so reluctant to take actions. 我多麼不想採取行動。

remain [rɪ`men] 動 保持
▶ She remains single for the rest of her life.
她保持單身來度過她的餘生。
動詞三態變化 remain - remained - remained

remark [rɪ`mɑrk] 名 評論，意見
▶ She always makes timely remarks. 她總能做出適時的評論。

remarkable [rɪ`mɑrkəbḷ] 形 非凡的
▶ It's remarkable that drivers here follow the traffic rules so well.
這裡的司機很遵守交通規則，令人感到驚奇。

remedy [`rɛmədɪ] 名 治療　　片 to prescribe a remedy 開出藥方

remember [rɪ`mɛmbɚ] 動 記住　　反 forget [fɚ`gɛt] 動 忘記
動詞三態變化 remember - remembered - remembered

R

remind [rɪˋmaɪnd] 動 提醒
▶ I'll write a note to remind myself.
我會寫張紙條來提醒自己。
動詞三態變化 remind - reminded - reminded

reminiscences [ˌrɛməˋnɪsnsɪz] 名 回憶錄
▶ The president will publish his personal reminiscences.
總統將出版他的個人回憶錄。

remorse [rɪˋmɔrs] 名 悔意
▶ He has not shown any remorse for his crime.
他沒有對犯下的罪行表現出任何悔意。

remote [rɪˋmot] 形 遙遠的
▶ I plan to live in a small town remote from the big city.
我打算住在遠離大城市的小鎮。
相關衍生字彙 close [klos] 形 接近的、near [nɪr] 形 近的、far [fɑr] 形 遙遠的、distant [ˋdɪstənt] 形 遠離的

remove [rɪˋmuv] 動 移開，脫掉
▶ It was so hot that he removed his tie.
天氣太熱了，所以他把領帶解開。
動詞三態變化 remove - removed - removed

renaissance [rəˋnesns] 名 文藝復興
片 the Renaissance（義大利）文藝復興時代

renew [rɪˋnju] 動 更新，使續期
▶ Remember to renew your membership yearly.
記得每年去更新會員身分。
相關衍生字彙 revive [rɪˋvaɪv] 動 復甦、refresh [rɪˋfrɛʃ] 動 更新，使恢復、kindle [ˋkɪndl] 動 激起（熱情等）、reanimate [riˋænəˌmet] 動 始恢復生氣
動詞三態變化 renew - renewed - renewed

renounce [rɪˋnauns] 動 聲明放棄
▶ The prince renounced his wealth for love.
王子為了愛情放棄財富。
動詞三態變化 renounce - renounced - renounced

renowned [rɪˋnaund] 形 著名的
▶ He was renowned for his talents. 他以才華著稱。

rent [rɛnt] 名 租金　　片 for rent 出租

repair [rɪ`pɛr] 動 修理

▶ Your car is too old to repair.
你的車舊到無法修了。

動詞三態變化 repair - repaired - repaired

reparation [ˌrɛpə`reʃən] 名 賠償，補償

▶ He promises to make reparation for the damage. 他允諾賠償損失。

repatriate [ri`petrɪˌet] 動 遣返

▶ The criminal will be repatriated back to his country.
這名罪犯將被遣返回他的國家。

動詞三態變化 repatriate - repatriated - repatriated

repay [rɪ`pe] 動 償還

▶ Please repay me the money.
請把錢還我。

動詞三態變化 repay - repaid - repaid

repeat [rɪ`pit] 動 重複

▶ Would you please repeat what you said?
請重複你說的話好嗎？

動詞三態變化 repeat - repeated - repeated

replace [rɪ`ples] 動 取代

▶ No one can replace you in my heart.
沒人能取代你在我心中的地位。

相關衍生字彙 substitute [`sʌbstəˌtjut] 動 代替、switch [swɪtʃ] 動 使轉換、exchange [ɪks`tʃendʒ] 動 交換，調換、interchange [ˌɪntɚ`tʃendʒ] 動 互換

動詞三態變化 replace - replaced - replaced

reply [rɪ`plaɪ] 動 回覆

▶ I hope you can reply to me immediately.
我希望你可以立刻回覆我。

動詞三態變化 reply - replied - replied

report [rɪ`port] 動 報告

▶ I already reported the incident to our manager.
我已經跟經理報告這個事件了。

動詞三態變化 report - reported - reported

reporter [rɪ`portɚ] 名 記者　　回 journalist [`dʒɝnəlɪst] 名 新聞從業人員

represent [ˌrɛprɪ`zɛnt] 動 代表

▶ My husband represented me to attend the meeting.
我先生代表我去開會。

動詞三態變化 represent - represented - represented

R

representation [ˌrɛprɪzɛn`teʃən] 名 陳述，抗議
片 to make representations to 向～提出抗議

---

reprimand [`rɛprəˌmænd] 名 譴責
▶ He has received lots of reprimands.
他已經收到很多譴責了。

相關衍生字彙 condemn [kən`dɛm] 動 責難、blame [blem] 動 責備、censure [`sɛnʃɚ] 動 譴責、criticize [`krɪtɪˌsaɪz] 動 批判、praise [prez] 名 稱讚

---

reproach [rɪ`protʃ] 動 責備
▶ The boy was reproached for not handing in his homework.
男孩因為沒交作業而被責備。

動詞三態變化 reproach - reproached - reproached

---

repugnant [rɪ`pʌgnənt] 形 不一致的
▶ We find the teacher's attitude towards students extremely repugnant.
我們覺得這位老師對學生的態度非常令人反感。

---

reputation [ˌrɛpjə`teʃən] 名 聲望
▶ He owns a good reputation. 他擁有好名聲。

---

request [rɪ`kwɛst] 動 請求，要求
▶ I request a loan from the bank.
我從銀行申請貸款。

動詞三態變化 request - requested - requested

---

require [rɪ`kwaɪr] 動 需要，要求
▶ If you require any further information, go to the student center.
需要進一步資料可洽學生中心。

動詞三態變化 require - required - required

---

requirement [rɪ`kwaɪrmənt] 名 要求，條件
▶ A foreign language is the basic requirement for our job.
我們的工作至少要求會一種外國語言。

相關衍生字彙 necessity [nə`sɛsətɪ] 名 必要性、essential [ɪ`sɛnʃəl] 形 不可缺的，必要的、imperative [ɪm`pɛrətɪv] 名 必要的、qualification [ˌkwɑləfə`keʃən] 名 賦予（或取得）資格、condition [kən`dɪʃən] 名 條件

---

rescue [`rɛskju] 動 救援
▶ Luckily, the cat was rescued from the fire.
很幸運地，小貓有被救出火場。

動詞三態變化 rescue - rescued - rescued

---

research [rɪ`sɝtʃ] 名 動 研究
▶ He devoted his life to the academic research. 他終其一身投入學術研究。

動詞三態變化 research - researched - researched

resemblance [rɪ`zɛmbləns] 名 相似　　　　● MP3 18-08
▶ You have a resemblance to the superstar. 你跟那個超級巨星有神似。

resemble [rɪ`zɛmbl] 動 相似
▶ The two designs resemble closely.
　　這兩件設計非常相似。

動詞三態變化 resemble - resembled - resembled

resent [rɪ`zɛnt] 動 怨恨
▶ She resented bitterly her stepfather.
　　她很痛恨她的繼父。

動詞三態變化 resent - resented - resented

reservation [͵rɛzɚ`veʃən] 名 預定，保留
▶ Before your vacation, you have to make a hotel reservation in advance.
　　度假前，你要事先預訂飯店。

相關衍生字彙 reserve [rɪ`zɝv] 動 保留、reservoir [`rɛzɚ͵vɔr] 名 水庫、keep [kip] 動 保留、
　　hold [hold] 動 保留、book [bʊk] 動 預定

reside [rɪ`zaɪd] 動 居住
▶ All his family reside in Paris.
　　他的家人都住在巴黎。

相關衍生字彙 residence [`rɛzədən] 名 居住、resident [`rɛzədənt] 名 居民、inhabit [ɪn`hæbɪt]
　　動 定居、live [lɪv] 動 住

動詞三態變化 reside - resided - resided

residual [rɪ`zɪdʒʊəl] 形 殘留的　　● residual odor 殘留的臭味

resign [rɪ`zaɪn] 動 辭職
▶ He resigned and started a new company of his own.
　　他辭掉工作，創辦自己的新公司。

動詞三態變化 resign - resigned - resigned

resignation [͵rɛzɪg`neʃən] 名 辭職　　● to submit the resignation 遞上辭職書

resist [rɪ`zɪst] 動 抵抗
▶ How can I resist the temptation?
　　我要如何抵抗這誘惑？

動詞三態變化 resist - resisted - resisted

resolute [`rɛzə͵lut] 形 堅決的
▶ Keep resolute in your decision. 自己的決定要堅持。

resolution [͵rɛzə`luʃən] 名 決心
▶ He lacks resolution. 他缺乏決心。

R

resolve [rɪˋzɑlv] 動 決心，決定

▶ I resolve to make my dream come true.
我決定讓夢想成真。

相關衍生字彙 decide [dɪˋsaɪd] 動 決定、determine [dɪˋtɝmɪn] 動 決定、confirm [kənˋfɝm] 動 證實，確定、conclude [kənˋklud] 動 推斷出，結束、settle [ˋsɛtḷ] 動 確定，決定

動詞三態變化 resolve - resolved - resolved

resort [rɪˋzɔrt] 動 訴諸

▶ Never resort to violence.
絕對不要訴諸於暴力。

動詞三態變化 resort - resorted - resorted

resource [rɪˋsors] 名 資源　片 natural resources 天然資源

respectable [rɪˋspɛktəbḷ] 形 值得尊敬的

▶ He is a respectable hero.
他是個值得尊敬的英雄。

相關衍生字彙 respectful [rɪˋspɛktfəl] 形 恭敬的、respective [rɪˋspɛktɪv] 形 各自的、respect [rɪˋspɛkt] 動 尊重、adore [əˋdor] 動 敬慕、reverence [ˋrɛvərəns] 名 尊敬，崇敬

respond [rɪˋspɑnd] 動 反應

▶ He always responded, "I don't know."
他總是回答：「我不知道」。

動詞三態變化 respond - responded - responded

response [rɪˋspɑns] 名 回應

▶ I need your response as soon as possible. 請儘快給我你的回答。

responsibility [rɪͺspɑnsəˋbɪlətɪ] 名 責任　片 to take the responsibility 負起責任

responsible [rɪˋspɑnsəbḷ] 形 負責任的

▶ You should be responsible for what you do.
你要為你所做的負責任。

相關衍生字彙 duty [ˋdjutɪ] 名 責任、obligation [ͺɑbləˋgeʃən] 名（道義上或法律上的）義務，責任、burden [ˋbɝdṇ] 名 負擔、load [lod] 名（精神方面的）負擔、job [dʒɑb] 名 職責

rest [rɛst] 名 動 休息　片 to take a rest 休息一下

動詞三態變化 rest - rested - rested

restaurant [ˋrɛstərənt] 名 餐廳　◉ MP3 18-09

▶ Running a restaurant is not easy. 經營餐廳不容易。

restore [rɪˋstor] 動 恢復
▶ She hasn't been fully restored to health.
她還沒完全恢復健康。

動詞三態變化 restore - restored - restored

restrain [rɪˋstren] 動 限制，控制
▶ You should learn to restrain your greed.
你應學習控制自己的貪婪。

相關衍生字彙 restraint [rɪˋstrent] 名 約束、restrict [rɪˋstrɪkt] 動 限制、restriction [rɪˋstrɪkʃən] 名 限制、limit [ˋlɪmɪt] 動 限制

動詞三態變化 restrain - restrained - restrained

result [rɪˋzʌlt] 名 動 結果
▶ His death resulted from drug abuse.
他的死起因於藥物濫用。

動詞三態變化 result - resulted - resulted

resume [ˋrɛzjuˌme] 名 履歷
▶ Before the job interview, remember to prepare a resume.
求職面試前，記得先準備好一份履歷。

retail [ˋritel] 動 零售　反 wholesale [ˋholˌsel] 動 批發
動詞三態變化 retail - retailed - retailed

retire [rɪˋtaɪr] 動 退休
▶ After retiring, she works for the orphanage as a volunteer.
退休後她在孤兒院當志工。

相關衍生字彙 retirement [rɪˋtaɪrmənt] 名 退休、retired [rɪˋtaɪrd] 形 退休的、retiree [rɪˌtaɪəˋri] 名 退休人員、quit [kwɪt] 動 辭職、resign [rɪˋzaɪn] 動 辭職

動詞三態變化 retire - retired - retired

retreat [rɪˋtrit] 名 撤退
▶ The soldiers carried out the retreat immediately.
軍隊立即執行撤退任務。

動詞三態變化 retreat - retreated - retreated

retrospect [ˋrɛtrəˌspɛkt] 名 回顧
▶ In retrospect, my university days are the happiest ones.
回顧往事，我的大學生活最快樂。

return [rɪˋtɝn] 動 返回　片 in return for 用以報答
動詞三態變化 return - returned - returned

R

reunion [ri`junjən] 名 重聚
▶ Since graduating from college, we have had a reunion yearly.
自從大學畢業後，我們一年聚一次。

reveal [rɪ`vil] 動 洩漏
▶ Who revealed the secret?
是誰洩漏祕密的？

相關衍生字彙 disclose [dɪs`kloz] 動 揭發，透露、uncover [ʌn`kʌvɚ] 動 揭露，發現、display [dɪ`sple] 動 顯露、expose [ɪk`spoz] 動 揭露、conceal [kən`sil] 動 隱藏、hide [haɪd] 動 隱藏

動詞三態變化 reveal - revealed - revealed

revenge [rɪ`vɛndʒ] 名 報仇
▶ He set fire in revenge for the loss of his job. 他縱火是為了失去工作而報復。

revenue [`rɛvəˌnju] 名 歲入，稅收　　片 government revenue 政府的稅收

reverberate [rɪ`vɝbəˌret] 動 回響
▶ The laughter reverberated through the party.
笑聲迴盪在派對裡。

動詞三態變化 reverberate - reverberated - reverberated

reverse [rɪ`vɝs] 名 挫折，失敗
▶ No one never suffers a reverse. 每個人都經歷過挫折。

review [rɪ`vju] 動 複習
▶ To pass the exam, she reviews her lessons every day.
為了通過考試，她每天複習功課。

動詞三態變化 review - reviewed - reviewed

revision [rɪ`vɪʒən] 名 修訂　　片 to make a revision 作修訂

revolution [ˌrɛvə`luʃən] 名 革命　　片 the industrial revolution 工業革命
相關衍生字彙 revolt [rɪ`volt] 動 反叛，造反、revolutionize [ˌrɛvə`luʃənˌaɪz] 動 徹底改革、reform [ˌrɪ`fɔrm] 動 改革、innovate [`ɪnəˌvet] 動 創新

revolve [rɪ`vɑlv] 動 旋轉
▶ The Earth revolves around the Sun.
地球繞著太陽轉。

動詞三態變化 revolve - revolved - revolved

revulsion [rɪ`vʌlʃən] 名 強烈的反感　　◎ MP3 18-10
▶ I walked away in revulsion. 我反感地走開。

reward [rɪˋwɔrd] 動 獎賞
▶ The brave boy was rewarded in public.
這名勇敢的男孩被公開表揚。
動詞三態變化 reward - rewarded - rewarded

rewrite [riˋraɪt] 動 重寫
▶ Please rewrite your assignment, where there are too many mistakes.
你的作業錯誤太多，請重寫。
動詞三態變化 rewrite - rewrote - rewritten

rhyme [raɪm] 動 押韻
▶ Spain rhymes with rain.
spain 和 rain 兩個字有押韻。
動詞三態變化 rhyme - rhymed - rhymed

rhythm [ˋrɪðəm] 名 節奏
▶ The kids danced to the rhythm of the music. 孩子們跟著音樂的節奏跳舞。

rich [rɪtʃ] 形 富有的
▶ The rich are not always happy.
有錢人並不總是快樂。
相關衍生字彙 riches [ˋrɪtʃɪz] 名 財富、fortune [ˋfɔrtʃən] 名 財富、poor [pʊr] 形 貧窮的、poverty [ˋpɑvɚtɪ] 名 貧窮

rid [rɪd] 形 除去的　片 to get rid of 除去～

riddle [ˋrɪdḷ] 名 謎語
▶ They enjoy guessing the riddles. 他們很喜歡猜謎語。

ride [raɪd] 動 騎乘　片 to go bike riding 騎腳踏車
動詞三態變化 ride - rode - ridden

ridicule [ˋrɪdɪkjul] 名 嘲弄
▶ You can ignore their meaningless ridicule. 你可以不要理會他們無意義的嘲笑。

ridiculous [rɪˋdɪkjələs] 形 荒謬的
▶ It's ridiculous that we received an empty box. 我們收到一個空箱子，真可笑。

right [raɪt] 名 權力　片 the right of free speech 言論自由權
相關衍生字彙 righteous [ˋraɪtʃəs] 形 正直的、rightly [ˋraɪtlɪ] 副 公正地、right [raɪt] 形 正確的，右邊的、rightful [ˋraɪtfəl] 形 正當的

rim [rɪm] 名 邊緣
▶ Be careful! The rim of the cup is broken. 小心！杯口是破的。

ring [rɪŋ] 名 戒指　片 a diamond ring 鑽戒

R

riot [`raɪət] 名 暴動
▶ A riot broke out in that city. 那個城市引發了暴動。

ripe [raɪp] 形 成熟的
▶ The fruit is not ripe for picking. 這水果還沒熟到可以摘。

ripen [`raɪpən] 動 變成熟
▶ Finally, their friendship ripened into love.
終於，他們的友誼發展成愛情。

相關衍生字彙 raw [rɔ] 形 生的、mature [mə`tjur] 形 成熟的、immature [ˌɪmə`tjur]
形 未成熟的、unripe [ʌn`raɪp] 形 未成熟的、full-grown [fʊl`gron] 形 成熟的

動詞三態變化 ripen - ripened - ripened

ripple [`rɪpl̩] 名 漣漪
▶ You can throw a stone across the lake, and then you can see ripples.
你可以從湖面丟石頭，就可看到漣漪。

rise [raɪz] 動 升起
▶ The sun rises in the east.
太陽從東方升起。

動詞三態變化 rise - rose - risen

risk [rɪsk] 名 危險
▶ Don't run any risk! 別冒任何危險！

rival [`raɪvl̩] 名 對手 ◎ MP3 18-11
▶ I have confidence in beating my rival. 我有信心打敗我的對手。

river [`rɪvɚ] 名 河流
▶ There is a bridge across the river. 有座橋跨過這條河流。

road [rod] 名 道路
▶ All roads lead to Rome.
（諺語）條條大路通羅馬。

相關衍生字彙 roadside [`rodˌsaɪd] 名 路邊、street [strit] 名 街道、roadblock [`rodˌblɑk]
名 路障

roam [rom] 動 漫步
▶ At night, many lovers roam along the river.
在夜晚，很多戀人沿著這條河流漫步。

動詞三態變化 roam - roamed - roamed

roar [ror] 動 吼叫
▶ Wow! The lion is roaring.
哇！獅子正在吼叫。

動詞三態變化 roar - roared - roared

roast [rost] 動 烤
▶ We roast a turkey on Thanksgiving.
　我們會在感恩節烤火雞。
動詞三態變化 roast - roasted - roasted

rob [rɑb] 動 搶劫
▶ Help! I've been robbed! Call the police!
　我被搶了！請打電話報警！
動詞三態變化 rob - robbed - robbed

robbery [`rɑbərɪ] 名 搶劫　　片 bank robbery 銀行搶案

rock [rɑk] 名 岩石
▶ The mountain is formed from rocks. 這座山是岩石構成的。

rocky [`rɑkɪ] 形 多岩石的
▶ It's dangerous to drive on the rocky road. 在這條岩石路上開車很危險。

role [rol] 名 角色　　片 to play an important role 扮演重要角色

roll [rol] 動 滾動
▶ A rolling stone gathers no moss.
　（諺語）滾石不生苔。
動詞三態變化 roll - rolled - rolled

romance [ro`mæns] 名 羅曼史，愛情故事
▶ Most girls like to read romances. 大部分女孩喜歡讀愛情故事。

romantic [rə`mæntɪk] 形 羅曼蒂克的，浪漫的
▶ Their love story is very romantic.
　他們的愛情故事很浪漫。
相關衍生字彙 story [`storɪ] 名 故事，（短篇）小說、tale [tel] 名 故事，傳說、
　　　　　　fairy tale 片 神話故事，童話、legend [`lɛdʒənd] 名 傳說、novel [`nɑvl]
　　　　　　名 （長篇）小說、epic [`ɛpɪk] 名 史詩、fiction [`fɪkʃən] 名 （總稱）小說、
　　　　　　myth [mɪθ] 名 神話

room [rum] 名 房間，空間
▶ There is room to improve your writing. 你的寫作仍有改善的空間。

root [rut] 名 根　　片 the root of evil 罪惡的根源

rotation [ro`teʃən] 名 交替，輪流
▶ In a year, the four seasons follow each other in rotation.
　一年有四個季節輪流交替。

rotten [`rɑtn̩] 形 腐敗的，腐爛的　　片 rotten fruit and vegetables 腐爛的蔬果

R

rough [rʌf] 形 粗糙的
▶ Mom's hands are rough with housework. 媽媽的手因為做家事而粗糙。

roughly [`rʌflɪ] 副 大略　　片 roughly speaking 大略説來

route [rut] [raʊt] 名 路線　　◎ MP3 18-12
▶ I am trying to find the shortest route from my place to the school.
我正試著找出從住處到學校最近的路線。

routine [ru`tin] 名 例行工作
▶ I have a fixed routine at work.
我上班有固定的例行事務。
相關衍生字彙 rule [rul] 名 規則、habit [`hæbɪt] 名 習慣、pattern [`pætɚn] 名 模式、
custom [`kʌstəm] 名（社會，團體的）習俗，慣例

row [ro] 名 排，行　　片 in a row 連續地

royal [`rɔɪəl] 形 王室的　　片 the royal family 王室家族

royalty [`rɔɪəltɪ] 名 版稅
▶ The publisher should pay the royalties. 出版社需支付版稅。

rude [rud] 形 粗魯的
▶ Don't be so rude to your friends. 不要對朋友如此粗魯。

ruffle [`rʌfl̩] 動 弄亂
▶ What ruffled your hair?
什麼東西把你的頭髮弄的這麼亂？
動詞三態變化 ruffle - ruffled - ruffled

ruin [`rʊɪn] 動 毀壞
▶ The heavy rain ruined our plan.
大雨毀了我們的計畫。
動詞三態變化 ruin - ruined - ruined

rule [rul] 名 規定　　片 traffic rules 交通規則

rumor [`rumɚ] 名 謠言
▶ I will find out who is spreading the rumor. 我會找出是誰在傳播謠言。

run [rʌn] 動 跑　　片 to run out of 用完
相關衍生字彙 runaway [`rʌnəˌwe] 名 逃亡、rundown [`rʌnˌdaʊn] 名 逐條核對、
runner [`rʌnɚ] 名 跑者、runaround [`rʌnəˌraʊnd] 名 迴避話題
動詞三態變化 run - ran - run

rural [`rurəl] 形 田園的，鄉村的
▶ Few young men can get used to the quiet rural life.
很少年輕人能習慣安靜的鄉村生活。

rush [rʌʃ] 名動 奔，匆忙　　片 in a rush 匆匆忙忙地
動詞三態變化 rush - rushed - rushed

rust [rʌst] 名 鏽，鐵鏽
▶ I keep my mind from rust by reading every day.　我藉由每天閱讀讓腦袋不生鏽。

MEMO

R

一網打盡「英語小知識」| Trip v.s Travel v.s Journey ————

▶ **Trip:** 往返一個地點（時間不長）。

▶ **Travel:** 前往某一個地點，或單指旅遊；travel 本身可能會包含很多段
的 journeys。

▶ **Journey:** 一地到另一地的過程，或指生命歷程（時間偏長）。

S sacred ~ systematic

★一網打盡 1086 個英文單字 ｜ 一網打盡 264 句英語會話句

sacred [`sekrɪd] 形 神聖的
▶ For the locals, the temples are sacred. 對當地人而言，這些廟宇是神聖的。

---

sacrifice [`sækrəˌfaɪs] 名 犧牲
▶ Many women make sacrifices for their family. 很多婦女會為了家人做犧牲。

---

sad [sæd] 形 傷心的
▶ I was so sad when she said goodbye to me.
當她跟我說再見時，我好傷心。
相關衍生字彙 sadly [`sædlɪ] 副 傷心地、sadness [`sædnɪs] 名 傷心、sorrowful [`sarəfəl]
形 悲傷的、unhappy [ʌn`hæpɪ] 形 不開心的

---

safari [sə`farɪ] 名 狩獵旅行
▶ Many travelers go on safari in South Africa. 很多旅人會到南非狩獵旅行。

---

safety [`seftɪ] 名 安全
▶ For your safety, please fasten your seatbelt.
為了你的安全，請繫上安全帶。
相關衍生字彙 safe [sef] 形 安全的、safely [`seflɪ] 副 安全地、safeguard [`sefˌgard]
名 安全裝置，保護措施

---

sagacious [sə`geʃəs] 形 睿智的，有遠見的
片 a sagacious choice 有前瞻性的抉擇

---

sake [sek] 名 緣故
▶ For the sake of God, I forgive you. 看在上帝的份上，我原諒你。

---

salary [`sælərɪ] 名 薪水
▶ With the salary, I can purchase a gift for my mother.
有了這筆薪水，我就可以買禮物給媽媽了。

---

sale [sel] 名 賣，銷售　　片 to make a sale 做買賣

---

salesman [`selzmən] 名 業務員
▶ The salesmen play important roles in the marketing department.
業務員在行銷部門是很重要的。

---

sail [sel] 動 航行
▶ Mark plans to go sailing this weekend.
馬克這個周末打算去航行。
相關衍生字彙 sailing [`selɪŋ] 名 航行、sailor [`selɚ] 名 水手、mariner [`mærɪnɚ]
名 水手、seaman [`simən] 名 海員
動詞三態變化 sail - sailed - sailed

salon [sə`lɑn] 名（營業場所）廳，院，廊　　片 a beauty salon 美容院

salt [sɔlt] 名 鹽巴
▶ Don't forget to put some salt into your soup.
別忘了放點鹽巴到湯裡。

salute [sə`lut] 動 敬禮
▶ The soldiers saluted the general.
士兵向將軍敬禮。
動詞三態變化 salute - saluted - saluted

same [sem] 形 相同的　　反 different [`dɪfərənt] 形 不同的

sample [`sæmpl] 名 樣品
▶ Here are some free samples of shampoo. 這些都是免費的洗髮精試用品。

sanction [`sæŋkʃən] 名 批准　　片 to get official sanction 取得正式批准
相關衍生字彙 permit [pɚ`mɪt] 動 允許，許可、license [`laɪsn̩s] 名 許可，特許、permission [pɚ`mɪʃən] 名 許可，同意、admission [əd`mɪʃən] 名（學校、會場、俱樂部等的）進入許可、certificate [sɚ`tɪfəkɪt] 名 證明書，執照

sand [sænd] 名 沙子　　片 a grain of sand 一粒沙子

sandwich [`sændwɪtʃ] 名 三明治
▶ I ate a sandwich for lunch. 我吃三明治當午餐。

sanitary [`sænə͵tɛrɪ] 形 衛生的
▶ The sanitary facilities in the area are very bad. 這個區域的衛生設備很差。

sarcasm [`sɑrkæzm̩] 名 諷刺　　MP3 19-02
▶ Sarcasm is the lowest form of humor. 諷刺是最低級的幽默。

satellite [`sætl͵aɪt] 名 衛星　　片 an artificial satellite 人造衛星

satisfy [`sætɪs͵faɪ] 動 使滿意
▶ I have been satisfied with my job.
我對我的工作感到滿意。
相關衍生字彙 satisfaction [͵sætɪs`fækʃən] 名 滿意、satisfactory [͵sætɪs`fæktərɪ] 形 令人滿意的、unsatisfactory [͵ʌnsætɪs`fæktərɪ] 形 令人不滿意的
動詞三態變化 satisfy - satisfied - satisfied

Saturday [`sætɚ͵de] 名 星期六
▶ She has a date on Saturday night. 她周六晚上有約會。

sauce [sɔs] 名 醬汁
▶ Give me some tomato sauce. 給我一些番茄醬。

S

savage [`sævɪdʒ] 名 野蠻人
▶ According to the history, our ancestors were savages living on wild animals.
根據歷史，我們的祖先都是原始人，靠野生動物維生。

save [sev] 動 拯救
▶ To save his business, he worked day and night.
為了挽救他的生意，他日以繼夜的工作。
相關衍生字彙 saving [`sevɪŋ] 名 儲蓄、savior [`sevjɚ] 名 救世主、savor [`sevɚ] 名 滋味
動詞三態變化 save - saved - saved

saying [`seɪŋ] 名 諺語　　片 as the saying goes 如諺語所說

scale [skel] 名 規模　　片 a large / small scale 大規模／小規模

scandal [`skænd!] 名 醜聞
▶ The scandal forced the mayor to resign. 這個醜聞迫使市長辭職。

scar [skɑr] 名 傷疤
▶ The fire left the boy with a scar. 這場火災留給男孩一個傷疤。

scare [skɛr] 動 使驚嚇　　片 be scared to death 嚇死了
相關衍生字彙 scarecrow [`skɛrˌkro] 名 稻草人、scared [skɛrd] 形 嚇到的、frighten [`fraɪtn̩] 動 使驚嚇、frightened [`fraɪtn̩d] 形 驚嚇的
動詞三態變化 scare - scared - scared

scatter [`skætɚ] 動 使消散，散佈
▶ He scattered his books all over the floor in his room.
他房間裡的書散落了一地。
動詞三態變化 scatter - scattered - scattered

scene [sin] 名 幕
▶ This is scene one of the play. 這是戲劇的第一幕。

scenery [`sinərɪ] 名 景色　　片 picturesque scenery 如畫的風景
相關衍生字彙 scenic [`sinɪk] 形 風景的、view [vju] 名 景色、picture [`pɪktʃɚ] 名 畫面

scent [sɛnt] 名 氣味
▶ The room is filled with the scent of flowers. 屋內充滿花的味道。

schedule [`skɛdʒul] 名 日程表，時間表
▶ I will have a tight schedule next week. 我下周的時間表很緊湊。

scheme [skim] 名 計畫
▶ The coach creates a training scheme. 教練擬定了一個訓練計畫。

scholarship [`skɑlɚ͵ʃɪp] 名 獎學金
▶ Luckily, I gain a scholarship for my graduate school.
很幸運地，我獲得了研究所的獎學金。

相關衍生字彙 school [skul] 名 學校、scholar [`skɑlɚ] 名 學者、schoolmate [`skul͵met]
名 同校同學、schooling [`skulɪŋ] 名 學校教育

science [`saɪəns] 名 科學　　片 science fiction 科幻小說
相關衍生字彙 scientific [͵saɪən`tɪfɪk] 形 科學的、scientist [`saɪəntɪst] 名 科學家、art [ɑrt]
名 藝術、artist [`ɑrtɪst] 名 藝術家

scissors [`sɪzɚz] 名 剪刀　　◎ MP3 19-03
▶ May I use your scissors? 我可以用你的剪刀嗎？

scold [skold] 動 責備
▶ Please teach him how to correct his bad habit instead of scolding him.
請教他如何改正壞習慣，不要只是責備他。

動詞三態變化 scold - scolded - scolded

score [skor] 名 分數
▶ Attitudes are more important than scores. 態度比分數更重要。

scorn [skɔrn] 名 藐視，輕視
▶ I need your respect, not scorn. 我要你的尊重，而非藐視。

scrape [skrep] 動 刮除
▶ It took me a while to scrape the chewing gum off the floor.
我花了不少時間刮除地板上的口香糖。

動詞三態變化 scrape - scraped - scraped

scream [skrim] 動 尖叫
▶ On seeing the spider, she screamed.
一看到蜘蛛，她就大叫。

動詞三態變化 scream - screamed - screamed

screen [skrin] 名 螢幕　　片 the small / big screen 小螢幕（電視）／大螢幕（電影）

screw [skru] 名 螺絲
▶ He helps me tighten the screw. 他協助我把螺絲鎖緊。

script [skrɪpt] 名 腳本
▶ Who will be responsible for the script? 誰要負責寫劇本？

S

sculpture [ˈskʌlptʃɚ] 名動 雕刻

▶ The famous sculptures were displayed in the museum.
這些有名的雕刻作品正在博物館展出。

相關衍生字彙 sculptor [ˈskʌlptɚ] 名 雕刻家、statue [ˈstætʃu] 名 雕像、creator [krɪˈetɚ] 名 創作者、sculpt [skʌlpt] 動 雕刻，造型

動詞三態變化 sculpture - sculptured - sculptured

search [sɝtʃ] 動 尋找

▶ The police are searching for the lost kid.
警方正在尋找失蹤的小孩。

動詞三態變化 search - searched - searched

season [ˈsizn̩] 名 季節

▶ Of all the four seasons, I prefer fall. 四個季節中，我比較喜歡秋天。

seaside [ˈsiˌsaɪd] 名 海邊

▶ We spent a holiday at the seaside.
我們在海邊度假。

相關衍生字彙 sea [si] 名 海、seal [sil] 名 海豹、seashore [ˈsɪˌʃor] 名 海岸、seasick [ˈsiˌsik] 形 暈船的、seagull [ˈsiˌgʌl] 名 海鷗

seat [sit] 動 使就坐 名 座位

▶ Be seated, please.
請坐。

動詞三態變化 seat - seated - seated

second [ˈsɛkənd] 名 秒

▶ There are sixty seconds in a minute. 一分鐘有六十秒。

secondary [ˈsɛkənˌdɛrɪ] 形 第二的   ⚑ secondary education 中等教育

secretary [ˈsɛkrəˌtɛrɪ] 名 祕書

▶ My secretary is a wise girl.
我的祕書是個聰明的女孩。

相關衍生字彙 secrecy [ˈsikrəsɪ] 名 祕密狀態、secret [ˈsikrɪt] 名 祕密、secretly [ˈsikrɪtlɪ] 副 祕密地

section [ˈsɛkʃən] 名 部分

▶ The book is divided into four sections based on different topics.
這本書依照不同的主題分為四部分。

security [sɪˈkjurətɪ] 名 安全性

▶ When I choose a house, security is the most important factor.
我找房子時，安全性是最重要的考量。

seek [sik] 動 尋找
▶ To seek for freedom, he escaped to America.
　為了尋求自由，他逃到美國。
動詞三態變化 seek - sought - sought

seem [sim] 動 似乎　　　　　　　　　　　　　　　　ⓞ MP3 **19-04**
▶ He seems a reasonable boss.
　他似乎是個講理的老闆。
動詞三態變化 seem - seemed - seemed

segregation [ˌsɛgrɪˋgeʃən] 名 隔離　　⒫ racial segregation 種族隔離

seize [siz] 動 抓住
▶ He seized my arm and asked for help.
　他捉住我的手臂要我幫他忙。
動詞三態變化 seize - seized - seized

seldom [ˋsɛldəm] 副 很少
▶ I seldom exercised before. 我以前很少運動。

select [səˋlɛkt] 動 選擇　　⒞ choose [tʃuz] 動 選擇
相關衍生字彙 selection [səˋlɛkʃ nɛ] 名 選擇、elect [ɪˋlɛkt] 動 選舉、election [ɪˋlɛkʃən]
　　　　　　　名 選舉、choice [tʃɔɪs] 名 選擇
動詞三態變化 select - selected - selected

selfish [ˋsɛlfɪʃ] 形 自私的
▶ A selfish person is not popular with friends. 自私的人不會受朋友的歡迎。

sell [sɛl] 動 賣，出售
▶ I decided to sell my car.
　我決定賣掉我的車。
動詞三態變化 sell - sold - sold

seminar [ˋsɛməˌnɑr] 名 研討會
▶ Every Wednesday afternoon, we have to attend a seminar.
　每周三的下午我們都得出席一場研討會。

senator [ˋsɛnətɚ] 名 參議員
▶ All the senators voted for the bill. 全數的參議員投票贊成此法案。

send [sɛnd] 動 送出　　⒫ to send away 把人送往～，送走
動詞三態變化 send - sent - sent

senior [ˋsinjɚ] 形 年長的　　⒫ a college / university senior 大學四年級生

sensation [sɛnˋseʃən] 名 轟動
▶ Their performance caused a sensation. 他們的演出引起轟動

S

427

sense [sɛns] 名 感官　　🅟 a sense of responsibility 責任感

sensible [`sɛnsəbl̩] 形 明智的，理智的
▶ The sensible answer is acceptable, of course.
這合理的答案當然可接受。
相關衍生字彙 practical [`præktɪk] 形 實際的、reasonable [`riznəbl̩] 形 合理的、
rational [`ræʃən] 形 合理的

sensitive [`sɛnsətɪv] 形 敏感的
▶ Don't discuss sensitive issues in the office. 辦公室內不要討論敏感話題。

sentence [`sɛntəns] 動 判刑 名 句子
▶ He was sentenced to ten-year imprisonment.
他被判十年監禁。
動詞三態變化 sentence - sentenced - sentenced

sentimental [ˌsɛntə`mɛntl̩] 形 多愁善感的
▶ She has been sentimental. A sad song can make her cry.
她一直很多愁善感，一首悲歌都可以讓她哭。

separate [`sɛpəˌret] 動 分離
▶ I was separated from my family for months.
我跟家人分開好幾個月了。
動詞三態變化 separate - separated - separated

September [sɛp`tɛmbɚ] 名 九月
▶ The Moon Festival falls in September this year. 今年的中秋節適逢九月。

sequence [`sikwəns] 名 順序　　🅟 in sequence 依次地

serene [sə`rin] 形 安詳的，寧靜的　　◎ MP3 19-05
▶ The serene night comforts my mind. 這寧靜的夜晚安撫了我的心。

series [`siriz] 名 系列　　🅟 a series of 一系列的

serious [`sɪrɪəs] 形 嚴重的
▶ AIDS is a serious disease. 愛滋病是很嚴重的疾病。

servant [`sɝvənt] 名 僕人　　🅟 a public servant 公僕，公務員
相關衍生字彙 serve [sɝv] 動 服務、service [`sɝvɪs] 名 服務、server [`sɝvɚ] 名 侍者、
serviceable [`sɝvɪsəbl̩] 形 可供使用的

set [sɛt] 動 設定
▶ A new factory will be set up here.
一家新工廠將設立在此。
動詞三態變化 set - set - set

setback [`sɛt‚bæk]名 挫折　🅟 a serious setback 嚴重挫敗

settle [`sɛtl]動 安置，解決
▶ He finally settled down to family life.
他終於定下來過家庭生活。
動詞三態變化 settle - settled - settled

several [`sɛvərəl]形 幾個的，一些的
▶ Several of them are my friends. 他們當中有好幾個是我的朋友。

severe [sə`vɪr]形 嚴重的　🔁 serious [`sɪrɪəs]形 嚴重的
相關衍生字彙 severely [sə`vɪrlɪ]副 嚴重地、severity [sə`vɛrətɪ]名 嚴重

sew [so]動 縫
▶ Mother taught me how to sew.
媽媽教我如何縫紉。
動詞三態變化 sew - sewed - sewed

shabby [`ʃæbɪ]形 破舊的
▶ It's hard for me to image that he lives in a shabby house.
很難想像他住在破舊的房子裡。

shade [ʃed]名 陰涼處
▶ The dog is lying in the shade. 小狗躺在陰涼處。

shadow [`ʃædo]名 影子　🅟 under the shadow of 處在～的陰影下

shake [ʃek]動 搖晃
▶ Before drinking, shake the bottle first.
飲用前，先搖晃一下瓶身。
相關衍生字彙 shiver [`ʃɪvɚ]動 發抖、quake [kwek]動 顫抖、tremble [`trɛmbl]動 發抖、vibrate [`vaɪbret]動 顫動
動詞三態變化 shake - shook - shaken

S

shallow [`ʃælo]形 淺的
▶ Swimming in the shallow of the pool is safer. 在池子的淺處游泳比較安全。

shame [ʃem]名 可惜，遺憾
▶ What a shame! The game was cancelled. 真可惜！比賽被取消了。

shameful [`ʃemfəl]形 可恥的
▶ The high rate of crime is very shameful. 高犯罪率是可恥的。

shape [ʃep]名 形狀
▶ These cups are all different shapes. 這些杯子都是不同形狀的。

share [ʃɛr] 動 分享
▶ Thanks for sharing everything with me.
感謝你跟我分享一切。
動詞三態變化 share - shared - shared

sharpen [`ʃɑrpn̩] 動 使銳利
▶ Please help me sharpen my pencil.
請幫我削鉛筆。
動詞三態變化 sharpen - sharpened - sharpened

shave [ʃev] 動 刮鬍子　　　　　　　　　　　　　◎ MP3 **19-06**
▶ My husband shaves in the morning before going to work.
我先生都是早上上班前刮鬍子。
相關衍生字彙 shaver [`ʃevɚ] 名 理髮師，刮鬍鬚的用具、beard [bɪrd] 名 山羊鬍、
moustache [məsˋtæʃ] 名 八字鬍、whisker [`hwɪskɚ] 名 連鬢鬍子
動詞三態變化 shave - shaved - shaved

shed [ʃɛd] 動 流出，散發，脫落，去除　　片 to shed tears 掉下眼淚
動詞三態變化 shed - shed - shed

sheep [ʃip] 名 綿羊
▶ Whenever I can't fall asleep, I count sheep. 每次我睡不著，我就會數羊。

shelter [`ʃɛltɚ] 名 躲避處
▶ Animals seek shelter from storms.
動物在暴風雨時會找躲避處。
相關衍生字彙 shepherd [`ʃɛpɚd] 名 牧羊人、shield [`ʃild] 動 保護、protect [prəˋtɛkt]
動 保護、protection [prəˋtɛkʃən] 名 保護

shift [ʃɪft] 動 轉移
▶ The typhoon will shift to the north.
颱風將北轉。
動詞三態變化 shift - shifted - shifted

shine [ʃaɪn] 動 照耀
▶ The sun shone all morning.
整個早上太陽高照。
動詞三態變化 shine - shone / shined - shone / shined

ship [ʃɪp] 名 船　　片 to launch a ship 讓船下水
相關衍生字彙 shipping [`ʃɪpɪŋ] 名 海運業、shipwreck [`ʃɪpˌrɛk] 名 船難，海難、
shipment [`ʃɪpmənt] 名 裝運

shirt [ʃɝt] 名 襯衫　　片 a short-sleeved shirt 短袖襯衫

shiver [ˋʃɪvɚ] 動 顫抖
▶ The cat is shivering.
這隻小貓一直在發抖。
動詞三態變化 shiver - shivered - shivered

shock [ʃɑk] 動 震驚
▶ The bad news shocked me.
這則壞消息使我震驚。
動詞三態變化 shock - shocked - shocked

shocking [ˋʃɑkɪŋ] 形 令人震驚的
▶ The murder is shocking for the local people.
對當地人而言，這命案太令人震驚了。

shoe [ʃu] 名 鞋子　　片 a pair of shoes 一雙鞋

shoot [ʃut] 動 開槍　　片 to shoot at 朝～開槍
動詞三態變化 shoot - shot - shot

shop [ʃɑp] 動 購物　　片 to go shopping 去購物
動詞三態變化 shop - shopped - shopped

shortcut [ˋʃɔrtˏkʌt] 名 捷徑
▶ There is no shortcut to learning.
學習無捷徑。
相關衍生字彙 short [ʃɔrt] 形 短的、shortage [ˋʃɔrtɪdʒ] 名 短缺、shortcoming [ˋʃɔrtˏkʌmɪŋ]
名 缺點、shorten [ˋʃɔrtn̩] 動 使變短、shortly [ˋʃɔrtlɪ] 副 馬上

shoulder [ˋʃoldɚ] 名 肩膀
▶ The rain keeps falling on my head and shoulders.
雨水不斷打在我的頭和肩膀上。

shower [ˋʃauɚ] 名 淋浴　　片 to take a shower 淋浴

shrink [ʃrɪŋk] 動 退縮
▶ Never shrink from your responsibility.
不要逃避你的責任。
動詞三態變化 shrink - shrank / shrunk - shrunk / shrunken

shuttle [ˋʃʌtl̩] 名 接駁車
▶ The school shuttles carry students every day. 校車每天載送學生。

sickness [ˋsɪknɪs] 名 生病
▶ Because of mountain sickness, I stopped climbing.
因為高山症，我就沒再爬山了。

S

siege [sidʒ] 名 包圍　　　　　　　　　　　🔘 MP3 **19-07**
▶ The castle was in a state of siege. 城堡被包圍了。

sight [saɪt] 名 視力
▶ Out of sight, out of mind. （諺語）眼不見心不念（離久情疏）。

sightseeing [`saɪtˌsiɪŋ] 名 觀光　　🅟 to do sightseeing 觀光遊覽
相關衍生字彙 sightsee [`saɪtˌsi] 動 遊覽，觀光、sightseer [`saɪtˌsiɚ] 名 觀光客

sign [saɪn] 名 跡象
▶ She shows no sign of sadness. 她沒有任何悲傷的跡象。

signal [`sɪgnḷ] 動 發信號
▶ They signaled for help.
　他們發出求救信號。
動詞三態變化 signal - signaled - signaled

signature [`sɪgnətʃɚ] 名 簽名
▶ The check needs your signature. 這張支票需要你的簽名。

significant [sɪg`nɪfəkənt] 形 重要的　　🔵 important [ɪm`pɔrtṇt] 形 重要的

silence [`saɪləns] 名 沉默
▶ Sometimes, silence is gold. 有時候沉默是金。

silent [`saɪlənt] 形 安靜的，沉默的
▶ If you don't know how to answer, keep silent. 如果不知如何回答，就保持沉默。

silly [`sɪlɪ] 形 愚笨的，傻的
▶ Don't be silly! 別傻了！

silver [`sɪlvɚ] 名 銀　　🅟 pure silver 純銀

similar [`sɪmələ] 形 相似的　　🅟 be similar to 與～相似

sincerely [sɪn`sɪrlɪ] 副 真摯地
▶ I express my appreciation sincerely. 我誠摯表達謝意。

sincerity [sɪn`sɛrətɪ] 名 誠摯　　🅟 in all sincerity 非常誠懇地

sing [sɪŋ] 動 唱歌　　🅟 to sing a song 唱首歌
動詞三態變化 sing - sang - sung

single [`sɪŋgḷ] 形 單身的
▶ She is a jobless single mother. 她是一位失業的單親媽媽。

sink [sɪŋk] 動 沉沒
▶ The ship is sinking.
　船隻正在沉沒。

動詞三態變化 sink - sank / sunk - sunk / sunken

sister [`sɪstɚ] 名 姊妹　　 反 brother [`brʌðɚ] 名 兄弟

situated [`sɪtʃuˌetɪd] 形 座落在～的，位於～的
▶ The hospital was situated near the train station.
　醫院坐落在車站旁。
相關衍生字彙 locate [lo`ket] 動 使～座落於、place [ples] 動 放置，安置、position [pə`zɪʃən]
　　　　　　名 位置，地點、sit [sɪt] 動 座落於，位於、perch [pɝtʃ] 動 把～置於（較高或較險處）

situation [ˌsɪtʃu`eʃən] 名 情況
▶ Now is an emergency situation. 現在是緊急狀況。

skating [`sketɪŋ] 名 溜冰　　 片 figure skating 花式溜冰　　　　 MP3 19-08

skeleton [`skɛlətn̩] 名 骨骼
▶ A doctor should be familiar with the human skeleton.
　醫生要非常熟悉人體的骨骼。

skeptical [`skɛptɪkl̩] 形 懷疑的
▶ I am still skeptical about the good news. 我還是對這個好消息存疑。

sketch [skɛtʃ] 名 素描
▶ He drew a sketch of his girlfriend. 他畫了女朋友的素描。

skill [`skɪl] 名 技術
▶ It takes practice to master a skill.
　要掌握技術需要練習。
相關衍生字彙 skillful [`skɪlfəl] 形 熟練的、skilled [skɪld] 形 有技能的、expert [`ɛkspɝt]
　　　　　　名 專家、unskillful [ˌʌn`skɪlfəl] 形 不熟練的

skim [skɪm] 動 瀏覽，略讀
▶ Every morning, I skim through the newspaper quickly.
　我每天早上都會快速地瀏覽報紙。
動詞三態變化 skim - skimmed - skimmed

S

skin-deep [`skɪn`dip] 形 膚淺的
▶ Beauty is skin deep. 美貌是膚淺的。

sky [skaɪ] 名 天空
▶ Stars are shining in the sky. 星星在天空閃爍。

slander [`slændɚ] 名 誹謗
▶ If you continue to say so, I will sue you for slander.
　如果你繼續這麼說，我會控告你誹謗。
相關衍生字彙 insult [ɪn`sʌlt] 動 侮辱、defame [dɪ`fem] 動 毀謗、rumor [`rumɚ]
　　　　　　名 謠言，傳聞、humiliation [hjuˌmɪlɪ`eʃən] 名 羞辱

slang [slæŋ] 名 俚語
▶ When you are learning a foreign language, you will find the slang hard to understand.
學習外語時，你會發現俚語很難懂。

---

slaughter [ˋslɔtɚ] 動 大屠殺
▶ Countless people were slaughtered during the war.
數不盡的人們在戰爭中被屠殺。
動詞三態變化 slaughter - slaughtered - slaughtered

---

slavery [ˋslevərɪ] 名 奴隸制度
▶ Slavery once existed in America. 奴隸制度曾經存在於美國。

---

sleepy [ˋslipɪ] 形 昏昏欲睡的　　片 to feel sleepy 覺得昏昏欲睡
相關衍生字彙 sleep [slip] 動 睡覺、asleep [əˋslip] 形 睡著的、drowsy [ˋdrauzɪ] 形 昏昏欲睡的、tired [taɪrd] 形 疲憊的

---

sleigh [sle] 名 雪橇
▶ Sleighs are usually pulled by dogs. 雪橇通常是小狗在拉的。

---

slender [ˋslɛndɚ] 形 纖細的
▶ Her slender waist is very attractive. 她纖細的腰很迷人。

---

slogan [ˋslogən] 名 標語，口號
▶ The advertising slogan is very popular with the teenagers.
這個廣告標語非常受青少年的歡迎。

---

slow [slo] 形 緩慢的
▶ I was often slow to react.
我常常反應很慢。
相關衍生字彙 slowly [ˋslolɪ] 副 慢慢地、slowdown [ˋslo͵daun] 名 減速、fast [fæst] 副 快速地、quickly [ˋkwɪklɪ] 副 快地

---

sluggish [ˋslʌgɪʃ] 形 懶散的，蕭條的　　片 a sluggish market 蕭條的市場

---

small [smɔl] 形 小的　　反 big [bɪg] 形 大的

---

smart [smɑrt] 形 聰明的
▶ I am not smart enough to fix the laptop by myself.
我還不夠聰明無法自己修電腦。

---

smash [smæʃ] 動 猛撞　　　　　　　　　　　　　MP3 **19-09**
▶ The truck suddenly smashed into the car.
卡車突然猛撞上汽車。
動詞三態變化 smash - smashed - smashed

smell [smɛl] 動 聞到

▶ I smelled something burning in the kitchen.
我聞到廚房有燒焦味。

動詞三態變化 smell - smelled / smelt - smelled / smelt

smile [smaɪl] 動 微笑

▶ The girl smiled sweetly at me.
女孩對我甜甜地微笑著。

動詞三態變化 smile - smiled - smiled

smoke [smok] 動 抽菸　　片 No smoking! 禁止吸菸！

相關衍生字彙 smoky [`smokɪ] 形 冒煙的、smoker [`smokɚ] 名 抽菸者、cigarette [ˌsɪgə`rɛt]
名 香菸

動詞三態變化 smoke - smoked - smoked

smoothly [smuðlɪ] 副 順利地

▶ We finished the project smoothly. 我們順利地完成這項計畫。

smuggle [`smʌgl] 動 走私

▶ It's illegal to smuggle goods across the border.
將貨物走私過境是違法的。

動詞三態變化 smuggle - smuggled - smuggled

sneak [snik] 動 偷偷進入

▶ John sneaked into the meeting room through the back door.
約翰偷偷從後門進入會議室。

動詞三態變化 sneak - sneaked / snuck - sneaked / snuck

sneeze [sniz] 動 打噴嚏

▶ The cold air made me sneeze.
冷空氣讓我打噴嚏。

動詞三態變化 sneeze - sneezed - sneezed

snow [sno] 動 下雪

▶ Suddenly, it snowed.
突然間下起雪來。

相關衍生字彙 snowball [`sno,bɔl] 名 雪球、snowy [snoɪ] 形 下雪的、snowman [`sno,mæn]
名 雪人、snowflake [`sno,flek] 名 雪花，雪片

動詞三態變化 snow - snowed - snowed

S

soak [sok] 動 浸泡

▶ In winter, I like to soak in a hot bath.
在冬天，我喜歡泡熱水澡。

動詞三態變化 soak - soaked - soaked

sob [sɑb] 動 啜泣
▶ The boy sobbed and said he wanted to see his mother.
這位男孩啜泣著說要見他的媽媽。
動詞三態變化 sob - sobbed - sobbed

---

social [ˋsoʃəl] 形 社會的　　片 social work 社會福利工作
相關衍生字彙 socialist [ˋsoʃəlɪst] 名 社會主義者、society [səˋsaɪətɪ] 名 社會、
sociology [ˏsoʃɪˋɑlədʒɪ] 名 社會學

---

sock [sɑk] 名 襪子　　片 knee socks 及膝襪

---

soft [sɔft] 形 柔軟的
▶ The pillow was so soft that I fell asleep soon.
枕頭好柔軟，所以我很快就睡著了。
相關衍生字彙 soften [ˋsɔfn̩] 動 軟化、software [ˋsɔftˏwɛr] 名 軟體、softly [ˋsɔftlɪ]
副 柔軟地、softball [ˋsɔftˏbɔl] 名 壘球

---

soil [sɔɪl] 名 土壤
▶ The farmer fertilizes the soil. 農夫為土壤施肥。

---

solar [ˋsolɚ] 形 太陽的　　片 the solar system 太陽系

---

soldier [ˋsoldʒɚ] 名 士兵
▶ His father is a professional soldier. 他爸爸是個職業軍人。

---

solid [ˋsɑlɪd] 形 固體的　　反 liquid [ˋlɪkwɪd] 形 液體的

---

solution [səˋluʃən] 名 解決
▶ All the engineers in the office are finding a solution to the problem.
辦公室的工程師正在找尋此問題的解決方案。
相關衍生字彙 solve [sɑlv] 動 解決、answer [ˋænsɚ] 動 回答、explain [ɪkˋsplen] 動 解釋、
fix [fɪks] 動 修理

---

song [sɔŋ] 名 歌曲　　片 to write a song 寫歌

---

soothe [suð] 動 安撫　　　　　　　　　　　　　MP3 19-10
▶ I don't know how to soothe his sadness.
我不知如何安撫他的悲傷。
動詞三態變化 soothe - soothed - soothed

---

sophisticated [səˋfɪstɪˏketɪd] 形 世故的，練達的
▶ She is a sophisticated career woman. 她是個處事練達的職業婦女。

---

sorrow [ˋsɑro] 名 悲傷
▶ I won't mention my personal sorrow.
我不再提及個人的傷心事。
相關衍生字彙 sorrowful [ˋsɑrəfəl] 形 傷心的、sorry [ˋsɑrɪ] 形 難過的、sad [sæd] 形 悲傷的、
grief [grif] 名 悲傷

sort [sɔrt] 名 種類　　⑩ kind [kaɪnd] 名 種類

soul [sol] 名 靈魂
▶ Religion saves my soul. 宗教拯救了我的靈魂。

sound [saʊnd] 形 健康的，健全的　　㊉ safe and sound 安然無恙

soup [sup] 名 湯　　㊉ thick soup 濃湯

source [sors] 名 來源
▶ The news comes from a reliable source. 這消息來自可靠的來源。

south [saʊθ] 名 南方　　㊏ north [nɔrθ] 名 北方

souvenir [`suvəˌnɪr] 名 紀念品
▶ How sweet of you to bring me a souvenir! 你真好，還幫我帶紀念品！

sovereignty [`savrɪntɪ] 名 主權
▶ A country's sovereignty can't be violated. 一個國家的主權不能被侵犯。

space [spes] 名 空間，太空　　㊉ outer space 外太空
相關衍生字彙 spacecraft [`spesˌkræft] 名 太空船、spaceship [`spesˌʃɪp] 名 太空船、spaceman [`spesˌmæn] 名 太空人、spacesuit [`spesˌsut] 名 太空衣

span [spæn] 名 一段時間　　㊉ a life span 壽命

spare [spɛr] 形 額外的，多餘的 動 騰出　　㊉ a spare room 客房
動詞三態變化 spare - spared - spared

spark [spɑrk] 名 火花
▶ A spark may lead to a fire. 小火花也可能釀成火災。

speak [spik] 動 說話
▶ Actions speak louder than words.
（諺語）事實勝於雄辯。
相關衍生字彙 spokesman [`spoksmən] 名 男發言人、spokeswoman [`spoksˌwʊmən] 名 女發言人、spokesperson [`spoksˌpɝsn̩] 名 發言人
動詞三態變化 speak - spoke - spoken

species [`spiʃiz] 名 物種
▶ Pandas are an engendered species. 貓熊是瀕臨滅絕的物種。

specific [spɪ`sɪfɪk] 形 特定的
▶ The course is offered for a specific age group.
這個課程是設計給特定的年齡族群上的。

specimen [`spɛsəmən] 名 樣品，樣本　　㊉ a blood specimen 血液樣本

S

special [`spɛʃəl] 形 特別的　　片 special delivery 限時專送
相關衍生字彙 specialize [`spɛʃəˌlaɪz] 動 專攻、specially [`spɛʃəlɪ] 副 特別地、
specialty [`spɛʃəltɪ] 名 專長

speculation [ˌspɛkjəˈleʃən] 名 猜測　　　　　　　◎ MP3 **19-11**
▶ There has been a great deal of speculation about their marriage.
他們的婚姻還是存在很多疑點。

speech [spitʃ] 名 言論，演講
▶ The writer will make a speech to the students. 這位作家將對學生做演講。

speed [spid] 名 速度　　片 speed limit 速限
相關衍生字彙 speedy [`spidɪ] 形 快速的、rapid [`ræpɪd] 形 快的、fast [fæst] 形 快的、
hasty [`hestɪ] 形 匆忙的、swift [swɪft] 形 快速的

spelling [`spɛlɪŋ] 名 拼字
▶ My computer can correct my spelling. 我的電腦會幫我校正拼字。

spend [spɛnd] 動 花費
▶ I spent my savings on travelling.
我把儲蓄都花在旅遊上。
動詞三態變化 spend - spent - spent

spill [spɪl] 動 撒
▶ I'm so sorry I spilled my coffee on your skirt.
真的很抱歉，我把咖啡灑到妳的裙子上。
動詞三態變化 spill - spilled / spilt - spilled / spilt

spirit [`spɪrɪt] 名 精神，活力　　片 in high / low spirits 開心／傷心

spiritual [`spɪrɪtʃuəl] 形 精神的，心靈的
▶ Reading fulfills my spiritual needs. 閱讀滿足我的精神需求。

splendid [`splɛndɪd] 形 燦爛的
▶ The queen is wearing a splendid necklace.
王后戴著燦爛的項鍊
相關衍生字彙 splendor [`splɛndɚ] 名 光輝、glory [`glorɪ] 名 燦爛、brightness [`braɪtnɪs]
名 光亮

spoil [spɔɪl] 動 寵壞
▶ Spare the rod and spoil the child.
（諺語）不打不成器。
動詞三態變化 spoil - spoiled / spoilt - spoiled / spoilt

sponge [spʌndʒ] 名 海綿
▶ A sponge can absorb a lot of water. 海綿可以吸很多水。

sponsor [ˋspɑnsɚ] 動 贊助
▶ Our club was sponsored by a big company.
我們的社團是由一家大公司所贊助的。
動詞三態變化 sponsor - sponsored - sponsored

spoon [spun] 名 湯匙　　🈁 a soup spoon 湯匙
相關衍生字彙 spoonful [ˋspun͵ful] 名 一匙的量、teaspoon [ˋti͵spun] 名 茶匙、fork [fɔrk] 名 叉子、knife [naɪf] 名 刀子

sport [sport] 名 運動
▶ I enjoy team sports, such as football. 我喜歡團隊運動，如足球。

sportsmanship [ˋsportsmən͵ʃɪp] 名 運動家精神
▶ Although we lost the game, we displayed sportsmanship.
儘管我們輸了，但我們仍展現了運動家精神。

spot [spɑt] 名 斑點，地點　　🈁 on the spot 當場

spotlight [ˋspɑt͵laɪt] 名 聚光燈　　🈁 in the spotlight 備受矚目的

sprawl [sprɔl] 動 伸開手足躺或坐著
▶ After work, he sprawled on the sofa.
下班後，他攤開四肢懶散地躺在沙發上。
動詞三態變化 sprawl - sprawled - sprawled

spray [spre] 動 噴灑　　🈁 to spray chemicals 噴灑化學藥劑
動詞三態變化 spray - sprayed - sprayed

spread [sprɛd] 動 傳播，擴散
▶ The rumor spread so quickly.
謠言很快就傳開來了。
動詞三態變化 spread - spread - spread

spring [sprɪŋ] 名 春天　　◉ MP3 **19-12**
▶ Easter comes in spring.
復活節在春天。
相關衍生字彙 spring [sprɪŋ] 動 彈跳、spring [sprɪŋ] 名 泉水、springboard [ˋsprɪŋ͵bord] 名 跳板

spur [spɝ] 動 刺激
▶ What spurred you to do so?
是什麼刺激你這麼做的？
動詞三態變化 spur - spurred - spurred

S

spy [spaɪ] 動 祕密收集情報，當間諜
▶ He risks his life to spy for the government.
他冒著生命危險替政府從事間諜活動。
相關衍生字彙 detective [dɪ`tɛktɪv] 名 偵探、investigator [ɪn`vɛstə͵getɚ] 名 調查者、
procurator [`prɑkjə͵retɚ] 名 檢察官
動詞三態變化 spy - spied - spied

squash [skwɑʃ] 動 壓扁
▶ I accidently squashed your container.
我不小心壓扁你的容器。
動詞三態變化 squash - squashed - squashed

squeeze [skwiz] 動 擠壓　　片 to squeeze the toothpaste 擠牙膏
動詞三態變化 squeeze - squeezed - squeezed

stability [stə`bɪlətɪ] 名 穩定，穩固
▶ With the emotional stability, they fall in love soon.
有了穩定的情感，他們很快的就墜入了情網。

stadium [`stedɪəm] 名 體育場
▶ The stadium is full of fans watching the game.
體育場擠滿看比賽的球迷。

staff [stæf] 名 全體員工
▶ There are more than one hundred staff in the school.
這所學校員工超過百人。

stage [stedʒ] 名 舞台　　片 stage fright 怯場

stagger [`stægɚ] 動 搖晃，蹣跚
▶ He staggered into the house carrying a heavy box.
他搬著大箱子蹣跚進屋。
動詞三態變化 stagger - staggered - staggered

stair [stɛr] 名 樓梯
▶ I have to climb the stairs to the fifth floor every day.
我每天得爬樓梯到五樓。
相關衍生字彙 staircase [`stɛr͵kes] 名 樓梯間、upstairs [`ʌp`stɛrz] 副 上樓、
downstairs [͵daʊn`stɛrz] 副 下樓

stammer [`stæmɚ] 動 結巴
▶ When she is nervous, she always stammers.
她緊張時，總是會結巴。
動詞三態變化 stammer - stammered - stammered

stamp [stæmp] 名 郵票　　片 stamp collecting 集郵

standard [`stændɚd]名 標準
▶ The standard of living keeps rising. 生活水準持續攀升。

standstill [`stænd‚stɪl]名 停止，停頓
片 to come to a complete standstill 完全停止
相關衍生字彙 stand [stænd]動 站立、standpoint [`stænd‚pɔɪnt]名 立足點，立場、standby [`stænd‚baɪ]形 備用的

stare [stɛr]動 凝視
▶ Don't stare at me!
別一直看著我！
動詞三態變化 stare - stared - stared

start [stɑrt]動 開始　　同 begin [bɪ`gɪn]動 開始
動詞三態變化 start - started - started

startle [`stɑrtḷ]動 吃驚
▶ The noise startled me out of my sleep.
噪音使我從睡夢中驚醒。
動詞三態變化 startle - startled - startled

starvation [stɑr`veʃən]名 飢餓
▶ Many people are still facing the problem of starvation.
仍有很多人面臨飢餓的問題。
相關衍生字彙 starve [stɑrv]動 挨餓、starving [`stɑrvɪŋ]形 飢餓的、hungry [`hʌŋgrɪ]形 飢餓的、hunger [`hʌŋgɚ]名 飢餓、appetite [`æpə‚taɪt]名 食慾，胃口

statement [`stetmənt]名 陳述
▶ Please judge which statement is wrong. 請判斷哪一個陳述是錯誤的。

station [`steʃən]名 車站　　片 a train station 火車站　　◉ MP3 19-13
相關衍生字彙 stationary [`steʃən‚ɛrɪ]形 不動的、stationery [`steʃən‚ɛrɪ]名 文具、stop [stɑp]名 站牌、railway [`rel‚we]名 鐵軌，鐵道

S

statistics [stə`tɪstɪks]名 統計
▶ Statistics show that men get higher salary than women.
統計顯示，男人薪水比女人高。

statue [`stætʃʊ]名 雕像　　片 the Statue of Liberty 自由女神像

status [`stetəs]名 地位
▶ To seek status, he gives up his love. 為了追求地位，他放棄愛情。

stay [ste] 動 停留
▶ I will stay here waiting for you.
我會待在這裡等你。
動詞三態變化 stay - stayed - stayed

steadily [`stɛdəlɪ] 副 穩定地
▶ The prices of houses keep rising steadily. 房價穩定地升高。

steal [stil] 動 偷
▶ His car was stolen last night.
他的車子昨晚被偷了。
動詞三態變化 steal - stole - stolen

stereotype [`stɛrɪəˌtaɪp] 名 刻板印象　　片 to break the stereotype 打破刻板印象

stimulate [`stɪmjəˌlet] 動 刺激　　片 to stimulate the economy 刺激經濟
動詞三態變化 stimulate - stimulated - stimulated

stir [stɜ] 名 騷動
▶ The actor's love affair causes a stir. 這名演員的緋聞引起騷動。

stock [stak] 名 股市　　片 a stock exchange 證券交易所
相關衍生字彙 stockbroker [`stakˌbrokɚ] 名 股票經紀人、stockholder [`stakˌholdɚ] 名 股東

stomach [`stʌmək] 名 胃
▶ The dirty food upset my stomach. 不乾淨的食物讓我的胃不舒服。

stoppage [`stapɪdʒ] 名 停工，罷工
▶ There was a stoppage at the airport.
機場有罷工。
相關衍生字彙 stop [stap] 動 停止、strike [straɪk] 名 罷工、stopover [`stapˌovɚ] 名 中途停留、
stopwatch [`stapˌwatʃ] 名 碼錶

stormy [`stɔrmɪ] 形 暴躁的
▶ Our boss has a stormy temper. 我們老闆的脾氣很暴躁。

story [`storɪ] 名 故事
▶ It's a long story. 說來話長。

straight [stret] 形 直的 副 直地
▶ Go straight along the road, and you will find the market.
沿著這條路直走，就會找到市場了。

straighten [`stretn̩] 動 整理　　片 to straighten something up 把～弄乾淨
動詞三態變化 straighten - straightened - straightened

strange [strendʒ] 形 陌生的
▶ The environment is strange to me.
這環境對我而言很陌生。
相關衍生字彙 stranger [`strendʒɚ] 名 陌生人、familiar [fə`mɪljɚ] 形 熟悉的、
unfamiliar [ˌʌnfə`mɪljɚ] 形 不熟的

---

stray [stre] 形 迷路的，走失的　　片 stray cats / dogs 流浪貓／狗

---

stream [strim] 名 溪流，流動
▶ Customers came to the store in streams. 客人川流不息地來這家店。

---

street [strit] 名 街道　　◎ MP3 **19-14**
▶ Both of us live on the same street. 我們住在同一條街上。

---

strength [strɛŋθ] 名 力氣
▶ I don't have enough strength to carry the heavy box.
我沒有足夠的力氣來搬這個大箱子。

---

strengthen [`strɛŋθən] 動 強化
▶ Knowledge can strengthen your competitive ability.
知識可以強化你的競爭力。
動詞三態變化 strengthen - strengthened - strengthened

---

strenuous [`strɛnjuəs] 形 奮力的
▶ I made strenuous efforts to improve my life. 我很努力的改善生活。

---

stress [strɛs] 名 壓力
▶ I won't be weighed down by the stress of work.
我不會被工作的壓力給壓垮。
相關衍生字彙 force [fors] 名 力量，影響、pressure [`prɛʃɚ] 名 壓力，壓迫、
tension [`tɛnʃən] 名（精神上的）緊張、burden [`bɝdn̩] 名 負擔

---

stretch [strɛtʃ] 動 伸展
▶ You can relax yourself by stretching your arms.
你可以伸展手臂放鬆一下。
動詞三態變化 stretch - stretched - stretched

---

strict [strɪkt] 形 嚴格的
▶ The teacher is very strict with her students, but she is very kind.
雖然老師對學生很嚴格，可是她非常善良。
相關衍生字彙 strictly [`strɪktlɪ] 副 嚴格地、harsh [hɑrʃ] 形 嚴厲的、generous [`dʒɛnərəs]
形 慷慨的、kind [kaɪnd] 形 善良的

---

strike [straɪk] 名 罷工　　片 to go on strike 進行罷工

S

strip [strɪp] 動 剝除
▶ On seeing the river, kids stripped off their clothes and jumped into it.
一看到河流,孩子們便脫掉衣服跳進去。
動詞三態變化 strip - stripped / stript - stripped / stript

stripe [straɪp] 名 線條
▶ She wore a dress with red stripes. 她穿了件紅色條紋的洋裝。

strive [straɪv] 動 奮鬥,努力
▶ More and more women strive to be successful career women.
愈來愈多婦女努力要當成功的職業婦女。
動詞三態變化 strive - strived / strove - strived / striven

stroke [strok] 名 一次努力,中風   片 at a stroke 一舉,一下子

stroll [strol] 動 散步
▶ I enjoy strolling along the path in the woods.
我很喜歡沿著樹林裡的小徑散步。
動詞三態變化 stroll - strolled - strolled

strong [strɔŋ] 形 強壯的   片 strong winds 強風
相關衍生字彙 forceful [`fɔrsfəl] 形 強有力的、powerful [`pauɚfəl] 形 強有力的、mighty [`maɪtɪ] 形 強大的、sturdy [`stɝdɪ] 形 健壯的,堅固的、solid [`salɪd] 形 堅固的

structure [`strʌktʃɚ] 名 結構
▶ The structure of the building is very strong. 這棟建築物的結構非常堅固。

struggle [`strʌgl] 動 掙扎
▶ They struggled for their ideal that everyone was born equal.
他們為了人人生而平等的理想而奮鬥。
動詞三態變化 struggle - struggled - struggled

stubborn [`stʌbɚn] 形 固執的
▶ He is so stubborn that his friends don't want to communicate with him.
他是如此固執,所以他的朋友都不想跟他溝通了。

stuff [stʌf] 名 東西
▶ Before I moved, I got rid of all the old stuff. 在搬家前,我丟掉所有的舊東西。

stumble [`stʌmbl] 動 絆倒
▶ I stumbled on a stone and got hurt.
我被石頭絆倒而受傷。
動詞三態變化 stumble - stumbled - stumbled

stupid [`stjupɪd] 形 愚蠢的
▶ How stupid of me to trust him! 我怎麼會笨到去相信他！

sturdy [`stɝdɪ] 形 結實的　　　　　　　　　　　　MP3 **19-15**
▶ You need a pair of sturdy walking boots if you like hiking in the mountains.
如果你喜歡到山區健行，你需要一雙耐用的靴子。

style [staɪl] 名 風格
▶ A black dress is always formal and in style.
黑色洋裝永遠都是正式且時尚的。

相關衍生字彙 stylish [`staɪlɪʃ] 形 時尚的、fashion [`fæʃən] 名 流行，時尚、
popular [`pɑpjələ] 形 流行的、designer [dɪ`zaɪnə] 名 設計師

subject [`sʌbdʒɪkt] 名 主題
▶ The subject of my thesis is about globalization. 我的論文主題是關於全球化。

subjective [səb`dʒɛktɪv] 形 主觀的　　反 objective [əb`dʒɛktɪv] 形 客觀的

sublime [sə`blaɪm] 形 崇高的
▶ I admire his sublime goal in life. 我很讚賞他崇高的人生目標。

submarine [`sʌbmərin] 名 潛水艇　　片 a nuclear submarine 核能潛艇

submerge [səb`mɝdʒ] 動 淹沒
▶ The flood submerged the whole village.
洪水淹沒了整個村莊。

動詞三態變化 submerge - submerged - submerged

submit [səb`mɪt] 動 提交
▶ We are all asked to submit our assignments on time.
我們都被要求要準時繳交作業。

動詞三態變化 submit - submitted - submitted

subscribe [səb`skraɪb] 動 訂購，訂閱
▶ I subscribed to the magazine for my daughter.
我幫我女兒訂閱了雜誌。

相關衍生字彙 subscription [səb`skrɪpʃən] 名 訂閱、order [`ɔrdə] 動 訂購、buy [baɪ] 動 購買、
purchase [`pɝtʃəs] 動 購買、shop [ʃɑp] 動 採購

動詞三態變化 subscribe - subscribed - subscribed

substance [`sʌbstəns] 名 物質
▶ The coat is made of a waterproof substance. 這件外套是防水材質製成的。

substitute [`sʌbstə،tjut] 動 代替
▶ Our English teacher was absent today and Mark substituted her.
我們的英文老師今天缺席，由馬克來代課。

動詞三態變化 substitute - substituted - substituted

S

subtle [`sʌtl̩] 形 微妙的　　片 a subtle change 微妙的變化

subtract [səb`trækt] 動 減去　　反 plus [plʌs] 動 加上
動詞三態變化 subtract - subtracted - subtracted

---

suburb [`sʌbɝb] 名 郊區
▶ We decided to buy a new house in the suburbs. 我們決定要到郊外買新房子。

---

subway [`sʌbˌwe] 名 地下鐵
▶ Many commuters depend on the subway system every day.
很多通勤者每天依賴此地鐵系統。

---

succeed [sək`sid] 動 成功
▶ She finally succeeded in passing the exam.
她終於成功通過考試了。
相關衍生字彙 success [sək`sɛs] 名 成功、successful [sək`sɛsfəl] 形 成功的、
successfully [sək`sɛsfəlɪ] 副 成功地、successor [sək`sɛsɚ] 名 繼任者
動詞三態變化 succeed - succeeded - succeeded

---

suck [sʌk] 動 吸吮
▶ The baby is sucking his thumb.
這嬰兒一直吸他的大拇指。
動詞三態變化 suck - sucked - sucked

---

sudden [`sʌdn̩] 形 突然的　　片 all of a sudden 突然地

suddenly [`sʌdn̩lɪ] 副 突然間
▶ All the things happened so suddenly. 所有的事情都發生得太突然了。

---

suffer [`sʌfɚ] 動 受苦於
▶ I have suffered from chronic diseases since I was young.
從年輕開始，我就一直為慢性疾病所苦。
動詞三態變化 suffer - suffered - suffered

---

sufficient [sə`fɪʃənt] 形 足夠的　　◎ MP3 **19-16**
▶ The food my mother prepared should be sufficient for the class.
我媽媽準備的食物應該夠全班吃。

---

suffocate [`sʌfəˌket] 動 使窒息
▶ The smoke almost suffocated me.
這煙霧差點讓我窒息。
動詞三態變化 suffocate - suffocated - suffocated

---

sugar [`ʃugɚ] 名 糖　　反 salt [sɔlt] 名 鹽巴
相關衍生字彙 sauce [sɔs] 名 醬汁、vinegar [`vɪnɪgɚ] 名 醋、pepper [`pɛpɚ] 名 胡椒粉、
seasoning [`siznɪŋ] 名 調味料

suggest [sə`dʒɛst] 動 建議
▶ I suggest you try the Italian restaurant.
我建議你們試試這家義大利餐廳。
動詞三態變化 suggest - suggested - suggested

suggestion [sə`dʒɛstʃən] 名 建議　　片 to make a suggestion 提出建議

suggestive [sə`dʒɛstɪv] 形 性暗示的,挑逗的
▶ There are many suggestive words in his letter. 他信裡有很多性暗示的文字。

suicide [`suə͵saɪd] 名 自殺
▶ It's a pity the famous writer committed suicide when she was young.
很可惜,這位有名的作家在年輕時就自殺了。

suitable [`sutəbl] 形 適合的
▶ Short shorts are not suitable for a job interview.
面試工作時,不適合穿著超短短褲。
相關衍生字彙 suit [sut] 名 套裝、swimsuit [`swɪmsut] 名 泳裝、suitcase [`sut͵kes] 名 行李箱

sultry [`sʌltrɪ] 形 悶熱的,酷熱的
▶ I hate the sultry weather in summer. 我討厭夏天悶熱的天氣。

sum [sʌm] 動 總結　　片 to sum up 總之
動詞三態變化 sum - summed - summed

summary [`sʌmərɪ] 名 簡述,概要
▶ Please give me a summary of your plan. 請給我你的計畫概要。

summit [`sʌmɪt] 名 高峰會　　片 a summit meeting 高峰會議

summon [`sʌmən] 動 召喚,鼓起,喚起
片 to summon up the courage 鼓起勇氣
動詞三態變化 summon - summoned - summoned

sunbathe [`sʌn͵beð] 動 做日光浴
▶ Many people enjoy sunbathing at the beach.
很多人喜歡在沙灘做日光浴。
相關衍生字彙 sunshine [`sʌn͵ʃaɪn] 名 陽光、suntanned [`sʌntænd] 形 曬黑的、
sunrise [`sʌn͵raɪz] 名 日出、sunset [`sʌn͵sɛt] 名 日落、sunscreen [`sʌn͵skrin]
名 防曬乳
動詞三態變化 sunbathe - sunbathed - sunbathed

superficial [`supɚ`fɪʃəl] 形 外表的,表面上的
▶ The twins have superficial similarities. 雙胞胎在外表上有相似處。

superior [sə`pɪrɪɚ] 形 高級的
▶ The bag was made of superior leather. 這包包是高級皮製品。

S

superiority [sə͵pɪrɪ`ɔrətɪ] 名 優勢
▶ We can expect the superiority of our company.
　我們可以期待公司的優勢。

相關衍生字彙 supermarket [`supɚ͵markɪt] 名 超市、superman [`supɚ͵mæn] 名 超人、
　　superb [su`pɝb] 形 極優的、superbug [`supɚ͵bʌg] 名 超級細菌、
　　superstition [͵supɚ`stɪʃən] 名 迷信、superstar [`supɚ͵star] 名 超級巨星、
　　supernatural [͵supɚ`nætʃərəl] 形 超自然的

---

supervise [`supɚ͵vaɪz] 動 指導，管理
▶ The general manager supervises all the departments in the company.
　總經理管理公司的所有部門。

動詞三態變化 supervise - supervised - supervised

---

supper [`sʌpɚ] 名 晚餐　　同 dinner [`dɪnɚ] 名 晚餐

---

supplement [`sʌpləmənt] 名 補充品　　片 vitamin supplements 維他命補充品

---

supply [sə`plaɪ] 動 供應　　　　　　　　　　　　　　　MP3 19-17
▶ All the students will be supplied with lots of reading materials.
　大量的閱讀資料將會提供給所有學生。

動詞三態變化 supply - supplied - supplied

---

support [sə`port] 名 動 支持
▶ Without your support, it's impossible for me to fulfill my dream.
　沒有你的支持，我不可能完成夢想。

動詞三態變化 support - supported - supported

---

suppose [sə`poz] 動 認為可能，猜想
▶ I don't suppose that he would propose to me.
　我不認為他會向我求婚。

動詞三態變化 suppose - supposed - supposed

---

suppress [sə`prɛs] 動 鎮壓，封鎖
▶ News should not be suppressed.
　新聞不該被封鎖。

動詞三態變化 suppress - suppressed - suppressed

---

supreme [sə`prim] 形 至高的
▶ The Pope is regarded as a supreme leader. 教宗被視為是至高的領袖。

---

sure [ʃur] 形 確定的
▶ I am not sure if he will attend the meeting. 我不確定他是否會出席此會議。

---

surface [`sɝfɪs] 名 表面　　片 the surface of the Earth 地球表面

---

surgeon [`sɝdʒən] 名 外科醫生　　反 physician [fɪ`zɪʃən] 名 內科醫生

surgery [ˋsɝdʒərɪ] 名 手術
▶ The surgeon suggests my father have surgery on his heart.
外科醫師建議我爸爸動心臟外科手術。

----

surmount [sɚˋmaunt] 動 克服　　片 to surmount the obstacles 克服障礙
動詞三態變化 surmount - surmounted - surmounted

----

surname [ˋsɝ͵nem] 名 姓　　同 last name 名 姓氏

----

surpass [sɚˋpæs] 動 勝過
▶ His achievement has surpassed the previous world record.
他的成就已經超越先前的世界紀錄。
動詞三態變化 surpass - surpassed - surpassed

----

surplus [ˋsɝpləs] 名 剩餘
▶ Many countries have a surplus of food, while some are facing the starvation.
很多國家食物有剩餘，然而有些國家正面臨飢荒。
相關衍生字彙 extra [ˋɛkstrə] 形 額外的、leftover [ˋlɛft͵ovɚ] 形 殘餘的、additional [əˋdɪʃən] 形 額外的，附加的、remaining [rɪˋmenɪŋ] 形 剩下的

----

surprise [sɚˋpraɪz] 動 使驚訝
▶ I feel so surprised at the news that my son won the prize.
我兒子獲獎讓我好驚訝。
動詞三態變化 surprise - surprised - surprised

----

surrender [səˋrɛndɚ] 動 投降
▶ The thief finally surrendered himself to the police.
小偷終於向警察投降了。
動詞三態變化 surrender - surrendered - surrendered

----

surround [səˋraund] 動 包圍
▶ The house is surrounded by a rose garden.
在房子的四周是一座玫瑰花園。
動詞三態變化 surround - surrounded - surrounded

----

surroundings [səˋraundɪŋz] 名 周遭環境
▶ When you choose a house to buy, its surroundings are very important.
當你想買房子時，周遭環境是很重要的。
相關衍生字彙 environment [ɪnˋvaɪrənmənt] 名 環境、neighborhood [ˋnebɚ͵hud] 名 鄰近地區、border [ˋbɔrdɚ] 名 邊界

----

survey [ˋsɝve] 名 調查
▶ A recent survey shows that only twenty percent of people are satisfied with their jobs.
最近的調查顯示，只有百分之二十的人滿意他們的工作。

S

survival [sə`vaɪv̩] 名 存活　🔗 chance of survival 存活機會

survive [sə`vaɪv] 動 存活
▶ I was struggling to survive in such a terrible working environment.
在如此糟糕的工作環境，我仍努力存活著。
動詞三態變化 survive - survived - survived

suspect [sə`spɛkt] 動 懷疑　🎧 MP3 19-18
▶ We suspected that one of our coworkers did it.
我們都懷疑是某位同事做的。
動詞三態變化 suspect - suspected - suspected

suspend [sə`spɛnd] 動 中斷，中止
▶ The relationship with that country was suspended twenty years ago.
與那個國家的關係早在二十年前就中斷了。
相關衍生字彙 stop [stɑp] 動 停止，中止、interrupt [ˌɪntə`rʌpt] 動 打斷（講話或講話人）、halt [hɔlt] 動 停止，終止、standstill [`stænd‚stɪl] 名 停頓
動詞三態變化 suspend - suspended - suspended

suspicion [sə`spɪʃən] 名 猜疑　🔗 mutual suspicion 互相猜疑

suspicious [sə`spɪʃəs] 形 可疑的
▶ I am aware that her behavior was a little suspicious.
我有察覺到她的行為有點可疑。

sustain [sə`sten] 動 支持
▶ The belief has sustained me for a long time.
這個信念支持我很久了。
相關衍生字彙 maintain [men`ten] 動 維持、support [sə`port] 動 支持、uphold [ʌp`hold] 動 支持
動詞三態變化 sustain - sustained - sustained

swallow [`swɑlo] 動 吞下　🔗 to swallow one's words 承認自己說錯話
動詞三態變化 swallow - swallowed - swallowed

swarm [swɔrm] 名（昆蟲類的）群　🔗 a swarm of bees 一大群蜜蜂

sway [swe] 動 搖擺，動搖
▶ It's hard to make a final decision. I sway between two options.
很難做最後的決定，我在兩個選擇之間搖擺。
動詞三態變化 sway - swayed - swayed

swear [swɛr] 動 發誓
▶ I swear that I didn't tell you a lie.
我發誓，我沒有說謊。
動詞三態變化 swear - swore - sworn

sweat [swɛt] 名 汗水　　🅟 no sweat 毫不費力

---

sweater [`swɛtɚ] 名 毛衣
▶ A sweater can keep you warm. 毛衣可以保暖。

---

sweep [swip] 動 打掃
▶ I sweep my room regularly.
　我定期打掃我的房間。
〔相關衍生字彙〕 vacuum [`vækjuəm] 動 用吸塵器清掃、clean [klin] 動 做清潔工作、mop [mɑp]
　　　　　　　動 用拖把拖洗、wipe [waɪp] 動 擦拭
〔動詞三態變化〕 sweep - swept - swept

---

sweet [swit] 形 甜的，甜美的　　🅡 bitter [`bɪtɚ] 形 苦的

---

swell [swɛl] 動 腫脹
▶ My index finger started to swell. It must be broken.
　我的食指開始腫脹，它可能斷了。
〔動詞三態變化〕 swell - swelled - swelled

---

swift [swɪft] 形 快速的

---

swiftly [`swɪftlɪ] 副 快速地
▶ He is able to respond swiftly to the change of the markets.
　他總能迅速地對市場的改變作出反應。

---

swim [swɪm] 動 游泳
▶ The kid is good at swimming.
　這個孩子很擅長游泳。
〔相關衍生字彙〕 swimming [`swɪmɪŋ] 名 游泳（運動）、rafting [`ræftɪŋ] 名 泛舟（運動）、
　　　　　　　diving [`daɪvɪŋ] 名 潛水，跳水、lifeguard [`laɪf͵gɑrd] 名 救生員、
　　　　　　　snorkelling [`snɔrklɪŋ] 名 使用水下呼吸管潛泳、surfing [`sɝfɪŋ] 名 衝浪、
　　　　　　　sailing [`selɪŋ] 名 航海，航行
〔動詞三態變化〕 swim - swam - swum

---

switch [swɪtʃ] 動 開，關　　🅟 to switch on / off 打開開關／關掉開關
〔動詞三態變化〕 switch - switched - switched

---

sword [sord] 名 刀，劍
▶ The pen is mightier than the sword.（諺語）文勝於武。

---

syllabus [`sɪləbəs] 名 教學大綱
▶ All the professors prepare their syllabus of this semester for their students.
　所有的教授都會幫學生準備好這學期的教學大綱。

S

symbol [ˋsɪmbḷ] 名 象徵

MP3 **19-19**

▶ The red heart is used as the symbol of love. 紅色的心型代表愛情。

symmetry [ˋsɪmɪtrɪ] 名 對稱

▶ The design of the coat has a perfect symmetry.
這件外套的對稱性設計得很完美。

sympathize [ˋsɪmpəˏθaɪz] 動 同情

▶ I really sympathize with the kid whose parents were killed in that accident.
我非常同情這孩子，他的父母在意外中雙亡。

相關衍生字彙 sympathy [ˋsɪmpəθɪ] 名 同情心、sympathetic [ˏsɪmpəˋθɛtɪk] 形 有同情心的、
compassionate [kəmˋpæʃənɪt] 形 有同情心的

動詞三態變化 sympathize - sympathized - sympathized

symphony [ˋsɪmfənɪ] 名 交響曲，交響樂

▶ The symphony played by the top orchestra was so touching.
這首由頂尖管弦樂團所演奏的交響曲，實在太動人。

symptom [ˋsɪmptəm] 名 症狀

▶ One symptom of the disease is high fever. 這種疾病的症狀之一是發高燒。

synonym [ˋsɪnəˏnɪm] 名 同義字　　反 antonym [ˋæntəˏnɪm] 名 反義字

system [ˋsɪstəm] 名 系統　　片 the immune system 免疫系統

systematic [ˏsɪstəˋmætɪk] 形 有系統的

▶ The boss is always systematic in dealing with any problem.
老闆總是很有系統的在處理問題。

MEMO

一網打盡

T

字母

table ~ tyrant

一網打盡「英語小知識」| Beautiful v.s Pretty

▶ **beautiful** 可以用來形容人、事、物的美（內在外在皆可），尤其這樣的美能夠感動心靈或是愉悅感官。

▶ **pretty** 通常用來形容「有吸引力」的美，但不一定是真正的 **beautiful**，形容人或物皆可，而對象通常指年輕女性或小孩。

table ~ tyrant

★一網打盡 329 個英文單字 ｜ 一網打盡 124 句英語會話句

◎ MP3 **20-01**

table [`tebl̩] 名 桌子　　片 to set the table 擺好餐桌

---

tablet [`tæblɪt] 名 藥片
▶ Without taking a sleeping tablet, he can't fall asleep. 沒有吃安眠藥，他睡不著。

---

tackle [`tækl̩] 動 處理
▶ To tackle this problem, we need an engineer.
　要處理這個問題，我們需要一位工程師。
動詞三態變化 tackle - tackled - tackled

---

tag [tæg] 名 標籤
▶ Look at the price tag! The scarf is so expensive.
　看看這標價！這條圍巾真貴。

---

tail [tel] 名 尾巴
▶ Dogs express their happiness by wagging their tails. 小狗搖尾巴表示開心。

---

take [tek] 動 拿　　片 take care of 照顧，處理
動詞三態變化 take - took - taken

---

takeover [`tek͵ovɚ] 名 收購　　片 to make a takeover bid for sth 競價收購

---

talent [`tælənt] 名 天份
▶ Obviously, the kid has a talent for languages.
　很顯然地，這位孩子有語言天份。
相關衍生字彙 talented [`tæləntɪd] 形 有天份的、gifted [`gɪftɪd] 形 有天份的、
　　　　　　 genius [`dʒinjəs] 名 天賦

---

talk [tɔk] 名 動 談話
▶ I don't like to talk politics.
　我不想談論政治。
動詞三態變化 talk - talked - talked

---

tall [tɔl] 形 高的　　反 short [ʃɔrt] 形 矮的

---

tame [tem] 形 溫馴的
▶ The lion is very tame. 這隻獅子很溫馴。

---

tangle [`tæŋgl̩] 動 使糾纏
▶ The cat tangled the yarn.
　貓咪把毛線弄亂了。
動詞三態變化 tangle - tangled - tangled

---

target [`tɑrgɪt] 名 目標　　片 to hit the target 射中靶子

相關衍生字彙 goal [gol] 名 目標、object [ˋabdʒɪkt] 名 目標，對象、aim [em] 名 目標、
destination [ˏdɛstəˋneʃən] 名 目的地，目標

task [tæsk] 名 工作，任務
▶ A new employee only deals with some simple tasks.
新員工只處理簡單的工作。

taste [test] 名 味覺，一小口
▶ Please have a taste of the cake I made.
請嚐一下我做的蛋糕。

相關衍生字彙 tasty [ˋtestɪ] 形 美味的、smell [smɛl] 名 嗅覺、touch [tʌtʃ] 名 觸摸、
hearing [ˋhɪrɪŋ] 名 聽力

taxation [tæksˋeʃən] 名 課稅，稅收，稅額
▶ The government announced that taxation would be increased.
政府宣布稅收要增加。

taxi [ˋtæksɪ] 名 計程車
▶ Taking a taxi to work is costly. 搭計乘車上班花費太高。

tea [ti] 名 茶
▶ Would you like something to drink, tea or coffee? 你要喝點什麼？茶或咖啡？

teach [titʃ] 動 教導
▶ Mom taught me how to cook.
媽媽教我如何煮飯。

相關衍生字彙 teacher [ˋtitʃɚ] 名 老師、professor [prəˋfɛsɚ] 名 教授、
education [ˏɛdʒuˋkeʃən] 名 教育、educator [ˋɛdʒuˏketɚ] 名 教育家

動詞三態變化 teach - taught - taught

team [tim] 名 隊伍 　片 team work 團隊合作

tear [tɛr] 動 撕下
⊙MP3 20-02
▶ Some pages were torn out of the dictionary.
這本字典有好幾頁被撕下來。

動詞三態變化 tear - tore - torn

tease [tiz] 動 戲弄
▶ I was only teasing the dog. I didn't hurt it.
我只是在逗弄小狗，並沒有傷害牠。

動詞三態變化 tease - teased - teased

technical [ˋtɛknɪkḷ] 形 技術的，專門的
▶ The job needs technical skills. 這項工作需要專門的技術。

technique [tɛkˋnik] 名 技術
▶ It takes time to develop a new technique. 發展新技術需要時間。

T

tedious [`tidɪəs] 形 冗長乏味的　　片 a tedious lecture 冗長的演講

teethe [tið] 動 長牙齒
▶ The baby is teething.
小嬰兒正在長牙齒。
相關衍生字彙 tooth [tuθ] 名 牙齒、dentist [`dɛntɪst] 名 牙醫、toothpaste [`tuθ,pest] 名 牙膏、toothbrush [`tuθ,brʌʃ] 名 牙刷、toothache [`tuθ,ek] 名 牙痛
動詞三態變化 teethe - teethed - teethed

temper [`tɛmpɚ] 名 脾氣　　片 to lose one's temper 發脾氣

temperate [`tɛmprɪt] 形 有節制的，溫和的
▶ His behavior used to be temperate. 他的行為過去一向很溫和。

temperature [`tɛmprətʃɚ] 名 溫度
▶ A sudden drop in temperature may cause a stroke.
溫度突然下降，有可能會引起中風。

temporary [`tɛmpə,rɛrɪ] 形 暫時的　　反 permanent [`pɝmənənt] 形 永恆的

temptation [tɛmp`teʃən] 名 誘惑
▶ How can I resist the temptation of ice cream? 我怎麼抵擋得了冰淇淋的誘惑？

telephone [`tɛlə,fon] 名 電話
▶ House telephones are gradually replaced by cellphones.
家用電話逐漸被手機取代。
相關衍生字彙 telescope [`tɛlə,skop] 名 望遠鏡、television [`tɛlə,vɪʒən] 名 電視機、telegram [`tɛlə,græm] 名 電報

tenant [`tɛnənt] 名 房客
▶ I am just a tenant and my landlord is not in now. 我只是房客，房東現在不在家。

tendency [`tɛndənsɪ] 名 傾向
▶ I do have the tendency towards optimism. 我確實是樂觀的。

tender [`tɛndɚ] 形 溫柔的　　片 a tender look 溫柔的表情

tense [tɛns] 形 緊繃的
▶ The relationship between the two countries seems tense.
這兩國的關係似乎很緊繃。

tension [`tɛnʃən] 名 緊張
▶ I felt the tension when Father stepped into the living room angrily.
當爸爸生氣地走入客廳時，我可以感覺到緊張的氣氛。

term [tɝm] 名 學期
▶ At the end of this term, we will have exams. 在學期末時，我們將會有考試。

terminal [ˋtɝmən!] 名 航廈
▶ My flight will take off at Terminal 1.
　我的班機從第一航廈起飛。

相關衍生字彙 pilot [ˋpaɪlət] 名（飛機等的）駕駛員、attendant [əˋtɛndənt] 名 服務員、captain [ˋkæptɪn] 名（飛機的）機長、Customs [ˋkʌstəmz] 名 海關、boarding card 片 登機證、gate [get] 名 登機門、claim [klem] 動 認領，索取

terminate [ˋtɝməˏnet] 動 終結
▶ The singer's contract was terminated.
　這位歌手的契約已被終止。

動詞三態變化 terminate - terminated - terminated

terrible [ˋtɛrəb!] 形 糟糕的　　　　　　　　　　MP3 20-03
▶ The terrible weather ruined my holiday. 這糟糕的天氣毀了我的假期。

terrific [təˋrɪfɪk] 形 極好的
▶ Wow, you look terrific in this dress. 哇，你穿這件洋裝好漂亮！

terrify [ˋtɛrəˏfaɪ] 動 驚嚇
▶ I was terrified by your crazy idea.
　我被你瘋狂的點子嚇到了。

相關衍生字彙 frighten [ˋfraɪtn] 動 使驚嚇、scare [skɛr] 動 驚嚇、shock [ʃɑk] 動 使震驚、horrify [ˋhɔrəˏfaɪ] 動 使恐懼

動詞三態變化 terrify - terrified - terrified

territory [ˋtɛrəˏtorɪ] 名 領土
▶ The general was killed in enemy territory. 這位將軍喪命於敵軍的領土。

terror [ˋtɛrɚ] 名 恐怖　　反 counter-terror 反恐的
相關衍生字彙 terrorism [ˋtɛrɚˏrɪzəm] 名 恐怖主義、terrorist [ˋtɛrərɪst] 名 恐怖份子、attack [əˋtæk] 名 攻擊、suicide bomber 片 炸彈客

test [tɛst] 名 測驗，考試
▶ I took an English listening comprehension test. 我做了英文聽力測驗。

testify [ˋtɛstəˏfaɪ] 動 作證
▶ The brave witness testified for me.
　這位勇敢的目擊者替我作證。

動詞三態變化 testify - testified - testified

testimony [ˋtɛstəˏmonɪ] 名 證詞
▶ The judge believed in the witness' testimony. 法官相信證人的證詞。

textbook [ˋtɛkstˏbuk] 名 教科書
▶ The professor is just like a walking textbook.
　教授像是個活教材。

相關衍生字彙 dictionary [ˋdɪkʃənˏɛrɪ] 名 字典、encyclopedia [ɪnˏsaɪkləˋpidɪə] 名 百科全書、notebook [ˋnotˏbuk] 名 筆記本、reference book 片 參考書

T

459

thankful [ˋθæŋkfəl] 形 感謝的
▶ I was so thankful for your timely help. 我非常感謝你及時的幫助。

theater [ˋθɪətɚ] 名 劇院　🅟 a movie theater 電影院

theft [θɛft] 名 偷竊，盜竊
▶ There were several thefts happening in our neighborhood recently.
我們鄰近地區最近發生很多竊案。

theme [θim] 名 主題
▶ The theme of the seminar is business management.
這個研討會的主題是商業管理。

相關衍生字彙 topic [ˋtɑpɪk] 名 主題，論題、subject [ˋsʌbdʒɪkt] 名 主題、issue [ˋɪʃju]
名 爭議，問題、outline [ˋaʊt͵laɪn] 名 要點，提綱、point [pɔɪnt] 名 要點，中心思想

theory [ˋθɪərɪ] 名 理論
▶ Theories can help us organize some ideas. 理論可以幫我們統整想法。

therapy [ˋθɛrəpɪ] 名 治療
▶ Listening to music can be seen as a therapy for sadness.
聽音樂可以是悲傷的療癒。

thereby [ðɛrˋbaɪ] 副 因此　🔄 therefore [ˋðɛr͵fɔr] 副 因此

thermometer [θɚˋmɑmətɚ] 名 溫度計，體溫計
▶ I used a thermometer to test my body's temperature. 我用溫度計量我的體溫。

thesis [ˋθisɪs] 名 論文　🅟 a doctoral thesis 博士論文

thick [θɪk] 形 厚的，粗的　🔄 thin [θɪn] 形 薄的，細的

thief [θif] 名 小偷
▶ The thief was caught on the spot. 小偷當場被抓。

thinking [ˋθɪŋkɪŋ] 形 有理性的　🎧 MP3 **20-04**
▶ A thinking person won't make such a decision.
有理性的人不會做這種決定。

相關衍生字彙 think [θɪŋk] 動 思考、thought [θɔt] 名 思考、thoughtful [ˋθɔtfəl] 形 思考周詳的

thirst [θɝst] 名 口渴，渴望　🅟 to have a thirst for 渴望獲得

thirsty [ˋθɝstɪ] 形 口渴的
▶ Exercise makes me thirsty. 運動使我口渴。

thorough [ˋθɝo] 形 徹底的
▶ I have to take a thorough rest. 我得徹底的休息一下。

thousand [ˋθaʊznd̩] 名 千　🅟 ten thousand 一萬

thread [θrɛd] 名 線
▶ I helped my mother put the thread through the needle.
我幫媽媽把線穿過針。

相關衍生字彙 needle [`nidl] 名 針、pin [pɪn] 名 別針、scissors [`sɪzɚz] 名 剪刀、iron [`aɪɚn] 名 熨斗、sew [so] 動 縫合

threat [θrɛt] 名 威脅
▶ A computer is never a threat for me, but a good tool.
電腦對我而言，不是威脅而是好工具。

threaten [`θrɛtn̩] 動 威脅
▶ He threatened to commit suicide.
他威脅要自殺。

動詞三態變化 threaten - threatened - threatened

thrift [θrɪft] 名 節儉，節約
▶ My parents taught me the value of thrift. 父母教導我節儉的價值觀。

thrill [θrɪl] 動 使興奮
▶ I was thrilled by getting the invitation.
我很興奮收到這個邀請。

動詞三態變化 thrill - thrilled - thrilled

thrive [θraɪv] 動 繁榮，興盛
▶ He that will thrive must rise at five.
（諺語）五更起床百事興旺。

動詞三態變化 thrive - thrived - throve

throb [θrɑb] 動 悸動
▶ I can hear my heart throbbing clearly.
我可以很清楚的聽到我的心在跳動。

動詞三態變化 throb - throbbed - throbbed

throughout [θruˋaʊt] 介 遍佈
▶ The rumor has spread throughout the country. 謠言已經傳遍全國。

throw [θro] 動 丟擲
▶ He threw a ball to the dog.
他丟球給小狗。

動詞三態變化 throw - threw - thrown

thunder [`θʌndɚ] 名 雷聲
▶ The thunder always comes after the lightning.
雷聲總在閃電後到來。

相關衍生字彙 thunderstorm [`θʌndɚˌstɔrm] 名 大雷雨、hailstone [`helˌston] 名 冰雹、lightning [`laɪtnɪŋ] 名 閃電、shower [`ʃaʊɚ] 名 陣雨

T

ticket [ˋtɪkɪt] 名 票
▶ The tickets to the concert were all sold out. 音樂會的票全賣光了。

tide [taɪd] 名 潮汐
▶ Time and tide wait for no man.（諺語）歲月不饒人。

tidy [ˋtaɪdɪ] 形 整齊的
▶ The books on his desk are so tidy. 他桌上的書很整齊。

tighten [ˋtaɪtn̩] 動 弄緊　　片 to tighten one's belt 勒緊褲帶節約度日
相關衍生字彙 tight [taɪt] 形 緊的、firm [fɝm] 形 牢固的、loose [lus] 形 鬆的、fasten [ˋfæsn̩]
動 繫上
動詞三態變化 tighten - tightened - tightened

timber [ˋtɪmbɚ] 名 木材
▶ The ship was made of timber. 這艘船是木頭做的。

time [taɪm] 名 時間　　　　　　　　　　　　　　　　　　　　　◎ MP3 20-05
▶ Time is money.（諺語）時間就是金錢。

timetable [ˋtaɪmˌtebl] 名 時刻表
▶ You can take the train according to the timetable. 你可以依據此時刻表搭火車。

timid [ˋtɪmɪd] 形 膽小的
▶ I am too timid to try anything new. 我太膽小，不敢嘗試新事物。

tip [tɪp] 動 給小費
▶ In America, we have to tip the taxi driver.
在美國，是要給計程車司機小費的。
動詞三態變化 tip - tipped - tipped

tiptoe [ˋtɪpˌto] 名 腳指尖　　　片 on tiptoe 踮著腳尖，悄悄地

tire [taɪr] 動 使疲憊　　　片 to be tired out 累垮了
動詞三態變化 tire - tired - tired

tired [taɪrd] 形 疲憊的
▶ I am so tired that I don't want to move.
我累到都不想動了。
相關衍生字彙 tiresome [ˋtaɪrsəm] 形 令人疲憊的、tire [taɪr] 名 輪胎、tireless [ˋtaɪrlɪs]
形 不知疲倦的、exhausted [ɪgˋzɔstɪd] 形 精疲力竭的

tissue [ˋtɪʃu] 名 衛生紙
▶ The tissue in the bathroom is running out. 廁所裡的衛生紙快用完了。

title [ˋtaɪtl̩] 名 標題　　　片 the title page 書名頁，扉頁

token [`tokən] 名 象徵
▶ I sent a card to her as a token of my appreciation.
我寄了卡片給她以表示我的感謝之意。

tolerant [`talərənt] 形 忍受的
▶ I can be tolerant of different criticisms.
我可以忍受不同的批評。
相關衍生字彙 tolerable [`talərəbl] 形 可容忍的、tolerance [`talərəns] 名 容忍、
tolerate [`talə‚ret] 動 容忍、stand [stænd] 動 容忍

toll [tol] 名 損失，傷亡人數　片 the death toll 死亡人數

tongue [tʌŋ] 名 舌頭
▶ English is not my mother tongue. 英文不是我的母語。

tooth [tuθ] 名 牙齒　片 clench one's teeth 咬緊牙關

top [tap] 形 一流的，最好的 名 頂尖
▶ His goal is to get the admission from the top university, such as Harvard.
他的目標是拿到像哈佛這樣頂尖大學的入學許可。

topic [`tapɪk] 名 主題
▶ The topic of the discussion is about warming. 討論的主題是暖化。

torch [tɔrtʃ] 名 火把　片 torch relay 聖火傳遞

torment [`tɔr‚mɛnt] 名 痛苦
▶ The child has suffered the torment of abuse from his father for years.
這孩子已經忍受他父親虐待的痛苦好幾年了。

tornado [tɔr`nedo] 名 龍捲風
▶ A tornado is a strong dangerous wind. 龍捲風既強烈又危險。

torture [`tɔrtʃɚ] 動 折磨
▶ Many black slaves were tortured to death at that time.
在當時，很多黑奴被折磨致死。
相關衍生字彙 agonize [`ægə‚naɪz] 動 折磨、afflict [ə`flɪkt] 動 使痛苦、disturb [dɪs`tɝb]
動 妨礙，擾亂、trouble [`trʌbl] 動（疾病）折磨、pain [pen] 動 使痛苦
動詞三態變化 torture - tortured - tortured

total [`totl] 名 總數　片 in total 總共　◎ MP3 20-06

tough [tʌf] 形 嚴格的
▶ The law should be tough on drunk drivers. 法律應對酒後開車者嚴懲。

tour [tur] 名 旅程　片 a tour guide 導遊

tourist [`turɪst] 名 觀光客　片 a tourist attraction 觀光景點

T

tournament [ˈtɝnəmənt] 名 錦標賽
▶ The tournament will be held in New York. 錦標賽將在紐約舉行。

---

trace [tres] 名 痕跡
▶ I didn't show any trace of my sadness. 我沒有露出任何悲傷的跡象。

---

track [træk] 名 蹤跡　　片 to keep track of 掌握～的動態

---

trade [tred] 名 貿易　　片 international trade 國際貿易

---

tradition [trəˈdɪʃən] 名 傳統
▶ We should cherish and hand down a good tradition.
我們應該珍惜並傳承好傳統。

相關衍生字彙 traditional [trəˈdɪʃənḷ] 形 傳統的、custom [ˈkʌstəm] 名 風俗、
folklore [ˈfokˌlor] 名 民俗

---

traffic [ˈtræfɪk] 名 交通
▶ During rush hour, the traffic jam gets serious.
在尖峰時間，交通阻塞的很嚴重。

---

tragedy [ˈtrædʒədɪ] 名 悲劇　　反 comedy [ˈkɑmədɪ] 名 喜劇

---

tragic [ˈtrædʒɪk] 形 悲慘的
▶ We are so shocked by the tragic news of the kid's death.
那個孩子去世的悲慘消息令我們感到相當震驚。

---

trait [tret] 名 特徵，特性
▶ One of his personality traits is generosity.
慷慨是他的人格特質之一。

相關衍生字彙 feature [ˈfitʃɚ] 名 特色，特徵、characteristic [ˌkærəktəˈrɪstɪk] 名 特色、
property [ˈprɑpɚtɪ] 名 特性

---

tranquil [ˈtræŋkwɪl] 形 寧靜的
▶ The old woman always shows her tranquil look. 老婦人總露出安詳的面容。

---

transaction [trænˈzækʃən] 名 交易
▶ Our company has lots of business transactions with Mark's.
我們公司跟馬克的公司有很多商業上的往來。

---

transcription [ˌtrænˈskrɪpʃən] 名 抄本　　片 to make a transcription 做謄本

---

transfer [trænsˈfɝ] 動 轉移
▶ She was transferred to the headquarters.
她被調職到總公司。

動詞三態變化 transfer - transferred - transferred

transformation [ˌtrænsfɚˈmeʃən] 名 改革
▶ Our educational system is undergoing a transformation.
我們的教育系統正經歷改革。

transition [trænˈzɪʃən] 名 過渡期
▶ He is a teenager in transition. 他是正處於過渡期的青少年。

translate [trænsˈlet] 動 翻譯
▶ Please translate the sentences into English.
請把這些句子翻譯成英文。
相關衍生字彙 translation [trænsˈleʃən] 名 翻譯、interpret [ɪnˈtɝprɪt] 動 詮釋、
interpreter [ɪnˈtɝprɪtɚ] 名 口譯人員
動詞三態變化 translate - translated - translated

transmit [trænsˈmɪt] 動 傳達，遺傳　　　　　　　　　　◉ MP3 20-07
▶ Genes are transmitted from generation to generation.
基因會代代相傳。
動詞三態變化 transmit - transmitted - transmitted

transparent [trænsˈpɛrənt] 形 透明的
▶ The girl's shirt is kind of transparent. 那個女孩的襯衫有點透明。

transplant [trænsˈplænt] 動 移植　　片 an organ transplant 器官移植
動詞三態變化 transplant - transplanted - transplanted

transport [trænsˈpɔrt] 動 運輸
▶ The goods will be transported to the retailers.
這些貨品將運給零售商。
動詞三態變化 transport - transported - transported

transportation [ˌtrænspɚˈteʃən] 名 運輸
▶ The public transportation in Sydney is very convenient.
雪梨的大眾運輸很方便。
相關衍生字彙 cargo [ˈkɑrgo] 名 貨物、airplane [ˈɛrˌplen] 名 飛機、truck [trʌk] 名 卡車、
subway [ˈsʌbˌwe] 名 地下鐵、train [tren] 名 火車

trap [træp] 名 陷阱
▶ An animal fell into the trap set by the hunter. 有隻動物掉入獵人設下的陷阱。

trauma [ˈtrɔmə] 名 創傷
▶ To get rid of the psychological trauma is not an easy job.
要抹去心理創傷不是一件容易的事。

T

travel [`trævl̩] 動 旅遊
▶ One of my dreams is to travel all over the world.
我的夢想之一是環遊世界。

相關衍生字彙 traveler [`trævlɚ] 名 遊客、journey [`dʒɝnɪ] 名 旅程、trip [trɪp] 名 旅遊

動詞三態變化 travel - traveled / travelled - traveled / travelled

tread [trɛd] 動 踩踏
▶ I am so sorry I trod on your foot.
很抱歉踩到你的腳。

動詞三態變化 tread - trod - trodden

treason [`trizn̩] 名 叛國，通敵　　片 high treason 叛國罪

treasure [`trɛʒɚ] 名 寶藏
▶ The sunken treasures at the bottom of the sea were found by a diver.
沉在海底的寶藏是被一位潛水員發現的。

treat [trit] 名 款待
▶ It's my treat today! 今天我請客！

treatment [`tritmənt] 名 治療
▶ I am receiving a new treatment.
我正接受新的治療。

相關衍生字彙 remedy [`rɛmədɪ] 名 動 治療、cure [kjur] 名 治癒、therapy [`θɛrəpɪ] 名 療法、medication [ˌmɛdɪ`keʃən] 名 藥物治療

treaty [`tritɪ] 名 條約，協定　　片 to sign a treaty 簽訂條約

tree [tri] 名 樹木
▶ Planting trees can help improve the quality of air. 種樹可以改善空氣品質。

tremendous [trɪ`mɛndəs] 形 巨大的　　片 a tremendous amount of 大量的

trend [trɛnd] 名 趨勢
▶ As a designer, I have to follow the trend. 身為設計師，我得追隨趨勢。

trespass [`trɛspəs] 動 擅自進入
▶ You shouldn't trespass into my lab.
你不該擅自進入我的實驗室。

動詞三態變化 trespass - trespassed - trespassed

trial [`traɪəl] 名 測試
▶ The trials show that air pollution does harm to people's health.
測試結果顯示，空氣污染的確有害人體健康。

triangle [`traɪˌæŋgl] 名 三角形　　片 a triangle love 三角戀情

相關衍生字彙 square [skwɛr] 名 正方形、oval [`ovl] 名 橢圓、circle [`sɝk] 名 圓形的東西、rhombus [`rɑmbəs] 名 菱形、trapezoid [`træpəˌzɔɪd] 名 梯形

trick [trɪk] 名 把戲　　🔊 MP3 **20-08**
▶ The naughty boy often plays tricks on his classmates.
　這個頑皮的男孩常常捉弄他的同學。

trifle [`traɪfl] 名 小事，瑣事
▶ The quarrel resulted from a trifle. 這個爭吵起因於一件小事。

trigger [`trɪgɚ] 動 引起，引發
▶ The racial issue triggered a violent attack.
　種族議題引發了暴力攻擊。
動詞三態變化 trigger - triggered - triggered

triple [`trɪpl] 形 三倍的
▶ With smart investment, she earned triple money.
　因聰明的投資，她賺得三倍的資金。

triumph [`traɪəmf] 動 獲勝，戰勝
▶ I believe that I can triumph over my weakness.
　我相信我可以戰勝我的弱點。
相關衍生字彙 triumphant [traɪ`ʌmfənt] 形 勝利的、victory [`vɪktərɪ] 名 勝利、success [sək`sɛs] 名 成功、achievement [ə`tʃivmənt] 名 成就
動詞三態變化 triumph - triumphed - triumphed

trivial [`trɪvɪəl] 形 瑣碎的
▶ The trivial things wasted lots of my time. 這些瑣碎的事浪費我很多時間。

troop [trup] 名 軍隊　　片 to deploy troops 佈署軍隊

trophy [`trofɪ] 名 獎盃，戰利品
▶ Our team was awarded a trophy. 我們的隊伍獲頒獎盃。

tropic [`trɑpɪk] 名 回歸線　　片 the tropic of Cancer / Capricorn 北回／南回歸線

tropical [`trɑpɪkl] 形 熱帶的
▶ Countless wild animals are living in the tropical rain forest.
　數不盡的野生動物住在熱帶雨林中。

trouble [`trʌbl] 名 麻煩　　片 to get into trouble 惹上麻煩
相關衍生字彙 troublesome [`trʌblsəm] 形 令人煩惱的、troublemaker [`trʌblˌmekɚ] 名 麻煩製造者、troubled [`trʌbld] 形 心煩的

true [tru] 形 真實的
▶ He finally makes his dream come true. 他終於讓夢想成真了。

T

467

trust [trʌst] 動 信任
▶ Why should I trust you?
　我為何要相信你？
動詞三態變化 trust - trusted - trusted

trustworthy [`trʌst‚wɝðɪ] 形 值得信任的
▶ He is a trustworthy doctor. 他是一個值得信賴的醫生。

truth [truθ] 名 真實　　片 to tell the truth 說實話

try [traɪ] 動 試驗，嘗試　　片 to try one's best 盡個人所能，盡全力
動詞三態變化 try - tried - tried

tulip [`tjuləp] 名 鬱金香
▶ The Netherlands is famous for tulips.
　荷蘭以鬱金香聞名。
相關衍生字彙 rose [roz] 名 玫瑰、jasmine [`dʒæsmɪn] 名 茉莉、lily [`lɪlɪ] 名 百合、
　　　　daffodil [`dæfədɪl] 名 黃水仙、orchid [`ɔrkɪd] 名 蘭花、carnation [kɑr`neʃən]
　　　　名 康乃馨、sunflower [`sʌn‚flaʊɚ] 名 向日葵

tumble [`tʌmbl̩] 動 跌倒，被絆倒
▶ Tom tumbled over the chair.
　湯姆絆到椅子而跌倒。
動詞三態變化 tumble - tumbled - tumbled

tune [tjun] 名 曲調
▶ I take a walk humming a tune. 我邊散步邊哼著曲子。

tunnel [`tʌnl̩] 名 隧道
▶ The tunnel bridges the two countries. 這條隧道連接兩個國家。

turbulence [`tɝbjələns] 名 騷動，動盪　　　　⊙ MP3 **20-09**
▶ He apologized for causing the social turbulence.
　他為引起社會動盪不安而道歉。

turn [tɝn] 動 轉動　　片 to turn down 拒絕
相關衍生字彙 turnover [`tɝn‚ovɚ] 名 人員流動率、turnaround [`tɝnə‚raʊnd] 名 歸航、
　　　　turnout [`tɝn‚aʊt] 名 到場人數
動詞三態變化 turn - turned - turned

tutor [`tjutɚ] 名 家庭教師
▶ On Sunday, a private tutor comes to my home. 星期天，會有家教老師來我家。

twilight [`twaɪ‚laɪt] 名 黃昏時刻
▶ Birds fly back to their nests at twilight. 在黃昏時刻，鳥兒飛回巢。

twinkle [ˋtwɪŋkl̩] 動 閃爍
▶ Stars twinkle in the sky.
　星星在天空閃爍。
動詞三態變化 twinkle - twinkled - twinkled

---

twist [twɪst] 動 扭轉　　片 to twist a towel 擰乾毛巾
動詞三態變化 twist - twisted - twisted

---

typical [ˋtɪpɪkl̩] 形 典型的，有代表性的
▶ The poem is typical of the poet's early work.
　這首詩是這位詩人早期的代表作品。
相關衍生字彙 representative [rɛprɪˋzɛntətɪv] 形 典型的、standard [ˋstændɚd] 名 標準、
　　model [ˋmɑdl̩] 名 典型、criterion [kraɪˋtɪrɪən] 名（判斷、批評的）標準，準則

---

tyrant [ˋtaɪrənt] 名 暴君
▶ The cruel tyrant was finally overthrown. 這名殘忍的暴君終於被推翻了。

MEMO

T

詞性說明

名 名詞	副 副詞	介 介系詞
動 動詞	形 形容詞	連 連接詞
代 代名詞	助 助動詞	

內文圖示說明

片 片語　　反 反義字　　同 同義字

一網打盡「英語小知識」│ Change v.s Transformation

　　當我們經歷到某部分不太一樣時，我們就可以使用「change」這個字了，像是某種心態的改變或是天氣的變化……等。而「transformation」指的是整體完全的改變。

U ultimate ~ utterance

★一網打盡 240 個英文單字 ｜ 一網打盡 43 句英語會話句　　◎ MP3 21-01

ultimate [`ʌltəmɪt] 名 終極，極限
▶ For me, the house is the ultimate in luxury.
對我而言，這房子已經是超級奢華了。
相關衍生字彙 ultimately [`ʌltəmɪtlɪ] 副 最後，終極地、ultimatum [ˌʌltə`metəm]
名 最後通牒，基本原理、terminal [`tɝmən!] 形 末端的，終點的，學期的、
conclusive [kən`klusɪv] 形 決定性的，確實的，最終的、eventual [ɪ`vɛntʃuəl]
形 最終發生的，最後的，結果的

---

umbrella [ʌm`brɛlə] 名 雨傘　　片 under the umbrella of 在～的保護傘下

---

umpire [`ʌmpaɪr] 名 裁判
▶ All the players should respect umpires' decision.
所有球員都要尊重裁判的判決。
相關衍生字彙 umpireship [`ʌmpaɪrʃɪp] 名 裁判之職權、moderator [`mɑdəˌretə]
名 仲裁者、arbitrator [`ɑrbəˌtretə] 名 仲裁人，主宰人、mediator [`midɪˌetə]
名 調停者，中介物

---

unable [ʌn`eb!] 形 沒能力的
▶ I am unable to join the marathon. 我沒能力參加馬拉松賽。

---

unaccountable [ˌʌnə`kauntəb!] 形 無法解釋的，難以理解的
▶ Feelings are unaccountable.
感情是無法解釋的。
相關衍生字彙 unaccountably [ˌʌnə`kauntəblɪ] 副 不能說明地，不可解釋地、
unaccounted [ˌʌnə`kauntɪd] 形 未說明的，行蹤不明的、unaccounted for
片 下落不明的，未予解釋的、unaccounted-for [ˌʌnə`kauntɪdˌfɔr]
形 不明的，未予解釋的

---

unanimous [ju`nænəməs] 形 一致的
▶ All members are unanimous in supporting the idea.
所有會員都支持這個想法。
相關衍生字彙 unanimously [ju`nænəməslɪ] 副 無異議地，全體一致地、
concurrent [kən`kɝənt] 形 同時發生的，協力的

---

unaware [ˌʌnə`wɛr] 形 沒察覺到的
▶ I was unaware of your presence.
我沒察覺到你的出現。
相關衍生字彙 unacceptable [ˌʌnək`sɛptəb!] 形 不能接受的、unaccustomed [ˌʌnə`kʌstəmd]
形 不習慣的、unaffected [ˌʌnə`fɛktɪd] 形 不受影響的、
unattractive [ˌʌnə`træktɪv] 形 無吸引力的

unbearable [ʌnˋbɛrəbḷ] 形 無法忍受的
▶ The coldness is unbearable.
這寒冷是無法忍受的。
相關衍生字彙 unbearably [ʌnˋbɛrəblɪ] 副 不能忍受地，無法容忍地、intolerable [ɪnˋtɑlərəbḷ] 形 難耐的，不能忍受的、insufferable [ɪnˋsʌfərəbḷ] 形 不可忍受的，氣人的

unbelievable [ˌʌnbɪˋlivəbḷ] 形 難以相信的
▶ It's unbelievable to me that he quit such a good job.
我無法相信他會辭掉這麼好的工作。
相關衍生字彙 incredible [ɪnˋkrɛdəbḷ] 形 不能相信的，難以置信的、doubtful [ˋdaʊtfəl] 形 懷疑的，令人生疑的、dubious [ˋdjubɪəs] 形 猶豫不決的，可疑的，含糊的、questionable [ˋkwɛstʃənəbḷ] 形 可疑的，靠不住的、unconvincing [ˌʌnkənˋvɪnsɪŋ] 形 不令人信服的、suspicious [səˋspɪʃəs] 形 猜疑的，疑心的

uncertainty [ʌnˋsɝtn̩tɪ] 名 不確定性
▶ We have to accept the uncertainty of life.
我們都必須接受人生中的不確定性。
相關衍生字彙 uncomfortable [ʌnˋkʌmfətəbḷ] 形 不舒服的、unconscious [ʌnˋkɑnʃəs] 形 未察覺的、undecided [ˌʌndɪˋsaɪdɪd] 形 未決定的

undeniable [ˌʌndɪˋnaɪəbḷ] 形 不可否認的
▶ This is an undeniable fact.
這是不可否認的事實。
相關衍生字彙 undeniably [ˌʌndɪˋnaɪəblɪ] 副 不可否認地、demonstrable [ˋdɛmənstrəbḷ] 形 可論證的，顯而易見的、unquestionable [ʌnˋkwɛstʃənəbḷ] 形 毫無疑問的，確鑿的、decisive [dɪˋsaɪsɪv] 形 決定性的，確定的，果斷的、decided [dɪˋsaɪdɪd] 形 無疑的，果斷的

underestimate [ˋʌndəˋɛstəˌmet] 動 低估
▶ The government underestimated the rate of unemployment.
政府低估了失業率。
相關衍生字彙 undervalue [ˌʌndəˋvælju] 動 低估，輕視、underrate [ˌʌndəˋret] 動 低估，輕視、misprize [mɪsˋpraɪz] 動 輕蔑、misjudge [mɪsˋdʒʌdʒ] 動 判斷錯誤，輕視、miscalculate [ˋmɪsˋkælkjəˌlet] 動 算錯，誤估
動詞三態變化 underestimate - underestimated - underestimated

undergo [ˌʌndəˋgo] 動 經歷
▶ Before I succeeded, I underwent many failures.
在成功前，我經歷過許多失敗。
動詞三態變化 undergo - underwent - undergone

undergraduate [ˌʌndɚˋgrædʒʊɪt] 名 大學生
▶ He is an MIT undergraduate now.
　他現在是麻省理工學院的大學生。
相關衍生字彙 undergraduate student 名 本科生、freshman [ˋfrɛʃmən]
　　　　　　名 （大學等的）一年級生，新生

underground [ˋʌndɚˌgraʊnd] 形 地下的
片 a underground passage 地下通道
相關衍生字彙 underground economy 片 地下經濟、subterranean [ˌsʌbtəˋrenɪən]
　　　　　　名 在地下生活（或工作）的人 形 地下的、hypogeous [ˌhaɪpəˋdʒɪəs]
　　　　　　形 地下的，生長在地下的、sunken [ˋsʌŋkən]
　　　　　　形 沉沒的，下陷的，低於地面（或樓面的），沮喪的、nether [ˋnɛðɚ]
　　　　　　形 下面的，地下的、underfoot [ˌʌndɚˋfʊt] 副 在腳下面，踐踏地，礙手礙腳地

understand [ˌʌndɚˋstænd] 動 瞭解
▶ I can understand all the teacher taught.
　我懂老師所教的內容。
相關衍生字彙 understandable [ˌʌndɚˋstændəbl] 形 可理解的，能懂的、
　　　　　　understandably [ˌʌndɚˋstændəblɪ] 副 可理解地、
　　　　　　comprehend [ˌkɑmprɪˋhɛnd] 動 理解，領會、realize [ˋrɪəˌlaɪz] 動 瞭解，認識到、
　　　　　　misunderstand [ˋmɪsʌndɚˋstænd] 動 誤會，曲解
動詞三態變化 understand - understood - understood

undertake [ˌʌndɚˋtek] 動 承擔
▶ Bill promised his father he would undertake the business.
　比爾承諾爸爸願意承接事業。
動詞三態變化 undertake - undertook - undertaken

underwear [ˋʌndɚˌwɛr] 名 內衣
▶ Underwear should be kept clean.
　內衣要保持乾淨。
相關衍生字彙 petticoat [ˋpɛtɪˌkot] 名 襯裙、underskirt [ˌʌndɚˋskɝt] 名 襯裙，裙子、
　　　　　　undergarment [ˋʌndɚˌgɑrmənt] 名 貼身衣、lingerie [ˋlænʒəˌri]
　　　　　　名 女用貼身內衣褲，女睡衣

undeveloped [ˌʌndɪˋvɛləpt] 形 未開發的
片 an undeveloped country 未開發國家

undo [ʌnˋdu] 動 解開　　　片 to undo the package 解開包裹
動詞三態變化 undo - undid - undone

uneducated [ʌnˋɛdʒʊˌketɪd] 形 未受教育的　　　◎ MP3 **21-02**
反 well-educated [ˋwɛlˋɝnd] 形 受良好教育的

相關衍生字彙 naive [nɑˋiv] 形 天真的，幼稚的、ignorant [ˋɪgnərənt]
形 無知的，不學無術的，沒有受教育的、illiterate [ɪˋlɪtərɪt] 名 文盲，無知的人
形 文盲的，未受教育的

unemployment [ˌʌnɪmˋplɔɪmənt] 名 失業 片 rate of unemployment 失業率

unfair [ʌnˋfɛr] 形 不公平的
▶ The punishment is unfair.
這處罰不公平。

相關衍生字彙 unfamiliar [ˌʌnfəˋmɪljɚ] 形 不熟悉的、unfinished [ʌnˋfɪnɪʃt] 形 未完成的、
unhappy [ʌnˋhæpɪ] 形 不開心的、unhealthy [ʌnˋhɛlθɪ] 形 不健康的、
unfriendly [ʌnˋfrɛndlɪ] 形 不友善的、unimportant [ˌʌnɪmˋpɔrtṇt] 形 不重要的

unfold [ʌnˋfold] 動 打開 片 to unfold a letter 打開信件
動詞三態變化 unfold - unfolded - unfolded

unforgettable [ˌʌnfɚˋgɛtəbl] 形 難以忘懷的
▶ Those days are unforgettable sweet memories. 那些日子真是難忘的甜美回憶。

unfortunate [ʌnˋfɔrtʃənɪt] 形 不幸的
▶ All the volunteers are trying their best to help the unfortunate people.
所有的志工正傾全力在幫助這些不幸的人。

相關衍生字彙 unfortunately [ʌnˋfɔrtʃənɪtlɪ] 副 不幸地，遺憾地，可惜、unlucky [ʌnˋlʌkɪ]
形 不幸的，倒楣的、unluckily [ʌnˋlʌkɪlɪ] 副 不幸地，不湊巧地、ill-fated [ˋɪlˋfetɪd]
形 惡運的，不幸的、disastrous [dɪzˋæstrəs] 形 災害的，悲慘的、
accursed [əˋkɝsɪd] 形 應受詛咒的，可惡的，不幸的、wretched [ˋrɛtʃɪd]
形 不幸的，悲慘的，惡劣的、unsuccessful [ˌʌnsəkˋsɛsfəl] 形 不成功的，失敗的

uniform [ˋjunəˌfɔrm] 名 制服
▶ In Taiwan, students wear uniforms at school.
在台灣，學生在學校要穿制服。

相關衍生字彙 uniformed [ˋjunəˌfɔrmd] 形 穿著制服的、uniformity [ˌjunəˋfɔrmətɪ]
名 一致，單調，統一、uniformly [junəˋfɔrmlɪ] 副 一致地，均勻地、
costume [ˋkɑstjum] 名 服裝，尤指（女子）套裝、outfit [ˋautˌfɪt] 名 全套裝備

uniformity [ˌjunəˋfɔrmətɪ] 名 一致性
▶ You and I have the uniformity of interests.
你和我有一致的興趣。

相關衍生字彙 consistency [kənˋsɪstənsɪ] 名 （液體等的）濃度，堅硬（度），一致，符合、
similarity [ˌsɪməˋlærətɪ] 名 類似，相似、conformity [kənˋfɔrmətɪ]
名 順從，相似，一致、correspondence [ˌkɔrəˋspɑndəns] 名 一致，符合，相當、
equality [iˋkwɑlətɪ] 名 相等，均等

U

unique [ju`nik] 形 獨特的

▶ Her style of dancing is very unique.
她跳舞的方式很獨特。

相關衍生字彙 uniquely [ju`niklɪ] 副 獨特地，唯一地、uniqueness [ju`niknɪs]
名 獨一無二，獨特性、infrequent [ɪn`frikwənt] 形 罕見的，不多的、
particular [pɚ`tɪkjəlɚ] 形 特殊的，獨特的，細緻的、
quintessential [ˌkwɪntɪ`sɛnʃəl] 形 精髓的，典型的、unheard-of [ʌn`hɝd͵av]
形 前所未有的，不尋常的、
extraordinary [ɪk`strɔrdn͵ɛrɪ] 形 異常的，非凡的

unit [`junɪt] 名 單元

▶ There are ten units in the book.
這本書有十個單元。

相關衍生字彙 chapter [`tʃæptɚ] 名（書籍的）章，回、section [`sɛkʃən] 名（文章等的）節、
part [part] 名 部，篇、volume [`valjəm] 名 冊，卷、paragraph [`pærə͵græf]
名（文章的）段，節

unite [ju`naɪt] 動 團結

▶ All the countries should unite to fight against the disease.
所有的國家都應該團結起來對抗此疾病。

相關衍生字彙 united [ju`naɪtɪd] 形 聯合的，團結的，一致的、unitedly [ju`naɪtɪdlɪ]
副 聯合在一起地，團結一致地、unity [`junətɪ] 名 單一（性），團結，一致（性）

動詞三態變化 unite - united - united

university [ˌjunə`vɝsətɪ] 名 大學

▶ The University of Sydney is the oldest university in Australia.
雪梨大學是澳洲最古老的大學。

相關衍生字彙 multiversity [ˌmʌltə`vɝsətɪ] 名 聯合大學、college [`kalɪdʒ] 名 大學，學院、
campus [`kæmpəs] 名 校園，學院

universe [`junə͵vɝs] 名 宇宙

▶ Is the Earth the center of the universe?
地球是宇宙的中心嗎？

相關衍生字彙 universal [ˌjunə`vɝsl] 形 普遍的，宇宙的，通用的，完整的、
universally [ˌjunə`vɝslɪ] 副 普遍地，一般地，到處、
universality [ˌjunəvɚ`sælətɪ] 名 普遍性，（興趣等的）多方面性

unless [ʌn`lɛs] 連 除非

▶ I will arrive on time, unless there is a traffic jam.
除非塞車，否則我一定準時到。

相關衍生字彙 unlikely [ʌn`laɪklɪ] 形 不太可能的、unlucky [ʌn`lʌkɪ] 形 不幸的、
unpopular [ʌn`papjəlɚ] 形 不受歡迎的、unsure [ˌʌn`ʃur] 形 不確定的

unload [ʌnˋlod] 動 卸貨
▶ The workers are busy unloading goods.
工人正忙著卸貨。

動詞三態變化 unload - unloaded - unloaded

unnatural [ʌnˋnætʃərəl] 形 反常的
▶ Snowing in summer is unnatural.
夏天下雪是反常的。

相關衍生字彙 unnaturally [ʌnˋnætʃərəlɪ] 副 不自然地，違反習俗地、grotesque [groˋtɛsk] 形 奇形怪狀的，可笑的、abnormal 形 不正常的，反常的、hypocritical [ˏhɪpəˋkrɪtɪkl̩] 形 虛偽的，偽善的

unnecessary [ʌnˋnɛsəˏsɛrɪ] 形 不需要的
▶ It's unnecessary for you to get involved in the quarrel.
你沒有必要捲入此爭吵中。

相關衍生字彙 unnecessarily [ʌnˋnɛsəˏsɛrɪlɪ] 副 不必要地，多餘地、needless [ˋnidlɪs] 形 不必要的，不需要的、unessential [ˏʌnəˋsɛnʃəl] 名 不重要的事物 形 不重要的，非本質的、superfluous [suˋpɝfluəs] 形 過剩的，多餘的、uncalled-for [ʌnˋkɔldˏfɔr] 形 不必要的，不恰當的、extraneous [ɛkˋstreniəs] 形 外來的，無關的

unreasonable [ʌnˋriznəbl̩] 形 不講道理的，不合理的
▶ It's unreasonable to ask your workers to work overtime every day.
要求員工每天加班是不合理的。

相關衍生字彙 unpleasant [ʌnˋplɛznt] 形 不愉快的、unprepared [ˏʌnprɪˋpɛrd] 形 沒有準備的、unstable [ʌnˋstebl̩] 形 不穩定的、unsuitable [ʌnˋsjutəbl̩] 形 不適合的

until [ənˋtɪl] 連 介 直到
▶ He didn't get married until he bought a house. 直到買了房子他才結婚。

unusual [ʌnˋjuʒuəl] 形 不尋常的
▶ It's unusual for him to stay out overnight.
他整晚沒回家是很不尋常的。

相關衍生字彙 unusually [ʌnˋjuʒuəlɪ] 副 非常，不尋常地、uncommon [ʌnˋkɑmən] 形 不尋常的，非凡的、rare [rɛr] 形 稀有的，傑出的，稀薄的、odd [ɑd] 形 奇特的，零散的，臨時的

unwilling [ʌnˋwɪlɪŋ] 形 不願意的
◎ MP3 21-03
▶ I am unwilling to help you.
我不願意幫你忙。

相關衍生字彙 unwillingly [ʌnˋwɪlɪŋlɪ] 副 勉強地，不情願地、unwillingness [ʌnˋwɪlɪŋnɪs] 名 不情願，勉強、reluctant [rɪˋlʌktənt] 形 不情願的，頑抗的、involuntary [ɪnˋvɑlənˏtɛrɪ] 形 非自願的，無意的，不由自主的

U

upset [ʌpˋsɛt] 形 坐立難安的，心煩意亂的
▶ I am so upset over my son's illness. 兒子的病情讓我坐立難安。

---

upside [ˋʌpˋsaɪd] 名 上面　　片 upside down 上下顛倒，亂七八糟

---

upstairs [ˋʌpˋstɛrz] 副 上樓　　反 downstairs [ˌdaʊnˋstɛrz] 副 下樓
相關衍生字彙 upside-down [ˋʌpˌsaɪdˋdaʊn] 形 顛倒的，混亂的、upside-down cake
片 水果蛋糕

---

up-to-date [ˋʌptəˋdet] 形 時髦的，流行的　　反 out-of-date [ˋautəvˋdet] 形 過時的
相關衍生字彙 vogue [vog] 名 時髦、fashion [ˋfæʃən] 名 時尚、popularity [ˌpapjəˋlærəti]
名 普及，流行、style [staɪl] 名 風格，（衣服等的）流行款式

---

urban [ˋɝbən] 形 城市的，都市的
▶ Living in the urban area is convenient, but costly.
住在市區很方便，但是很貴。
相關衍生字彙 urbane [ɝˋben] 形 都市化的，高雅的、urbanity [ɝˋbænəti] 名 都市風格，雅致、
urbanize [ˋɝbənˌaɪz] 動 使都市化，使文雅、urbanized [ˋɝbənˌaɪzd]
形 城市化的，都市化的、urbanization [ˌɝbənɪˋzeʃən] 名 都市化、
urban decay 片 城市衰落、urban forest 片 城市森林、urban renewal
片 城市重建計畫、urban sprawl 片 城市擴張、urbanedge [ˋɝbənɛdʒ]
形 鄰接於城市的、urbanism [ˋɝbənˌɪzm] 名 都市生活，都市集中、
urbanologist [ɝbənˋalədʒɪst] 名 都市問題專家，都市學家、
urbanology [əbəˋnalədʒɪ] 名 都市問題學，城市學、urbiculture [ˋɝbɪˌkʌltʃɚ]
名 都市生活特有的習俗

---

urge [ɝdʒ] 動 強烈要求
▶ The president urges that the bill be passed.
總統要求通過這項法案。
動詞三態變化 urge - urged- urged

---

urgent [ˋɝdʒənt] 形 緊急的
▶ Please pay attention to the urgent situation.
請注意此緊急狀況。
相關衍生字彙 urgency [ˋɝdʒənsɪ] 名 緊急，迫切，催促、urgently [ˋɝdʒəntlɪ]
副 緊急地，急迫地、pressing [ˋprɛsɪŋ] 名 按，壓，壓制 形 緊迫的，懇切的、
compelling [kəmˋpɛlɪŋ] 形 強制的，令人信服的

---

use [juz] 名 使用
▶ It's no use crying over spilt milk.
（諺語）覆水難收。
相關衍生字彙 useful [ˋjusfəl] 形 有用的、useless [ˋjuslɪs] 形 沒用的、used [ˋjuzd] 形 使用過的、
usage [ˋjusɪdʒ] 名 用法

usher [`ʌʃɚ] 動 引領
▶ The secretary ushered the visitors to the reception room.
祕書引領訪客到接待室。
動詞三態變化 usher - ushered - ushered

usual [`juʒuəl] 形 **尋常的**　　反 unusual [ʌn`juʒuəl] 形 不尋常的
相關衍生字彙 usually [`juʒuəlɪ] 副 通常地，慣常地、customary [`kʌstəmˌɛrɪ]
形 慣常的，按慣例的、ordinary [`ɔrdnˌɛrɪ] 形 平常的，普通的，差勁的、
typical [`tɪpɪkl] 形 典型的，獨特的

utensil [ju`tɛnsl] 名 **器皿**　　片 household utensils 家庭用具

utilize [`jutlˌaɪz] 動 **利用**
▶ Students should learn how to fully utilize the library.
學生應該學會如何充分的利用圖書館。
相關衍生字彙 use [juz] 動 使用、apply [ə`plaɪ] 動 應用、employ [ɪm`plɔɪ] 動 使用，雇用、
hire [haɪr] 動 雇用
動詞三態變化 utilize - utilized - utilized

utmost [`ʌtˌmost] 名 **最大努力**
▶ I already did my utmost to prepare for my interview.
我已經盡最大的努力去準備面試了。
相關衍生字彙 utmost purpose 片 最高宗旨、supreme [sə`prim] 形 最高的，極度的，至上的

utter [`ʌtɚ] 動 **發出聲音**　　片 to utter a sigh 發出嘆息聲
相關衍生字彙 utterly [`ʌtɚlɪ] 副 徹底地，完全地、express [ɪk`sprɛs] 動 表達，陳述
動詞三態變化 utter - uttered - uttered

utterance [`ʌtərəns] 名 **發聲，表達**
▶ You are brave to give utterance to your opinion at the meeting.
你很勇敢，在會議裡表達自己的看法。

U

一網打盡

字母 V

vacancy ~ vulnerable

詞性說明

名 名詞　　　副 副詞　　　介 介系詞

動 動詞　　　形 形容詞　　連 連接詞

代 代名詞　　助 助動詞

內文圖示說明

片 片語　　　反 反義字　　同 同義字

一網打盡「英語小知識」｜你不知道的「手指頭祕密」I ————————

「thumb」為「大拇指」，與中文相應的是，英語的 all (fingers and) thumbs 表示「笨手笨腳」的意思。

「forefinger」又稱「index finger」即「食指」。從排位上來說，「forefinger」應為「第一指」；從功用上來看，此手指伸出時有標示或指向的作用。

vacancy ~ vulnerable

MP3 22-01

★一網打盡 276 個英文單字 | 一網打盡 48 句英語會話句

vacancy [`vekənsɪ] 名 空缺　　片 a job vacancy 職缺
相關衍生字彙 vacant [`vekənt] 形 空白的，未被佔用的、vacate [`veket]
動 空出，使撤退，取消、vacantly [`vekəntlɪ] 副 神情茫然地

---

vacation [ve`keʃən] 名 假期
▶ I spend a vacation abroad annually.
　我一年出國度假一次。
相關衍生字彙 vacationist [ve`keʃənɪst] 名 休假者，度假者、vacation deprivation
片 假期剝削、vacation hangover 片 度假後遺症、vacation rental 片 度假租賃、
holiday [`hɑlə‚de] 名 節日，假日、furlough [`fɝlo] 名（軍人等的）休假，暫時解雇

---

vaccinate [`væksn‚et] 動 接種疫苗
▶ Kids are all vaccinated against some serious diseases.
　孩童都接種疫苗以對抗一些嚴重疾病。
相關衍生字彙 vaccination [‚væksn`eʃən] 名 接種疫苗、vaccine [`væksin] 名 疫苗、
injection [ɪn`dʒɛkʃən] 名 注射
動詞三態變化 vaccinate - vaccinated - vaccinated

---

vacuum [`vækjuəm] 名 吸塵器
▶ I use a vacuum to clean my house.
　我用吸塵器來打掃房子。
相關衍生字彙 vacuum-packed [`vækjuəm`pækt] 形 真空包裝的、vacuum bottle
片 熱水瓶，保溫瓶、vacuum cleaner 片（真空）吸塵器、vacuum crystallization
片 真空結晶、vacuum flask 片 保溫瓶、vacuum gauge 片 真空計、vacuum tube
片 真空管

---

vague [veg] 形 模糊的，不明確的
▶ Most teenagers are vague about their future.
　大部分的青少年對自己的未來是茫然的。
相關衍生字彙 vaguely [`veglɪ] 副 模糊地，茫然地、vagueness [`vegnɪs] 名 含糊，茫然、
unclear [ʌn`klɪr] 形 不清楚的，含糊不清的、indistinct [‚ɪndɪ`stɪŋkt]
形 模糊的，難以清楚辨認的、misty [`mɪstɪ] 形 有霧的，朦朧不清的

---

vain [ven] 形 徒勞的　　片 in vain 徒勞無功地
相關衍生字彙 vainly [`venlɪ] 副 徒勞地，自負地、vainness [`vennɪs] 名 徒勞，自負、
ineffectual [‚ɪnə`fɛktʃuəl] 形 無效果的，徒勞無益的、fruitless [`frutlɪs]
形 不結果的，無益的、

---

valid [`vælɪd] 形 有效的
▶ Before you go abroad, make sure your passport is valid.
　在出國前，要確定你的護照是有效的。

相關衍生字彙 validate [ˋvæləˌdet] 動 使有效，確認，證實、validity [vəˋlɪdətɪ] 名 正當，效力、effective [ɪˋfɛktɪv] 形 有效的，起作用的、cogent [ˋkodʒənt] 形 使人信服的，切實的、authorized [ˋɔθəˌraɪzd] 形 經授權的，公認的，經認可的

valley [ˋvælɪ] 名 山谷

▶ Living in the valley is like living in paradise.
　住在這山谷中如天堂般。

相關衍生字彙 river basin 片 江河流域、ravine [rəˋvin] 名 溝壑，深谷、strath [stræθ] 名 寬廣的（河）谷、cleft [klɛft] 名 裂縫，裂口 形 劈開的，裂開的、concavity [kɑnˋkævətɪ] 名 凹面、valley filling 片 河谷填積、valley glaciation 片 河谷型冰蝕、valley glacier 片 山谷冰川

value [ˋvælju] 動 珍視，重視

▶ I value the friendship between you and me so much.
　我非常重視你我之間的友誼。

相關衍生字彙 valuable [ˋvæljuəb!] 形 貴重的、cherish [ˋtʃɛrɪʃ] 動 珍惜、treasure [ˋtrɛʒɚ] 動 珍愛、valueless [ˋvæljulɪs] 形 沒有價值的

動詞三態變化 value - valued - valued

vanish [ˋvænɪʃ] 動 消失

▶ All my worries vanished into thin air.
　我所有的煩惱都消失得無影無蹤。

相關衍生字彙 disappear [ˌdɪsəˋpɪr] 動 消失，不見，滅絕、perish [ˋpɛrɪʃ] 動 消滅，枯萎，腐爛、vanishing point 片 消滅點，消失階段、vanishment [ˋvænɪʃmənt] 名 消失

動詞三態變化 vanish - vanished - vanished

vanity [ˋvænətɪ] 名 自負，虛榮　　片 a vanity fair 浮華世界

vapor [ˋvepɚ] 名 蒸氣　　片 water vapor 水蒸氣

相關衍生字彙 vaporize [ˋvepəˌraɪz] 動 使蒸發、vaporizer [ˋvepəˌraɪzɚ] 名 蒸餾器，噴霧器、vaporous [ˋvepərəs] 形 多蒸汽的，空想的、vapor lock 片 汽塞現象、vapor trail 片 飛機的凝結尾，飛雲、vaporable [ˋvepərəb!] 形 可氣化的、vaporarium [ˌvepəˋrɛrɪəm] 名 蒸汽浴室、vaporific [ˌvepəˋrɪfɪk] 形 產生蒸汽的，似蒸汽的、vaporization [ˌvepərəˋzeʃən] 名 蒸發（作用）、vaporless [ˋvepɚlɪs] 形 無水蒸氣的、vapory [ˋvepərɪ] 形 蒸汽多的，空想的

variety [vəˋraɪətɪ] 名 多樣化　　片 a variety of 各式各樣的

相關衍生字彙 various [ˋvɛrɪəs] 形 各式各樣的、vary [ˋvɛrɪ] 動 變化、varied [ˋvɛrɪd] 形 變化的、variable [ˋvɛrɪəb!] 形 可變的、variation [ˌvɛrɪˋeʃən] 名 變化

vault [ˋvɔlt] 名 保險庫，地下儲藏室　　片 a wine vault 酒窖

vegetable [`vɛdʒətəbḷ] 名 蔬菜
▶ We plant some vegetables on our balcony.
我們在陽台上種了些蔬菜。

相關衍生字彙 legume [`lɛgjum] 名 豆科植物，豆莢、herb [hɝb] 名 草本植物，藥草、
vegetative [`vɛdʒə,tetɪv] 形 植物的，有生長力的、vegetal [`vɛdʒətḷ]
名 植物，蔬菜 形 植物的，有關植物生長的

vegetarian [,vɛdʒə`tɛrɪən] 名 素食者
▶ Mary never eats meat. She is a vegetarian.
瑪莉不吃肉，她是位素食者。

相關衍生字彙 vegetation [,vɛdʒə`teʃən] 名（總稱）植物、plant [plænt] 名 植物、
vegetarianism [,vɛdʒə`tɛrɪənɪzəm] 名 素食主義、vegetal [`vɛdʒətḷ] 形 植物的

vehicle [`viɪkḷ] 名 交通工具
▶ Cars, buses, and trains are vehicles. 汽車、公車和火車都是交通工具。

vein [ven] 名 靜脈　　反 artery [`ɑrtərɪ] 名 動脈

vend [vɛnd] 動 出售，販賣　　片 a vending machine 自動販賣機
動詞三態變化 vend - vended - vended

vendor [`vɛndɚ] 名 小販，叫賣者
相關衍生字彙 seller [`sɛlɚ] 名 銷售者，賣方、salesman 名（男）推銷員，業務員、
peddler [`pɛdlɚ] 名 小販、vendor scheduler 片 採購計劃員、vendor scheduling
片 採購計劃法

venerable [`vɛnərəbḷ] 形 令人肅然起敬的，德高望重的，令人尊敬的　　 MP3 22-02
▶ He is a venerable scholar.
他是一位德高望重的學者。

相關衍生字彙 venerate [`vɛnə,ret] 動 尊敬、respect [rɪ`spɛkt] 動 尊敬、
veneration [,vɛnə`reʃən] 名 尊敬、respectable [rɪ`spɛktəbḷ] 形 值得尊敬的

vengeance [`vɛndʒəns] 名 報復
▶ Heaven's vengeance is slow but sure.
（諺語）法網恢恢，疏而不漏。

相關衍生字彙 vengeful [`vɛndʒfəl] 形 復仇心重的，報復的、vengefully [`vɛndʒfəlɪ]
副 復仇心切地、revenge [rɪ`vɛndʒ] 名 動 報復、retaliation [rɪ,tælɪ`eʃən]
名 報復、reprisal [rɪ`praɪzḷ] 名 報復、avengement [ə`vɛndʒmənt] 名 報仇

ventilate [,vɛntḷ`et] 動 使通風
▶ Open the window and let fresh air ventilate the room.
打開窗戶讓新鮮空氣流通。

相關衍生字彙 ventilation [,vɛntḷ`eʃən] 名 通風，流通空氣、ventilation system 片 通風系統

動詞三態變化 ventilate - ventilated - ventilated

venture [ˋvɛntʃɚ] 動 冒險
▶ Nothing ventured, nothing gained.
（諺語）不入虎穴，焉得虎子。

相關衍生字彙 adventure [ədˋvɛntʃɚ] 名 冒險、attempt [əˋtɛmpt] 動 試圖，企圖、enterprise [ˋɛntɚˏpraɪz] 名 冒險精神、risk [rɪsk] 動 冒險於

動詞三態變化 venture - ventured - ventured

---

verdict [ˋvɝdɪkt] 名 裁決
▶ The jury will announce their verdict ten minutes later.
十分鐘過後，陪審團將宣布裁決結果。

---

verge [vɝdʒ] 名 邊緣　　片 on the verge of 瀕臨～，快要～

---

verify [ˋvɛrəˏfaɪ] 動 證實，查證
▶ The teacher is verifying what the kid said.
老師正在查證孩子所説的內容。

相關衍生字彙 verifiable [ˋvɛrəˏfaɪəbl] 形 可驗證的，可檢驗的、verification [ˏvɛrɪfɪˋkeʃən] 名 證明，核實、confirm [kənˋfɝm] 動 證實，堅定，批准、certify [ˋsɝtəˏfaɪ] 動 證明，擔保，保證、substantiate [səbˋstænʃɪˏet] 動 證明～有根據，使實體化

動詞三態變化 verify - verified - verified

---

version [ˋvɝʒən] 名 版本
▶ The novel was adapted to a movie version.
這本小説已被改編為電影版本。

---

vessel [ˋvɛsl̩] 名 船艦　　片 to launch a vessel 讓船下水

---

veteran [ˋvɛtərən] 名 退伍軍人
▶ The government has the duty to take care of the disabled veterans.
政府有責任照顧傷殘的退伍軍人。

---

vibrate [ˋvaɪbret] 動 震動
▶ Leaves are vibrating in the wind.
葉子在風中擺動。

相關衍生字彙 vibration [vaɪˋbreʃən] 名 震動、vibrant [ˋvaɪbrənt] 形 震動的、quiver [ˋkwɪvɚ] 動 顫動、tremble [ˋtrɛmbl̩] 動 震顫

動詞三態變化 vibrate - vibrated - vibrated

---

vicinity [vəˋsɪnətɪ] 名 鄰近
▶ My house is in the close vicinity of the school. 我的房子緊鄰學校。

485

vicious [ˋvɪʃəs] 形 邪惡的，惡毒的
▶ Your vicious remarks did harm to my feelings.
你惡毒的言論傷害到我的感受。

相關衍生字彙 viciously [ˋvɪʃəslɪ] 副 邪惡地，敵意的、vicious circle 片 惡性循環、
viciousness [ˋvɪʃəsnɪs] 名 惡意，邪惡、spiteful [ˋspaɪtfəl] 形 懷恨的，惡意的、
malicious [məˋlɪʃəs] 形 惡意的，蓄意的、ruthless [ˋruθlɪs] 形 無情的，殘忍的、
inhumane [ˏɪnhjuˋmen] 形 無人情味的，殘忍的

victim [ˋvɪktɪm] 名 受害者　　片 earthquake victims 地震受害者
相關衍生字彙 victimize [ˋvɪktɪˏmaɪz] 動 使犧牲、victimization [ˏvɪktɪmɪˋzeʃən]
名 犧牲，欺騙、scapegoat [ˋskepˏgot] 名 代罪羔羊

victory [ˋvɪktərɪ] 名 勝利
▶ The football team had a sweeping victory.
足球隊獲得全面性的勝利。

相關衍生字彙 victor [ˋvɪktɚ] 名 勝利者、victorious [vɪkˋtorɪəs] 形 勝利的、winner [ˋwɪnɚ]
名 勝利者、win [wɪn] 動 贏

view [vju] 名 觀點　動 看待
▶ I view him as my opponent.
我視他為我的對手。

相關衍生字彙 viewer [ˋvjuɚ] 名 觀看者，參觀者、viewless [ˋvjulɪs] 形 不表示意見的、
viewable [ˋvjuəbl] 形 看得見的，值得一看的

動詞三態變化 view - viewed - viewed

viewpoint [ˋvjuˏpɔɪnt] 名 觀點
▶ From my viewpoint, you are a promising young man.
就我的觀點，你是個前途無量的年輕人。

相關衍生字彙 perspective [pɚˋspɛktɪv] 形 透視的，透視畫的、sentiment [ˋsɛntəmənt]
名 感情，情緒，意見

vigil [ˋvɪdʒəl] 名 守夜
▶ The nurses take turns keeping a vigil over the patient.
護士輪流值夜班照顧病人。

vigor [ˋvɪgɚ] 名 活力
▶ A leader should be a man of great vigor.
領導人必須是充滿活力的人。

相關衍生字彙 vigorous [ˋvɪgərəs] 形 充滿活力的、energy [ˋɛnɚdʒɪ] 名 體力、
energetic [ˏɛnɚˋdʒɛtɪk] 形 充滿活力的

violate [ˋvaɪəˏlet] 動 違反
▶ A good doctor never violates the medical ethics.
好醫生絕對不會違反醫德。

動詞三態變化 violate - violated - violated

violation [ˌvaɪəˋleʃən] 名 違規　　片 to commit a violation 違反規定　　 MP3 **22-03**

相關衍生字彙 violate [ˋvaɪəˌlet] 動 違犯，侵犯、violator [ˋvaɪəˌletɚ] 名 違背者，侵犯者、
delinquency [dɪˋlɪŋkwənsɪ] 名 懈怠，違法行為、invasion [ɪnˋveʒən]
名 入侵，侵犯

violence [ˋvaɪələns] 名 暴力
▶ I am against answering violence with violence.
我反對以暴制暴。

相關衍生字彙 violent [ˋvaɪələnt] 形 暴力的、violently [ˋvaɪələntlɪ] 副 暴力地、
powerful [ˋpaʊɚfəl] 形 強而有力的、mighty [ˋmaɪtɪ] 形 強大的

violinist [ˌvaɪəˋlɪnɪst] 名 小提琴家
▶ Being a well-known violinist is her dream.
她的夢想是成為知名的小提琴家。

相關衍生字彙 violin [ˌvaɪəˋlɪn] 名 小提琴、violinistic [ˌvaɪələˋnɪstɪk] 形 小提琴手的、
violinmaker [ˌvaɪəˋlɪnˌmekɚ] 名 小提琴設計人或製造人

virtue [ˋvɝtʃu] 名 美德
▶ My husband is a man of great virtue.
我先生是個品格高尚的人。

相關衍生字彙 virtuous [ˋvɝtʃʊəs] 形 有道德的、virtuously [ˋvɝtʃʊəslɪ] 副 合乎道德地、
virtueless [ˋvɝtʃʊlɪs] 形 無美德的，無效力的

virus [ˋvaɪrəs] 名 病毒　　片 common cold virus 普通的感冒病毒

visible [ˋvɪzəbl̩] 形 看得到的
▶ The dust is visible to the naked eye. 灰塵是肉眼所看得到的。

vision [ˋvɪʒən] 名 視力
▶ Keeping watching the computer screen will make your vision blurred.
一直看電腦螢幕會讓你的視力模糊。

visit [ˋvɪzɪt] 動 拜訪
▶ During the vacation, I will visit several friends in Europe.
這次假期，我將拜訪幾個歐洲朋友。

相關衍生字彙 visitor [ˋvɪzɪtɚ] 名 訪客、traveler [ˋtrævlɚ] 名 旅行者、commuter [kəˋmjutɚ]
名 通勤者、guest [gɛst] 名 客人

動詞三態變化 visit - visited - visited

V

vital [`vaɪtl] 形 致命的，重要的
▶ I made a vital mistake.
我犯了致命的錯誤。
相關衍生字彙 vitality [vaɪ`tælətɪ] 名 活力，生命力、vitalize [`vaɪtə,laɪz] 動 賦予～生命，激勵、vitally [`vaɪtəlɪ] 副 充滿活力地，極其，十分、necessary [`nɛsə,sɛrɪ] 形 必要的，無法避免的、essential [ɪ`sɛnʃəl] 形 不可缺的，本質的、fundamental [,fʌndə`mɛntl] 名 基礎的，根本的、required [rɪ`kwaɪrd] 形 必須的

vitamin [`vaɪtəmɪn] 名 維他命
▶ I take some vitamins to keep healthy. 我吃點維他命來保健。

vivid [`vɪvɪd] 形 鮮明的，活潑的
▶ Lily is a vivid girl.
莉莉是個活潑的女孩。
相關衍生字彙 vividly [`vɪvɪdlɪ] 副 生動地，鮮明地、vivify [`vɪvə,faɪ] 動 (使) 有生氣，(使) 生動、vividness [`vɪvɪdnɪs] 名 (色彩，光線等) 鮮豔，活潑

vocabulary [və`kæbjə,lɛrɪ] 名 字彙
▶ I enlarge my vocabulary by reading.
我藉由閱讀來擴大單字量。
相關衍生字彙 lexicon [`lɛksɪkən] 名 詞典，語彙、dialect [`daɪəlɛkt] 方言、idiom [`ɪdɪəm] 名 慣用語、jargon [`dʒɑrgən] 名 行話，胡言亂語、vernacular [və`nækjələ] 名 本地話，方言，行話、terminology [,tɝmə`nɑlədʒɪ] 名 (總稱) 術語，專門用語、phraseology [,frezɪ`ɑlədʒɪ] 名 語法，措辭

vocal [`vokl] 形 聲音的　　片 vocal cords 聲帶
相關衍生字彙 vocal chords 片 聲帶、vocalic [vo`kælɪk] 形 母音的，含母音的、vocalist [`vokəlɪst] 名 聲樂家、vocalization [,vokələ`zeʃən] 名 發聲，有聲化、vocalize [`vokl,aɪz] 動 發聲，喊叫、vocally [`voklɪ] 副 發聲地，用語言表達、vocals [`voklz] 名 聲樂作品，聲樂節目

vocation [vo`keʃən] 名 職業
▶ I choose to be a teacher as my vocation.
我選擇當老師為我的職業。
相關衍生字彙 vocational [vo`keʃənl] 形 職業的、occupation [,ɑkjə`peʃən] 名 職業、job [dʒɑb] 名 工作、profession [prə`fɛʃən] 名 專門職業

vogue [vog] 名 時尚　　同 fashion [`fæʃən] 名 時尚

voice [vɔɪs] 名 聲音　　片 with one voice 異口同聲地

volcanic [vɑl`kænɪk] 形 火山的　　片 volcanic ash 火山灰

volcano [vɑl`keno] 名 火山
▶ Experts predict that the dormant volcano will erupt soon.
專家預言這座休火山將很快爆發。

---

volleyball [`vɑlɪˌbɔl] 名 排球　　片 beach volleyball 沙灘排球

---

volume [`vɑljəm] 名 音量
▶ The volume of your music annoys me. 你音樂的音量吵到我了。

---

volunteer [ˌvɑlən`tɪr] 名 志工　　◎ MP3 **22-04**
▶ Our society needs more kind-hearted volunteers.
我們的社會需要更多善心的志工。

相關衍生字彙 voluntarily [`vɑlənˌtɛrəlɪ] 副 自願地、voluntary [`vɑlənˌtɛrɪ] 形 自願的、
willing [`wɪlɪŋ] 形 願意的

---

vomit [`vɑmɪt] 動 嘔吐
▶ The stale seafood made me vomit.
那不新鮮的海鮮讓我作嘔。

動詞三態變化 vomit - vomited - vomited

---

vote [vot] 動 投票
▶ She was voted to be our class leader.
她被票選為我們的班長。

相關衍生字彙 voter [`votɚ] 名 選舉人，投票人、voting [`votɪŋ] 名 選舉，投票、
ballot [`bælət] 名 選票、投票權、referendum [ˌrɛfə`rɛndəm] 名 公民投票、
selection [sə`lɛkʃən] 名 選擇，選拔

動詞三態變化 vote - voted - voted

---

vow [vau] 名 誓約，誓言
▶ The marriage vow is so touching.
婚姻的誓約真感人。

相關衍生字彙 promise [`prɑmɪs] 動 承諾、guarantee [ˌgærən`ti] 名動 保證、swear [swɛr]
動 發誓、pledge [plɛdʒ] 動 保證，誓言、oath [oθ] 名 誓言

---

voyage [`vɔɪɪdʒ] 名 航海，航行
▶ She joined a round-the-world voyage.
她參加了環遊世界的航行。

相關衍生字彙 voyageable [`vɔɪɪdʒəbl] 形 可航行的、voyager [`vɔɪɪdʒɚ]
名 航行者，航海者，旅客

---

vulgar [`vʌlgɚ] 形 粗俗的，粗魯的
▶ Speaking loudly in public is vulgar. 在公共場所大聲喧嘩是很粗俗的。

vulnerable [`vʌlnərəbl̩] 形 易受傷的，脆弱的

▶ She is a girl who is vulnerable emotionally.
她是個在情感上容易受傷的女孩。

相關衍生字彙 vulnerability [ˌvʌlnərə`bɪlətɪ] 名 易受傷，弱點、vulnerably [`vʌlnərəbl̩ɪ]
副 脆弱地，易受傷害地、unprotected [ˌʌnprə`tɛktɪd]
形 無保護的，未受關稅保護的、defenseless [dɪ`fɛnslɪs] 形 無防禦的，無保護的

| MEMO |

MEMO

詞性說明

名 名詞	副 副詞	介 介系詞
動 動詞	形 形容詞	連 連接詞
代 代名詞	助 助動詞	

內文圖示說明

片 片語　　反 反義字　　同 同義字

一網打盡「英語小知識」| 你不知道的「手指頭祕密」II ————

　　「middle finger」為「中指」，此指居中，名正言順，且與中文說法也一致。

　　「ring finger」是「無名指」，從世界各地的婚俗習慣來說，「wedding ring（結婚戒指）」戴在這一手指（通常指左手）上，表示已婚。

　　「little finger」顧名思義為「小指」。在美國和蘇格蘭，人們又賦予它一個名稱「pinkie / pinky」，有「小巧可愛」之意。

 wage ~ write

wage [wedʒ] 名 薪水

▶ To get a decent wage, he works very hard.
為了拿到不錯的薪水，他很認真工作。

相關衍生字彙 payment [`pemənt] 名 支付，付款、salary [`sælərɪ] 名 薪資 動 給～薪水、
remuneration [rɪˌmjunəˈreʃən] 名 酬勞，償還，薪資、
compensation [ˌkɑmpənˈseʃən] 名 補償金，津貼

wail [wel] 動 痛哭

▶ All the players wailed for losing the game.
球員們因輸球而痛哭。

相關衍生字彙 wailful [`welfəl] 形 悲嘆的，哀悼的、shriek [ʃrik] 名 尖叫聲 動 尖叫，喊叫、
squeal [skwil] 名 尖叫聲 動 發出長而尖的叫聲、howl [haʊl] 名 動 怒吼，嚎啕大哭

動詞三態變化 wail - wailed - wailed

wait [wet] 動 等候

▶ I am so sorry to keep you waiting so long.
很抱歉，讓你等這麼久。

相關衍生字彙 wait-and-see [`wetənˈsi] 形 靜候的，觀望的、wait behind 片 留下、wait for
片 等候、wait on 片 伺候、waiter [`wetɚ] 名（男）侍者，服務生、
waiting [`wetɪŋ] 名 等候，服侍 形 等待的，服侍的、waiting game
片 伺機而動的策略、waiting room 片 等候室、waitress [`wetrɪs] 名 女服務生

動詞三態變化 wait - waited - waited

wake [wek] 動 醒來　　片 to wake up 醒過來

相關衍生字彙 wake a sleeping dog 片 惹事生非、wake up to 片 認識到，意識到、
wakeful [`wekfəl] 形 不眠的，覺醒的，警覺的、wakefully [`wekfəlɪ]
副 睡不著地，提高警覺地、wakefulness [`wekfəlnɪs] 名 不眠，覺醒，警覺、
waken [`wekn̩] 動 睡醒，覺醒，喚醒、wakening [`wekənɪŋ] 名 喚醒、
waking [`wekɪŋ] 形 清醒的，未睡著的

動詞三態變化 wake - waked / woke - waked / woken

walk [wɔk] 動 走路

▶ He walked away without saying anything.
他沒說任何話就走開了。

相關衍生字彙 walker [`wɔkɚ] 名 步行者、walkout [`wɔkˌaʊt] 名 罷工、walking [`wɔkɪŋ]
名 散步

動詞三態變化 walk - walked - walked

wall [wɔl] 名 牆壁

▶ On the wall is an old clock.
牆上有個老時鐘。

相關衍生字彙 wall map 片 掛圖、wall off 片 用牆隔開、wall painting 片 壁畫、wall plug 片 牆上插座

---

wallet [ˋwɑlɪt] 名 錢包
▶ His wallet was bulging.
　他的皮夾鼓鼓的。

相關衍生字彙 billfold [ˋbɪlˏfold] 名 皮夾子、purse [pɝs] 名 錢包，（女用）手提包

---

wander [ˋwɑndɚ] 動 漫遊，閒晃
▶ He wandered in the streets alone at night.
　他在夜晚一個人在街上閒晃。

相關衍生字彙 wanderer [ˋwɑndərɚ] 名 流浪漢，迷路的動物、wandering [ˋwɑndərɪŋ] 形 徘徊的，蜿蜒的，錯亂的、wanderingly [ˋwɑndərɪŋlɪ] 副 徘徊地，流浪地，迷路地、wanderings [ˋwɑndərɪŋz] 名 漫遊，閒逛

動詞三態變化 wander - wandered - wandered

---

wane [wen] 名（月）虧
▶ The moon is on the wane today. 今天月亮由盈轉虧。

---

want [wɑnt] 動 想要　　片 the wanted 被通緝者
動詞三態變化 want - wanted - wanted

---

ward [wɔrd] 名 病房
▶ It's hard work to work in the emergency ward. 在急診病房工作很辛苦。

---

wardrobe [ˋwɔrdˏrob] 名 衣櫃
▶ I hang all my clothes in the wardrobe.
　我全部的衣服都掛在衣櫃裡。

相關衍生字彙 wardrobe dealer 片 舊衣商、wardrobe mistress 片 戲裝女保管員、clothes [kloz] 名 衣服，寢具、closet [ˋklɑzɪt] 名 壁櫥，衣櫥、robe [rob] 名 長袍，浴衣

---

warehouse [ˋwɛrˏhaʊs] 名 倉庫　　片 warehouse supermarket 倉儲式超市
相關衍生字彙 warehouse club 片 批發店，大型零售商店、warehouse supermarket 片 倉儲式超市、warehouseman [ˋwɛrˏhaʊsmən] 名 倉庫管理人、warehousing [ˋwɛrˏhaʊzɪŋ] 名 入庫，儲倉、wareroom [ˋwɛrˏrum] 名 商品陳列室，商品儲藏室

---

warfare [ˋwɔrˏfɛr] 名 交戰狀況　　片 biological / chemical warfare 細菌戰／化學戰
相關衍生字彙 war [wɔr] 名 戰爭、warhorse [ˋwɔrˏhɔrs] 名 戰馬，老兵、warlike [ˋwɔrˏlaɪk] 形 好戰的，軍事的

---

warm [wɔrm] 形 溫暖的
▶ Aunt Vicky is a warm woman.
　薇琪姑媽是個溫暖熱情的人。

相關衍生字彙 warm-hearted [ˋwɔrmˋhɑrtɪd] 形 熱心腸的、kind-hearted [ˋkaɪndˋhɑrtɪd] 形 善良的、cold [kold] 形 冷的、cool [kul] 形 涼的、warmth [wɔrmθ] 名 溫暖

warn [wɔrn] 動 警告

▶ Mothers warn their children not to talk with strangers.
媽媽都會警告孩子們別跟陌生人說話。

相關衍生字彙 warn off 片 通知離開，警告～不得靠近、warner [`wɔrnɚ] 名 警告者、
warning [`wɔrnɪŋ] 名 警告，告誡 形 警告的，引以為戒的、warning sign
片 警告標誌，警告牌、caution [`kɔʃən] 名 小心，謹慎 名動 警告，告誡、
notify [`notəˌfaɪ] 動 通知，告知

動詞三態變化 warn - warned - warned

warrant [`wɔrənt] 名 授權

▶ The police is waiting for the court to issue a search warrant.
警方正在等法院發出搜查令。

相關衍生字彙 warrant officer 片 美國陸軍准尉，海軍士官長、warrantable [`wɔrəntəbl]
形 可保證的，可承認的、warrantee [ˌwɔrənˈti] 名 被保證人、
warranter [`wɔrəntɚ] 名 保證人、warranty [`wɔrəntɪ] 名 保證書，擔保，授權

warship [`wɔrˌʃɪp] 名 軍艦

▶ The warship was commanded by a general.
這艘軍艦由一位將軍所指揮。

相關衍生字彙 corvette [kɔrˈvɛt] 名 輕武裝快艦、battleship [`bætlˌʃɪp] 名 戰艦、
battlewagon [`bætlˌwægən] 名 戰鬥艦、frigate [`frɪgɪt] 名 驅逐艦，護航艦

wash [waʃ] 動 洗   片 a washing machine 洗衣機

相關衍生字彙 washable [`waʃəbl] 形 可洗的，耐洗的、washboard [`waʃˌbord] 名 洗衣板、
washing [`waʃɪŋ] 名 洗滌（劑）

動詞三態變化 wash - washed - washed

waste [west] 動 浪費

▶ Don't waste your life on playing video games.
別浪費生命在電玩上。

相關衍生字彙 waste away 片 消瘦、waste disposal 片 廢物處理，廢料處理裝置、waste pipe
片 廢水管，排水管、waste sorting 片 垃圾分類、waste time 片 浪費時間、
wastebasket [`westˌbæskɪt] 名 廢紙簍、wasteful [`westfəl]
形 浪費的，揮霍的、wastefully [`westfəlɪ] 副 浪費地，揮霍地、
wastepaper [`westˌpepɚ] 名 紙屑、wastebin [`westˌbɪn] 名 垃圾桶、
wasted [`westɪd] 形 浪費的，荒蕪的、wastefulness [`westfəlnɪs]
名 浪費，揮霍無度、wasteland [`westˌlænd] 名 荒地，未開墾地、
wasteness [`westnɪs] 名 荒涼，浪費、wasteplex [`westˌplɛks]
名 廢棄物回收設施、waster [`westɚ] 名 浪費者，荒廢者、wasting [`westɪŋ]
形 荒廢的，消耗性的

動詞三態變化 waste - wasted - wasted

watch [watʃ] 動 觀看　　🅟 to watch out 小心　　◉MP3 **23-02**

相關衍生字彙 watch for 片 等待、watch out 片 小心，當心、watch over 片 監視、
watchdog [`watʃˌdɔg] 名 看門狗，監視人、watchful [`watʃfəl]
形 警惕的，注意的、watchfully [`watʃfəlɪ] 副 注意地，警覺地、
watchable [`watʃəbl] 形 悅目的，值得一看的、watcher [`watʃɚ]
名 看守人，視察者、watchfulness [`watʃfəlnɪs] 名 警覺（性）、
watchman [`watʃmən] 名 夜間看守人，警備員、watchtower [`watʃˌtauɚ]
名 瞭望台

動詞三態變化 watch - watched - watched

---

waterproof [`wɔtɚˌpruf] 形 防水的
▶ A raincoat is of course waterproof.
　雨衣當然要防水。

相關衍生字彙 water [`wɔtɚ] 名 水、waterfall [`wɔtɚˌfɔl] 名 瀑布、watercolor [`watɚˌkʌlɚ]
名 水彩、waterway [`watɚˌwe] 名 水路

---

wave [wev] 名 浪　　🅟 to make waves 興風作浪

相關衍生字彙 wave band 片 （電訊之）波帶、wave guide 片 波導管，波導器、wave pool
片 衝浪池、waveband [`wevˌbænd] 名 波段、waved [wevd]
形 波浪型的，有波浪的、waveform [`wevˌfɔrm] 名 波形、
wavelength [`wevˌlɛŋθ] 名 波長，波段、waveless [`wevlɪs]
形 無波的，平靜的、wavelet [`wevlɪt] 名 小浪，微波、wavelike [`wevˌlaɪk]
形 副 波浪般的（地），波狀的（地）

---

weak [wik] 形 虛弱的
▶ The spirit is willing but the flesh is weak.
　（諺語）心有餘而力不足。

相關衍生字彙 weak acid 片 弱酸、weak holdings 片 短期持股、weaker sex 片 婦女，女性、
weaken [`wikən] 動 削弱，減少、weak-headed [`wik`hɛdɪd]
形 易醉的，怯懦的，遲鈍的、weakhearted [`wik`hɑrtɪd] 形 無勇氣的，怯懦的、
weakish [`wikɪʃ] 形 有弱點的，稍淡的、weak-kneed [`wikˌnid]
形 雙腿無力的，軟弱的、weakling [`wiklɪŋ] 名 懦弱者 形 虛弱的、weakly [`wiklɪ]
形 副 虛弱的（地），軟弱的（地）、weak-minded [`wik`maɪndɪd]
形 懦弱的，優柔寡斷的、weakness [`wiknɪs] 名 虛弱，病弱

---

wealth [wɛlθ] 名 財富
▶ He is seeking his wealth all his life. 他終其一生在追求財富。

---

wealthy [`wɛlθɪ] 形 有錢的　　🄸 rich [rɪtʃ] 形 富有的

相關衍生字彙 moneyed [`mʌnɪd] 形 有錢的，金錢上的、well-heeled [`wɛl`hild] 形 富有的

---

weapon [`wɛpən] 名 武器　　🅟 a nuclear weapon 核子武器

497

wear [wɛr] 動 穿戴

▶ She is a middle-aged woman wearing a pair of glasses.
她是位中年婦女,戴著一副眼鏡。

動詞三態變化 wear - wore - worn

wearisome [`wɪrɪsəm] 形 令人厭煩的,令人疲倦的

▶ What a wearisome meeting!
多令人討厭的會議!

相關衍生字彙 weary [`wɪrɪ] 形 疲憊的、tired [taɪrd] 形 疲憊的、fatigued [fə`tigd] 形 疲憊的、exhausted [ɪg`zɔstɪd] 形 精疲力竭的

weather [`wɛðɚ] 名 天氣　　片 under the weather 身體不舒服的

相關衍生字彙 weather bomb 片 天氣炸彈、weather centre 片 氣象中心、weather forecast 片 氣象預報、weather forecaster 片 氣象報告員、weather map 片 天氣圖,氣象圖、weather report 片 氣象報告、weather vane 片 風向計、weather-beaten [`wɛðɚ`bitən] 形 飽經風霜的、weatherboard [`wɛðɚ`bord] 名 擋雨板 動 給~裝擋雨板、weatherboarded [`wɛðɚ`bordɪd] 形 有風雨板的、weatherbound [`wɛðɚ`baʊnd] 形 被風雨困住的、weathercast [`wɛðɚ`kæst] 名(廣播電台或電視的)氣象報導、weatherglass [`wɛðɚ`glæs] 名 晴雨表,溼度計、weathering [`wɛðərɪŋ] 名 風化(作用)、weatherman [`wɛðɚ`mæn] 名 氣象預報員、weatherology [ˌwɛðə`rɑlədʒɪ] 名 氣象學、weatherwise [`wɛðɚ`waɪz] 形 善於預測天氣的

weave [wiv] 動 編織　　片 to weave a lie 編織謊言

動詞三態變化 weave - wove / weaved - woven / wove / weaved

wedding [`wɛdɪŋ] 名 婚禮

▶ Their wedding reception will take place soon.
他們的婚宴很快就要舉行了。

相關衍生字彙 wedded [`wɛdɪd] 形 已婚的、divorced [də`vɔrst] 形 離婚的、married [`mærɪd] 形 已婚的、engaged [ɪn`gedʒd] 形 訂婚的

weekday [`wik.de] 名 工作天

▶ A weekday is any day from Monday to Friday (inclusive).
工作天是指包含周一到周五的任何一天。

相關衍生字彙 weekdays [`wik.dez] 副(美)在平日、week [wik] 名 一星期、weekend [`wik`ɛnd] 名 周末 形 周末的 動 度周末、weekends [`wik.ɛndz] 副 每周末地、weekend box office 片 周末票房、weekender [`wik`ɛndɚ] 名 周末旅行者(袋)、weekly [`wiklɪ] 名 周刊,周報 形 每周的 副 每周、weeknight [`wiknaɪt] 名 周日夜晚

weep [wip] 動 哭泣
▶ We all wept for joy.
我們都喜極而泣。
動詞三態變化 weep - wept - wept

weigh [we] 動 秤重
▶ Before you make a decision, remember to weigh the advantages and disadvantages.
做決定之前，記得權衡利弊得失。
動詞三態變化 weigh - weighed - weighed

weight [wet] 名 重量　片 to gain weight 變胖

well-off [`wɛl`ɔf] 形 富裕的
▶ His family is very well-off.
他的家境很富裕。
相關衍生字彙 well-known [`wɛl`non] 形 出名的、well-being [`wɛl`biiŋ] 名 幸福

welcome [`wɛlkəm] 動 歡迎
▶ You are welcome.
不客氣。
動詞三態變化 welcome - welcomed - welcomed

welfare [`wɛl,fɛr] 名 福利
▶ Our government is improving the social welfare.
政府正在改善社會福利。
相關衍生字彙 welfare benefits 片 福利金、welfare capitalism 片 福利資本主義、welfare state 片 福利國家、welfare work 片 福利事業、welfarism [`wɛl,fɛrɪzəm] 名 社會福利政策

west [wɛst] 名 西方　反 east [ist] 名 東方
相關衍生字彙 western [`wɛstɚn] 形 西方的、westward [`wɛstwɚd] 副 往西、eastern [`istɚn] 形 東方的、eastward [`istwɚd] 副 往東

wet [wɛt] 形 濕的　反 dry [draɪ] 形 乾的 ◎MP3 23-03

wheel [hwil] 名 輪子　片 behind the wheel 在駕駛
相關衍生字彙 wheel clamp 片 車輪固定夾、wheel horse 片（馬車）後馬、wheelbarrow [`hwil,bæro] 名 獨輪小車，手推車、wheelbase [`hwil,bes] 名 軸距、wheelchair [`hwil`tʃɛr] 名 輪椅、wheeler [`hwilɚ] 名 車夫，有車輪之物、wheelhouse [`hwil,haus] 名 舵手室，駕駛室、wheelman [`hwilmən] 名 舵手，騎腳踏車的人、wheelwork [`hwilwɜk] 名（機器中的）齒輪轉動裝置、wheely [`hwilɪ] 形 輪子的，輪狀的

W

whip [hwɪp] 動 鞭打
▶ The rider whipped his horse.
騎師鞭打著馬匹。
動詞三態變化 whip - whipped / whipt - whipped / whipt

whisper [`hwɪspɚ] 動 耳語
▶ He leaned over and whispered in my ear.
他靠過來在我耳邊說話。
相關衍生字彙 murmur [`mɝmɚ] 名 低語聲、mutter [`mʌtɚ] 名 咕噥 名 動 抱怨、
mumble [`mʌmbl̩] 名 咕嚕 動 含糊地說
動詞三態變化 whisper - whispered - whispered

whistle [`hwɪsl̩] 動 吹口哨
▶ He whistled a song.
他用口哨吹著歌曲。
動詞三態變化 whistle - whistled - whistled

whole [hol] 形 全部的　　片 on the whole 大體上，一般說來

wholesale [`hol͵sel] 名 批發　　反 retail [`ritel] 名 零售
相關衍生字彙 wholesome [`holsəm] 形 有益健康的、wholegrain [`holgren] 形 全麥的、
whole-hearted [`hol`hartɪd] 形 全心全意

wicked [`wɪkɪd] 形 邪惡的
▶ I never did anything wicked. 我從不做壞事。

wide [waɪd] 形 寬的　　片 far and wide 到處
相關衍生字彙 wide-awake [`waɪdə͵wek] 形 完全清醒著的，機警的、
wide-angle [`waɪd`æŋgl̩] 形 寬角度的、wide-angle lens 片 廣角透鏡、
wide-bodied [`waɪd`badɪd] 形（飛機）機身寬大的，寬體的、
wide-eyed [`waɪd`aɪd] 形 驚奇的，天真的、widemouthed [`waɪd͵mauθt]
形 大口的，高聲說出的、widen [`waɪdn̩] 動 加寬，擴大、
wide-open [`waɪd`opən] 形 完全開放的，取締不嚴的、
wide-ranging [`waɪd`rendʒɪŋ] 形 廣泛的、wide-screen [`waɪd`skrin]
形 畫面寬闊的，寬銀幕的

widely [`waɪdlɪ] 副 廣泛地
▶ He read widely, from literature to science. 他廣泛地閱讀，從文學到科學。

widespread [`waɪd͵sprɛd] 形 廣泛的
▶ The information from the Internet is in widespread use.
網路上的資訊被廣泛使用。

widow [`wɪdo]名 寡婦　　反 widower [`wɪdoɚ]名 鰥夫

wife [waɪf]名 太太　　反 husband [`hʌzbənd]名 丈夫

wild [waɪld]形 野生的
▶ There are fewer and fewer wild animals.
野生動物愈來愈少了。
相關衍生字彙 wilderness [`wɪldɚnɪs]名 荒野、wildly [`waɪldlɪ]形 野生地、
wildfire [`waɪld͵faɪr]名 野火、wildlife [`waɪld͵laɪf]名 野生動物

willing [`wɪlɪŋ]形 願意的
▶ I am willing to do anything for you.
我願意為你做任何事。
相關衍生字彙 willing to 片 樂意，願意、willingly [`wɪlɪŋlɪ]副 樂意地，願意地、
willingness [`wɪlɪŋnɪs]名 樂意，自願

win [wɪn]動 贏　　片 a win-win policy 雙贏的政策
相關衍生字彙 win acceptance with 片 被接受，受歡迎、win an advantage over 片 勝過、
win over 片 說服，爭取、winner [`wɪnɚ]名 獲勝者，優勝者、winning [`wɪnɪŋ]
名 獲勝，勝利 形 獲勝的，贏的、winningest [`wɪnɪŋɪst]形 贏得絕大部分的、
winningly [`wɪnɪŋlɪ]副 迷人地，嬌媚地、winningness [`wɪnɪŋnəs]
名 動人，吸引力、winnings [`wɪnɪŋz]名 贏得的錢
動詞三態變化 win - won - won

windy [`wɪndɪ]形 有風的
▶ It's a windy day.
今天是個有風的日子。
相關衍生字彙 windmill [`wɪnd͵mɪl]名 風車、windshield [`wɪnd͵ʃild]名 擋風玻璃、
wind [wɪnd]名 風

window [`wɪndo]名 窗戶
▶ I just went window shopping without buying anything.
我只是逛逛街，沒有買東西。
相關衍生字彙 window cleaner 片 門窗清潔工、window curtain 片 窗簾、window frame
片 窗框，窗架、window seat 片 靠窗座位、window shade 片 遮光窗簾、
window shopping 片 流覽商店櫥窗、windowless [`wɪndolɪs]形 無窗的、
windowy [`wɪndəwɪ]形 多窗的

windowsill [`wɪndo͵sɪl]名 窗台
▶ A bird is perching at the windowsill. 窗台上有小鳥棲息著。

wine [waɪn]名 酒　　片 a glass of wine 一杯酒

wing [wɪŋ] 名 翅膀

◎ MP3 23-04

▶ Children are under their parents' wing till they grow up.
孩子會在父母的保護下直到長大。

相關衍生字彙 winged [wɪŋd] 形 有翼的，迅速的，高尚的、wing-footed [`wɪŋˌfʊtɪd] 形 迅速的，健步如飛的、wingless [`wɪŋlɪs] 形 無翼的、winglet [`wɪŋlɪt] 名 小翼、wingmanship [`wɪŋmənˌʃɪp] 名 飛行術、wingover [`wɪŋˌovɚ] 名（飛機的）橫轉、wingspan [`wɪŋˌspæn] 名（飛機或鳥的）翼展、wingspread [`wɪŋˌsprɛd] 名 翼幅、wingy [`wɪŋɪ] 形 有翅膀的，迅速的，翼狀的

---

wink [wɪŋk] 動 眨眼

▶ He winked at me as a sign for greeting.
他對我眨眼表示問候。

動詞三態變化 wink - winked - winked

---

wipe [waɪp] 動 擦拭

▶ I wiped my table with a piece of tissue.
我用衛生紙擦桌子。

動詞三態變化 wipe - wiped - wiped

---

wisdom [`wɪzdəm] 名 智慧

▶ Mother often advises me and gives me words of wisdom.
媽媽常給我意見並給我智慧之語。

相關衍生字彙 wise [waɪz] 形 有智慧的、wisely [`waɪzlɪ] 副 聰明地、wit [wɪt] 名 機智、clever [`klɛvɚ] 形 聰明的

---

wish [wɪʃ] 動 希望

▶ I wish I were a bird.
我願我是隻小鳥。

相關衍生字彙 wish on 片 把～強加於，塞給、wish to goodness 片 極其希望、wishbone [`wɪʃˌbon] 名（鳥禽胸部的）叉骨、wishful [`wɪʃfəl] 形 願望的，渴望的、wishful thinking 片 一廂情願的想法、wishfully [`wɪʃfəlɪ] 副 渴望地，希望地、wishing well 片 許願池、wishlist [`wɪʃlɪst] 名 希望得到的東西的清單

動詞三態變化 wish - wished - wished

---

withdraw [wɪð`drɔ] 動 抽回，提（款）　　反 deposit [dɪ`pɑzɪt] 動 存（款）

動詞三態變化 withdraw - withdrew - withdrawn

---

wither [`wɪðɚ] 動 乾枯，枯萎

▶ The flowers withered soon in hot weather.
花朵遇上熱天氣很快就枯萎。

動詞三態變化 wither - withered - withered

withstand [wɪð`stænd] 動 反抗，抵擋
▶ Can the old house withstand the storm?
　這老舊房子承受的了暴風雨嗎？
相關衍生字彙 endure [ɪn`djur] 動 忍耐，持久、resist [rɪ`zɪst] 動 抵抗，抗拒、oppose [ə`poz]
　　　　動 反對，妨礙
動詞三態變化 withstand - withstood - withstood

witness [`wɪtnɪs] 動 目擊
▶ I witnessed the car accident.
　我目擊了車禍。
動詞三態變化 witness - witnessed - witnessed

woeful [`wofəl] 形 悲哀的　　　同 miserable [`mɪzərəb!] 形 悲傷的
相關衍生字彙 woefully [`wofəlɪ] 副 悲哀地，令人遺憾地、woe [wo] 名 悲哀，災難

wolf [wulf] 名 狼　　　片 wolf in sheep's clothing 披著羊皮的狼（假好心的人）

wonder [`wʌndə] 動 想知道　　　片 no wonder 難怪
動詞三態變化 wonder - wondered - wondered

wonderful [`wʌndəfəl] 形 棒極了的
▶ I have two wonderful kids.
　我有兩個超棒的孩子。
相關衍生字彙 incredible [ɪn`krɛdəb!] 形 難以置信的、extraordinary [ɪk`strɔrdṇ͵ɛrɪ]
　　　　形 非凡的、exceptional [ɪk`sɛpʃən!] 形 卓越的、superb [su`pɝb] 形 極好的、
　　　　marvelous [`mɑrvələs] 形 了不起的、remarkable [rɪ`mɑrkəb!] 形 值得注意的

woolen [`wulɪn] 形 羊毛製的
▶ The woolen scarf keeps me warm. 這條羊毛圍巾很保暖。

word [wɝd] 名 字，語言　　　片 in a word 總而言之

workaholic [͵wɝkə`hɔlɪk] 名 工作狂
▶ He is a workaholic. 他是個工作狂。

workbook [`wɝk͵buk] 名 練習簿
▶ The teacher hopes we can use workbooks to practice.
　老師希望我們用練習簿做練習。
相關衍生字彙 exercise [`ɛksə͵saɪz] 名 練習，習題、practice [`præktɪs] 名（反覆的）練習，學習、
　　　　rehearse [rɪ`hɝs] 動 排演、train [tren] 動 訓練，培養、educate [`ɛdʒə͵ket]
　　　　動 教育，培養

worldwide [ˋwɝldˏwaɪd] 副 遍及全球地
▶ The food is sold worldwide.
　這種食物銷往世界各地。
相關衍生字彙 international [ˏɪntɚˋnæʃən] 形 國際性的、extensive [ɪkˋstɛnsɪv]
　　形 廣大的，大規模的、universal [ˏjunəˋvɝs] 形 普遍的，宇宙的，完整的

worry [ˋwɝɪ] 動 擔心
▶ Don't worry about me.
　不必擔心我。
相關衍生字彙 worry about 片 擔心，焦慮、worry at 片 一心想要克服、worryingly [ˋwɝɪɪŋlɪ]
　　副 令人煩惱地、worrywart [ˋwɝˏwɔrt] 名 杞人憂天者、worried [ˋwɝɪd]
　　形 擔心的，發愁的、worrisome [ˋwɝɪsəm] 形 令人煩惱的，悶悶不樂的
動詞三態變化 worry - worried - worried

worship [ˋwɝʃɪp] 動 敬奉，信奉，崇拜
▶ In different religious ceremonies, people worship different gods.
　不同的宗教儀式中，人們敬奉不同的神祇。
相關衍生字彙 worshiper [ˋwɝʃɪpɚ] 名 禮拜者，參拜者、worshipful [ˋwɝʃɪpfəl]
　　形 虔誠的，崇拜的、worshipingly [ˋwɝʃɪpɪŋlɪ] 副 崇敬地
動詞三態變化 worship - worshiped / worshipped - worshiped / worshipped

worthwhile [ˋwɝθˋhwaɪl] 形 值得做的　　◎ MP3 23-05
▶ It's worthwhile to learn English. 學英文是很值得的。

worthy [ˋwɝðɪ] 形 值得的　　片 to be worthy of 值得～

wound [wund] 名 傷口
▶ It's a wound to my pride.
　那是對我的自尊的一種傷害。
相關衍生字彙 injure [ˋɪndʒɚ] 動 傷害、bruise [bruz] 名 傷痕，青腫、hurt [hɝt] 動 使受傷、
　　fracture [ˋfræktʃɚ] 名 骨折，折斷、bleed [blid] 動 流血

wrap [ræp] 動 包裹
▶ I wrapped the package and mailed it.
　我把包裹包好就寄出去了。
動詞三態變化 wrap - wrapped / wrapt - wrapped / wrapt

wrath [ræθ] 名 憤怒　　同 anger [ˋæŋgɚ] 名 憤怒
相關衍生字彙 wrathful [ˋræθfəl] 形 憤怒的、wrathfully [ˋræθfəlɪ] 副 憤怒地、wrathy [ˋræθɪ]
　　形 憤怒的，激怒的

wreck [rɛk] 名 失事遇難
▶ Along the beach all were the plane wrecks.
　沿著沙灘都是飛機殘骸。

相關衍生字彙 wreckage [`rɛkɪdʒ] 名（船隻等的）失事，（失事船或飛機等的）殘骸、 wrecker [`rɛkɚ] 名 使船失事的人，救難船，救援人、wrecking [`rɛkɪŋ] 名 失事，遇難，營救

wrench [rɛntʃ] 動 扭傷

▶ I wrenched my ankle while I was dancing.
我跳舞時扭傷腳踝。

動詞三態變化 wrench - wrenched - wrenched

wrinkle [`rɪŋkl̩] 名 皺紋

▶ There are wrinkles on Father's face.
爸爸的臉上有了皺紋。

相關衍生字彙 wrinkled [`rɪŋkl̩d] 形 有皺紋的、wrinkling [`rɪŋklɪŋ] 名 起皺紋，皺起、 wrinkly [`rɪŋkl̩ɪ] 形 有皺紋的，易生皺紋的

write [raɪt] 動 寫字　片 to write back 回信

相關衍生字彙 write down 片 把～寫下、write down as 片 把～描寫成、write off 片 勾銷，取消、 write out 片 寫出、writer [`raɪtɚ] 名 作家，記者、writing [`raɪtɪŋ] 名 書寫，筆跡，文件、written [`rɪtn̩] 形 寫下的，書面的

動詞三態變化 write - wrote - written

MEMO

W

505

一網打盡

字母

X-ray ~ zoom

詞性說明

名 名詞	副 副詞	介 介系詞
動 動詞	形 形容詞	連 連接詞
代 代名詞	助 助動詞	

內文圖示說明

片 片語	反 反義字	同 同義字

一網打盡「英語小知識」│ 距離 v.s 長度 ———————————

foot
英尺

hectare
公頃

diameter
直徑

acre
英畝

yard
碼

circumference
周長

 **X-ray**

X-ray [`ɛks`re] 名 X 光
▶ The doctor decided to take an X-ray of my leg.
醫生決定幫我的腿照 X 光。

Y **yacht ~ youthful**

yacht [jɑt] 名 遊艇
▶ The rich man owns a private yacht. 這名有錢人擁有一艘私人遊艇。

----

yard [jɑrd] 名 院子
▶ I planted lots of flowers in the yard. 我在院子裡種很多花。

----

yawn [jɔn] 名 呵欠
▶ You must be tired because you keep giving yawns.
你一直打呵欠，一定是累了。

----

year [jɪr] 名 年　　　片 year by year 年復一年
相關衍生字彙 yearbook [`jɪr͵bʊk] 名 年鑑，年刊、yearly [`jɪrlɪ] 形 每年的、
year-end [`jɪr͵ɛnd] 名 年終 形 年終的、monthly [`mʌnθlɪ] 形 每月的、
month [mʌnθ] 名 月

----

yearn [jɝn] 動 思念，渴望
▶ I yearn for letters from you.
我渴望你寫信給我。
相關衍生字彙 desire [dɪ`zaɪr] 動 渴望、long for 片 渴望、wish [wɪʃ] 動 但願、hope [hop]
動 希望、crave [krev] 動 渴望獲得
動詞三態變化 yearn - yearned - yearned

----

yell [jɛl] 動 吼叫
▶ I heard someone yelling inside the room.
我聽到有人在房間裡吼叫。
動詞三態變化 yell - yelled - yelled

----

yellow [`jɛlo] 名 黃色　　　片 the yellow race 黃種人

----

yield [jild] 動 生產，讓步
▶ He didn't yield an inch.
他一點都不退讓。
動詞三態變化 yield - yielded - yielded

youthful [ˋjuθfəl] 形 年輕的
▶ Papa is still full of youthful energy.
　爸爸仍然充滿年輕人的活力。

相關衍生字彙 youth [juθ] 名 青春時代、youngster [ˋjʌŋstɚ] 名 年輕人、young [jʌŋ] 形 年輕的

 zeal ~ zoom

MP3 **26-01**

★一網打盡 13 個英文單字 ｜ 一網打盡 5 句英語會話句

zeal [zil] 名 熱忱
▶ No matter how old you are, you should have the zeal for learning.
　無論年紀多大，你都要永保學習熱忱。

相關衍生字彙 zealous [ˋzɛləs] 形 熱心的、zest [zɛst] 名 熱情、enthusiastic [ɪn‚θjuzɪˋæstɪk] 形 熱心的、passion [ˋpæʃən] 名 熱情、passionate [ˋpæʃənɪt] 形 熱情的

- - - - - - - - - -

zero [ˋzɪro] 名 零，（攝氏）零度
▶ Water freezes at zero. 水在零度時會結冰。

- - - - - - - - - -

zone [zon] 名 區
▶ Here is a parking zone. 這裡是停車區。

- - - - - - - - - -

zoo [zu] 名 動物園
▶ Many parents take their kids to the zoo on the weekend.
　很多父母會在周末帶孩子去動物園。

相關衍生字彙 zoology [zoˋɑlədʒɪ] 名 動物學、zookeeper [ˋzu‚kipɚ] 名 動物園管理人、zoologist [zoˋɑlədʒɪst] 名 動物學家

- - - - - - - - - -

zoom [zum] 動（相機、攝影機）鏡頭拉近或拉遠
▶ At the end of the film, the camera often zooms out.
　在電影的最後，鏡頭常常會拉遠。

動詞三態變化 zoom - zoomed - zoomed

X-Z

用「句子」背GEPT
全民英檢初級單字

從句子去記單字才是王道！
用句子去學英文才能同時學好「聽力」和「會話」！

超詳細！絕對合格！

《用句子背GEPT全民英檢初級單字》
1書＋1別冊＋1MP3 定價／**349**元

專為考生量身打造的學習方案！
全民英檢聽、說、讀、寫一次到位！

國家圖書館出版品預行編目（CIP）資料

一網打盡英文單字15,000 / Victoria
Lin 著. -- 初版. -- 臺北市：我識,
2015.07 面；公分

ISBN 978-986-5785-67-3（精裝附光碟）

1. 英語 2. 詞彙

805.12 　　　　　104009037

一網打盡
英文單字
15,000
Vocabularies

書名 / 一網打盡英文單字15,000
作者 / Victoria Lin
發行人 / 蔣敬祖
編輯顧問 / 常祈天
主編 / 戴嬿凌
執行編輯 / 謝昀蓁
校對 / 許祐瑄
視覺指導 / 黃馨儀
內文排版 / 健呈電腦排版股份有限公司
法律顧問 / 北辰著作權事務所蕭雄淋律師
印製 / 金濱印刷事業有限公司
初版 / 2015年07月
出版單位 / 我識出版集團－我識出版社有限公司
電話 / (02) 2345-7222
傳真 / (02) 2345-5758
地址 / 台北市忠孝東路五段372巷27弄78之1號1樓
郵政劃撥 / 19793190
戶名 / 我識出版社
網址 / www.17buy.com.tw
E-mail / iam.group@17buy.com.tw
facebook網址 / www.facebook.com/ImPublishing
定價 / 新台幣 449 元 / 港幣 150 元（附1MP3）

總經銷 / 我識出版社有限公司業務部
地址 / 新北市汐止區新台五路一段114號12樓
電話 / (02) 2696-1357 傳真 / (02) 2696-1359

地區經銷 / 易可數位行銷股份有限公司
地址 / 新北市新店區寶橋路235巷6弄3號5樓

港澳總經銷 / 和平圖書有限公司
地址 / 香港柴灣嘉業街12號百樂門大廈17樓
電話 / (852) 2804-6687 傳真 / (852) 2804-6409

I'm

我識出版社
17buy.com.tw